THE COURT MEN
Their greatest strength was pride!

Sir Simon—driven to bequeath his family a glittering legacy; determined to destroy the one man who stood in his way. . . .

Geoffrey—to win love he did his father's bidding, and discovered—too late—just what it cost. . . .

North—a Court by marriage, he had all the advantages but was rarely faithful to the woman who made them possible. . . .

THE COURT WOMEN
Their tragic flaw was passion!

Honey—vibrant, vulnerable, she surrendered everything to the man who became her father's enemy. . . .

Susan—bored by provincial pleasures, she let a casual affair shatter everything she cherished. . . .

Angela—an artist of genius, a devastating beauty, she pledged her love to a man who promised her nothing. . . .

PRIDE'S COURT
THREE GENERATIONS OF FIERCE LOYALTIES AND SHOCKING BETRAYALS

Pride's Court

Joy Carroll

A DELL BOOK

Published by
Dell Publishing Co., Inc.
1 Dag Hammarskjold Plaza
New York, New York 10017

Copyright © 1980 by Joy Carroll

All rights reserved. No part of this book may be
reproduced or transmitted in any form or by any
means, electronic or mechanical, including photocopying,
recording, or by any information storage
and retrieval system, without the written permission
of the Publisher, except where permitted by law.

Dell ® TM 681510, Dell Publishing Co., Inc.

ISBN: 0-440-17088-5

Printed in the United States of America

First printing—March 1980

For my parents—
John Robert and Elsie Holroyd

As well as the dozens of authors consulted to bring to life the social and political backgrounds for this story, a number of people shared memories, private papers, and professional expertise with me. For example, His Majesty's Theatre is gone now, and it is due to aficionados like Herbert Whittaker, Charles Rittenhouse, and John H. Victor that I was able to recreate an opening night in 1921. Mary L. Fraser, Chief Librarian, Cape Breton Regional Library, contributed accounts of conditions in Nova Scotia coal mines, and Jean Armstrong provided me with descriptions of how the funicular functioned in Quebec City during the early thirties. I have Peter C. Holdroyd to thank for his grasp of how Canadian gold mines were financed and for some fine points about the stock market. From Gillis Purcell and Charles H. Peters, I was able to glean subtle details about the decor of the St. James's Club in the early twenties. Bill McVean (broadcaster) and C. Wallace Floody advised me on bush flying and rescue operations. Eric Kruger and Brian Dixon, Forensic Services Center (Toronto), along with Ralph Percy, provided information about train accidents. James Lovisek, an assistant in herpetology, Royal Ontario Museum, told me more about snakes than I could find in any textbook. M. Jacques L'Ecuyer, Comptroller, Ritz-Carlton Hotel, Montreal, provided details about the elegant Palm Court in 1930. Jean O'Heany, M.D., gave me valuable medical advice, as always. My researcher, Joan Coleman, tracked down every subject, no matter how difficult or obscure, with enthusiasm and persistence, and I am grateful for her help. Finally, I am indebted to my editors, Linda Grey and Kate Duffy, for creative support and infinite patience.

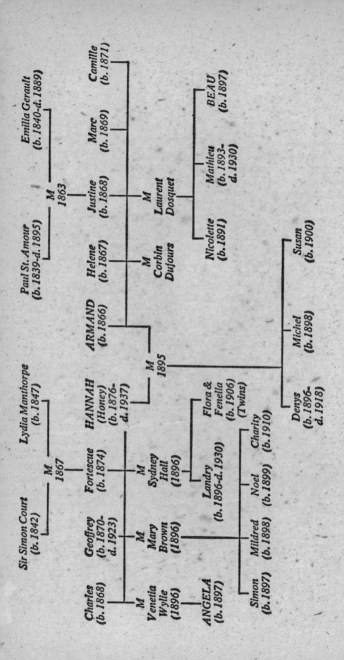

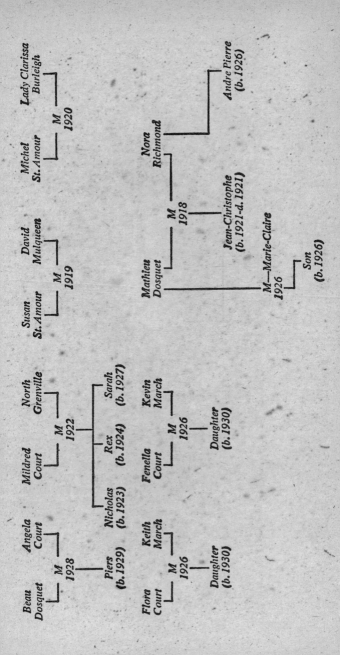

Part One

1921–1925

CHAPTER ONE

Half an hour before curtain time a platoon of gleaming limousines gathered in the cool September night outside His Majesty's Theatre on Guy Street. They tyrannized all the surrounding roads while they let loose a glittering flock of first-nighters; plump matrons awash in mink and diamonds, slim young things in wisps of pastel chiffon and feathery aigrettes, men of all ages in the starched statement of white tie and tails.

Herbert Marshall, the young English actor and war hero, was opening in a play called *Fedora*, and everybody who was anybody, or even pretended to be anybody, in the English community of Montreal had turned out to see and be seen. The entire house, from the orchestra up through the dress circle on the second level to the family circle and the "gods" on the third, was sold out. Those in the best seats wore full dress. An opening was always a welcome excuse for a touch of pomp.

Sir Simon Court had taken the Royal Box. With his exceptional height, bulky form, trim white beard, and flashing blue eyes, not even a stranger from the farthest corner of the provinces would have mistaken him for anything but what he was—a very important person. Knowing this, he always felt compelled to occupy a prime position in any public gathering.

As a typical Court gesture of family solidarity Sir Simon was personally escorting his young granddaughter, Mildred (his son Geoffrey Court's daughter), and with them in the chauffeur-driven Rolls-Royce was his eldest son, Charles. (Sir Simon had yet another son, Fortescue, but he was not present on this particular occasion.) Along with the party was a favorite granddaughter, Susan, with her husband, David Mulqueen. While Sir Simon was in railroads, shipping lines, and mining, the Mulqueens were in textile mills.

Sir Simon, as head of the powerful and prolific Court clan, had much on his mind besides the frivolity of playgoing. Among his fellow moguls in Montreal there had been a great deal of whispering lately that Sir Simon was getting too old to be a natural leader. He was only seventy-nine and, dammit, he *wasn't* old. He had never felt better in his life, he assured himself now, and he fully intended to put a stop to these senseless rumors. Let everybody see tonight that he was in excellent health and still as strong as Atlas and as rich as Croesus.

That wasn't his only problem, of course. (He always had a list of urgent matters to be dealt with, but he accepted that as his lot. Noblesse Oblige, after all.) His grand-daughter, Mildred, must have a proper husband, and at present there was nobody in sight. She was an heiress, yes. Prominent socially, yes. From the best family, yes. But physically she was large, rather plain (he admitted this to himself grudgingly), and definitely without a sense of style. In the latter regard, it was a pity she had not taken after the Courts; her mother (who had married his son Geoffrey) had been a Brown from Bootle, Lancashire, and there you had it. What more could one say? If only poor Mildred had resembled the handsome, elegant Courts, there would have been no problem in finding her a husband. He shook his head as he mulled these dreary thoughts over in his mind, but he did not despair.

No, Sir Simon decided, he would never give up the quest. There must be a perfectly eligible young man *some-where* in this city! And if not in Montreal, then in New York or London. Actually it was to this end that he some-times ventured out to public affairs that he found incredibly boring. What logic was there, for example, in going to a play? In watching a bunch of actors mouthing lines about situations that did not exist? What could people possibly see in such an exhibition? The pleasure had always escaped him. With the possible exception of some Shakespeare, which he had been dragged to see as a child in England. Now, when it came to kings, conquerors, emperors, it might be worth a few minutes of a man's time to find out what they had to say. But that was rare. Mostly, he ap-peared at an opening such as the one tonight on the slim chance that he might find a suitor for Mildred. God knows, neither of her parents took the slightest interest in the problem, and so he had assumed full responsibility. Otherwise, the Courts might become extinct, and he shud-dered to think of such a disaster.

As he walked into the theater, he gave an approving glance at his other granddaughter, Susan Mulqueen, and noted that she was more to his liking. Odd, though, how things had turned out when you considered her lamentable heritage on her father's side. Sir Simon's only daughter, Honey (a ravishing beauty when she had eloped twenty-five years earlier), had borne Susan by a renegade Frenchman called St. Amour. Even after all this time, the mere mention of St. Amour's name brought a painful twinge to the area somewhere between Sir Simon's heart and his stomach. Yes, his scurrilous son-in-law might be the death of him yet, Sir Simon decided, if he didn't stop thinking about the blackguard. But Susan, now, had style despite her unfortunate father. Reared among foreigners, pagans, and dangerous heretics, she had somehow managed to escape the Church and had been clever enough to find an acceptable Protestant husband for herself. No girl could do better than marrying a Mulqueen, unless, of course, she married a Court.

As Sir Simon shepherded his brood down the side aisle of the theater and up into the Royal Box, he acknowledged the presence of old acquaintances, giving them a brief nod as if he were indeed royalty. He noted a small rustle of interest when people saw Susan in his party. He had so publicly disowned her mother, Lady St. Amour. (Even the fact that Armand St. Amour had been knighted for his contribution to the war effort had not softened Sir Simon's heart. He thought it a disgrace to give a perfectly good knighthood to an obvious charlatan.)

The Court party seated itself carefully, appropriately, as they did all things social. In the front row of chairs Sir Simon sat with a granddaughter on either side. His son Charles and David, Susan's husband, took up a place behind them. The curtain was late going up (why could these people never be on time?), and Sir Simon picked up his antique opera glasses, a pair that had belonged to his father, Sir Cathmor, and peered about the theater to see who else had been foolish enough to attend.

A flutter of opening-night fever consumed the audience. There was a great deal of moving about, waving to friends, whispering, consulting of programs. The actual star, Marie Löhr, was internationally famous, and she was supported by two men who were already making a name for themselves. The rose velour curtain had been pulled back to reveal the asbestos act curtain with its pretty Victorian landscape. The magnificent chandelier, all brass and crystal, twinkled overhead. Painted cupids with no visible means of support floated on the ceiling. In the midst of this comfortable ambience Sir Simon felt free to sweep his glasses about the house, finishing up on the two boxes situated directly across the theater from his own.

One box was noticeably empty. In the other sat a woman he did not know, accompanied by Kingsley Whyte, a member of Parliament whom he privately referred to as a "silly pansy." The woman who caught his eye in this way was tall, with a cap of shining blond hair and a rather prominent bosom. She had an assured, almost imperious air, which appealed to him. Her face was strong, chiseled, and she had no-nonsense eyebrows (not like the plucked absurdities he had begun to see on giddy young girls around the city). Her smile, he noticed, was complete and attentive.

Sir Simon felt a sudden, unfamiliar urge to know more about the woman. He spoke to Susan.

"Who is the woman in the box across the way?"

"Let me see," Susan said, taking the opera glasses from her grandfather and training them on the couple he indicated. "Tulah Horne. Don't you know her?"

"If I knew her, I wouldn't ask," Sir Simon said crossly. "Which Hornes, then? The lumber people?"

"Yes, I think so. Tulah lives in the family house on Maisonneuve."

"Do you know her well?"

"Not really, I just keep reading about her in the newspapers. She's a suffragette. She's working for the vote for women."

Sir Simon allowed himself a protesting grunt.

"Rubbish!" he said, grinding his teeth. "Absolute rubbish. She looks intelligent enough, however." (As if womens' votes and brains could not possibly go together.)

Susan giggled.

"The Suffrage Association is trying to get Judge Emily Murphy made a senator," she said. "I read it in the *Star*."

"A *senator*?" The old man was frankly appalled.

"Yes, why are you so surprised?" Susan asked.

"They must be mad," Sir Simon said.

Charles, having heard this exchange and smiling at Susan's provocation, leaned forward.

16

"I know her, Papa. Do you want to meet her?"

Sir Simon was not sure. Watching him, Susan could not help baiting him a little more.

"They're terribly serious about the vote, Grandfather," she said. "They marched on the premier's office recently. Every so often a delegation of women goes to Quebec City to see him. You must have read it in the papers."

"I never read stories about idiots."

"Oh, well, you've missed the ones about suffragettes then."

"If you want an introduction," Charles said, still amused at his father's dilemma, "just say the word. We can go round at intermission if you like."

"If you insist," Sir Simon said, retrieving the opera glasses from Susan and taking another look for himself.

Charles and Susan exchanged conspiratorial glances. Behind the old man's back Susan rolled her eyes because at first she found his new interest extremely funny. As the idea took hold, however, it became less and less amusing. What if he became seriously interested in this woman, Tulah Horne?

Before she had time to dwell upon the awkward possibilities, the curtain went up and she sat back to enjoy the play. But even as she watched Mr. Herbert Marshall's delicious limp (from a war wound, the newspapers had reported) and the somewhat overblown dramatics of Marie Löhr (described in the program as "the Flower of the London Stage"), the importance of her grandfather's whim nagged at the back of her mind. When it came to Sir Simon and Pride's Court, the great house over which he reigned in Montreal, Susan had certain ambitions of her own. And they certainly did not include a new Lady Court. Her grandmother had been dead three years, and Susan now realized that it was possible that Sir Simon might remarry.

At intermission Sir Simon stood up to stretch his legs. Charles looked at him questioningly. Sir Simon's face reflected a certain air of indecision, but in his own mind he still found the idea of meeting Tulah Horne rather tempting. Despite her insane political ideas, he might be able to save her from herself. He had never been a man to deprive others of his good counsel when it was needed.

"Do you want to go over and meet her, Papa?" Charles inquired.

Sir Simon hesitated.

"Who's coming to the smoking room?" David asked. "I'd like a cigar."

"We'll go over to meet Miss Horne as soon as the crowd moves a bit," Sir Simon allowed to Charles. "You go along, David."

By the time they had made their way around the dress circle, Tulah Horne and her escort, Kingsley Whyte, were standing in the box. Sir Simon barely acknowledged Whyte but smiled generously upon Tulah, who, at close range, was even more fetching than she had been in the distance. He made a bluff and hearty reference to womens' votes, but not in his usual thundering, sarcastic manner. This surprised even Charles. Next, he made an astonishing offer. He invited Tulah to dinner at Pride's Court the following week and, going even farther, explained his household arrangements, a thing he never did.

"My granddaughter, Susan, will be hostess," Sir Simon said, grandly ignoring Whyte, whom he would never have countenanced at his table because of his odd reputation. "It used to be Charles's wife, Polly, who did all that. But she's ill. My granddaughters often help out on social occasions."

Such an elaborate explanation was so unlike his father that Charles could not think of anything to say. Tulah Horne encompassed both of them in her ample smile and accepted. Charles wondered how his father would look to such a woman. Tulah herself must be at least forty-five, but she was vivacious, with a driving, forceful smile that revealed white, hard teeth. Watching her, Charles decided that she was terribly impressed with his father. The lights dimmed as first warning.

Sir Simon, restless as always, said they must be getting back to their own box and took his leave. As he walked behind the curtains, he almost ran headlong into Honey and Armand St. Amour. He saw that his daughter, though fiftyish, still looked elegant; her pale hair streaked with gray was smooth and stylish, her fine blue eyes still sparkled, her face still had the contours of the great beauty she had once been. He glared at her.

"Papa!" she said, with an involuntary little cry of surprise.

He froze. So *they* were the ones who occupied the empty

box next to Tulah Horne! Naturally St. Amour would be late. A man like that was totally irresponsible. Couldn't expect him to able to tell time or make the necessary effort to get anywhere when he was due. Sir Simon gave Honey a cold look and did not speak. He turned his most ferocious look on his son-in-law and swept by.

Charles, coming along behind his father, stopped to talk. He had always been friendly with Honey, and in fact, she had often come to his assistance in the past concerning urgent family matters.

"Hello, Honey. You're looking well."

"Papa doesn't think so, evidently," Honey said lightly. But she was hurt, just the same. She had never been able to destroy completely her love for her father, although there had been times when she had actually felt hate.

"Don't pay any attention to him," Charles said consolingly. "He's preoccupied with his own problems. Hello, Armand."

"I was going to call you," Honey said quickly, "to ask about Polly. I hear she's been quite ill."

The lights dimmed again. Charles said hastily, "Polly is very ill. I'm driving her up to the sanitarium—there's one at St.-Jovite, you know—probably next week."

"Oh, I am sorry, Charles," Honey said.

(That could mean only one thing, Honey realized. Polly had tuberculosis. It was frequently fatal, and at the very least, it meant that the victim would be an invalid for some time.)

"I'll give you a call, Honey. I've got to go now, or Papa will be furious. You know how he hates being disturbed when he's in his box."

He managed to arrive back in the Royal Box before the curtain went up. Sir Simon had just finished describing Kingsley Whyte to Susan as "a sickly dairy maid" but broke off that conversation to bestow his most odious stare upon his tardy son. The accidental meeting with Honey and Armand had utterly destroyed the genial mood generated by his introduction to Tulah. After the play, which Sir Simon thought imbecilic, the party was safely stowed in the Rolls-Royce with Dodgson, the chauffeur, at the wheel. Sir Simon could not get over the stupidity of the actors, particularly Marie Löhr. "Why couldn't she figure out what was happening right in the beginning?" he demanded.

"Saved us all a lot of trouble. The woman was absolutely cretinous!" There was no use trying to explain to him that if she had known the plot, there would have been no play.

After Sir Simon had dropped Susan and David at their own house on Pine Avenue, they waved off the Rolls with a sigh of relief. Family outings were all very well and in a good cause, but they could be extremely wearing. Riding in the enclosed limousine was a bore, too, after the Hispano-Suiza Susan drove. (She had traded in the silver Rolls-Royce the Mulqueens had given as a wedding present, in favor of a long, low lemon-colored Hispano.) She adored driving the car; it was so startling, and it gave her a rare feeling of power.

Once inside, Susan stood still and listened for sounds from the upper part of the house. But only the ticking of the hall clock disturbed the silence. Baby Anthony must be sound asleep in the third-floor nursery under the watchful eye of Rose Starkey. Starkey had been with the Courts for years, and Susan had inherited her as a nanny. Feeling relaxed, she tossed her purple velvet cape onto a hall chair, where it promptly slid to the floor. She left it. The maid could pick it up in the morning. David was locking up.

"Let's have a drink, darling," Susan said. "I'm not sleepy."

"All right. Just wait until I get rid of my hat and coat."

"I put whisky in the small sitting room before we left."

"Good. We'll listen to music."

They drifted toward the small sitting room at the rear of the house, where Susan had installed a new console gramophone and a collection of jazz records. After the Hispano-Suiza, the gramophone was the love of her life, and she played it at all hours of the day and night. Susan switched on a small table lamp, a bronze mermaid holding up an orange globe. She began to shuffle through the cabinet where she kept her records. David mixed them each a whisky and soda.

"What do you think of Grandfather's interest in Tulah Horne?" Susan asked, still crouched on the floor searching for the right piece of music.

"Definitely peculiar. I've never known him to show an interest in women. But men are like that, darling. Never say die. Never give up the ship. England expects every man—"

"Oh, shut up, David! It may be serious."

"What do you mean, serious? He only went over to her box. Surely that isn't a confession or a crime, is it? You women make everything into a crisis."

"I have dire feelings, David. Dire."

"What difference does it make, anyway?"

"How can you be so stupid? A new Lady Court? Why, the whole family would be upset!"

"I wouldn't worry. He only asked her to dinner, didn't he?"

"Do you suppose an old man like that could . . . well . . . could . . ."

"Make love? Why not? I expect to be doing it when I'm ninety."

"David, you're revolting. Give me a minute to put this thing on and then we'll dance. Here's the one I want."

"I suppose you think you might become hostess of Pride's Court yourself? Is that it?"

"Why not? Nobody else wants to do it, and I love the house. I'd adore to live there, run it, have guests. I don't lie about that, David."

"Well, get the music on." He sat watching her, his manner a bit languid, the droop of his mouth suggesting incipient boredom.

"Here it is. My favorite."

David slumped lower in the chair. Even in the half-darkness, his blond hair, bleached almost white by the summer sun, shone like a beacon. His skin was golden from days of tennis, riding, golf. His voice was world-weary, and his eyes roved restlessly over his wife's slim figure while the rest of him remained motionless.

"So what's the news on poor old Polly, anyway?" he asked next.

"Bad, I'm afraid. Doctor Glossop says she has . . . they think it's tuberculosis. Ugh. You know what *that* means!"

"Well, I gathered it was pretty critical. Charles said something about taking her to St.-Jovite, but I didn't like to spoil the evening by asking exactly what was wrong. So depressing."

"Grandfather refused to believe Glossop at first, so he

called in other doctors. You know how he goes on about things."

"Your family never fails to astonish me. Always great tragedies, great dramas. We Mulqueens just browse along—"

"Let's browse through this tango. Come on." She pulled him to his feet.

"Give me a chance to finish this drink, will you?" He drained the glass and set it down.

"Listen to this part, it's exciting. Hurry up."

"Always in a rush."

He stood up to face her, and they smiled at each other lazily in the peculiar glow of the lamp. The tango thumped encouragingly, offering an underlying sexuality to the atmosphere. Susan responded to the music, eager to find some excitement in a world that had somehow diminished after marriage. Only two years earlier everything had seemed magical, they were both physically attractive, they had money and position. Surely that would shield them from the flat, tedious life they observed around them. But now they were bored. There was, apparently, no shield. No magic. There was just life.

Susan had thought having a baby might help. David had taken up horses, breeding racing thoroughbreds, searching for some thrill by way of competition, gambling, high stakes. Recently he had bought an expensive yearling that they could not afford and was at present boarding the mare at a friend's farm. Susan still rode to hounds, drove the big yellow car, bought clothes in New York, traveled to Paris. Nothing helped, not really.

She stood poised before him now, ready to lend her body to the hypnotic rhythm, slim in gold tissue cut like a tube over a mauve satin skirt embroidered with the golden beaks of purple parrots. She looked desperate, her eyes bright with need, her head set on a long, graceful neck, rather like that of a fashionable doll.

"Wait. I'm going to take off this goddamned jacket. Who invented these suits, anyway?"

He tore off the long-tailed jacket, the tie. The stiff shirt was uncomfortable. He took it off and hurled it on a chair. Now he was wearing only his trousers and underwear.

"Lucky me, to have so little on," Susan said sweetly.

22

"Shocking, is more like it. Every man in the theater was ogling you."

"David really." But she was pleased that David had noticed other men looking at her. The low neck of her gown was held up by narrow string straps, the gold material just barely rose above the warm, pink nipples.

The music caught them and they began to dance, breast to breast, then thigh to thigh, breaking apart, dipping, pressing, tantalizingly close, flesh on flesh. Under the thin icing of violins a tuba growled a dirty, pulsating beat. Susan and David danced well together, and she followed him smoothly through the dance, finally feeling the first welcome throb of fire in her thighs. She looked up into David's face trying to imagine him as a stranger she had picked up in a foul waterfront bar. Turning him into a soiled, drugged, evil man who carried a knife, perhaps, and was probably a dangerous pervert. When she and David touched now, she felt him harden. If only they could recapture that sweet delirium of the first few times, she thought, so long ago—the very first day, in fact, when they had picnicked with champagne by the river. David was the first man ever to touch her secret places, and he taught her the delights of the flesh. If only they could feel like that again! It had seemed to Susan then that it would never end. David had promised that.

The record stopped. Susan wound up the machine and put the needle back at the beginning. But they had only danced a few steps when David pulled her down upon the carpet.

She pretended to resist, to be shocked.

"Not on the Royal Persian carpet!"

He ignored that and pushed his hand down the front of her gown and pulled out one of her small breasts and began to fondle it. She wondered if he wanted her to take off the gown, but he made no attempt to do so. Nor did he take off any more of his own clothes. So it was to be like *that*, she thought. Sly David. It always seemed much more wicked when they made love with their clothes on, snatching at stolen pleasure. Daring somebody (but who, now that they were married?) to find them, punish them. Susan wore nothing under the gown, there was nothing but the single layer of silk between her body and the world. She always found it exhilarating to walk around like that, and it amused her to think of how men would react if they knew. David thrust his hand up her skirt, then hiked it a little over her thighs. It was easy to find the warm, damp nest between her legs.

"Devil! You go out practically naked!"

His fingers probed the golden thicket, driving up the pitch of her fever. She lifted her lips to him. "Now, David. Now, please!" The record scratched on and finally came to a halt as he thrust into her and they heaved violently, deliciously, upon the antique carpet.

CHAPTER TWO

On the long drive down from St.-Jovite (after he had settled Polly in her room in the sanatarium and made every possible arrangement for her comfort), Charles became more and more depressed. Committing his wife to a hospital had been a step toward loneliness, another sad event in a personal life that had been plagued with disappointments.

After all his agonizing years with Venetia, watching her fabulous beauty devastated by smallpox, her mind slowly waste away from a self-inflicted seclusion, and her eventual dreadful suicide, Charles had welcomed the stability of his second wife, Polly. He had brought Polly to Pride's Court, where she had been kind to his only daughter, Angela, and had earned the respect of his difficult father, Sir Simon. After his mother, Lady Court, died, Polly had taken over management of the house and had done a wonderful job of it, too. Now, she was critically ill. Perhaps she would never return to Pride's Court. Certainly she would never be fit to run it again.

These melancholy thoughts led him to memories of Angela, and he wanted to see her again. But she was in England, living with a penniless French Canadian musician. They were not even married. Her behavior had scandalized Sir Simon. Yet Angela belonged at Pride's Court, he told himself angrily, as he guided the big Rolls-Royce down the almost-vacant road. She was part of the Court ménage, and perhaps she wanted to come back just as much as he wanted her to return. The house was empty most of the time. The more he thought about this, the more determined he became to approach his father about the matter. The idea of Angela's return grew and fastened on his mind more firmly with every mile.

By the time he arrived at the wrought-iron gates of Pride's Court, it was evening. Myriad windows in the mansion were aglow in the chilly October darkness. The house was half Gothic, half Italian Renaissance—an architect's whimsy; it was covered with deep bay windows, inexplicable porticos, and sudden balconies and was topped with a four-story tower, from which Sir Simon used to watch his own ships come upriver to the busy docks of Montreal. Magnificent though it was, Pride's Court now seemed lifeless, haunted by memories and whispers of the past, of a time of greatness that might never be seen again. Charles, putting away the car himself rather than call for Dodgson, felt a wave of nausea as he made his way into the huge and empty front foyer.

Peters took his coat and hat to the cloakroom. As he was walking away, Charles asked, "Where is Sir Simon?"

"In the Red Sitting Room, sir," Peters said. "He's waiting for you, sir. He told Cook to hold dinner until you arrived, I believe."

"Thank you, Peters."

As he walked across the broad expanse of the Great Hall, he could hear the unnaturally loud click of his heels upon the polished parquet between the huge Turkey carpets. Above him the vaulted ceiling was deep in shadows. He could not recall feeling so low in years. If only there were family in the house—people coming and going, parties, laughter, the gaiety of youth.

He found his father, glass in hand, examining his latest acquisition, a clock made in the Federal period. Collecting clocks had long been one of Sir Simon's hobbies.

"A beauty, isn't it?" he asked when Charles came in. "They call them banjo clocks. The face is shaped like a banjo, you see. Doesn't really fit in this room, but I took a fancy to it."

"Very nice," Charles said, pouring himself a stiff scotch and soda. "Well, I've done it, Papa. Polly is settled in."

"Don't feel badly, Charles, it had to be done. Best thing for her. Doctors all said so. When you *have* to do something, do it quickly and get it over with. Mooning about over a decision always makes it harder."

"Yes, Papa, I realize that." (Pause) "The house seems so empty. I sometimes wonder why we keep it up."

"*Why we keep it up?*" his father bellowed, catapulted out of his serene position by such a treasonous suggestion. "Where else would we live?"

Charles did not reply.

"I hadn't noticed that it seemed empty," Sir Simon said coldly.

But he had, of course. He often caught himself thinking of the days when Lydia had been alive, when the children had been young, when they brought friends home, when Lydia gave great dinner parties. Especially when Christmas was approaching. Lydia had always made such a fuss about Christmas. But it didn't do to give way to these things. He poked at the fire sternly.

Charles sat down in one of the maroon leather chairs before the fire. As he watched the dancing flames, it seemed to him that he could see Angela's lovely face there. A terrible longing to be with his daughter swept through him. Yes, he decided, he would bring the matter up with his father. There was a time to be silent and a time to speak.

"Papa, I've been thinking a lot about Angela," Charles began hesitantly. "I'd like her home again. I'd like to have her back in the family with us."

"It was *her* choice to run away," Sir Simon said gruffly.

"But she was encouraged by my daughter, Lady St. Amour. It wasn't all Angela's fault. She was young. How was she to know that becoming a friend of the St. Amour family was lethal?"

"Honey was fond of Angela, and after all, Angela was lonely when her mother was so ill. You know that, Papa."

"My daughter"—he refused to call her Honey, which was her fond nickname in the family—"lured Angela to England. Then she encouraged her to run off with that penniless musician. After all I did to stop such a thing!"

(This was not entirely accurate. Honey had taken Angela to England two years before, when Armand was knighted. Sir Simon had forgotten, conveniently, that he had encouraged Honey's daughter, Susan, to be married at Pride's Court when her parents were absent. But the feud between father and daughter was one of long standing.)

26

"Perhaps Angela feels differently now. It can't have been much fun for her, living with Beau. They haven't any money. She is used to much better things. Life can't possibly seem so romantic as it once did," Charles pointed out.

"You think Angela might give up that gypsy life?"

"It's possible."

"And the idea of becoming a painter?"

"I don't know about her career, Papa. She seemed quite set on being an artist."

Sir Simon had made it very clear on several occasions that being a woman painter and being a whore were much the same in his eyes. He frowned upon the idea that Angela might be saved from the arms of the Frenchman yet still be in the clutches of the muse.

"And what about the scandal?" Sir Simon went on. "Everybody in Montreal knows she was living with that man. What are we to do about that? Who will receive her? It's infamous!"

Charles had expected this. He walked across the room to the commode where the bar tray sat and replenished his drink. Then he returned to the fire. He had an instinct about how to approach this thing with his father, but he had to be cautious.

"If *you* told people . . . the right people . . . that Angela had been under her grandmother's wing—after all, Lady Twickenham *does* live in London, doesn't she? So it's possible—if *you* said that, people would believe you."

Sir Simon was not displeased with this view of his personal power, for he had always seen himself as an opinion maker. But lying was another thing. He digested the notion with the aid of more scotch.

"That may be so. People listen to me."

It was perfectly true that if he announced it, if he told people at the club, at certain gatherings, that Countess Twickenham had been supervising Angela's career in London, they would accept it.

"It won't do to send a letter, though. Or a cable," Charles pressed on, seeing that his father was mellowing. "Somebody must go over and talk to Angela . . . convince her to return."

"Um. Yes. Well, nobody has time for gallivanting

27

around the globe saving fallen women. You're too busy. I'm too busy. Fort is too busy. Geoffrey is too busy. So there's nobody."

"I think there is," Charles said, playing his next card carefully (if his father accepted this idea, there was some hope, but it depended heavily upon how Charles presented the scheme). "I have a suggestion that has some justice in it."

"You have? I'd like to hear it."

"Honey."

"Honey?"

He might as well have suggested Satan. It would have produced about the same explosive reaction from his father. But he pursued the thought quickly before his father's anger set like fresh cement.

"Look at it this way, Papa," Charles went on hastily. "You blame Honey for taking Angela to England in the first place. You blame her for introducing Angela to Beau. So why wouldn't it make sense to ask Honey to bring Angela back? Surely that would make up for her mistake —her guilt, if you want to put it that way."

"She *ought* to feel guilty."

"Honey always had a lot of influence with Angela."

"Too much. Obviously too much."

"I'm sure Honey had no idea when she introduced Angela to Beau that it would turn out like this. They were only children, and Beau was living with Honey. She is his aunt, after all. How could she foresee that they'd fall in love?"

"Fall in love? That's the trouble with the world. Too much nonsense and not enough sense. Honey has been a traitor to this family ever since the day she met that Frenchie!"

"Perhaps Honey wouldn't have time to go. But I thought it would be a chance for her to correct the mistake—"

"She isn't that busy!" Sir Simon protested in his usual perverse way. "Why hasn't she time to go? Just because she calls herself the publisher of that rag *Le Monde*—"

"I could ask her."

"It would be *her* time being wasted and not ours," Sir Simon went on, mulling it over. "God knows, she ought to pay for her mistake. She owes the family that much."

"Why don't I speak to Honey, then? She might be willing to take a trip over. Michel is still there, you know." Michel was Honey's son. He had married an English girl after the war.

"Do as you like. But Lady St. Amour is not easy to deal with."

"Still, it's worth a try. The house is empty. It would be good to have some life around the place again."

Sir Simon reluctantly conceded that he had been thinking much the same thing. It was all very well to bring in Susan as a hostess, occasionally, or to invite Mary or Sydney, his sons' wives, to act for him. But it was definitely makeshift. Peters announced dinner on this note, and the two men went into the small dining room together.

When Honey St. Amour arrived at Taunton, it was late afternoon and already raining. Out in the station parking lot she felt the penetrating dampness despite her nutria coat and was relieved when at last she spotted a crumpled Daimler with a hand-printed sign stuck in the windshield announcing it was for hire. The car had seen better days.

She banged on the window until the driver peered at her through the streaming glass, not deigning to hurry, although he must have been able to see Honey was getting wet. Finally he got out rather slowly and came round to open the door for her. She handed him the small leather case she carried and climbed gratefully inside.

The driver, heaving himself behind the wheel, commented on the foulness of the weather and asked where she would like to go.

"A place called Cricket House. I have a map," Honey offered. In London she had found Angela and Beau Dosquet's friend John Leach, who had given her directions.

"Aye, I know Cricket House. Over Pyecroft way. I've an aunt lives nearby."

His speech was spiced with local dialect and he wore a navy pea jacket that hinted at an earlier, more lively career at sea.

"Good, then you won't need my map."

"No, mum. I'll find 'er."

He started the car with a horrendous lurch forward and steered it ponderously into traffic. After this rather ill-starred beginning, however, he made a furious, concentrated attack upon the road. He drove as if he were going into battle, not yielding an inch to other cars or horse-drawn vehicles but forging ahead at a relentless pace. Fortunately, the size of the Daimler demanded respect from passing drivers and nervous horses, and nobody was prepared to argue. The hired car swept grandly through the wet evening.

Thinking back to London, Honey considered what John Leach had told her. Beau was now in France and Angela was alone in the country house. Honey did not like the sound of this, although her mission was to bring Angela back to Montreal and to her family. If Angela was lonely and unhappy, it would make Honey's task easier, but she had always been fond of Angela and could not take pleasure in that kind of victory.

Honey sighed as she thought about the situation that might confront her at Cricket House. After all, it wasn't entirely Angela's fault that she was so high-strung and imaginative. Her upbringing had been strange—a beautiful mother who had eventually killed herself, a tyrannical grandfather, and an indulgent father. What could one expect?

When the Daimler finally thrust its nose between the dilapidated stone gates of Cricket House, night had fallen. The grass was a sleek shadowed green carpet, the clumps of cedar were dripping, and the house glimpsed between rolling hills turned out to be a great gray stucco pile with Gothic windows. When they were very close, Honey could see that the front steps were crumbling at the edges and the enormous tree that covered some of the windows had been strangled long before with ivy.

Even the portico seemed to have lost hope; it sagged to one side. The house looked empty; there wasn't a light in any of the windows. Just as Honey was on the point of deciding that Angela had somehow escaped her, she was encouraged by the sight of smoke coming from one of the chimneys.

"I thought crickets were cheerful," the driver observed, "but this 'ere place is a bit spooky-like."

"It isn't very cheerful, is it?" Honey agreed. An air of general disuse hung over the whole house and was now intensified by rivulets of rain pouring through breaks in the eavestroughs. "Pull right up by the porch, please, and wait until I make sure there's somebody at home. Otherwise, I'll go back to Taunton with you."

He nodded somewhat glumly, and it was apparent that he had little faith in his passenger's arrangements. Honey got out and hurried to the shelter of the porch. She was just going to bang on the door when it flew open and Angela cried, "Aunt Miel!" She used the French for "Honey," as she had done when she was a child. "What on earth are you doing here?"

Honey kissed her niece on the cheek.

"I'll explain everything after I've paid the driver." Angela was holding up a kerosene lamp. Was there no electricity, then? Honey shivered at the uncomfortable prospect.

Once he had seen that his passenger was relatively safe, the driver got out and placed her luggage on the steps. Honey paid him, tipping generously for safe delivery, and he touched his cap respectfully.

"Good night, m'um. If you're sure everything is all right."

"Yes, thank you, everything is fine. Will you come back for me tomorrow afternoon? Let me see, about three o'clock? I shall want to catch an evening train back to London."

Considering the tip in his hand, he was quite amenable to the idea of returning to Cricket House. Angela led the way into the front hall and closed the door on the sound of the retreating car. The place fell silent except for the splash of rain on the windows.

In the glow of Angela's lamp the square hall with its high ceiling and broad oak staircase looked dark and rather forbidding. The chandelier was a ghost, bulbless and mute. Passageways leading in several directions were all masked in shadow.

"No electricity, I'm afraid," Angela said, guessing her aunt's thoughts. "But it must have been quite an impressive house in its day. No heat now, either, except what we burn in the fireplaces. I only use the drawing room when it's so cold because that's more practical. It's not much more than camping really, but the rest of the house is impossible, damp as a tomb."

She led the way down one of the halls to a heavy, closed

31

door. When she opened it to reveal the drawing room and a small fire burning in the grate, Honey said, "It's a ghastly house."

"I knew you'd say that," Angela said with a smile. "And of course, you're right, Aunt Miel. Come inside, it's a bit better by the fire."

The drawing room had an unsavory, gypsy air about it. Like a cave, it was crammed with objects of every kind—a grand piano cluttered with sheet music, an unmade sofa-bed, and a large easel holding an unfinished painting. Scattered about the room were various chairs almost obliterated by books, papers, and tubes of paint and a small side table covered with a tin tea tray. Out of this strange mélange an elegant mantelpiece emerged: alabaster decorated with three carved heads. On a small mat before the fire lay a short-haired black cat, which turned to look curiously upon the humans and then went back to sleep. Honey shivered with cold and distaste. How could she survive a whole night in such a place?

"Sit down, please, Aunt Miel," Angela said, sweeping some books off a chair and pulling it closer to the fire.

Honey did so but kept her coat on. She opened her single bag and brought out a bottle of sherry, which she had belatedly picked up at Fortnum and Mason. Looking at the tea tray with its plate of half-eaten biscuits and no sign of bread or jam or cakes, she began to wish she'd had the foresight to pick up a liberal food hamper.

Angela followed her glance. "Tea will be pretty Spartan, I'm afraid. Would you like some of the sherry, then?"

"I would very much like it," Honey said, handing over the bottle.

"How did you find me?" Angela asked when she had located two glasses and poured them each a portion.

"I talked to your friend John Leach in London."

"I suppose you've come to fetch me and take me home," Angela said, giving her aunt a sulky look.

"That's one reason, yes."

"And what other reasons, please?" Angela looked alarmed. "Is somebody ill, or . . . dead?"

"Not dead, darling. But Polly is very ill."

"I'm sorry to hear that. I liked her."

Angela turned away to put a kettle on an iron hook and swing it into the fire. Honey studied her niece. Angela was

32

thin and had taken no particular care with her clothes or hair. She wore a long green woolen skirt and three sweaters piled one on top of the other. A smudge of paint stained the collar of the outer sweater. The long black hair, parted in the center, was caught in a thick braid, but it looked as if a thorough brushing wouldn't be amiss. The heart-shaped face, so delicate, so perfectly balanced, was like white silk, and the huge gray eyes were grave. The mouth, full and potentially sensual, had become taut. Angela somehow managed to look like a fallen angel.

"Is she very ill? What happened?" Angela demanded. "Is it something terrible?"

"Charles has taken her to a sanatarium in the Laurentians."

"Then she has . . . tuberculosis?" Angela hesitated at the word. It was almost a death sentence.

"I'm afraid so, darling. Your grandfather and your father both doubted poor Doctor Glossop's original diagnosis. Papa insisted on getting several opinions, but in the long run it made no difference. Glossop was right. Polly is very ill."

"I'm sorry," Angela repeated. "Poor Father, he's had such bad luck with his wives, hasn't he?" She made a comic little *moue* to cover up her distress. "He must be lonely."

"He's very lonely. That's partly why I agreed to come here to talk to you."

"I think I'll have another sherry," Angela said, refilling her aunt's glass. "Going back to Pride's Court is something I haven't thought about seriously."

While Angela made tea, they talked about relatives. Michel, Honey's son, was living with his English wife and was involved in testing airplanes near London. Landry, her Uncle Fort's son, was at Oxford on a Rhodes Scholarship.

"My goodness, I *am* out of touch! If I'd known where Landry was, I could have visited him. I've never been to Oxford. Beau and I lead such introverted lives. We never go anywhere. How about the terrible twins? They must be out of Miss Greenshield's school by now, aren't they?"

She was referring to Fort's two daughters, Flora and Fenella.

"They've put the girls in a Toronto private school.

33

Bishop Strachan. It's considered to be academically acceptable, and your grandfather thought the English atmosphere would be good for them."

"I can't imagine any school keeping the twins in line," Angela said, rolling her eyes, "They frighten me to death half the time. They're so fey."

"Well, I don't see them, but from what I hear, you're quite right. They're strange."

"How did you find time to leave your newspaper to come over here?" Angela wanted to know. "You must be very busy."

"There was a conference of editors, so I took the opportunity when I could. I promised Charles I would talk to you. And I wanted to see Michel, too."

"I'm grateful for the visit, Aunt Miel. It's lonely here."

"Now, Angela, let's talk about this seriously," Honey said, glancing around the room as if it were a pesthouse. "How long have you been here alone? I understand Beau is in France."

"He's been gone about three weeks," Angela said, shrugging. "Beau has a commission from Sir Thomas Beecham to write a war symphony. He's visiting the battlefields. I suppose John told you that."

"He did mention it. Have you no servants, nobody to clean or shop, not even a companion?"

"I go to town with a neighbor sometimes for food. We have no money for servants. Life here is very simple."

"You mean you have no money at all?"

"A few pounds, I think. I earned some doing magazine illustrations and I've had an advance from a publisher for a children's book. But most of it's gone. I'm not good with money. Neither is Beau."

Over tea Honey became increasingly irritated.

"You can't live like this, Angela! When I think of your upbringing . . . Pride's Court . . ." She trailed off as if she could not begin to describe the situation. "You should have gone back to London while Beau was away."

"I can't afford to live in London. We get this place rent-free for looking after it."

"When is Beau coming back?"

"I have no idea. You know what he's like. He lived with you long enough. You must remember how vague he can be. Especially when he's composing. He hasn't written."

34

Angela picked up the cat rather absentmindedly and stroked it.

"I call her George," Angela said. "After George Sand."

"Really, Angela, you're behaving like a child. You're twenty-four years old, don't you realize that? Do you and Beau think you can behave like children forever? Do you both sleep and work in this—this *room*?"

"Yes, I'm afraid so. Does it seem terribly decadent?"

"*Stupid* is the word I'd use. And unnecessary."

"I'm sorry it offends you."

"I'm more worried than offended. You're going to get very ill. You look thin and tired."

"How is Father?" Angela said, changing the subject while she poured tea.

"He's well enough, but he misses you. That house must be very empty without any young people in it. When I was growing up, it was so different. After all, there were four of us, and our friends. And Mama entertained a lot. You must think about coming back, Angela. Living in this way is very selfish."

"I suppose it must look selfish, but I can't live without Beau. Though I do think he should have written . . . that he should have let me know how he is and told me his plans."

Honey saw the first signs of uncertainty in her niece and pressed her small advantage.

"You could paint at Pride's Court," she said. "And not worry about money."

"But I wouldn't have Beau."

"Do be reasonable! Beau's whole family is in Montreal, or around it. He'll come back. You could fix up a studio in the house, or even rent one somewhere else. Perhaps if you and Beau were separated for awhile, you might be able to decide what to do with your lives. You might be ready to marry, for example."

"Grandfather wouldn't like me to marry Beau. Look how he treated you when you married Uncle Armand! You've been an outcast ever since. Anyway, I hated living in Pride's Court when I was a child. I know the rest of the family thinks it's the most gorgeous house in the world, but not for me it isn't. I was lonely and frightened. After Mother died, I used to think she haunted the little sitting room beside my apartment. Did I ever tell you that?"

"Angela, that's terrible!"

"Well, it's true just the same. I used to go in there and sit in the cold waiting for her to speak to me. Sometimes I thought I felt her presence."

"I'd like to look at your paintings," Honey said abruptly, standing up. "Do you mind?"

"No, of course not. Go ahead if you like."

Honey walked over to the easel. As soon as she moved from the fire, she felt the intense cold in the room. She bent to move some canvases that were stacked against the wall. Many of the pictures were large, portraying dream-like landscapes with distant horizons filled with classical architecture in the Greek style. Here and there were odd-ments of machinery. Several figures inhabited each painting, women draped in togas with faces like cannibals and men in loincloths or nothing at all, with deep, burning eyes.

"I don't understand them," Honey said. "But they do make a person stop and think."

"I've worked hard here," Angela said. "Life has been wonderful in so many ways, but since Beau left for France, I feel lost. He seemed eager to get away by him-self. I suppose he needs his freedom," Angela confessed.

"All you creative people seem so eccentric," Honey said.

"I suppose we must seem that way to other people. But I'm not as selfish as Beau. I'd have given up my painting for him if he'd asked me. But Beau wouldn't give up any-thing at all for me, not a single thing."

"When he lived with me as a child, it didn't matter. I guess I didn't pay much attention. He was always studying his music, composing, and practicing the piano."

"I could leave here, I suppose, if I knew Beau would find me again. What if he came back suddenly and I was gone?" Angela said thoughtfully.

"We'll tell John Leach where we're staying in London. Beau will get in touch with him, surely. I'm at the Savoy, by the way. I couldn't get into the Ritz."

"I can't abandon the cat," Angela said suddenly.

"We'll take the cat with us. They allow small pets in the hotel. I've often seen women walking their poodles."

"I might get a letter from Beau in the morning," Angela said quickly. "And that might help me decide what to do."

"Why don't you think it over tonight?" Honey decided it

36

was time to retreat a little. Angela might react badly if she were pushed too hard.

"All right, I will. And thank you for coming all the way out here to tell me about Polly."

"I wanted to see you, darling. That's all right. But why don't you find out exactly how much money you have?"

Angela searched in a tin tea caddy for the remainder of her cash. She had exactly two pounds and three shillings. Honey was shocked. She could not imagine living in a cold, empty house with only two pounds between her and the world.

"Would you like to show me the bathroom?" Honey ventured. "I'm feeling rather tired. I suppose we'll have to find a place for me to sleep."

"I could bring a cot in here where it's warm," Angela said doubtfully, gazing at her elegant aunt. "And I'll show you where the bathroom is now. It works, but I'm afraid there's no hot water. Wait—I'll light another lamp, because we'll both need one."

Honey was almost overcome with dismay. The combination of washing in icy cold water and sleeping on a hard cot in this dreary room was almost too much for her. But she was more than ever determined to take Angela home before the child died of pneumonia or starvation, or both.

CHAPTER THREE

Honey awoke to stare at a strange ceiling. She did not recognize the white plasterwork pattern of elongated women springing out of pineapples. The effect of the design was so bizarre first thing in the morning—they looked like truncated mermaids with blind eyes—that it was some time before she could recall exactly where she was. Then it came to her. Cricket House. *Cold* Cricket House, she amended testily.

Angela was already up and clattering around the hearth. Honey could hear the welcome crackle of flames on dry wood. Soon a drift of warm air would change the frigid chemistry of the room, but she still felt resentful of the discomfort. Even in the borrowed flannel nightgown and woolen wrapper, she had shivered in the night.

"Oh, you're awake," Angela said as Honey threw off the blankets and got out of bed. "It's bound to warm up soon. I've got a good blaze going now."

"Did you learn to make fires in self-defense?"

"And bring in wood as well. Beau could never remember that wood had to be carried in from the shed. I've filled a copper boiler to heat water for you."

"That's kind of you, Angela." Honey felt guilty for being so impatient.

Sensing her aunt's displeasure, however, Angela was apologetic.

"I'm really sorry things are so messy, Aunt Miel, but you *did* come unannounced, you know."

"What difference would it have made to all *this* if you'd known I was arriving?" Honey asked, gesturing at the untidy room. "What possible difference?"

"None, I suppose."

"Whatever you decide, you'll have to do something about the way you live. You'll fall sick soon if you don't. You look very pale and thin."

Honey searched in her bag for the tube of Mer toothpaste, her brush, and a facecloth. She wished now that she had thought to bring a towel. The towels she had seen in the bathroom the night before made her uneasy. Regular laundry, she was certain, would be at the bottom of Angela's list of chores.

Over breakfast tea Honey managed to relax a little. Angela looked weary and dispirited. The lovely face was thin, and violet shadows swept under the huge gray eyes. Her fingers trembled as she spread marmalade rather absently on a piece of half-burned toast.

"Do you have a traveling suit?" Honey inquired.

"There must be something around that I can wear. If I decide to go," Angela said noncommittally. "I'll look upstairs later."

"I hope you've been thinking about what I said."

"All night. I couldn't sleep."

Angela left the table to feed the cat with water and a bit of toast. All the fresh milk was gone. The cat sniffed the bread, licked the butter, and then marched off haughtily.

After they had cleared away the breakfast things, Angela began to pick up paint tubes in a desultory way and put

38

them in a box. She examined brushes and soaked them in a glass jar of turpentine while Honey, having nothing better to do, tended the fire.

"What time does the postman come?"

"At noon. Perhaps I'll get a letter from Beau today and that will help me decide."

"Beau doesn't seem to worry about you half as much as you worry about him," Honey said with regret. Beau, after all, was her nephew on Armand's side of the family, and she felt some responsibility for introducing Angela to him in the first place. "If you don't hear from him today, will you come back to London?"

"I don't know what to do. Or what I really want," Angela said miserably.

"Stop considering Beau first."

"After all, you left Pride's Court for love," Angela said accusingly. "And you haven't regretted it. How can you be so harsh about what I'm doing?"

"That was quite different."

"Because you got married?"

"Partly, yes. Armand was never as selfish as Beau," Honey said. But there was a slight reservation in her voice as she said the words. They were true. But there had been another woman, once. And it had hurt her terribly when she found out.

"Anyway, I can't live in London," Angela said, reverting to an earlier argument. "What about my paintings? I'm preparing for a show. I can't leave them here, they'll mildew."

"We'll send somebody out to pack them. Meanwhile, you can stay in my suite at the Savoy."

"I haven't any money, you know that."

"Angela, don't be stupid!" Honey said, quite exasperated. "I'll look after the finances. When you make up your mind to return with me to Canada, I only have to cable your father for money. There's no problem."

"Was that part of the plan? You wave your magic wand and my life becomes beautiful again? Like a fairy-tale princess?"

"You are a Court," Honey said.

"Yes, I am a Court."

"Then I won't say more. Everything you could possibly

want is waiting for you if you leave this ridiculous way of life. If you leave this episode with Beau behind you."

"Episode! It's a bit more than that!"

"All right, it is. But Beau will come back to Montreal . . . you know that. His mother is there. The whole family is there. You'll see Beau again, no matter what you decide. When you're both more mature, perhaps you'll marry."

"Grandfather wouldn't like me to marry a Frenchman. He's never forgiven you, Aunt Miel."

"I'm sure he'd prefer marriage to *this*."

"Don't you remember how sick I was that first Christmas after Beau left Montreal for London? I couldn't paint, or eat, or sleep. I was going mad. All because I missed him so terribly—"

"You're older now and you've lived with him for two years. Surely you can see life is more real, more difficult than you thought?"

"Yes, it is a bit," Angela admitted.

"Why don't you look for a carrying basket for the cat?"

"And what if Beau arrives one day after I leave here?"

"He can find us. We'll tell John Leach our plans. Beau is sure to contact him."

Angela found a picnic basket with a lid for the cat and after a quick search in her closets located a winter suit, which, with a little pressing, would be good enough for the journey into town.

"Do you think this will get me by your doorman?" Angela asked. "I have so few clothes. I never dress."

"I'll press the suit if you heat the iron," Honey offered. "And you can finish packing your paints."

When the noon post arrived, there was a letter, but it was not from Beau. Honey could see that at once by the gloomy look on Angela's face. The envelope was long and bore an embossed crest upon the back flap. Angela read the handwriting without recognizing it.

"I don't know who it's from," she said. "But it has a London postmark."

"Well, open it. It looks very interesting."

"Perhaps it's from some friend of Beau's . . . with news," Angela said. But after reading a few lines she exclaimed, "But this is amazing, Aunt Miel! It's from Julia. You know, my mother's mother! I've never seen her, of course, but Mother used to talk about her. She sounded so

40

worldly, so rich and romantic. She's in London and she wants to see me."

Angela handed the letter to Honey. Looking at the frail tracery on the thick linen paper, Honey could almost see the aging, elegant writer.

My Dear Angela—[it began]

I have only just found out you are in England. Quite by accident—a mutual friend, Sir Thomas Beecham. Imagine our surprise when we discovered we both had a connection with you! I must see you as soon as possible. After all, you are Venetia's daughter and my only grandchild.

Are you like your mother, I wonder? She was so lovely but so impractical. I long to hear about her life in the wilderness, poor darling. It was all so unfortunate!

Do come and see me at my town house if you can. I shall be here two weeks longer. But if not, my country place. I want to hear about poor dear Venetia so much. Did you get her jewels, darling? She had some pretty ones.

I'm quite lonely as the earl has left me to run away to Argentina with a Parisian dress designer. Can you imagine the horror of that? But so like Twickenham. He never did have sense about women. Please write and say you'll visit . . .

> Julia

Angela began to giggle.

"What are you laughing at?" Honey asked.

"That bit about the wilderness. How they'd love that in Montreal!"

"You must visit your grandmother, Angela," Honey said encouragingly. "She sounds fascinating."

"Yes, I'd like to. But there's no letter from Beau."

"Perhaps you could look for a decent piece of luggage," Honey suggested quickly. "One bag will do for now."

When the big Daimler rolled up the driveway at last, Honey felt relief. She hurried out to inform the driver that there would be two passengers for Taunton. She entrusted him with stowing the cat in the basket in the backseat.

"I'll be out with the other passenger in a moment," Honey said. "Wait, please. I'll find out what's keeping her."

She had left Angela to lock up the house. She found her

still in the drawing room leaning on the piano, her fingers clutching a piece of manuscript on which the beginnings of a musical score had been scratched.

"It's a serenade. He was writing it for me," Angela said, beginning to cry over the piece of paper. "Oh, Aunt Miel, I don't think I can go. He might come back tomorrow."

"And he might not. If he does, he'll find you, my dear. Stop worrying and come along. The driver is waiting."

Angela allowed herself to be led at last to the car. Once inside, she flung herself into one corner and began to weep over the crushed manuscript. When they boarded the train, she was still sniffling. Several people stared at her while Honey searched for an empty compartment. Halfway to London, however, Angela calmed herself and began to tidy up. The thought of arriving at the Savoy in such a disheveled state terrified her so that by the time they reached Victoria Station, she was at least presentable.

For her part, Honey felt as if a tremendous load had been lifted from her shoulders once they were established in her suite in the hotel. There were adjoining bedrooms and a pleasant sitting room. When a tea tray with sherry arrived, Honey thought (as she had often done in the past) how civilized London was. It always seemed to put things right when one came to London. A small miracle.

CHAPTER FOUR

Angela had dutifully replied to Julia's note and had received by hand an invitation to tea on Upper Grosvenor Street. Honey quite rightly pointed out that Angela had nothing to wear for such an occasion, and so the shopping began.

For three days Angela allowed herself to be trailed through Bond Street shops and after that, Harrod's. Honey was clearly uninterested in shopping (her own clothes were usually made for her, and so she was more accustomed to patient fittings than to the wear and tear of in-store buying), but she was determined to see Angela outfitted properly.

"She's probably very grand," Honey said of Julia. "That's what the family understood, anyway."

"You don't think the earl left her penniless, then?"

"I wouldn't think so. Her letter doesn't sound poor. She's probably as rich as ever."

"I'm nervous about meeting her."

"Whether you are or not, you can't allow her to see you looking so tatty. The family would be appalled if you did. She's bound to say it's because you're a colonial. That isn't fair, since you had lovely clothes when you lived in Montreal."

"Clothes. What do clothes mean?" Angela said with a shrug.

They had spread Angela's few things out upon the bed during this early discussion, and Honey had waved her hand over them scornfully.

"This is the result of living in England with no money. Your underthings, Angela, are quite impossible!"

"Money does make a difference, doesn't it?" Angela said with a sigh. She could recall the days when all her clothes had indeed been fine, but that had ceased to matter long ago. Now she stared out of the window at the Thames below. It came to her that she would like to paint some river scenes. The traffic patterns were fascinating and the people seemed to have stepped straight out of a stage play. She could use some of the color in her own work. Her attention was brought back forcibly by Honey's voice.

"Naturally money is important," Honey was saying. "Without it human beings are degraded. It's impossible to be spiritually uplifted when you're dirty or hungry or cold. I've never believed those stories of martyrs for a minute."

"Beau never seemed to care what I wore," Angela said.

"All very noble. You can paint in rags if you like, darling, but there's no need to live like a gypsy when you've finished work."

"All right, Aunt Miel, if you want me to, I'll buy some clothes, but only because of the family. I don't want to shock Julia. But I haven't actually decided to go back to Montreal, you know. I hope you haven't cabled Father for money."

"I haven't cabled anybody yet. I saw some pretty French lingerie in a small shop on Bond Street . . . crepe de Chine inset with georgette, beautiful handwork. And your hair, Angela. Perhaps a trim? It desperately needs shaping. It's so thick, darling."

They finished that first crucial chat on a rather uncertain note. Honey mentioned that there was no use looking at furs in London, since the best furs were in Canada, and Angela quickly caught her up.

"I haven't agreed to return to Pride's Court. I won't need an expensive fur if I stay here in London."

Honey dropped the matter, but by the time Angela took a taxicab to Upper Grosvenor Street to see the countess, she was properly coiffed and gowned to meet the situation.

As she rang the bell, she glanced quickly down the row of classic white houses. It was a quiet, sedate street. So quiet she could hear the bell echoing inside the house and then the footsteps of the butler as he approached. The elderly servant who answered her ring was six feet of cold disdain. She told him who she was. "Lady Twickenham is expecting you, madame," he said. But he made it clear that she somehow fell short of the mark. Angela followed him up the stairs to the second-floor drawing room as if she were a docile child. Patrician faces stared at her from ancestral portraits, and she wondered if some of them were her own forebears or if they were all Twickenhams. She was shown into a mellow room of golds, browns, and soft beiges, highlighted by bronzes and warmed by massive vases of fresh flowers, so that the whole atmosphere was a caramel wash of calm.

Her eyes were drawn to the woman standing in the center of the room, posed carefully next to one of the marble-topped boulle tables.

Julia, Countess of Twickenham, was tall and slim and straight as a ruler. No hint of approaching age was allowed to bend her shoulders in the slightest degree. She was sheathed in a gray silk tea gown that matched her eyes as well as the delicious petal-curl of her chrysanthemum-cut hair. Pale, unlined skin was still stretched tightly over high cheekbones, and the once-sensual lips were precise and determined. Her nose was still as chiseled as a sculptor's creation. She wore long pearl pendants to accent the shape of her face, and a triple strand of giant pearls wound around her neck. She was at the same time startling and sad, a polished and well-preserved antique.

Face to face with her maternal grandmother at last, Angela was merely a variation on the same theme. Her own hair had been cut and curled around her white face.

Her gray pansylike eyes performed the same reflecting trick so cleverly rehearsed by her grandmother, they reflected the gray wool of her gown. Her nose was almost identical, but Angela's mouth was still soft, unembittered by time. They stared at each other for a few silent moments, transfixed by surprise and mutual pleasure.

"Venetia!" Julia cried involuntarily.

"It's Angela."

"Yes, yes, of course. Just for a moment I was confused. You look so like your mother."

"Everyone says that."

"My dear, I could stare and stare. It takes one's breath away just to look at you. Your mother was like that, too, you know. It was all so sad . . . so unfortunate that she went to that awful place. She was so unhappy there . . ."

"It wasn't the place, you know. It was her disfigurement that made her unhappy," Angela amended.

"Such a waste, such a beauty," Julia went on, ignoring the correction. "She ought to have married the prince of Wales! Instead, she threw herself away on a colonial nobody!"

They had somehow managed to sum up Venetia's tragedy in a few words: her exquisite beauty, her unsuitable marriage to Charles Court, her illness and disfigurement and subsequent seclusion and suicide. It was all encapsulated in those few sentences, in the very tone of their voices, but then, they both knew Venetia's story and there was no need to go over every detail, to extract more from the pool of pain.

"Well, Father isn't exactly a nobody. The Courts are very powerful over there, you know. Still, it wasn't a comfortable background for me as a child. Long after she died, I used to believe that I could sense her presence in Pride's Court, particularly in one room. I'd sit there in that cold room waiting for her to speak to me."

"My poor darling child!" exclaimed the countess sympathetically.

They spoke as if they had picked up a conversation dropped only a few moments before. The air was infused with complete rapport, and no long, dreary histories were needed to patch together Angela's story. They had both wept for Venetia many years before, and it only remained

45

to make up for the time they had been apart. Julia moved forward gracefully to take Angela's hand in her own.

"Seeing you is a miracle. If only I'd found you sooner, my dear, but I didn't know. How could I? Nobody told me you had come over here and I couldn't possibly go to Canada." She pronounced *Canada* as if it were some obscure African protectorate seldom mentioned by civilized people. "And that ridiculous grandfather of yours, Simon Court, wouldn't receive me. Something about my being divorced. It was all so terribly difficult."

"He's very stuffy. But in a way, I'd like to see you two together," Angela said, grinning for the first time since she had come into the room. "You'd be a shocker, Grandmother."

Julia looked startled.

"Don't call me Grandmother! Call me Julia, please. Your mother always called me Julia except when she was angry. We were more like friends than mother and daughter. I suppose I never felt much like a mother."

"I'm sure she loved you very much."

"I suppose she did. I was always busy when she was a child. Perhaps too busy to spend much time with her. I always had a new husband, it seemed." Julia sighed.

In this regard, Angela thought silently, she was not much like Julia. She could not imagine loving anybody but Beau.

"We'll have tea and talk about your life, Angela," Julia said. "I imagine you're much like your mother, rather vague about your arrangements. I had to think for her, you see. Still, I was never sure she did the right thing when she accepted Charles Court."

She rang for the butler and ordered refreshments, then indicated that Angela should sit beside her on the sofa before the fire. Without further fencing she announced that she had found Angela's whereabouts quite by accident when talking with "Beecham," as she called Sir Thomas. Beecham was enchanting, of course, but quite mad, and they had both been absolutely amazed to discover the connection Angela had with both.

"From what Beecham said, Angela," Julia began seriously once she had prepared her tea exactly as she liked it, "you must give up this living arrangement immediately. It's totally unsuitable. Quite without style or

46

meaning. It won't do at all. I'm astonished that Sir Simon would tolerate such a liaison."

"He didn't. He disowned me," Angela said.

"Good. Now, all you have to do is repent and we can fix it all up. Or if you don't want to go back there—frankly, I can't imagine what they *do* in Montreal—you can live with me."

"That's kind of you, but—"

"I can't think why great beauties like you and your mother persist in throwing yourselves away. I never did. It's incomprehensible. No, I admit I made too many marriages, but I always had a good settlement and I didn't find myself in a disastrous situation at any time. Milo has left me now—I daresay I mentioned that in my letter—but I've plenty of money, and the position is unassailable. Those things last, my dear, but passion never does. Take my word, Angela, and don't indulge yourself in passion. It's like a drug."

"I'm sure you're right," Angela agreed.

"I've not only lived it, I've watched my friends. Men always take advantage of women if they can. When Beau gets tired of you, *his* reputation won't suffer. People just laugh and say that's the way men are. But you will look like a fool and you'll be hurt. Believe me, Angela, you must end this liaison quickly before any more damage is done."

Over tea Julia went on at length in the same vein. She asked Angela to consider living with her at Much Hadham, her Sussex estate. "Twickenham didn't want to live there, so I took it over. The old fool thinks he can live like a king in Argentina with this tart, and perhaps he can. But I prefer to live among civilized people, not aborigines. I spent a month in South America many years ago, and it's very rough. The men are impossible. There is no decent food. There are no theaters. There are no roads. It's quite dangerous. Absolutely filled with foreigners of every kind."

Angela found her grandmother entertaining as well as fascinating. Julia promised to introduce her to several eligible men (wedding bells rang in her voice as she described several candidates) and said that she personally had no worries about money.

"Milo was generous. Did you take your mother's jewels?

She had some quite good ones, you know. You ought to look into it. If Charles gave them to his second wife, you must get them back. Men have to be watched."

"In a way, I think I ought to see Father. Now that Polly is sick, he's lonely. That's why Aunt Miel came to get me, really."

"Oh, you can go home and visit, that's quite all right," Julia said generously. "But then you sail straight back to London. We can live in both houses, I keep them up anyway. And there's always Paris, and the Riviera if you like."

Later in the conversation she became nostalgic and sentimental. She wanted to hear about Venetia's death in the fire that swept through a wing of Pride's Court, and later about Charles's second wife, Polly.

"Polly came from a good family, I believe, but she was quite plain. Poor Charles." And that was Julia's summing up of the situation.

Angela stayed two hours and left her grandmother with a firm promise to come to dinner the following Tuesday, before she considered sailing.

"Bring your aunt along, too. I daresay I can find a partner for her at table. There are plenty of unattached fellows around. I long to meet her. Everybody said she was such a romantic girl, and I suppose she was, running off and leaving all that behind. But *I* wouldn't have done it."

Beau Dosquet dismissed the taxicab and walked the last six blocks to Waterloo Bridge. Through the gathering mist of early evening he could see the soft star-pools of street lamps in the distance and, nearer, the turbulent shape of traffic as it wound along the banks of the Thames. He moved with his customary impatience, leaning slightly forward as if willing himself to reach his destination before it was physically possible.

The combination of soft dark hat, long flowing cape, and angular face with its slanted green eyes, aristocratic nose, and sensual mouth gave him a theatrical air. He might have been taken for a famous stage star or dissolute poet rather than a struggling unknown composer. He was never conscious, however, of his effect upon others. Most people (and there were a few notable exceptions) were unimportant to him, merely part of the landscape.

He crossed the road swiftly to reach a spot near the end of the bridge, where he was to rendezvous with Angela. He had deliberately chosen the place to isolate her from family influence. Much better to meet Angela outside on somewhat foreign ground than in the easy smugness of the Savoy Lounge or the suite she shared with Aunt Miel.

As he made his way through the moist half-darkness, he saw Angela suddenly materialize out of the fog, a vision of the heart. The old familiar desire struck him like a pain in the chest. For weeks he had thought of nothing but his music (sleep, food, drink, even love had been ignored). All impulses of the flesh had been sublimated to the drive of creation. Now, every hunger surfaced at the sight of Angela.

Desire fought with anger. It was obvious that he and Angela belonged together. He had known that since they were children, since the first day they had met in the nursery of Aunt Miel's house on St.-Denis. He had been playing Chopin when Angela first walked in—he could recall exactly the way the light from the high windows fell on her dark hair and the way she stood transfixed by his music. Her face had not been so lovely—it was imperfectly formed because she was so young—but the huge gray eyes held reservoirs of wonder and curiosity and imagination, even then.

He knew almost instantly that Angela was the only woman he would ever love. He had (it seemed) known her forever. He had understood her without sharing a single thought—as if their minds and hearts were linked together. Why, then, had she foolishly run away from the house in Devon, why had she fled back to the luxury of money and family position? Why was she so impatient? Surely, as a fellow artist she could comprehend his single-minded concern with creating music?

He hurried forward to meet her, raising his voice against the intrusion of city sounds.

"Angela!"

His voice carried, cut through the wet air. She halted a moment and then threw herself toward him. Her huge eyes were like bruised petals, her mouth was open, the full lips

49

a pink sulk. Her whole facial expression was so familiar, so desirable, that he shivered.

"Beau!"

Her voice was soft, warm with the old cadence of love.

She will always love me, he thought fiercely as he put his arms around her. *Always. She can't change that.*

They clung together paying no attention to people passing by. Then she pulled herself loose to look into his face, to offer the tentative, weary smile of a person who feels used.

"Let's walk across the bridge," Angela suggested.

"If you like. I suppose this is as good a place as any to talk."

He pulled her arm through his possessively, his gloved fingers intertwined with hers. He could feel her body warmth through the heavy cloth, could feel the flow of life.

"How was your tour of France?" she asked.

"Worthwhile. I felt something . . ." he shrugged.

"Have you seen Beecham since you got back?"

"Yes, I told him all about my tour. I did spend quite a bit of time roaming about on the battlefields—they're cleaning them up now, of course, planting grass, putting up headstones. I caught cold, it was terribly damp."

"You don't take care of yourself!" she protested automatically. "I suppose you haven't eaten—"

"Oh, hell, I'm fine. Sir Thomas was most encouraging. He's subsidizing me while I actually write the symphony, and he's promised to premiere it right here in London."

"That's wonderful, Beau!"

"I got a check from him, too. John Leach said I should insist. You know how eccentric Beecham is. He's quite likely to forget the entire project in a month."

"I know. What about the music, though? Have you begun to write anything?"

"A little. I have one of the main themes, at least . . ." He trailed off inadequately. He could never discuss the actual labor of writing music. Instead he looked down at her and noticed that she wore a jacket he had never seen before. It had a mink collar. She had been shopping with Court money, he thought angrily. He glared at the fur as if it were alive and could grasp his meaning.

"I'm sorry you went down to Devon first. Did you get my note?"

"I got your note," he flung out, his fingers clenching around hers so that it hurt. "Naturally I went down to Cricket House as soon as I'd completed my business in London. I had no idea you'd come back from the country."

She quickly sensed the violence in him, could trace the spread of growing anger. Even in the night shadows his face looked pinched and wild. An explosion was near, she knew, because it was impossible for Beau to do anything, even become enraged, without complete dedication.

"I'm sorry you had the trip for nothing. I came back with Aunt Miel—"

"It was stupid."

"It was stupid of you not to write!" she flared. "I had no money left. I was lonely out there, and cold. It's a horrible house to be alone in."

"You have your work, haven't you? If you want to be taken for a serious painter, then behave like one. Do you need a nursemaid? Stop acting like a child. I had no money to send, so how could I have given you any?"

"You never have money. I never have money. I'm tired of it and I'm ill. I need comfort for a change instead of cold-water baths and tea in cracked cups. Aunt Miel says I'll get really ill if I don't change my habits."

"*Aunt Miel says?*" he leaned heavily on the words. "So you're back taking orders from the family, are you?"

"Can't you understand anything? I was alone, I was cold, I was hungry. I was living on tea and biscuits. Don't you understand I don't want to live like that?"

"I only understand we belong together," he said stubbornly.

"Try to see it my way, Beau!" She wondered if it were possible for him to live in a dream where realities did not penetrate. It was all so clear to *her*.

"You knew I'd be back soon," he said next.

"The only thing I knew was that you didn't care enough to write a single letter. Or to tell me how you were. Or to ask how *I* was! I could have died out there and you wouldn't have known. I hate being alone and cold."

"It was only temporary. You knew that. But you couldn't wait for me, could you? You had to let one of *them* talk you into leaving me. I expected it. I just didn't think it would be Aunt Miel. I didn't think she'd be Judas."

"Father asked Aunt Miel to bring me home. Back to Montreal. Back to Pride's Court."

"She's come to buy you off. To make you live like *them*."

They were the enemy. The powerful Courts, who had separated Beau from Angela. Unless he acted, they were about to succeed again.

"I'm eating properly, sleeping in a warm bed, taking hot baths, wearing clean clothes, if that's what you mean by being bought off."

"And shopping for trinkets."

"It's nice to be warm."

"You don't need fur to be warm."

"I do need coal to be warm. Can't you see that? Aunt Miel was worried when she saw me. She says I'll be sick again—"

"You've forgotten how sick you were when you lived in Montreal and I was in London. All the comforts of Pride's Court didn't help you. You almost starved to death while your precious family fed you everything money could buy. You have a short memory, Angela."

"Your memory is even shorter. You can't remember to write a single letter in three weeks. You don't care a damn about anybody but yourself and your music. You aren't real."

"For God's sake, Angela, *you're* not real. Do you think *this* is real?"

He stopped abruptly and grabbed the mink collar of her jacket, tearing out a piece of fur. She began to weep. It had happened. The thing she feared most. She was giving in to him again, he was weakening her resolve just as Aunt Miel had predicted. She ought to have refused to see him. He always had this effect on her, making the most ordinary comforts of life seem sinful. Making everybody else in the world seem frivolous, while only he, Beau, understood the true values of life. She ought never to have left the safety of the hotel.

"Stop crying and listen to me. You want to paint . . . you want to paint marvelous things . . . to reach into your mind and bring out beautiful fantasies. Do you think you can do it in a cosy, conventional, prissy place among that bunch of moneygrubbers you call a family? Money is all they know. Tea at precisely five thirty every afternoon, appointments at the bank, to discuss which piece of what company your grandfather, or your father, or one of your uncles will buy next. They're straw men and you know it! Propping themselves up with their whiskies and their clubs—"

"There has to be something in between," she cried tearfully. "I don't see how feeling cold can produce good painting, or good music either, for that matter."

They had come to a full stop on the bridge. A strong wind was sweeping up the mist and carrying it out of sight.

"It's a hell of a lot more conducive than wearing Paris rags. I know *that*! Do you honestly think you'll paint better because you ride in a Rolls-Royce? Or because you have an expensive horse in the barn? What in hell's gone wrong with you? We settled all this when we were children."

"We only settled that you're incredibly selfish."

He grabbed her shoulder roughly, peered down into her face, and said in a voice boiling with anger, "Will you, for Christ's sake, listen before you make a fatal mistake? Think of your own mother! Was she happy living in that huge house with all the money, the clothes, the food, the wine— was she happy? She killed herself, that's how happy she was. They're all unhappy, every one of them. They produce nothing and they understand nothing but money. In the old days you used to sneak away from them, over to Aunt Miel's house to paint in the nursery. Aunt Miel seemed to understand. After all, she ran away from Pride's Court herself. Now, she's changed too. But you had more sense as a child than you have now. Going back to the Courts is death."

She trembled desperately. Part of her wanted to surrender to Beau because she loved him so much. She looked up into his eyes and felt the same stab of longing she always felt when they were close. Her fingers itched to touch his face, and she could taste his kisses without actually putting her lips on his. He was passionate, eager, the dream made flesh after all the lonely weeks. Why could the two of them not agree on a reasonable way of life? What was this stupid argument about, anyway?

As if to reply to her unspoken question, he began to kiss her. The wind was so chilling that her teeth rattled, but inside her head she heard again her clever grandmother's urbane voice telling her that life with Beau would end disastrously and that she would regret it forever if she went on living with him.

Beau pressed his cold cheek against hers and whispered in her ear, "Come back with me, Angela, and forget about your family. We'll make music and love. You'll paint wonderful things. Life will be better——"

"Not to Cricket House. I won't go back to the country." She could feel her tears drying in the harsh wind.

"All right, back to London. You can paint. John will help us find a place to live. A studio for you."

"My paintings are all packed and ready to ship." (She was wavering. She was actually listening to what Beau was saying.)

"That doesn't matter. We'll unpack them. I'll arrange a show for you, you don't need your grandmother for that. Angela, you know I can't live without you. Stop being such a fool . . ."

"And you wouldn't leave me again?"

It was so very close. Everything she wanted was so very close. Beau only had to say the words.

"I won't leave for a while, no," Beau said hurriedly. "I can't promise how long I'll be in London. You know I can't commit myself too far ahead."

He had become vague again. His eyes were lost to her as he stared over her shoulder at the river.

"Beau, let's get married and settle it. We're both twenty-four years old. We're not children any longer."

This was her true surrender. She had tossed away all the good advice from Aunt Miel and from Julia, her grandmother. She wanted only to listen to Beau, to his pleasant voice, and to feel his warm kisses (what could they know about that, anyway?), to have his strong hands on her cheek, to hear his music, to share his talent. She wanted to be first to hear this new symphony, the poignant melodies of songs unwritten.

"We can't marry yet, Angela. You know that."

His voice was cold, almost as cold as the November wind. She recognized that formidable retreat, the way he would disappear from her field of influence. She had watched him do it so often in the past. He would, at those times, become unreachable. Then the glow faded, the light was snuffed out of their mutual space.

"Why can't we get married? It's only a year before I inherit the money Grandmother Court left. I'll be twenty-five then, and we can manage just fine—"

"It isn't the money."

"Oh. Then nothing has changed."

"I have to be free. It would be a handicap to marry. We're both serious artists, darling, and we don't need to worry about this middle-class nonsense. I refuse to be tied to other people's rules, you know that. What good did marriage do my mother?"

That was the key. He was caught in the trap of his *own* family. His mother had had an affair with a farmhand while she was still married and Beau was their child. When the truth came out, the family was shattered. Even though Beau's mother and the farmhand eventually married, Beau did not forgive either of them. He carried the shame of it with him still, and the word *marriage* drove him into a rage. What point was there in marriage (he asked) when it could so easily be destroyed and bring so much pain?

"Marriage is mindless," Beau said now.

"Oh, stop living in the past!" she cried.

"The past is part of me. I can't forget."

She had lost him. His face was hard, and he did not seem to see her. The flow of love between them had stopped as if it had been turned off. Again she heard her grandmother's voice urging her to be sensible, to restore her dignity as a woman, to cherish her beauty, her position, and—yes—her money as well. Her grandmother saying, "I don't understand why great beauties like you and your mother persist in throwing yourselves away! *I* never did."

"Don't turn away from me like that," Beau said, but she was already leaving him. He reached out to grasp her wrist, but she was quicker and began to run along the wet pavement.

Beau took after her, crying, "You don't know the truth about that old grandfather of yours! I just found out from Beecham. Your grandfather deliberately created the scholarship I won just to get me out of Montreal. Do you realize what a lethal old fraud he is? Do you hear me, Angela?"

His voice sailed off in a gust of wind as she flung herself into a taxicab. The door slammed. She gave the driver the name of her hotel, and he started up just as Beau came alongside.

"Did you hear what I said about that old pirate? Did you hear?"

She looked straight ahead, not letting herself worry about the fact that he was in the roadway and might get run over. She steeled herself not to look back.

Beau ran across the bridge looking for another cab, but it had begun to rain and every one that came by was occupied. Angela's taxicab had actually disappeared from sight, and he knew she could easily reach the Savoy before he could catch up.

For the remainder of her stay in London, in the few days before the *Lady Lydia* sailed for Halifax, Angela accepted no telephone calls. She tore up Beau's letters unread. And within a week she was on the Atlantic, her face pale and set, the light in her eyes completely dead. She spent the days walking the deck wearing her aunt's mink overcoat and huddled into it, as if it would protect her from everything she feared. The coat was a reminder of home. She was going back to the vast reaches of Pride's Court—to all the ritual, luxury, splendor, pomposity, and, above all, the indestructible security of the family fold.

CHAPTER FIVE

When she first caught sight of Pride's Court after her two-year absence, Angela felt a slight tingle of apprehension. As a child she had disliked the huge house, perhaps even hated it at times, but today she could not deny that in the chill November afternoon, its outlines softened by a thin drift of snow, Pride's Court was truly magnificent.

Even the lighted windows seemed to bid her welcome. The four-story center tower was as impressive as ever, offering, as it did, a view of the St. Lawrence across the rooftops of the lower town. Each wing angled off with graceful balance and disappeared into the depths of a silent winter garden. It might have been a fairy-tale castle.

When she rode through the heavy iron gates, sitting beside her father in the black Rolls-Royce, the house seemed to be waiting for her return. She knew her father was immensely pleased by her decision to come back. He hadn't spoken much on the drive from Windsor Station (she had taken a boat to Portland, Maine, because the St. Lawrence was frozen, and then a train into Montreal), but she could feel his pleasure and his anticipation that she would renew the life and youth of Pride's Court.

Actually he hadn't changed much, Angela thought, although perhaps he was a bit heavier. He'd grown a thick, military moustache, too, which made him look more like Sir Simon. The brilliant blue Court eyes were sad. *He's thinking of Polly,* Angela decided, *or perhaps he's going back even farther, and I remind him of my mother. Yes, that's likely it.*

Charles got out of the car underneath the spread of the limestone portico. A strong wind blew snow against his face, sprinkling his hat brim with tiny diamonds. The door burst open and Dodgson, Sir Simon's chauffeur, sprang out into the cold muffled in an enormous overcoat.

"Put the bags just inside and then Peters can take them up. You can put the car around, Dodgson."

"Right, sir. Welcome home, Miss Angela."

"Thank you, Dodgson, I'm glad to be here."

Despite the gust of wind and whirl of snow that blew them through the door and into the reception hall, Angela realized that she truly meant what she said. It was good to be home. She drew in her breath sharply at the beauty of the rooms that stretched out before her. In earlier days she had been too close to the house, too deeply involved in her own problems to appreciate the proportions, the exquisite details. Now she knew, at least for a brief spell, why so many family members adored the place.

It was as if she were seeing the house for the first time: the eight perfect walls of the reception hall, with the four niches housing pure white marble statues. Beyond that first room was the Great Hall itself, with its high vaulted ceiling and huge Turkey carpets. Over the grand staircase hung the portrait of great-grandfather Cathmor Court watching over all of them. One almost expected a flourish of trumpets upon entering.

Peters took her coat and brushed off some snowflakes. Charles removed his own coat and hat and handed them over. After Peters had disappeared in the direction of the cloakroom, Charles said, "We're having a small family dinner tonight to celebrate your return, Angela. Just your Uncle Fort, Aunt Sydney, Uncle Geoff, Aunt Mary, and Mildred. She's the only one of your cousins in the city, I'm afraid. Everyone else is away."

"Are we having fatted calf?"

"No, I think Mrs. Kennedy said something about saddle of lamb."

"Oh, Father," Angela said, smiling in spite of herself. He had no sense of humor and she ought not to have been so frivolous. Still, she was glad no more family members were coming to dinner. Things would be difficult enough as it was; no doubt they regarded her as a "scarlet" woman.

She and her father had not moved when Peters returned to pick up her luggage, and she watched him climb the broad sweep of marble stairs, a bag in each hand. Suddenly she felt tired. But there was still so much to do—a gown to have pressed for dinner, unpacking, tea.

"Is Grandfather home now?"

"I doubt it. He works late. So you won't have to brave the lion's den yet, my dear."

"Thank goodness! I feel tired after that train ride. I think I'll need a good bracer before I face up to Grandfather."

Charles patted her shoulder and gave her an understanding smile.

"How would it be if I have a word with Mrs. Kennedy and ask her to send your tea up on a tray? Then you won't have to come down before dinner. Perhaps you'd like a whisky along with it?"

"Father, that would be marvelous! Such luxury. I'd forgotten what it was like to be civilized. Do you think Mrs. Kennedy will mind?"

"Leave her to me. And when you do see your grandfather, don't make any silly remarks, Angela. After all, he's seventy-nine years old. Though I often find that hard to believe. No matter what he says, he's delighted to have you back. Remember that."

"Don't worry, I haven't the strength to bait him. I could never stand up to him, anyway. I'm not at all like Aunt Miel, you know. *She's* not afraid of him, but I always was."

"Honey was always a rebel," Charles said, his tone fond when he spoke of his sister. "Anyway, let's not think about the past but go on with the present. We'll begin again."

"All right. I'll promise to behave." She reached up to kiss his cheek. "And I *am* glad to be back. I guess I did miss Pride's Court, after all."

At precisely eight o'clock Angela stood on the landing of the grand staircase and looked down. Her relatives clustered below around Sir Simon. They all looked up expectantly as she appeared. *For all the world as if they think I'll be a freak,* Angela thought, stifling a giggle.

Her grandfather looked quite fit, even from this distance. His eyes were bright with anticipation, his white beard was perfectly trimmed as always, and his suit a dream of careful tailoring. For a man of seventy-nine he was truly a wonder.

Uncle Geoffrey looked a little more smug and self-assured than she remembered, but Aunt Mary was as mousy-brown as ever. As for Aunt Sydney, she was still a Rosetti model in her flowing olive-green gown and soft, light-colored hair. Uncle Fort, still a bit devilish-looking, wore his beard shorter and more narrowly trimmed. Behind all the others stood her cousin, Mildred, Geoffrey and Mary's daughter.

Mildred had not (unfortunately) inherited the blue Court eyes nor their customary intense coloring. Rather she favored her mother, so her hair was an undistinguished brown, her eyes a hazel shade, and her whole frame rather awkward. She wore a plaid woolen dinner dress that did absolutely nothing to enhance an already dull appearance.

Oh, dear, Angela thought sadly. *Poor Mildred. She's plainer than any woman has a right to be.*

As Sir Simon Court stood at the foot of the stairs looking up, he had an alarming sensation of déjà vu, as if this scene had taken place before. Angela proceeded down the stairs, extraordinarily beautiful. (Why, *why* had this lovely girl thrown herself away on that despicable Frenchman? What was the absurd reasoning behind these family defections?) It could have been another night, twenty-five years before, when Angela's mother, Venetia, made her first appearance at Pride's Court. Angela had unwittingly chosen a cerulean silk gown with a finely pleated skirt. She wore her mother's sapphire pin at the throat. (Venetia, too, had been a vision in blue and wore the same jewel.) Sir Simon heard Charles gasp beside him. It was uncanny.

The way the light from the huge chandelier struck the silky skin, picked out the gray shadowed eyes, and touched the thick dark curls with a shimmer of light. The house fell quiet as Angela reached the bottom step. Then suddenly everything came to life again, and the bizarre moment passed.

Sir Simon, oddly moved, bent to kiss his granddaughter.

"My dear, we're all happy to have you back."

Angela threw her arms around him and hugged him. Tears were close, but she blinked them back. Just for a moment she forgot about her grandfather's tyrannies, his vengeful nature, even the newly discovered fact that he had parted her from Beau by creating a false music scholarship. She kissed all her relatives enthusiastically, even her cousin Mildred. Then Sir Simon offered Angela his arm and they went in to dinner, followed by the others.

Seated in the long, green-carpeted dining room with its panels of English country scenes and wide fireplace, where a twelve-foot log crackled comfortably, Angela stared at the Court coat of arms to remind herself that she was truly home. Yes, there it was (erasing any lingering doubts), two golden lions salient, red and white shield, three crossed lances under a crested helmet. She was back in the family. The cold Devon landscape receded and almost vanished. Life with Beau became dreamlike: Perhaps it had never happened. She was succumbing to the vast security of the Courts. To the warmth, the comfort, even the power.

Sir Simon had placed Angela on his right so that he could chat with her during the meal.

"Your cousins are up in northern Ontario," he explained. "Noel travels back and forth between the city and Kirkland Lake, but Simon is living up there. He loves it!" (He was referring to Geoffrey's two sons.)

"Are you in mining, then?" Angela had lost track of the varied Court interests in her two-year absence.

"Didn't you know? We've staked a big claim on the shore of Kirkland Lake. Gold. There's a fortune in the ground. We're having a bit of trouble with our neighbors, but the boys are looking into it."

His eyes glittered with a fresh challenge.

"How is Simon?" Angela asked, thinking of her young cousin's condition when she had left for England. At that time Simon II had been suffering from shell shock and spent a great deal of time in the hospital. His war service had left him seriously disabled.

"The rough life up there is good for him. Can't say I'd like it, especially in this weather. Gets even colder than here, you know, and the wind is vicious, they say. But Simon seems to thrive on it."

"It's better than the pressure of business down here," Mary observed quietly.

"Yes, my dear, you're quite right," Sir Simon said. "He's a different boy."

Despite his attempt at chattiness during dinner, Sir Simon had another and even more pressing problem on his mind. He had a riveting announcement to make to the family, and it was a question of just when he ought to make it. Should he tell them at dinner? Or ought he to wait until they were all gathered in the Red Sitting Room after brandy and cigars, when he and his sons had rejoined the ladies for a nightcap? A hard, uncompromising expression crossed his face as he thought of the possible reaction to his news. But his mind was made up, and he intended to have his way. As he had so often said in the past, it didn't do to show signs of weakness with one's children or one's inferiors. (Or with one's own peers, if it came to that!) People were so quick to take advantage. It always became the thin edge of the wedge, and before you knew it, you had another Indian Mutiny on your hands.

Even now he held a tight rein on the multiple family enterprises as well as the personal lives of his children and grandchildren. He might be slightly stooped with age, but his energy was still high and his eyes gimlet sharp. He could meet a challenge with almost as much enthusiasm as he had in the past. His voice (which had been favorably compared with that of a demented drill sergeant) was a little diminished, but when he was in good form, it was still potentially dangerous to the average eardrum.

He gazed fiercely down the table at his sons. Certainly he could look upon them proudly. They wore the easy confidence of inherited position and they were all handsome in a large, regular-featured, fair-skinned way. They exuded good health, fine fabrics, and expensive cigars. All three had been successful in business, although occasionally they had given him trouble by disagreeing with his ideas.

61

He could not honestly say that any one of his sons had the same intense drive or wild imagination as himself. Nevertheless they were fine men and a credit to him. Wherever Court men went, even in foreign countries among complete strangers, they commanded respect. Sir Simon, savoring a rather generous helping of English trifle drenched in whipped cream (which had specifically been forbidden by his doctors), made a decision. He would tell them the news with brandy. Everybody would feel more mellow then.

So it was in the Red Sitting Room, Sir Simon's favorite spot in the entire fifty rooms of Pride's Court, that he finally stood before them, back to the fire, and announced, "I have something important to tell all of you. Could I please have your attention?"

A wave of expectancy passed over the group. Glasses paused in midair. Eyes turned toward him automatically.

"Some news about the gold mine?" Geoffrey asked hopefully.

"No, this is personal. In fact, highly personal."

Now a ripple of uneasiness flowed over the group. They all stared at him candidly, looking for a clue. Was he ill? Was there some fresh family scandal about to break just after they had successfully recaptured Angela and brought her back into the fold?

"I may as well take the bull by the horns," Sir Simon said.

They waited in silence. Only the ticking of the Louis XV clock disturbed the heavy air.

"I'm going to get married."

If he had announced that he was ascending into heaven, they couldn't have been more astounded. Fort managed only a croaking "*What?*" As for the others, they continued to stare at the old man, goggle-eyed.

"Getting married, Papa?" Charles managed, at last.

"Yes, getting married. You've heard of the custom, haven't you?"

"Married to *whom?*" Geoffrey asked in a ghostlike voice.

It suddenly struck the rest of them that Geoffrey had hit upon the second most important point. To *whom?*

"I was about to tell you that," Sir Simon said, enjoying the sensation he had caused. "To a bright, intelligent, active young woman. She'll be able to run this house, I can tell you!"

"Not French, I hope?" Fort said, introducing a note of grim humor.

Sir Simon was instantly furious.

"Do you think I'm senile? She's very English, I assure you. She has some rather odd ideas . . . about votes for women . . . but I intend to point out the error of her ways."

"You don't mean she's part of that franchise committee . . . the Montreal Women's Club?" Sydney asked, beginning to see the light.

"Well, yes. But she'll give that up. This whole question of the vote for women is sheer nonsense. You might as well give the vote to the horses. But Tulah is spunky. Misguided but spunky."

"You don't mean Tulah Horne, surely?" Sydney asked.

"Do you know Tulah Horne?" Charles said, turning to his sister-in-law. "Papa met her at the theater . . . about two months ago."

"Yes, I know her," Sydney said. "I met her at the Montreal Women's Club. I've been a member for some time."

"I didn't know that!" Fort said, bursting into the conversation with his own point of view. "You didn't mention that, Sydney."

There was an accusing tinge to Fort's voice.

"Knowing how the Court men feel about women who try to obtain equal rights for themselves, I neglected to mention it," Sydney said coolly. "But yes, I was active in the campaign this year when we tried to have Judge Emily Murphy made a senator."

"A woman senator!" Sir Simon cried, temporarily derailed by a monstrous vision. "Is there no limit to this insanity?"

"If you feel so strongly, how can you plan to marry a woman who wants the vote?" Fort asked. He was annoyed that Sydney had confessed something in front of his family—something he had not been told privately.

"Ah, that shows how shortsighted you are," Sir Simon said, always eager to point out how much more he knew about life than anybody else. "First, I admit to disagreeing with Tulah's political ideas. What man wouldn't? Second, I intend to convert her. Ha. Ha. Yes, convert."

"Whew!" This from Mildred, who so far had remained silent but who was, nonetheless, mesmerized by the prospect of a new grandmother, a new Lady Court, and a suffragette into the bargain. "A grandmother who marches on Parliament! That's exciting!"

Sir Simon grandly ignored this unseemly interruption.

"Under my wing Tulah will learn what is right and proper. I'll be helping her and helping the government at the same time. It's a good work, but one that will benefit me, too. You see?"

They saw. They saw very clearly. And the road ahead looked rocky.

"Does Miss Horne know you plan to reeducate her?" Fort asked, smiling in spite of his own annoyance. "Or will it come as a shock to her, do you think?"

"Certainly she knows. Do you take me for a fool? We'll see who gives in, Tulah or me."

"I think this calls for another drink," Charles said, moving toward the brandy decanter. "Anyone care to join me?"

"Yes, please, definitely," Geoffrey said. "And when are we to expect this wedding, Papa?"

"Yes, when?" Almost everybody asked that.

Sir Simon held up his glass and examined it before the light as if the color were of great importance. He paused, looked about him, and said slowly, "New Year's Day."

New amazement. So soon, and on a holiday, too. Really, he was outdoing himself in both style and shock. It was Charles who finally introduced a rather dampening note. "I imagine you want me to move out of Pride's Court, Papa?"

Sir Simon was startled into a booming denial.

"Don't be foolish, man! This house is big enough for all of us, as you well know. You just keep the apartment you have. I like the family around me, you know that. I want this house filled with people for a change. Tulah will be delighted. Wonderful woman, except for this peculiar political idea she has, of course. But that's something we can cure."

When the first wave of astonishment had passed, everybody began to talk about a holiday wedding in Pride's

Court. It added a dash of excitement to life, for the Courts had always celebrated weddings, Christmas, birthdays, and funerals with much pomp and circumstance. Even Mary, who was usually phlegmatic, joined in the discussion and became concerned about arrangements that must be quickly made.

Angela stood back and observed them. They had forgotten about her in the temporary flurry of Sir Simon's news. The first flush of happiness she had felt at being safely back in the harbor of her family had vanished. Now she felt outraged by this latest whim of Sir Simon's; it seemed to infringe upon her own life and that of her father. Why had they brought her back? The Courts led such a selfish, introverted life—they cared nothing for the outside world, nor for painting, nor music, nor theater. Money and social position were the only things they worshipped. This house, to which she had returned so willingly, was to be taken over now by a complete stranger—a woman who would turn all their lives upside down. Even her own father felt he ought to move out. But it was like Grandfather to consider only himself. She felt betrayed.

I can't bear any of them, really, she thought grimly. *I do hate this house, just as I remembered. I always hated it. What made me think it would be different this time?*

As she slipped out of the Red Sitting Room without saying good night, she longed desperately for Beau. He was the only one who understood the way she felt, her values, her emotions. These people might be family, but they were strangers. Out in the cold emptiness of the Great Hall, she looked toward the marble staircase where Sir Cathmor gazed down from his Olympian position. She shivered. Yes, she hated Pride's Court. She remembered now why she had left.

In Mellerstain Sydney went upstairs first. On the drive to their own house from Pride's Court she and Fort had barely spoken. That was the way they lived, though, so there was nothing different about it. Yet that little outburst before the family, her admission that she had done something that Fort did not know about, had made him angrier than usual. She was aware of it.

Sydney pushed aside the heavy curtains that covered the

65

French windows of her bedroom and looked down upon the cold, still garden below. A thin frosting of moonlight covered the hedgerows and bits of foliage stuck in the dry claws of the bushes. An icy breath pressed hard against the windowpanes to remind her that winter was here. She shivered in spite of the warm air behind her. The delicate silk nightgown was, suddenly, totally inadequate.

A fresh cloud of sweet tobacco smoke informed her of Fort's arrival. She made no sign that she knew he was in the room.

"Sydney." Fort spoke gently, trying to capture her attention. "I'm sorry if I jumped on you about the Women's Club. I was so surprised by Papa's behavior that I guess I sounded angry."

"It doesn't matter."

"Yes, it matters. You have every right to belong to any club you believe in. After the way you and Polly worked in hospitals during the war, you earned it. Do you forgive me?"

He waited patiently for her reply. She refused to acknowledge this speech, however. From his tone she knew he wanted to talk about the family, to discuss endlessly the coming marriage and Angela's arrival. The Courts loved to pick over every detail. Nothing interested a Court as much as another Court.

"I hope you'll be part of Papa's wedding. We ought to support him, if this is what he wants."

She heard his soft step on the carpet and turned her head slightly to catch his outline in the dim room.

"You might think about *our* marriage, too," Fort suggested.

"I stopped thinking about *our* marriage when you broke your promise to me two years ago."

"For God's sake, Sydney, be reasonable!" Fort cried, suddenly losing his temper. "I found out who your father was to set your mind at rest! So you could stop wondering about your background, stop agonizing. You were damned worried he might have been a drunkard or a criminal, you know that."

"So that *you* could stop agonizing, you mean."

"That isn't fair."

"It's perfectly fair. You only cared about the children, the question of heredity . . . I know that. You didn't

66

care about me or how I feel about this. What if you'd found out my father was a criminal? Then what would you have done? Left me? Would you have killed the children because they had bad blood?"

"I knew it would turn out all right. That if you knew who your father really was, you'd find peace. It was *not* knowing that was harmful, Sydney. Believe me."

"You Courts always know what's best for everybody. I made my position clear when we married and you accepted my terms. You were not to ask questions about my past. I told you I'd left all that behind me. You promised not to inquire or press me. I believed you."

"Look, Sydney, I thought I could do it. But after the children came, I felt differently about things. I admit it. But how could I know that? You didn't know who your father was. There was concern. . . . I felt we'd be happier if the whole thing were cleared up."

"First you dug around in my past until you found out the truth about my poor, pathetic mother . . . a common London streetwalker. No wonder I wanted to forget! I left that kind of life when I was little more than a child so I could do better for myself. *I* escaped, but you couldn't leave well enough alone, could you? You had to find out about my father, just in case the well-bred Courts now had some strange wild blood in the family. What if my father had been black? Or Oriental? What would you have done then? Thrown us all out?"

"Sydney, that isn't true."

"Why do you lie?"

"Your father was a perfectly decent man, probably brilliant. Your mother was a victim of bad luck, that's all. Finding that out is the best thing that could ever have happened to you. You ought to be grateful to me . . . you ought to thank me. You ought to go to England and look up your father."

"Stop it! I have no intention of seeing my father."

"That's just being pigheaded. Anyway, let's forget about all of it and start over. Let's be friends."

"Friends? You're selfish and dishonest like the rest of your damned family. It's as simple as that."

"I broke my promise. Have you never done that? Are you so perfect, then?"

"That's really begging the question. You ought to join

the Catholic Church with arguments like that. You'd make a good Jesuit."

"I tried to help. Let's begin again, Sydney, and . . ."

His voice cracked with strain. He wondered why he continued to storm this particular bastion when there were so many women around for the taking. He'd had other women since he married Sydney, of course, quite a number: young ones, older ones, intelligent ones, stupid ones, pretty ones, and ones not quite so pretty. He had once made love to two women at a time. The memory of that night flashed across his inner vision, and he saw again the two white bodies sliding over each other, lying beside him on the flat acres of the bed. He thrust the vision away.

He stood close to her now, forcing her to turn around and face him directly. His hot palm rested on her bare shoulder and the scent of rich tobacco enveloped them. He stared down into her eyes: eyes that looked blank in the magic of night sculpture. He twisted away from her to place his pipe carefully in an ashtray. She looked away.

Apart, they paused, both unsure, it seemed, and the room grew still. Life had slowed as if they were underwater—two people hanging suspended, graceful, mesmerized by the moment. Fort broke the spell when he grasped her arm and swung her violently about to face him again. His grip was a declaration of war.

"Look at me, damn you!"

She tried to pull away from him, but a sense of hopelessness engulfed her. Faint moonlight from the windows traced the fine lines of her husband's face, and she saw the sensual looseness that had taken possession of his mouth.

"Don't touch me."

But he refused to be thrust aside. Sydney fell back on one of her old defenses: complete immobility. On most nights that was enough to discourage Fort when pride took over from passion. Not tonight. She could see that he had already changed his clothes, and through the soft and yielding silk broadcloth of his pajamas she felt him harden.

"Please go back to your room and leave me alone," she whispered, trying to shake free. "Please, don't force me!"

"Why not? You're my wife. I love you."

"And I *despise* you."

"Then I've nothing to lose, have I? I might as well behave badly."

He pressed his moist mouth on hers, forcing her lips apart. She endured and let her body go limp as if every bone had suddenly melted. He picked her up roughly and carried her across the room to the bed, then tossed her unceremoniously down so that she sprawled awkwardly on her back. Before she could gather herself together in defense, he kneeled over her. He became a stranger. Hulking. Menacing. Dimly, she could make out his face; it was swollen with anger and lust. While he straddled her, he somehow managed to tear off his own pajama top and open the front of his trousers. She knew it was useless to resist.

"Let me see you naked," this stranger's voice was saying. "Let me see you, Sydney."

She closed her eyes to shut him out. He tore at her silk gown, ripping it down the front so that her white, thin body was exposed. From his crouching position over her he stared hungrily at the small firm breasts, the flat stomach, and the dark intrigue below. He ran eager hands over her neck and shoulders, scooping at the unresponsive nipples.

"You belong to me, Sydney. I bought you. Don't forget that."

With a harsh cry he drove into her. She lay like a stone statue beneath him—utterly cold and unmoving. Even her breath stopped. From a great distance she heard his mumbled cries as his craving exploded in a desperate crescendo. During his final cruel thrust, when his body arched in its own conclusive triumph, she grimaced with pain and nausea. Suddenly he let all his weight down on her and she struggled to breathe. He began to cry. His hot tears fell against her hair. She was stunned, but even this show of vulnerability did not touch her heart. When he flung himself away at last, she did not speak.

CHAPTER SIX

Sir Simon was lunching at the St. James's Club on Dorchester Boulevard. This was something of a departure from his recent daily routine. In the past few years he had been frequenting the St. James's less and less and the Mount Royal Club more and more, but today a wave of nostalgia (an unfamiliar emotion) had come over him, and he favored a visit to his first Montreal club.

Perhaps it was not all that extraordinary that he would go back. A new era in his life was about to begin, and he was feeling some apprehension. The announcement of his engagement to Tulah Horne had appeared in the social columns of the *Montreal Star*. As it happened, he had received an early edition before he left the office. By now the whole business community would know his plan. His mind began to turn on memories of his long and eventful life, and it seemed entirely fitting that he retreat to one of his earlier haunts.

Sir Simon climbed the steps of the club, huddling into his overcoat against the stiff wind. He decided once more that the old building was indeed impressive. And it was good to know that the amenities were available. Once he was inside, the hall porter (who had been with the club ever since Sir Simon could remember) helped him off with his coat and hat and then ushered him into a comfortable room on the main floor where members often took a quiet drink before lunch.

He nodded to three men he knew and then settled himself in a chair close to the fire. When he had ordered a scotch and soda, he allowed his eye to rove with approval over the green marble and mahogany mantelpiece, the oversize mahogany table covered with magazines like *Blackwood's*, *Field and Stream*, and *Country Life*. He liked the *feel* of the room. A man knew where he was here: secure in a padded brown leather chair studded with brass tacks engraved with the club's badge. There was a reassuring smell of well-kept wood and expensive books. Not that anybody read the books, mind you, except for an occa-

70

sional dip into DeBrett's to check on an English connection.

Thus it was purely a coincidence that he ran into North Grenville. Grenville was by himself, sitting in one of the deep armchairs, when Sir Simon entered. Grenville crossed the room and spoke.

"Congratulations on your engagement, sir," he said politely. "I saw the announcement in the paper."

Sir Simon was startled. Few club members approached him unless he invited them to do so, and at first he did not recognize the boy. Yet he had a faintly familiar air. Sir Simon was trying to sort it out when North explained, "You don't remember me, but you know my father, Henry Grenville."

Sir Simon appraised the young man bent over out of deference to an older, sitting clubman. He was the dark type of Anglo-Saxon, fashionably clean-shaven, expensively tailored, completely self-confident. His skin was well-fed, his brows pleasingly thick, his nose straight and well-proportioned in a large, square face. Everything about him (including the rich baritone voice, private school inflection, English handmade shoes) marked him as "belonging."

"I know your father well," Sir Simon admitted.

Despite his credentials North felt nervous. Was he about to be rudely cut in front of a dozen men who knew him? If so, it would be a black mark against him in his search for a job.

"How is your father, by the way? Haven't seen him at the club lately," Sir Simon said, his voice still gruff and noncommittal.

"He's retired," North said. He felt hot and wished he'd had the good sense to remain in his own chair on the other side of the room. To ease the tension Sir Simon mellowed and waved to the empty chair beside him.

"Sit down and tell me what Henry's doing since the bank merger."

A blissful relief swept over North. He had smelled social disaster. He had ventured where most angels would have feared to tread, but somehow the gods had been with him and he had triumphed. He sank gratefully into the proffered chair and turned his warmest, most charming smile upon Sir Simon.

"Thank you, sir. It's a pleasure. Well, Father's playing

a little golf, and he does some shooting at Long Point. . . ."

Sir Simon had no time for dilly-dallying at country clubs no matter how exclusive, but on the other hand, he completely sympathized with a man who liked to shoot. His feelings on a club such as Long Point were therefore mixed.

"Good club, Long Point. Lot of Americans in it, though. They're everywhere these days. I don't go off weekends, I have too much work to do. That's what keeps a man young. I doubt if I'll have time to attend my own funeral." This being Sir Simon's idea of a witty remark, he allowed himself a half-guffaw.

North joined him.

"Well, you're a legend. Everybody knows that," North said in his extraordinarily deep voice.

Sir Simon was pleased. He had long seen himself as a giant among men, working against fearful odds, helping bumpkins and fools, an unsung hero of the little man. He could never be sure that people recognized him for what he was. So it was doubly encouraging to hear this kind of remark from such a young man. After ordering one more scotch for each of them (that was Sir Simon's quota at lunch), he gave his opinions on the state of the economy, business in Montreal, the absurdity of holding an election in December, and the general degradation of the Liberal party. He touched briefly on the bank merger two years earlier that had led to Henry Grenville's retirement: when Grenville's Bank had been swallowed by the ever-growing Bank of Montreal.

"As for this election," he said, coming back to the crucial issue of the day, "if we don't return Arthur Meighen as prime minister, this country will go to the devil! Who are the Liberals offering as party leader? William Lyon Mackenzie King. Descendant of a rebel and made of the same bloody stuff. The man's a raving communist. Look how he fooled old Rockefeller down there in Denver over the miners' walkout. Actually got Rockefeller to meet with the organizer of the United Mine Workers of America. And do you know who *that* was? Mother Jones. A woman! Just another example of how the world's gone mad. Rockefeller ended up shaking the old biddy's hand—the man must be in his dotage. And who is this man King? Nobody but an opportunistic pirate, a former bum boy for Laurier. And that says it all. Do you realize this *King* could be our next prime minister? We're on the brink of hell!"

After this explosion Sir Simon finished his scotch, inquired about the Grenville family house, and found out Henry had sold the larger house for a smaller one on McTavish. He then began to muse about the vast amounts of money that had poured into Conservative coffers. All the while, he resumed scrutiny of his new acquaintance.

North had presence. That came from breeding (the Grenvilles were from good English stock) and the right schools. The boy's voice was an asset: He ought to run for Parliament with a voice like that. Wouldn't matter much what he said, but it would *sound* good. Perhaps the party could use the fellow in some way in a later election. It was too late now to recruit.

"Why did Henry retire, anyway?" he now demanded.

"He seemed to lose interest in the bank after the merger."

"A man shouldn't retire. Bound to kill him in the end."

"You're right. Father is only sixty-three now. That's what I told him."

"Well, we agree on that. What are you in, then?"

Sir Simon thought he might be interested in Grenville. He could always use a good man, a man he could trust, one who belonged. It came to him, too, that Mildred was still a problem. Twenty-three years old and no husband in sight. God knows, he'd brought around plenty of beaux, but nothing had worked out. Mildred was a bit dull, he admitted, but she was a Court, goddammit, and a suitable mate had to be found for her. On top of everything else, Geoffrey and Mary didn't seem to be concerned. No feeling for dynasty.

North Grenville suddenly became alert to the fact that Sir Simon was interested in him as an employee and that in this old man was an awesome concentration of power. What the Courts did not control or have a share in these days was scarcely worth mentioning. This meeting might be the break he needed.

"I'm not in anything at present. I'm looking around," North said, fixing his dark eyes upon Sir Simon's sharp

73

blue ones. "There are several areas that interest me. I had expected to join my father in the bank, of course."

"Naturally. My sons have all come into one of my companies," Sir Simon said with genuine feeling. "I suppose you were too young to work in the bank, then?"

"I graduated the year of the merger."

"Where from?"

"Harvard Business School."

"Excellent. Couldn't be better. Look here, North . . . by the way, are you married?"

North was surprised by this abrupt turn in the conversation but replied quickly,

"No, I'm not married, sir. I wouldn't consider marriage until I know what my career will be . . . where I'm going."

"Sensible fellow. Now, it just occurred to me while we were chatting that I have an opening at the Empire Bank. A spot for a man who's looking for hard work, a solid opportunity. A man I could trust."

North brightened. The Courts controlled so many different areas of business that even if he didn't like banking, he might find another niche.

"I'd appreciate the chance to talk about it."

"Why don't we have lunch right now?" Sir Simon said heartily, heaving himself up out of the chair. "Unless you have other plans? I have a table waiting upstairs."

"Yes, I'd like that very much, sir. I have no plans for lunch. I wandered in here on the spur of the moment."

As they walked up the great staircase to the dining room, North was aware that several members were watching. Lunching with Sir Simon was a point in his favor. Even if nothing came of the talk, the very fact that he had shared a table with the old man would be a plus factor in some other situation.

Over a hot consommé madrilène au sherry and rare roast beef North listened assiduously. At first Sir Simon raved on about the election, again revealing sums he had spent on the campaign. The election was to be held in ten days and he found it difficult to push it aside. But eventually they moved to other topics: mutual friends, schools, clubs, and marriages between families they both knew. Over a dish of hard imported strawberries covered with clotted cream they reached banking and, during coffee, the particular position

Sir Simon had in mind. By the time brandy came, Sir Simon had offered North the job and invited him to Pride's Court for Saturday night dinner.

Stowing thoughts of Mildred's future in the back of his mind along with other family problems, Sir Simon fixed his attention on more important matters at hand. Aside from the election (which would influence contracts and assorted government plums) there was the huge claim the Courts now had in the gold fields of northern Ontario. Business problems were as pressing as always: Parts were slow in coming from Detroit for the car factory at Lachine, and one of his sons would have to go to Edinburgh immediately after Christmas about ships for the Court line that were already on order. There was plenty to keep a man occupied. Still, he felt that the luncheon had been worthwhile. As the old saying went, for want of a nail the shoe was lost, and so on; he had always believed that attending to details as well as the big issues was the key to success. Today's meeting might be fortuitous.

Sir Simon had deliberately defused the tension of the Saturday night family dinner, when he intended to introduce Tulah Horne to the whole family, by inviting another newcomer, North Grenville. He was providing a side attraction to lure some of the attention from the main event. *I ought to have been a showman,* he thought gleefully. *It'll be a two-ring circus! That's the stuff to give 'em. It'll keep 'em from staring at Tulah all night.*

He was well aware that his family disapproved of his coming marriage. A new Lady Court reigning over the family seat was bound to create fresh problems. Especially when that woman was as vital and as opinionated as Tulah. Nobody cared what *he* wanted, of course, nobody wanted *him* to be happy, but he was used to such ingratitude. It had followed him all the days of his life. So in a way it was biblical.

However, when the moment came—when Peters announced that Tulah had arrived—Court courtesy was not lacking. Both Charles and Angela accompanied Sir Simon to the reception hall to welcome her. She entered, blown on a wintry breeze and bundled in a black seal coat that had seen better days. She wore a rather old-fashioned tuque of the same fur on top of her short blond hair, and she seemed to be tied together like a rather shapeless bundle by a long white wool scarf. Her black cloth overshoes were rather ugly, and when the wrappings were removed, she stood revealed in a military-style blue serge dinner dress decorated with brass buttons.

Nothing diminished her energy, and at forty-five, Tulah Horne was still a lodestar. Vitality seemed to shoot out from every pore, from every movement, drawing attention to the smallest thing she said or did. She was exceptionally tall, almost six feet. She towered over Angela and stood eye to eye with the Court men. Her rather high-riding bosom appeared to need no support, yet her waist was as tiny as that of a young girl. Most women would have looked frumpy in the straight-cut dress, but Tulah managed to emerge from her black pumps like a phoenix rising from the ashes. She smelled fresh and cool, and as soon as she entered the Red Sitting Room, where the family was gathered, she became the center of attention.

After the introductions and congratulations, Geoffrey dispensed drinks. The warm aura of the Red Sitting Room, always so dependable, helped smooth the way. Sir Simon had just purchased an eight-day striking mantel clock by James Cox (he had a small but distinguished clock collection) brilliantly painted with Battersea enamels and housed in a rich ormulu case. He showed it proudly to Tulah.

"Absolutely charming, Simon," she said, flashing her electric smile. "But I don't know anything about clocks, I'm afraid."

"I'll instruct you," he said, undaunted. "And after dinner we'll have a short tour of the important rooms. We'll have to wait for a complete tour, I'm afraid. Afternoon's best for some of the rooms. Light is so important."

"I can't wait! I've always wanted to see inside this house," Tulah cried, giving off sparks and treating everybody to another show of her magnificent teeth.

Sir Simon beamed. The Courts were, in general, amused. It was not often that anyone came to Pride's Court with as much charisma as themselves, let alone more. Mary, never able to shine in the family, managed to fade into obscurity, and Mildred stood in a corner. The others might have been watching a stage play, and despite their basic ill humor about the wedding, they watched the scene as an entertainment.

In Mildred's case it was quite different. She was lacking in the Court aplomb, and now she sulked over her sherry. The drink seemed to curdle in her glass while she awaited with some trepidation the next onslaught from a new young man her fierce old grandfather had found as a dinner guest. No doubt he would be as dreary a bore as all the others Sir Simon had brought around. Why couldn't she have been beautiful like the others, like Angela, or striking like this Tulah Horne? Life was cruel.

Sir Simon was now showing off his prize. Looking less than his age but still heavy and a bit red in the face, he was saying to his sons, "Tulah was a nursing sister in France, you know. Worked right up there with the troops under fire."

"Not quite at the front, Simon, but quite close enough to be shot at," Tulah amended happily. "I was behind the lines when the Germans stormed Verdun. We were terribly close to the fort of Douamont when it was overrun. The Huns broke right through. There were times we didn't know where they were, behind us, around us. But we were always ready."

I wouldn't have wanted to be a Hun if Tulah got hold of me, Angela thought crossly. *In fact, I wonder if I want to live in this fortress if she's going to run it.*

While Tulah might be brave, charming, lovely, and energetic, and just what Pride's Court needed, she was definitely not what Angela needed. It was like being caught in a whirlwind when you planned to have an afternoon nap. Angela looked at her grandfather to see how he was taking it. After all, Tulah was upsetting the traditional roles; women did not fight wars, men did. But when she saw Sir Simon's blue eyes bright with excitement, she realized with a sinking heart that he was enjoying a good war even when it was being verbally fought by somebody else. Tulah was a fresh challenge. That must be the secret of this ridiculous match!

"She was right in the thick of it!" Sir Simon cried cheerfully. "Only wish I'd been there myself. Tell them how you nearly got murdered by a Hun, but you got him first, Tulah."

"It was self-defense," Tulah protested.

"You mean you actually killed a man?" Mildred demanded, startled out of her sulk by this alarming bit of information. She could not imagine herself killing a rabbit.

"Had to, I'm afraid. It was him or me. I was helping a wounded soldier off a litter and the German came from behind a bush. He was pointing a gun at me, so I shot him."

"You were allowed to carry a gun?" Geoffrey inquired, his tone a veiled suggestion that all was not well with the nursing corps.

"Well, we weren't supposed to," Tulah acknowledged. "But in war you take whatever steps are necessary to protect yourself. It was a .32-caliber handgun."

"Very brave, very brave," Sir Simon said, looking outrageously pleased. "Tulah's quite a woman. Lives on Maisonneuve at the moment, in the house her mother owned. All by herself. Runs the estate like a lawyer."

Sir Simon went on to regale them with stories of Tulah's political activities, which (he pointed out) would cease once she was mistress of Pride's Court. She wouldn't have time to parade around City Hall looking for votes for women or go gallivanting off to Quebec City to make a nuisance of herself with Premier Taschereau. Tulah said she had no intention of giving up her committees and that Quebec was the only province where women did not have the municipal or provincial vote.

"We *can* vote federally, and I hope there'll be a good turnout on election day," Tulah said.

"And *I* hope there won't," Sir Simon said emphatically. "What do women know about politics?"

"Just as much as you do, and often more," Tulah said. "What you need, Simon Court, is somebody who'll stand up to you."

The family waited in anticipation of a temper tantrum but he merely chuckled into his scotch.

Angela thought, *So that's the secret! He's found a new sparring partner. Honey's served her useful time and Tulah's the new incumbent.*

Sir Simon looked at his watch. He checked it with the mantel clock. It was almost time for Peters to announce dinner and North Grenville had not arrived. Just as he was speculating that North might be one of those irresponsible young people infesting the earth today, Peters came in and announced North's arrival. Sir Simon felt relief. He hated to be wrong and he had taken rather a liking to the fellow.

When North Grenville walked into the Red Sitting Room, he was first drawn to Angela—she stood aside, wearing gray silk to match her eyes, and he could not help but be attracted by her beauty. He was soon distracted by Tulah, the real guest of honor, who always seemed to dominate any room in which she stood. It was some moments before he could give his attention to Mildred. Sir Simon had handed him a drink and taken him around to be introduced. When that was over, he left North with Mildred, saying, "This is Geoffrey's daughter. She's an excellent rider. Do you hunt?"

"I have ridden a bit, but I don't hunt."

"You can always join the Montreal Hunt," Sir Simon said helpfully. "What do you do for exercise?"

"I play golf," North said somewhat defensively.

"Silly game," Sir Simon pronounced and walked away.

Mildred and North were beached then in one corner of the room, each clutching a drink. Mildred smiled tentatively. North, having sensed that Sir Simon approved of him talking to Mildred, even though he did not subscribe to the game of golf, brought a portion of his charm to bear upon her. He smiled.

"You ride? Every day?" The voice was low, resonant.

"That's about all I do in the summer," she said. "Are you out of university?"

"Yes, I graduated last year. I'm going to work for your grandfather in the bank."

"Oh, yes, I remember now. He offered you a job. I expect we'll see you around here often, then."

"If you invite me."

While they talked, North took careful inventory. She was tall and rangy, which he did not mind, but her coloring was dull. She did not look like her cousins in the least. She lacked the Court style. But she might be improved. It wouldn't hurt to take her about anyway, just because she *was* a Court.

At dinner he was seated next to Mildred, but since Tulah dominated the table, they had little chance to talk. Following a substantial raspberry fool, Sir Simon gave Angela the signal to take away the women and leave the men to their brandy and cigars. Tulah was indignant.

"You're not still going along with that abominable English custom, are you, Simon? Frankly, I despise it.

When I'm hostess here, I won't put up with it. As if women couldn't understand business if they were allowed to hear about it! Ah well, Angela, we must endure, I suppose."

Sir Simon looked pained but rallied quickly.

"We've always done it that way. Perfectly civilized, too. Good enough for my father and good enough for me."

"Your father lived in a drafty English castle, but I don't see *you* doing that, Simon," Tulah said.

Sir Simon shook his head in wonderment. She was an extraordinary woman. Still, he did not linger over brandy and cigars as he usually did, and the men soon rejoined the ladies in the Red Sitting Room. Before taking Tulah off on a tour of some of the rooms, he grasped North's arm and led him to a corner where Mildred had once more ensconced herself.

"Here's a chap who wants to learn how to play backgammon," he said. "Take him along to the card room, Milly. I had a fire laid and there's whisky and soda if he wants it. She's an expert player, North, so see if you can put her in her place."

Realizing that her grandfather was placing his personal stamp of approval on North, Mildred felt a sting of mixed excitement and fear. The thought that she might attract this man left her almost paralyzed. Of all the men her grandfather had shoved in her direction, North was the first to interest her seriously. She found him devastatingly attractive, and consequently she became so nervous that her childhood stammer returned.

"Do you p-p-play the game at all?" she asked as they sat over the backgammon table.

"I've played, but not too well. Perhaps you can teach me."

She was so conscious of North's brown eyes watching her every move that she shook the dice with trembling fingers. For an awful moment, everything she knew about the game fled from her mind, but with an enormous effort she handed the dice to North.

"You move first," she said when he had rolled.

As the game progressed, North watched the large hands hovering over the board and began to assess her features and how she could be improved. From merely taking her out as a casual companion, his mind leaped forward to the fantastic possibilities open to him if she should marry him. If he became part of the Court domains. He began to dwell on whether or not he could actually fall in love with her or, at the least, find himself attracted to her enough to perform as a husband.

Mildred, playing badly and continuing to stammer, did not outshine North as her grandfather had predicted, but she had ceased to care about the game. What would it be like to have North making love to her? To feel those well-kept hands on her face, stroking her neck? She flushed at the thought.

"Is it too warm for you?" North asked. "Shall we pull the table away from the fire?"

"N-n-n-no. I'm fine."

North rose from the table and poured himself a second glass of whisky and soda. He ought to be careful how much he drank under the circumstances, he decided. Usually, he liked the sharp edges of reality to be softened and blurred, but tonight he could not afford to look sloppy or out of control. He would make this drink last for the rest of the evening.

Taking his seat again, he dared to lean across the board and seize one of Mildred's hands and press it between his palms. He felt her fingers quiver. He took the other hand with a deliberate, slow movement and twined his fingers through hers and leaned his elbows on the table so that their arms touched from wrist to elbow. In the firelight, her face had taken on a slack almost sensuous look. He let his eyes shift from her face to her neck and then released one of his fingers to touch the inside of her bare wrist. To barely touch it. A whisper of skin on skin.

Mildred gave an involuntarily little shiver. Her mouth was open slightly and looked moist. He allowed himself to lower his eyes to the plump breasts outlined in lavender wool. He could imagine that she was a virgin. Yes, he was sure of that. He thought about uncovering those breasts, offering certain delights that he had lately come to understand. His mouth formed a suggestive opening, and he took in one of her fingertips ever so lightly, wetly. She was wilting, sliding down in her chair, and then she retrieved the damp finger, but she did not protest.

Under the table North felt the first sinuous flow of desire turn embarrassingly hard. He squirmed, temporarily uncomfortable, but knowing now that he could make love to

Mildred, that he actually wanted her. That was important. Like a voyager getting his bearings in a dark river, he now knew the way that he must go.

He leaned farther across the table, willing her with his eyes to meet him, join him. He wanted to taste her mouth as a lustful child wants a rich dessert and feels he must have it instantly or he will fly into a rage. His tongue moved restlessly over his teeth. Mildred swayed above the backgammon board toward him, eyes closed, lips parted. He let his indulgent mouth rest on hers, nudging her lips farther open, forcing her to take in his tongue. She opened her mouth to let him in, and he slid his tongue over hers and then under it, playfully but with enough titillation to make her want more. Finally, she took in his whole tongue —a symbolic, delicious gesture of surrender.

They sat still, half-drugged with wine and lust, gorged with barely tasted desire. At once innocent (after all, there was a table between them and their hands were merely clasped) and riddled with luscious guilt. When they allowed their mouths to separate, cheeks pressed together, and Mildred could still smell the scotch on North's breath, a new ache seized her—began in her chest and traveled downward to her thighs, forced her legs apart ever so little as if to ease the distress. A sense of abandon that was entirely unfamiliar spilled over her, drowning all reason.

Noises from the next room lapped at the shores of their private world, and they pulled apart, sensing danger.

"I must see you tomorrow," North said, still hanging onto Mildred's hand.

"Yes, come for tea."

"Do you think your grandfather will mind?"

"No, he's given his approval. I knew that when he sent us in here to play backgammon. That's his way. Please come. Come early."

North shifted in his chair, still aroused. He was passionate by nature, a sensualist in the experimental stages, and he had learned in the locker room that he was generously endowed.

"What were we doing? Oh, yes, playing a game," he said with a forced smile. He would have liked another drink, but that wasn't wise. It would be just like the old man to notice such things.

"Let's stop, anyway," Mildred said. "I d-d-don't feel like p-p-playing anymore, anyway." Her stammer was more noticeable.

North agreed and was surprised to find how much he wanted Mildred. She was hardly what he would have described as beautiful. But he supposed the attraction had something to do with the whole situation—the house, the new job, his own visions of becoming part of the Court clan.

"God, I can't concentrate on anything. You've excited me too much." He stood up and stretched a little. Then he turned to look at her. "You ought to wear blue, you know."

Rendered in North's deep tones, this sounded like some magical pronouncement. Mildred responded eagerly, thrilled that he was taking such an interest.

"D-d-do you really th-th-think so?"

Mildred stared down at the nondescript gown she was wearing and realized that it had no style; it was neither long nor short, and suddenly it seemed to be covered with buttons and frills. She felt ill and discouraged. North must think she was a fool.

"Will you be an attendant at your grandfather's wedding?" North was asking.

"Only as a member of the family, not in the wedding p-p-party," Mildred said. "Nobody likes the idea much, you know. And now that we've m-m-met her . . ." she trailed off expressively.

"I can understand why you aren't too keen," North said. He spied a porcelain humidor with a brass collar sitting on one of the side tables. He opened it to select an Uppmann. He waved the cigar at Mildred in a belated effort to inquire with his eyebrows whether she minded if he smoked it. Mildred indicated that she did not mind. Everything he did seemed perfect to her.

They walked back to the Red Sitting Room, and as they did so, North touched the palm of Mildred's hand with the tip of his finger, tracing a circle lightly on the flesh. Sharing their secret, shaking inside with their private discovery, they found Sir Simon sailing on a sea of wild enthusiasm: He was spinning vast projects involving the redecoration of Pride's Court. Tulah was cheering him on. Mildred felt exhausted just listening to him. Despite the lateness of the hour both Sir Simon and Tulah were still generating high-voltage energy in every direction.

CHAPTER SEVEN

They met in Sir Simon's huge office in the Empire Bank overlooking busy St. James Street. Sir Simon hunched expectantly at one end of the long, polished boardroom table, neatly posted beneath his own image. He looked a good deal older and heavier than the portrait, of course, but no less fierce. Geoffrey and Noel sat on one side of the table, on his left, while young Simon II took a place on his right. An air of mixed gloom and excitement hung over the meeting. Gloom for the shattering results of the election, excitement at the smell of gold.

Sir Simon was not in an affable mood. Things might be going fairly well in his personal life, but the damned Liberals had taken all 65 Quebec seats in the federal election. In five of the nine provinces, the Conservatives had failed to take a single seat. In total, the Liberals were sending 117 members to Ottawa, while the Conservatives had barely managed an even 50. And these 50 did not include Arthur Meighen, the party leader. It was a rout. Complete and simple. The country was in the hands of infidels, and the most sinister infidel of them all was William Lyon Mackenzie King, the new prime minister. Sir Simon frankly despaired for the human race. How much was due to women having the vote, he was not prepared to say, but that some blame must be attached to that unsavory fact, he was certain.

"So you've brought good news about the claims, have you?" he asked in his high-volume voice. "God knows, we need some good news after this shocking election. At least in Ontario they had the sense to vote Tory. Bunch of cretins here . . . what can I say? Give fools the vote and you get foolish government. The Romans had the right idea when they invented the oligarchy. Or was it the Greeks? No matter, it was the right idea."

Sir Simon's classical education was sketchy to say the least, but he knew what an oligarchy was, and that such an elitist situation was totally correct. It puzzled him how foreigners had come to think of it, but then, you couldn't give the English credit for *everything*, more's the pity.

He reached for the mahogany humidor, especially designed for the oversize cigars he had had made in order to outwit his personal physician. One cigar a day, the maniac had prescribed, so Sir Simon had ordered custom-made, huge cigars manufactured to his liking. One lasted several hours, but he was able to say with a clear conscience that he smoked only one a day.

"We've got a fantastic strike," Noel said, anxious to impress his grandfather with developments in the north. He was much like his father had been at that age; reddish-blond hair, light blue eyes, and fair complexion, roughened now by the outdoors, and rather solidly built. He wore a navy blue serge suit with a vest and his school tie. "In fact, we're absolutely certain that these two claims—they're almost side by side—will develop into something as big as Porcupine or Hollinger."

"Definitely," Simon II agreed quickly. "But we need your complete backing, Grandfather. All the way. We don't want to go public. Let's keep the shares in the family."

This notion, along with Simon's enthusiasm, cheered the old man slightly. The north country had agreed with the boy, and he'd really taken hold of this project. After a great deal of time in and out of hospitals he was over the shell shock, it seemed. His hands no longer trembled when he lighted a cigarette, but Sir Simon did not know how a loud noise would affect him. It was when a gun went off in the drawing room and young Simon had scuttled under a table in a terrified reflex action, that they had first discovered the severity of his illness. Unlike his brother he was dressed casually in a cashmere sweater under a heather tweed jacket. The typical bright blue Court eyes looked clear now and the shadow had passed from them. Sir Simon shelved his anger at the election, temporarily, and was pleased with his two grandsons.

"Fire away! Tell me what it's all about. You look healthy, Simon. Good northern air agrees with you, does it?"

"I love it up there. I plan to live in Kirkland Lake, at least until the mine is well underway."

"That's a switch," Sir Simon cried, but he wasn't angry. Anything that confirmed masculinity was a definite plus. "What about you, Noel?"

"I have no intention of living up there, but I don't mind going back and forth by train. Right now, though, it will take both of us to organize things properly."

"Let's hear your story, then. I guess you know all about it, Geoff?"

"I've heard it more than once," Geoffrey said, "but the boys are so fanatical about it, I find the whole thing catching."

"It's an Aladdin's cave, that's what it is," Simon began, banging his fist on the edge of the desk. "The quality of ore is unbelievable, and from other data we have, we know that down there—deep, mind you—there's so much gold. . . . You see, they've only sunk the shafts about a hundred feet. We bought it out because the owner ran out of money—hit a fault at about one hundred feet—but we have to get much deeper."

"Could you begin at the beginning?" Sir Simon asked a little impatiently. "What exactly do we *own*?"

"Two large claims. But they aren't exactly adjacent, and that's a problem. We have to get hold of the small claim that almost splits them down the middle. We bought shares in one at thirty-two cents and the other at thirty-nine cents. I know they'll be worth a hundred times that in two years. Maybe five hundred. I don't want to raise money by selling shares to deepen the shaft. I want to keep it a Court enterprise," Simon said.

"Do you agree, Noel?"

"Yes, basically. I don't want to sell public shares, but we need your support. Sure, there's some risk, but everything we know about the area, about the geology of this particular strip, backs up our belief. Look at Harry Oakes! He's rich, but he could have been richer if he'd hung on. Instead he sold some shares. We want to avoid that."

"All right, suppose I agree, and your father and your uncles agree . . . but what's this about a small claim in the middle of our mine? You'd better explain that."

"Slight snag, yes," Geoffrey said, interrupting. "As the boys see it, they need this wedge of land . . . only about seven acres, but it almost splits the two claims down the middle. For security, and to avoid future trouble, we've got

86

to get that claim. They need capital immediately to purchase it and for developing the claims we already own."

Simon II pushed a sheaf of reports, maps, and documents across the desk toward his grandfather.

"It's all here. You can study it, and I think you'll agree it's a risk worth taking."

"Yes, but give me more details."

He spoke roughly, but actually he was pleased. The boys were true Courts, chips off the old block. Surprising, when you came to think of it, that Geoffrey would produce the sons to carry on the Court enterprises. No use waiting for Landry, Fort's son. He was a scholar and bookworm. Charles had no sons, only Angela.

"Go ahead, tell me the worst!" Sir Simon said encouragingly. "Who owns this piece of land?"

"First, let me try to explain the geography to you, Grandfather," Simon began. "Both our claims are on the south shore of Kirkland Lake. That's quite a bit south of the big mines already bringing out top-grade ore like Hollinger and Porcupine. One claim has been worked minimally. There's a small mill on it, and the quality of the ore is superb. My gut feeling is that it's just the tip of the iceberg. Now we must get this patch of seven acres—"

"Wait a minute. Where in hell is Kirkland Lake?"

"Just inside the Ontario border from Quebec. About three hundred miles northwest of Ottawa. Rough country."

"What railroad goes in there?"

"The Timiskaming and Northern Ontario. You can get to a small place called Swastika and walk a few miles east to Kirkland Lake. Nothing there now but a few shacks, but soon it'll be as busy as a beehive."

"How much money are you asking for?" Sir Simon said, coming to the point.

"Half a million dollars. Maybe more," Noel said, taking over from his brother.

"All right, come to the crux of the matter. Who owns this wedge of land?" Sir Simon demanded. "I think you're keeping something from me."

"It's a bit tricky," Geoffrey said.

"Right. Armand St. Amour has the claim," Noel admitted.

"My son-in-law?" Sir Simon asked incredulously. "That damned Frenchman, St. Amour?"

"That's right," Geoffrey said.

"How in blazes did he get into this?"

"Through that American partner of his, Max DeLeon. Evidently DeLeon had this stake for years and St. Amour has taken over much of the old man's business now that DeLeon is dead. I don't know what arrangements he's made with the widow, but in any case he has this land, and we've got to get our hands on it. We can't have St. Amour controlling a valuable chunk like that right in the middle of our mine. But we've got to get it before the mine turns into a big producer or he'll hold us up."

"Ah, now I begin to see how things stand," Sir Simon said. Still, it was a fresh challenge. "We'll think of a way to get it. Anytime the Courts can't outsmart a pack of Frenchmen, it's time to call it quits."

Both Noel and Simon felt great relief. They had been afraid before coming to the meeting that Sir Simon might decide he wanted no part of a deal with St. Amour.

"I'll study these reports first," Sir Simon said, shuffling the papers on the desk. "But unless I've lost my wits, we'll get that land—and cheap. We'll drive St. Amour out of business. He won't know what hit him. I won't have some French upstart interfering in my plans. Use a front man. We must have several we could use." Then: "Who knows about your buying the two major claims?"

"A few people. Not many," Simon said.

"Better make it quick, then."

"He'll no doubt try to get a high price. He'll smell what's going on," Geoffrey said. "The man's no fool—"

"Yes he is!" Sir Simon interrupted with a bellow. "The brute is a complete idiot!"

This, of course, was not true, but there was no use in arguing with the old man about Armand St. Amour. He had committed the cardinal sin when he ran off with Sir Simon's only daughter and married her. It was a battle of long standing.

"Whether he is or not," Geoffrey said placatingly, "we have to buy that land before he finds out the value of *our* claims."

"Anyway, Grandfather, we plan to build a town on the minesite. There's nothing there at the moment but shacks, tents, and trees. We'll build a town right from scratch!" Simon said.

"We're going to call it Courtsville," Noel added.

Sir Simon was staring out of the window. Temporarily his vision had been clouded by the memory of his beautiful but wayward daughter throwing herself away on a foreigner all those years ago. And he couldn't seem to get rid of the swine, St. Amour. The man kept cropping up in the oddest places. It was cruel, it was unjust.

Noel's words brought him abruptly back into the room. "Courtsville? A town?" The idea caught his fancy. Funny he'd never thought of naming a town after the family before. *"Courtsville."*

He rolled the word over his tongue as if it were fresh honey and his eye took on a bright, hard look of triumph.

"I like that! Our town. Courtsville."

Noel and Simon II knew then that they had gained their objective, all the support they would need from the most powerful source in Montreal.

Angela sat alone in the drawing room staring at the colored tree lights. It was the first time the Courts had used electric lights on the huge tree, and she found it fascinating, although she wasn't sure whether or not she really approved of the innovation. Red, blue, white, and green bulbs shimmered in metal reflectors making the tree look like a moving, living thing. All the old ornaments had been hung, too, and the usual tinsel and the star at the top. But it was the lights that gave it the extra touch.

The drawing room was seldom used by the family except on special occasions. It was considered too large, too overpowering. The forest green walls were gilded with enormous portraits of Sir Simon's ancestors and those of Lady Court—the Manthorpes. Sir Simon's title was English and he could trace it back many generations. One of his ancestors had supported William of Orange when that monarch first landed on English shores in 1688.

Tonight, almost the entire Court family would be present. It was Christmas Eve. Only Charles would be absent. He was spending Christmas in St.-Jovite with Polly. Angela, feeling rather insignificant in the huge room, moved toward the blazing fire framed by a Siena marble mantel. Nearby was a mahogany settee (very valuable, Sir Simon had always told the children, and not to be treated roughly) covered in deep green and crimson brocade. Behind the settee were two massive marble-topped boulle tables, one bearing a Meissen bowl of fresh white chrysanthemums, the other two huge Sevres vases. The room was furnished with various other antiques, a smattering of comfortable chairs, and many not comfortable at all.

For some reason Angela found herself first downstairs after tea. She had had a rest in her room, bathed, and changed, and she fully expected that several family members would be in the drawing room first. But everyone was late, it seemed. Tonight there would be no dinner—that was part of the Christmas Eve ritual—but instead, eggnogs, brandies, wines, hot mince pies, rich dark fruit cake, and shortbread. Not that she cared much about the food; she wasn't hungry. She had no reason to look forward to this evening. Since Beau was not here, life was dull.

No doubt the rest of the family felt differently. *They* had each other, and Grandfather was so excited about his coming marriage he could almost ignore the disastrous election. But Angela had nobody; even her father was away. If only she could have spent Christmas with Aunt Miel and Uncle Armand, she thought wistfully, that would have made Beau seem closer. Here in Pride's Court each group had moved in bringing the children along. The whole house was as busy as a resort—until this moment. She knew that the stillness would soon be broken, however, when the Courts came down and began Christmas celebrations.

When she heard someone coming, at last, Angela turned eagerly to see who it was, hoping it was one of the relatives she liked. She was delighted to find that it was her cousin Landry. Of all her cousins, he had always been her favorite —from as far back as those days when all Court children spent their summers at Drake House on the South Shore.

"Landry! How nice to see you again. Merry Christmas!"

He came toward her and bent to kiss her cheek. She had not seen him in two years and he was suddenly a grown-up, lanky and with a hint of moustache. *He must be twenty-five,* she thought. *A man. And so tall!*

"You're just as beautiful as ever," he said shyly.

She had chosen a soft pink woolen dress with a high collar and long sleeves (remembering that some corners of the drawing room were cool). The hems this year were neither one thing nor another, ending vaguely at mid-calf. On her, however, the gown looked attractive.

"Thank you," she said. They held hands for a moment. "I'm so relieved it's you, Landry. I thought it might be one of the others, and I'd have to struggle to make conversation."

He squeezed her fingers. They had always shared some kind of special communion. They were misfits in the family despite their engaging looks and bright minds. Standing in front of the fire, they were silent for a little while, lost in memories. Landry's eyes were like his mother's, wide-spaced and dreamy. Angela, observing him, thought he had a strange, vulnerable look. As if he were afraid of something.

"I thought I might be alone with the prospective Lady Court. I haven't met her yet, you know."

"Oh, my, Landry, better stiffen your spine. She's rather frightening, all right. Bursting with energy! Pretty, though. I can't imagine how Grandfather's going to handle her."

She giggled. Landry blushed as if she had said something faintly lewd.

"How are things at Oxford?" Angela asked quickly, sensing she had embarrassed him. "Do you like it? You must be clever to be a Rhodes scholar, Landry. Only a few are chosen from Canada each year, isn't that right?"

"Yes, but we aren't too popular. English fellows are pretty stuffy. They stick together and talk about families and people they know. Though I've met a few friendly ones. To tell the truth, I'm not sure whether I like it or not."

"I expect you'd rather be in your lab anyway. Still trying to find a new winter wheat?"

"I had to abandon that for the time being. But I'd rather be in a lab than anywhere else."

"Explain it to me again, Landry. About your experiments."

"It's not that interesting, just that everyone's keen on finding an early-maturing wheat for northern Canada . . . like northern Manitoba and the Peace River country. Red Fife takes too long to ripen, so the frost kills it. We have Marquis and Thatcher, but even *they* don't ripen fast enough. But it's not interesting to other people."

"I like to hear what you're up to, don't be silly."

"And what about your painting?"

"Not much to tell. I was getting ready for a London

show, but when I decided to come home, my work stopped. So far, I haven't found a studio here in Montreal."

"Don't ever stop painting, Angela," Landry said solemnly. "I always thought your flowers and birds were beautiful."

"I paint more difficult things now," she said. "We've all grown up since those days."

"How about a drink? A sherry?" He began looking for the drinks tray he knew must be in the room. "Ah, here it is."

While he poured, she asked, "Do you like the tree lights?"

"I'm not sure. It's a change," Landry said, handing her a glass. "Here's to us, the different ones! I find it hard to remember we're cousins."

"We *are* cousins, aren't we? Is that bad?"

They were so engrossed they didn't hear the door open. It was only when Flora spoke that they realized someone had joined them.

"Is *what* bad?" she asked.

Landry turned on his twin sisters to reprimand them.

"Why are you sneaking up like that? And don't snoop on other people's conversations."

A knowing look came into both pairs of wide green eyes. They stood together, twin creatures, with long, straight hair caught at the nape of the neck with green velvet ribbon, perfect oval faces, pouting mouths. Every detail was the same from the white lace collars on navy velvet gowns to the neat patent slippers. They smelled of lavender. They looked oddly old-fashioned, like models from an antique print. Each wore a small brooch of rubies on the left shoulder, a gift from some previous Christmas. They were poised like sentinels, curious, watchful, alert.

"Is *what* bad?" Flora repeated.

"Yes, tell us. We love to hear bad things," Fenella said. Landry looked cross.

"Are you girls allowed to drink sherry? If so, I'll get you a glass. Do you remember your cousin Angela?"

"We're allowed sherry on special occasions," Flora said.

"Of course we remember Angela, how could we forget?"

"Isn't it sherry people put poison in all the time? To get rid of unwanted relatives?" Flora asked.

"That was Amontillado," Fenella said. "But let's have some anyway."

"Stop gaping," Landry said, handing them each a glass.

"We're only gaping because we haven't seen Angela since she became a skeleton in the closet. We've been away at school."

"Mind your manners, or I'll have you sent up to bed," Landry admonished.

"Just try it, and see what happens. Poison in your drink, Landry. Don't think we wouldn't, because we would. Anyway don't blame us, blame *her*. Have you ever seen anyone quite so gorgeous, Fenella?"

"Only in English magazines."

"It's what comes from having you-know-what," Flora said knowingly. "I read it somewhere. It always improves a woman's looks."

"Stop being rude, this instant!" Landry cried.

"It doesn't bother me," Angela said calmly. "Sit down, girls, and stare away."

"Thank you, Angela. It's such a novelty for us, you see, leading the sheltered lives we do," Fenella said, pretending to be grateful.

They sat side by side on a settee, posed with straight backs as if a photographer in the wings were about to take a picture. Each held her glass precisely and crossed her ankles gracefully. Two pairs of eyes searched Angela's face (probably for traces of dissipation), and yet they somehow managed to look innocent and untouchable.

Their scrutiny did not last long. In a few minutes the intimate atmosphere was shattered as various relatives swept into the drawing room: some in couples, some alone, crying out greetings, exchanging peck-kisses, admiring the lighted tree. Tulah and Sir Simon came together. Geoffrey and Fort tended bar. Charity, Geoffrey and Mary's youngest child, had arrived with her parents and two brothers, Simon II and Noel. She was a precocious pixie with huge defiant eyes and light-colored hair.

While the Court men talked endlessly about the election just past, North and Mildred buried themselves in one corner of the room. North held Mildred's hand or brought her drinks or offerings of food. Angela could not help looking at them with envy. She felt terribly alone and unloved. Yet she sensed that Mildred would have a difficult time with North. She could feel his restlessness, his taste for women, which he tried hard to conceal. *She's fallen madly in love,*

Angela thought with sympathy, *and he's likely to dump her. He's far too good-looking, too fascinating, to be satisfied with poor Mildred for very long, money or no money.*

Angela spent most of the evening chatting with Landry. The air was filled with the scent of hot mulled wine, evergreen, and cigar smoke. There were piles of gifts wrapped in colored tissue under the tree. Tulah flew around the room like a butterfly, alighting here and there to shine and chat. Sir Simon looked terribly pleased.

Just after midnight Charity (being the youngest in the family) was sent off to bed. The twins followed almost immediately but only after haggling with their father about the time. Sir Simon eventually announced that if Tulah insisted on sleeping in her own house, he would walk her home right away.

"I can't stay up all night, at my age, you know. I'll ring for Peters to bring your coat."

Once Sir Simon and Tulah had gone, the party gradually broke up. Angela found herself alone in the Great Hall with Landry, so that they climbed the stairs together. As they walked along the dimly lit upper corridor, Angela felt that the wine and food had done very little to relieve Landry's tension. She could tell he wanted to linger, but she was tired.

"Good night, Angela, sleep well," he said, stooping to kiss her lightly on the forehead.

She opened her bedroom door. He hovered uncertainly in the hall, staring at her.

"Good night, Landry. Try to get some sleep. Tomorrow is going to be hectic. You know how much Grandfather likes Christmas. See you at breakfast."

He still seemed to pause.

"Go along, Landry," Angela said in what was almost a motherly tone of voice. "You've had enough wine to make you sleep hours."

"I'm used to drinking wine. We drink a lot in digs."

"You may be, but I'm not." And she yawned.

He walked away slowly. She watched him, saw his shoulders droop so that he looked old. Then she closed her door with a sense of relief. For a little while, she had thought he might prove difficult, and she did not feel able to deal with anyone else's problems at the moment.

A fire had been lighted in the grate, giving off a pleasant crimson glow. Here in Pride's Court a fire was a luxury, she thought, while at Cricket House it had been a necessity. She sat for a little while thinking about her homecoming, and in the safety and warmth of her room, it once more seemed a good thing.

Eventually, she wandered to her dressing room and selected a white crepe de Chine nightgown with a fine lace top. It was all she needed here; no more sleeping in sweaters just to survive! After washing and brushing her teeth, she sat on the edge of the bed, ready to turn out the light and collapse.

There was a faint knock. Angela frowned.

"Who is it?"

"Please, may I come in?"

"I'm just about to go to sleep."

Without paying any attention to her reply, Landry opened the door.

Angela stood up, alarmed. What if someone had seen Landry coming here? Anyone might be wandering about, there were so many people staying in the house. She felt cold with fear. Her hands flew to the neck of her silk gown where the lace was cut low, revealing too much of her breasts. She felt incredibly naked, aware that Landry could see the outline of her nipples as he walked slowly across the carpet toward her. He looked excited, flushed, his eyes too bright to be natural. When he spoke, his voice shook.

"Don't be angry, Angela, I had to come. I must talk to you."

"But it isn't safe, Landry. You know that."

"I m sure no one saw me. Please listen to me."

She hesitated, catching his need, afraid to let him stay, afraid to let him go.

"All right, Landry, but only for a moment."

Sir Simon and Tulah reached the house after a fifteen-minute walk under a silent, starry sky. He was puffing from exertion, his breath steaming and then freezing to form a rime around his beard. He stamped the snow off his boots while Tulah fitted her key into the Yale lock. He heard it turn slowly in the cold air. The heavy oak door swung inward, letting them enter a square vestibule designed to cut drafts and provide a place for boots, rainwear, and umbrellas. Sir Simon hurriedly pushed open the inner doors, which led to the main hall. A colored glass lamp, left on by Tulah earlier, was still burning, decorated in seasonal pieces of tinsel. The house seemed shrunken after the great spaces of Pride's Court.

"Sure you won't change your mind and come back with me?" Sir Simon asked, peering upward from the bottom of the stairs. "Seems so damned lonely here. Not too late to change your mind, you know. Plenty of bedrooms made up and ready."

Tulah was already taking off her coat. Sir Simon began to grumble. "You need a new fur, Tulah, this is past a joke. Positively scruffy."

"Darling, there's plenty of wear in this one."

"I'm buying you a new coat next week."

He put the coat on the hall bench while Tulah removed her overshoes.

"Are you staying a little while to warm up? Would you like a brandy, Simon?"

"No thanks, I'll just take a quick look around," he said with an edge in his voice. "I can't afford to stay up half the night worrying. Hard enough to sleep these days, without adding more problems."

"Very well, but I locked everything before I left today. And I'll put on the night bolt when you leave. You can hear me do it."

Sir Simon checked the drawing room. The curtains had been left open and a light patch of sky was clearly stamped against the darker color of the walls. All was quiet. Next, he climbed a few stairs, glancing at the upper hall, where Tulah had left a tiny wall light burning.

"All right," he said at last, "I'll be on my way."

Tulah merely laughed. She knew his moods and found him completely predictable, but she was fascinated by his brilliance in business and by his spirit. His stubbornness could be handled quite easily and she had become extremely fond of him.

She walked with him back to the vestibule.

He stopped with his hand on the knob.

"I want to hear you put on the night bolt," he said testily.

"Yes, darling."

Showing affection was difficult for him, but he kissed her cheek.

"They liked you," he said gruffly. "The family liked you."

"I'm glad. I liked them, too."

She put her arms around his neck, touching the still-cold fur of his coat collar and pressed her cheek to his.

"Now, don't walk too fast. Take care of yourself."

"Yes, yes, I know how to do that. How do you think I reached this age?"

But he was pleased, just the same, to have someone make a fuss about him.

"Well, I'd better get myself out there and walk home. It's late."

She closed the door and shot home the bolt so that he would feel comforted. Then she heard the crunch of his footsteps on packed snow. He was gone.

Sir Simon trudged through the still night, walking faster because it was almost all downhill. Before long, he was back in Pride's Court and, as was his custom, double-checking on the way Peters had locked up for the night. Finally, satisfied, he made his way to his own apartment. In the upper corridor, as he was about to turn toward his own wing, he caught a muffled sound. Yet the house appeared to have settled down for the night. He walked slowly along the corridor in the wing where his tribe was temporarily in residence.

Just as he reached Angela's door, he heard strange sounds. All his forebodings about Tulah now surged to the fore but in a different context. There was someone in Angela's room!

Yes, he heard unmistakable sounds of movement, of low voices, even of sobbing. What in hell? Perhaps a burglar had gotten into Angela's room and was molesting the girl! He yanked the door open and burst in, prepared to save her. Instead, he saw two of his grandchildren rolling about on the bed stark naked. Landry, of all people! And sniffling. Sir Simon roared like a bull that has just been stuck by a sharp-eyed picador.

"What in hell is going on?"

His eyes traveled swiftly from the clothes dumped on the carpet to the naked young bodies on the bed. Rage consumed him. He could scarcely speak, but with a monumental effort he pulled his voice into control and cried, "Get up, you slut! How dare you turn Pride's Court into a bawdy house!"

His fury was directed toward Angela. He merely shriveled Landry with a scornful glance. Landry disentangled himself, leaving Angela completely exposed. She tried to cover herself with her arms.

"You incestuous trollop! I sinned against God the day I forgave you and took you back. Get out! Be out of this house before breakfast and don't tell me where. I don't want to know. I won't have your filth in this house another day!"

He wheeled about, still quivering with anger, and slammed the door behind him. Landry began to cry in earnest now, dragging on his clothes with trembling hands. Angela went to the bathroom to be devastatingly, methodically ill.

CHAPTER EIGHT

Tulah decided to leave the downstairs hall lamp burning. As she reached the landing and turned at right angles for the final short flight to the second floor, the house seemed uncannily silent. Like the Christmas poem, she thought, "not a creature was stirring, not even a mouse." Still, she was not in the least nervous. After her war experiences civilian life seemed tame.

The Horne place, though spacious enough, was only a third the size of the Pride's Court. But she found it comfortable after an evening with the voluble Courts. They would take some getting used to.

Once inside her own bedroom, she saw that the fire had sunk to a bed of glowing embers. A night lamp beside the bed spread a small, pink circle of light on the carpet, but the corners of the room were dark. The arch to the dressing room and bathroom beyond was barely discernible at first, but soon her eyes became adjusted to the semidarkness. Her nightclothes were in the dressing room, and she walked toward it but stopped almost instantly. She heard a faint creak. A shiver of apprehension passed through her.

In France men had told her they could feel the presence of another human close at hand, even though no one was in sight. She had heard soldiers discussing this when they talked of ambush. In her own experience there had been that awful day when she had killed the German. She had known there was someone hiding nearby, though she could see no sign. Now, the same electric, prickle wave crept along her scalp and down her neck. Another faint creak, the sound of a careful tread on thick carpet perhaps, came from the direction of the dressing room.

She gave herself a brief but stern lecture. Old houses always complained at night when there were fewer distracting sounds from the street. It was natural to hear beams shifting and loose panes rattling in the wind. On the other hand, she distinctly remembered a creak in the dressing room floor that she had meant to have repaired. Well, there was no use worrying about that now, she must investigate and satisfy herself that everything was in order. Despite this resolution, she was tempted to rush out of the room, down the stairs, and out into the night. In one sharp, clear moment she was poised for flight—like an animal that has scented danger.

Her practical nature quickly assumed control. She could not leave like a coward! So instead, she moved softly toward the night table, where she kept a pistol hidden in the drawer. The drawer made a sound that shivered through the dark room, but she located the gun and clasped it firmly.

As she swung toward the dressing room archway, a bulky figure appeared like a huge shadow. He came toward her so that she could make out a heavy overcoat and a rough cap. He was dangling something from one hand that picked up the fire's dying glow and flashed—one of her necklaces. In the other hand he held a gun.

"What are you doing here?" Tulah demanded.

She was ashamed of the tremble in her voice. She was more frightened in her own house than she had been that day in France. Then she had been primed for trouble, but here, in the solidly built mansion with its thick stone walls and double-glass windows, she felt cut off. Even if she screamed, it was unlikely that anyone out on the street would hear.

The intruder did not answer. For an endless moment they stared at each other, both speechless, both threatening. She raised her gun carefully and pointed it at him. She heard his little gasp of surprise when he realized that she was armed. Waves of hostility and fear shot across the room.

"Put down the necklace and get out," Tulah said, trying to erase any hint of nervousness, "or I'll shoot you!"

He hesitated, moved toward her so that the faint light from the lamp revealed his expression. He looked haggard, pathetically thin, but his eyes were brutal. She had seen faces like that many times during the war and recognized the look: desperation, ignorance, and hatred.

"The likes of you don't care if I starve," he said coarsely. "You got plenty. What's a necklace to you?"

"Put it down," Tulah repeated, "and get out. I warn you."

"No woman's likely to frighten *me*."

He was so close now that she could smell the rum on his breath. Probably he was drunk.

"I'm going to call the police if you don't leave immediately. Get out of my house and put the necklace down before you go."

"Not bloody likely."

To her horror he lurched, still clutching the jewelry, and raised the gun.

"You know what I look like. If I get caught, what chance do I have? Not with somebody like you as a witness. Be damned if I'll let you do that!"

Tulah knew that she had started a series of events she could not stop. She felt his angry eyes through the gloom, saw the menace of the gun he held, but she was frozen, unable to move a muscle. When the sharp crack shattered the room's pulse, the blow struck her just above the left breast, and she reeled back against the bed. Instinctively she held onto her gun. He turned his back on her to escape, and with a tremendous effort she raised herself up high enough to fire.

He dropped across the doorway, blocking the entrance. She saw the bright necklace skitter across the carpet out of his reach, but his right arm, the one holding the gun, was pinned beneath him.

Tulah fainted. When she became conscious again, her dress was clammy with blood and she realized she must get help quickly. She was already too weak to stand up, and on hands and knees she crawled across the carpet. It was useless to try to move him, she thought, to retrieve his gun. She could only hope that he was incapable of following her downstairs. Dragging herself over his body, she reached the hallway and paused to catch her breath before the long journey down the stairs. Then, half-crouching, holding the bannister with one hand and taking one careful step at a time, she made the slow descent. She could feel the spread of blood across the front of her gown, seeping into the sleeves and down the front of her skirt. Every second increased the risk of her bleeding to death; her only chance lay in reaching the telephone.

Thank God, she had left the hall light on. At least she could see where she was going. Once downstairs, however, she collapsed again. The single telephone was located in a small library facing the street. She willed herself to reach it, to lift the receiver and get the operator's attention.

Despite her struggle she fainted again. This time when she awoke, she could not be sure whether minutes or hours had elapsed. Her instinct for survival was still strong, and she began to creep once more along the hall when she heard sounds from upstairs. He was moving! And he was still armed.

She pushed herself toward the library, clutching the gun tightly. From behind came the unmistakable sounds of someone slowly coming down the stairs. He might be severely wounded, but he was still able to stumble in her direction. Once inside the library she could see a patch of sky and thought wildly of throwing the gun through the glass to the street in the hope that it might attract the attention of some passerby. He was getting nearer, painfully but inevitably dragging himself along. Her face was so close to the patterned carpet that she could see the lotus flowers woven there and wondered if they were the last things she would see on earth. She edged across the room and at last reached the telephone table in the broad bay window. Using a chair, she hoisted herself to her knees, terribly aware that she would be silhouetted against the clear night sky. He was in the doorway now, she could hear his rough breathing. There was no time to call the operator, he would never just stand there and let her do it! If she tried to stand, he'd shoot. She pitched her own gun at the center of the glass, and it cracked the cold pane but fell back into the room.

She turned to look at the doorway and saw him leaning there, a drunken shadow, still wearing the coat but without his cap. He was cursing. He raised his arm, tried to steady it with his other hand, but could not quite manage to do so. She flattened on the floor, found her gun, and picked it up again. With a tremendous effort she raised herself to her knees and turned to fire at him.

He sagged as the bullet hit him. Sure that he would fall to the floor, she managed to stand up, pick up the telephone from the table, and hurl it at the window. It struck low, just above the sill. Glass shattered across the carpet, icy shards glittered on the edge of the frame. A blast of frost cut into the room, tearing her breath away. With hands on the sill, she tried to scream across the spike-rimmed opening. A second crack of gunfire cut across the library.

The bullet hit her in the back, just above the hips. Her legs folded and she fell forward into the broken window. Her neck was almost severed. Her blond head hung, scarcely attached, and she drowned in blood, impaled on icicles of glass. Blood dripped and froze, hideous stalactites above the white snow.

Inside, the intruder fell upon the exquisite carpet, blending his blood with hers.

Angela had slept very little, and when she struggled out of bed on Christmas morning, she wondered if she could face the day. She pulled open the heavy curtains. Fat gray clouds moved across the sky like huge, slow blimps. Her mood matched the weather. She must leave Pride's Court as soon as possible, before there was any chance that she would have to face either her grandfather or Landry.

The house was quiet, but she knew that far below in the kitchens tea trays were being prepared by Cook and would be brought up by maids. Already the staff would be setting in motion elaborate preparations for the big Christmas dinner. She would have loved a cup of hot tea, Angela thought, but the longer she stayed in the house, the greater the risk. The best thing to do was pack a bag and flee to Aunt Miel's house.

The terrible misfortune that had led her grandfather into her bedroom—a whim, some unfamiliar sound, she did not know what it was—would have severe effects upon life in Pride's Court. Poor Landry was likely to be affected forever. She had no idea what might have happened if they had not been interrupted, but she was sure he would have even more serious doubts about his masculinity now. She could not face Landry, it would only embarrass him more.

As for Grandfather, she shuddered to think of such an

encounter. His anger always cooled slowly, and even when people crossed his will in small ways, he could remain infuriated for days. A moral offense (*crime* was probably the word Sir Simon would use) such as she and Landry had committed might bring on an eternity of rage.

At this moment she longed for Beau. If only she had Beau to comfort her in this desperate time. She felt so alone. It was the kind of thing she could tell no one, not even Beau, so there was no use thinking of that. Oh, it was all so awful: Why had she felt sorry for Landry last night? Why had she allowed sympathy to get the better of her judgment? But it was too late to change things. She had always been fond of Landry, and the combination of that, the wine, and her own loneliness had been too much. She had wanted to *help* Landry, not harm him.

There was no time to sit down and indulge herself in regrets, however; she must think. Should she telephone Aunt Miel first? That would mean risking a meeting with Grandfather because the single telephone was in the library. No, that wouldn't do. There was bound to be someone at home at the St. Amours' on Christmas Day. They couldn't lock the house in winter, even if they had gone to the farm.

If Aunt Miel pressed her for reasons, she would have to fall back on her choice of career. Everybody knew Sir Simon didn't approve of her painting. Sir Simon would tell his own story within Pride's Court, and he would protect Landry. Men always stuck together, and even in his rage, Angela remembered, *she* was the one he had attacked.

She threw some clothes into a small bag, put on the red fox coat her father had given her, and went downstairs to find Peters. She heard him in the dining room.

"Find me a taxicab, Peters," she said, looking about nervously for any sign of her grandfather. "I'm going to Lady St. Amour's if anybody asks."

"But Miss Angela . . . on Christmas morning?"

"Please, Peters, don't ask questions. Just get me a cab."

"I could order one of the cars, miss."

"No, no, I don't want one of the cars. Just a taxicab."

Peters went off shaking his head. Angela retreated to the reception hall to wait. There was less likelihood of her grandfather appearing there, she decided. After what seemed like hours the taxicab arrived and Peters took her out, still looking puzzled. It was a bitterly cold morning.

103

Peters helped her in and closed the door. Then he gave the driver the St. Amour address.

As she sat back in the car, her mind became fixed on the events of the night before. She could not get the scene out of her mind. It was so ugly, so frightening, so shaming.

"What if someone saw you come in here?" she had said to Landry when he refused to leave. "Grandfather may still be wandering about. He walked Tulah home."

"I'm sure no one saw me," Landry said.

"What do you want? It's very late. I'm tired."

"Please Angela, you're the only one I can talk to. I'm desperate, please listen to me. I have a problem . . . I think I have, anyway . . . and you're the only girl I could ever love in the whole world. You must help me. Please."

"Don't say that, Landry!" She had truly been shocked and had backed away from him. "We're cousins, you can't love me."

"Will you listen to me?"

She saw the haggard, searching look. He was shaking.

"How can I help you, Landry?"

They were whispering, although sounds did not travel too well in Pride's Court, the walls were so thick. Yet if someone happened to be going by, they might possibly catch voices through the door.

"Sometimes I think I'll kill myself."

"Don't be a fool, Landry." She had touched his arm then, wanting to shake sense into him. "Nothing is that bad."

But his agony seemed real. She could see he needed sympathy. All evening the feeling had grown that Landry had a strong attachment for her, but she had hoped her instincts were wrong. Apparently she had been right all along. And this was the result.

He moved closer to her, his eyes examining her face. She thought there were tears in his eyes. He looked down from her face to her neck, and his eyes came to rest upon the dark stain where her nipples pressed against the open lacework of her gown. She was surprised to find herself responding slightly to his mood. When she did not back away or become angry, he gave a soft, wounded cry and then threw his arms around her. He buried his face in her thick dark hair. She could feel his tears upon her cheek. His mouth moved hungrily down the curve of her shoulder.

She tried half-heartedly to push him away.

"Landry, for God's sake, stop it."

"You must help me."

He pulled her toward the bed and they both collapsed upon the turned-down quilt. He kissed her so urgently that she detected the bitter scent of an emotional crisis.

"Save me, Angela, save me," Landry whispered, taking his mouth away long enough to plead. "Save me."

"From what?" She could not understand what he was saying. She felt drawn to him, but she felt afraid, too.

"You won't laugh? Angela, I can trust you, can't I? You won't make fun of me. We've always been good friends. I've always loved you."

His hands slid over her breasts to find the tip of one nipple through the lace pattern. He leaned back, jerking at his tie, then tearing off his shirt, and throwing both on the floor. He was panting and sobbing. His eyes were almost closed now, and he began to whisper in her ear, but she could not make out the words or what it was he found so difficult.

"You'll have to tell me if you want me to help."

"I'm afraid, don't you see? I'm afraid I'm one of *them*. But I love you, Angela, so if I can love you, then I'm not one of *them*. That's right, isn't it?"

Angela was so appalled by his suggestion that she said nothing. Landry took her silence for consent. He stood up and tore off the rest of his clothes. She protested, but he did not listen. He lifted her to her feet and tried to slip the gown over her head. She let him do it. She stood there, all graceful curves sculpted from rubescent flesh, shimmering in the firelight. He gasped as he looked at her and pushed her down on the bed once more, this time as if he were clutching at his last hope of salvation. They rolled over and over on the broad bed, Landry in a mindless frenzy and Angela submissive but stunned. They rolled until their bodies were fiercely entwined, wound miraculously into an ecstatic braid.

Even in this extremity Angela realized that Landry's whole future as a man might hang in the balance, and she could not bear to reject him. He was too fragile, too tender to survive such a blow. She wanted so much to help him, not because she felt passionate about him but because theirs was a special friendship. They pressed together in a damp embrace, but although his lips consumed her skin from face to thigh and his fingers twitched eagerly across her body, it was futile.

It was at that very moment that Sir Simon had burst into the room and begun his tirade. As the cab ground into the snow piled in front of the St. Amour house, Angela was jarred out of her reverie.

She paid the taxi driver and rang the front doorbell. A girl whom Angela had never before seen answered and did not recognize her.

"Is Lady St. Amour at home?" Angela asked. "I'm her niece."

"Oh, yes, yes, mademoiselle, I'm sorry, I didn't know . . ." the girl said in French. "Please come in."

Once inside, however, the maid looked doubtful. People simply did not come calling on Christmas morning without notice. As Angela brushed snow from her boots, she said briskly, "Please tell my aunt I'm here."

"Yes, mademoiselle."

Angela looked around the hall and felt that the house welcomed her. She had always loved the house in a strange way, partly because she had first met Beau here. She watched the maid disappear upstairs to speak to Honey.

When Honey rushed down the stairs and hugged Angela, she felt safe and loved for the first time in months.

"Whatever's happened, darling? Trouble with Papa?"

Angela felt tears coming—tears of relief and gratitude that Aunt Miel understood and would not ask too many embarrassing questions.

"You know what he's like," Angela said.

"What's the old ogre been up to? And at Christmas? Does he never give up? I suppose it's something about this new wife. I never did think you and Charles could live with that. I remember Tulah from club meetings. A very strong character."

Angela took off her coat and boots. She was satisfied to let her aunt think that was the problem. The truth couldn't be told and she'd had no time to think up a plausible story.

"You look pale, darling. Have you eaten breakfast?"

"I've had nothing. I had to get out before I ran into Grandfather."

"Well, come along up. I'm just having mine. Hortense

will bring another cup and some hot water. There are muffins and toast."

Over tea in Honey's pretty green and pink sitting room they talked around the problem. Honey did not press for details; she felt Angela would tell her sooner or later. Now was not the best time to force the issue when the girl was so obviously upset.

"Is anybody staying in the nursery?" Angela asked.

"Not at the moment. You're welcome to move in if you wish. I don't want to interfere with your father's plans for you, though."

"Father doesn't know about this. He's up in the Laurentians with Polly."

"I didn't know. I haven't spoken to any of the family for some time. When he gets back, you'll have to discuss your plans with him . . . arrange for an allowance . . . but in the meantime, don't worry. We can look after you. Next year you come into your inheritance from your grandmother."

"Yes, things should be better then. I'm sorry I didn't visit after we got back," Angela said apologetically. Her aunt was being so generous and so unquestionably loyal she felt badly about her behavior. "I kept meaning to. But I've been so mixed up. I miss Beau so much—"

"Angela, of course I understand. But this love affair between you and Beau has to be resolved. You're making yourself ill over him. It's no good."

Angela said meekly, "I know. But I can't seem to stop loving him."

"Did you and Papa quarrel over Tulah moving into Pride's Court?"

"I don t see how Father and I can go on living there," Angela said evasively. After all, it was partially true, and no doubt she would eventually have come to some disagreement with Tulah. "You've met her, so you know what a dynamo she is."

Honey laughed.

"I know. She makes everybody else seem half-asleep. She'll make Papa jump, and it serves him right, the silly old fool. I was rather pleased when I heard he'd dug himself into such a stupid situation. But from your point of view, and from your father's, it's quite different."

"Are you and Uncle Armand the only ones living here now?"

"Yes, for a while. My real news is that we're giving up this house. Armand has taken a house on Pine Crescent. It will be a while before we move, of course, but I'll be back on the Mountain after all these years."

"Oh, Aunt Miel! That means we'll lose the nursery!"

"That *is* a pity. I know how you loved that room. So did Marc and Camille; they always stayed up there when they were guests in the house. Strange how a room becomes so important."

"That was where I first saw Beau. He was playing Chopin on the piano, and the light was so beautiful. Do you remember?"

"Very well. I had no idea things would turn out this way . . ." Honey said with some regret, "or I wouldn't have introduced you to Beau in the first place."

"It wasn't your fault. How could you know?"

"You must get over this passion for Beau," Honey said decisively, "and get on with your life. If you work hard and don't see him, perhaps you'll forget. Work has saved my sanity on more than one occasion, I can tell you."

Angela, who had thought her aunt was always happy, looked surprised.

"Don't look so amazed," Honey said, smiling. "We all have troubles. Now, tell me some gossip about Pride's Court."

For a little while, Angela forgot her own frustrations as she recounted Tulah's visits and how much Sir Simon doted. They both giggled a lot about that. And then there was Mildred's new suitor, North Grenville.

"The Grenvilles," Honey said, frowning. "Henry Grenville was head of a bank. It merged with one of the larger ones. He was a little older than Armand. What is the son like?"

"Oh, dashing! Charming, and all the rest. Mildred's quite dotty with love. You ought to see them holding hands and mooning all over the house. I just hope he doesn't chuck, that's all. It's the first time poor Milly has ever had such luck."

"And what about the boy? How does he feel?"

"He seems to like her quite a lot. He certainly pays plenty of attention to her."

"And does Papa approve of all this?"

"He thinks North is a godsend. Gave his blessing from the start. North works for him at the bank, you know. Grandfather thinks he's found the ideal husband for poor old Milly. So I think it will all come off in fine style, Probably sometime in the spring. Oh dear, Aunt Miel, why is life so simple for some people and so difficult for others?"

CHAPTER NINE

Despite the fact that she had not planned on guests and thoroughly expected to dine *intime* on Christmas night, Honey had set the table with her George III cutlery and brilliantly colored Worcester dessert plates. She had bought them in London when Armand was knighted. Angela was forced to admire her aunt's style and the care she took with appointments, although she herself would not have bothered with such details.

Sitting solemnly, eating delicious stuffed goose by candlelight, Angela realized how fond she was of her aunt and uncle, how much she had missed them. Aunt Miel was still slim, in a fashionable gown with a silver sheen. She wore the necklace her mother had given her the day she died. Her fine, gray-gold hair was brushed carefully into a sleek chignon, not so fashionable these days as the short cuts so many women favored but flattering nevertheless. Uncle Armand, wearing a dinner jacket and black tie, was distinguished, handsome, deftly sure of himself. What a handsome pair they must have been when they eloped all those years ago, Angela thought with an artist's appreciative eye.

"Welcome back to the St. Amour side of the family," Armand said, raising his glass of hock to his niece.

"Thank you, Uncle Armand. It's kind of you to take me in. You and Aunt Miel always seem to be rescuing runaways and strays. That's how I met Beau in the first place."

"Well, Beau wasn't happy on the farm," Honey said. "And he needed to be in Montreal to study his music. We were glad to do it."

"What you need to do," Armand said with a friendly smile, "is to get right to your painting, Angela. Why don't you go out after Boxing Day and buy all the supplies you need, my dear? Don't worry about money. Miel will talk to Charles when he returns, and we'll make some arrangements. You have all the space you need in the nursery, no need to go out to rent a studio."

"Is there any point in writing to Charles?" Honey asked. "Or will he be back too soon for a letter to reach him?"

"No use, he'll be home in a week," Angela said. "I'm going to start work immediately, yes. Though I'm not sure just what I want to paint."

"You know we're moving out of this house next summer, don't you?" Armand inquired. "I wonder if we could commission you to do some paintings of this house. You could begin with your favorite room, the nursery."

"What a wonderful idea, Uncle Armand!" Angela said, offering a genuine smile for the first time. Her face turned lovely again, quite illuminated with a flash of joy.

"How clever of you, darling," Honey said fondly to her husband. "Would you, Angela?"

"Of course. I'd adore to paint the nursery. The light is so special. . . . You know how I've always loved it. I'll begin as soon as I can get my materials together."

This was the first notion that had caught her fancy in some time; for the rest of the meal, part of her mind was already working on the project. Capturing the mood of the nursery would be a challenge . . . so beautiful, so otherworldly, the light shimmering through the dormers, the space, the hint of times past, of memories still alive. Even the toys. . . . She was seized with a grip of creative energy. For the first time since her return to Montreal she was desperate to paint, felt she *must* paint or she would explode. In these few moments she was more like herself than she had been since the first happy days at Cricket House.

They took coffee in the small sitting room. Honey had replaced some of the drearier paintings. One of the new acquisitions was a family portrait by a minor English painter, Arthur Devis, which she had bought at Christie's for only seventy-five pounds. She had her father's taste in objets d'art. Angela felt the room had definitely improved since her last visit.

"Have you told Angela we'll be going to the farm a couple of days before New Year's?" Armand asked.

"Not yet, darling, I was waiting until she settled in. It is a bit of a problem."

Angela could not be taken to the farm. Beau's mother, Justine Fitzgerald, had not approved of them living together in England and would have made it most uncomfortable. The family gatherings were difficult enough, and this was an extra burden Honey could not add. This meant that Angela would be alone in the house, with only a reduced staff of servants.

"I know, Aunt Miel, don't worry," Angela said quickly, "I understand perfectly. Beau's mother wouldn't receive me very graciously."

"She's very much the religious fanatic, I'm afraid," Honey said. "Well, I don't have to tell you how complicated the family scene is, even without you."

"I'll be perfectly all right," Angela said cheerfully. "By then I'll have my paints and be started on something, and I won't want to leave the nursery. Just don't think any more about it."

"Actually, we'll leave two days before. We want to be at the farm for *réveillon* supper." This was the traditional French New Year's Eve heavy meal, served after a church service. Very much a family affair.

"Perhaps you could go to Mellerstain," Honey said.

Angela, thinking of her disastrous scene with Landry, knew she could not face Aunt Sydney, Uncle Fort, and Landry himself over the New Year's holiday.

"Really, I'll be fine. Please don't worry."

"We'll think of something. I thought you liked Sydney."

"I do like Aunt Sydney. She's always been good to me," Angela said noncommittally.

They could hear the telephone ringing from the far corner of the house, where Armand had a small study.

"I wonder if that could be Michel," Honey said, brightening. "But it's rather late over there to be calling, isn't it?"

"I'll see, darling," Armand said, getting up to take it. "But don't get your hopes up, *chérie*. I think Michel and Clarissa would have called much earlier."

He was gone only a few moments, but when he returned, he looked grave.

"What is it, Armand?" Honey said quickly, rising from her chair. "Is it for me?"

"Yes, it's Gabriel. About a story. He needs to talk to you. A dreadful thing has happened, *ma chérie*, and he wants to know how to handle it."

"Someone is dead? Not family?" Honey said, grasping the strange air Armand had about him. "No . . . . Not *Michel*?"

"No, darling, not Michel."

Honey had a constant fear that Michel, because he was flying, would be killed in an accident.

"It's Tulah Horne," Armand said. "She's been killed."

"How awful!" Angela cried. "But how could that happen?"

"I don't know the details. Gabriel wants to speak to you, Honey," Armand said. "I think you'd better take the call. It's important how the story is handled in the press."

"Yes, of course," Honey said.

When she had gone, Armand poured himself a brandy. "Angela, would you like a drink, my dear?"

"No thank you, Uncle Armand."

"I hope she decides to play down the story," Armand said. "This constant duel between Miel and her father is bad for everybody."

"Aunt Miel has good sense. She'll know what to do," Angela said. "But what kind of accident could it have been? Grandfather walked her home last night, I know it. And she must have been all right when he left her."

"It will all come out," Armand said philosophically, "but I gathered from Gabriel's attitude that it was . . . particularly horrible."

In the end, Honey decided that *Le Monde* would not try to sell newspapers on the sensationalism of Tulah's death. Armand was pleased at her decision. She found out later, when she talked to Fort, that Sir Simon had gone into complete seclusion and would see nobody but his doctor. The rest of the family had retired to their own houses and were not answering the door or the telephone. The Courts had vanished, at least temporarily, from the limelight.

Looking up from her easel, Angela saw that the afternoon light was fading quickly. In the dormers, where snow edged the small panes of glass, a lemon sky was tempered with shifting gray clouds that changed the nursery's bright morning mood to one of late afternoon wistfulness. She would have to stop painting. It was the childlike, gay quality of the nursery, tinged with nostalgia, that she wished to capture. She felt happy about her work. It was, definitely, the best thing she had painted for some time.

Downstairs Hortense would be preparing tea (which would also serve as supper) in the small sitting room. Afterward Angela planned to read in front of the fire; she had begun John Buchan's *History of the War*. It was a link with Beau's pilgrimage through France.

Impatiently she put down her palette and began to clean her brushes in a pail of turpentine. (It was just the right size, having once contained Heinz's plum butter; the paper label was stained and ragged with use.) She removed her painting smock and stood back to judge of the effect of her work. Yes, it was shaping up nicely; she felt a tingle of pleasure at the thought that she was working well again. The picture seemed to be working *with* her, taking off on its own.

The shadows in the nursery deepened. She turned on a single lamp and walked toward the corridor where the bedrooms and bathroom lay. Even if there was no one else in the house, she wanted to wash up before tea. She always felt messy after painting seriously. Not that she minded being in the house alone. There were still three servants about, anyway, and in many ways it made things easier. She did not have to make meaningless conversation. And as far as Tulah's death was concerned, she felt sad but grateful that she had escaped Pride's Court before the discovery was made. She could imagine the mood of that great house under these circumstances.

She would have liked tea up here, she reflected, after washing and brushing her hair. By herself, in the safety of the nursery surroundings. She well understood why Marc and Camille liked it so much and why Beau had chosen it as his studio. But it wasn't fair to ask Hortense to carry a tray up to the fourth floor on a holiday. Perhaps she ought to go down and bring it up herself.

How lovely it was that Aunt Miel had preserved the nursery just the way it had been when she'd come to this house as a bride! The rocking horse still stood in the corner with a glint in its eye, the miniature furniture, the blackboard, the books filled with fairy tales and pictures, the shelves of toys, all were there. The first day she had seen

Beau had been right here in this room. How painful it was but how sweet to recall the days when she and Beau had been so close—the first time she had heard him play Chopin, sitting at the piano with the summer light falling on his thick dark curls, his slim body tense with effort. He had been so truly beautiful. You could say that about Beau and still know that he was masculine. He was much more than handsome. There was an ethereal quality about him that suggested some other plane. They had been so close then (almost like the Court twins), never quarreling, encouraging each other creatively, vowing always to be together. Who would have believed that all those promises would turn to ashes?

And then in England everything had been truly perfect at first. But the days began to go awry somehow. Beau was essentially a solitary man; music came first. She loved him still, everything about him—his face, his voice, his unique talent, even that same need to be alone. He was not like other men. The passion in him ran through his blood and bones. But they were apart again, intensely angry. Every day without Beau seemed to hurt, but there was nothing she could do.

With a tremendous effort she turned away from the nursery fire, from staring at the silent piano, and prepared to go downstairs. Hortense would be cross if there were any later. But before she could move, she heard somebody coming up the nursery stairs. Hortense, she thought with an irritated shrug. Now the maid would look put upon for the extra effort.

It was done now. She waited for the door to open. But it was not Hortense who stood in the open doorway. It was a phantom from the past; unbelievable, a ghost, a dream she had somehow caused to come alive.

He stood still staring at her. Then he turned swiftly and closed the nursery door. His restless green gaze once more took in her face, then her whole being. His shaggy curls were unfashionably long, over his collar. His sensual mouth was pink, full, open, as if about to speak. He brought with him the scent of cold air, disturbing the snug womb of the nursery. She saw that he wore dark green corduroy trousers and a heavy hand-knitted sweater. He was terribly thin and boyishly fierce. He held out his arms.

She ran to him, all resolutions gone in the glory of the

moment. Beau swept her up in a hard, hungry embrace both hurting and sensuous, pressing his cheek against hers until the bones seemed about to crack. She began to cry. Beau was crying too, and the taste of tears lingered in their kiss. Then they collapsed in a heap upon the carpet by the fire, thoughts of tea and maids, of long separations, of old rages, utterly forgotten. It was like the first time they had made love with the mystery, the newness, the excitement of a first experience, and it was like the last time they had made love, as if they were dying and the funeral drums were beating in their ears. It tasted of eternity.

Afterward, lying before the fire, Beau said, "I knew everything would be all right if I could just see you, touch you. Imagine how amazed I was when Hortense told me you were living here, that you were up in the nursery! I thought I was going to have to break into Pride's Court to find you, and instead you're here."

"Our room, really. Beau, I've always loved it. When I left Pride's Court—and don't ask about that right now—I was so lucky to find the nursery empty. But they're moving from this house next summer. Uncle Armand has bought a house up on the Mountain."

Beau looked downcast.

"What a shame! Someone else in our room!"

"I'm painting it for them so there'll be a record. That's what I'm working on right this minute."

"Angela, what a wonderful idea."

"Uncle Armand thought of it. Beau, I can't believe you're here. Why did you come back in the middle of winter?"

She expected him to say he had come for her. That he couldn't live without her. She waited for the words, smiling, expectant. But her mood pitched downward as he said, "I'm appearing with L'Orchestre de Québec as soloist next week. It isn't a particularly strong group, but they've been importing talent lately. As a native of the province, I felt I ought to give them a hand. It was a chance to come back for a couple of weeks anyway."

"Oh. That's splendid."

"I thought I'd see if Mother would like to go with me to Quebec City for the concert. I'll ask her tomorrow."

"*Tomorrow?*"

"Well, yes, I'm taking the noon train to St.-Cloud. I'm just staying here tonight, you see. That way I can visit the whole family at once. And be there for the New Year's Eve dinner."

"But darling, you know very well *I* can't go to the farm. Your mother won't receive me. That's why I didn't go with Aunt Miel, that's why I'm alone. Surely you won't leave me on New Year's Eve now that you're here?"

"Sweetest darling, I'm here *tonight*. That's what's important surely. You weren't expecting me. So you can see how sensible it is to go out to the farm and see everybody at once. Saves all sorts of dreary visits. I haven't seen any of my family for two years after all."

"Beau, that's so selfish of you. How can you even think of leaving me so soon? It's your fault, anyway, that your mother won't have me in the house. If we were properly married, she'd have to receive me whether she wanted to or not. You don't care that much for your family. . . . You never did."

"I want to be home at *réveillon*," he said stubbornly. She recognized instantly the familiar self-centered look—like a small child about to have a tantrum if he did not get his own way.

"Why, suddenly, do you insist on being at a family dinner? It never bothered you before."

"It's something I want to do, that's all. I'm sure Mother would like it."

"I'm sure she would."

Angela's face had turned a dead white, and her eyes had become a flat gray. She now took refuge in the commonplace.

"Tea will be cold. Let's go down."

"To hell with tea."

"Dear God, you sound just like Grandfather."

"So what? I don't care about tea, I care about you, and right now."

"Oh yes, you care, all right. All you can think of is taking a train to St.-Cloud to eat oysters and turkey."

"That's stupid. I want to see my family. We both know you can't go. It's quite simple."

"That's why you're being so horrible."

"Don't be a child. You were alone when I arrived."

"Me a child?" she screamed at him, her Court temper surfacing at last. "How can you say that, Beau Dosquet?

116

You're acting like a spoiled, selfish brat. You're the worst brat I've ever met. You're nothing but an infant!"

"And you're a spoiled little rich girl."

"If we were married," she said, bringing her voice down with an effort, "then I could go with you. As it is, your mother regards me as a fallen woman. A scarlet woman."

"Married? We've been over this marriage thing a thousand times. So will you stop it? What in hell is the use of going over it again?"

"Stop shouting!" she shouted. "The maid will hear you."

"Let her hear. I don't give a damn!"

"Monster! I should never have let you touch me. What a fool I was. That's all it is with you, sex, sex, sex, and nothing else. Now that that's taken care of, you don't give a damn about me. Have you no feelings?"

She began to sob, anger mixed with disappointment and hurt.

"You let me use you if it comes to that. Don't try to pretend you have no appetites of your own. Are you saying I raped you?"

"I thought everything was different."

"Nothing's different. Why would it be? We belong together and that hasn't changed, but I'm not getting married. Why do you have to behave like some bourgeois housewife? Like the rest of the sheep. I thought we were better than that. We don't need these ridiculous rules. That's for people like Hortense. They need to be told what to do, how to behave. We don't."

"Obviously you do need to be told how to behave," she cried, slamming out of the nursery and down the stairs. "Why don't you go back where you came from?"

She went directly to the sitting room and found tea laid out. She heard Beau come down and disappear into the kitchens at the back, probably looking for Hortense and his own private tea tray. She shut the sitting room door firmly to keep him out. At one point she was sure he had gone out because she heard the front door open and shut. *He's gone*, she thought with a terrible pang, *good riddance*. But she knew that she would die if he didn't come back. Oh, what was the use of all this? Why couldn't she get over this passion for Beau? Why did she let him treat her so badly?

Sipping tea disconsolately and not touching the meat sandwiches so neatly cut upon the fine china plate, she listened for sounds of Beau's return but heard nothing. She could not imagine where he would go. All his relatives would now be out at the farm. He could go to a hotel, of course, but that was stupid. Why was he like this? Over and over the question turned in her head until she had a monumental headache. It wasn't as if he had another woman, or she another man. The incident with Landry had been quite separate, nothing to do with lust or love but merely an act of pity. She did not count that. She drank two cups of tea and a glass of port and rang for Hortense.

"Did Mr. Dosquet go out?"

"I don't know, mademoiselle." The maid looked at her strangely.

I suppose she knows what we were doing up there, Angela thought crossly, *but I don't care. Let her think what she likes.* "Well, I'm going up to the nursery. So there'll be nothing else tonight, Hortense. And don't bother ordering food for tomorrow. Take the day off. Just leave some cold food for me in the kitchen. I'll get it myself."

"*Merci, mademoiselle.* Do I have permission to go to my mother's for the day?"

"Please do, Hortense. I shall be fine."

She climbed the stairs as if she were crippled. The old house was quiet, the stairs shadowed, but she was delighted to be so far up, in her eyrie, away from the world. Being on the fourth floor was like being in another world—away from street sounds and servants and the sounds of other people's lives. She could not have borne having to talk to anybody tonight, or to listen, either.

She walked through the dimly lit nursery to her bedroom. She was so exhausted that she thought she might read in bed rather than in front of the nursery fire as she had planned. She did not bother to turn on the bedroom light, but the patch of sky in the dormer outlined the furniture. She had not taken two steps into the room before she heard a sound, and then saw him standing there, and she gasped, not sure just for a moment who it was.

"Beau! You frightened me!"

"Did I? I'm sorry."

He was wearing a dressing gown. She assumed from this that he had moved his luggage up to one of the other nursery bedrooms.

"What do you want now? Why are you back?"

She had wanted him back, but now she felt resentful and angry again. Why must she go through all the emotional pain once more? Her voice grated unnaturally.

"You didn't really think I was going, did you?"

His voice was low this time. Coaxing. He crossed the room to where she stood uncertainly, passed her, and closed the bedroom door. Then he took her shoulders in his strong hands and forced her to turn to him. His fingers were digging fiercely into her flesh, hurting, but she did not protest. Relief that he was here drowned anger, hurt, and resentment.

"I thought you'd gone."

"I wanted you to think that."

"But I heard the front door——"

His fingers lingered on her face, lightly, lovingly outlining the fine bones, the voluptuous mouth, the great deep eyelids.

"I thought I'd die," she whispered.

"Come, Angela, let's begin again."

She softened before his lack of pretense. How like a little boy he was! She let him undress her slowly; precise movements undid the buttons of her sweater one by one and removed it, hands found the skirt hook and let it fall to the floor. She stood shivering in her silk chemise and step-ins, dry-mouthed with relief and desire, and trembling with want. A sword cut through her heart at the idea that she wanted him so much she would give in without a word after his cruelty. She let him unfasten her stockings. What if he should leave again? What if he should stop making love to her now? The faint light of night fell on her white skin, her smooth shoulders, and slender neck, the elegant outline of her face with its perfect nose, shadowed cheekbones, huge eyes.

She did not speak as he slid the chemise from her, or the flimsy silk away from her hips. His hands, so skilled at coaxing music from cold ivory, were just as apt on her breasts and on the narrow hips harboring a perfect triangle of dark down. He studied her for a few moments, letting his eyes enjoy her, though he saw that she was shaking in the cool air.

They walked to the bed, hands gripping tightly, and then fell upon each other starving, crying, shouting, kissing each other into oblivion. The feel of love rolled up over her to enclose her, and she reached for that top of the elusive wave until it finally crashed and she was back in shallow water. Afterward they lay together damp and spent, but snug beneath the blankets, saying nothing. They both slept, but it was still night when they awoke again, and Beau was pressed up against her, once more urgent, shaking her shoulder a little to make sure she was going to respond. She turned sleepily to him, "Beau, I never want to leave you again."

"That's what I've been saying. You just don't listen."

"Darling, I do listen. I'm sorry I've made such a fuss. We waste so much time arguing. It's as though we don't really want to be together."

"That's an odd thing to say."

He was kissing her nipples, running his hands over her slender waist.

"Still, it's true."

"Now, darling, don't start all that marriage stuff again," Beau said, still nibbling. "We have this beautiful night together. Let's just make love again. I'm desperate for you. Can't you feel it?"

"Yes, I know, I do feel it. Lovely, darling."

They were lying side by side, and she lifted herself up on one elbow to look down on him. He looked so vulnerable she felt like crying. Like a small boy who has found some fantastic joy and isn't sure it's real. His face was at once innocent and desirous. Years had vanished without a trace, leaving him like a living statue; it seemed almost indecent to touch him. Her lips traced his hairline, nudged across his eyebrows and across the closed petals of his slanted eyes. *He is as beautiful as an angel,* she thought. *How fragile he looks!* She wanted to wrap her arms around him and protect him forever from life's terrible blows. She ran her lips down his chest across the dark hair, lower and across his stomach, where the hair twined down toward his loins. Her lips foraged over his hard penis and the twin fonts until she felt him groan with anticipation. Luxuriously he stretched and tightened. This time they made love slowly, exquisitely, savoring every moment, balancing on the rim of urgency until they sank into peace.

They fell asleep again.

At eight o'clock in the morning Beau got up and began to dress.

"Are you going to find some breakfast?" Angela asked sleepily.

"I can make coffee. You stay here. I'll bring it up to you."

"All right, darling. But it's so early."

"Well, go back to sleep, then. I've got to pack a few things in a small bag before I catch the train."

She sat up then, rigid with surprise. An emotional wave struck her, bringing her fully out of dreams and into the harsh light of morning.

"You mean you're still leaving today, after last night?"

"Of course." He looked amazed.

"Beau, I thought— You're *evil*!"

"Evil? Angela, for God's sake, you're hysterical. I'll bring up some coffee and we'll talk."

"There's nothing to talk about. I hate you! Get out of my life. Take your stupid clothes and get out. You don't know the meaning of love. You only love yourself. You are the most selfish, hateful man in the whole world!"

He swore at her.

She picked up a lamp and hurled it at him. He dodged, swearing again.

"If you go to the farm today, I never want to see you again as long as we live."

He dressed. Then he stood staring at her.

"If this is blackmail, Angela, forget it. I'm not ready to get married. I think you'd better understand that right now."

"You're a selfish, pigheaded brat. You want everything and you give nothing."

"My trouble is, I'm brutally honest. Women can't stand honesty. Do you want me to lie to you?"

"I want you to get out." This time she spat the words at him. "And I want you to understand that what you think is love is nothing but lust. And I want you to understand that I never want to see your face again, or hear your name again, or touch you, or—or—"

She was still sobbing when he left the house. On the long train ride to St.-Cloud, he raged inside, but he had settled nothing when he arrived at the station. And soon he was engulfed by his family. His mood, however, did not lighten.

CHAPTER TEN

Not every member of the St. Amour family was able to come to the farm for New Year's Eve *réveillon*. Ottawa was fermenting with political and social activity since the election, and as a senator, Corbin Dufours was very much involved. He was invited to the governor general's exclusively male New Year's Day levee, and Helene was looking forward to a number of holiday parties that included both of them. The prime minister had been sworn in three days earlier, and a certain amount of social activity centered around that. Helene had never been too friendly with her brother Armand or her sister Justine, so she was not much missed.

Marc St. Amour, Armand's only brother, could not leave Montreal because of his pressing duties at Notre Dame Church. As vicar general he carried a heavy responsibility. Rumor had it that he was within shouting distance of the bishopric. His sister Camille was still his housekeeper and she would not go to the farm without him. Justine's daughter, Nicolette, was staying in the city to await the birth of her first child. It was an unpleasant fact that not a single member of the family regretted her absence.

Those family members who did arrive in time for *réveillon* attended mass in the small, unheated church in St.-Cloud. New Year's Eve always lured a full congregation out of the surrounding countryside so that the narrow pews were crowded with farmers and their families. In the uncertain flicker of candlelight the worshippers took on a medieval look as they huddled in shapeless sheep-lined coats, dark leather jackets, and hand-knit tuques. They might have been figures in a faded oil painting as they clasped their missals and doggedly followed the service.

Beau found himself wedged in a front pew between his bulky stepfather, Timothée Fitzgerald, and his brooding mother, Justine. Why was it, he wondered idly, that she always turned mass, *any* mass, into a personal ritual? As if the priest were conducting the service just for her. Beau glanced quickly from one face to the other and realized

122

with a twinge of regret that he had escaped from Angela's impossible demands only to be caught up once more in his family's special brand of warfare. One day, many years before, it had been exactly the reverse. He had fled to Angela, to Montreal, to get away from all this. What had drawn him back? Some vague thread of nostalgia, he supposed. He let out his breath slowly and decided to immerse himself in the solemn dignity of the church service. It was a way out of reality, at least.

A strong scent of freshly cut evergreen boughs mixed oddly with billows of sweet incense. Beau allowed the service to envelop him so that he slipped easily backward in time. He stared up at the familiar face of the carved wooden Virgin over the altar. Her sad, lidless eyes caught and held his own. He found himself drowning in chants and the hum of Latin phrases.

The blurred music produced by untrained voices washed away his own pain. Then, through a miracle of some kind, he detected in his inner ear a simple, poignant melody. In those first moments he felt faint from the strong whiffs of incense and wondered if he were hallucinating. The melody sang through the private reaches of his mind. It was silvery and sad: a curve that touched the heart and made his eyes damp with grief. A simple enough theme yet one he could build upon; tentative now but surely the roots of something grander. He knew he could weave it into his War Symphony. Curious, too, that the cry that he had not been able to pick up from ghosts on the battlefields of France was printing itself upon his consciousness through the sound of church music! The problem was to retain it until he could get home and write it down. It was slightly elusive still, threading finely in the deep tracks of his awareness.

He gazed into the Virgin's eyes, praying for assistance and straining to hear again the agonizing sound. It began to fill his mind and he lost touch with his surroundings. He was frozen in time. The chants flowed and swirled around him, the faces of his family faded, and he felt dizzy with creative joy, with orgasmic ecstasy. He had his theme.

When the service ended, he ran out of the church, pushing past people roughly, without speaking. Then he huddled into a back corner of the sleigh, wordless and unseeing on the drive home. His family ignored him. At the door of the house he leaped out and ran into the kitchen and up the stairs to slam the door against intruders. In the poorly lighted dormer bedroom he began to scratch furiously on a piece of manuscript paper, his sole purpose to capture the vibrant pith of the thing. Later there would be harmonies: the intricacies of orchestration.

The others trooped in, stamping off snow and throwing cold wraps into a corner. The smell of turkey drifted amiably through the air, and everyone looked forward to the late night supper. At Christmas they had celebrated in the city with Honey and Armand in the old family house on St.-Denis, but it was the custom for everybody who could travel to go out into the country for New Year's. Timothée dispensed drinks, and without waiting for Beau to come down, he took his place at the head of the long table. The aromatic turkey was ready to be carved. It was stuffed according to Justine's special recipe: a dressing of minced veal and pork, chopped turkey innards, bits of bacon, chopped onion and herbs, milk-soaked bread, egg yolk and Armagnac. There was a rough pâté and rich cake baked to look like a yule log. Justine had lined up four heavy silver sconces, each holding four candles, the length of the table.

When Beau finally appeared, everybody was seated at the table. Honey and Armand occupied one side, with an empty space between them for Beau. On the other side, Mathieu, his wife, Nora, and Nora's friend, Rose, were sitting in uncomfortable silence.

Justine looked up crossly from her place at the foot to remonstrate, "Really, Beau, you might be a little more thoughtful on New Year's Eve! What have you been doing?"

She was still a handsome woman with black hair pulled back from a large dark-eyed face that scarcely seemed able to conceal her impatience and energy. The black hair had two splendid wings of white at the temples.

"I'm sorry, Mother," Beau said without much conviction, "but I had to write something down quickly. I had an idea for a theme while I was in church."

He poured himself wine from one of the decanters set at intervals along the table.

"Beau, that's wonderful," Honey said enthusiastically. "It's so good to see you again and know you're working.

Will you be in Montreal for awhile? We've plenty of room if you want to stay."

"I know. I saw Angela," Beau said tersely.

"You did? You visited the house?"

"Yes. I stayed overnight."

"I see." Honey was uncertain about the wisdom of pursuing this. She had not counted on Beau's arrival in her absence. No one had expected him. She saw Justine's disapproving glare, Timothée's suddenly rigid posture. They blamed her, of course, for bringing Angela and Beau together. But it had all seemed so harmless when they were children.

Armand interceded quickly,

"The turkey smells delicious, Justine. It's amazing the way you make it just like Mother did."

"Thank you," Justine said, glancing over her shoulder toward the servant girl. "Bring the vegetables now, Marie-Claire."

They passed the dishes around informally. It was Justine who introduced the unfortunate subject of the baby.

"Have you checked on Jean-Baptiste?" she asked Nora. "I mean since we came back from church?"

"Yes, he's about the same."

"You mean the fever is still high?"

"And his breathing is difficult. Yes," Nora said without adding any detail. They seldom spoke of the baby. "I'll go up and see how he is directly after supper."

"Take your time," Mathieu said nastily. "It won't make very much difference to the baby."

"I worry when nobody is checking up on him," Nora said gently. "I realize there isn't much we can do."

"Nothing changes, when it comes to *him*," Mathieu said and his voice was extremely unpleasant. "So let's not talk about it."

"I prayed for him," Justine said fiercely. "He's innocent. He'll go to heaven. We can be thankful for that, at least."

Beau, sensitive to every mood that blew around a room, could not tolerate talking about the baby. It was a hidden, terrible family secret. He asked himself, as he looked about him, why he had come back. Why had he thought it necessary to leave Angela in the city and expose himself to the small tyrannies of his mother, to his natural father's bitterness, to his brother Mathieu's stormy anger?

"You've certainly improved the heating system with that furnace," he said to Timothée. "I was able to work in my bedroom without gloves."

"Are you ready for the concert in Quebec City, darling?" Honey changed the subject. "You must be missing your practice time."

"They've arranged a practice hall for me when I arrive. I'll have to work like the devil."

"What are you playing?" Armand asked.

"Rachmaninoff's Second Concerto," Beau said. "It suits me. I like the romantics, you know."

"Imagine, a celebrity in the family!" Nora said.

"Not quite yet," Beau corrected. He did not feel Nora belonged. She had been a governess, after all. "When my symphony premieres in London, then perhaps you will be able to say I'm a celebrity." The symphony was to be a milestone in his career. A major work. It had been commissioned by one of the leaders in the world of music, after all.

"Well, are you coming with me to Quebec City, Mother?" Beau asked, refilling his wine glass. "The trip might do you good. It would be a change."

"What do you think, Timothée? Can you manage?" Justine asked, turning to her husband. "Shall I go?"

"Yes, yes, go if you want."

Timothée spoke roughly, although he did not mean to do so. He was always uncomfortable around Beau. It was so obvious that Beau was his natural son: the slanted green eyes, the full mouth, the shape of the head. Though Timothée was now white-haired, Beau's black, renegade curls fell in the same pattern about his face. The two men had the same intensity of expression.

"You have plenty of help at the barns, haven't you?" Beau demanded, looking directly at Timothée. "And Marie-Claire will feed you and manage the house. I don't see any problem."

"There's no problem. Justine can go if she likes."

Justine was reluctant to make a decision. She did not wish to appear to be indulging herself, to be having a good time. Her role as martyr suited her better: a great deal of prayer, work, and abstinence from pleasure was part of the image she had created for herself. As if by this, she could wipe out the error of twenty-five years earlier.

Timothée now stood up and raised his wine glass. He looked toward his stepson, Mathieu.

"I'd like to propose a toast to the new member for Lachine!"

They all stood, grateful for the switch in conversation, and raised their glasses. Mathieu was one of the sixty-five Liberals elected from Quebec.

When they were seated again, Justine brought up the question of Mathieu's plans for the future. He would have to spend a great deal of time in the capital.

"Will you move to Ottawa, Mathieu? Sell the house in Montreal?" she asked.

"No, no. Nora will continue on in the house. I'll travel back and forth."

"But that's so exhausting," Justine protested. "And Nora will be alone so much."

"I'll take the train," Mathieu said.

"A godsend for drivers on the road," Beau muttered. Mathieu's wild driving was legend in the family, and in fact all over Montreal. It was a miracle he had not yet killed himself or somebody else.

Nora, upon hearing of Mathieu's plan, was washed with sweet relief. Until this moment he had not confided in her. The idea that Mathieu would be away most of the time was so appealing that she had difficulty controlling her expression. She paid a heavy price for security. Especially since the baby had come. Before, Mathieu had been scarcely tolerable; he had the appetites and consideration of an animal. But after Jean-Baptiste was born, he had added accusation to his other unpleasant characteristics. He blamed Nora for the dark, unmentionable problem that must always be kept hidden. And he swung wildly from never wanting to touch her again in case they had another child like Jean-Baptiste, to demanding another baby as soon as possible to correct the flaw.

"Nora will be alone so much," Justine said again.

"I'll visit her as much as possible. Especially on my day off," Rose volunteered.

"You can always visit me," Honey said to Nora. "And bring the baby if you like. I can send a car around for you."

"Thank you, Lady St. Amour," Nora muttered. She had never been able to call Honey anything else, despite the connection through marriage. Long years as a Court governess had accustomed Nora to keeping her place.

As the wine flowed, conversation became more general. The results of the election were the main topic. Mathieu had begun to eye Marie-Claire each time she leaned over the table to scoop up dishes or replace the wine. She was definitely a disturbing influence in the room—like a warm monsoon passing over the table. A stir of sensuality clung to her like musk.

Justine's arrangements for household help had always been questionable. She depended on local farmgirls. However, with the arrival of Marie-Claire she had managed to outdo herself. The girl had smooth olive skin and a thick dark braid hanging enticingly down her back. Her shoe-button black eyes were tilted and sly under deep-set lids, her eyebrows thick, her nose short and turned up michievously. She had a wide mouth that seemed to be perpetually open, as if she were expecting something, like a hungry child. It was not that she was exactly pretty but rather that she held out a vague and highly disturbing hope—undefined, undefinable.

At seventeen Marie-Claire was nubile with full breasts, a smallish waist, and rolling hips. When she was older, she would turn stout (one could see that instantly), but now, at her peak, she was tempting. Her clothes were incredibly gauche: a boyish woolen sweater in a blue and beige pattern over navy serge gym bloomers. Her woolen stockings ended in canvas shoes. The whole effect was incongruous and, but for the face and the obvious breasts, would have been as asexual as a nun's habit.

It was only Mathieu who appeared to notice the girl. Timothée had long been used to the sight of her, Beau was preoccupied, and Armand had never cultivated a taste for servants. Mathieu, however, was mesmerized. Every time she leaned into the table, his eyes followed her every movement. Marie-Claire knew he was watching her and gave him sidelong glances from her dark eyes. Once she accidentally brushed his shoulder and they exchanged looks.

After the special cake and coffee Justine suggested they move into the kitchen. It had always been a family custom to do that in the days before the furnace was installed. The kitchen, then, was the warmest room in the house, furnished in one corner with comfortable chairs. The group now rose (some unsteadily) from their places in the dining room to sip brandy around the generous kitchen fire.

The conversation continued to turn on the election. Honey was keen to discuss it because *Le Monde* was naturally involved in political issues. Like most Quebecers, Honey knew little about the new prime minister, Mackenzie King.

"We now have three parties," Mathieu was explaining to his elders as if they didn't know. "That's the important issue here. The new party, the Progressives, are a bunch of communist western farmers. But that doesn't make them any less dangerous to our position. With sixty-four seats in the house—more than the Tories—they ought to be the official Opposition. That's the real danger, right there, and I hope King knows it."

"King can get around that," Armand said cautiously. "All he has to do is absorb them. Their leader, Crerar, is new at the political game. It ought to be possible."

"Well, it's how he dishes out the Cabinet posts," Mathieu said. "Just wait and see."

"Why are they so dangerous? Because they're westerners or because they're farmers?" Timothée wanted to know, his voice edgy. "I'm a farmer myself, and I don't think it makes me dangerous."

"They're *western* farmers, and that means they're communist," Mathieu said. "There's a great deal of difference between them and us. They're red."

"Poor Papa," Honey said, thinking of Sir Simon and how much money he must have donated to the Conservative cause. "He must be raging. Though of course with Tulah's death, he's likely mourning and still in shock. Perhaps he doesn't care so much about the election."

Mathieu was anxious to avoid any dreary discussions about family tragedies. He had enough when he thought about the baby upstairs. More than enough.

"King might invite Crerar into the Cabinet," he offered quickly.

"Possibly. It would be a good move if he did," Armand agreed.

"I think I'll go upstairs now and look at the baby," Nora said, getting up from the table.

"If you like," Mathieu said without interest.

Rose rose from her chair and followed Nora out of the

.room. They climbed to the second floor, where, at the end of one wing, an adjoining bedroom to the guest room Rose occupied had been turned into a makeshift nursery. This arrangement suited Mathieu. Nora could spend the night with him in the large bedroom they shared further down the hall. But Nora usually got up some time in the night, anyway, and checked upon the sleeping baby.

After Nora and Rose had gone, Mathieu became more aware of the clatter of dishes from the scullery, where Marie-Claire was cleaning up. He glanced from time to time at the heavy wooden door in one corner of the kitchen that led to the maid's bedroom. During the past year Timothée had installed a small bathroom for the hired help, and this was considered a great bonus when Justine was seeking servants.

Even while he talked politics with his relatives, Mathieu's mind fermented with visions of Marie-Claire. How could he get into her room after everyone else had gone to bed without attracting attention to his behavior? The girl might be stupid and kick up a fuss. How could he be sure that those looks she'd given him were really meant to encourage?

As he rolled these considerations around in his mind, his cigar kept pace in his mouth. He sucked steadily at his brandy glass as well, drawing in the burning liquid as if it would give him assurance.

The night was country-dark, country-silent. The entire family had gone to bed and there was only an occasional protest from the embers as the fire settled, a hint of wind around the kitchen door, a creak from some ancient rafter.

Drunk as he was, Mathieu knew the house intimately, and he was able to find his way to the maid's room without much difficulty.

He opened the door to Marie-Claire's room cautiously. Still, it creaked. A shattering noise in the terrible quiet of the night. A little shock of fear ran through him, but he slipped inside the room and, with the awful deliberateness of the drunk, shut the door behind him, led on by that terrible tyrant, his sex. He heard Marie-Claire whisper from the other side of the room.

"Who's there?"

"Only me, Mathieu."

"What do you want?"

"To talk. Just to talk."

"I'm in bed."

"I know that. Don't be frightened."

"I'm not frightened."

Her whispered French hissed at him across the cool air. He knew that she was not frightened. He sensed her calmness. As he moved toward the bed, he caught his hip on a chest of drawers and swore. But he remembered to keep his voice down. In the lessening blackness of the room he saw her faint outline against the window. She was clutching the bed covers to her chin.

He reached the bedside, staring down at her, wanting to rip away the covers and see her body.

"You're beautiful . . ." he began awkwardly. He reached out to her with a shaking hand and tried to take away the covers gripped in her strong fist. His mind dwelled lovingly on the large breasts he had savored all evening and his tongue moved over his lips as if he could already taste her flesh. But Marie-Claire still held tight to the bedclothes.

"I know what you want," she said softly.

He felt the old familiar prickle of anticipation. Even in his drunkenness he stiffened so that his trousers became extremely tight.

"You knew I'd come."

He bent over, his hand on her hand loosened the large peasant fingers from the material.

"No, no, it isn't right." Her voice held no conviction.

He thought he would go mad if he did not adjust the front of his trousers and free the despot into the cool night air. His hand fell away from Marie-Claire's, and he fumbled with his clothes. She released the covers slowly, and with his free hand he pulled them away from her. He was flushed, painfully roused. He could see more clearly since his eyes had grown accustomed to the room. She wore a man's flannelette nightshirt with buttons down the front.

He forgot, temporarily, his own discomfort, and using both hands, he began to unfasten the nightshirt. His fingers were stiff with haste, but somehow he managed to free the springy, luscious flesh. She did not protest. She seemed to have stopped breathing. Her breasts were dark, the nipples so large, so spread over those rolling surfaces that he gasped and his mouth opened in anticipation.

"Let me—let me—" he began, bending his dark head over her.

"No—no—you mustn't," Marie-Claire whispered. He recognized a coldness in her response. It was almost businesslike, but he dismissed it as nervousness. Instead of questioning her, he pressed his hot face to her breasts, suffocating himself in the pliant flesh. His tongue licked out to run wild over the smooth brown surface.

Marie-Claire allowed this for a few moments, but at last she said, "We can't do it . . . because I'm sick. Do you understand what I mean? I'm sick."

He froze, his mouth still agonizingly poised over one hard nipple. Reluctantly he drew back, a waterfall of repugnance washing down his throat, through his stomach, to his loins. He drew away, slowly but with a primitive reaction he could not have explained. He let the heavy breasts fall as if they had burned him. His eyes glazed with longing, and yet, the note of vulgarity had punctured his manhood.

"When I'm well again . . ." she whispered, as if to humor him, "then we could do it. But I'd have to come to Montreal, wouldn't I?"

He could not understand what she was saying. It seemed so irrelevant. His flattened hopes were reflected only in his flaccid sex, and not in his mind. With an effort he tried to reply, but his eyes were still caught by the mounds of flesh, which she had failed to hide. His mind sank lower to the dark place between her thighs. Another place, another time. What was that that she was saying? He struggled to comprehend. A future time. Montreal. His voice scraped as he said, "Montreal. . . . But how will you come to Montreal?"

"I thought you might need a maid," she said.

"You mean, work for me? For me and Nora?"

"Well, you should have a maid. Especially if you're going to be away so much. I heard you talking about being in Ottawa."

He and Nora had a general cleaning woman. They did not have an actual full-time maid. Nora did the cooking. However, with so much time spent on the baby, it had become difficult. He supposed he could spare five dollars a month for a maid. Yes, he could afford that. His mind veered to the idea of Marie-Claire sleeping in the attic. This voluptuous body stored like a piece of luggage in the box room, waiting for him to take it out, to pack it with his urgent desires. Yes, that would be convenient. And Nora wouldn't care. She didn't like making love; Marie-Claire might be the answer to some of his problems.

"You want me to take you to Montreal? But what about my mother?"

"Oh, she can get another maid. There are lots of girls around who want to work in a place like this."

"Yes. I suppose so."

He could probably talk Justine into accepting the idea. He had been able to get around his mother in one way or another most of his life. She might balk at first, but with a little persuasion she could usually be brought around.

"You could arrange it, then?" she insisted.

He approached closer, once again. He nodded and decided that he would take another small sample of future delights. Why not? She was offering herself to him in exchange for something she wanted. It was difficult to believe that he could not have it right this minute. He pressed his head to her breasts once again, tasting, touching, becoming excited again until he reminded himself that he must wait.

He stood up.

"I'll make some arrangements." His voice slurred over the words.

"That's good. That would be nice."

She began to fasten the front of her gown as if she were putting away her wares. He stumbled toward the door, opened it, and let himself out into the kitchen.

After he had gone, the smell of brandy hung in the air. Marie-Claire did not like the smell but she lay quiet, staring into the spaces of the room. She smiled a satisfied smile. She had made a bargain. She had followed the advice she had heard from women who chatted with her mother. Once a man had his way, they had said over and over, you could get nothing from him. You had to hold out. You had to bargain. And you had to bargain when he was still hard. That was the time.

Marie-Claire wanted to go to Montreal more than anything in the world. To live in the country for the rest of her life was impossible. She would not be buried here. It was death. What better way than to have a man with Mathieu's poisition in life find her a job? If she had to humor him, well, she would have to humor *some* man, anyway, so it might as well be in exchange for something she wanted.

She was not sick, of course. She had never been in better health in her entire life. But Mathieu would never know that. She thanked God that she had judged him right . . . that he would not touch her if he thought she was unclean. Her mother had been right about that, too. Some men were unable to have sex when a woman was ill. She had won her little game. She continued to smile into the night until she fell asleep.

CHAPTER ELEVEN

Nora had not fallen asleep. She lay rigidly in the big double bed with the covers pulled up smoothly under her armpits to create a kind of shield. The wintry sky was outlined by the single dormer. As she lay there listening, she heard Mathieu's footsteps coming along the hall, then the door opened and he came in. She pretended to be asleep. He ignored her and went into the adjoining bathroom, came out again, and after hesitating by the door, went once more into the corridor.

Mathieu's attitude toward her had been erratic ever since Jean-Baptiste was born. At times he demanded his conjugal rights so they could have another child. On other occasions he was shrill and spiteful, berating her for the disgrace she had brought upon the family and threatening to ignore her forever.

Nora had intermittent guilt feelings. She was not deeply religious despite her recent conversion to Catholicism, but it had often occurred to her that she might be suffering punishment for her unnatural relationship with Rose Starkey. What if Jean-Baptiste's deformity was really her fault, as Mathieu said? Could that be possible?

Mathieu did not blame her for *that* reason, of course. He had no idea how she and Rose felt about each other.

Mathieu must find somebody to blame other than himself, since he could not face the idea that a defective birth had anything to do with *him*. When she was not feeling guilty herself, Nora wondered if the sin was Mathieu's: his lust, his selfishness, his ambition. Lust was one of the seven deadly sins, after all. He was a cruel, thoughtless man. Was the punishment due to his behavior, then?

The baby was now two months old, so there had not yet been time for signs of another pregnancy. Again, Nora was divided on whether or not she wanted another baby. To have a healthy, beautiful boy would surely cancel out the disastrous birth of Jean-Baptiste. Perhaps then Mathieu would be calmer and kinder. Yet at other times she was smitten with fear. Suppose it happened again? What if she had another—she scarcely tolerated the word even in the depths of her own mind—monster? Oh, it was all so terrible. Why had she married Mathieu in the first place? She had never loved him. But she knew perfectly well that she had married him for security, to escape being a servant all her life. Even Rose envied her that.

She lay in the bed, debating whether or not she ought to go to the improvised nursery and look at the baby. Rose and she had done so only half an hour before, and Jean-Baptiste was still feverish. His breathing was labored. They had carefully turned him over on his other side—he could not turn his head himself—to prevent bedsores. She noticed that he had not taken much of the milk from the feeding bottle.

She might as well get up and walk down the hall, Nora reflected. She could not sleep, and leaving the room would eliminate any possibility of a drunken sexual encounter with Mathieu. She got out of bed and found her slippers and a long velvet wrapper Mathieu had given her for Christmas. She walked across the hand-hooked rug toward the door, opened it, and went out into the cool corridor.

There were no sounds from below, so perhaps Mathieu had passed out on a downstairs sofa. She walked swiftly along the hall toward the end rooms where Rose and the baby slept. No noise came from any of the bedrooms, so she assumed the entire family was asleep.

When she entered the nursery, a small night-light was

burning. Rose was standing by the crib. The baby gave a high, piercing cry, a kind of howl. Nora and Rose looked at each other helplessly. It was such an awful cry that they had learned to dread it. In the dead of night it was eerie.

"He looks worse," Rose said.

Nora walked to the crib. She steeled herself to look in, to see again the huge, long head, the bulbous forehead, the flat cranium. He lay helplessly on his right side, breathing with a slight rasp. Nora stared at Rose.

"I felt his forehead. He's hot," Rose said. Rose was brave, Nora thought. She never did shrink from touching that frightful head. The skin over the top of the huge skull was stretched thin. There seemed to be nothing between the skin and the poor brain beneath. Nora shuddered.

"Where's Mathieu?" Rose asked in a conspiratorial tone.

"Downstairs. He may have fallen asleep."

"Or he may be after the hired girl," Rose said.

In the lamplight, in the night shadows, she looked welcoming and generous. Her dark red hair clung in small curls to her forehead and temples, her round face was soft, her eyes sympathetic.

"I watched him at dinner. He couldn't take his eyes off her."

"I know, but I don't care," Nora said grimly.

"I've turned Jean-Baptiste over on his other side," Rose offered. "He won't eat. There's nothing more we can do. Why not forget about the problem for a little while?"

"I wish to God I could forget it forever," Nora said.

"Come into the bedroom so we can talk without disturbing him. If he starts crying again, he'll wake up the whole house."

Nora hesitated. As she stood guard for a moment over the dreadful little creature lying so pitifully on its side, she remembered the day she had first found out about Jean-Baptiste's illness. It was three days after his birth and she still hadn't seen him. On the fourth day, when Nora was feeling stronger, she sensed the nurse's apprehension. It almost amounted to terror. But she demanded to see the baby, and the nurse scurried off, saying, "I'll call Doctor Gagnon, madame."

The baby had been born at home, with a midwife and doctor in attendance. Nora lay in the guest room, which had been fitted as a delivery and convalescent room, and awaited Doctor Gagnon's arrival.

She knew there was something radically wrong. Though she had not seen the baby, she had heard the sharp, odd cry from down the hall. It struck her that it was an animal cry. But she rejected that thought as soon as it came into her mind.

"The baby isn't . . . well, normal, madame," Dr. Gagnon said, spreading his hands and shrugging in the effort to make his words more digestible. "These things happen."

"What things?"

"A problem, at birth, you see. When there is something missing, as it were—"

"Missing? A hand? An arm?"

She had heard of births like that. People whispered about them. Many families had children hidden away, idiots, deformed creatures. She thought she would cry, even before Doctor Gagnon explained what the trouble was.

"No, you can't actually see what's missing, madame. But there is a spinal fluid secreted in all of us that passes up and over the cerebral hemispheres—that is, the brain. Do you understand? A kind of system that keeps the brain from being dry and brittle. Now, this fluid is pumped up and then reabsorbed into the system."

"You mean there's something wrong with his brain?"

"Yes, that's right. This spinal fluid must be absorbed into the cranial venous sinuses. Any pathological process that interferes with this absorption causes the fluid to collect on the brain. Pressing down on it. The baby's cranial bones are not locked together at birth, and the fluid collects and pushes them apart. The head grows larger . . . it continues to grow larger . . ."

"You mean my baby . . . has a large head?" Nora's words were a mere whisper.

"It was a difficult birth on that account. You've not been well, madame."

She had thought it difficult, but since it was a new experience, she had wondered if she were merely imagining the horrendous tearing and stretching. She recalled her own sharp cries, echoing through the house. She shuddered now, remembering.

"These babies do not usually live long," he began again, obviously wishing he had some other message to convey but plunging ahead because he must. "The brain is defective. The child is apt to succumb to infection. Often pneumonia. There is nothing we can do. Any experiments to tap the fluid have been unsuccessful so far. I hope you will try to understand that the baby would not be normal if he lived. Therefore . . ." he broke off.

It was a week before she was able to see the baby. He was kept in a crib with a firm mattress, and the hired nurse changed him, fed him, and turned him from side to side. The huge head was unsupportable. When at last she saw the baby, she was alone. Mathieu refused to go with her into the room.

"I never want to see that baby again!" Mathieu had cried out sharply. "What have you done to me?"

Numbly Nora went to the bedroom where the baby lay. She stared down at her son. She saw the paper-thin skin stretched over the top of the monstrous head, looking as if it would split like an overripe fruit. The head was as large as the entire body . . .

Now, in the blackness of night, Nora pushed away the memories and walked from the crib into Rose's bedroom. She felt utterly alone. If only Mathieu had been loving, had been gentle, had been understanding. But he was none of those things. He had reacted in a cruel, callous way. He had blamed her.

Rose was taking off her wrapper.

"I'm going to lie down," Rose said. "It's very late. Why don't you stay here, Nora? Then if the baby cries, we'll both try to keep him quiet so the rest of the family won't be disturbed."

Nora felt so tired that she thought she might not be able to walk back to her own bedroom. She looked at Rose standing in a pink nightgown that clung to her every curve.

"Mathieu won't come in here," Rose said. "Come and lie down, Nora. The way we used to do. Remember, when we lived together at Mellerstain? Before you married?"

Nora remembered only too well the comfort of those days in the warm, cosy third-floor apartment. How Rose had waited on her when she came home from the Court office, where she helped with war shipments. How Rose had tea ready on a tray. How Rose ran her bath. How devastated Rose had been when Nora decided to marry Mathieu.

"Yes, I know how it used to be."

"Come to bed, Nora. We'll hear the baby if he cries."

Slowly, Nora removed her wrapper. The long-sleeved gown she wore hung on her loosely. She was thinner than she had been years before, her hips sculpted in bone, her stomach flat again since the baby's birth, her breasts small and tight.

"Oh, Nora," Rose said softly. Her voice trailed across the space between them, looping Nora in a soft net, bringing her closer into Rose's moist, warm orbit.

Nora felt herself sinking. She had sworn to herself after Jean-Baptiste's birth that she would never let Rose touch her again. It was a sin to do what they had done, and she had been punished. She must stop. She must change her attitude. Yet, nobody but Rose cared for her. Nobody but Rose wanted to hold her, stroke her, wipe away her tears, offer some balm to her heart. Rose was so kind, so warm, so loving.

Nora was drawn to Rose, enchanted by her luminous look, by the outstretched arms. She felt the need for comfort, for more than comfort, for release. She saw how Rose ran her tongue, just the tip of it, over her lips, and how her plump breasts pushed out under the thin gown.

"Nora, you needn't stay here if you don't want to," Rose said. But her hands touched Nora's shoulders, and ran down her arms, lightly, caressingly.

Surely it would not be sinful to let Rose touch her and kiss her? What could be wrong with that? There was so much coldness in the world, so much harshness in life with a man like Mathieu. Was she doomed to live forever without love? Her heart pounded with the possibility of grasping at this moment, of letting Rose press her naked body up against her own, of feeling those soft curves, damp creases, sweet plumes in secret places.

"Come, Nora," Rose said, whispering in Nora's ear so that her breath stirred Nora's blond hair. Rose let her lips graze down the smooth neck to the curve of shoulder where the gown took up sentinel duty. She opened Nora's gown at the neck and thrust one hand down to the neat, pointed little breasts, and the nipples sprang to life under her touch. Then she kissed Nora on the lips and they pushed together, breathing like twins, breast pushed against breast, mound against mound, until their legs trembled so they could no longer stand. Rose led Nora to the bed. There was no turning back now.

Rose unfastened Nora's gown completely so that she could step out of it. Her hands, shaking now, ran over the small breasts again, over the thin hips, through the short crop of crisp pubic hair. Then she took off her own gown and stood naked so that Nora could see the silken haven she offered and take refuge there.

It was dawn. Nora had fallen into such a deep sleep that she had no idea how long it was since she had last looked at Jean-Baptiste. She got up wearily, letting Rose lie under the covers with her reddish curls half-hiding her face.

Pulling on her robe, she padded into the nursery and forced herself to peer into the crib. In the grayish light the baby lay still, a paler version of his former flushed self. The eyes were closed and the lids waxy. The rasping had ceased.

Nora bent over, fear seizing her stomach and twisting it into a knot. She touched the ugly face and found it cold. Dead. Yes, dead. Even while she slept in Rose's arms. She began to scream and Rose came running. Suddenly the room was filled with her St. Amour and Dosquet relatives.

"He's dead!" Nora shrieked over and over. "I let him die!"

The only member of the household who did not come was Mathieu. And he barely wakened long enough to be told the sad news before he fell back into his wine stupor. But his last waking thought was that life would be much easier now. And whether Nora liked it or not, the Dosquets were about to hire a maid from the country.

CHAPTER TWELVE

Sir Simon grieved through the dark months of January and February. Winter's cold hand seemed to have seized on his heart: even *his* resilience had failed and he was

140

spiritually paralyzed. Visits from his sons, business opportunities that normally would have challenged him, a call from his granddaughter Susan—nothing cracked the stony robe he wore to protect himself against the world.

Actually, it was Fort and Charles who made arrangements for Tulah's funeral. Sir Simon seemed incapable of making any decisions, however small. He was lost to the pain of others as he struggled with the knife edge within his own soul.

By choice it was a small funeral, held without formal notice in order to keep away the curious. With his family as support, Sir Simon appeared in his full-length beaver coat looking like some melancholy king with a mourning retinue. He moved in a mindless, speechless dream, looking neither left nor right. He appeared not to notice the few passersby who accidentally stumbled upon the service. He did not see his own relatives nor hear the droning of the archdeacon who performed the brief service.

Afterward Pride's Court became a ghost palace. The rooms were hollow, disturbed only by a whisper of wind around the window panes, a door slamming somewhere in the distance. Servants walked softly over thick carpets performing the necessary duties, cooking Spartan meals and serving them to Charles and Sir Simon, dusting, polishing, arranging fresh linen—but no one ever came. No visitors rang the front doorbell these days and no automobiles pulled up under the broad limestone portico. No lights blazed from the great dining room, no logs burned in the immense fireplace under the Court coat of arms, and no watcher stood in the tower overlooking the St. Lawrence. Sir Simon did not go out. He did not visit Fort and Sydney in Mellerstain nor the more ordinary house on McGregor Avenue where Geoffrey and Mary now lived.

Although all three sons tried to interest their father in various projects, they met with failure each time. They found their own taste for entertaining shrinking almost as much as the old man's. Temporarily, at least, the Courts had retired from center stage in the city of Montreal and had taken on an unusual protective coloring. For months no one heard much about them. Certainly, nothing was printed about them in the social columns. It was June, a hot and humid day, before any real dent was made in

Sir Simon's lethargy, and then it came in the disguise of gold.

Reports from the Court mine showed a superb grade of ore. Shafts had been sunk lower; already they were at nearly three thousand feet, and a lateral cut was made, running under Kirkland Lake. They had struck a fabulous vein and the ore was testing at twelve hundred dollars a ton.

In these circumstances Noel and young Simon became increasingly tense about the fact that Armand St. Amour held a seven-and-a-half-acre lot in the very center of their property. Something must be done and quickly. Sir Simon would have to be prodded into action.

With this in mind both boys came down to Montreal to meet with their grandfather. It occurred to them that he might find it inspiring to see pictures of the village of Courtsville, growing steadily now east of the lake. When they had first suggested naming a town after the family, Sir Simon seemed to like the idea. Perhaps this would jar him out of his dream world. Armed with a few photographs that Noel had taken with a new Kodak camera, they traveled by train down to the city.

Sir Simon had long since stopped going to his office in the Empire Bank, except on those rare occasions when it was absolutely necessary. To ease things Fort called the meeting in the conservatory at Pride's Court.

Noel and Simon were shocked when they first caught sight of their grandfather. The old man was sitting in the sunlight filtered green through palms and ferns in the conservatory. There was a smell of dying jasmine blossoms in the air. Sir Simon looked a hundred years old. He had lost weight and his face sagged around the jowls. While his grooming was still meticulous, his suit hung on him.

Fort had seen his father from time to time over the spring months, but even he was startled to realize that his father was mortal. He felt a cruel jab of fear as if a pit were opening up beneath him; death already shadowed the warm glass walls. Fort pulled himself together with an effort.

"Papa, the boys want to talk about the gold mine," Fort said in a more buoyant voice than his mood dictated.

Sir Simon was sitting in a cushioned bamboo armchair.

He was smoking the eternal cigar and was armed with a huge marble ashtray at his elbow.

"I thought we were making money up north?"

"We soon will be. That's the problem. Our gold mine is a gold mine," Fort said, trying to lighten the mood. He noticed that both his nephews were a bit frightened by the sight of their grandfather. The family might rage against Sir Simon's many tyrannies, but not one of them could imagine life without him.

"*That's* a problem? What in the hell's the matter with you?"

"It's a problem because—" Fort began.

But Sir Simon interrupted him with a shout.

"I thought you were going to tell me we'd struck fool's gold!"

"It's real gold, best quality anybody's hit for decades," Fort said. "Do you recall hearing about the fact that Armand St. Amour owns a piece of land right in the middle of our mine?"

"Of course I remember, you idiot! Do you think I'm in my dotage?"

"Well, something's got to be done about that, and fast, Papa," Fort said, running interference for Noel and young Simon.

Sir Simon's blue eyes took on a fresh gleam. A touch of interest crossed his face and his muscles tightened.

"Is that the small claim that swine owns? Is that the one you mean?" he cried, like a wounded bull. "St. Amour has given me nothing but trouble since the day he first entered this house! He's stolen my daughter and my grandchildren, and now he's stolen my gold mine."

"Now, Papa, he hasn't stolen it. Before we bought the two claims, there was an overlapping stake. A man can only stake out forty acres. That's the law. Somebody in St. Amour's outfit found out about the overlap and bought it up. Part of St. Amour's claim is actually under the lake. That's why I'm so worried. The vein we've cut into underwater has the best-quality ore."

"Well, why don't you make him an offer? Buy him out?"

"He won't see me," Fort said simply. "I rather suspect he's holding out to talk to you."

Sir Simon ground his teeth.

"The cur! That's about what you'd expect from him, isn't it? He wants me to beg, does he?"

"I'm only guessing," Fort said with a shrug.

"I won't go down on my knees to that Frenchie, you can't expect me to! I ought to shoot him!"

Fort turned away to hide the first smile that had made its way across his face since the meeting began.

Noel said, quickly, "Look, Grandfather, we brought some pictures of the town to show you. Courtsville. Here's the hotel we own." He thrust a handful of snapshots at the old man.

Sir Simon stopped long enough to look at the pictures. As he glanced from them to his grandson, the perfidies of Armand St. Amour temporarily fled his mind. He began to leaf through the pictures again.

"Courtsville, eh? Our town. That's wonderful. I'm proud of both of you. I'll come up one day and inspect the mine and the town."

"That would be a real morale booster for the men," Simon said with enthusiasm.

"But first," Sir Simon said, "we'd better settle this problem with St. Amour. Does he just want to be difficult?"

"Probably," Fort said, "but he won't refuse to see *you*, Papa. He couldn't resist a meeting. That's why we want you to handle it."

Sir Simon allowed himself a grunt of satisfaction.

"Is it time for a drink?" He took out his gold pocket watch and gazed at it. "I need my glasses to see this thing, although the numbers are as big as you can get. Damned eyes! What time is it?"

They assured him it was after five o'clock. Sir Simon did not take his predinner drink until that hour, no matter what the stress and strain of the moment. Fort rang for the butler.

"We'll make him an offer," Sir Simon said.

"And if he refuses?" Simon II asked quickly. "What do we do then?"

"In this game, you think up alternative plans. I have a military mind, that's why I'm so successful. If plan A fails, you must have plan B ready. Now, if he refuses a perfectly legitimate offer, even a generous offer—although I hate to pay him too much, it might kill me—if he *refuses* even that . . . we must have something *he* wants. You take my meaning?"

"Barter?" Noel suggested.

"Exactly. We must find out what St. Amour needs. Put somebody on it right away, Fort. But wait until I give it some thought, will you? Let me see . . ." Sir Simon closed his eyes and appeared to dredge up bits of information from the depths of his mind. "He has a mine down at Thetford. But he's also in coal in Nova Scotia. Or he might be short of money again. The man hasn't much of a head for business, you know. Perhaps he wants to sell."

"Let me know when you want me to move on that," Fort said. "What about insurance? Perhaps we ought to look into that side of things."

"Mmmm. Maybe. I haven't been around to Canada Assurance for some months. I'd better find out what McGillvray is up to." Ian McGillvray was the president of the company, but Sir Simon was the chief stockholder.

"Armand may refuse to see me, but he'll see *you*, Papa," Fort said again, handing drinks around from the tray.

"Well, I'll ask him to lunch. At the Windsor. Wouldn't want to take a man like that to my club . . . sets a bad precedent for others. Wouldn't do at all."

"Make it as soon as you can," Fort added.

"Don't worry about me, Fort. I'll have a call put in to him tomorrow. We don't want a man like that connected with the mine. Might as well take in that bloody Italian fellow . . . calls himself a Fascist. That hound will be running Italy next, if old King Victor doesn't look out. I don't like the way things are going."

Thus having satisfactorily equated his son-in-law with a dangerous new politician named Mussolini, Sir Simon felt better.

"By the way, we don't want to pay him off in shares, whatever the deal is," Fort reminded his father. "If we split the shares later on, Armand might hold too much power. We want to pay a flat sum."

Sir Simon had not even contemplated such an idea. Now he turned deep red with rage.

"Pay him off in shares?" he cried as if a murder had been suggested, or at the least, a lashing. "I wouldn't let that man have a share in a mousetrap factory!"

"I just thought I'd mention it," Fort said.

"Make me another drink," Sir Simon said, in evident need of immediate support. "The idea . . ."

Fort complied with his father's request. He had long since given up encouraging the old man to follow doctor's orders. Sir Simon was allowed only one drink before the evening meal.

"It would be a favor to the country," Sir Simon said, swallowing a mouthful of scotch, "if St. Amour were shot."

"Let me tell you about the mine, Grandfather," Noel offered.

"Yes, let's talk about that," Sir Simon agreed grimly.

The four Court men settled down among the potted palms to plan the promising future of the Court mine. There was the added spice of outmaneuvering Armand St. Amour. Sir Simon had a reason to live again.

They met on neutral ground. The dining room of the Windsor Hotel was sumptuous, and the service was excellent. The food was better, of course, than that served at his club, although Sir Simon did not much care about such a fine point when it came to being in the right place at the right time.

Sir Simon was already seated when Armand arrived. He had taken up a position in a corner table with his back to the wall, like a sensible military man. This way, there could be no surprise attack. And he could see everyone else who came in, as well. He nodded curtly when Armand took his seat, but of course he did not get up. He was not meeting Armand so much as he was giving him an audience.

"You're late," Sir Simon said, looking at his watch ostentatiously, although without his glasses he could not read it. "Four minutes late."

"I'm sorry. I trust you're keeping well?"

"I am fit as a man of forty. So if you're waiting for me to die, you're wasting your time."

Armand concealed a smile. He had expected an attack, and therefore he was not surprised. His own situation was secure, for he did not want to sell. And he knew that Sir Simon was desperate to buy.

"I'll tell Honey you're well," Armand offered. "Are we having a drink before we order?"

Sir Simon did not particularly want to drink with his son-in-law. It showed a certain camaraderie that pained him exquisitely. On the other hand, he did not know whether he could face the man across the luncheon table without a comforting potion. He hesitated. Then, realizing that the strain of keeping up a conversation with Armand St. Amour minus any soothing agent might kill him, he said tersely, "Scotch and soda."

Armand raised his hand almost imperceptibly and a waiter appeared. He studied the menu while Sir Simon gazed haughtily about the room.

"Tell him J and B," Sir Simon said, deliberately holding off until the waiter had left the table and thus causing Armand to call him back.

When the drinks came, Sir Simon said, "We may as well get to the point."

"Of course, sir. I thought you might like to order first."

"Tell him," Sir Simon said as if Armand were his personal servant, "I will have the lamb."

Armand did as he was told. If his father-in-law had behaved in any other way, it would have been cause for alarm. As it was, everything seemed to be normal.

"Holding that piece of land is an untidy bit of business," Sir Simon began. "It doesn't hinder us in any way. Doesn't stop us mining. We're going ahead. But it isn't good business. That's what I don't like about it."

"It's awkward, I'll admit."

"You have no access to your claim," Sir Simon went on. "Unless we give you access. So it's no good to you."

"Well, it is *some* good," Armand amended. "In that I expect some revenue from the portion of the vein you're mining that runs under my claim."

"Hard to prove."

"But worth the attempt if rumors are true. The ore is first grade. You're taking out fifty tons a day."

"It's not that good," Sir Simon said.

"Perhaps, but I like what I hear. And some of that gold rightfully belongs to me."

Sir Simon did not care for the phraseology. Nothing that belonged to a Court could possibly have any connection with anybody else. He did not like Armand's rather flat position, his lack of respect. On the other hand, he argued silently with himself, what could you expect from a barbarian?

After two drinks Sir Simon felt somewhat calmer, but when the lamb arrived, he sent it back because it was too pink. There was no way that the luncheon could be smooth, or a success. The mere sight of St. Amour upset his digestive system. His head ached with anger. Finally, at the end of his patience, he said, "I know you don't want to sell. But what is your price?"

"Rent. I am thinking of charging you rent."

"*Rent?*"

The word suddenly became profane. Sir Simon's spontaneous bellow startled diners around them.

"Why not?" Armand asked politely.

Sir Simon was infuriated. What would this upstart think of next? Visions of firing squads danced through his head, and he thought longingly of the good old days when brigands could be summarily killed without a second thought. Shooting was too good for him. Perhaps hanging would be better.

"Rent?" he repeated, as if the word were foreign and therefore inexplicable.

Armand was amused, but he did not dare show any signs of it. He had merely thrown out the idea of rent as a beginning, to see what his belligerent old father-in-law would say. Really he wanted something quite different.

"It was only a suggestion," Armand said mildly.

"I wish to buy," Sir Simon said as firmly as he could. "It's the only sensible approach and you know that. What do you want for the land?"

"I don't want to sell."

"But I want to buy. The land's no good to you if you can't get at it, and part is in the water. What are you going to do, swim over it? Drop in by airplane?"

"Let's go back to rent, then."

"Load of rubbish," Sir Simon pronounced and ordered himself a Grand Marnier. "You're witless. I'm not surprised, leading the kind of life you do." This rather dark hint about Armand's playboy years was outdated, and Sir Simon knew it. Yet he managed to imply that irreparable damage had been done by Armand's dissolute ways in his youth.

Armand ignored the thrust and sipped his brandy.

"All right, all right, what's your price?" Sir Simon said

finally. "I haven't got days to spend on this. I'm a busy man."

"Thirty thousand dollars and two hundred thousand shares."

If Armand had turned into a beast before his eyes, Sir Simon could not have been more shocked. For several moments he stared at his son-in-law, and then he managed to say several things one on top of the other. Was Armand a lunatic? Was he determined to waste Sir Simon's valuable time? Was this whole luncheon a joke?

"It's a fair price. You're no doubt familiar with what Harry Oakes paid for a similar claim?"

"Harry Oakes is an upstart."

"I only mention it as a guide, that's all."

"I don't think we can do business."

"You're mining under my property right this minute," Armand assured Sir Simon. "So I'll be forced to pursue the idea of rent."

"Madness. Unheard of."

But Sir Simon's mind was on something else. He must hurry the investigation he had begun. He must find something Armand needed—something he needed desperately and that Sir Simon could provide. St. Amour must be brought to heel.

"There's always room for a new idea in business."

"I will not pay you in shares," Sir Simon said loudly and with great firmness. "That is the last thing I would do. I assure you that I would rather perish. And that's final."

Armand shrugged and ordered another brandy. Sir Simon rose, leaving his son-in-law to pay the bill. He swept grandly from the room, barely acknowledging the greetings of two acquaintances at a table near the door. The thing must be solved, and there was only one way to solve it. Find out what the Frenchman wanted and then be in a position to offer it. Sir Simon's mind moved forward toward his insurance company and the possibilities it offered. He ordered his chauffeur to take him to the offices unannounced. There was no time for ceremony. The situation was acute.

CHAPTER THIRTEEN

North was surprised when he received the summons. It came at four thirty on a warm June afternoon. Every fan in the Empire Bank Building was whirring steadily, and every desk was decorated with a paper cup from the water cooler. North would have liked to take off his jacket, but that was not allowed. When he was called to Sir Simon's office, he left his desk hurriedly and made his way to the men's washroom. After he had washed his hands and brushed his thick hair into place, he made sure that his tie was straight and that his fly was done up. What could the old man want of him so suddenly at the end of a dreary, humid afternoon?

He was alternately assailed with thoughts of glory and gloom. Perhaps he had made some mistake in his work, some glaring error that Sir Simon had found. On the other hand, perhaps he had insulted Mildred and she had reported him. Although this seemed unlikely. She appeared to be mad about him, if he could judge women. Could it be a promotion? He had done nothing spectacular, not really. He had tried to work hard, to be on time, to learn the business. He had made no unpleasant scenes. Of course, rumors might have reached Sir Simon about one or two things. There had been other women (only to protect Mildred, he assured himself) and he had been thrown out of a questionable club one night. Still, young men were known to do these things. Sir Simon would surely not hold that against him.

As he stepped into the cage elevator for the rise to the top of the building, North thought about Mildred. He did not love her—that is, he did not love her in the romantic way suggested by poetry and novels. She was not beautiful, witty, or stylish. Since they had met, North had encouraged her to buy better clothes and have her brown hair cut in a fashionable way. She had bought a chic little Stanley Roadster with a pale green body and blue leather upholstery.

It was a comfort to know that he desired her physically and that this would not be a problem, but he was realistic enough to admit secretly that much of her charm lay in the Court wealth and the prestige attached to escorting Sir

Simon's granddaughter. He liked the parties to which they were invited, the houses to which they had access, the new respect people gave him.

And though she was not beautiful, she was young, fresh, and eager. He had been careful, diplomatic to the point of priggishness, about his approaches to her, skirting daringly around the edges of dangerous flirtation. No matter how torrid their kisses and his exploratory embraces, he drew back. It was too risky. Too much hinged on his position at the bank and on Sir Simon's good opinion. Mildred would have let him make love to her, he knew that, but he refused staunchly. Sometimes he paid a girl to sleep with him; once in a while he managed to find a partner who was simply out for a good time. It helped him keep his sexual drives in check.

The past six months had been a hiatus in the lives of all the Courts; a long pause in family affairs while everyone marked time. Even an outsider like North had felt it. Nobody actually said so, but each Court was waiting until Sir Simon took complete charge once again.

As he approached the secretary's desk (a new dragon had been installed at the gates), he was assaulted by a mixture of fear and guilt. Was this summons good news or bad? Was Sir Simon about to give him something or take something away?

He was ushered in to the huge private office that doubled as a board room. The old man stood with his back to the door, staring down upon St. James Street. The money street. The street of power. A portrait of Sir Simon in his younger, more vigorous days hung at one end of the long, polished board table. The room was redolent of cigars, despite the open windows.

"Good afternoon, sir," North said politely. "You wanted to see me?"

Sir Simon turned. He wore a fierce expression, his blue eyes questioning. North stood uncertainly just inside the door. The room was humid and he felt sweaty and a little untidy. It was like waiting for a Court sentence, he thought, making a pun for himself to lessen the impact of the meeting.

"You're looking fit," Sir Simon observed. His voice was stern, however.

151

"Thank you, sir. So are you. We're all glad to see you back at the bank."

"I'm back all right and in fighting trim. You can rely on it. I've a lot of plans, North. It's time for an old man to take a firm hand again."

"It certainly is. Everyone has been waiting."

Sir Simon looked pleased.

"I've checked into your work. You've been doing well. Do you like it here?"

"Definitely. I certainly hope to continue on here at the bank."

"How are you and Mildred getting along?"

The quick switch put him off guard. He stammered as he said, "Fine, sir. We're getting along fine. At least, I think so. Mildred is . . . a very attractive girl, you know . . ."

Sir Simon looked skeptical. North felt his position weaken, his credibility melt before that sharp blue stare. Perhaps he had said the wrong thing. Sir Simon was known for trickery and for violent swings of mood. Perhaps he was just a temporary escort for Mildred in Sir Simon's eyes and a stopgap at the bank.

"What are your intentions?"

Sir Simon's forceful question came as a shock. North stared at Sir Simon a little helplessly, falling back on his natural charm and courtesy with a tentative smile. Making any decision was difficult for him. He always postponed it as long as he could.

"You mean about Mildred, sir?"

"Of course I mean about Mildred! You haven't been mooning about with any other female in my household, have you?"

"No, no. Of course I haven't."

Sir Simon waved his arms impatiently.

"Sit down," he said, taking his own chair at the head of the board table and under his portrait. "I'm going to have a serious talk with you."

North felt his security slipping away. He had done well enough at the bank, but it seemed to him, as he faced the stern and bearded face across the table, that he was about to be put in his place. He had no money by Court standards and Sir Simon would doubtless consider him a fortune hunter when it came to Mildred. The Grenvilles were completely acceptable socially, of course. They had been bankers, originally, in Yorkshire, and Henry had emigrated to Montreal to begin a new bank in the city under a government charter. The fact was that North Grenville would himself have been a perfect catch for Mildred if Henry had not lost most of his fortune a few years before. Now North had all the tastes of the rich without any means to support them. He was already in debt to his tailor and his wine merchant, and he had run up a considerable gambling debt. Learning to live on the modest salary he earned at the bank was not really one of North's strong points. Had Sir Simon gotten wind of these things?

"We both know where we stand on the matter of your background," Sir Simon said a little cruelly. "No need to go into that. You have no money. But the Grenvilles are good, solid people. I like Henry. Always did. I like you, too, North. And so I'm going to give you an opportunity to show what you can do."

North breathed again. At least he was not about to be dismissed summarily. Not to be told, evidently, that he must stop seeing Mildred. And not to be reminded of his debts. He relaxed a little and took out a gold cigarette case from which he extracted a Player. He lighted the cigarette with a matching gold lighter from Cartier's.

"I have a special assignment for you," Sir Simon began. "Absolutely top secret. Only my sons know about this. I'm trusting you as if you were one of the family. Also, I'm in a hurry. And I want results."

"I'll do my best," North said quickly, trying not to let either relief or fear leak through his voice into the smoky atmosphere of the room. "You can trust me, you know that, sir."

"Yes, I know that. You're ambitious."

North shrugged his shoulders a little to indicate that he was but that it was not something he would care to discuss. Sir Simon went on talking.

"I want information of a certain kind. It may be hard to get, but everybody has his price, everything has its price. And when I explain it to you, you'll understand. At all times, you must be discreet. The amount of money you can spend is not a consideration. I want the information and I'm willing to pay. In fact, let me stress that I *must* have it."

"I'm anxious to hear what it is."

"We'll get to that," Sir Simon said, puffing heavily on his cigar. "First, I want to tell you that if you complete this assignment to my satisfaction, there'll be a big promotion for you. Not only in business, but if you want to marry Milly and if she'll have you, I will not only approve, I will offer you Pride's Court as your home."

North was so astonished by this speech that he could think of no reply. He simply stared.

"I don't mean to move out," Sir Simon said hastily. "But you know the size of the place. You and Milly will have one wing and she can run the house. Put some life into it. That's what I hoped to do with my own marriage"—he paused for a moment and his voice softened—"but that wasn't meant to be. I realize that. Milly's not beautiful, but she's been brought up to this way of life, and she's sensible. She could handle Pride's Court. I'm sure of it."

"I don't know what to say."

This was true. He hoped to God he could successfully bring off the job Sir Simon has asked him to do. The idea of living in Pride's Court, making it his address, was almost too much to digest. He had entertained ambitions ever since he'd met Sir Simon that day in the club, he had craved the Court connections and all that went with it, but he had never quite visualized the situation that confronted him now. Who could have foreseen this offer when the family relationships were so complicated? Charles still lived in the house, and sometimes the family spoke of bringing Polly back. He had detected in Susan a greed that matched his own. And she, after all, was more nearly Sir Simon's ideal than Mildred. The idea had struck him often that Susan and David Mulqueen might be invited to move into the great house if Polly died. But that he and Mildred should be the ones . . . it was incredible!

"I want you to agree to take the assignment," Sir Simon was saying testily. "I want to get on with it. You do want to marry Milly, don't you? God knows, you're always hanging about. It's enough to make a man ill the way you two moon over each other. I'm not blind, you know."

North, who had never for moment doubted Sir Simon's ability to observe, shook himself mentally. He heard his own voice saying, "Yes, I want to marry Milly."

154

"Does she want to marry you? If she doesn't, she gives a damned good imitation of it."

"I haven't asked her. I think so."

"*Think* so? You must be an idiot! I've never seen such lollygagging around in all my life. I'll be glad when the two of you are over this stage. It's enough to give me an ulcer. In my day people didn't carry on like that. It's all this *jazz*—that's what does it. Brings out the worst in people. Flappers! What, may I ask, is a *flapper*? You'd better marry Milly before there's some kind of scandal." With an effort, Sir Simon stopped himself from delivering a long lecture on declining morals. "Let me explain what I want."

He proceeded to describe the situation at Kirkland Lake with the overlapping claims and St. Amour's intransigence. He allowed himself several tasty expletives to describe his son-in-law and then brought up the question of insurance.

"Insurance may not be the answer. We need to find out about his mine in Nova Scotia, somewhere around Sydney. I hear he wants out of it. Too much trouble, not enough profit. Look into it, find out if he really wants to sell and what his price is. We'll offer him something reasonable to take it off his hands if he'll sell the claim up at Kirkland Lake. He may grab at the chance. But I have to know as much as possible before we can make the offer."

When Sir Simon had finished explaining what he wanted, he swung back to the problem of Mildred.

"If you do marry Milly, I'll pay all the expenses at Pride's Court. That's understood. Upkeep, servants, everything. No need to worry. There's plenty of room for Charles in the east wing, where I am. You and Milly could take the west wing. House is big enough for a regiment. It needs people in it. No good with just the two of us rattling about."

"I'm overwhelmed."

"You get this bit of work done, and then we'll decide on a wedding day. I think August would be suitable. Weather's usually fairly good in August."

"Yes. I'll get on this immediately. You can depend on it. I'll consider my connections—people I can talk to without giving anything away."

"All right, North. I leave the details to you. Report

to me as soon as you can. How would you like a big wedding in Christ Church? Biggest wedding this city has ever seen? Eh? We could show them how to do it! Just short of a royal wedding, that's what I'd like to see! Nobody has the style anymore. But we could show 'em a thing or two about weddings!"

Sir Simon had added one more challenge to his list. The most fantastic, the costliest, the most elaborate wedding the city would ever know. Pomp and circumstance. That's what life needed. A good jolt of pomp and circumstance.

CHAPTER FOURTEEN

Sir Simon was pleased with the results of North Grenville's investigations. By mid-June he had the information he needed; he knew where he could strike to bring Armand St. Amour into line. Seeing a tremendous personal victory just over the horizon, he was more than ever in the mood to stage an ostentatious wedding.

Sir Simon Court selected Saturday, August 19, as the wedding day. The ceremony was scheduled to take place in Christ Church Cathedral at seven o'clock in the evening. Sir Simon regretted that the church was so small—it seated only about 850—but there was no suitable alternative. Candlelight, he decided, would add to the beauty of the occasion, since the nave was a bit stark. The service would be followed by a reception, dinner, and ball in Pride's Court.

Accordingly, Sir Simon commanded his new secretary, Miss Barber, to find all the accounts she could put her hands on of both royal and great American weddings. Extravaganzas, that's what he was looking for. He wanted ideas, models from which he could borrow spectacular effects.

He had already made a special request, through influential friends in Ottawa, for the appearance of the governor general at the ceremony. The ambassador from the Court of St. James's to Washington happened to be a personal friend, so he had expedited that invitation by telephone. He had also rounded up three generals and an admiral. It was regrettable that the prime minister could not be in-

156

vited, but he was, unfortunately, not only a Liberal but a nobody. So much the worse for him. In addition to all those guests, Sir Simon had sent cables to two close comrades in London, peers of the realm, to offer them free passage on a Court ship if they would attend. A little British elegance, he thought, could not do any harm.

In the English community of Montreal, where rumors flew whenever a great occasion arose, North Grenville emerged as a fresh and fascinating figure. Several matrons with marriageable daughters regretted the fact that they had overlooked him. Obviously, there was more to Grenville than immediately met the eye. If Simon Court had put his seal of approval upon Grenville, then he was, without doubt, a catch. How could they have missed such a prize? At the club the men looked at him with a sharper eye, concluding over scotch and soda that he was deeper than he appeared.

Elaborate arrangements for the wedding moved forward inexorably, but North Grenville was seldom if ever consulted. Most of the time he felt as if he were watching a parade of somebody else's life. Sir Simon was in charge of almost everything, and what was left Mildred and her female relatives absorbed. As the prospective groom, North felt totally unnecessary. Sir Simon had ordered masses of flowers from Connecticut—shunning Ontario as a place not to be trusted—and had talked the bishop of Montreal, John Farthing, into performing the ceremony with the assistance of the rector of the cathedral, Archdeacon Carlisle.

No sooner had the date been set than Sir Simon called a council of matrimonial arrangements at Pride's Court. Family members gathered in the conservatory, open now to the gardens, where thousands of roses scented the humid June breeze.

Mildred's parents were present, but they did not count. Sir Simon, with his sure instinct for delegating authority, had chosen his granddaughter, Susan Mulqueen, as a consultant. She was the only avant garde woman in the family—sleek, assured; a touch risqué perhaps. She arrived in a shortish, flip skirt that revealed most of her calf and carried a long black cigarette holder, which she flourished rather too obviously. Her husband, David, lounged about as a spectator, basking in his wife's panache.

Sir Simon came to the point as soon as a round of drinks had been served.

"We have a problem," he began, his voice loud among the jasmine blossoms. "The wedding gown. Everything else is under my supervision and coming along well. Champagne from New York, not enough on hand here in Montreal and we can't depend on a new shipment from France, far too risky. Bishop Farthing will perform the ceremony." Here he coughed and gave them all a conspiratorial smile. "He's not in favor of so much pomp—Low Church, always was—but I've promised a sizable donation to the building fund. The steeple is leaning badly and the foundations need work, so they're eager for contributions. Archdeacon Carlisle will assist. But Mildred has no gown. I want something splendid . . . something . . ." He struggled to find the right word. They all knew what he meant. Magnificent. Memorable. Breathtaking. A gown to make the guests gasp.

"I don't care about expense," Sir Simon added.

Susan became the center of attention. She placed a cigarette in the holder and smiled winningly at her grandfather. She wore a geometrically designed blouse of white silk with points caught on a jet necklace and emphasized with jet diamond-shaped buttons. Her small head sported a new, extreme hairstyle: polished cap pulled back into a tiny cluster of curls, flat curls fringing her cheeks. She had a rather long neck, so that she looked like a dancer, her whole body neat and smooth and precise. The other Court women looked awkward in comparison.

Sir Simon glared at the offending cigarette.

"Disgusting! Must you smoke, Susan?"

"You smoke smelly cigars," she said sweetly. "We've all put up with it for years. Where's the harm?"

"David, she's out of hand!" Sir Simon said, turning to David Mulqueen. "Can't you do something with your wife?"

David, tall and blond, lean from tennis, glazed in rich tan from sailing, smiled indulgently.

"Afraid not, sir. She does exactly as she pleases."

"Hmph! The world is going to hell in a breadbasket. Well, Susan, you seem to know about clothes. Somebody told me you shop in Paris. Is that right?"

"I have bought some things there. When I happen to

be over there. Anyway, I know how to solve this problem. But it will cost money."

"I told you that doesn't matter!" Sir Simon said huffily. "Now, remember, Mildred is a big girl."

Mildred was not pleased with this description. Standing close to North, her arm linked through his possessively, she gave her grandfather and her cousin Susan an angry look.

Susan returned the look calmly. Inwardly, however, she was furious. She had always wanted to reign over Pride's Court herself, and now that was out of the question. As well, she rather envied Milly her groom. North looked exciting. He and Mildred had the first flush of romantic and sexual involvement to look forward to, whereas she, Susan, was already bored. Even the horses failed to make up for that feeling of anticipation, of undiscovered thrills. Marriage had become quite dreary. David was rather tedious. She spoke directly to Mildred in her flat, cutting voice.

"Well, you *are* tall, Milly. That's just a fact of life."

"I'm not a g-g-giant," Mildred said, her fingers digging into North's arm. Susan didn't like her, and she didn't like Susan. They were cousins, but Susan had always made Mildred feel large and untidy.

"I didn't say you were a giant," Susan said sweetly. "But you aren't exactly petite. What's the difference, anyway? Grandfather wants to know where we can find a suitable wedding gown. I happen to have a suggestion."

"I knew you would, Susan," Sir Simon said, looking pleased.

"There's a designer in Paris called Erté. He exports to shops like Altman's and Bendel's and others. He does covers for *Harper's Bazar*. His things are the last word."

"Erté? Never heard of him," Sir Simon said. "I suppose we can't find an Englishman? Or even an American? Do we have to have a Frenchman?"

"Actually, he's Russian. He changed his name," Susan said. "But if you want something stunning, something everybody will remember, he's the designer to get. You asked me, and that's my advice."

"I knew we ought to consult Susan," Sir Simon said, willing to accept even so preposterous a person as a Russian if it would produce the right costume for Mildred.

"I'll call Altman's," Susan said, "and find out how to contact Erté. He could design the clothes and make them up in Paris and send them for final fittings over here. He'll have to do the bridesmaids' dresses, too, or the thing will look ghastly."

"Can you find me some pictures of what he's done?" Sir Simon inquired, not a man to buy anything blind if there was an alternative.

"I'll show you some copies of *Harper's*," Susan said. "I'll send them around to your office in the morning."

"It must be white," Sir Simon went on thoughtfully, making sure the wrong impression wasn't about to be created at the start. "I like a bride in white. You can have color in the rest of the women. And in the flowers."

Nobody asked Mildred. North watched the scene with growing concern. He felt like a stranger who had wandered in by accident. Except for the odd glance the Courts paid no attention to him.

"That's what I want," Sir Simon continued, warming to his task. "Color for the rest of the girls, but *rich*. The men'll be in tails, of course. If North had been a military man, we could have a military wedding. A great pity to miss that. So there'll be no decorations. I know the governor general—Lord Byng was a friend of my cousin's. Lady Byng is half Greek, but she can't help that. She came from a good family, I believe. Now, I want all the Court women to wear beautiful gowns. And jewels. Bring out all the family pieces—nothing must be spared. North, do you have decent tails? Better order new ones, anyway. To be safe."

"I have tails," North said.

"Get new ones. Go to *my* tailor. Then we can be sure."

North felt beleaguered. It was clear that marrying into the Court family had certain disadvantages. The family was everything, the individual nothing. He'd be spending the remainder of his life doing as he was told—either by Sir Simon, or by whoever succeeded him. And for what? He looked at Mildred standing beside him, still clutching his arm as if she were in terror, and realized that she was just as much in awe of the old man as he was, as they all were. For some reason Mildred looked especially plain today. Probably because Susan looked so elegant. It was mean of them to discuss Mildred's size and make her nervous, and she had begun to stammer again just when she seemed to have improved so much. A feeling of uneasiness spread through his veins like a vague, enervating infection.

Suddenly, Mildred spoke up in a sharp, short flurry of rebellion.

"What if I d-d-don't like this Erté?"

"Do you have an alternative idea?" Susan asked.

"You're stammering again," Mildred's mother said.

Mildred subsided. Sir Simon rang for more drinks, and when they came, he held up his glass and smiled at his family.

"To the bride and groom. To the biggest wedding this city will ever see!"

Everybody drank to that. Then Sir Simon announced without warning, "I've decided to have two trumpeters."

"Trumpeters?" North bellowed, shocked into action by such a bizarre prospect. "Good God, what next?"

"What's wrong with trumpeters?" Sir Simon asked. He glared at North like some ancient chieftain whose most reasonable order has been questioned by an ignorant lackey.

"But it sounds like a circus," North protested.

"Nonsense! Royalty do it all the time. You've only to think of the Coronation. Trumpeters add a nice touch. It alerts everybody to what's going on, what's about to happen. Wakes them up a bit. We ll get a couple of trumpeters from a military band and dress them up. Susan, your friend whatever-his-name-is, can design something for them, too."

Susan grinned. How like Grandfather to transform a Paris designer into a personal friend! But North was not amused. He gripped his glass and then drained it rather rudely.

"Haven't *I* anything to say about this wedding?" he demanded. Sir Simon was astonished.

"If there's anything you seriously object to . . ." he began, but then he quickly turned away, leaving North without an opportunity to reply. "We must get on with some other decisions."

It was now or never, North thought. He would have to assert himself immediately, or he'd be a puppet for the rest of his life. He looked into Mildred's eyes and read there her silent request for his surrender. He sighed and decided to find another drink.

* * *

The day before the wedding a heavy rainstorm drenched the city of Montreal. The spacious gardens of Pride's Court were spongy underfoot and everyone was delighted to think that Sir Simon had had the foresight to plan an indoor wedding. Sir Simon took credit with becoming modesty. (He also took full credit within the family circle for arranging with the bishop and the archdeacon to wear their robes and conduct the elaborate service. The bishop was Low Church and did not, normally, abide anything that smacked of Papism. Neither did Sir Simon, but when it came to pageantry, *his* religious scruples were more flexible than those of the church dignitaries.)

Thousands of red and white roses (the Court colors) banked the front of Christ Church Cathedral and large candelabra flamed on either side of the chancel steps. Each carved pew along the center aisle of the nave was garlanded with masses of tiny red rose buds spiked with arum lilies. A red carpet stretched the length of the church and special prie-dieux were set out to the right of the chancel to accommodate the governor general and his party.

Eight hundred and fifty guests were seated in the nave itself, while another fifty were seated in each transept. (These were not the choice seats, of course, because the view was limited, but the guest list had been carefully pruned to make sure the right people were in the right pews.) The choir, seated in the chancel itself once the processional was completed, was thirty-five strong.

Promptly at seven, when all the guests were seated, two trumpeters heralded the arrival of the governor general's party. While the congregation stood, the verger led the party from behind the choir stalls to special chairs that had been set out and provided for them. The organist played "God Save the King." When the processional march resounded with a flourish, the pageantry continued.

From the back of the church the crucifer led the choir down the main aisle. He wore a longish white surplice over a vermillion cassock and carried the cross high, with extra care. Behind him the choir was dressed in blue cassocks, over which they wore short white surplices. They walked majestically to the choir stalls on either side of the chancel.

Next came the archdeacon, who was also rector of the cathedral, wearing a black cassock. From his shoulders hung a floor-length white silk cope ornamented with silver tracings. The bishop's chaplain followed, carrying the bishop's crozier. Then came the bishop himself, resplendent in purple cassock and white satin cope embroidered with gold thread. He wore the white miter of his office, its tall arch adding a gracious dignity. A deep cleft severed the hat from side to side. The bishop took his place at the top of the chancel steps flanked by the archdeacon. The chaplain stood behind, facing the pews.

Then North and his best man, Simon II, emerged from the vestry and made their way behind the choir stalls to a position at the foot of the chancel, slightly to the right. A faint rustle of approval spread through the cathedral when North appeared. In the glimmer of candles North looked extraordinarily handsome. He was dark, romantic, remote. (Actually, he was nervous and wondered for the hundredth time why he had agreed to such an extravagant affair. The idea of making a mistake terrified him. He wondered if his voice would suddenly fail during the responses and if he would drop the ring. It was like being the star in an opera without knowing the lines or the plot.)

Still, he and young Simon stood like perfectly structured men slightly angled to the pews in order to allow room for the ushers, who would eventually proceed up the side aisle. He knew that the governor general was watching him. He was thankful for the flickering light from the candles.

Now the actual wedding party came up the aisle in the quaint, doll-like step favored on such occasions. Charity came first, wearing lavender organza. She wore a silver crown on her short, shining hair and carried a huge muff of parma violets. Then came the twins, Flora and Fenella, walking side by side with solemn oval faces framed in bonnets made of fresh pink and blue daisies. The gowns they wore touched the floor: moss green silk with wide panniers entirely covered with tiny silk violets. Behind them the six bridesmaids (all recruited from among Mildred's school friends) wore vast hoops of rustling taffeta encrusted with ribbon loops in colors graduating from baby pink to deepest plum. The tall, pointed hennins of a romantic medievalism were draped with swoops of sheer silver tissue. They were a trifle mad, these hats, but nothing seemed too far-fetched now. A single diamond was suspended by a silver chain over each girl's forehead (they were gifts from the bride).

And at last there was Mildred, floating down the tunnel

of curious, expectant faces. She might have been an empress from Byzantium. She wore white satin folded finely over her bosom and caught tightly at the waist in a silver girdle. The skirt exploded in a pristine tent weighed down by a twelve-inch hem of handmade silken rosebuds with silver hearts. Her white orchid muff dripped blossoms to the floor and her veil, a mist of white mousseline held in place by a diamond-studded tiara, fell into waves of silver embroidery. The train was held up by two small girls and stretched six feet behind her.

When Mildred joined North at the chancel steps and the bishop towered over them surrounded by his own impressive retinue, they made a fantasy couple. They were larger than life, richer than imagination. From the first pew, on the bride's side of the church, Sir Simon gazed fondly upon his handiwork. Mildred, beautiful as all brides are beautiful, had become splendorously barbaric. North, the royal consort, was a worthy addition to the Court clan.

For the reception and ball, Pride's Court was crammed with summer flowers and alight with the jewels of the elite. In the Great Hall, which had been cleared especially for the occasion, an orchestra straight from London's Savoy Hotel (brought over on a Court ship at Court expense) played the latest fox-trots and tangos from their spot on the marble staircase. Tables set up in the spacious dining room tottered under mounds of oysters on ice beds, salmon mousse, filet de boeuf with truffles, turkey in hollandaise sauce, *riz de veau à la Toulouse*, various pâtés (one in an artichoke sauce), cheeses, fruits, and Nesselrode puddings. Champagne flowed in an endless stream.

The governor general led Mildred in the opening waltz while North squired Lady Byng. Landry and Charity, Fort and Sydney, Charles and Noel and Simon II with girls carefully selected for the evening took the floor.

Flora told Lord Stanhop that she would have married North in a minute if only dull Mildred hadn't snagged him first and said she thought he was divine. Fenella predicted darkly to Viscount Glyn that no good would come of the marriage, since North was a fortune hunter of the most delicious variety, and Mildred was too plain to be described, and wasn't it all sad? Both gentlemen reported the remarks to Sir Simon. They had found (like everybody else) that the twins were unfathomable. No one was sure whether or not they took themselves as seriously as they appeared to do. No one knew whether they had a sense of humor or whether they were a bit odd. Nobody knew very much about Flora and Fenella, and that included their mother.

North drank a great deal of champagne. At times he watched the grandeur of the ball with a spectator's detachment. Most of the time he tried to be attentive to Mildred, but there were moments when he wanted to flee. Between drinks he felt trapped, and he soon abandoned wine in favor of scotch. He managed to dance a few times, but late in the evening, wandering in the conservatory, he fell into a potted palm and was rescued by Fort. By two o'clock he was falling asleep, and still later he was ill in the bathroom off the servants' hall.

Sir Simon was oblivious to any flaws in his spectacular arrangements. He was supremely confident that the wedding had been a sensation. There had been photographers from every newspaper, including that scurrilous rag *Le Monde*. But he did not turn the fellow away. On this occasion, let them print the pictures, for nothing (he felt certain) but good could come of such a magnificent occasion. Let Honey see the photographs and weep once again, knowing what she'd missed by eloping with the despised Frenchman.

He did suffer a slight setback when he took a moment alone in the conservatory and found young Landry sitting with a young man he had met in Oxford and who had returned to Montreal at the same time for the summer. Just for a moment Sir Simon thought they were holding hands, but that was so ridiculous he decided his eyes were going on him. Landry said quickly that his friend had been dizzy and he was trying to help him. Sir Simon thrust out the seed of doubt. He comforted himself with the thought that North and Mildred were a fine pair. He had seen North kissing Mildred on the neck just a few moments earlier, and though he normally deplored public exhibitions, it was encouraging to know that North was fond of the girl. He congratulated himself on his choice of Mildred's husband.

The *Lady Lydia* was tied up at one on the piers regularly used by Court ships. She was fully staffed, although she was not scheduled to sail for France until early Monday morning. The damp velvet of August enfolded her quiet decks, and only a faint whisper of wind disturbed the red and white colors of her house flag.

Sir Simon had arranged for Mildred and North to spend their wedding night and the remainder of the weekend on board. By the time they reached the dock, driven by young Simon, there was little darkness left. Already a hint of light threatened to break open the smothering blackness in the east. Mildred and North were escorted to the Royal Suite by a smirking steward, given a tray of drinks and sandwiches, which they did not need, and left alone.

North escaped to the deck while Mildred undressed. She had exchanged the elaborate wedding gown for a simple silk suit before leaving Pride's Court, so it was easy enough to prepare for bed. She put on a lemon-colored chiffon nightgown that scarcely concealed her plump breasts and, dizzy with wine and expectation, stood nervously by the bed. She had longed for this night, had been desperately afraid something terrible would prevent the wedding from taking place. She had never wanted anything so much in her life as she wanted this marriage.

North came back in, walking unsteadily. He gave her a smile and a wave, and went into the bathroom and shut the door. She heard water running. He seemed so slow that she wondered if she ought to go in and see if he were all right; she knew he had been drinking a great deal.

Finally North emerged naked. He walked with the extreme care of the drunk across the maroon carpet. His dark hair was mussed, giving him a boyish, mischievous look.

He reached out with his finely made hands to grasp her bare arms.

"Sweetheart, take that nightgown off."

His throaty voice was encrusted with wine and the first vague stirrings of desire.

"Yes, in a moment."

She was whispering. She had no idea why she was doing that. Her stammer had disappeared and that was a relief, but being so close to having exactly what she wanted, to having North make love to her after all these months, made her fearful. What if it should all slip away? What if this were really some kind of dream?

"Do you love me, darling?" North asked. "It's important that you love me. Say you love me."

"Of course I love you, North. You know I love you!"

She was surprised at his diffident approach, at his need for reassurance. Her voice caught in her throat so that she could not speak. Her inner core of sensuality thickened and spread.

"Tell me you love me," he repeated. When his mouth came down on hers, he groaned—a muffled, rich, craving groan that shook her.

"I love you, North," she said when he took his mouth away. "I love you."

"Take that damned thing off, will you, sweetheart?" North said. "It's scratching hell out of me."

She glimpsed the angry, childish expression that flitted over his face and obediently took off the nightgown. She did not want North to be cross or frustrated. She wanted him to have everything he wanted. She wanted to spoil him.

He thrust himself against her smooth body so that Mildred's face was in his shoulder. She could smell his clean, male flesh. A honey-tide of hunger flooded her, and she sank upon the huge bed, pulling North down with her. They lay side by side, legs locked together, while his lips ventured across her cheeks and his teeth nipped her ear playfully. He searched her mouth with his tongue—a textbook on the production of delicious responses, North had been born knowing how to kiss a woman; his own sensuality spanned the long, slow trek across aching nerve ends. Slowly, oh so slowly, his lips moved around the edges of Mildred's prickly desire.

"I adore you," he murmured, his face pressed into the cleavage between her breasts. "I adore being with you, I adore kissing you, I adore making love to you."

As she swam in the warmth of his lust, Mildred thought briefly of the formality of the wedding, the glitter, the beauty, the mad extravagance, and how it had all led to this. This flow of flesh on flesh that was more exciting than any ball, any event that could be imagined. She wanted to be adored by North. What sweetness it was! She could have listened forever to his words.

But North stopped kissing her then and rolled away, lying on his back, staring at the ceiling. His need had vanished as quickly as it had arisen.

"Too much wine," he said, making a wry face.

"Yes, you did have a lot of champagne," Mildred said indulgently.

"And why not?" he demanded, glancing toward her.

Lying there, with Milly's large receptive body waiting for his pleasure, he took a moment to enjoy his triumph. The victory he had won over his father, who had predicted he would be a failure. And over the people who had refused to hire him earlier, the ones who had neglected to invite him to intimate dinners or choice weekends in the country. The men who had forgotten to ask him for a game of golf. To hell with all of them! They had come out to see him today, the crown prince. And here was the key to it all, the princess herself, stretched out for his delight. What was it all due to? Oh, partly his success with Sir Simon, and yet, he must not overlook the fact that he had something Mildred wanted. He looked down the plane of his chest, across his stomach to the dark patch of pubic hair, and the recalcitrant member began to stiffen before his gaze. Yes, she lusted after him. He would be only too happy to oblige, for making love was one of his greatest talents. He put his hand on himself and knew that he was indeed ready.

"And why not?" he asked again, turning on his side and putting one hand on Mildred's thigh, the other on himself. "Come here, sweetheart, and we'll make love. Oh, God, Milly, I've wanted to get inside you for so long!"

Milly surrendered. Years of accumulated yearning, of romantic ideas gradually transformed into sexual drive, had gathered in a heavy pool somewhere near her center. North kissing her greedily from his position above her, slid away from her mouth, traveled her body, and buried his head between her thighs. Her ache spilled over his dark head fitted so neatly in the supplicating wedge. When he sat up, she saw the stiff and unrepentant flesh large, absolutely desirable.

"Am I big enough for you?"

"Oh, darling, you're magnificent."

"Are you sure I'm big enough? I want to be the best lover you could ever have, Milly. Are you sure I'm big enough?"

She pulled him toward her roughly, so moist that he could thrust inside without struggle. She lay there under him, slack, spread like a downed bird for his pleasure. And despite the champagne, he made love to her for over an hour. That night Mildred caught a fever of dependence on North that settled in as a chronic condition.

CHAPTER FIFTEEN

Honey was working late. In fact, all the offices on the editorial floor of *Le Monde* were alight as staffers took telephone calls, telegrams, cables, and worked on stories concerning the latest international crisis. The world was on the edge of another explosion.

This time, the issue was the neutrality of the Dardanelles, those straits that were a vital transportation link between Europe and Asia Minor. At the moment a small contingent of British troops along with a smattering of French and Italian soldiers were isolated at a garrison called Chanak while Turks and Greeks seesawed back and forth in bloody battle.

As she wrote, Honey thought crossly that it was all that wild Turk's fault. How dare an obscure army officer bring the world to the brink of destruction once again? He had been sent to Gallipoli to keep the peace while the Greeks took over the territory from the Turks. Instead, he had rebelled against his own government and sworn to drive out the Greeks forever.

A year of carnage had followed Mustafa Kemal's revolt while Turk slaughtered Greek and Greek slaughtered Turk. Finally, the British could hold still no longer. The Dardanelles was a lifeline of trade, and they could not afford to see their own and Europe's economy threatened because a Turkish officer had begun a slapdash form of tribal warfare. To this end they had demanded military support from the dominions around the world. New Zealand had responded instantly with a resounding "Yes!" Not so Canada. Unfortunately, Colonial Secretary Winston Churchill had indiscreetly released a press statement about the matter before sending off official cables to the various dominions. In Canda Prime Minister Mackenzie King was miffed. He refused to move on the issue without the consent of Parliament.

169

This came as a surprise to London. But King was stubborn. Was London still making Canada's foreign policy, he demanded to know? Had the magnificent sacrifices made by Canadians during the Great War been for nothing? As a result of his stand the Cabinet met hour after hour while Canadian newspapers printed fierce statements pro and con. Lines were clearly drawn. In Toronto the Liberal *Globe* announced sternly: "If Turk attacks Constantinople, he attacks Canada." The Conservative *Montreal Star* had in essence agreed. But in Ottawa *Le Droit* (no doubt reflecting a French Canadian viewpoint) demanded outright refusal to the request to send troops to foreign soil. Honey was about to take the same line in *Le Monde*. While her English blood would have dictated otherwise, she knew instinctively that the French would not stand for yet another rally to the English flag.

She was frowning over the copy, stuck in the bulk of an Oliver typewriter, when her attention was drawn to a figure who now thrust himself into her open doorway. It was Charles Court, and she saw at once that something was seriously wrong.

"Charles!" she cried, rising from her chair to greet her brother. "Whatever is the matter?"

He stared at her, rather dazedly.

"Not Papa?"

Charles seemed not to hear her. He was a tall, slightly paunchy man in a well-cut gray woolen suit. His thick hair almost matched the material except for underlying streaks of dark left from his youth. He wore steel-rimmed glasses, which gave him an intellectual look but did not quite effectively screen the sharp blue Court eyes.

"Not Papa?" Honey repeated.

"No."

He came into the room and took a chair in front of her desk. She sat down, a flutter of fear in her stomach. Then she rose again and went around her brother to close the door on the noise outside.

"I saw the lights on. I thought you might still be in your office," Charles said.

"We're all working late because of this Dardanelles problem. It's terrible. I'm awfully worried about it, Charles. The whole world is quite likely to be at war again."

He did not seem to hear her but stared at his hands, folded in his lap. Then he pulled himself up and looked at her with a more direct focus.

"I had to talk to you."

"Would you like a brandy?" Honey offered. "I keep a bottle here for emergencies."

"Yes, please."

She poured out the brandy in a drinking glass and handed it to Charles. He took it with a shaking hand and drank it off quickly.

"Polly?" she asked now.

He took off his glasses and passed his hands over his eyes as if that would brush away the difficulty. Without looking at Honey, he said numbly, "Polly's dead. I got a telephone call tonight."

"But . . . she wasn't that ill! I thought you were planning to bring her back to Pride's Court soon."

"I was. It was a hemorrhage. Sometimes that happens. I was planning to visit her next week. Now, they're sending Polly back in a coffin."

"Does Papa know?"

"Not yet. The message came to my office."

She walked around the desk and placed her hand gently on his shoulder. She did not know how to offer him comfort. Charles was alone. It was odd that he always seemed to come to her when he was in trouble.

"Pride's Court is so empty," Charles said. "But you know, I was looking forward to bringing Polly back again."

"Mildred and North will be back from their honeymoon soon, won't they? The house will be more lively then."

"Yes."

He did not say that the house had often been lonely for him. When he was a child, it had seemed so vast, and much of it had been cold. Even forbidding. The first few days after he brought his first bride home, before Venetia fell ill, had been wonderful. Then, the house had been truly alive and welcoming. He had tried to get close to Angela when she was a baby, but it had been difficult, and somehow he had never quite established a warm and loving relationship. While Polly was well, they had been quite happy, but then the house turned cold again when she left. Yet he had never seriously thought of moving. Pride's Court was so much a part of him.

"Angela ought to be with you, Charles. I'm going to speak to Papa about asking her back for a little while, even if he *is* angry with me. He must think about you for a change."

"Oh, Papa won't have her back," Charles said hopelessly. "I don't know what happened between them, do you?"

"No, she won't tell me. Still, I'm sure it can't be so bad. You know how Papa gets into a rage over something trivial. Perhaps this time he'll relent."

"I wanted to be close to Angela," Charles said. There was a dull tone to his voice that struck Honey as peculiar. She had never seen Charles behave this way before. Even when things were so terribly difficult with his first wife, he had never let down. His face had a pale, unhealthy look, and his features were slack. He was more like an orphan than the scion of a great family, the heir to a title, the manipulator of millions of dollars, and the employer of thousands of men.

"Angela has had a difficult life in many ways," Honey said, still puzzled at her brother's odd way of speaking. "That's partly why I took her in. I had no idea she and Beau would fall in love. You know that. I was as surprised as anybody. And I have never approved."

"I understand, Honey. Papa never did, you know."

There was a short silence. Then Charles, polishing his glasses on a large white linen handkerchief, began to weep. Honey was appalled. She had never seen her brother cry, and she did not know what to say that would help. Tears washed down his cheeks and he shook with sobs.

"My—God . . ." he said.

Honey realized that she would have to get Charles home. He could not drive in his present condition. She could always have Papa send the chauffeur to pick up the Rolls-Royce later. The real difficulty lay in getting Charles out of the building without attracting attention.

Somehow she spirited him down the backstairs to the street, where her huge gray Packard touring sedan sat in elegant splendor. Charles had completely broken down and was still sobbing by the time they reached Pride's Court. He made some effort to straighten up as they drove under the limestone portico.

She helped Charles out of the car into the mild September night. He leaned heavily on her arm as if he had suddenly become crippled. There was a pleasant smell of autumn in the air; the bitter scent of chrysanthemums and marigolds still blooming amid the blackened leaves of less hardy flowers, a touch of smoke, dampness sifting down the mountain.

She rang the front doorbell and Peters opened it. His face, usually impassive, reflected astonishment.

"Why, Mr. Charles, are you ill?"

"Help me in with him, Peters, will you? And then find Sir Simon."

They walked slowly through the reception hall into the Great Hall. Honey saw a light in the Red Sitting Room and steered Charles there.

"Sit down here, Charles, and I'll get you a drink," she said and looked around for the drinks tray. She found it and poured straight whisky and handed it to him. He took it without speaking.

Sir Simon came in as Charles drained his glass. He saw his daughter and, not realizing that something was wrong with his son, cried, "What are you doing in my house?"

'Oh, Papa, how *could* you?" she cried, exasperated beyond endurance by his pigheadedness. "Can't you see Charles is unhappy? It isn't a question of what I'm doing here, it's what to do for Charles."

"Unhappy? What's going on?" he shouted as if they were all deaf and several blocks distant.

"He's had a call about Polly. She's dead."

Sir Simon stopped for a moment, arrested in mid-anger.

"I'm sorry, Charles."

Charles did not speak but held out his glass to Honey. She refilled it. Sir Simon's eye gleamed in a terrible way. The whole scene was somehow out of his hands, and his wayward and arrogant daughter appeared to be in command. It was unthinkable.

"You must pull yourself together, Charles. We must decide what to do—" he began.

"He can't decide anything tonight. Can't you see that?" Honey cried.

"How dare you come in here and attempt to dictate to me in my own house!" Sir Simon shouted, whirling on his daughter. "Get out, *Lady* St. Amour!"

But Honey was not yet ready to capitulate. There was

something else she wished to say and all her father's insults would not prevent her.

"You ought to bring Angela back to be with her father," she declared. "If you like, I'll go home and speak to her. I could drive her over. And you'll have to send Dodgson for the car. It's parked by the newspaper building, where Charles left it. I drove him home."

This was too much for Sir Simon. His temper exploded in an angry burst and his voice rattled the windowpanes.

"Don't tell me how to behave, you tart!"

"Papa!" They had had violent words in the past, but he had never before said anything so shocking to her.

"That's what you are, and you've encouraged Angela to be the same. I can't tell you what went on here, but believe me, I won't have that girl in the house again. Not under any circumstances. My mind can scarcely come to grips with what I've seen—what I know. Angela is no better than you are, a common trollop, and it's more than ever a sin upon your head that Charles cannot have his own daughter with him in his hour of need!"

"How dare you say that to me!"

Honey could not imagine what Sir Simon was talking about. Since nobody had seen fit to tell her what the quarrel was that had driven Angela out of Pride's Court, she could not understand her father's wrath.

"I dare to say anything in my own house. You're not welcome here! I told you that before. Now get out. Go to your Frenchies if that's what you want. If that's what Angela wants, let her have them. Just don't set foot in here again."

The scene he had witnessed between Angela and Landry still seared his vision. Sometimes he awoke in the middle of the night, and it reappeared again before his eyes. His beautiful granddaughter, whom he had so generously forgiven for her mistake, was a whore. Naked in the arms of her own cousin. And in *his* house. It was unthinkable!

Worse, almost, was the brazen behavior of his daughter, the woman responsible for every sorrow that had beset Pride's Court since the dreadful day when she had eloped and had thrown her life away upon a foreign rake.

"Get out!" he cried again.

This time Honey turned and, unable to bear any more, ran from the room. As she fled toward the front doors of the great house, Sir Simon bellowed, "I'd rather send for the devil than for Angela Court!"

Charles set down his glass and, with the glazed look of a sleepwalker, followed his sister from the room. As she slammed the front doors of the house, Charles began the long walk up the marble staircase to his apartment. He was, for the time being, very, very old.

Sir Simon, watching this impossible scene, raised his fist to the ceiling and shook it. Silently he swore that St. Amour would be punished. He would be made to pay in full for the terrible wrongs he had done to the Court family. Nothing had ever been the same in the vast and beautiful house since the day Armand St. Amour had set foot in it. That was twenty-seven years ago. Revenge was long overdue.

CHAPTER SIXTEEN

Angela's first exhibition was to be held the following May. She worked furiously during the winter and spring months in the nursery on St.-Denis Street. Meanwhile, she corresponded regularly with her grandmother in London. Lady Twickenham eagerly seized the opportunity to sponsor Angela's work and took charge of all details connected with the show as well as expenses.

The countess chose a gallery on Brook Street in Mayfair—not too large but with a long history of successful artists who had exhibited there. Anything outside Mayfair would have been out of the question, since Lady Twickenham had only the vaguest ideas about other areas of London.

Julia took a firm hand in everything from the guest list to the choice of frames. Only champagne would be served. "It's no use asking people what they want, just put a drink in their hand and they're perfectly happy. They don't come to make choices but to see the pictures. No food. People spill bits of cheese and caviar, and it's ghastly. If they can't drink without eating, they ought not to come," she told the gallery owner.

This edict did not prevent her from persuading a certain critic to attend, even though he was a notorious drunk. Julia's theories were gloriously flexible. In fact, when it came to the guest list, Julia was ruthless. She pulled every string she could, and no telephone call or personal note was too much trouble. She went so far as to ring up friends of Lord Twickenham if she thought they might help or if they had any influence with the critics or dealers. The earl had at one time collected antique Georgian tureens and saltcellars and had come to know quite a number of London dealers in this way. Julia made contact with every one.

It was the critics, however, who received her special attention. One of the most difficult, a man who wrote for the *Times*, was known to ignore newcomers, and if they were women, they might never have lived and painted at all. Angela was a double hurdle. But Julia was undaunted. She maneuvered the critic into luncheon at Claridge's three days before the opening. Over a bottle of Château Margaux, she begged him to tell her the truth about Angela's work when he saw it. She must know, she confessed in a conspiratorial whisper, whether to encourage the girl in her career. Or was it hopeless? Would it be the kindest thing in the end to withdraw support from her ambitious granddaughter? She appealed to him to come to the exhibition just to give her the benefit of his experience. She sealed it with an even more touching plea.

"Just because she's Canadian," Julia confided over Armagnac and coffee, "people like us ought not to ignore her."

Finding himself placed so neatly on the same level as the countess, the critic murmured assent.

"The king depends upon us to be generous to colonials, you know," Julia went on, not giving him time to reason. "They fought in the war. We must give them our support."

So in the end even King George and the fate of the British Empire seemed to rest upon the critic attending Angela's exhibition. He left the luncheon with a sense of mission. Julia left with a headache. But in a good cause, she felt.

Honey and Armand arrived in London for the opening and took a suite at the Ritz. As well as giving moral support to Angela, they were anxious to visit with Michel and his wife, Clarissa. Michel was in the process of detaching himself from a small British company manufacturing light aircraft. He had managed to secure a berth with the United States Navy. Rear Admiral Moffett, the United States Navy's energetic chief of aeronautics, was a friend of the Duke of Burleigh, Clarissa's father. Through this kindly connection Michel had been promised a place on the first flight of the airship ZR-1, presently being constructed in Philadelphia along lines established by earlier German zeppelins. The United States had an active program in airships, and the Navy felt there was a great future for them.

Clarissa would have followed Michel anywhere and was quite happy to accompany him to Lakehurst, New Jersey, where the dirigible would be tested sometime in the fall of 1923.

Honey and Armand were delighted to attend Angela's opening along with Clarissa and Michel's young friends. Fortunately, it was a glossy, warm London evening, and no wraps or umbrellas were needed. It seemed a night to dress elegantly.

As they turned off Piccadilly, heading for Brook Street, they joined an impressive cavalcade of expensive motorcars all making for the gallery. Upon arrival, they found both Julia and Angela receiving near the door. Angela looked nervous but stunning in gray chiffon—her huge eyes exactly matched her gown. Honey gave her an encouraging hug.

Not long after her relatives had arrived, Angela began to circulate round the room, afraid to hear what anyone said but tempted to listen just the same. She spotted a couple of the critics and lost her nerve; she really did not want to know what they might say.

Privately, Julia had admitted that Angela's work was strange. The pictures were dreamlike landscapes of forests and classic temples, all with deep perspectives that appeared to stretch for miles. Any humans who might have strayed onto the canvas were either voluptuous naked women or fully clothed old men who looked vaguely embarrassed.

The fact that she had no idea what the paintings were

about did not deter Julia. It was enough to sponsor the show, to cajole the critics; certainly she did not feel compelled to analyze the work. She was very grand in purple silk with gold-fringed hem, and she displayed every diamond she owned somewhere on her person. Her gray petal hair swept upward while her eyes ranged about in an appraising manner. She glittered like a chandelier from each beringed finger, up her arms stiff with brilliant bracelets, to the choker around her neck.

Julia was much heartened by the arrival of several loyal friends who had not appeared in Mayfair for months: men who had not come down to London to sit in the House in recent memory and still others thought dead by their peers. It was quite touching, Julia decided, but then, breeding always did tell. She had lived by that precept all her life, and the theory did not come unraveled simply because Sir Ranulf Cherwell-Ross arrived dead drunk. She forgave him instantly and had him spirited away to safety. After all, she had hunted with Sir Ranulf when he had been Master of the Quorn (one of the oldest Hunts in England), and one did not allow old friends to make fools of themselves.

The critic upon whom she had lavished so much attention at Claridge's admitted warily that Angela had "possibilities." He would, he promised the countess, discuss the whole project with her after his review had appeared. Julia cleverly invited him to yet another luncheon. She knew when he accepted that she had won. She could see the Union Jack reflected in his eyes.

Michel and Clarissa brought a party of young people. They swarmed in a tight, noisy little band, some smoking Turkish cigarettes, and all of them underdressed for the occasion. They laughed a great deal at nothing. Julia did not like them much, but since Clarissa was a duke's daughter, she knew that the girl could not be all bad.

Despite her concern for her exhibition, Angela furtively watched the door all evening. As the time spun out, her mood sank lower. She had hoped, she had been *sure*, Beau would come. In the beginning she had fully expected him to arrive with Aunt Miel and Uncle Armand. When that didn't happen, she thought he might slip in casually. Aunt Miel had seen Beau earlier in the week and reported that he was back on Half Moon Street working on his symphony.

This longing to see him come into the gallery alternated with the stern warning to herself that it would be better if Beau did not show up at all. Why start the whole affair again unless Beau had changed? She was making a recovery. It would be shattering to suffer the same pains again for nothing. Much better not to see him, even for a moment. Still, she found herself looking hopefully toward the door and was angry when she recognized her own lack of logic.

She watched the crowd mill about her, glasses in hands, mouths chattering, voices rising. There was a sense of enthusiasm, of excitement in the room. She could feel the strong undercurrent of expected success. Several paintings had sold and she knew that most critics had shown up. She knew, too, that viewers found the pictures sexually arousing. Especially when they realized that the artist was female and young. She sometimes overheard comments.

"My dear, I'm afraid to look!" cried a woman in a dress like an Arabian tent who was staring fixedly at the naked bodies. "One can see almost everything! Isn't that—?" She left the question hanging in midair.

"What exactly is the artist trying to say?" a thin man demanded of his elderly companion. "That women are sad because men are lacking?"

"I don't follow it," somebody else said, "but I don't mind trying."

"Miss Court is too pretty," one woman commented sourly, summing up the thoughts of many viewers. "It will be downhill all the way."

Angela enjoyed their reactions, but she could not rid herself of her terrible longing for Beau to appear. Eventually Clarissa swept up beside her with a young man in tow.

"Here's a man who wants to meet the artist," Clarissa said. "You're such a success, darling! This is Dorian Fraser. He's vaguely related to me."

Angela turned her glance toward a fair-skinned young man who smilingly acknowledged the introduction. He was tall and slender and had a good tailor. Clarissa was explaining that he was a successful architect while Angela

179

took inventory. His light brown hair was well cut, and he had a strong, direct gaze. His features taken separately were not memorable, but they seemed to blend rather nicely. He had a pleasant, genial face.

"I can vouch for him," Clarissa said.

"She told me you were beautiful, and you are," Dorian said to Angela, ignoring his cousin. "Are you coming with us afterward? We're all going to a club I know."

"Julia expects me to join her," Angela said doubtfully. "She has taken two tables at the Savoy."

"We'll come, too, and then we can all go somewhere later. Mustn't disappoint Julia, she's done so much for you," Clarissa said.

Angela nodded, although she was still distracted by the idea that Beau might show up at any moment. In that case she would no doubt foolishly surrender and go off with him. If only she could be stern and cool and tell him how nice it was to see him but that she had other plans. But that was stupid, because why did she care if he came if she didn't intend to see him alone? She noticed that Dorian was still talking.

"You must come with us," he was saying a little tipsily. "Or I shall drink too much and die of alcohol poisoning. You wouldn't want that on your conscience, would you?"

"Dorian, shut up and leave Angela alone," Clarissa said impatiently. "We'll work it out."

Angela thought Dorian a bit silly, but at the same time it was nice to have some attention paid to her. Beau had not seen fit to come, and soon the show would be over and she would be off with Julia and her other relatives. Beau's chance would be gone. How *could* he? She would have gone to a premiere of his symphony if she had to be taken in an ambulance, she thought with an edge of anger. But that was like Beau. He thought of nobody but himself.

"I insist you promise," Dorian said.

He saw her look away from him, followed the direction of her eyes to the door, and recognized the problem.

"You're expecting somebody." It was almost an accusation,

"Yes, I am."

She was impressed that he was sensitive enough to pick up her distress signals. She felt a small rush of warmth toward Dorian.

"Oh, Angela, you're not waiting for Beau?" Clarissa asked in a pained voice. "Aunt Miel says he isn't coming. Didn't you know that?"

"No, I didn't. Aunt Miel didn't mention it."

She felt suddenly distraught, as if the whole show had collapsed around her ears. She would have liked to run away from all these chattering people. She wanted to cry.

"Who is this Beau you're talking about?" Dorian wanted to know.

"He's a relative by marriage. I can't explain. It's much too involved, Dorian, so just forget it." Clarissa pulled Dorian away, leaving Angela by herself once more.

More people streamed in. Angela was only vaguely aware of them. The evening had become a nightmare, and when at last Julia came to take her away, she felt relieved. Only a few stragglers were left and the gallery owner and attendants would take care of them. Clarissa and her friends swore to join Julia's party at the Savoy, and they all drove off.

At one point during supper, Angela found Dorian sitting beside her, although that had not been the original plan. He said in her ear, "Don't worry about that fellow, don't waste yourself. There are hundreds of men in the world who would care enough to come to your exhibition. For example, I care. I care very much."

"Thank you."

She liked Dorian and found it pleasant to be reassured, but she could not talk to him seriously. Her mind was still trailing off toward Half Moon Street, where she could visualize Beau sitting at the piano, Beau getting himself tea in the kitchen, Beau upstairs in the bedroom. She shook her head as if to clear away these visions.

"May I see you tomorrow? May I take you out to dinner? I have tickets for a play . . ."

She agreed to see Dorian, more as a distraction than because she found him fascinating. If she were out socializing, she would not fall into a depression over Beau.

By a stroke of luck Beau had found that the house on

Half Moon Street was for rent. He had given it up when he moved to the country with Angela, and it had been taken over by a music teacher, an elderly man who gave piano lessons. But by the time Angela fled back to Montreal, the house was unoccupied again. Since it was familiar to him and conveniently situated, Beau snapped it up.

Very little had changed. The same green brocade sofa, assortment of upholstered chairs of uncertain pedigree, Oriental carpet, and hunting prints were in evidence. The grand piano stood in the window. On the evening of Angela's show Beau paced about the house, opening windows to let in the warm evening air, pouring a glass of gin and tonic for his friend John Leach, settling at the piano only to leap up again without playing.

Beau glanced restlessly at the clock on the mantelpiece as he had been doing every few minutes for the past hour. It was now well after eight o'clock.

"I suppose the damned place is filled with ridiculous people all chattering about nothing," he said crossly. "They never look at the pictures. I don't see the point of openings, do you?"

John Leach sat on a nondescript chair with one leg thrown over the arm. He was intensely thin, with a narrow face and hair already receding at thirty. His skin was ruddy, and at times he developed patches of eczema. He was not attractive physically and he knew it. He had managed to secure a position as a music critic for the *Express*, but in actuality he thought of himself as a failed flutist never quite able to catch on with one of the reputable symphony orchestras or chamber groups.

John Leach had a somewhat symbiotic relationship with Beau Dosquet: He was a hanger-on, a man who fed off Beau's electric energy, off the scent of genius. For his part, Beau used John as a sounding board for musical ideas, as an errand boy, as link with a reality he sometimes felt had escaped him.

They were opposites in almost every way. It was inevitable that John would become jealous of Beau. That pain was something he had to endure in order to remain in Beau's orbit. He recognized the fact that Beau was physically attractive to both men and women: not just handsome like some of the current movie idols—John Barrymore, or Ramon Navarro—but much more masculine and dangerous. Beau had a haphazard, fiery charm that sprang from his searching green eyes, disheveled black curls, and sensual mouth. If John Leach looked in the mirror and compared himself with Beau, he could only despair. He seldom indulged in that whimsy, however.

Watching Beau pace, John said, "What difference does it make what either of us think of art openings? You aren't *going* to the opening, remember?"

"Aunt Miel was wrong to make me promise not to go," Beau said angrily. "Angela may expect me."

"Did Angela call you?"

"No, but then, I didn't call her, either."

"Forget it. Settle down. We'll go out to dinner somewhere. Have a drink."

"I don't want a drink. Her family has put pressure on Angela. They've done everything they can to keep us apart."

"And when you were together, you went off to France. My God, Beau, I watched the whole thing. You and Angela aren't good for each other, that's all."

"That's what Aunt Miel says."

Beau moved to the piano and pulled out the stool. He positioned it carefully before he sat down. The top of the piano was propped up to increase the volume. He glanced across at his friend before he began to play.

"I have something extraordinary to tell you."

Leach looked surprised. What next? his eyes seemed to say.

"Sounds as if I'd better throw some more gin into my glass."

"Help yourself. You know where it is."

Leach shouted from the dining room as he fixed his drink, "Is it about the symphony?"

"Yes, of course. I've had a breakthrough. A flash of inspiration. I want to tell you about it. Come and sit down."

Leach did as he was told.

"In the third movement . . . you know I've never been satisfied with the middle of it. I think the climax is effective and I think the opening of the third movement is right, but the middle . . . well, it's come to me. I'm going to introduce a section in the jazz idiom."

"*The jazz idiom?*"

If Beau had said he was turning it into a jig, Leach could not have been more surprised. Seeing this, Beau spoke quickly, defensively.

"A few composers are experimenting along these lines. Gershwin, for one. Eva Gauthier is going to sing three of his popular songs in a classical concert this fall. Right in Aeolian Hall. Think of it! Satie has been playing around with the classical style for years. Making jokes. Ravel was influenced by him and now Ravel's "La Valse" is a kind of deification of the waltz form. I feel a revolution coming even in symphonic form. Why not?"

Leach groaned.

"I'm glad I poured myself more gin. You're crazy. Do you really think Sir Thomas will go for it?"

"If he doesn't, somebody will."

"Ah, but you need the money he owes you on completion of the work. Also, who could better premiere the symphony than Sir Thomas himself?"

"I have to take risks sometimes."

"Why not wait until you're more established?"

"It's *right*, John."

"You're a lunatic. You're letting personal problems interfere with your work."

"Listen."

Beau began to play. A rocking, slightly jarring rhythm was superimposed on a theme that was inherently dignified. It was disturbing. Leach found himself mesmerized. It was a daring idea, no doubt about that. He wondered if it could be made to work with a symphony orchestra reared on the precision of Mozart, the drama of Brahms and Beethoven.

Eventually, Beau stopped playing.

"Well?" he demanded.

"Fantastic," John Leach said. "It's your problem, of course, if you want to take the risk with Sir Thomas. But if he liked it, he'd be the person to do it."

"A chance I have to take."

Beau began to pace again, looking quickly at the clock from odd angles, as if he hoped Leach wouldn't notice what he was doing. He could imagine the scene on Brook Street, the gallery all lighted, the people coming, Angela looking like a dream creature, probably wearing gray to match her eyes. Aunt Miel, Angela's grandmother, Julia. All of them, spectacular and secure.

"I think I'll have a drink after all. Pour me some brandy, will you?"

Leach got up slowly, as if he might refuse to obey the request. He did not like to be treated like a servant, although he knew that Beau was scarcely conscious of the way he spoke at times. He got the brandy and handed it to Beau.

"You want to watch this stuff," he said, referring to the brandy. "Especially before you eat."

"Oh, God, don't lecture me. I don't want to eat anyway. I don't feel like food. I feel like—"

John Leach gave him a half-leer, half-smile.

"I know what you feel like," he said.

"And don't be suggestive." But his heart wasn't in correcting Leach's manners. He did not hear him fully, he was so distracted. He thought about walking to the gallery.

"Will you forget about Angela and her show?" Leach said next. "Let's go somewhere for dinner."

"Do you mind if I don't go for dinner?"

"Yes, I mind. You invited me."

"I'm sorry. I'm not going. I think I'll work."

They both knew this was a lie. John was annoyed. He had nothing to do if Beau decided not to go to dinner. He would have to eat alone.

"Like hell you're working. You're going off to that bloody opening."

"No, no. I'm not."

"Don't lie. Your aunt will be furious with you. So will the dotty old countess. They'll all hate you for showing up and upsetting the artist. Why do it, anyway? You know you don't intend to marry Angela."

Beau waited impatiently for Leach to leave. As the moments spun out, he became more rude and eventually, unable to withstand the atmosphere any longer, Leach walked out into the street, leaving Beau alone. Beau poured himself another brandy and went over the problem in his mind, arguing both sides and knowing perfectly well that he was about to give in. She would probably still be there, he thought, conjuring up a vision of her pale heart-shaped face and columbine eyes. He ought to have called her, anyway, and not listened to Aunt Miel. Why had he done that? What difference could it possibly make to anybody else what he and Angela did? Angry, he strode out into the night, walking toward Brook Street with a knowing, purposeful step.

When he reached the gallery, it was still brilliantly lighted and he could see a few people scattered about with wine glasses in their hands, talking loudly, gesticulating. He went in and his mood plummeted. Angela was not there. None of his relatives were there either, and he knew they must have gone on to supper somewhere. He spoke to the attendant.

"Has the artist left?"

"Oh yes, sir, she left about fifteen minutes ago."

"I must look around."

"We'll be closing in ten minutes, sir."

"Yes, I won't be long."

The first thing that struck him was the size of the paintings. They were larger than he had expected. She had accomplished a massive amount of work since she had returned to Montreal. He was impressed. Even a little awed, knowing how meticulously she worked. The pictures all had a dreamlike air with naked women, breasts like ripe pears, walking along formal paths lined with classic pillars and steam engines wildly intermixed. In the distance there was sometimes an interminable flight of stairs or a distant city, but the huge-eyed ladies did not appear to see anything beyond their immediate range. Their bodies were sensual, but their eyes were dark pools of despair. Men who appeared intermittently on the landscape were either very old and dry or very young and mesmerized. In either case, men and women ignored each other with Olympian grandeur. The overall effect was, nevertheless, one of intense eroticism. Rolling curves of enticing flesh, suggestive, inchoate, bloomed like lush flowers on leg stalks. One picture was different. Obviously, it was a self-portrait. Angela's face, misty but unmistakable, was wreathed in a nunlike headgear. Her hands were crossed on her breast, her eyes distinctly melancholy. Beau wanted the painting, but even as he formed the notion, he knew he could not buy it himself. He would not want Angela to know he was the owner of the painting. How was he to get around it? Providing it was not purchased between now and closing time, he thought, he could find somebody else

186

to purchase it in his name. His mind skipped nimbly over certain possibilities, and then he thought of an antiques dealer he had met through Sir Thomas Beecham, who had been buying an old but elegant piano the year before. Yes, he would telephone the dealer, a Mr. Brackam, in the morning. Commission him to buy the painting—that was it.

This idea comforted Beau. Having at least done *something*, he felt better. A bittersweet mood overcame him as he walked back into the night: It was as if he had acquired part of Angela. A silent, obedient, totally amenable part. A little of his restlessness evaporated. He returned to Half Moon Street to compose.

CHAPTER SEVENTEEN

The exhibition was a decided success. Three out of four London critics praised it and half the paintings were sold during the first week. Four pictures of Angela appeared in various daily newspapers, and *Country Life* sent a photographer to Julia's London house to catch Angela's beauty for the next issue. Julia was ecstatic.

The countess noticed how much time Angela spent with Dorian Fraser. However, if she had any reservations, she did not mention them. Dorian was an improvement over Beau Dosquet (*that* man was quite impossible), and Dorian's family was more than socially acceptable. Dorian's mother had once been a lady-in-waiting to the queen, and Dorian himself had been a member of the Palace Guard. The Frasers were not titled but were related to a number of aristocrats. Though not exactly rich (Julia always knew these things or could lay hands on the facts when necessary), they appeared comfortably well off. Their houses were ancient, their horses excellent, the two hunts to which they belonged were impeccable. As well, Dorian's career as an architect was assured; he had the right connections and showed considerable talent. He was good-looking in the upper-class English fashion, courteous and well tailored.

If Julia had bigger game in mind for Angela, she could only have looked in the direction of royalty or vast wealth.

Julia was the first to admit, when under the influence of good wine, that a great fortune was a pleasant addition to a man's other qualities. And she had reason to know. But she was clever enough not to interfere with Angela and Dorian, for he obviously was rapidly replacing the awful Beau in Angela's thoughts. Once Angela was cured, Julia reasoned, other steps could be taken. She intended to give the whole question of Angela's marriage a great deal of study. She might even consult Twickenham, who was terribly good about introductions to the right people.

In fact, the show had been hanging two weeks when Dorian took an afternoon off in the middle of the week to go walking with Angela in Green Park. A somewhat watery sun was still struggling through gloomy clouds as they strolled along the paths and shared vital information about their families and aspirations. When they were out with Clarissa and Michel and their friends, it was always too noisy and the parties far too distracting for serious talk. Consequenly, they still knew only sketchy details about each other's backgrounds.

"Where exactly is your family seat?" Angela asked.

"The country place is near Sidmouth, in Devon. Do you know that village? I believe you lived in Devon once."

"Yes, yes, I did. But I didn't get about much."

The word *Devon* gave her a distinct twinge of hurt and nostalgia. Why did Dorian's family place have to be in Devon? Must she be reminded of Beau and Cricket House just when she was beginning to feel happy again? A sudden wave of longing for those past days of love and wine swept through her. She thrust the visions away. *Not now*, she thought angrily, *not now*. *Not when I like Dorian so much, when we're having such a warm, wonderful walk.* Beau hadn't cared enough to come to the opening. He had not telephoned. He was selfish, cruel, horrible—just as she had said when she left him. He was out of her life. She would go on and make a life without him.

The sun had completely disappeared and the air was gray with threatening rain. She pulled up the collar of her lightweight coat and tugged at the cloche clamped upon her head. Dorian was carrying an umbrella, so they wouldn't get soaked.

"Then you don't know that part of England?" Dorian persisted, still talking about his family place. "It's quite lovely. I'm sure you'll like the house. It's part Elizabethan, part Georgian, part Victorian, part nothing. Perhaps that's why I became an architect, there was a bit of everything to study at Grange. I love the place, though. I want to show it to you, Angela."

"That would be nice, Dorian," Angela said, struggling to recapture the gaiety she had felt when they'd started on the walk.

"Tell me about Pride's Court, and your grandfather, and your mother. Wasn't she a great beauty?"

"Yes, she was. Well, you've seen Julia. *She* must have been fantastic in her day, too. Mother was supposed to be the most beautiful woman in England."

"You're more beautiful than either, I'm sure," Dorian said, taking her arm and squeezing it. "It's a good feeling to be seen with you. I suppose other men have told you that?"

"I don't much like being an ornament."

"You aren't. How could you be when you're so talented? But you must know men are proud to be seen with you. If you didn't know that, I'd consider you stupid."

"I don't think about it."

"Were you lonely when you were a child?" he asked, switching quickly to a safer topic.

"Very lonely. It's lonely to be an only child. Then when you're brought up in a huge house, with a mother who's a recluse and a grandfather who's a tyrant, it's just that much worse."

"Poor darling. I'm going to make up for all that."

"Are you, Dorian?" She turned to look at him, to appraise him again as if she had never seen him before. His assurance was engaging. He was honest, and that was something. Direct, too. *He's very sweet*, she thought, *and loving*. He stopped and his lips fell lightly on her cheek. In all their times together he had done no more than kiss her. He was holding back, politely, considerately, and she was glad.

"You were an only child, too," Angela pointed out. "So you must have had much the same experience."

"In some ways, but for a boy in my sort of family it had other features. As soon as I was old enough, I went shooting with my father. Then I was shipped off to school early and stayed there as long as possible. After that, the army.

Those things are all arranged, you know. I wasn't alone too much."

"It's beginning to rain." She held up a hand to feel the first drops. "Put up the umbrella, Dorian."

They pressed together under the protective black tent and scurried toward the traffic of Picadilly.

"Time for lunch," Dorian offered. "Do you have any preferences? Or shall I decide?"

"Wherever you like. I'm not hungry."

"Not wasting away over that rude fellow who didn't show up, are you?" Dorian said, and then, not wanting an answer, continued talking quickly: "Let's not go where we might meet Clarissa and her friends. I know a good seafood place in Soho."

Taxicabs were scarce, but Dorian managed to flag one down and they climbed inside gratefully, pulling the dripping umbrella behind.

"Deliciously wicked, taking the day off," Dorian said. "Makes everything more fun."

He took her hand and kissed the palm.

"You're a romantic," Angela said, pleased. Still she had not recovered from the memory of Cricket House, and it was difficult to return to her earlier gay mood. She looked fixedly at Dorian in the hope that she could erase her inner vision of Beau. *He has a really nice face*, she thought, *dependable and kind. He seems to care.*

They found the restaurant Dorian had in mind and made their way up perilously narrow stairs to the second floor. Once they had taken off wet coats and shaken out the umbrella, the maître d' seated them at a window overlooking the street. The tables were small and square and covered with stiff white cloths. A faint odor of cooked fish hung in the air.

Dorian ordered dry white wine and they both decided to have Dover sole. At first they talked about general things: Clarissa and her horses, the farm she lived on with Michel, and Michel's ambition to be on a dirigible crew in the United States. But after two glasses of wine, Dorian leaned forward eagerly and seized her hand. He was intense and forced her to pay attention.

"Look at me, Angela, don't look away. Tell me what you see."

"I see a tall, dark stranger," she said, trying to turn the conversation back to unimportant things.

But she knew he would not accept this. He was determined to be grave and she felt afraid. The idea had come to her (perhaps it was in the air) that he was going to propose. Once he did that, they would not be able to turn back. Either the relationship would crack or she would have to accept Dorian.

"Can you hear me, Angela?" he insisted. "It's a bit noisy in here."

As if to emphasize his words, an unlucky waiter dropped a tray. There was the clatter of broken crockery, and they both felt the shock from an unexpected sharp noise.

"You see?" Dorian said and laughed. "We're on stage. And that's the sound effect. The waiter must have known what I was about to say."

"Don't say it now."

"I'm sorry, but I have to say it now."

"Really, Dorian—"

"Angela, will you marry me? I must know. I must know today."

He looked so desperate that she felt instant sympathy.

"Dorian, it's impossible to know what I want. We've only known each other—"

"Two weeks," he broke in. "I realize that. I can count. It doesn't matter. I love you. I need you. I can help you, I can do things for you, and you need to be protected."

"From what?"

"Everything. Life. You're so vulnerable."

Yes, he's stumbled on the truth, she thought, *I am vulnerable. So terribly vulnerable. With Beau, I felt used. How nice it would be to have somebody care about my interests for a change, to do what I want, to listen to what I have to say!*

"I'd have to paint, Dorian. I couldn't give my full time to running a house—"

"Is that all that worries you? We'll have servants. You don't need to do anything but give orders."

Could life be reduced to such order and simplicity? Could she escape her obsession for Beau by attaching herself to this amiable, courteous, apparently loving man? It would be like a cure. How wonderful to be free to paint and still be protected and cherished, without arguments about where they would live, and where the next check was coming from. Free from worry about whether she would be left alone to create and at the same time cope with loneliness and the awful realities.

"You do understand that painting is the most important thing in my life?"

"I know. Don't worry about that, Angela. I'm proud of your work. And I have my own career, so I wouldn't be jealous. I'm ambitious myself, you must know that."

"I know you're good at your work, Dorian. Everybody says so."

"We can live anywhere you like. In the country, in one of the houses my parents own, or we can buy another house. We can take a place in London if you feel that would help your work. Whatever you want to do, darling. I'm not rich, not like Julia or Clarissa's father, but there's no shortage of money. We can see my friends or your friends or both. You'll decide things like that. I guarantee I won't interfere and you'll be free to make decisions."

She stared at him, hovering on the brink of acceptance. Then like a drowning person, she snatched at the lifeline.

"All right, Dorian. I'll marry you."

Her voice seemed to come from a distance. Yet she knew she had said the words because Dorian broke into a flashing smile. He grasped her hand over the table and crumpled her fingers in his strong ones and then kissed the inside of her wrist.

"There's one thing I must tell you."

Dorian stopped talking to signal the waiter. After a short consultation he ordered champagne. It was a celebration. The waiter beamed upon them while Angela watched, still entranced by the impetuous thing she had done.

But Dorian's words sent a current of fear through her body. So there *was* a flaw. She might have known there would be a flaw. What was Dorian hiding?

"What's your terrible secret?" she asked brightly when the cork had been eased out of the champagne bottle, the glasses filled, and they had touched glasses.

"Not so terrible. Just tedious, I'm afraid."

"You're not a Bluebeard? You haven't got several wives hidden somewhere in the country?"

"Bluebeard didn't have several wives. It was little boys he had hidden behind locked doors, my darling. And some of them were quite dead. But no, I don't have hidden wives."

"Divorced? You're worried that we can't be married in a church, is that it?"

"It's about the wedding, but that isn't the reason. I hope you haven't got your heart set on a huge wedding. That your father, and Julia, and Clarissa, and your Aunt Miel—all your relatives—aren't going to storm down on my head about this."

"As it happens, I don't want a big wedding either but what is *your* reason? You'd better tell me, Dorian."

"Sure you don't want all the fuss and trimmings?"

"Absolutely sure."

Dorian allowed a small sigh to escape and looked hard at Angela in the washed-out light of the rainy afternoon. It was a great pity there couldn't be a big wedding because Angela would have made a stunning bride. He would have liked the attention, too, but he knew he could not face it. Even the thought of it chilled him and made his champagne taste flat.

"I'll explain. Although I'm ashamed of it. The memory is so humiliating. I guess that's why nobody mentioned it to you, not Clarissa, nor any of them. They knew how awful it was for me."

She could not imagine what he meant. She saw the stirrings of defeat cross the smooth, ordinarily bland features. Odd that he looked more human in that moment than he had at any other time since she'd known him, Angela thought distractedly.

"Last year I was about to marry Lady Maryanne Gosse. Perhaps you've heard of the family?" Dorian began, bringing himself to the point of revelation with an effort. "The wedding was to be in St. Margaret's, of course. The Gosse family love that sort of thing. If you haven't seen a picture of Lady Maryanne in *Tatler* or *Country Life*, I'll tell you that she is beautiful. No denying it. I thought I was very much in love. She thought she was, too. Our families were pleased. The invitations went out, the gifts arrived, gowns were made—oh, the whole bloody works. You see?"

"I'm beginning to see. But go on."

"I arrived at the church. It was sunny. I remember thinking what luck it was to have such a glorious day for such an elaborate affair. We were having a garden

reception at the Gosse house. My best man was with me
. . . fellow I went to school with . . . Peter ffrench-
Hodges . . . we came into the church at the appointed
hour, standing there at the front. You know how it is.
Like a stage. The church was packed, of course, and overflowing. The organ played unmercifully. We stood and
stood and stood until I was perspiring like a galley slave.
A thing I never do. I could feel the sweat running down
my neck. She didn't come. I became a bad joke . . . left
waiting at the church. I wanted the floor to open up and
swallow me. I was dying of humiliation. Since then, I've
never been to a wedding, people don't talk to me about
friends' weddings . . . it was all so painful. Until I met
you, Angela, I thought I'd never risk marriage again. But
if we eloped . . . if people didn't know . . . do you
see?"

Angela reached across and took his hand.

"Poor darling," she said, feeling genuine sympathy,
"how awful for you!"

"She ran off with an army officer," he added irrelevantly.

Dorian emptied his glass. The waiter came to refill it.
They sat in silence for a while. Then Angela said, "We'll
elope. But I'm afraid I don't know the rules. You'll have
to arrange everything, Dorian. Where could we go?"

"I thought out to Grange. My parents are in London
now, and there are only a couple and a few outside servants
in the place. Oh, and sweetheart, I brought this. In case.
I hope you don't mind."

Inside the lid of the blue velvet box was the name
Asprey. He took out a diamond solitaire set in platinum, the
size of a crocus. Angela's gray eyes filled with tears as he
placed it on her finger.

"Really, I can't say anything." She sniffed a bit.

"Well, don't then. Just wear it now and drink up your
champagne. But darling, don't let Julia see it. Not yet. The
idea that she or somebody else will interfere terrifies me.
Do you understand?"

"Nobody will know."

"Just between us, Angela. I love you."

"Because I'm beautiful?" She asked this harshly, forcing
him to answer.

"That's part of it. But that's not everything, Angela, you know that."

She was a replacement for Maryanne. Beautiful Maryanne, who had humiliated him. And one day soon he could present her to his friends, to the world, this second beautiful lady and say, "See? I've done it." And all his shame would be erased. She was about to protest to Dorian when a flash of insight stopped her. Why should she upbraid Dorian, when she was doing exactly the same thing? Dorian was a replacement for Beau. She sank back in the chair, weakly, and stared down at the dazzling diamond. She twisted it a little on her finger. It was a fair exchange, after all.

They managed to keep their secret. On the day Angela's show closed, they drove down to Devon where Dorian had arranged for the marriage in the parish church. The rector had promised to provide witnesses and not to tell a soul about the ceremony. The couple who looked after Grange were alerted to expect Dorian and a house guest for the weekend. Angela concocted a story for Julia about a weekend with friends of Clarissa and, although Julia was disappointed, having wanted to take Angela to the country herself, she made no protest.

The actual wedding ceremony was brief. The rector, wearing his surplice and stole, performed it in the tiny church with its ancient windows, memorial tablets studding the walls, and twin sarcophagi in the center aisle. As she walked toward the chancel rail with Dorian, Angela stopped for a moment to admire the marble figures stretched out upon the coffins. A Crusader and his wife, hands folded upon breasts, chiseled faces white and cool. Completely accepting of fate, untouched by time. Angela shuddered. Inside the marble coffins the bodies would be shriveled, "dust to dust." Someday she would be like that. What a dreadful thought to have on one's wedding day!

Dorian and Angela took a glass of sherry with the rector and his wife. (A fanciful piece of money had changed hands, and the rector was thinking of what he might do with the unexpected bonus. A new winter coat, or a comfortable reading chair?) It was a short drive from the church to Grange, up the winding gravel road, across a small stream festooned with willows, past hedges of azaleas, to the classic Georgian front door.

"Here it is," Dorian said unnecessarily. "I'll send Hawkins out for the bags."

The central hall was a huge rectangle filled with light from two glass panes, one on either side of the front door. A setting sun poured pink-gold on a polished refectory table bearing two tall acorns of inlaid wood, and on mellow Aubusson carpets and ancient wall paneling. At the far end a square, perfectly proportioned dark wood staircase led up to the second floor. Though not grand, the house was elegant, understated as if its design and ancestry made it ridiculous to be pretentious.

In the drawing room after dinner Dorian showed Angela his newest toy, a radio. A tinny sound hardly identifiable as "Songs My Mother Taught Me" and sung by a quavering tenor came over the airwaves.

"Not worth listening to, is it?" Angela said, thinking of Beau's piano and the music she had once taken for granted.

"Only because it's so astonishing," Dorian said, flicking it off. "It's a miracle that the man is actually singing from miles away."

He looked a little put out that she did not appreciate his gadget and then asked if she liked Grange (she had seen little of it so far) and if she thought they ought to live in London. Angela did not know what she wanted and the discussion drained away. She sensed that Dorian was nervous and blamed it on his terrible experience the year before. Still, they were truly married and safe here.

"Shall we go upstairs now?" Dorian asked finally.

Angela rose, feeling exhausted. She had taken rather too much wine.

As they walked hand in hand up the beautifully proportioned staircase, with Dorian's ancestors glowering down upon them, Angela reminded herself that she was beginning an exciting new life. She must not think of Cricket House or Beau ever again. She must forget the magic days in the nursery on St.-Denis Street, the passionate nights in London. All that part of her life must be erased.

The bedroom she and Dorian now shared was a huge square with a bathroom off one corner. Two enormous deep windows were equipped with painted wooden shutters as well as heavy green drapes, pulled now against the night air. The Fraser coat of arms was carved into the mantelpiece, the broad bed was crowned with a circular canopy and swags of crimsom silk.

Tired as she was, Angela disappeared to run a hot bath. She lay in it for a long time, calming herself. She thought of Dorian and the fact that she was about to give herself to him. He was sweet and she loved him. He was right for her. Dorian loved her. Everything he said and did proved that. She fondled the diamond ring, the matching wedding band of platinum that now encircled her finger. When she came back into the bedroom Dorian was in bed, naked.

"Used the bathroom down the hall," he explained. "I couldn't wait for you."

His eyes stared at her brightly from the bed, where he was propped up on fat, frilled pillows. He lifted the cover.

"Take off the nightgown, darling, and get in beside me. I want to hold you."

Staring at her from the safety of the bed, Dorian was pale and his hands, holding up the covers as an invitation, were trembling. Angela stood for a moment, letting him see her. It was his privilege, after all. In a sense, she felt excited, acutely conscious of the need to forget the past and make a new life. This was not the passion she had felt for Beau, not the wild surge that demands immediate fulfillment. Rather it was a tentatively sensual feeling that sprang from the idea that it was correct to make love to her husband and that he was an attractive man.

"Put the light off," Dorian said, his voice strained so that Angela felt the first pang of apprehension. Still, she obediently crossed the deep green carpet to the dressing table and snapped off the twin lamps. The room was velvet-black until her eyes adjusted a little and she began to see shapes again.

Slipping into bed, she felt Dorian's warm, smooth skin. His arms reached around her and he began to kiss her. He was really very good at kissing, and she lay back luxuriously to enjoy it. His hands began to search her body and she waited, aroused now, for the replenishment she had always experienced when Beau had loved her. Nothing happened. It dawned on her that Dorian was not ready to make love and that all this petting and fondling was leading nowhere. An icy fear made her stomach muscles contract.

"Help me, Angela," he said, his voice rasping with frustration. "You must help me."

She was slipping back in time, she thought hysterically. Her life was unreeling backward and she was once more with Landry that awful night when her grandfather caught them. Why was this happening to her again when her intentions were so good? It was cruel. Not again, don't let it happen again! she thought over and over.

"You must help me!" Dorian was saying. "I knew as soon as I saw you that you were the only woman who could . . . I've never been the same since that day . . . when Maryanne made a fool of me . . ."

She was listening through her own panic. What could she do? Communicating love and desire when it was mutual was something she knew instinctively. This other problem was strange to her. Dorian's anger and resentment were being transmitted through his hands which turned hard and rough. He thrust her head down toward his thighs.

"Don't you know what I mean?" he cried.

She knew, but she felt ill. She took the flaccid flesh in her mouth, and the idea gripped her that when you did not really love a man, this act could be revolting. It was not the same thing at all. It was animalistic. But Dorian was so insistent that she was afraid to refuse. She suffocated on soft flesh pleading, somewhere in the reaches of her mind, with it to harden. To bring this travesty to an end in the only way that would pacify Dorian. Nothing helped.

"Don't stop!" Dorian shouted.

She took up the unresisting member and tried to stroke it, to instill tenderness when she felt revulsion. It did no good.

At last, completely frustrated, Dorian rolled away from her, pounding the bed with his fists.

"It's no use!" he cried. "I can't make love!"

He leaned over her then, and she could smell a sharp, astringent odor. For a moment she thought he was going to kill her and she pushed at him with all her strength.

"Dorian, stop it. For God's sake, stop it!"

He threw himself back on the bed away from her. He began to sob great rending sobs. Angela, folded up like a fetus on her own side of the great bed, prayed for morning.

* * *

She must have fallen asleep, although it had seemed as she crouched on the very edge of the bed that she would never sleep again as long as she lived. When she got up, Dorian was gone. She washed and dressed and went downstairs feeling like an old woman. The sun was shining, but she could take no pleasure in the morning and didn't even have a taste for tea. She would go out for a walk, she decided, and perhaps that would clear her mind. For she had a problem and she did not know how to face it. Though she didn't know the property, she followed paths leading in the general direction of a copse on a slight hill.

As she walked slowly, admiring the old trees, and the vines and wildflowers under them, the morning air was shattered by a loud shot. A new terror seized her for a moment, as she thought Dorian might have . . . but no, she then realized with relief that wasn't the answer. In the country they were always shooting something. As she rounded a slight bend in the path, she spotted him poised, gun raised. Then he saw her, lowered it, and waited for her to catch up.

"Good morning," Dorian said awkwardly. "I'm potting at blackbirds. They steal from the garden."

"So I see. Have you eaten breakfast?"

"I had tea. I'll go back with you, if you like, and have some eggs."

"I'm not hungry."

"Angela, we must try again. I'm sure I can . . . that it will be all right. Last night I was nervous. I'm sorry if I sounded angry . . . you can't think what it's like for a man . . ."

"Let's not discuss it right now."

A small gray squirrel appeared without notice. He scampered along the path toward them, then stopped with the abruptness of a toy that has wound down. His sharp black eyes darted furiously from side to side, wild with alarm. Every nerve in his body quivered.

Angela was about to smile, but it set like cement upon her lips. Before she could speak, Dorian had raised his gun and the small body writhed in a puddle of blood.

"Why did you do that?"

"They damage the trees."

The sun, at that moment, disappeared behind a cloud. Angela turned from Dorian and ran toward the house. She heard a second shot. "I'm just making sure he's finished off!" Dorian called after her. But she did not answer.

Back in the house she flung a few things into a small bag. Her one thought was flight, and she knew that she could walk to the village. It was less than a mile down a narrow, shaded lane. If she could get there, she reasoned, she could hire a car. Something, anything, ask the way to the nearest train station, beg a lift. *I'll go back to Julia*, she thought. *Or Aunt Miel. Yes, I'll go back to Montreal with Aunt Miel and Uncle Armand. They'll know what to do.*

CHAPTER EIGHTEEN

Upon his retirement ten years before, Eustache Lavergne had removed himself from the bishop's palace and taken up residence in a house of his own choosing. He selected an enormous brick pile on Côte-des-Neiges that had some years before been the pride of a wealthy tanner. It bore many traces of the tanner's middle-class taste, but though the decor was deplorable, the floor plan appealed to Bishop Lavergne.

This was because two wings of red brick, joined by a short front section consisting of two main rooms, formed a tight U. The space between the two wings was no more than ten feet, so that a person standing in a window of one of the inside guest rooms in the northwest wing could peer into the window of a matching servant's room in the northeast wing. The tanner may or may not have noticed this. In any event the guest rooms were seldom used anymore and the servant wing was almost all empty except for storage and the pantries and kitchens on the main floor. Therefore no particular inconvenience resulted from the house's peculiar design.

Bishop Lavergne was intrigued. He saw in it certain possibilities that probably had not occurred to the tanner or his family. There were many other good features: five working fireplaces, an efficient heating system, a well-appointed den with built-in glass-fronted bookcases imported from England, and a well-proportioned square staircase with mahogany balustrades. Taken on the whole, the house fitted the bishop's needs very well indeed.

As he grew frailer, Bishop Lavergne relied more and more on sedentary pleasures. He had given up his long walks and restricted himself to a "constitutional" once a morning. He still ate well (his tastes leaned toward French sauces, which did not help his gout), he had a fine wine cellar, and he frequently read from his large store of ancient pornographic literature. Occasionally he went to auction sales, where he bought other people's lifetime collections of exotic beetles mounted in glass cases, human skulls, animal skeletons, fetishes from jungle cultures, and stuffed birds. He had become fascinated by death.

He had recently mounted a particularly gruesome specimen of the taxidermist's art in the central hall: a huge hawk with wings spread and a bloody wound in the neck. The appearance of the hawk had caused his housekeeper, Madame Jeanmaire, to break a long-suffering silence. She had been with the bishop for twenty years and his latest acquisitions alarmed her. The hawk caused her to ask for an interview. (Actually, she feared for the bishop's mind and had gone so far as to hint at this to her sister who lived in Lachine).

One windy March afternoon, shortly after the hawk's arrival, Madame Jeanmaire faced the bishop in his den. He sat behind the massive desk, leaning over an old manuscript that fluttered in his hands, brown and ragged with age. She spoke to the top of his head, explaining her aversion to the bird.

Finally, the bishop looked up, rested his elbows carefully upon either side of the paper he was reading, and folded his beautifully manicured hands. When he spoke, his voice was soft with wisdom.

"My dear woman," he said, "I keep these things about the house to teach myself *humility*."

Madame Jeanmaire blinked, taken aback. She saw almost instantly that she had made a serious error in judgment, but there was no way to beat a quick retreat.

"A man in my position"—he spread out his arms to indicate not only his material situation but his spiritual one as well—"is given a great deal of power. It would be so easy to become arrogant. After the seven deadly sins I count arrogance next."

Madame Jeanmaire felt she had been guilty of arrogance herself in presuming to judge the bishop. She longed desperately to flee. He fixed her with his faded brown eyes and she could not move.

"Even bishops are human. *I* am all too human, I'm afraid. And mortal. I wish to keep in mind, particularly, that I am mortal. Looking at these bones, at these signs of death, makes me pray. I pray, madame, for enlightenment and humility."

It was a rout. Every time she dusted a skull after that, Madame Jeanmaire reflected upon her own ignorance and the wisdom, the *goodness*, of her employer.

When the bishop was not reading salacious literature (he was pleased with the recent acquisition of a copy of *My Secret Life* by an anonymous Victorian, which, though not classical, was spellbinding), he sometimes listened to a crystal receiving set, which could pick up radiophone transmission for a distance of fifty miles. Most of the music was distorted and shaggy and consisted of fervent tenors and heavy divas, but he once accidentally heard some of the new "jazz" and a tango.

Perhaps it was this element that inspired in him the brilliant idea that Madame Jeanmaire required a young maid to help her with work about the place. A moldy smell of aged wood, paper, and repeated layers of wax and polish combined with the waft from bones, stuffed birds, and tropical artifacts. The very house had become ossified, he thought. It lacked the fresh touch. Something young, sweet-smelling, and gay. Contrast, as he had often told himself, was an important spice of life.

Madame Jeanmaire was both cook and housekeeper. Twice a week a general came in to wash and polish floors, push the new vacuum cleaner, and clean windows and bathrooms. But it was apparent that Madame Jeanmaire was falling behind. She needed more help.

It came to the bishop that a young girl, some child rescued from a poor family and then trained, was just what the place required. Such a girl could relieve Madame Jeanmaire of much running up and down stairs, errands at the shops, scrubbing of pots and pans.

He called Madame Jeanmaire into his den one day in early April.

"Madame Jeanmaire, I have decided to hire a maid."
She looked alarmed. Had her work not been satis-

factory? she began, but he hushed her protests and explained.

"I'd like to provide help for you and at the same time hold out the hand of mercy to some poor child, madame. A child who would otherwise go into factory work. A child who, coming under my influence spiritually, and your influence in the earning of a living, would benefit greatly."

"Yes, Your Excellency, I see what you mean."

Madame Jeanmaire rolled her eyes appreciatively as the bishop outlined the difficulties of some of the poorer members of the Church. Large families, a dozen or so people crowded into two rooms, inadequate bathrooms, bad health, early retirement from school to work at any job they could find.

"Don't you feel that any mother, given an opportunity, would feel it an advantage to place a young girl here? In this house?"

"Oh my, yes. Yes, indeed."

"What a lucky day for some poor waif, to be taken out of that environment and given the advantages we offer here. Under my wing. You could train her, and later, if we don't need help, she can find a job in another house. With my reference, of course. Meanwhile, she would be safe. We have plenty of rooms in the other wing, madame. Give her a suitable one. If she happens to be intelligent, I might help her with her reading."

Once she saw that this was not a criticism of her work but only another of the bishop's kindnesses, Madame Jeanmaire was all enthusiasm.

"A living miracle!" she exclaimed as he talked.

"Well," the bishop said, shrugging slightly so as not to make too much of it, "not quite that. But still, it could be a good work."

"Wonderful, Your Excellency. Only you could think of it."

He let that pass.

"Youth has boundless energy."

"How young do you have in mind?" Madame Jeanmaire inquired, screwing up her face in the effort to think. She was a thin woman in a conventional black cotton uniform reaching to mid-calf. She wore sturdy black tie oxfords and black stockings, and her hair was pulled back tightly into a severe bun held in place with brown bone hairpins. She had worn glasses so long that a red pinchmark on either side of her nose was a permanent disfigurement.

"Well, let me see." The bishop hesitated, evidently giving the matter his gravest consideration. "About thirteen, I think."

"Thirteen?" She was startled. Her voice squeaked a bit. "Isn't that a bit young, Your Excellency?"

"I don't believe so. Not when you consider the problems," the bishop said smoothly. "Large families do force the children out to work early despite laws covering education. Many a mother would be delighted to find such a haven for a young girl. Much better than a factory. Also, the child can be adequately trained if she hasn't learned bad habits. Easier for you, I'm sure."

"Still, it's a bit young. Having a girl like that under my care . . ." Madame Jeanmaire said dubiously. She allowed herself a wisp of a sigh.

"You can manage it all very well. I have great faith in you. It's worthwhile, remember that."

Madame Jeanmaire was greatly mollified by his remark and also impressed with his concern for others. She was constantly surprised by the bishop's Olympian view. She therefore began the very next day to look into the matter, and names chased each other through her head. Families she had met at church, unemployed fathers who were the heads of huge broods, widows struggling to survive. It was an important task and she did not shirk her duty.

Consequently, Madame Jeanmaire announced in less than a week that she had found a candidate and would like to bring the girl to him for an interview. Megan Malone was twelve and came from a solid but poor Catholic family. Altogether there were fourteen in the family, and Mrs. Malone was instantly taken with the bishop's offer. It was an opportunity sent from heaven, a blessed answer to her prayers.

The bishop looked forward to meeting the girl. When Megan first came into his study, however, he was disappointed. She was sulky and peaked, her skin pale, her face sharp with lack of filling meals, her dark hair straggly and unkempt. A bit like a character out of

Dickens, he thought with his usual literary leaning. Yet when he looked harder at the slightly soiled woolen skirt and white shirt she wore, he could see that she was remarkably developed for twelve. Her legs, in stockings riddled with runs and gaps, were long and slim. He raised his glance from the child's body to the face above, and by chance, the dying afternoon light from the study window struck Megan's countenance and lighted up her face. Her pale blue eyes were ringed with black around the iris. One did not see that often, the bishop realized, and it was fascinating. It gave the girl an exotic, almost fey look that pleased him.

He made up his mind right then that she could be cleaned up and fed. Her hair was doubtless thick enough when washed. Madame could arrange for uniforms and clothes for Sunday.

"Would you like to work here?" he asked in a kindly way.

"Oh, yes, Your Excellency," Megan said, having been instructed on how to address a bishop.

The truth was, she had been swept away by the grandness of the house, by the importance of her benefactor. She was in awe. She was frightened. But she wanted desperately to be accepted.

"Madame Jeanmaire needs extra help in the house. She's probably told you that. Would you like to take the job?"

"Oooh . . . yes," Megan said, her voice trailing stars of wonder. "I'd work hard. Very hard, Your Excellency."

"If you prove suitable, I might also help you with your reading," the bishop said, trying to figure out how long it would take to fatten the child up a bit. "Do you like to read?"

It did not take long to settle Megan in the house on Côte des Neiges. Every person connected with the project had a reason to be enthusiastic, and by June Megan was an established part of the household, slightly more nubile and smiling often. Once a week the bishop read with her in the study after dinner. She was willing but much in awe of him. That, he decided, was just as well. Nothing in this life should be hurried.

Always interested in the workings of his household and in the good of Megan, his new protégée, the bishop had instructed Madame to see that the child slept with her window open. She would not be brought up to do that, he pointed out, but in this house the location of her bedroom would insure privacy.

In early July a sullen summer storm hung over the city and the air in the bishop's house was muggy with damp and heat. The bishop ordered late tea on a tray in his study (Madame Jeanmaire had gone to see her sister in Lachine, and on these occasions he always dispensed with formality), and Megan brought it to him.

She had changed from her routine gray uniform to a white cotton jumper meant to be worn with a blouse. Megan had abandoned the blouse because she was so hot and the costume was like a sun dress. Her arms were bare, the yoke of the neck rather low. Under the light material her small breasts rose suggestively, but she seemed innocent of that.

Bishop Lavergne wore a summer suit and had taken off the jacket. When he was at home relaxing, he wore ordinary clothes. Tonight he was perspiring heavily despite the fact that he had installed overhead, tropical-style fans in the important rooms.

"Ah, iced tea. That was thoughtful. Just set the tray on this table, Megan."

"Yes, Your Excellency."

"I really think it's too hot to study tonight," he said next. "I wonder if you'd like just to finish up your work in the kitchen and then go up to your room. Perhaps you have something entertaining to read there."

"Yes, I do, Your Excellency."

"Fine. If you keep the window open, you'll get whatever breeze there is."

He smiled at her, looking at the smooth hands as they arranged things on the tray, the arms moving gracefully. She bent over slightly, to pick up a napkin that had slipped to the floor. He saw the stockings stretching upward.

"Once you've picked up my tray, you're free, then," he assured her.

During his tea he thought about Megan. Did she undress quickly once she got into her room? Did she sleep without benefit of pajamas or nightgown? He rather imagined so. The poor were not used to such luxuries. In this heat . . . He wiped his forehead with a handkerchief and finished his tea. Then he left the room, slowly, deliberately, walking upstairs with a slight edge of expectancy.

The bishop made slow progress along the upstairs hallway, where small wall brackets shed feathers of light upon the patterned carpet. Without hesitation he stopped before one of the guest rooms and, taking a key from his pocket, unlocked the door. It was dark inside. The curtains had been pulled since the last time the room had been cleaned. The musty smell of an old, enclosed space made him sneeze. He walked to the window, moved the curtains a fraction of an inch, and looked out. Megan's bedroom window was directly opposite and it was open. He could see into the room, distinguish clearly the bed, a chest of drawers, a wicker chair, a picture on the far wall. He stood still, waiting, his lips moist with anticipation.

He was a patient man, and the ten minutes he waited did not seem unduly long. Megan came across his vision, walking toward the bed. Almost immediately she began to remove her clothes. He could sense the heat in the other room, and rejoiced with her when she pulled the jumper over her head. She disappeared from his view then, but when she came back to stand in the window and breathe in the evening air, arms braced on the sill, she was absolutely naked.

His breath stopped. He choked, swallowed, steadied himself, eye pressed to the narrow opening he had created between the curtains. Her small breasts were like scoops of pale ice cream topped with plum-colored cherries. He made the comparison in his mind, letting the thought sink and rise again. Such dark rosettes! His hands trembled. He could almost feel the silken young flesh beneath his beautifully cared-for hands. His mouth filled with saliva. He saw the small face, the dark hair framing it, the strange eyes, with their sky-blue centers, their black hems. He saw the undeveloped mouth, not yet versed in the ways of love. The ledge cut across her body at the level of her thighs, and the thick dark patch of hair seemed to sit on it, as on a platter. The light was going, making shadows between her slim legs and around the delicious, tilted breasts. She stretched her arms upward (oh, delightful sight!), tightening the muscles of her arms, pulling up the small dark points. She smiled happily, drinking in the air. She stood like that for a few moments and then wriggled a little.

The bishop felt his own body move suggestively. He sternly forced himself to keep the curtain still for fear of alarming his little bird. He was rewarded with more than he could have hoped in his wildest dreams. For she stood there, not quite still, quivering a little, and let one hand fall to her hip. Then the hand slid across her shadowed leg toward the dark covert, and while his tongue ran eagerly across his lips, he watched mesmerized while the tips of Megan's fingers disappeared from sight. She began to sway in front of the window, back and forth, with a slight rotary motion. Her eyes were closed, her lips formed a sweet smile. As she accelerated her gyrations, the bishop was jolted into paradise.

The consecration service was to be held Sunday morning. The bishop-elect, Marc St. Amour, was presently vicar general of Notre-Dame church. He was both awed by his coming elevation and uneasy. Never in his career, and he was now fifty-five, had he expected to rise to such a rank. In fact, he would have been quite content to remain a working priest. His uncle, Bishop Lavergne, had always encouraged him to be more ambitious, except for a brief period during the election of 1896, when Marc had refused to follow the Church edicts and advise his congregation to vote Conservative. Outside that one period when he had been demoted but not defrocked, Marc and his uncle had enjoyed a respectful, if not entirely warm, relationship.

Marc was grateful to his uncle. At a time when Marc had despaired, had actually thought of leaving the Church altogether, Bishop Lavergne had set him straight. It was his duty to remain a priest and fight the devils that assailed him. After considerable soul searching, Marc had agreed. During the war he had been a chaplain, and when he returned, he was made vicar general. It had been whispered for a long time that he would be made a bishop, but despite this, he was not an ambitious or self-centered man.

On the Saturday previous to his consecration, Marc prayed for two hours. Still, his fear, his restlessness, persisted, and he felt the need for reassurance. The idea that he was unworthy refused to leave his mind, and only one man could help him. He had once confessed his worst sin to his uncle and had been absolved. His uncle would understand (without too much explanation) his present reservations, and so he telephoned for an appointment and was invited to take coffee after dinner.

The day was heavy with the promise of rain. Somewhere over the mountain thunder rumbled and announced its intention of arriving during the night. The lawns were already soggy with previous storms, the trees an emerald green lace against the houses. Marc felt as heavy as the air.

He pressed the doorbell and was welcomed by the housekeeper, Madame Jeanmaire.

"Ah, Father, come in. His Excellency is expecting you."

"Thank you, madame. I will. I trust you are surviving the heat?"

He was always formal with the housekeeper. She seemed to inspire it. He followed her to his uncle's study, and as they walked, he remarked upon the storm and the fact that it was about to rain heavily again. Madame Jeanmaire agreed with him.

She showed him in and he found his uncle sitting in a comfortable chair beside his desk, his feet up on a stool. The pale light of early evening made him look rather tired.

"Your Excellency," Marc began, keeping carefully to customary protocol.

"Don t bother with the formality, Marc, sit down," the bishop said, waving his hand toward a chair facing him. "How are you feeling about your consecration, eh?"

Marc sat down and smiled without much conviction.

"That's just it, Uncle Eustache, not too sure of myself."

"Well, we all have doubts."

"Did *you* have doubts?"

"Of course I did. We all do. It's a great responsibility. A bishop is, after all, more than a priest, he is a successor to the apostles."

"Yes, I understand that. It bothers me. I don't feel worthy."

Bishop Lavergne seemed totally unperturbed by his nephew's worry. He ordered iced tea and gave his opinion that iced tea was more refreshing in this weather than anything else. Actually he longed for brandy, but his doctor had forbidden it, since his gout was acting up again.

They chatted about relatives for a while. The bishop said he planned to attend the service next day (if his gout allowed) and that he looked forward to seeing family members. Marc assured him that Camille was well, that her eyesight had not improved (she had been blind since an attack of smallpox over twenty years before), but that she was cheerful.

"It was a blessing when she regained some of her sight," Bishop Lavergne said, referring to the fact that Camille could see faint shadows with one eye.

"Uncle Eustache, I had to see you. I've tried to work this out by myself. I've prayed and prayed for comfort, for assurance but I still don't feel that it's right for me to accept this elevation to the bishopric. I need not tell you again the reasons. I think you understand."

"Ah, so that's it. I was afraid of that."

"I'm not sure . . ." Marc shook his head. "I wish I could be sure of myself . . . of my strength but only last week—"

"Last week?" The bishop perked up. Over the years most confessions had become routine, a bit dreary. The same stories with only slight variations. But he had found in Marc's earlier confession several rather exquisite touches. His deep and long-lasting passion for his sister. And that sister's blindness, which made her so dependent.

"As recently as that, knowing about the consecration, I think I've fallen back. I would like to tell you about it . . . Will you bear with me, Uncle?"

"Now, Marc, I'll be happy to hear your confession, but you mustn't feel quite so guilty! I'm sure you've overcome your temptation! I'm positive of it."

"*I'm* not sure, though. That's the trouble. You know, Uncle Eustache, I never had ambitions to rise in the church."

"That's one of the good things about you, Marc. You're a humble man."

Marc shook his head and looked away from his uncle's face. He felt anything but humble. He was afraid. He was guilty of lust, there was no question of that, whatever else the bishop might say.

"It doesn't excuse everything," Marc said, shrugging as if to rid himself of the burden.

"The Church has seen fit to recognize your abilities, your potential goodness, and that cannot be denied."

"They don't know. You're the only one who knows."

The bishop gave his full attention to his nephew, seeing in him the thin, dark face that resembled his sister's except for one important thing: Marc's eyes burned in a fanatical way. It was surprising, thought the bishop, that no one in the Church had noticed this tension in Marc. How had they come to miss it? Still, the priest had done good works for many years, especially during the war.

"Well, my son, confess then. Tell me what happened so recently that disturbs you."

Marc began slowly to tell his story. He had decided (he told the bishop) one day last week, Tuesday as a matter of fact, to take Camille into the country for a picnic. Getting out of the hot city seemed a good idea, and he knew of a small lake on a farmer's land where they could go. Earlier in the year he had had occasion to visit the farmer and at the time had been invited to visit the lake. They packed a picnic lunch and drove out.

"Yes, yes, I can imagine all that," the bishop said, sipping on his iced tea and hoping Marc would soon get to the point. "Go on."

Marc conjured up the scene in his mind, painful, sinful. His heart began to pound alarmingly. They had found the lake and there was nobody around. It was quite far from the house and screened by woods. A narrow dirt road provided the only access. Camille had decided to wade in the water and Marc had allowed her to take off her stockings and shoes and hike up her skirts so they wouldn't get wet. The water was clear and cool. Marc had not realized that the lake, though small, was deep and fell off sharply quite near the shore. Camille had stepped into deep water and begun to flounder. Although it was easy to pull her out, her clothes were soaked. The gray summer dress was plastered to her body like a silken sheath.

Camille had stood before him dripping and pathetic. He

had fetched a blanket from the car and helped her off with her wet clothes. She had stood behind some bushes holding out her arms for the blanket. He had heard a cardinal whistle, that obscene half-human cry they were noted for.

Something inside suddenly gave way. He could feel the bitter barrier drop away and assumed a strange sense of freedom that he had believed completely destroyed by the demands of society and by his own fervent prayers. He soared with such ardor that he could no longer keep his hands from grasping Camille's full, white breasts. He put his mouth on one of them, crushing the other against his cheek. The softness drove him to behave like a starving baby. His arms slipped around her naked body and they both fell to the ground, eyes closed, making unfamiliar guttural sounds deep in their throats.

He, the celibate, was covering his sister with licentious kisses (he was mortified to remember!), he was fondling her still delightful breasts, and his hands wandered willfully to the forbidden place between her legs, where it was damp and beckoning.

Pain forced him to release himself from the constricting trousers and then he hovered over her as she lay exposed in the afternoon light. Camille, panting with a fresh madness he had not seen in years, took him in her two hands and pulled his stiffness into her dark, moist thicket. *He was about to thrust.*

At that point he came to his senses as a wave of terror assailed him. Poised to penetrate, he became suddenly limp. Nausea followed fear. He rolled away from her into the grass but still pressed his face into her breasts. His tears washed over her pink, hard nipples. She rocked him against her, but she was squirming with want, her legs spread out invitingly, her body lifted off the grass. He began to stroke her out of pity (or so he believed), telling himself it was only that. She moaned with gratitude. They had never come so close in any former encounters. It was this fact that disturbed Marc most, for he felt he was losing ground in his battle against temptation. He had after all these years almost committed the gravest of sins.

When he had finished his story, looking tired and haggard, the bishop said calmly, "That was a very close thing, Marc. But I'm proud of you."

"*Proud of me?*"

Marc straightened in his chair, gave his uncle an incredulous—almost savage—glare, and repeated himself.

"Proud of me?"

"Yes. To come to the edge of the fire like that and still have the strength to draw back. Remarkable! Very few men could have resisted temptation the way you did, Marc."

Marc was astonished.

"Uncle Eustache, your interpretation of the thing amazes me. I thought I had slipped so far back . . . had lost all the ground I worked so hard to gain over the years . . . I was distraught . . ."

"I sometimes think you don't remember the New Testament. That you haven't even read it," the bishop said with a smile.

"What do you mean?"

"I quote you James, chapter one, verse fourteen. 'Every man is tempted when he is drawn away of his own lust, and enticed.' "

"But still, Uncle Eustache, so close to my consecration!"

"Even Christ was tempted," the bishop said, placing his hands together in a manner that suggested prayer.

Marc fell silent.

"If Christ could be tempted, why not a bishop-elect?"

Marc could think of no answer to that. It seemed to him that anything he said would be fatuous. That he would be making himself out to be more important than he was.

"Let us pray together," the bishop suggested. "I won't kneel, Marc, because of my gout. I don't have a prie-dieu in here, as you can see. So perhaps if you kneel by the stool . . ."

They spent a great deal of time praying, and the bishop's soft, mellifluous voice melted like caramel over Marc's bowed head. In the end Marc was feeling strong again. He was ready now to assume his duties, to speak to the Virgin on his own behalf. He was cleansed.

From her place in a front pew of the cathedral Camille listened intently. Marc had described the service to her in infinite detail so that she would be able to see it in her mind and take part in the most important day of his life. She could feel the warm sun streaming through one of the church windows and falling upon her face. Surely that was a sign that she and Marc were truly forgiven?

Camille was surrounded by most members of the St. Amour family. Only Uncle Eustache was absent. He'd sent regrets and the message that he'd suffered an acute attack of gout during the night. This made it impossible for him to walk. But the others were all there: Armand and Honey; Justine and Timothée, who had come in from the farm; Mathieu and Nora; Helene and Corbin, who had come down from Ottawa; and Nicolette and Luc. Nicolette and her mother, Justine, were still cool, but it was an indication that they might resume civilized relations now that Nicolette had shown up. Marc, trying to bring the family together, had prevailed upon his niece to make up her long-time quarrel with her mother.

Leaning on Marc's account of the ceremony, Camille knew that the archbishop must have entered the church with his three chaplains. Armand touched her arm to indicate that she should stand. The shuffling and coughing of a large congregation getting to its feet confirmed this. The archbishop, she recalled, would be wearing his precious miter, that arched, embroidered cap that conferred extra stature and elegance upon his bearing. His vestments would be green because it was summer.

Marc, with two assisting bishops in their white miters, would proceed to special chairs set out for them in front of the altar. The archbishop would begin by kneeling before a special prie-dieu while he silently prayed. Then he would walk to his own special chair to the left of the altar.

Camille could easily conjure up a picture of Marc in his vestments: the amice for his head, the alb (a white linen garment with long sleeves), the cincture about the waist, the stole on his shoulders, and the long cope. White. After a few minutes she heard the senior assisting bishop ask that the bishop-elect be consecrated, and the mandate was read by a notary.

During prayers Camille thought of her brother's dilemma and how Bishop Lavergne had calmed Marc's fears. He was, truly, a wonderful old man. For it had seemed to Camille after that agonizing day by the lake, and her behavior, her unforgivable behavior, that Marc must renounce any thought of the bishopric.

Uncle Eustache had pointed out certain undeniable

truths, given examples from both the Old and New Testaments to support his argument. Temptation was one of the commonest problems of religious men. That was true, and she was grateful for her uncle's intervention in what might have been a tragedy. She would have killed herself if she had been the cause of Marc's downfall. But Marc was to be a bishop. She wanted to weep with relief and joy as she steadied herself by grasping Armand's arm. Armand patted her hand gently to indicate that he understood.

But he did not understand. Nobody could understand the anguish she and Marc had suffered over the years. Thank God nobody knew their distress except the bishop himself. If only she had not lost her sight! How often she had screamed that silently in her prayers. Then she could have left Marc, gone away somewhere to be a missionary or a nun in some reclusive order. Anything to save him from pain. As it was, she was dependent upon the family and especially dependent upon Marc.

The archbishop was now reading the examen, and Marc was answering the eighteen questions. She could hear his voice as it floated through the large building, sounding calm and accepting. Properly humble yet prepared also to perform his duties in his new role.

Mass began. Marc, led by the assisting bishops to his chair, removed his cope and was garbed in pontifical garments during prayers and Psalms. The mass reached the Alleluia.

The stately ceremony moved on, magnificent in its perfect rhythm, impressive as a coronation. Marc would be prostrating himself before the archbishop, Camille thought as she heard the Litany of the Saints. There would be the triple blessing from the archbishop as he stood alone wearing his miter and holding his crosier. Then the archbishop would open the Book of Gospels and impose it on Marc's shoulders and the back of his head. Two chaplains would hold it in place for some time. There would be the Laying On of Hands and more prayers.

She followed as best she could, sometimes losing the thread but picking it up again when the archbishop intoned the *Veni, Creator Spiritus*. After only one verse the archbishop would sit down, put on his miter, remove his gloves and ring, replace the ring, and then the chaplains would place the gremial (a cloth adorned with gold lace) in his lap. During further prayers the archbishop would anoint Marc's head with Holy Chrism (a consecrated oil), first using one large sign of the cross covering the whole head and then with three smaller crosses.

Then would follow a number of somewhat complicated prayers and rituals. Camille tried to remember all of them. A long linen stole would be placed around Marc's neck and joined together in front to hang like a sling. His hands would be anointed with Holy Chrism, the archbishop would bless the new bishop's crosier and ring, and place the ring on Marc's finger. During the whole time the Book of Gospels would be supported behind Marc's head by the two chaplains. After the Kiss of Peace from the archbishop and two assisting bishops, Marc would return to his chair to wash his head and hands. The long mass would proceed.

When they reached the *Te Deum* with its triumphant sound, Marc was led through the church by the assisting bishops while he blessed the congregation. *This*, she thought, *is the most precious moment of all.* At the end of the long service Marc thanked the archbishop and assisting bishops and spoke to the congregation. This was his first sermon as a bishop of the Church.

CHAPTER NINETEEN

Mildred had astonished the entire Court family by her vigorous interest in decorating. No sooner had she and North moved into the three-room apartment in Pride's Court than she was bringing in platoons of decorators, painters, furniture dealers, and drapers.

Sir Simon had offered the newlyweds a spacious and light-filled corner suite in the east wing. White broadloom and eggshell walls heightened the somewhat ethereal effect. The only accents of a richer hue were the wooden frame of the undulating Victorian sofa, a round walnut table on which books and magazines were piled, and a French clock with arched dial and white enamel face. It was inscribed *Le Roy et Fils*, and the boulle case was supported by gilt mounts. Mildred had designed a shelf between two of the sitting room windows especially to hold it.

It was a rather delicate landscape: perhaps a little *too*

delicate when one considered that it was supposed to be shared by a man. But Mildred had sought to provide herself with what she thought of as a "feminine" background. She was constantly irritated by her size and by the awkwardness of her frame. She wanted to please North, to retain his attention, and so she tried through clothes and atmosphere to seem more helpless and girlish than she truly was. Unfortunately, something in their combined chemistry worked against her.

The same pastel theme was carried through into the bedroom, where an Adam four-poster was draped with cream silk embroidered with tiny rosebuds. Fragile Sheraton armchairs with green silk covers picked up the leafy colors in country scenes by Claude. A Louis XVI marquetry and parquetry petite table de salon added a touch of gold-brown. It was round, with a delicate fence around the top and a sliding door concealing three small drawers. Nothing in the entire apartment indicated that a male ever entered the place.

A dressing table with a graceful oval mirror on a stand took up most of a single tower on one side of the bedroom. The tabletop was covered with a definitive collection of beauty aids: Hudnut's rouge, three boxes of various kinds of face powder, Pompeiian night cream, cold cream, a lipstick by Camille, a pair of eyebrow tweezers, an elaborate silver brush and comb set bearing Mildred's initials on the back, atomizers filled with Chanel No. 5 and patchouli and a number of swansdown powder puffs. There were no bureaus or chests of drawers. A walk-in dressing room provided racks, drawers, and shelves for all North's and Mildred's clothes. North kept his toiletries in the bathroom.

Mildred, gowned in pink crepe de Chine for a family dinner Sir Simon had planned for a week, sat before the mirror experimenting with rouge. It was a daring step, she knew, but necessary. Her complexion had gone quite sallow after the birth of baby Nicholas two months earlier. She frowned at her reflection, wondering if the rouge really did improve her appearance. Why, she asked herself for the thousandth time, did she not look more like the Courts instead of the Browns of Bootle, her mother's relatives?

She thought with frustration of her cousin Angela's beauty and of her cousin Susan, who was so elegant. The twins, Flora and Fenella, always managed to look like paintings that had somehow come alive. It was so unfair! (Even her young sister, Charity, might turn into quite a handsome girl.)

Mildred leaned closer to the glass to fix on a pair of gold earrings. As she did so, North's reflection appeared behind her. He was standing midway across the carpet, holding what was obviously the end of a drink of scotch and water. She gave an irritated sigh.

"Didn't you have enough to drink downstairs? Do you have to bring liquor up here?"

She regretted the words almost as soon as she had spoken. North looked hurt and then tilted his glass to empty it. He was no longer looking at her but gave the impression that his mind was far away.

"You know there'll be wine at dinner," Mildred began, and then to placate him, "Grandfather ordered Peters to bring up some Vaucrains. You know that's your favorite burgundy."

He wheeled about then, coming closer to her chair. She saw the fleeting petulance that disturbed North's features; the corners of his mouth turned down and an angry look flashed in the brown eyes. His thick black hair was slightly out of place over his forehead, giving him a boyish look.

"I simply wanted to finish my drink up here because I'm late. Your grandfather kept us talking."

This remark was meant to indicate that it was Sir Simon's fault and that North was trying to cooperate. Actually, Sir Simon had been ranting about the prime minister again. King seemed loath to do anything to stop the flourishing smuggling trade in liquor between Canada and the United States. Most Canadian businessmen would have found the practice quite acceptable, except that it had produced a return flow of smuggled manufactured goods. Trucks and boats did not arrive at the border empty when they came to pick up their cargoes. Sir Simon had recently become involved in a successful tobacco business, and this was one of the industries affected. Consequently, he was outraged at the Liberal government's easy attitude toward the whole affair. His solution was to shoot all smugglers at the border. But he knew King would never endorse such an efficient method of dealing with the problem. That was the trouble with the world today, he had told North and Charles in the library. Everyone was too soft. Instead of the firing squad Sir Simon and a number of other powerful Montreal manufacturers had formed a Commercial Protective Association in an attempt to force the government to tighten up on smuggling of all kinds.

"Whatever the case," Mildred said in a crisp voice, getting up from the table, "it isn't necessary to drink in the bedroom."

"The English send up trays of whisky and soda so civilized people can drink while they dress for dinner," North said.

"This isn't England."

"Obviously."

"North, will you please get ready?"

"Yes, sweetheart. I'm sorry." Suddenly he was obedient again. He set the glass down on a gilded gesso side table.

Mildred swept across the room and picked it up.

"Don't set it on there, it will mark."

"I'm sorry, darling. I wasn't thinking."

Was he listing slightly as he turned from her? Surely not so early in the evening, Mildred reasoned, unless he'd been drinking at lunch.

"Did you stop in to look at Nicholas?"

"Yes, darling, of course I did." North's deep voice soothed her, but his next words made her stiffen with irritation. "He didn't say a word. Just lay there staring up at me."

"Oh, North, don't be so stupid! You know why I want you to go into the nursery every day. I want Nicholas to know his father. It would be so easy for you to ignore him."

"Yes, darling." A touch of sarcasm.

"Did you work hard today?"

She ought not to ask, she knew. It implied that she didn't trust him to carry out his responsibilities to the family, to her.

"How the hell would I know?" North said, raising his voice for the first time. "What seems hard work to me doesn't seem hard work to your relatives. Ask somebody else if you want to know."

"Grandfather told me he was pleased with your work at the bank," Mildred said, making a belated attempt to patch things up.

"So I got a good report card, did I? Thanks, sweetheart."

This time he walked away from her completely and went into the bathroom. He slammed the door. Mildred paused, not able to make up her mind what to do. It was time she went downstairs to have a final word with Cook and Peters. Yet she disliked leaving North when the air was so hostile. She followed him to the bathroom, knocked, and entered. He was standing staring at himself in the full-length mirror. He was naked.

Mildred felt the familiar wave of sexuality that had begun on their wedding night. North was tall, not really broad-shouldered but well proportioned. He had attractive arms and legs, covered with a fine, light hair that did not match the dark hair on his head. He had very little hair on his chest, but Mildred rather liked his smoothness.

"North?"

He raised his eyebrows as if to inquire why she was invading his territory. They were miles apart, she realized. He was angry and very cool. My God, he's handsome, I do love him. I love him more than ever. What's wrong between us?

"You needn't be defensive about Grandfather. He only asks people to work as hard as he does himself. I know he likes you, North. It's always so obvious when Grandfather likes somebody and when he doesn't."

She would have liked to kiss him, but she held back. Perhaps he would be cross with her. He really should not object to working hard because they lived free in Pride's Court in exchange for her running the place. He was well paid at the bank and had been promoted twice. Naturally, Grandfather expected a great deal in return, and Mildred was certainly doing *her* share, between the house and the baby.

The fact that Mildred did not want to face was that North was essentially lazy. He lacked drive. It was heart-breaking to see somebody as bright as North wasting himself. Sometimes he demonstrated how brilliant he could be, but he didn't follow it up. She often had the feeling that only half of North was ever present at any one time. It was odd. She would have liked to lecture him about it but knew he couldn't accept criticism of any kind. That was one of his failings. The Court men were so intense, so busy, so ambitious. Nobody had ever had to drive them.

Her brothers, Noel and Simon II, appeared to take after their forebears. They were making slaves of themselves up at the gold mine, she knew. North, on the other hand, would have preferred to play golf, fish, or just drink at one of his clubs. Yet he liked the expensive clothes, the cars, the wonderful prestige the family had brought him. He had liked surprising his own father, she knew that. Why was North so difficult?

"If you want me to get ready, sweetheart . . ." North said coldly, letting the sentence trail off into nothing. He made no move to kiss her or touch her.

"Yes, I'm going right down now. Come as soon as you can, North. You know how Grandfather hates people to be late."

"It was his idea to dress," North pointed out. "Otherwise, we could have worn our business suits to dinner."

"He likes a formal dinner at least twice a week, you know that," Mildred said defensively.

North ignored her and stepped into the shower, closed the glass partition, and turned on the water. Mildred, feeling dissatisfied, left the bathroom and went down the main staircase and then back toward the servants' quarters to find Cook. She had ordered vichyssoise, although Grandfather wasn't fond of it, because the weather was hot. Mildred began to worry about dinner. She had decided on the Meissen porcelain dinner service with the blue motif and because of that, had told Peters to ask the gardener for bachelor buttons for the table. She wondered if Peters had managed to get enough flowers. Jenkins was so stingy with flowers. She remembered her mother saying that all gardeners hated to supply flowers for the house.

After she had consulted with Cook and rescued the roast beef from possible annihilation, Mildred surveyed the table arrangements. The flowers were adequate, though not generous. They made three bright blue splashes against the white damask and picked up the blue in the pieces of Meissen that were already in place. Peters had brought out the three pairs of George IV silver candlesticks, as Mildred had instructed. Sir Simon liked to see the silver used. Pride's Court had a magnificent collection of holloware as well as two sets of sterling flatware.

As she left the dining room, Mildred could hear voices from the conservatory and knew that her grandfather was downstairs and some guests had arrived. Then she heard her father's voice.

Mary Court was already sitting in a deep wicker armchair when her daughter came in. She was cooling herself with a Japanese fan, which she had recently taken to using. There was a glass of sherry beside her. She wore a gray silk gown of no particular distinction except that it covered as much bare flesh as possible.

Mildred dutifully kissed her mother's cheek, gave her father a brief peck and her sister, Charity, a perfunctory hug. She had never been demonstrative with her family, and the only person she had ever wanted to hug and kiss with any amount of passion was North.

Charity was wearing white cotton voile with a pale blue sash tied in a bow at the hip. Even Mildred, whose fashion sense was scarcely acute, thought it dreadful. Despite the dress, however, Charity looked quite pretty. She was slim, with blond hair cut in straight bangs across the forehead, huge brown eyes, and legs as long as a pony's.

"Where's North?" Sir Simon demanded, glaring at Mildred.

"He's coming, Grandfather. He won't be long."

"People ought to be punctual. It shows lack of respect when they keep other people waiting. North should have been in the army. Now that would have taught him something about the value of time."

It was Sir Simon's firm belief that the army cured all mankind's ills. He had fought in the Crimea and adored telling stories about his youthful exploits. Any man who had never served in the army or, failing that, the navy had been deprived in his view.

"May I please have some sherry?" Charity asked.

"Lemonade for you, my girl," Sir Simon said flatly, not allowing time for Charity's parents to give an opinion.

"The Rutherfords let Sally have a glass of sherry before dinner. Everybody in this family is hopelessly outdated."

She had a curiously flat, confident way of speaking. There was none of the usual hesitation or doubt of the thirteen-year-old girl in her manner. Sir Simon poured a glass of lemonade for her and she made a face at it.

"Where are the others?" Sir Simon asked, beginning to pace up and down. He was a punctual man and had never been able to understand tardiness. Waiting for relatives and businessmen was just one of the crosses he had been forced to bear all his life.

"Susan and David will arrive shortly," Mildred said.

Sir Simon gave a noncommittal huff and looked at his son Geoffrey. Now *he* was always on time. He looked at Geoffrey with approval.

Geoffrey had always been the least attractive of the Court men, but he had improved with age, as some men do. He was slightly heavier now but still far from paunchy, and he had taken on a patina of power, which added to his bearing. His reddish hair was quite gray, even white in places, but his blue eyes were still bright with ambition and his voice was more confident than it had ever been. Though not as handsome as Charles nor as dashing as Fort, he exuded a sense of stability and decisiveness. When he was younger, his father and brothers had treated him as some kind of errand boy and then later as a workhorse. Geoffrey got all the jobs nobody else wanted to do. Yet occasionally he came out with an original, even brilliant idea. Consequently he had earned their respect.

Sir Simon was about to launch into a political diatribe when he was brought to a halt by the arrival of Susan, David, and North. North had his hand under Susan's elbow. Mildred tensed when she saw them. She had never liked Susan—the girl was an interloper and a manipulator. It was shocking the way she cozied up to Grandfather, always scheming in some fashion and flattering him. Mildred did not like to see North's hand on Susan's arm. She had caught the look on his face when he gazed down at Susan's polished little head. Susan was extraordinarily chic as usual, wearing brown silk that bloused out at the waist and then fitted tightly to the knees and ankles. Very Parisian, Mildred thought crossly, and very expensive. Mildred would have liked to strangle her cousin.

Peters came in and announced dinner, and they all moved off toward the dining room. North was beside Susan, and they were laughing together about some private joke. Mildred seethed but said nothing. At table she sat at the foot while Sir Simon sat at the head, but North and Susan were effectively separated, and at least, she thought grimly, they could not whisper all through the meal.

Between courses Sir Simon discussed the Court mine and his latest acquisition of the piece of land Armand St. Amour had been holding.

"This calls for a celebration!" he cried to the table. "Finally we've got the better of that pirate. Oh, he held us up, but we've come out the victors just the same. Charles and Geoffrey know all the details, but I want the rest of you to hear the good news."

He proposed a toast.

"To victory!" he said, holding up his glass. "To the Court mines! They're ours now!"

He explained that he had managed to persuade St. Amour to sell the claim he had been holding by offering to take a failing coal mine off his hands.

"I didn't know he was in coal," David said.

"He only had one mine at Clover Valley. And it isn't much of a mine, I gather. Out in Nova Scotia. Never made a cent on it. North looked into it for me. St. Amour wanted to unload the thing because he wants to buy into sugar. The man's a bit demented. I made a tempting offer to St. Amour's partner, and I know we paid too much but it was on the understanding that they'd sell the mining claim to us at the same time. You see? I've got what I want. We'll see what to do about the coal mine—maybe we can make it pay. We'll investigate the possibilities."

"Clover Valley is where they had a bad cave-in about a year ago," North explained. "You may remember reading about it in the papers. Forty miners were trapped and only a few were rescued."

"No doubt they ran the thing badly," Sir Simon said, always willing to believe the worst about his son-in-law. "Not properly shored up, I imagine. What does St. Amour know about mining?"

"You may have to pour money into it," North warned.

"Geoffrey will find out. I'm sending him out there," Sir Simon said. "The main thing is we got the claim up north."

"How soon are you leaving?" Mary asked. This was the first she had heard about Geoffrey's projected journey.

"I meant to tell you later, Mary," Geoffrey said. "I'll know tomorrow. But it will probably be next week. Actually, I don't mind. I haven't seen much of the Maritimes and I've been studying reports about the mine. We may be able to make a profit. Everybody needs coal."

Sir Simon continued to gloat throughout dinner. He had managed (as he saw it) to outwit St. Amour. Now that the Court mine was safely in his grasp, it would be time to think about future punishment, of possible financial ruin, for St. Amour. He had never let the true depth of his hatred leak through to his sons or to the rest of the family. His determination to destroy *Sir* Armand was much too dangerous for discussion.

"I really talked his partner into the deal," he went on grandly. "The American, John Bead. Funny how St. Amour is tied up with the Yankees. Second time he's done that, too. I can't understand the fella's motives."

The fact was, he understood perfectly. St. Amour had needed money on more than one occasion and he had been able to raise it in New York. Sir Simon would not have been above the same maneuver if it had ever been necessary, but his own financial jugglings had kept him always in the black or able to raise money in Canada or England.

"Yes," he repeated, "the French and the Americans make strange bedfellows."

Put like that, it sounded definitely sinister. It would have been easier to believe (Sir Simon's tone implied) an alliance between a Zulu warrior and a Chinese rice harvester. Any relationship between people of differing races, especially those of non-British extraction, struck him as revolutionary. He had never been troubled by notions of equality and people to him were either princes or varlets. The vast middle class simply did not exist for him.

"What's his partner's name, again?" David inquired, egging the old man on. They all joked about his prejudices behind his back.

"John Bead. I told you. As in necklace. That's a very American name, don't you think? I don't think many foreign names make sense, do you?"

Having thus disposed of foreigners in one sweep, Sir

Simon was ready to tackle the diabolical workings of the Liberals in Ottawa and most particularly that arch-crook, Mackenzie King. The dinner conversation became totally political.

After dinner David offered to give Charity a game of Mah-Jongg in the card room. It was the newest fad, supposedly imported from China and played with colored tiles. Charity was a devotee and was delighted to find a partner.

On most occasions at Pride's Court the men retired to the library for coffee and brandy and a continuing discussion of their business problems. Tonight the plan was changed when Sir Simon announced rather portentously that he must speak to North alone. Geoffrey and Charles went along with the women to the Red Sitting Room, where they would have their after-dinner brandy.

Having indulged himself in a substantial amount of burgundy after his predinner scotch, North was not sure he could handle a private meeting with Sir Simon. What in hell could he want now? North wondered. He thrust back a stray fear with the thought that Sir Simon had been cheerful and friendly during dinner. So it could not be some terrible disaster. My God, not another special assignment, surely? Only luck had gotten him through the last one. He followed Sir Simon with some trepidation.

Peters had already placed a tray of coffee and brandy in the library, and Sir Simon took his glass but did not sit down. North felt compelled to stand, too, but Sir Simon waved him to a chair.

"Sit down and enjoy your coffee," he said expansively. "I'm a bit restless myself, but there's no need for you to stand."

North collapsed gratefully. He had not been sure he could stay on his feet for long without looking pained.

"I want to talk to you about something serious," Sir Simon began, "and it will require careful consideration on your part. Mind you, I don't intend to put any pressure on you, North. It's your decision."

Inwardly, North groaned. The very fact that Sir Simon had come up with some scheme was enough to demand a yes. What was he about to find himself saddled with now?

There were times when even the fantastic luxury in which he lived seemed scarcely worthwhile. Often he felt exhausted. He longed to relax and forget business, but the Courts never seemed to stop. It would have been fine if he'd been born with the incredible Court energy, but as it was, he found it almost impossible to keep pace.

"Yes, sir," he managed to say. As it happened, Sir Simon did not expect any other response at this time. He pressed on, brandy in hand.

"To me, North, you're one of the family."

"Thank you, sir."

"Yes, you're like one of my own grandchildren. And you've made me a great-grandfather. God bless you. Mildred seems very happy. You've made all of us happy, North."

North had never visualized himself as a bearer of happiness to anybody, except perhaps Mildred when he made love to her. This was a new role. He raised his eyebrows in unconcealed surprise.

Sir Simon went on, ignoring the expression as he ignored anything that did not particularly please him or fit in with his plans, "I'm satisfied with your work at the bank. Everything is fine except your regrettable habit of being late. However, we shall overlook that for the moment. I hope you feel happy?"

"Mildred and I are very happy. I can't think of an improvement."

He told the lie easily. It had come to him since he met the Courts that it was incredibly easy to lie. *If I didn't have to work*, he thought morosely, *life would be improved a great deal, but you can't say that to a Court. It's treason.*

"In view of the Court holdings," Sir Simon was saying, "which for the most part I control, and in view of the special place you and Mildred hold in the family, *I* have thought of an improvement. Only if you agree to the plan, North. There will be no pressure."

"And what is it you want me to do, sir?"

North roused himself and sat up straight in his chair. It was important that he appear interested, and God knows, he *was* interested. He was about to find out what Sir Simon had in mind. He swallowed brandy and steadied himself. Sir Simon swung around suddenly,

"What would you say to changing your name?"

North was staggered. Such an idea had never occurred to him, although he knew dimly that people had done so in the past.

"I've never thought of such a thing."

"I mean legally, of course. Everything legal. You could keep the Grenville and hyphenate the name. Grenville-Court. What do you think? Sounds good, eh?"

"I . . . don't know . . ."

It was such a novel idea, so unexpected that North had trouble shaking the wine mists from his head to consider it in the proper light. Sir Simon ploughed on relentlessly.

"It's done all the time in England."

"Yes, I realize that. Usually to preserve the mother's name, though, isn't it?"

"What difference does it make *why*?" Sir Simon demanded. "I see Mildred as a Court rather than a Grenville. You don't find yourself particularly attached to your father, do you? Therefore, the Grenville name can't be all that important. Mildred has shown her colors running this house and having a son. What about Nicholas? I want him to be a Court."

North, who had up to this point not given his son much thought, pictured the child and realized that he had, indeed, assumed Nicholas to be a Grenville. Now, he was to be something else. A Court.

"I've considered the question," Sir Simon continued, "and here's my position. I have three grandsons to carry on the name. Landry. Hmph! Not too sure about that—his brain is in a wheatbin. Noel and Simon II may well marry and produce Courts—I certainy hope so. And that's it. But here we are, certain of you and Mildred and the baby."

"It's unusual," North muttered.

"If we can name a town after the family, we can change your name to make it part of the family."

"That's right, I guess."

North had never been particularly introspective about either himself or the Courts, but he saw now that to Sir Simon the dynasty was everything. No idea was too far-fetched, no scheme too bizarre, if it perpetuated the Courts of Mount Royal. North felt more than ever like a pawn in a game, just as he had the year before, when everybody but himself planned the wedding at Christ Church. Yet, changing his name would cement him more securely into the

Court family so that he could never be ousted, no matter how little he worked, how happy or unhappy Mildred was. He would never be disowned or deported from the Court domains.

"You did well to produce a son so soon. I'm proud of you and Mildred. I know you can do it again. Eh?"

Sir Simon smiled conspiratorially. This was the closest he would allow himself to come to the topic of sex. He hurried on then, without waiting for a reply.

"North Grenville-Court. Do you like the sound of it? I plan to make you and Mildred a suitable gift, of course. What about Drake House? The deed in your new name, North."

Drake House was the Court summer place on the South Shore of the St. Lawrence. It was a huge frame mansion surrounded by acres of valuable land.

"Drake House? But—"

"You'll soon need it for the children in the summer anyway."

"Actually, since Nicholas in only two months old, I hadn't given the summers any thought . . . not with regard to children. But I suppose that would be ideal."

"All our children summered at Drake House. And the grandchildren, too. It's all settled, then?"

Sir Simon held out his hand. North accepted. They looked at each other with understanding, although North was still composing his face into the right expression.

"It's an honor, sir. Mildred will be happy. I know she will."

"Everybody will be. We all like you, North. Now let's go and tell the others. I'll have Peters bring out some Dom Perignon. This calls for a celebration."

As he climbed the marble staircase, North gave a half-drunken salute to Sir Cathmor Court hanging so solidly in his huge gilt frame above the landing. The old boy, by some miraculous turn of fate, had just become his ancestor. North was elated. Never in his wildest flights of fancy had he envisioned the events of tonight. He was to own Drake House and all the land surrounding it. He was to become more than an in-law to the powerful Court family, he was to be enveloped by it.

The importance of the price tag was rapidly diminishing.

As he forced himself up the steps, the first shock of Sir Simon's suggestion had evaporated, and he began to think a little disparagingly of his father, Henry Grenville. Why consider him? North had felt for years that his father despised him and that he had been astonished by the marriage North had made to such an influential heiress. What was there to remember about the Grenvilles, really, except the name of a defunct bank?

And in return for giving up the name Grenville, North was to share in "all this." He allowed his imagination to range swiftly over the vast Court holdings. Wealth. Power. Land. Wealth forever and forever for North Grenville-Court and his children. Yes, the change was worth almost any price. He did not regret his agreement.

It was gratifying, too, to find out how many of the family members accepted the idea. Charles. Geoffrey. Mary. They seemed to like him and welcome him into the Court family. All except Susan. That sly, hard-nosed little bitch was furious. He had seen the resentment in her eyes, the forced smile she had plastered on her pretty lips when Sir Simon made the announcement. Nevertheless, she was sexy. He would have liked to be taking Susan to bed. He sniffed her restless need for sexual variety. It was a social scent he had always been able to detect.

When he reached the apartment, Mildred was already in the bedroom. He found her pulling the silk bedcovers off the four-poster. She was wearing a filmy white nightgown that exposed a large part of her breasts. The urge to make love (never far below the surface even when he was drinking) now sprang to the surface. He smiled coaxingly at his wife. Better than nothing, even if Susan's neat little body would have been more appealing.

He reminded himself that he ought to be grateful to Mildred. Indirectly she was his benefactor and the source of his power. Mildred had brought him the prize, and Mildred had given him a son. She was essential to his well-being, and on top of that she was available. He must not overlook that. Lusting after Susan was a waste of time, at least for the present.

"Milly!" he said in his deepest, most persuasive voice, "you must be trying to excite me in that thing you're wearing. Look what you've done to me!"

He passed his hand suggestively across the front of his

trousers. He walked uncertainly to where his wife was standing and put his arms around her, then ran his lips smoothly down the deep cleavage that was, in its own way, rather attractive. He nuzzled her neck and made playful, lustful sounds.

Mildred, who up until this moment had been torn between pleasure at North's coup with her grandfather and the pain of his obvious flirtation with Susan, hesitated. She was a little drunk herself.

"Look what *I've* done to you? I'm not sure I'm the person responsible for your condition, darling. You've been ogling Susan all night."

He saw the danger and dropped his hands abruptly. He managed to look wounded, as if he had been unjustly accused. Then he wandered toward a chair, where he began rather ineffectively to take off his clothes.

"Susan? I hardly noticed Susan."

"Don't throw your dinner jacket on the floor," Mildred said, moving to pick it up. Then relenting, she added, "Here, let me help you undo that tie. You'll never manage. North, you've had too much wine."

He stood still then, like a small boy and waited for her to untie the black silk, to wrestle with the studs in his dress shirt, to unbutton the top of his trousers.

"Darling, when you touch me like that you make me so"—he was about to use a locker-room word but stopped himself in time, knowing it would offend her—"excited," he finished lamely.

"Do I? You're a spoiled brat, North. That's all you are." Her tone was fond rather than reprimanding. Even drunk, his skin smelled sweet. She had often noticed that about him. His face, sleepy, touched with lechery, was so handsome that she wanted to kiss him wildly. "You just want me to undress you and fuss over you. I think you're still a child."

"You think so?"

He was not displeased. He liked it when Mildred helped him off with his trousers. Being waited on, being the center of attention was exactly what he did like. It was one of the most bearable things about Mildred that she seemed willing to give him this attention. She was really in love with him, North thought, and it was something he could not

231

comprehend. Why? *But mine not to reason why*, he told himself silently. *Mine but to make love to the little lady.*

As Mildred helped North, she thought about Susan. She had felt so triumphant when her grandfather made the statement about Drake House. Susan had been mentioning that property to Sir Simon for ages, hinting how nice it would be for the racing stable she and David were about to build. How Susan must have raged inside when she found out that Mildred and North were to benefit. Served her right, she was a grasping, interfering little snob. And now she was making up to North. Well, she would find herself receiving fewer and fewer invitations to Pride's Court, Mildred thought vindictively, and that would be one of her first steps in the near future. To cut off Susan.

"Darling let's get that underwear off," Mildred said, weaving a bit as she helped North. "I think it's the unsexiest thing I ever saw." He wore mercerized cotton combinations.

"Um. All right, then, do that. Are you lusting after me?"

"Don't be so silly," Mildred said, blushing.

"Are you proud of me? Did I do the right thing?"

"The right thing. You're magnificent. Grandfather thinks so too."

North wavered over to the bed and collapsed on his back, his head propped up on two fat pillows. He began to fumble with a cigarette box on the night table.

"Take off that damned nightgown," he said.

Mildred obligingly pulled off the gown. Her hips were heavy and her legs had definitely suffered since the baby came, but the heavy, overblown breasts were lush.

"Come here, Milly," North said, suddenly wanting to touch her. "I love it when you do things to me. Come and do things to me, darling."

She joined him on the bed. North was sprawled out, legs wide apart, face at a peculiar angle so that his chin was on his chest, his penis indecently erect. She knelt between his legs on the bed and bent her head to kiss him.

"Mmmmmmm. More. I adore that. Do that some more."

He lighted a cigarette and began to smoke, with his eyes closed, as if he were a latter-day Roman emperor. Mildred, taking her mouth away for a moment, caught his expression. She felt used. She might as well have been hired, she thought, like some girl off the street. North was taking absolutely no interest in what was happening to her. Propped there against the pillows, blowing smoke lazily toward the ceiling, he was sinking into a blissful stupor. A small rebellion arose as her Court pride resisted the idea of being a mere object. North was nothing without her. Nothing but a well-born charmer. She doubted that he had any idea of love, certainly not of any great passion. He was utterly superficial. In a rare flash of insight, she realized he would be unfaithful to her. If not this week, then some other week. He was not as strong as she, nor as disciplined. Not even as intelligent, though God knows he was much, much better looking. But why did she let him run over her in this way?

North crushed out the cigarette.

"Make love to me, Milly. Sit on top of me and make love to me. You know how you do that sometimes. I adore it." His voice was a warm, dark waterfall that poured over her softly. She felt ill with the love that swept through her. "You know what I need, Milly. Do it that way, Milly, and I can kiss your breasts at the same time. Here . . ." He reached out and pulled her up toward his chest.

Milly obeyed. Even if North was not really making love to her, they were together, alone here. She enjoyed being with him, touching him, doing the things he asked her to do. North belonged to her and tonight he had been woven even tighter into the fabric of the Courts. It was comforting. No matter what he did, he would never leave her. And anything would be better than losing him.

She gave herself up completely to pleasing North. It was odd, she thought as she moved rhythmically on him, that she responded so well to the idea of being subjugated in the sexual act when she could never bear it in any other aspect of life. She felt exhilarated, though not sexually stimulated, as her body massaged his. It was possible to love his body, every inch of it, without being satisfied herself. A terrifying passion had seized her and if there was a cure for it somewhere, she did not wish to find it.

CHAPTER TWENTY

Geoffrey traveled by ship from Halifax to North Sydney and then took a local ferry into the dock at Clover Valley. It was ill named, being a scoop in the shoreline and entirely dependent upon coal for its existence. If the mine were forced to close, it would become another Nova Scotia ghost town, since almost every man worked either in the collieries or provided some service to the miners. About three thousand people lived in a haphazard collection of frame houses and shacks clustered around a single main street. There was one hotel, the Neptune, four churches, a brick bank, and a few shops.

When Geoffrey arrived, it was late afternoon and the town was steaming under a merciless August sun. Even the salt breezes were unable to provide much relief. Almost immediately Geoffrey felt depressed, and that was unusual, since he took a generally optimistic view of life. Surroundings seldom affected him; in the course of a varied business career he had been exposed to a great number of unpleasant and even cruel situations. But here, in Clover Valley, a pall hung over the place. It was like a town awaiting a death sentence.

He found the Hotel Neptune without any trouble and carried his own bag inside. He had concluded that there would be no bellboy, and he was right. His sight failed momentarily in the shadowy interior and then adjusted to the dim light. As he crossed the small lobby, he noticed the dismal gray linoleum, the brass spittoons, and the single spindly fern on a wooden stand. A few loungers in worn leather chairs looked up when he came in. No doubt they would recognize him, he decided. The arrival of the new owner would be the main topic of local gossip, and they needed no introduction—he was a stranger and he wore an expensive suit. He approached the desk clerk, who turned out to be a wizened little man with one arm; his empty sleeve was casually pinned up with a common safety pin. The man wore a green eyeshade and peered at Geoffrey from underneath.

"Mr. Court, isn't it? We've been expecting you. We have

the suite reserved." He pushed the register across the counter for Geoffrey's signature. Geoffrey did not have much hope that the "suite" would be luxurious.

"Yes, I'm Geoffrey Court. Webster told you I would be here today? I'll be here a few days."

"Bill Webster certainly told me, Mr. Court. We've tried to make things as comfortable as possible."

"What's your name?"

"Jake Renny, sir."

"Fine, Renny. Do you have a porter to take up my bag?"

"I'm the porter."

He came out from behind the desk and awkwardly picked up the bag. Geoffrey felt unreasonable annoyance. It always made him feel uncomfortable to be around the handicapped, especially when they were servants. Still, he made no attempt to pick up the bag himself. Instead, he followed Jake Renny up the plain wooden staircase, noticing that the carpet was in need of repair. The usual picture of Queen Victoria in her later, heavier years hung on the wall. If he'd seen that particular portrait once, he'd seen it a thousand times, and it was always singularly ugly.

Jake Renny unlocked the door to a corner room facing the sea. The curtains had been pulled back and the window opened to air the place and presumably encourage some breeze. The water lay below like a thin, shiny mirror. He could smell the salt.

"I'll put your bag down here, Mr. Court," Renny said, placing it carefully on a folding luggage stand. "Can I get you something? You must be thirsty."

"Yes, do you have scotch?"

"Might have some rye. Nobody here drinks scotch. Rum, now. They drink rum. And beer."

Geoffrey was irritated with himself for not thinking to bring a supply of decent scotch. There would be no drinkable wine either, he realized. He ought to have brought supplies with him. Not only did he feel like a drink himself, but he wanted to offer Webster one, too. The meeting did not augur well and the drink might help to ease things along.

"Bring rye if that's all you have. And ice and water."

"Yes, I'll be right back."

The suite consisted of a small bedroom and what passed

for a sitting room. The chairs were old and upholstered in brown fabric. A few scattered carpets were strewn about the linoleum-covered floor. Geoffrey decided not to think about the room; after all, that was the least of his problems. The mine was the important thing. What to do about it. Whether to close it or keep it open.

He stood by the window, taking in all the fresh air he could until Renny came back. A man he took to be Webster was behind Renny, who put a tin tray down upon the table.

"Is that all, sir?"

"Yes, I'll come down if I want anything else."

Jake Renny left them. Webster offered his hand.

"Welcome to Clover Valley, Mr. Court. I'm Bill Webster. Superintendent and general manager."

He spoke with a Scottish burr that was not unpleasant. Geoffrey recalled that he had noticed a great many Scottish, Irish, and English names on the payroll. Webster was a large shaggy man, badly in need of a haircut and shave. His nose was a little too red (as if he indulged in too much liquor too often), and he smelled heavily of tobacco. He had barely shaken hands with Geoffrey before he pulled out a pack of Players and began to light up. He wore no jacket, only a soiled blue shirt and ill-fitting trousers. Under one arm he carried a sheaf of papers and a binder filled with more papers. He put them down beside the tray.

"Sit down, Webster. We'll have a drink."

"Thank you, I will."

"That breeze isn't doing much to cool the place off," Geoffrey said as he poured rye into the two cheap glasses.

"Not today, no."

The ice was in an open bucket. It wouldn't last long, Geoffrey thought. He was generous with it in the drinks. He would have liked to remove his coat, but that would have suggested a degree of informality that the Courts did not allow. Letting down standards with employees only brought trouble in the end.

Geoffrey raised his glass.

"To the Clover Valley Mine!"

"To the future!"

When he had taken a mouthful of the drink and found

it bearable although not to his taste, Geoffrey took out his carefully folded handkerchief and wiped his forehead. He could not recall being so hot. But the drink helped.

"I don't think much of your ferry service from Sydney," he said to Webster. "It's not much of a boat. I had to wait three hours for it."

"It won't improve, either. Nobody in Sydney gives a damn unless you make a lot of noise. Nobody here is important enough to demand a decent ferry."

"If we keep the mine open, I'll make some noise. You can depend on that," Geoffrey said.

"If we keep it open," Webster said. He did not sound hopeful.

"Isn't the government interested in keeping the mine open? They don't want another thousand men on their unemployment rolls, do they?"

"Probably not, but they're too damned stupid to get off their asses. When did government do anything unless it was pushed? I guess they'd like to keep the mine going, all right, but . . ." and he shrugged and drank some of the rye with a grateful look.

Geoffrey made a mental note that he must pay a visit to the premier when he was next in Halifax. Perhaps he would make a special stop on his way back. When the Courts invested, they expected a little cooperation from the elected representatives.

"St. Amour took no part in politics down here, I guess. Didn't bother the premier or the Cabinet with requests for services?" Geoffrey suggested.

"His company—Arcan—only had the mine five years. During that time it was Bead who came here. Once before the accident and once after. Sir Armand never did show up."

"Tell me about the accident, Webster."

"You've read the reports, I imagine. It wasn't anybody's fault, you have to understand that. These things happen in coal mines all the time. We call them 'bumps'—a bit like an underground earthquake. Shakes everything for miles, blows stuff out of the shafts, timbers, fans, rocks, and worse. Then the tunnels cave in and the miners get trapped. It's often hell to get them out."

"I read everything I could about it, but I'd like to hear what you have to say."

"We had other problems at the time, too. Like the hoists weren't working properly because the electrical system failed. That caused a lot of delay. It cost lives because we couldn't get the elevators to work. The system often fails, but it never got fixed properly. That costs too much money."

"Weren't the men angry about that?"

"Sure, they were angry. But mostly they worry about their jobs. Where will they go if the mine closes?"

Webster polished off his drink. The ice rattled in his glass as he drained it. Geoffrey offered him another and Webster agreed to have one.

"Why don't you mix it the way you like it?" Geoffrey suggested.

"Thanks, I will."

"And what is the condition of the hoists now? The electrical system?"

"Well, the hoists need overhauling. And a lot of rewiring needs to be done. I've mentioned it in my report. But the profit margin is so low that nobody in his right mind wants to spend a dime. I know that. Bead knew that. We all know it."

"Haven't the miners got a union?"

"Sure, but the miners are fatalists here. You gotta understand, Mr. Court, that sense doesn't enter into this thing. The men know the danger. Bumps. Gas. Explosion. Fire. All part of the mining game, but that's all they know how to do. Sure, they'd like it to be safe, but . . ."

He trailed off and Geoffrey fixed himself another drink. He couldn't remember when he'd felt the need for a drink more than he did right now, despite the fact that he didn't like rye. He seemed to be catching despair from Webster like a contagious disease.

"Tell me about the problems . . . I want to know."

"Yeah, well, I have to tell you that before the accident happened last year, the mine was losing money. One hundred thousand dollars a year."

"Then it isn't surprising Bead didn't want to spend. Why didn't he close down the mine then?"

"Because the men begged him not to. We employed about eight hundred men at the time. Everything was worn out, needed fixing. There was no profit. The miners knew it. The union knew it. But the union didn't say anything. They were dead quiet."

"You mean the union didn't demand that safety measures be taken or the mine closed?"

"Far from it. The accident happened. Number Four Colliery collapsed and forty men were trapped down there, sealed at the two-thousand-foot level. Deep mining here, you know, under the ocean, a lot of it. St. Amour and Bead wanted to close the mine—oh yes, I know that, Bead said so. It was losing money and it was jinxed, he said."

"What changed his mind?"

"The miners. They petitioned the Arcan Company to keep the mine open. Even the mayor got in on the act. See, there's nothing else in this town. What were the men going to do? Move away? Where? With what money? To what jobs? We'd all be looking for work if the mine closed, including me. So they asked Bead not to close."

He shook his head. His glass was empty again. Faced with an ever-escalating sense of despair, he stared at the tray. Geoffrey waved toward it so that Webster did not hesitate to replenish his drink. Both of them were damp with perspiration.

"Well, Bead came out here," Webster went on, picking up the threads of his story wearily, "and met me and Charlie Stewart. He's the supervisor. We talked about it. Bead said, well, if they were going to keep the mine going they'd have to work the deepest colliery, Number Two Shaft. That had been closed two years because of the risk. The coal is better quality, though. So Bead figured there was a chance he could make it pay. Down to six thousand feet. Sometimes the deeper you go, the better the coal."

"So Bead put it to the men?"

"Charlie Stewart put it to the men. The two of us. We told them the truth, it was Number Two and deep or nothing at all. And no extra pay for the risk. Only a minimum amount of money spent on repairs to the hoist and a few other things."

"They accepted your terms?"

"They accepted all right. Number Four was sealed up like a tomb with fifteen bodies in there. Be there till Kingdom Come, I guess."

"And what about the quality of coal in Number Two? Was it better?"

"It made some difference, yes. We began to show a slight profit. But that'll only last until something happens. And if we don't spend any money. But it isn't safe, Mr. Court, I have to tell you. If you spend the money, there goes the profit."

Webster looked out to sea again as if he could actually envision the profits drifting away across the water. His craggy face seemed to have taken on deeper valleys with his consumption of alcohol, his eyes were filmed over from too much thinking and too much rye.

"You'll see it all in the figures," he repeated in a monotone. "The small profit. The way it works."

Geoffrey began to walk up and down on the worn patterned linoleum. Like Webster he was wrapped in gloom. A faintly ominous mood had now spread over the room. It was like a funeral, or at best, a wake. Geoffrey wondered absentmindedly why he had come all this distance, why his father had insisted that he see the mine for himself. Why could they not have decided the mine's fate from an office in Montreal?

"It's only a matter of time before there's another disaster, and I just hope it isn't worse," Webster said.

"Does your report include the absolute minimum investment we have to make to bring the mine up to some kind of safe level?"

"It's in the figures. I brought them with me."

He handed a sheaf of papers to Geoffrey.

"I'd like to keep the mine open," Geoffrey said without much conviction. "What's the daily wage rate?"

"A little over four dollars."

"I hope we can work miracles," Geoffrey said. "So everything is here that I need? I'll study it tonight. The payroll, shifts, equipment, cost of recent repairs, sick list, ponies . . . you use ponies?"

"We have two hundred ponies and horses. The stable is in fair condition."

"I see. That's practical, then, is it?"

"In the smaller galleries, yes. We haven't got electrical power in some of the farthest tunnels," Webster said. "I had Mrs. Moore prepare all the information; she knows more about it than any of us. We're lucky to have her. She took hold as soon as she came on the job. She's only been with us since the accident last year, but she's a big help just the same."

"Isn't that a bit unusual? Hiring a woman at the pithead?"

"I guess so. Her husband, Terry Moore, was killed in the accident. He was a foreman. Colleen Moore was left with two small children, and she could typewrite and keep books so I took her on. She asked for the job, and what could I say? We needed somebody."

"Oh, I wasn't being critical," Geoffrey reassured him. "You did the right thing, Webster. Well, I'm coming over to the pithead first thing tomorrow morning. I want to meet your supervisor and your foreman. Arrange for me to tour the lower levels, will you? I want to see Number Two."

"You want to go right down to the bottom?" Webster said, his voice rising. "You don't have to do that, Mr. Court. I can tell you exactly what the conditions are."

"I'm going down. I want to see for myself. My father expects me to do that."

"All right, sir. If you like. But it's hot and dirty and cramped. The men are used to it, but somebody like you—"

"That doesn't matter. Just make sure I can go down for a couple of hours. You'd better come with me. Now the other thing we could do before dinner is inspect the property owned by the Clover Valley Coal Company. I know we own this hotel, and it's in bad shape. There are other buildings, I take it, and some cottages. I want to see them."

"We own a store, a blacksmith's shop, some cottages." Webster opened the binder and brought out a sheet of paper. "Here's the list."

Geoffrey took the paper, scanned it, and put it in his pocket. Webster agreed to go with him on a walking tour, although he eyed the half-empty rye bottle rather wistfully. They toured the town, a collection of undistinguished buildings badly in need of paint. There were very few trees. The ground had a reddish tinge. A few miners had gardens and chickens, but it was the coal that kept the town going. The coal seemed to color life, as if it had seeped into the bloodstream of the people, giving it a dark and listless air. There was a whisper of spiritual decay. Geoffrey, viewing properties that now came under the vast umbrella of Court holdings, felt a surge of disgust. The idea that his family's name was attached to such a dilapidated project bothered

241

him considerably. He rejected the idea that the Courts would own anything run-down or shabby and made up his mind to improve the town if the mine were to be kept open.

Two of the company-owned cottages were empty. Webster said that the available renters could not afford them, although they were listed at only fifteen dollars a month. Geoffrey replied that the cottages must be repaired and rented, at a lower rate if necessary. That was preferable to leaving them empty. He made notes as they walked around.

"Is there a painter in town?"

"Not a good one. You'll have to hire somebody in Sydney. If you give Mrs. Moore instructions, she'll look after it. You can trust her."

"Mrs. Moore sounds very efficient."

"Sure. She's efficient, all right."

When they returned to the hotel, the sun was going down behind the rise of hills and the air had cooled slightly. Geoffrey began to think about dinner.

"How is the food here in the hotel?"

"Stick to the seafood, and it'll be eatable," Webster advised. "But it won't be great."

"What about wine? I suppose the hotel doesn't have a wine cellar?"

Webster allowed himself a sarcastic laugh. "Wine cellar?" he repeated as if it were some bizarre idea imported from another planet. No, there was no wine cellar, but he could get some of Mrs. Moore's foxberry wine. He would pick up a couple of bottles.

"Mrs. Moore is very enterprising."

"She's got to make a little extra when she can, with the kids to look after. Actually, she doesn't rent a house. She lives over at Sarah Galt's rooming house. That's all she can afford, but Sarah lets her use the backyard to grow raspberries and a few vegetables. Her kids pick the foxberries in the marshes; that's what she makes the wine from."

"Get me half a dozen bottles, Webster. Is it legal to make wine here?"

"Yeah, it's legal."

Geoffrey knew that the province was "wet," but there were so many individual regulations concerning wine, beer, and alcohol from province to province that nobody could possibly keep up. He sighed with resignation and told Webster to meet him in the hotel dining room in an hour.

Geoffrey did not sleep well that night. Still, he managed to get up early and was out at the pithead by eight o'clock. The buildings used as offices for the Clover Valley Coal Company looked as run-down as the rest of the town. Geoffrey added to his notes that the place must be cleaned up and painted if they stayed in business. When he entered the office, he found a woman working at a small desk. There was no sign of Webster, but he knew that it was not time for a shift change and he imagined the superintendent's hours were linked to the shifts. The woman bending over the set of books wore a neat black cotton dress with a white collar and cuffs. Her dark hair was tied back with a red scarf. She was very businesslike. She heard him come in and smiled up at him.

"Good morning, Mr. Court."

"You must be Mrs. Moore. Your wine was excellent. You saved my dinner from complete disaster."

"That's kind of you. I've been making it for years, but the foxberries are getting harder and harder to find, I'm afraid."

"Is Webster around?"

"He's down the pit. There's been some trouble with the electrical system again, and when that happens, some of the pumps don't work."

She got up to clear space at a desk and then offered him a chair. He saw that she was slim and that her face was a pleasant oval shape. Her gaze, which she directed at him quite calmly, was steady and came from dark brown eyes. She had healthy skin, rather shiny, as if she ate properly and took good care of herself. Although her whole manner was businesslike, she was genial and even warm. He liked her immediately and could understand why Webster had hired her. He could *not* understand how she had come to be married to a foreman in a mine.

"Is there anything I should inspect here on the surface?"

"Certainly, if you like. I can show you around."

They walked around the property and Geoffrey asked questions. She had the answers or she knew where to find an answer. He liked her cool, crisp attitude, her way of dealing so easily with him. At the same time, she was intensely feminine and much too pretty for a place like this.

"Do you know much about the pieces of property the company owns around town?" Geoffrey asked when they had finished the tour.

"I know all the properties and the tenants. Is there something you'd like to know about them?"

"If we keep the mine open," Geoffrey said, and saw her instant withdrawal, the cloud in her dark eyes. "If we do, then I'd like to make some changes. For one thing, I want to rent those two empty cottages. It's better to rent them cheaply and have somebody in them than leave them vacant."

"I agree. But nobody could afford that much rent."

"We'll lower the rent."

"And still make repairs? That's not very businesslike, is it?"

"It doesn't balance the books, if that's what you mean. But the Courts are never associated with run-down businesses and shabby property."

He asked her to join him for lunch so that they could discuss the properties in detail. She seemed hesitant but finally agreed when he stressed that it would save time and that he planned to return to Montreal as soon as possible. Over lunch they had some more of Mrs. Moore's foxberry wine and discussed each piece of property. She seemed to know them in great detail: what needed fixing and approximately how much it would cost.

"I know you have enough work, considering your salary," Geoffrey said over coffee, "but if you'll take on an extra job for me, I'll be glad to pay you. I'd like you to find a contractor, get estimates, and supervise the work on the cottages. Also, rent them and collect the rent."

"Extra pay? That would be wonderful!" Her eyes lighted up at the prospect. He thought how desperate she must be for money and found himself upset, although he scarcely knew her.

"How about a rent-free cottage? Would that be satisfactory? I'm sure with two children you could use the space."

"Mr. Court, that sounds like heaven to me."

He felt unduly pleased with himself for having struck such an agreeable bargain. He told her she could decide on the repairs for the cottage she chose and see that it was done the way she wanted it. This was one of the times he could remember actually using his power for somebody else's good, and it made him feel euphoric. The plan was so fitting: She was doing him a favor and he was in a position to do her a favor. What could be better? He would explain the plan to Webster so that there would be no misunderstanding when he had gone. Mrs. Moore would be in complete charge of the property side of the mine. Temporarily, the idea that he might have to shut down Clover Valley Mine had escaped him.

"You can even have a title," he said enthusiastically, his blue eyes cheerful at the idea. "How about property manager? Does that sound impressive enough?"

"Very grand," she said and laughed. "I'd love to take the job with or without the title. A cottage. I can't believe it! And I can have my own garden there."

Geoffrey consulted his watch. Before they went back to the pithead, he said, he would like her to take him to the seaside. So far, he had seen nothing but the dock and the town. She seemed hesitant once more but finally nodded agreement.

As they walked down toward the ocean, he felt younger, a bit irresponsible as if he were playing hooky. He thought how few times in his life he had made use of the extraordinary power of the Court name for his own pleasure, his own will. Will! They were all subject to Papa's will—that was the trouble. Subject to the demands of the family enterprises, family gatherings, weddings, funerals, catastrophes, and triumphs. Everybody feeding into that all-consuming, hungry dynasty that Sir Simon had created. Even Fort had finally succumbed and was woven as tightly into the fabric of the Court family businesses as the rest of them. And Papa, clever Papa, had netted a new recruit in Mildred's husband. North, too, was completely at the disposal of the Court empire.

Geoffrey realized that his thoughts were disloyal, almost as bad as Honey's defection. Yet she had at least been outspoken about it. He was hiding *his* disloyalty in a subversive way. He pushed the thoughts aside and looked at the sea and sniffed the cool wind now coming off the water.

They walked along the shore, skirting rocks and rushes of surf as if they were children. He wanted to take her hand but didn't dare disturb the easy mood they had established. He thought she might object and take off like a seagull if he tried to get too close. They sat on a rock to stare out to sea.

"I love the sea," Colleen said. "Though God knows it's greedy and dangerous. But it's hypnotic, don't you think?"

"Definitely. If I lived out here, I'd want a house over-looking the ocean. Up there, perhaps"—he turned to point up the cliff face—"so I could hear the pounding waves at night and watch the storms from a safe place."

"How beautiful that sounds!"

"With windows all across the front and a walk on top for pacing. And a telescope to sight the ships coming in."

She laughed. She had a pretty musical laugh.

"Why are you laughing?"

"Because it sounds so dreamlike, and yet, for you it could be a reality. For me, it would always be just a dream. That seems funny to me."

"I don't see why," Geoffrey said huffily. Still, when he dwelt upon it, he really did not care if she thought it humorous. He rather imagined she had little to laugh at in life.

"Have you ever thought of moving from this town?" Geoffrey asked as they walked back toward the road.

"Not seriously. And not unless the mine closes. I can't take risks when I have the children to care for."

"If you ever decided you'd like to work in Montreal, I could find you a job there." Then he added hastily, in case she took the wrong meaning from his words: "You seem so efficient, and good people are always hard to find. You'd do well in the city, I'm sure."

"Thank you. I've never thought about going to Mon-treal."

She ought to live in a more civilized place, he decided, where her intelligence and grace would be appreciated. What could the people here know of her worth? Whom could she possibly befriend? She was not like the others he had seen—her eyes held promises.

"I'll stay here until the children are out of school. Unless you close the mine."

"What will your children do for a living if you stay? They'll be miners like the others."

"Yes, that's probably what will happen."

It would be easy enough to find the girl a good job, he

decided. Either in one of the Court companies or in one of the offices run by his friends. They always helped one another, it was the unwritten, unspoken law. The network. Helping your own kind. You called somebody and asked for a favor. Someday you'd be asked for a favor in return, though not necessarily from the man who had granted you one. That didn't matter. There was no question about it. The network.

As he took her hand to help her up the rock face, he said again, "You really ought to consider Montreal."

"No, Mr. Court, I don't think I ought to. Perhaps I *never* should. Whether or not the mine closes."

He drew back, knowing he had shown his hand. That invisible wire of attraction between them had tightened and almost snapped. His mind raced onward to the vision of Colleen in Montreal, and even as he formed the dream, he knew that he would not be content just to help her get a job, that he would want to see her. He would not be satisfied with just a friendship, and the need to see her would grow and haunt him at night.

Geoffrey had never indulged in affairs, as Fort had done. He did not know, but he suspected that Charles had not done so either. Still, there was a strong current of sexuality in the Courts, and it surfaced more obviously in some members of the family than in others. Look at Honey and her flagrant elopement with Armand. Angela, too, who had practically done the same thing. Even Mildred, his own daughter, though plain and much too large for a girl, was besotted by her own husband. The waves of her sexuality were almost embarrassing when North was around.

Mildred had done everything right, though. She had married the right man and she loved him. Mildred was fortunate. In his own case, the drive had been slow to surface, and he had felt nothing even remotely approaching lust for his wife, Mary. She had come into his life at a time when he ought to marry, and he had found her suitable. The word *suitable* echoed in his mind: dull, flat, hideously dry. He was fifty-three years old and coming to the end of his life, and what had he ever done that was really exciting? He had money, all the money he could ever spend. He had played everything safe. Always.

By the time they reached the pithead, he had managed to push away all these upsetting ideas and was ready to settle down at the desk Mrs. Moore had offered him. There were reports to study. When Webster finally came up, it was to report considerable alarm for the safety of the miners. The pumps weren't working in Number Two Shaft and the men would have to surface unless the system could quickly be patched. That would mean Geoffrey could not go down the mine today. He would have to wait until the next morning at the earliest.

At five, Geoffrey could only look forward to a dull evening in the Hotel Neptune. He could go over all the information again and he could give the matter his undivided consideration. He could try to come to some sensible decision, and that was why he had come out to the mine in the first place, he reminded himself. Instead of accepting that verdict, his mind reverted to Colleen Moore and the cottage she would have. Which one would she want? He tried to remember the differences between them, but they seemed minuscule. Finally, he could resist no longer, and when he saw that she was preparing to leave, he spoke to her.

"Would you be free to work this evening?"

She stood rigid in the middle of the tiny office. Again, he thought of the seagulls he had seen perched on the rocks, stiff with apprehension before they flew off across the water.

"What did you have in mind, Mr. Court?"

"I'd like to go over the cottage properties more thoroughly. I'd like to have your opinion on the amount of work needed, on the possible tenants. I wondered if you knew which cottage you wanted for yourself."

"The one on Church Road."

"I'm not sure I remember it."

"It has a back porch," she said briefly.

"Is that important?"

"I could use it for a potting shed. For my garden supplies."

"Oh yes, that's fine. Well, what do you say? Could you get somebody to give your children supper?"

"That's no problem. We usually eat with Sarah anyway. All right, Mr. Court, if it will help you."

"I lost time today. I still have the tour of the mine to do, you know. I counted on doing that this afternoon."

"Yes, I'm sorry you were held up."

"Is there anywhere to eat except the hotel?"

"There is a private house . . . a woman there makes meals for people sometimes. Her place overlooks the sea, and she has a little verandah. That might be nice. She serves lobster."

"That sounds excellent. Can you arrange it, then? You'll have to come by the hotel for me, since I don't know where we're going. Is that all right? I'll bring the reports and the files with me."

They had steamed lobster in a cottage owned by a Mrs. O'Hara. It was properly prepared and so delicate that Geoffrey could not recall having eaten any in Montreal, or Paris, or London that was better. During dinner they chatted about a number of things besides mine property—about responsibilities to one's family, religion, work, love, and children. Geoffrey told Colleen about his own children, even mentioning how Simon had been shell-shocked. He seldom told anybody that and was surprised to find it was easy to talk to Colleen about the problem. He told Colleen about Mildred's wedding and the romance between her and North.

"It sounds like a fairy tale," Colleen said, her eyes bright with interest. "I wish I could have been there. They must have looked beautiful."

"Everybody said so. I guess it was very grand. It was all Papa's idea," Geoffrey said. "Still, I think it worked out fine."

"And does he love her?"

"Who? Oh, you mean North?" It was a moment before he could reply. He hadn't given the matter much thought. "Yes, I guess so. I assume so."

After he had said the words, Geoffrey decided it wasn't quite true. "No, I don't think he *does*, now that you ask. Mildred isn't like so many of the Courts. Not like her cousin, Angela, or my sister, Honey. Now, Honey was a great beauty in her day. And my brother's twins, Flora and Fenella, are lovely in a strange way. No, Mildred is rather a big girl. Not at all pretty." He made a deprecating gesture with his shoulders. "Like me, I guess. I was never good-looking like my brothers. North probably married her because of the Court family. His own father retired early, and the Grenvilles lost a great deal of money. North always had expensive tastes and he's considered quite handsome—women like him. Drinks too much, but Papa took to him from the beginning. And Mildred is . . . very much in love with him."

Geoffrey was surprised to hear himself go on like that. He had so far managed to ignore North Grenville's faults and the way he treated Milly. It was odd, therefore, to find himself discussing the subject with a perfect stranger. No, she wasn't a stranger. He felt close to Colleen.

"He'll probably break her heart," Colleen said.

"You think so? Yes, I suppose that could happen."

Suddenly he felt sorry for Mildred and realized the price of the passion that had seized so many Courts but that he had never felt. They walked back toward the hotel after dinner. Geoffrey, not wanting the evening to end, suggested they stop by the cottage on Church Road. Colleen had a set of keys in her bag, and when they went inside, it was still light enough to inspect the place. She showed him the shed at the back with its single small window.

"If only there were more windows!" Colleen exclaimed, "I might be able to turn it into a little greenhouse. But then that would mean heating it. No, that would be too expensive."

"If you had vegetables all year round, wouldn't that save money?"

"Oh, but the cost of heating it!"

"It's small. Surely the heating bill wouldn't be that much. You go ahead and have it glassed in, and properly lined. I want you to do that, please. You'll make it pay for itself, and it isn't a luxury at all, Colleen."

He had said her first name without thinking. Now it stopped the conversation, as if one of them had said something unspeakable. She began to write on her notepad, hastily putting down figures.

"Do you really think it's practical?"

"I insist. It's my cottage, after all, and I want that shed turned into a greenhouse." He made it into a joke.

She accepted that. The idea was too close to her heart to turn down.

"What will people think? That I've come into money?" she asked.

"The truth. You're doing an extra job and working hard," Geoffrey said quickly. "And that's worth a cottage, believe me. I want you to take full responsibility, Mrs. Moore. It will take time."

They walked through the cottage planning changes. A new floor in most of the rooms, wallpaper, new steps at the front, a new sink. For a few minutes it seemed that they were both going to live in the cottage and share their lives. They talked about color and price. And they laughed. Colleen continued to make notes in a businesslike way.

"I'll speak to Webster before we go down the mine tomorrow. I'll tell him you've taken on this job for me, so there'll be no trouble when I'm gone. You can send the estimates and the bills directly to me."

"I don't know when I've been so excited," Colleen said. "I never dreamed seriously of having a house again."

He wondered if she had ever considered remarrying but did not ask. If she *had*, he did not want to hear about it. By the time he left her at the boarding house, it was dark. He took her hand for a moment and held it, then crushed it between his two strong ones. The unspoken attraction between them flowed like a current in the air. For the first time he was conscious of how small she was and that he loomed over her. In his entire life he had never wanted to kiss a woman as much as he did now. His mind told him not to be a fool, but the flood of energy that their touch had released made him lean over and place his mouth on her forehead. He felt her stir and knew she responded. Then she turned away quickly.

"Good night, Mr. Court. And thank you."

She was gone. He was left standing in the warm night alone with an emotion that he recognized but had never experienced, an emotion that would be difficult for him to quell. His orderly, uneventful life had suddenly ceased and a new one had begun.

CHAPTER TWENTY-ONE

Geoffrey, wearing a regulation miner's overall on top of his own expensive underwear, rubber boots one size too large, and a hard hat with a battery-powered headlamp, stepped into the cage elevator. Four of them went down together: two "fire bosses," who were going to inspect some of the side galleries for dangerous gas, and Bill Webster along with Geoffrey.

The cage swayed alarmingly as it descended to the six-hundred-foot level. It seemed extremely fragile, Geoffrey thought, and he made a mental note to ask Webster about the safety of the elevator when they were alone.

At the six-hundred-foot level they would have to transfer to a train of eight cable-operated trolleys that would take them down a long slope into the earth under the ocean. Geoffrey felt claustrophobic; he would be glad to get off the small elevator. Two cages operated in tandem, one going up and one going down at the same time.

The elevator jolted to a stop and they clambered off. It was a fifteen-minute walk through a tunnel lighted by bulbs set in wall brackets. Three different collieries were operating at the moment, and Webster planned to take Geoffrey on a train down to the lowest level—Number Two Shaft. Even at this level some of the branch tunnels had carts pulled by ponies. In Number Two Shaft all the carts in the side galleries were operated by ponies and horses. As they rode through the narrow tunnels, Geoffrey could see that the ceiling was never higher than seven feet. He began to feel even more hemmed in. Already the air was heavy and damp. It clung to the skin like warm tea: invisible, but palpable.

The train came to a stop at a central point from which several tunnels branched off. Webster seemed to know exactly where he was going, and Geoffrey followed. Webster said he knew the colliery like the back of his hand. "The ponies never get lost either. I'll show you the stables if you like, so you'll feel satisfied that the animals are well cared for." Geoffrey asked if the horses didn't go blind from being underground so long.

"Not altogether," Webster said. "As we've pushed farther under the ocean, we've moved the stables forward so the ponies are as close to the mine face as possible. They never go above ground, though, unless they're sick."

"Where do you get the ponies?"

"From Newfoundland. The horses come from the west, mostly, from Saskatchewan, although a few are from Prince Edward Island. You'll see they don't have too far to go from the stables to the rail lines, and their maximum haul with loaded carts would be about fourteen hundred feet. They're not overworked, you know. That's not the problem. The problem is rats. Where you have feed for the ponies, you have rats. They're fed hay and oats, sometimes corn. That's what attracts rats."

As they moved along, Geoffrey took a more violent dislike to the hot and sticky air, to the patches of blackness that closed in upon him. He began to think about the ocean overhead and the fact that the chipped, muddy-brown ceiling, which sometimes showed in the light from his headlamp, was all that stood between him and millions of tons of water. Ahead he could hear the chip of men's picks against the rock face, and the whirring of the ventilating fans. Sometimes a man would shout at another or burst into a brief song.

The fire bosses went off together, leaving Geoffrey and Webster to tramp deeper into the tunnel. A track ran alongside them, and they stumped over the uneven floor into an ever-increasingly hostile air.

"There's always danger of gas," Webster was explaining as they walked. "Especially in these side galleries. It collects in pockets. You can't smell it. The men often say they *can* smell gas, but that's just superstition. They think it makes them feel cold and clammy. Well, maybe it does."

"Perhaps they have an instinct," Geoffrey said.

"Perhaps. In a place like this you can't blame men for having their little ideas, their funny ways."

As they pushed deeper into the gallery, Geoffrey felt more and more panicky. He could not recall ever having been so afraid. He had inspected various kinds of factories that the Courts owned or controlled, some of them extremely dirty and even dangerous, but nothing like this. Fort had gone north to inspect the gold mines at Courtsville, and at the time Geoffrey had been pleased that he hadn't been asked to do the job. He would never have dreamed of saying no to his father or his brothers, but on the other hand, he had been pleased that Fort was sent.

He could easily have sidestepped this tour of the mine. Webster had been against it and yet he felt compelled to see for himself. His father would expect a firsthand report. In a way, though, the tour would accomplish very little. As he followed Webster, he tried to imagine working down here in the dark heat and filth day after day, week after week, year after year. He shuddered at the idea that the lives of the miners were an endless parade of black and sooty hours —with all the additional hazards. He began to wish his father had not bought the mine, had stayed out of coal, but at the same time he understood why Sir Simon had made the deal. A rush of anger assailed him when he thought of trying to keep a mine open that might cost lives. Perhaps he did not want to solve Colleen Moore's problem by investing more money in Clover Valley. Better to face the prospect of moving her to Montreal if he could talk her into such a plan.

He was sweating heavily, and his face was running with moisture under the ill-fitting hat. His feet, unaccustomed to the draw of rubber boots, felt twice their normal size. The whole thing was rapidly becoming a nightmare, and he hoped he could remain calm so that Webster wouldn't see his reaction.

"I've told Mrs. Moore to take over the properties," he told Webster when they paused. "So I want you to back her all the way. She's to have the cottage rent free in payment for extra work. I've written a memorandum to that effect. It's in my papers back at the hotel."

"Certainly, you can depend on me to back her up. Now here"—he stopped to examine the coal face where there were some loose chips—"maybe you can see the quality of the coal. Take a chip and we'll compare it with some from another colliery later."

Geoffrey did as he was told and stuffed a chip into his overall pocket. The hat was gripping his forehead, biting into the flesh and giving him a headache. He could hear the ceaseless whirring of the fans.

"Is much water coming in? Is flooding a problem here?"

"As long as the pumps work, we're okay," Webster said.

Webster launched into a technical explanation of the pumping system, but Geoffrey's mind was fixed on the time when he could get back to the train and then to the elevator, which would take him to the surface. To the sunlight. They were now with a small group of men chipping at the coal face and in the crossed beams of their two headlamps they could see the picks swinging.

"We're about ready to blast again, Petrie," Webster said to one of the men. "You guys have pretty well cleaned out this gallery."

"Yeah, the next shift will have to blast."

"Only another three hours," Webster said encouragingly.

"Three hours and six minutes," the miner said, grinning.

"I'm showing Mr. Court around. He wanted to see how you fellows really work down here."

They passed the men, going ever deeper.

"The time must seem long to them," Geoffrey said.

"They're used to it," Webster said. "This is all they know. Want some coffee? I always bring a thermos along."

Webster gave him a cupful, and Geoffrey drank it. It tasted good down here in the darkness.

"Never know when you need coffee. I carry some rum, too, and aspirin. Even on a routine inspection."

They left the miners behind. Webster, standing so that his headlamp shone straight ahead, pointed out the end of the gallery. Another half-dozen men were at work there. It was the end of the world, Geoffrey thought, it was hell. He wanted to run back, but he fought down his panic.

Then it came.

Geoffrey was unaware of what was happening—the roar, the force, the deluge of rocks, bodies, and equipment were so sudden and so frightening! He was tossed upward in a hail of coal, rock, and timber. And he came down with such a thud that his bones felt shattered. The world was a mingled blackness where "up" could not be separated from "down," and there was no air. Only dust. He was choking on dust.

After what seemed like a lifetime of terrible noise and incredible dust and blackness, he found that he was sitting with his back against a rough wall. His hat had been knocked off and he could see nothing. There was no light. He pressed against the wall and knew there was stickiness on his hands. He assumed it was blood. At last, when the noise settled, he called out, "Webster!"

No reply. But in a few moments he heard a groan in the darkness without knowing from which direction it came.

"Webster!" he cried again.

"Over here."

A feeble, dust-choked voice.

"Are you all right, Webster?"

His eyes strained against the darkness, but still he could see nothing.

The sound of another human voice gave him courage. God, if he had been alone, he would have gone mad! He began to feel his legs and his body gingerly and decided he was intact.

"I'm stuck," Webster managed to say. "Can't move."

What in hell did that mean? He must find Webster. Webster would know what to do.

"You'll have to keep talking so I can find you," Geoffrey said.

Webster groaned. In the bitter black Geoffrey's nerve failed for a moment and he was afraid to move. Then he pulled himself together and began to crawl like a baby in the direction of Webster's voice. He heard a curious scuttling noise. But he knew that wasn't Webster, and he inched forward to the voice. Once he bumped his face on a piece of fallen timber and once something ran over his bare hand—clawlike, horrible. Rats. He remembered what Webster had said. There were rats because of the food for the ponies. He called again and Webster answered, but it was very deceptive.

"For Christ's sake, Webster, call out. I can't find you."

"Here, over here."

Geoffrey made agonizingly slow progress toward the voice. His right hand grasped a boot that he took to be Webster's foot, but when he explored the leg, it came to a clammy, horrible end. It wasn't attached to a body. A scuttling sound close by made him withdraw his hand quickly. He felt nauseated. But he crawled ahead toward the groans and cries Webster occasionally made.

He found Webster lying on his back. By exploring carefully with his hands he discovered that Webster's left arm was sandwiched between two pieces of timber, just above the elbow.

"Have you got a penknife?" Webster grated.

"No, but what for?"

"To cut off my arm."

He knew then that their situation was desperate. Webster said he could not stand the pain, that he wanted his arm cut off so he could be free. That he refused to lie here trapped in the dark and dust, with the rats running over his legs. But Geoffrey knew that even if he had a knife, he could not cut off the arm. The bone had to be sawed through. No, he could not free Webster unless he had help.

"That wouldn't work," Geoffrey said. "We'd have to

try to lift the timber. Where are your aspirins? And your flask? I'll give you something if I can find them."

"Yeah. First look for my headlamp. I've got an extra battery in my belt. We can put it in, if you find the lamp."

After a slow search Geoffrey found the hat and the headlamp and brought them back to Webster's side. Webster told him how to insert a new battery, and when he had it going, he shone it on Webster. Webster looked terrible, and there was no way that Geoffrey could lift the timbers by himself because of the rockfall. He gave Webster aspirin and some of the rum.

"Thank God for that," Webster said. "Save the light, though. Take a look around first and see how big this hole is. We'll figure something out. And get a stick or something to throw at those damned rats. We've got some in here with us."

Geoffrey flashed his headlamp around the hole to get an idea of the size. He saw the severed leg but no other sign of a human being. The bright eyes of the rats fixed him from one corner—sparkling and vicious. He gathered small rocks and a broken piece of wood and piled them beside Webster, ready to fend off the animals if they approached.

Gradually, the mine fell silent, and it was then that Geoffrey first heard faint voices from the other side of the rockfall that cut off one end of the tunnel. There were other survivors! He told Webster what he had heard and once more began his pilgrimage across the floor of the cave. It was hard to communicate, but he gathered there were four of them. They had a ventilator pipe on their side of the wall and were taking turns breathing through it. Also, they had found a small quantity of food—some cheese sandwiches, a squashed tomato, a bit of chocolate, and a can of water. With them were three dead miners. On his own side Geoffrey had already begun to notice the smell of death; it would not be long before the leg decayed in this heat and damp, he thought. He would try to cover it. But on the other hand, if the rats were hungry. . . . He gave up thinking about that. By shouting and pressing his ear to the rocks, he made a plan to excavate a hole at one end of the wall; they would work from their side and he from his. That way Geoffrey might be able to squeeze through.

There was nothing he could do for Webster but dole out the rum. Moving the rocks gave Geoffrey something to do. It was better than just sitting. He kept talking to Webster as much as he could, and he knew Webster was losing blood and getting weaker.

As the rocks were moved, he could hear the miners more clearly: They would sing a bit, joke, and pray. He figured that they spent four days like that. The water had run out by the time Geoffrey was able to get through the hole, but he breathed air from the ventilator pipe. All of them were reduced to drinking their own urine to moisten swollen mouths. Webster begged God to let him die. His cries (sometimes weak and sometimes stronger) broke through their time, punctured their thoughts. He apologized occasionally for making his friends miserable. The rum was gone.

On what Geoffrey took to be the fifth day, a miner called Jennings was making one more attempt to shout up the ventilator pipe. "For God's sake, somebody help us!"

Then the miracle occurred, for a thin sound came back down to them from above. Men were digging for survivors and had heard their cry. None of them could be sure how long it was after that (after those first tears of joy, those frail poundings on the back as they celebrated their rescue) that the copper tube was shoved down through the pipe. After the first flood of water, which Jennings caught in his hat, came coffee and then thin soup. They tried to obey instructions from above to drink slowly, but they were ravenous. They were galvanized by hope. Words came down to them from a disembodied spirit. They could hear banging and took that to mean that their friends on the surface were digging toward them.

That night Webster died.

They all grieved for Webster, but it was a relief not to hear his pitiful cries. Sounds of the approaching rescue team grew louder. They waited patiently now, only taking time to hurl a rock at one of the rats if it came too close. They sang a few songs. Jennings had taken over the job of catching whatever supplies came down the pipe because he seemed to be best at the trick.

As he sat with his back against the rock, Geoffrey began

to think again about keeping the mine open. He would have to find out how much damage the bump had done. He thought of Colleen and knew that the mine's closing would make her suffer. On the other hand, he could surely persuade her to travel to Montreal, and this kind of vision brought him a pleasant glow. To himself he swore that when he reached the surface, when he saw the sun again, his life would change. He would do more exciting things, he would be more affectionate, he would take risks. If only he could breathe again, up there, in the precious clean air above ground.

It was Jennings, sitting beside the pipe, who generated a fresh alarm.

"Does anybody else feel funny?"

"What do you mean funny?" somebody said. "We all feel terrible. How in hell would we know if we felt funny?"

"The place stinks, if that's what you mean," somebody else said.

"Christ, I don't mean that," Jennings said. "I feel cold. I feel cold in my bones."

Silence. They knew what he meant. A tension that had left them after the first flood of hope now returned in full force.

"Jennings, if this is some kind of joke, I'll kill you," one of the miners said.

"I wouldn't joke," Jennings said. "I feel cold."

"You mean gas? Is that what you mean?"

"Methane?" Geoffrey asked, sniffing the fetid air. But he could detect no new smell on top of the stench of filth and decay and dust. Coal gas had no odor. Everybody said that.

"I feel the coldness. Like snow in my veins. Do you see a kind of glow over there?"

They were sitting in the dark. The batteries had been dead a long time. The hush that had fallen deepened and spread, an invisible cloud in the blackness of the night. They all stopped talking. Sounds still filtered down from above, but in the tunnel a haze had begun to sap their minds, and the air grew as thick as cotton batten. Geoffrey could see pictures before his eyes—like dreams floating in a black sea. Strange pictures that flowed together, beautiful pictures of Colleen in Montreal and Geoffrey escorting her to a restaurant. How lovely she was!

He felt a damp and furry body slither over his hand. He paid no heed, not even attempting to strike the filthy thing with a rock he kept close by. Squeaks. And small bright eyes.

Colleen's face appeared before him.

"Colleen, come here. This way, Colleen!"

But she faded again, lost in the blackness, in the cold swamp of air that was rolling over him so slowly. He tried to move his hand, to grasp something real, and felt a furry body. It lay still. Of course, he thought in a moment of singular clarity, the rats would die first. It was some consolation to know that they would not live to gnaw on his body. A small triumph in this vast catastrophe.

He tried to cry out, to ask somebody for help. But in this pit there was no help, nobody to hear his plea. There were no more songs and no more prayers. Dimly, so very far away, he heard a banging noise. With a tremendous effort he tried to remember everyone he ought to pray for. That was the best thing to do. He was slipping away, floating softly into some outer darkness. The last vision that drifted through his mind was the vicious little eyes of the rats waiting for Webster to die. And there was silence in the tunnel.

CHAPTER TWENTY-TWO

Sir Simon had no hesitation in invading enemy territory when his cause was just. The armor of righteousness would protect him. He strode into the building that housed *Le Monde*, marched past the receptionist on the main floor and into the elevator. On the editorial level he bluffed past Honey's secretary, who sat outside the smallish cubicle she called an office, and flung open her door. He bawled out his case without preamble.

"When is this rag going to print the truth?"

His voice, scarcely diminished by age and weariness, bounced off the panes of glass.

"You call yourself a *publisher*?" he demanded.

Honey looked up sharply from the copy that lay on her desk, which she was reading for final approval. She had taken over supervision of all stories concerning the mine disaster, since it became known that her brother had been killed. Blame lay in some fuzzy area just beyond human reason. Since the mine had belonged once to Armand's holding company, she wished to be particularly careful about stories concerning dangerous conditions at Clover Valley.

The story she was handling was, in fact, the lead on Clover Valley scheduled for the front page, and the last person she expected to see materialize in her office on this hot August afternoon was her father.

"Papa!"

"Stop printing that garbage about the mine being *my* responsibility. You know godamned well the dangerous conditions were left over from your fancy husband's management."

"We didn't say that," Honey protested.

"You keep calling it a Court company! What the hell else do people think but that we ran some gimcrack operation? Well, it was your precious *Sir* Armand who ran a rotten ship. And if you don't put that in print, I'm going to find some newspaper that will!"

He was enraged now, his words flowing quickly, his face red, his eyes alight with the fire of his crusade.

"We haven't laid the blame—" she began.

"Your own brother was killed!" he cried. "Have you no feelings left at all? Have these heathens completely destroyed your soul? Well, I suppose they have. What can anybody expect? Some Court *you* turned out to be!"

"I'm no longer a Court. You saw to that, Papa." Honey was stung by his injustice. "You've made it clear every time we meet that I'm not a Court."

"Truth is truth," he said, shifting his argument. "And I expect you to have the decency to print it. Nothing else would have brought me to this office."

"We have a reporter at the scene. I read everything written about the disaster. What more can I do?"

"Your own brother!" Sir Simon said again, abandoning any rules of debate in favor of his temper. "What have you to say about Geoffrey?"

"I feel deeply about Geoffrey," Honey said, mustering her dignity. She had become pale. She felt terribly old and incapable of dealing with this intrusion. Although her skin was still good, tight over her cheekbones, her eyes had taken on a tired look, as if they could no longer bear to look on the world around her without sighing inwardly. Her blond-gray hair was stylishly cut, her mouth still wide and a trifle sensuous. She was a handsome woman, but she looked exhausted.

"You know that I feel deeply about Geoffrey," she repeated.

"Deeply enough to tell the truth to the world?" Sir Simon pressed, facing her across her paper-strewn desk like some elderly avenging angel. "It was Armand's fault. Every horror that has happened to my family seems to be Armand's fault. I think he's some devil sent to torment me. I sent Geoffrey out to Clover Valley to set things right, and this is the result."

"It has nothing to do with Armand. John Bead was looking after the company affairs out there."

"St. Amour knew the mine was in wretched condition when he sold it to me," Sir Simon went on remorselessly. "Did you know the electrical system failed the day before the disaster?"

"No, I didn't."

"Ha," he said triumphantly, "I thought you didn't. It has been faulty for years. Faulty when we bought it."

"You insisted on getting control of Clover Valley, even though you knew it lost money. I know that much. You demanded that Armand sell the stake at Courtsville, you—"

"I didn't want that stinking coal mine, you fool! But it was the only way I could get that crooked husband of yours to part with the piece of my gold mine he owned. He wanted to hold that property so he could torture me. Buying Clover Valley was a form of blackmail. Pure and simple. That's the kind of man he is. To think they made him a knight of the realm! Bah! Why don't they knight the savages in the South Seas? It would make just as much sense."

"Armand didn't blackmail you, and that is a terrible thing to say, Papa! You turn everything around to make it favorable to yourself."

"Armand is putting all his money in sugar," Sir Simon said, implying that this was illegal by the tone of his voice. "And I only hope he rots for it."

"How do you know that?"

"I make it my business to know these things. I tell you

it was blackmail. What would I want with a pit in Nova Scotia, at the end of the world? Poor-quality coal, unsafe mine, losing proposition. It just shows to what lengths your husband will go to make an old man miserable. But at least I intended to make it safe or shut it down, which is more than *he* did. That's why Geoff was there, as you very well know. And like a Court, he insisted on going down to see the conditions for himself."

"Armand left the mine's management to his partner."

"And why did they keep it open?"

"Because the miners begged them to. Did you know that? They begged John Bead to keep the mine going, even though they knew it wasn't safe."

"And why would an owner listen to a laborer? Tell me that if you can. Bead is an American, and *they'll* do anything. I always said so. No brains, no leadership. Do *you* ask your printer's devil what you should print in an editorial? I hope not. You don't ask the animals how to run the farmyard."

Honey pushed the copy away from her and stood up, as if to dismiss him. There was no use going on with the discussion. No argument with her father was ever resolved. He would always come back to the point he wished to make, despite all arguments from the other side.

"Let's get to the point," Sir Simon said, lowering his voice to what he fondly imagined was a pitch of reason. "Are you going to publish the facts or am I? Are you going to put the blame for this atrocity squarely where it belongs? On Arcan, your husband's company? Or am I going to have it printed somewhere else?"

Honey, wavering slightly before this fresh tirade, made a half-hearted reply.

"You know I can't print a story like that."

"Fifty men died in that disaster as well as Geoffrey. What about *them*? Whose responsibility is that? What about the widows and orphans?"

She was stung to remind him of his own guilt.

"And whose responsibility is it to look after the widows and orphans killed by *your* Ramsay rifle? I don't see you doing anything about that, Papa. What about my son? *Your* rifle cost my son his life! I didn't print that!"

But he blazed on, shameless in his use of other people's tragedy. War was war, and mining was mining, and this could have been prevented, he roared. It suited him at this moment to offer as a sacrifice the victims of the Clover Valley disaster. It did not suit him to think about the scandalous Ramsay rifles he had manufactured during the war. *These* widows and orphans were Armand's burden.

"Papa," she interrupted, shouting to make herself heard, "I must ask you to leave."

"Not before I get the satisfaction I came for. A woman publisher has no judgment. What can I expect? Why do I look for justice when there is only blindness? Well, I'm going to a decent newspaper and I'm going to make the facts public. Let your Sir Armand see what he can make of that!"

"I'm sure he can handle it. Now please go."

"A title for building a few miles of railroad," Sir Simon huffed, referring to Armand's contribution during the Great War. "What's it mean? Nothing. It's the same with Laurier. *Sir* Wilfrid Laurier! Just because he was a makeshift Frenchie politician. Any fool can get elected, God knows. That's the flaw in a democracy. You see it every day. We ought to rule by oligarchy. That's the only answer, rule by the elite, though how the Greeks ever thought of it is beyond me."

Honey was almost capable of smiling at this remark. Her father's chauvinism never failed to astound her even after all these years. He was frozen in time like a fossil in a rock. She supposed he would remain so until the day he died. Wars, famines, terrible calamities, would have absolutely no effect upon his opinion.

"You're impossible!" she cried.

"*I'm* impossible?" He was outraged.

"You're a bigoted old man, you're an antique. All you know is family and power. You think being an Englishman makes you divine. You're nothing but a relic, and a sad one at that!"

She thought she had gone too far. He turned purple with rage and looked very much as if he were going to have a heart attack.

"Don't tell me what I am, you treacherous vixen!" he managed through a breathless but still loud voice. "You're not even married, as far as I'm concerned. Churched by some pagan priest, in a heathen establishment! I don't call that marriage!"

"That makes your favorite granddaughter a bastard," she said, hurling at him the only piece of ammunition that came to mind.

"What?"

"Susan."

"How dare you say anything about Susan? She's a fine girl, though you wouldn't know. How she came to be that way, being raised among the Frenchies, I don't know. I can only assume that blood tells. Court blood."

Honey sank back in her chair, totally exhausted.

"Please leave. I'll print the facts as I understand them. That's all I have to say."

"And I'll print the facts if I have to buy a newspaper to do it!"

"Well, you've done that before, only it was to conceal the facts," she cried, referring to the purchase of *Le Monde* as her own wedding present. Afterward she had discovered Sir Simon gave her the newspaper because it was on the verge of printing a scandal about the Courts, and Sir Simon rightly decided that Honey would stop the story once she owned the paper.

"As for Geoffrey's funeral," he threw at her from the door, "you and your family are not welcome. Do not show up at the cathedral, or I'll have you thrown out. And that includes Angela."

With this, he took his leave, knowing that once again he had had the last word, that he had wounded her.

She thrust the story from her and sent for Gabriel, her editor. She turned the remainder of the work over to him, saying she felt ill. Gabriel, an old friend as well as employee, had seen Sir Simon leave and knew the cause of her distress, but he did not discuss it. And Honey knew that it was useless to try to make important decisions after the scene she had just been through. That whole problem, the stories and the editorial on the mine disaster, would be better done by Gabriel.

In the spring Honey and Armand had finally been able to move into their redesigned house on the Mountain. More than a year of planning and renovation had produced Edenbridge, a mock Victorian mansion. Although she was well aware that she could not duplicate the grandeur of Pride's Court, Honey had supervised the production of a gracious house with commodious reception rooms and elegant bedrooms and baths. She was reasonably well satisfied.

Edenbridge boasted a vast drawing room with two fireplaces, oak paneling, and finely worked plaster ceiling. It was not yet completely furnished, some pictures and antiques were still due to arrive from London and Paris. On one side of this main reception area was a sunny morning room facing east, filled with tropical plants and featuring two enormous antique breakfronts where the valuable china was kept under lock and key. Beyond that the Long Gallery stretched out to form a windowed room with a Steinway grand as its jewel. Honey saw it as a salon and thought that someday Beau might play there for his family and friends. At present, however, Angela occupied one end of it with her easel and some of her paints and equipment.

On the day of Geoffrey's funeral Honey retired to her apartment on the second floor. She could not keep her mind off the family gathering at Christ Church Cathedral, the crowds she knew would be there, her father's insistence on formal mourning, the whole dismal ritual of a great family tragedy. And though she knew it would be painful, she wanted to be part of the family in this terrible time. But she was an outcast.

In the pale blue bedroom with the cream furniture and woodwork, created to bring out the color of her eyes and hair, she undressed wearily in the late afternoon and ran a bath. She tossed a handful of expensive French bath salts into the sunken tub and the scent of roses permeated the room: sweet, insistent, deliciously heady. While she waited for the tub to fill, she pinned up her hair and looked with a certain amount of dismay at the colorless face, the expressionless eyes that confronted her. She wanted to weep, but tears had not come yet. As she lay in the perfumed water, she derived little comfort from the fact that her body was still good. Nothing helped settle the churning in her stomach. It was odd, she thought, how grief seemed to gather in that particular organ, and yet what had sadness to do with the stomach? It was ridiculous.

Yes, she ought to have been present at Geoffrey's funeral, in memory of their childhood years, in memory of their mother, who was dead, in memory of the whole

Court dynasty. It was wrong for Papa to have outlawed her like this. She could imagine them all: Sir Simon towering in his sorrow but leading the family into the pews in majesterial fashion; Mary, a wan black-veiled widow; Mildred, stark and imposing and no doubt clinging to North, who would follow Sir Simon like the crown prince. The twins, of course, mysterious and sly, sheltered behind veils that would only make them seem elusive and desirable; Charity (who, she had heard, was already causing concern with her wild behavior), trim and pretty and not as sad as she ought to be over her father's death. Noel and young Simon, stoic, solid, Courts to the core. Oh, she could see them all in her mind's eye. The great Court family, stared at and admired by curious strangers and staunch friends.

Yet, she longed to be part of it. Even if she could assess it somewhat dispassionately, there was an invisible cord that kept her attached to her relatives, though she seldom saw them. She had never felt close to the St. Amours. Her father's dire prediction that they were foreigners and would always remain so had come true.

When she stepped out of the bath, her mood had not improved, and in fact she was closer to crying than she had been before. In a way, she thought it would be better if she did cry; that would at least release her from this awful tension. But then her face would be a wreck for dinner. It would, as her mother had said years before, be "giving in." Instead, she put on a cerulean blue night-gown and negligee and lay down on the chaise longue.

As she lay with her eyes closed, she wondered if she should go to Angela. Angela had her painting and was probably working on a canvas in the Long Gallery at this very moment instead of pining away in her bedroom. Even Angela had better things to do than go over old wounds and dig up old memories. At this, Honey felt a surge of self-pity and the tears came under the lids and trickled down her cheeks. She thought of Geoffrey as a little boy who had always been pushed around by Charles and Fort. Even by Honey herself. She had often laughed at Geoffrey, teased him, frightened him, and manipulated him. He had been the dull one of the group, and she had given what love she had for siblings to Fort. *He* was the witty one, the brave one, the imaginative one. Fort could do everything better—swim, sail, ride, create games, and outwit the grown-ups. Poor Geoff had always trailed behind, looking for attention, trying to compete in a sternly competitive situation that was overwhelming. Even Mama had not liked Geoffrey very much, Honey thought upon reflection. The thought wounded her. Mama had done her best to be fair and kind—even, in her own manner, affectionate.

And so Geoffrey had lived a plain, uneventful life. Not a touch of romance anywhere. You could hardly call his marriage to Mary romantic. The children had been dull, as well, if one were honest about it. Although Mildred was showing considerable style now that she was married and running Pride's Court. (So Fort had told her when they last chatted on the telephone.)

In the midst of these thoughts she heard Armand come into the room. She did not open her eyes, but lay like some medieval effigy; pale, lusterless, half-dead. She heard his footsteps on the carpet and, though she tried, could not stop the tears.

"Chérie!"

He knelt beside her, taking her hands in his. His voice, as always, was soft and musical, flowing smoothly over her like a tropical stream. She felt slightly soothed by his presence and opened her eyes to look at him. *Dear God,* she thought, *how handsome he still is! How distinguished!*

"You are crying for Geoffrey?"

"Partly," she managed to say. There was no way she could explain to Armand all her regrets, the thousand sighs that had piled up over the years when she thought of her break with the Courts. "I should have been at the funeral."

"I know, darling, I know."

He kissed her fingers and then took out his folded white handkerchief and wiped at her eyes.

"You *are* kind, Armand," she managed to say, but there was still an edge of disaffection in her voice. She had been, mentally, at least, cut off from the St. Amours in her mind. She had been so completely immersed in thoughts of her own family that she felt he was an intruder. "I still miss them. Even Papa, although I hate him, too, for all the cruel things he's done."

He kissed her cheek, and she did not turn away from him. The kiss, beginning chastely, became more passionate and she resisted, but Armand would not free her from his embrace and slowly she slipped into the familiar comfort, drifting from the sharp shores of reality into a kinder, sweeter place. As Armand caressed her, she felt again the sweeping urgency that had always drawn her to him, shot through with waves of grief. As he picked her up to carry her to the bed, she gave herself up to him without reservation. And as Armand paid homage to her secret splendors, she knew that her passion for her husband was still the first thing in her life.

By early evening the sky had cleared. A short, violent shower had made it unwise to take supper in the garden, as Honey had planned, and she ordered it served in the Morning Room, which, for some reason, had become a room they used at all hours. It was always bright and welcoming no matter what the weather, and since it was not too large and was accessible to the kitchens, she had found it most useful.

Angela was still painting, working on a brilliant portrait of Beau. The subject made Honey nervous, a sign that Angela had not recovered from her obsession, but she had to admit that it was a gripping picture. Angela did not comment on it, and Honey wondered if she ever thought (instead of Beau) of her husband, who was still in England. Letters came from Dorian at odd intervals, in which he begged her to come back, promising her the world in return for her presence in his house. The letters were pitiful. Angela had shown a couple of them to Honey, and Honey had not been able to finish reading them. She did not like to see a man or a woman lose dignity. What else could this inane pleading be called?

"Why do I feel so depressed?" Angela asked, putting down her brushes and turning to her aunt. "Is it because of Uncle Geoffrey? I wasn't that close to him."

"Partly, darling. He was family. We're attached in an invisible way to family members whether we like to admit it or not. Look at me. I've been down all day about not being at the funeral, and yet if I'd been there, it would have been equally painful. I'm afraid we don't always make sense."

"Probably you're right. Perhaps I'm having a premonition about Dorian. I suppose I'm going to get another one of those awful letters."

"Well, you *did* marry him, Angela. You must take responsibility for that. You ought to see a lawyer about getting an annulment."

"It's the kind of private thing I can't bear to discuss—you know, the sort of thing I'd have to tell a lawyer."

"You'll have to face up to it sometime."

"If I go back to England . . . perhaps later it won't seem so distasteful. I thought I was solving something, marrying Dorian, but it didn't work," Angela said, sourly, cleaning her brushes. "I think I've done enough for today. Do you like the portrait? I've never done one of Beau that satisfied me, you know. He has such a marvelous face."

"It's easy to see why you'd want to paint him," Honey said noncommittally. "Come along, darling, and change for supper. We're only having something light in the Morning Room. Armand is home, so there's no need to wait."

Angela walked beside her aunt along the carpeted expanse of the Long Gallery. She could see across the drawing room through the adjoining doors and into the Morning Room. A lightness, a weightlessness that was dreamlike possessed the house in the late afternoon. It was a serene feeling, and she loved it. How fortunate she was to be taken in by Aunt Miel and Uncle Armand and allowed to live here! Angela thought. Fussed over and cared for despite the fact that she was a runaway (out of favor with her father, Charles, and her grandfather, Sir Simon).

"You know, Aunt Miel," she said as they walked toward the oak staircase that led to the second floor, "I'll always love Beau. It was foolish of me to try to live with another man. Beau is part of me. It's that simple and I ought to have known."

Honey felt her spirits plummet. So that was the way it was, then, and there was to be no end to this wild attachment between Beau and Angela. It was like waiting for a bomb to go off, she thought, merely a pause before another explosion that would shatter everyone's calm. She sighed and kissed her niece on the cheek and patted her arm.

"Go and change, dear, and come down in a few minutes."

"I've annoyed you. I'm sorry. I merely told the truth."

"Tonight isn't the night I want to think about it," Honey said.

When they were sitting at the table, Angela absent-mindedly pushed her food around her plate and stared intermittently out of the window. Honey, catching her distracted air, suddenly realized how thin the girl was. Her skin was translucent, like fine silk stretched tightly over bones one was not usually aware of. *She's consumed with thoughts of Beau,* Honey thought a trifle wildly, *and nothing has changed. Dorian doesn't even exist for her.*

Aloud she said, "Eat up your chicken, and your asparagus."

"Pardon? Oh, yes. I was thinking."

"Wine, Angela? I opened a bottle of Pouilly-Fumé. I thought it might cheer up your aunt, since she likes it so much," Armand offered.

"No, thank you, Uncle Armand. I don't care much for wine these days."

"Well, I won't press you. Can't waste it on people with no sense of appreciation."

Honey's attention was now drawn to her niece. "What are you doing this evening?" Honey asked.

"Reading, I guess," Angela said.

She had no friends her own age, Honey reflected, and that wasn't natural. Angela never seemed to need to go out with young people. She was, in a way, very old in spirit, although she did not look that way. All her time was consumed in painting, reading, or going for walks in the park.

Angela left them after supper, and Honey and Armand decided to take coffee and brandy in the library. Armand was reading reports and Honey was trying to read some poetry when Georgina, the maid on duty for the evening, brought a letter that had come by special delivery from *Le Monde*. Honey took it and gave Armand a look that indicated she was reluctant to read it. It could only mean trouble, she thought, and tonight she did not want to make any decisions about the paper. Especially if it had anything to do with a report of Geoffrey's funeral for the next day's edition or about Clover Valley Mine.

The postmark, however, was a London one. And a new fear intruded. Something to do with Beau? Michel and Clarissa were now established at Lakehurst, New Jersey, so it couldn't be from them. She tore it open, fear stirring in the pit of her stomach.

It was from John Leach in London, and his message was so frightening that she could not, at first, grasp it. She read the letter twice while Armand waited, and then she handed it to him, her mouth set, her eyes large with disbelief.

Armand read:

Dear Lady St. Amour:

I am writing to inform you of my arrival next Tuesday, September 3, bringing your nephew, Beau Dosquet. The circumstances are so critical that I have taken upon myself to bring him on the first boat without asking your permission. He will not go to his mother's farm and has agreed to come to you, or he will not leave London. He cannot stay here.

It is so tragic, and so difficult to explain. But he has gone deaf and the doctors call it "hysterical deafness," which I take to mean he has gone deaf from shock. Sir Thomas premiered the War Symphony four days ago, and I believe it was the reception of the work that put him into a state of hysteria. Unfortunately, the work is ahead of its time. The performance was poor (the whole thing reminds me of Rachmaninoff's experience in St. Petersburg, when his *Symphony No. 1* was introduced to the public by Glazunov—the performance was bad and nobody thought well of the work and Rachmaninoff had a nervous breakdown) and the audience actually booed the work in the jazz section. I don't know if you know what London audiences are like—they can be cruel.

Beau left before the symphony ended and walked apparently alone along the embankment. I gather he was frantic. He remembered a party being given for him and Sir Thomas at the Savoy and did manage to go there. The first thing he heard when he entered the room was criticism, so I gather. It was then he went deaf. Nobody knows how to cure this. They say another shock will do it, perhaps, but again, nobody knows what kind of shock. All very sad, and Beau is almost unmanageable. I probably don't need to tell you what kind of response he has had to this handicap. I fear at times he might kill himself. Therefore, I have made him promise to return to Montreal, and to you. This is the best I can do, Lady St. Amour, and I hope you understand my concern.

Yours sincerely,
John Leach

P.S. We are booked on the *Empress of Scotland*.

"This is terrible," Armand said, folding the letter and putting it down on a table nearby. "Thank God he has this friend Leach. He's so high-strung—"

"Oh, Armand, what a ghastly thing! This is the worst thing that could happen to a man like Beau. To be deaf! How on earth will he compose?"

Armand, searching for some gleam of hope, said, "Didn't Beethoven work when he was deaf?"

"Yes, but he was older. More secure. I think he actually wrote the Appassionata after he went deaf. But Beau . . . at his stage he might do anything. I'm thankful this Leach has enough courage and concern to bring him back here!"

"Honey, we must take him in. But what about Angela?"

"Oh, darling, I haven't had time to think about that. We can't have them under the same roof, surely? There are limits to what I'm prepared to accept."

"Anyway, we can't stop him from coming. We must be calm, and not worry about how they will behave until we see what condition Beau is in. He may have to go to a hospital."

"That's true. How shall we tell her?"

"Not tonight. Let her sleep tonight. Here, have a brandy. The occasion calls for it."

Honey, who did not usually enjoy brandy, took it gratefully.

"Perhaps it won't last," she said hopefully, referring to Beau's condition. "We must pray for a cure."

"I'll leave that to you," Armand said, making a wry mouth. "You can be in charge of it. My sisters have always been head of the prayer division in our family."

Honey slumped down into the plump, velvet-covered armchair. "It just shows we don't know when we're well off."

"Perhaps things will look better in the morning," Armand said without much conviction.

"You know perfectly well they'll look worse," Honey said, thinking of some way to tell Angela the terrible news. "God knows how Angela will take it."

"Have a nightcap," Armand said, proffering the decanter of brandy again. "It will help you sleep."

"Yes, I will. Sleep is going to be difficult."

In the Long Gallery Angela was concentrating fiercely on the portrait. Ever since she had been told of Beau's illness, a trance had overtaken her, cutting off the pain. (It was difficult for Honey to decide which was more worrisome, Beau's deafness or Angela's catatonic response to the news.) Angela continued to paint despite her mood, and the portrait steadily improved. She had caught Beau's elusive animality, the churning desperation at his feverish core. He glared back from the canvas as if he were slightly mad, a creature in flight from unnamed demons.

She stood with her back to the gallery, brush in hand, looking intently at her work. The door behind her opened and she heard it but did not turn to investigate. A sixth sense told her who it was; she could feel the waves of his presence reach out to her. She stopped breathing and bit her lip with the effort to remain still. Let him come to her. Even now she must exercise this small bit of restraint.

His steps on the carpet were muffled. When he was so near that the scent of him, his body warmth, touched her, she turned, knowing what she would see. The unruly black curls, the voluptuous mouth, the flaming green eyes.

"Beau!" she whispered.

"I can't hear you." His voice had taken on an odd tone now that he spoke without hearing his own words. It had diminished, was thinner, lacking resonance and timbre. They stared at each other like two statues, and the painting echoed Beau's face in a taunting manner.

They moved toward each other at the same time, arms wrapped about slender bodies, each of them as fragile as the other, it seemed. She felt the rigidity of his frame, a petrified living being. They both began to weep, pressing their cheeks together, running lips hungrily over the well-loved planes of beautiful faces from a happier past.

"Angela, what will I do?"

It was a muted scream of agony. She had no answer, and all she could do was hold him close and try to offer comfort. For him that was scarcely enough. Only perfection, only *everything* life had to offer, was enough for Beau. His art demanded it.

"It will be all right," Angela murmured over and over. But the words were empty, and a knife was turning somewhere in her body sending jagged little messages of pain in all directions.

"I can't hear what you're saying."

"We'll have to write messages," she said uncertainly.

"I can't hear my own music."

"Other musicians have composed when they were deaf, and blind, and ill."

"Stop talking," he said angrily. "Don't bother! Don't you understand? It only makes it worse!"

My God, how will I reach him? she thought in agony. *How will I offer comfort to him if he can't hear and won't try to communicate?* They stood like that for a long time. Angela had no desire to carry the passion to any conclusion. She sensed that Beau felt the same. This was a hiatus, and the truly physical side of their love was suspended. *There is relief in that,* she thought *because I don't think I could bear to have any intimate relationship with Beau when he's like this. Not here in this house.* It wasn't right, and it would not help. That much she understood.

Later, when she spoke to Honey, Angela explained this briefly. "We aren't living together, Aunt Miel. I want you to understand that. There's nothing like that going on. So you needn't worry. I can't explain it. We just don't . . . well, I suppose Beau is mortally wounded. And that part of his life doesn't exist right now."

Honey was forced to explain this later to Armand, who was concerned about a scandal. "After all, *chérie,* she is another man's wife. Nothing has changed in that regard."

"There's nothing physical in what they have now," Honey told him. "She told me so. Angela doesn't lie. I sensed that when I saw them together."

"That's rubbish," Armand said, speaking as a man.

"No it isn't! Every man isn't like you. You shouldn't judge others by your own appetites." She was angry.

"You've never objected to my appetites."

"That isn't the point."

275

"What *is* the point?"

"Beau is a genius. Now he's ill because of what has happened to him. The doctors apparently told him his hearing would come back, but it will take another shock."

"A success or a failure?" Armand asked skeptically.

"Don't be nasty," Honey said, still cross with Armand for his unforgiving attitude. "You don't understand. But don't criticize when you don't know what you're talking about."

"What about his mother? Is she to be told? Or are you planning to hide him here at Edenbridge?" Armand demanded.

"Beau will decide when he wants to see the family. He isn't ready at the moment. He'll tell me. Armand, I want to protect him as much as I can."

"Aren't you playing God?"

"Not if Beau asks for privacy. It's his decision, not mine. When he's ready to face Justine and Timothée, he'll say so."

Throughout the autumn Beau remained a recluse at Edenbridge. During the day he worked at the piano, trying to compose. His moods fluctuated wildly from hope to ferocious tantrums. He had taken to reading what Angela wrote on pieces of paper, but his own replies were usually abrupt and often ugly. His rage permeated the house.

When letters arrived from Dorian, Angela hid them. She knew that it would only excoriate the unbearable wound if Beau knew about Dorian's pleas. She had told him only that Dorian was in England and that the marriage was over. Beyond that, they did not talk about it. This other problem, Beau's handicap, was much more urgent. The marriage seemed a minor thing in comparison.

By Christmas Honey had convinced Beau that he ought to see his family, and when he reluctantly agreed, she made plans for a huge family party at Edenbridge. Everyone promised to come; even Helene and Corbin said they would make the journey from Ottawa and forego some of the festivities there that Helene still loved so much. But nothing had really changed with respect to Beau's problem. He was working on his abandoned opera, *Héloïse and Abélard*, and he went nowhere.

CHAPTER TWENTY-THREE

In the civic election of 1924 the political mood of Montreal had darkened and swung from the Liberal to the Conservative camp. Brash, antic, loquacious Mayor Médéric Martin, with his delightful public capers (he had once seized a platform paid for by his opponent to deliver his own flamboyant rallying cry), was out after ten years of power. In his place appeared a careful man. Excruciatingly dull and certainly no arch-Conservative, Charles Duquette was, nevertheless, a loyal right-wing lieutenant. He had once been in the shoe business, and now was president of the Alliance Nationale, a mutual insurance society. His appearance, his ability to sway an audience, left much to be desired in the way of entertainment, but at the polls, where it counted, Duquette won by a narrow margin.

For during his mighty reign scandal had blighted the fabled Martin image. The dancing, prancing political juggler, Man of the People, had himself become suspect. During his 1918 mayoralty campaign Martin had declared that he would "drive the money-changers from the temple" —there had been that little matter of men in high places reaping taxpayers' dollars from the sale of land for Maisonneuve Park, he pointed out repeatedly—yet after his election he fell strangely silent on the issue.

People in the street, readers of newspapers and periodicals, began to whisper that it was odd that Sir Lomer Gouin, key figure in the provincial Liberal machine, had appointed Martin a life member of the Legislative Council so soon after his last success at the polls. *Too* odd, you might say. *Too* convenient. This along with a pretty shove during the 1924 election from Conservative newspapers that persistently ridiculed Martin in editorials and cartoons, and from ubiquitous popular songs that derided him, brought him down at last.

The victory of Duquette in Montreal was hailed by Conservatives across the country as a rosy weathervane for the next federal election. In November 1924, there had been that regrettable incident of the contraband alcohol, all sixteen thousand gallons of it, passing duty-free from Quebec City to Montreal, where it would eventually be turned into drinkable whisky and shipped to the United States. Probably the cargo had originated on the French-owned island of St.-Pierre, just off the southern coast of Newfoundland. Nobody knew for sure. However that might have been, a federal customs officer named Bisaillon ousted the provincial investigators from the cargo vessel and took over the situation himself on behalf of Ottawa. The two Americans who said they owned the shipment escaped. The whole affair was mossy with decadence and connivance. Bisaillon was not fired by the ministry, as people had expected, and so the powerful Montreal Commercial Protective Association rose up in wrath, demanding justice. So did the Montreal Board of Trade and the Canadian Manufacturers' Association. What, exactly, were the Liberals doing up there in Ottawa? Had the prime minister no shame? But King wore blinders in many matters and would not listen.

Sir Simon, a noisy member of the Protective Association from its inception, watched all these performances with glee. To his way of thinking, the crooked Liberal prime minister, William Lyon Mackenzie King, was busily weaving his own noose, digging his own grave, and knocking nails in his own coffin. It was only a matter of time before the demagogue fell. The handwriting, he was wont to say, was on the wall.

Yes, from the point of view of Sir Simon and all the Courts, and of all their powerful financial allies, the pendulum was swinging back in the right direction. At his club Sir Simon said it, and his cronies agreed wholeheartedly. It was high time, too, before the wretched country sank from sight beneath the intolerable weight of scoundrels and influence peddlers, witlings and conjurers, pimps and pirates.

The Sunday before Christmas 1924 fell bright and clear. Sir Simon had summoned his entire family to Pride's Court for a significant dinner. He had been seething with excitement since the letter had arrived at his office in the Empire Bank Building, but he refused to make the announcement to his family without all the formal trappings the situation demanded.

More than a year had passed since Geoffrey's death. He

had taken that hard, but it had seemed to him during the hot, despairing August that he had borne so many terrible fateful stabs over the years he was becoming almost immune. He could not be expected to crumble now. He had remedies for pain. One was the delicious announcement he was about to make; everyone who counted would eventually know that at last he was to be recognized for what he was.

He was to be elevated to the position he had coveted for most of his adult life. It would be a bitter pill for some people to swallow, especially that brigand Armand St. Amour. Which brought him to one of his other remedies for pain: dwelling upon the ruin of his son-in-law. For Sir Simon now entertained the most vicious hatred for Armand St. Amour that it was possible for a man to harbor and still remain sane. It would take time, of course, to bring Armand down, but he was laying the groundwork. There were no lengths to which he was not prepared to go to see Armand punished. This man, this *French magpie*, had cost him more time and money, more anguish of soul, than any other single human being in his entire lifetime. St. Amour must be destroyed.

But that, for the moment, was in suspension. Revenge would wait. It grew sweeter by the year, like vintage port. This celebration he had in mind was one of peculiar triumph for Sir Simon, and he wanted every detail to be right—every arrangement made to enhance the moment.

All the Courts were home for Christmas. Sir Simon had insisted on it. A few relatives were staying in the great house, and a few in the coach house, where Mary had been living since Geoffrey's death. Even Susan and David had been prevailed upon to leave their own house in charge of servants and move into Pride's Court along with little Anthony and his nanny, Rose Starkey. (They shared the huge third-floor nursery with Nanny Redman and young Nicholas Grenville-Court.)

North barely managed to conceal his pleasure when Susan and David moved in. He was not exactly subtle, Mildred thought angrily, he was as transparent as glass. But North—easy, charming, nipping into the expensive scotch and fine wines provided by his lavish relative, ambling about Pride's Court like a crown prince, handsome, delightfully apt in every social situation, capable of catering to Mildred in the most heartwarming way most of the time and retreating into silence when he failed—*this* North could not be controlled with as hard a hand as Mildred would have liked. *She* was too passionate about him. *He* was too incapable of genuine passion.

Mildred was eight months pregnant, and Sir Simon (looking for an excuse to draw the family net closer about him) said he thought she needed assistance with such large-scale Christmas entertaining. It was his idea that Susan ought to be recruited.

No amount of protest on Mildred's part had swayed him, and she was overruled. But she was furious. She despised Susan and suspected her of all sorts of treacheries. She was jealous of Susan's beauty, her consummate style, her musical laugh; but most of all she was jealous of the way North looked at Susan every time she appeared. Mildred would have preferred to work herself into a stupor over the holiday arrangements than take help from Susan or have the woman as a guest in her house. But the difficulty was, Pride's Court was her home without quite being her castle. As long as Sir Simon was alive, she would never have the final word about anything.

For many meals there would be eighteen people at table. The accompanying strain on the servants or on the nerves of various family members did not disturb Sir Simon. He had never considered such things. On top of the ordinary requirements he had piled a heavy, nostalgic demand. He had, in his moment of triumph, harked back to the days of his childhood in England with his father, Sir Cathmor, and his mother, Lady Court. He longed for a touch of the true Victorian spirit. Special dishes must be prepared for the Sunday feast. Difficult things to make, magnificent foods to look at and savor. Mildred had had her instructions and she had worked with the cook to produce the dishes Sir Simon demanded.

Not all the family was housed in Pride's Court, of course. Fort, Sydney, the twins, and Landry, along with an English friend from Oxford who had come out on a Court ship for Christmas, were remaining in Mellerstain. They would attend all important dinners. Mary had sold their house and now lived in the coach house, which Sir Simon had enlarged and modernized. Charity was still at home for holidays, naturally, and Noel stayed with his mother when he was in Montreal. Simon II made his home in Kirkland Lake and Courtsville. He had become engaged in the autumn to a girl called Chris McLeary, whom Sir Simon found totally unsuitable. But Mary, with her usual complacency, did not seem to mind. And Noel refused to comment, merely shrugging his shoulders and saying it was young Simon's business.

In the frosted air of late afternoon Pride's Court rose like a fairy-tale castle. Blue shadows made sculpture of the deep snowbanks in the garden and behind the towers, the last feeble rays of winter sun picked out diamonds on the roof. Dozens of windows were alight on every floor of the house. In some, wreaths were hung, or garlands of holly. In the great drawing room the enormous tree bloomed with rainbow lights, shimmering little halos of ethereal color.

The Courts gathered in the Red Sitting Room for pre-dinner drinks and to await the latecomers, or they stood about admiring the tree. Mildred had done a marvelous job of decorating, everyone agreed. Sir Simon compared it favorably to the lavish preparations Lady Court had made when she was alive, which was, after all, the greatest compliment he could pay. Despite her heaviness, and her exhaustion, Mildred was pleased. She wanted to be a credit to her grandfather and to North. She wanted, especially, to have North realize how much she contributed. Oh, perhaps she wasn't beautiful the way Angela was, or pretty the way Susan was, or grand the way the famous Aunt Miel was. But she had managed, in a short time, to pull all the strings of Pride's Court, to make it work, to keep life smooth and easy for Sir Simon, for Uncle Charles, and—most particularly—for North.

They knew he had important news. He simmered with it. No one, not even Charles, knew exactly what it was. While the old man was out of the room, there was speculation, but as soon as he appeared, they stopped talking. He had his own way of doing these things and they respected that. Still, some kind of momentous announcement hung in the air.

Sir Simon, always the showman, insisted on waiting until they were all at dinner before giving out the secret he had been hoarding so happily for several days. At the table, where he could gaze upon his entire family with one sweeping glance, he would convey the reason for the celebration and not until then. The Courts of Mount Royal. All together, strong, loyal, powerful, successful. That's what he loved to see!

The family trooped into the huge dining room as soon as Peters announced dinner at seven. Since the immense table could accommodate twenty-four with ease, any fewer produced no hint of overcrowding. Sir Simon took up his position at the head, as befitted his station, and Mildred, as official hostess, at the foot. The remainder of the family members were distributed with some strategy, especially North and Susan. Mildred had made sure that they were separated.

The menu to be served was whimsically archaic. The wines the best Sir Simon had in his cellar, chosen with love and care, to be brought out with simplicity for people who had (he knew) the educated taste to appreciate their worth.

"Sit down, all of you," he began, just as if he were chairing a meeting. "I have an announcement to make. This is an occasion. A happy occasion. And for it I have asked Mildred and Cook to prepare a special dinner. We are having my favorite champagne first, since I expect you to toast me. I'm confident you'll *want* to when you hear the news. Peters, open the Veuve Cliquot-Ponsardin. I prefer it to Dom Perignon."

That sealed it. It was a great occasion. For Sir Simon was never prodigal with his fine wines. He had a scale in his head for every kind of wine and chose them according to his own viewing of the event. Even his usual distaste for things foreign went by the board when it came to wine, for even *he* had to abandon the cause when it came to suggesting that England could produce the best of everything. Secretly, this had fostered many a giggle among his children and grandchildren as they watched him struggle to explain how the French, and the Germans, and even the Italians had grown fine wines and liqueurs. An accident of climate, he insisted, and that was all. But it didn't sit well with him just the same. It was an admission of defeat and one he swallowed almost every day of his life. He liked his wine. He liked his scotch—and everybody knew who made *that*.

Peters eased the corks out expertly so that only the faintest pop heralded the opening of a bottle. When all the glasses were filled, Sir Simon waited for the full attention of his brood.

"You see before you," he began, coughing a little, even turning pink with pleasure above the line of his thick white beard, and with his blue eyes flashing like a victorious general, "you see before you, the new Viscount Court of Mount Royal. It's on the New Year's Day Honors List."

They stood and cheered. They raised their glasses in toast after toast so that Peters was kept busy opening the precious bottles of champagne. Mary wept, the first time anybody had seen her show such emotion over a happy event. Mildred was oddly touched, proud of the old man despite his difficult nature, proud to be the hostess at this gracious, wonderful occasion. Charles and Fort beamed, knowing how much it meant to Sir Simon. How long he had wanted this honor, how many times he had been disappointed in the past (particularly after the war, when he had contributed so much). North was, for him, genuinely moved. It was not often he felt deeply about anything, but he now experienced a certain vicarious pride in the white-haired old man with the flashing blue eyes. And he thought fleetingly of how lucky he had been to marry Mildred and become part of this impressive scene. The younger ones laughed, not quite knowing what it meant but affected by the scene just the same. Sir Simon gazed upon them fondly.

In the welter of congratulations, the burst of toasts and cheers, he glowed like a beacon. He was flushed with excitement and the blue eyes flashed almost as they had when he was a young man. He had coveted a peerage for many, many years. He could not even recall when he had first decided that his title should be upgraded, that he would make that mark upon the Court family history. It had become his constant dream, in the midst of his many other dreams of glory and acquisition, and he had never lost sight of it for a moment. He had hoped the new title would come from his soldiering in the days when he was young; from his exploits in finance and politics when he was old. After the war he had expected to be elevated at least to baron, which would have entitled him to be called Lord Court. It had not happened. When his damnable son-in-law had become a knight and styled himself Sir Armand, he had felt the bitter taste of hemlock in his mouth. Not that Armand's title equaled his own; it didn't. Armand's was only a lifetime honor, not to be passed to his son. In contrast, Sir Simon's was hereditary and went back to the seventeenth century. But ordinary people didn't know that. A "Sir" was a "Sir" to them. Ignorance was rampant, Sir Simon realized. You couldn't go around explaining that sort of thing to people, and who would want to? Vulgar, in the extreme. But it rankled.

He had waited, and he had waited. He had donated huge amounts of equipment and money during the Boer War, and later in the Great War. He had been unstinting with his time and with the time of his sons. Yet he had not been given the nod. Just knowing Armand was called "Sir" had spurred him on, perhaps, as much as a sense of injustice. He had found out (God knows when it was, years before) that titles could be purchased through an honors broker with an office in Whitehall. He was a man called J. Maundy Gregory, and he had a monopoly on such things. Selling honors raised money for party coffers, whichever party happened to be in power at the moment. Each of the leading parties had encouraged it. Lloyd George had done it and had been exposed, but the practice continued. Stanley Baldwin was still doing it, although without quite so much brazen fanfare. Sir Simon had bowed to the inevitable and taken himself to London, where he lunched quietly with Maundy Gregory. He had disliked the bounder instantly and intensely, but they had come to an agreement. The viscountcy had cost him two hundred thousand pounds. It was worth every penny.

Five days before this dinner of celebration, the letter had arrived, inviting him to accept the honor and suggesting the style of address that he had discussed while in London. Viscount Court of Mount Royal had been found acceptable by the Garter Principal King of Arms, who by virtue of his office was advisor to the Crown on these matters. The stationery was embossed with a gold royal arms ensigned with a crown. It came from the prime minister's office.

It was not as if he didn't deserve the honor, Sir Simon reasoned. It was his secret, of course—this little transaction with Maundy Gregory. His family would know nothing about that. But he had done more than his share for king and for country. And of all the things he wanted before he died, the most important was to be called Lord

Court. He had rolled it over his tongue in the dead of night, and in the depths of despair. He had heard the happy ring of it in his times of triumph. Now it was his. Viscount Court of Mount Royal. *Lord Court.*

The meal began with mulligatawny soup, a chicken broth spiced heavily with curry. It steamed into the nostrils and encouraged Sir Simon in dreams of his youth. Then came the droll fish course: stargazey pie, a fanciful concoction of herrings seasoned with spices, chopped herbs, onions, bread crumbs, and bacon, and baked in egg custard. It was topped with a short-crust pastry from the center of which herring heads (mouths stopped with parsley) gazed at the ceiling. Their tails decorated the outer rim of the crust. He smiled affectionately upon it as Peters carried the pie around the table for the admiration of all the guests. Charity made rude noises of disgust and was shushed halfheartedly by her mother. The twins rolled their eyes simultaneously but were forced to have a portion just the same.

With the entrées came a fine white Bordeaux: Château d'Yquem. There was baked ham filled with apricots, and there was turkey elaborately garnished with truffles, mushrooms, and watercress, swimming in white wine and stuffed with garlicky force meat.

"A bit sweet," Sir Simon said, holding up the white wine, "but I do like the taste. It's the most expensive of the Bordeaux, you know. In 1847 the brother of the emperor of Russia bought four barrels of the stuff for three thousand pounds. It just shows."

Everyone had heard this story at least ten times over the years, but they were tolerant of Sir Simon now, in his glorious victory. (As a rule, he would not have respected the choice of the brother of the emperor of Russia, since he was obviously Russian, but in the case of wine he made many exceptions.)

The dinner had taken on a festive air. Sir Simon was encouraging a free-drinking atmosphere, which he usually deplored. Moderation was the thing, he often said. But not tonight. Fort, still stinging under the continued defeat of his marriage, was glad enough to drink good wine with congenial members of his family. He liked North and found him a good solid drinking companion. They had an unspoken bond of venturesome, slightly questionable morals and a love of the good life. Even proper Charles was consuming wine at a fearsome rate. The youngsters had to be watched. They had caught the wave of excitement from their elders and were pushing their wine glasses toward Peters whenever they thought no adults were looking. Landry and his friend, Miles Flanders, were not rationed, of course.

Desserts were equally exotic, after the parade of main courses. Mildred and her cook had somehow created an old-fashioned gooseberry tansy, sitting sweetly green in a huge glass bowl, spiked with the dark maroon of cinnamon sticks and topped with maidenhair fern. When the syllabub arrived, the whole table clapped. It was orange-pink frozen whipped cream permeated with wine. And it was covered with crystallized flowers of mauve, pink, orange, yellow, blue, and green. It looked too exquisite to eat. There was a mountain of hot mince pies, and there was brandied fruitcake.

"We'll take our port at table tonight," Sir Simon announced. "At least the first glass so the ladies won't have to retire to their coffee. Tulah didn't approve of that custom, you know. Well, I suppose customs change."

As if to confirm the importance of the dinner, the port was vintage—1912—which by this time had reached its peak. A great deal of port was consumed.

"When do we call you Lord Court?" Miles Flanders asked, drawing attention suddenly to himself.

"Not until after New Year's Day," Sir Simon said, pleased at the question. "Then it'll be Lord Court this, and Lord Court that, I suppose."

"You'll get used to it, Papa," Charles offered.

"I imagine so." Sir Simon would have been willing to get used to it immediately.

When they finally left the dining room, the children wanted to play backgammon, while Sydney, Mary, and Mildred began a game of bridge. They retired to the Red Sitting Room, for the card room was reserved for a poker game among the men. Sir Simon did not usually indulge in gambling, especially if the stakes were likely to be high, but tonight was different. The men were quite intoxicated, but still functioning, as hard drinkers always do. Fort, Charles, David, and Sir Simon began a game while North watched. He did not feel he could participate. He preferred to be a spectator, especially when he saw how much money was at stake.

Around eleven o'clock Landry asked permission to walk home with Miles. They were both tired, Landry said, and needed some fresh air. Sydney was pleased. Landry had been alone so much, and there were no girl friends in his life. She felt that he had a good friend at last. Miles was a bit mannered, but she put that down to his Englishness.

"Go along, then. Have you a key? I expect everything is locked up by now, Landry. We'll be along shortly, as soon as I find out what your father proposes to do about his poker game."

The twins were looking a bit droopy, Sydney thought, and she herself was almost ready to call a halt to the evening. But Fort, when she looked into the card room, was deeply involved and shook his head at her. That was useless, she thought, and momentarily regretted the fact that she had turned down Sir Simon's invitation to sleep at Pride's Court. It would have been a good idea because she did not want to leave without Fort. It would look bad, somehow.

Mildred was exhausted, too. She had stopped playing cards and sipped listlessly on some port. She had worked so hard to make the dinner a success, and it certainly had been a success, that Sydney felt compelled to praise her, to cheer her up. Mary and Noel, Simon and his fiancée, were saying good night. They only had to cross the courtyard, and that created no problem. Sydney said, "I'd like to go, Mildred, really. But Fort looks as if he's dug in for the night."

"We could find somebody to drive you if you want to go," Mildred said. "North isn't playing cards."

"No, no, it isn't fair to force him out into the cold just because Fort wants to stay," Sydney protested.

"Why don't you sleep over here, then? All the rooms are ready. I thought it best to be prepared. Really, Aunt Sydney, it wouldn't be any trouble."

Sydney hesitated. The boys had already left for Mellerstain, but at their age it wouldn't hurt for them to be in the house alone. The housekeeper would be asleep on the third floor, at any rate, since she hadn't yet left for her short holiday. Sydney saw that the twins were yawning.

They had had too much wine, and even on normal occasions they required a great deal of sleep.

"If you're sure, Mildred, I'll tell Fort."

"Definitely, Aunt Sydney. No trouble at all. We can sort out the rooms, I'll go with you. I'm ready to go to sleep standing right here."

Mildred saw Susan wandering aimlessly about, glass in hand, restless as a cat. She was aware that North, too, was unattached to the card game. And she did not like that, but by this time she was too tired to make a scene. Surely the two would behave in Pride's Court, she reasoned.

After a discussion about bedrooms and nightclothes, Sydney went to the library to telephone Landry about the change in plans. Then she went to the card room to tell Fort, who actually looked grateful. He had no wish to leave the card game and no desire to sober up enough to drive home.

Miles and Landry crunched their way over the packed snow toward Mellerstain, breathing damp smoke into the clear night air. Even in the borrowed overcoat (one of Landry's) lined with muskrat, Miles looked like a leprechaun. He was slim; his white face, surrounded by thick red curls, had oddly tilted eyes the color of toasted almonds and unusually rosy lips. A scattering of freckles on the bridge of his nose testified that he was human enough, but little else did.

Landry had met Miles in his final year at Oxford. Despite the fact that Miles was a year younger, he was the dominant one. Elusive in his friendship, just dancing on the perimeters of intimacy but never quite coming close. After Landry had left England to work on an agricultural experimental farm in western Canada, he wrote to Miles and was surprised and pleased to get a reply. They began a rather poetic correspondence filled with bits of philosophy, imagery, notions based on little experience, and veiled suggestions.

When Landry invited Miles Flanders to come to Mellerstain for Christmas (his own plans were to return from Manitoba to his family for the season, anyway), he was delighted to receive an acceptance. He asked his father to provide a ticket for Miles on a Court ship. It was arranged and the boys arrived in Montreal from opposite directions on the same day.

Now, as they walked through the frigid air, Miles huddled into his coat and complained in his soft, musical voice.

"How do people put up with this cold? It's beastly! You might have warned me, Landry."

"Wouldn't you have come, then?"

"I don't know. But at least Mellerstain is comfortable. Thank God for that."

"If there isn't a fire in our rooms, I'll make one," Landry said generously.

"Good. Do you think you can dig up some wine?"

"I expect so. I've had quite a lot, though."

"Well, I need some more."

Landry was not at all sure how much Miles could drink without becoming either sick or obnoxious, but since he was a guest, he felt compelled to humor him. Miles was used to the very best of everything. His family had been enormously rich, and he was an only child. At fifteen, when his parents had died, he'd inherited a fortune. A guardian managed his affairs. He was extraordinarily blasé and his tastes leaned to the exotic. Even then, he did not seem to find much that was exciting in life. Or so he said. Landry did not know when to believe Miles or how to assess him, which was probably one reason he found him so enchanting. Miles was mysterious and could not be easily possessed.

When they arrived at Mellerstain, the telephone was ringing. Landry took the call.

"It's Mother," he said when he came back to the front hall, where Miles was carelessly tossing his overcoat on a chair. "She isn't coming back here tonight. They're all sleeping over at Pride's Court."

"Good, then they won't know about the wine we plan to drink."

"Yes, I suppose that's good. Old Mrs. Fulford is up on the third, asleep, I should think. But she won't hear anything. Deaf as a post."

"Well, you find the wine. I'll go and see if there's a fire in my room," Miles offered. "Bring a corkscrew. And glasses."

When they were in Miles's room and a fire was going

and Landry had poured out the Chablis he found, Miles said, "We don't need the lights. Let's just have the fire. That's much more restful, don't you think?"

"Yes, why not?"

"And I'm going to take off this monkey suit. How I hate dressing for dinner. I wonder why people insist on torturing themselves like this."

"That's a good idea. So will I."

Landry went to his own room, undressed, and put on a fine cashmere dressing gown his mother had bought for him. But when he came back to Miles's room, Miles was wearing a rich silk gown embroidered with dragons. It was maroon in color, with gold thread, and golden tassels on the tie belt. Landry felt gauche in his own dressing gown.

"That's pretty drab," Miles observed with a slight sneer. He tasted the wine. "But this is excellent."

"I'm glad you like the wine," Landry said uncertainly.

"I say, go into my closet there and help yourself to one of my other dressing gowns. Silk feels so nice against the skin. You must try it. It slithers over you, quite stimulating."

Landry felt vaguely out of his depth. He did not want to offend Miles or to seem less experienced. After all, he was older. However, he had never thought about silk in that way. His clothes were inclined to be practical.

"Oh, go ahead," Miles said impatiently. "What are you afraid of?"

Landry went to the closet and found a dark blue silk gown, thin, soft—almost like a woman's, he thought. But he did not say that. He hesitated to take off his own dressing gown, since he wore nothing underneath. He felt Miles watching him from the armchair. There was a smile on his face, and the dark eyes were mysterious, remote.

"Go ahead and change," Miles said. "Do you think I'm an ogre or something? What do you think I'm going to see, something I haven't seen a thousand times?"

Put like that, it sounded childish to resist. Landry undressed again, turned slightly away from Miles and slipped into the silk gown. When he walked across the carpet, he understood what Miles meant. He felt the silken, ever-so-whispered feel of fine material slide across his body. He responded to it in an unexpected but sensual way.

They sat by the fire, and Miles had let the maroon silk slide away from his legs. They were slim but well shaped. A fine cast of reddish down picked up highlights from the fire.

"Do you still own your house?" Landry asked. He had been in Miles's house once, a peculiar, luxurious little mansion in St. John's Wood, a suburb of London.

"My, yes. I wouldn't give it up! Too much privacy, you know. Did I ever tell you about my famous green dinner?"

"What on earth is a green dinner?"

"I got the idea from that famous black dinner described by Huysmans. Did you ever read that book? Where all the decor was black, the pool, the baths, the furniture, the plants, everything. Even the food was black. So I decided to have a green dinner. I had the dining room painted green, and the furniture, too, and all sorts of green plants brought in for decoration. The tablecloth was green, the candles, the dishes, even the lights. We all wore green clothes and green wigs. It was bizarre. As for the food, I managed fine with green turtle soup, asparagus, artichokes, green olives, avocado salad. But the entrée was difficult. Finally, I decided on whitefish swimming in parsley and watercress sauce. We drank green chartreuse, of course. It was a wonderful success. The guests talked about nothing else for weeks."

When they had finished the first bottle, Miles insisted that Landry go down to the wine cellar for a second one. Landry felt quite drunk and slipped once on the stairs.

Miles complained, upon his return, of the lack of music. He could not live without music, Miles said, and he wished he had a guitar or a recorder. "It adds so much to the mood, don't you think?"

"I don't know. I haven't thought about it."

"Really, Landry, you're so . . . primeval," Miles said.

Landry could think of no reply to a remark like that, but he found Miles intriguing.

"I also play the flute," Miles offered, smiling faintly.

That seemed appropriate, Landry thought. The pipes of Pan. Miles had become more pixieish, more intriguing, his presence as strong as perfume in the room. Landry felt himself in thrall to Miles, as if he would do anything Miles asked. Would obey him in anything.

"You have such dreamy eyes," Miles said next. "You must be a Pisces. That's a water sign."

"I don't know."

"You don't seem to know much," Miles said, but his voice was gentle, like a slow stream polishing rocks.

The fire was dying. There was very little light now, only a faint, warm glow. It made Miles's white skin rubescent.

"Shall I poke up the fire?" Landry asked.

"No, I think the embers are lovely. As a matter of fact, I was thinking that it's too warm in here. Do you mind if I take this off?"

Already he was unfastening the belt of the dressing gown. Landry, sitting motionless as a Buddha, stared at his friend. Miles stood before the fire now, all pink in the dark shadows of the room. He was almost hairless, except for the down on his legs and forearms, the darker fringe around the loins. He turned slowly toward Landry and moved softly across the carpet. Silent, like a dancer. He stood squarely before Landry, then, so that Landry could not look anywhere but at that coral flesh.

"Take off your dressing gown," Miles said. "You don't want your guest to feel uncomfortable, do you?"

Mesmerized, Landry stood up and began to untie the belt that held his gown together at the waist. He could feel his heart pounding with excitement, his mouth wet with an unfamiliar hope. For one awful second his failure with Angela and his grandfather's fury clouded his memory. The vision faded as Miles moved a tiny bit closer to him so that he could smell the scent of some spicy lotion on the warm flesh. Waves of it assailed him, emanating from the darker hair of Miles's thighs. His fingers trembled with the need to touch. His voice had gone. He could not speak.

"Kneel down on the carpet," Miles said. "Kneel down before me, Landry. I want to feel your lips. Right here, my dear."

Landry knelt down, shaking like a leaf, so that he thought he must surely fall over. He felt faint with a surge of desire that swam up to his brain, turned him hot, then cold, then warm. A perfect warmth. His hands reached up toward Miles, toward the long, narrow, rocklike phallus.

"Kiss me, my dear," Miles said, in a voice as sweet as a child's. "Kiss me."

The floodtide offered up Landry's own manhood. It rose. He bent his head to pay homage to the new god.

Susan was bored with poker. She took her drink into the Red Sitting Room and sat sulking by the fire. David was so deeply involved in the stupid game that he didn't care whether she was still awake or had gone to bed. Everybody else had retired, it seemed. But she was restless, wide awake, wanting *something*, some excitement, some personal contact that would make life worthwhile. What was the good of money, or clothes—of titles, even— if you were still bored most of the time? There was no answer. She stared moodily into the mixture of port and soda water she had concocted.

"Thank God, somebody's still up." A deep voice intruded into her thoughts. She looked up to see North standing there, tipsily handsome, swirling his drink about in a glass, raising his eyebrows at her in a most flirtatious manner.

"They've all gone. I'm very bored," Susan said.

"Join the club." He laughed. "I've joined the club, and it hasn't helped change the boring part of life." And he laughed again.

"What's the answer, do you think? I love to dance. And ride. I love the horses we've got. You must come out to the farm and see our new horse, Sundance."

"I'd like that."

"Well, come anytime. I'm often there during the week. Call me first and find out. How about Wednesday? Can you drive over Wednesday?"

"I think so. I'll telephone you from the office. Can I get you a drink?" North asked.

"No, thanks, I've had more than enough. I feel I'm sailing as it is."

"I've got to walk around and check the locks," North said, hovering near the door. "Do you want to come around with me?"

"Oh, yes. That would be better than sitting here alone or watching the poker game. I don't know what they see in gambling."

North saw quite clearly why everyone was addicted to gambling, but he had so often run up debts in the past that Mildred had made him promise to stop playing for money.

It was difficult for him to resist, but he was trying. It was one of the reasons he was drinking so much tonight, he told himself. Mildred was always putting some new restriction on him.

They began the rounds of the doors and windows. North took her hand, and they swung their arms like children.

"You must have a route for doing this," Susan observed. "Like a postman."

"Sure. This is quite a house, isn't it? I guess you know that. You used to be here quite a lot before Mildred and I got married."

"Yes, you must adore living here," Susan said, a slightly grim note entering her voice. My, how North had fallen into the lap of the gods when he wooed poor old Milly! Who would have expected such good fortune?

"It has its price," North said, his voice taking on the same grim note, but for a different reason.

Their mood had subtly changed. They continued to walk, but the fun had gone. Susan was sorry she had allowed that to occur. This stroll with North was the first exciting thing that had happened all evening. She thought to inject a note of mystery into it now by telling him her secret.

"I know something about this house that I'll bet you don't."

He was alert, turning to her, smiling at her.

"What's that, Miss Detective?"

"Is there a prize if I reveal a secret you don't know?"

North laughed, the deep, echoing laugh that was part of his charm.

"Naturally, there's a prize. In a contest like this there's always a valuable prize."

"All right, then."

They went through the green baize door into the kitchens, pantries, utility rooms that served to keep the big house running. North checked doors and windows casually. Peters was reliable, and he only did this as a concession to Sir Simon.

"When do I find out your secret?"

"Now. Come with me."

She tugged at the sleeve of his dinner jacket playfully. He followed her, saw the amber velvet of her gown disappear around a corner then caught her in one of the sculleries that was no longer used.

"See this door?" Susan said, pointing to a door that obviously was never opened. There was no need for this particular little cul-de-sac nowadays. Mildred had reorganized the staff, the way work was accomplished. There were many labor-saving devices now, too. Vacuum cleaners, electric irons, carpet sweepers, all sorts of appliances, and the staff was actually smaller than it had been twenty years earlier.

"I see the door. Where does it lead?"

They were standing close together. He had caught her hand again, automatically, for holding hands was one of the things he liked to do. He liked touching women. He loved to kiss them. In fact, he liked all the delicious bits of foreplay, all the frills of sexual contact. He could smell her perfume.

"What's the perfume?"

"L'Heure Bleu."

"Mmmm . . . nice."

"Thank you. You know how Grandfather has always kept Grandmother s apartment just the way it was when she died? Like a shrine? It's locked, as I'm sure you know. And he only opens it for the maid who cleans it. Her clothes are all there, in the closet. Everything on the dresser, hairbrushes, bottles of scent, creams. Even her jewels are still in their cases."

"How do you know so much? Have you been in?" He was curious. He detected in her voice a note of mystery, a wisp of excitement.

"Yes, but Grandfather doesn't know that. So don't give me away, will you?"

"And I suppose you're going to tell me that this door, unopened for years, leads up there?" He was being sarcastic.

"There's a staircase behind the door that leads straight up to Grandmother's apartment! There, what do you think of that? Isn't that worth a prize?"

"But locked. Forever locked."

"I know where the key is."

"My, you are the clever one. Where is the key?"

"On top of the door. I guess Grandfather forgot, or he thought nobody would ever find it. It was purely by accident that *I* found it, you know. I was snooping in those cupboards up there, hunting for treasure, one day. Found the key, the light switch, everything. So do you want to see in there? It's perfectly safe."

He hesitated. Even in his cups, he wasn't sure that it would be all that safe to trespass into territory that Sir Simon clearly wished to keep for himself. And with Susan. What if they were caught?

"You're afraid," Susan said, her eyes taking on an accusing, faintly wicked air. "What an adventurer *you* are, North! Are you afraid of Sir Simon or of me?"

"I'm not afraid, don't be silly. Let's go if you want to."

He wasn't sure why he was doing this, unless it was to be alone with Susan, where nobody would find them, where they wouldn't be interrupted. He followed her after she inserted the key in the lock and turned on the dim wall light that showed the stairs. She closed the door behind her, and led him up, up, into darkness.

She found a switch at the top, and it lighted up a small dressing room, which in turn, led to the bathroom.

In the bedroom, dominated by the big four-poster with its blue satin spread, Susan turned on the dressing table lights. The air was still, heavy, depressing. The shutters were closed, the curtains pulled. No light came in from outside. He saw that she was right, and that all the jars, bottles, brushes were set out on the dresser.

She stood near him and looked up into his face. A touch of sin hung as heavy as the air between them. North looked down at the slim body pressed into the shiny velvet gown. He could see down into the neck where the pleasant hillocks of her small breasts pushed up in a beckoning way. He would have liked to put his hand down there. He was sure she wore nothing under the dress. Was that possible? he wondered with a quick thrill of desire. Well, Susan was different. What if she wore no underwear at all? The idea moved him oddly, stirred his sexuality.

A crazy idea struck him.

"Let's turn out the lights and play hide-and-seek."

"Oh, you're such a child." But the words were only half-chiding. He sensed that she wanted something, that if she were coaxed, if she were teased a little, she might . . . He could not quite bring himself to hope what she might do.

"You hide on me. I'll try to find you."

"Is that my prize? For showing you the secret?"

"In a way."

She snapped off the lights. The room was suddenly, shockingly dark. He stood still, teetering slightly from all the alcohol he'd consumed, unsure of his next step. He heard her move away from him.

Susan ran swiftly to the closet where the rows of musty clothes hung in lavendered seclusion. She stood among them, wanting to giggle but waiting for North to find her. Waiting to complete the game in the only way possible now; for she knew that he was aroused, just as she was. They might never again find such a secret, delightful, dark, and wondrous place for an assignation. She wanted North. She wanted him to kiss her and fondle her, and she wanted to find out what he was like. What Mildred had in the way of a lover. Was he really that good? That exciting?

Under her gown she wore nothing. The idea of walking around like that, when she thought about it, titillated her. She moved a little restlessly in the closet, wanting him to come to her, wanting his hands to run over her smooth flesh beneath the golden dress. She heard him cautiously approach the closet; his hand came through between the dresses. He swore, muttering about the thickening scent of clothes and lavender.

"Hey, are you in there?"

She held her breath for a minute, making him wait. A hand, unseen in the dark, touched her bare neck.

"There you are! I've found you, Susan, come out. I've got your prize waiting." His voice hissed with desire.

"Thank God you found me. I was suffocating."

His hands did not leave her, but slid down her arm, to her hand, leading her out into the room once more. Then he pulled her into his arms, and his right hand slid down over her breasts. "God, Susan, come here. I can't wait."

He began to kiss her in the blackness. They wrapped themselves together in the blackness, hands moving in exploration, lips and tongues entwined. She tasted his mouth, sweet despite the alcohol, felt the smoothness of his lips and the hard chin roughened by a first fuzz of night beard.

He thrust her away while he took off his clothes.

Then, naked, he pushed his hands down into the top of

her dress, seized a breast, and drew it out. He bent in the darkness to take it in his mouth. Coming up for air, as she let him do whatever he wished, he said, "You don't wear much underneath, do you?"

"Nothing at all."

"Christ, Susan, *really?*" His hands left the pleasant country of her bosom for lusher fields. He lifted the narrow velvet skirt, found the roundness of her stomach, and then the thick hair beneath. His fingers probed the damp, divine bed, so springy and receptive to him. His sex was hard, and she was begging him to enter now, lost in her own fantasies. He took her on the carpet, and, breathing hard, waited for a second wind. He was ready again so quickly that she gasped. He took her against the cold, biting edge of the dressing table, and she found that as exciting as the first time. When they were done, dripping with perspiration in the motionless air, she said breathily, "You'd better tidy yourself up, darling. Before you go to bed. Or dear Milly might suspect something."

Standing in his own bathroom, he stared into the mirror. My God, but he looked terrible. He had circles under his eyes, and his skin looked parched, his mouth was dry, his eyes glazed. He wondered if it would help to have another drink. He kept a bottle of scotch in his bathroom against emergencies. Just what emergencies, he had never quite figured out. He took it out now and added scotch to some water in a toothbrush glass.

He washed. He washed carefully, trying to erase any sign of sin, any hint of wickedness. (He did not dare shower.) Once he was in his pajamas, he padded over the carpets in the dark, toward the bed, where Mildred lay, a huge hulking heap.

"Why have you been so long? I've been ill."

"Ill? You mean, really ill?" He tried to feign concern.

"I feel nauseated. I feel awful. I'm exhausted. I hope I haven't done the baby any harm by working myself to death over the dinner."

"Now, Milly, now, sweetheart, don't worry." He summoned up every ounce of charisma, let his voice sink as low as it would go, painted upon its surface a veneer of deep interest.

"Where have you been?"

"Locking up. You know your grandfather likes me to check everything. Ugh. I've got a headache. I think I need something for it. What have we got for headache?"

"I don't know," she said crossly. "There's some Bromo seltzer in my bathroom, take that."

Instead, he climbed into bed and lay down. Mildred turned awkwardly toward him. Then she said, "You smell of perfume. Oh, my God, North, you smell of perfume!"

There was a hysterical note in her voice.

"That's only my own lotion. I just washed."

But he thought, *Susan's perfume is in my hair. It's in my skin, even though I washed. It's sticking to me.*

"No, it isn't your lotion. Do you think I don't know what your lotion smells like? You've been with Susan. You've been with that bitch Susan, haven't you? Answer me! No, don't bother, North, you'll only lie. Oh, my God!"

She began to weep. It seemed to her that the bottom had fallen out of her world. Her stomach lurched with the terror of her knowledge. North had made love to Susan, and if he would do it now, he would do it again, and he would go on and on doing it. He might even run away from her and leave her, and then she would die. There would be no point in living if she did not have North. She lived for him, she loved him so much she would have died for him, but he did not love her. He didn't know the meaning of the word, she told herself, but that didn't make any difference. *Oh, North, I adore you so, I love you so, and you've loved somebody else! I'll never trust you again, not ever! I know how you want other women, I've seen you looking at them!*

She began to weep in earnest, great heaving sobs that wracked her from head to foot. She made herself sick and went to the bathroom to be violently ill, wretching and throwing up all the rich food and wine she had consumed. She continued to cry. Nothing North said made the slightest bit of difference; she was impervious to his words and continued to cry and cry and cry. By morning North was hollow-eyed from watching, from listening, from feeling guilty. Mildred was in labor.

At the Royal Victoria Hospital Mildred's second son was born, the day after Sir Simon's triumphal announcement. He was called Rex. Sir Simon insisted upon it. The baby was a king, he said, and should have a royal name.

Part Two

1925–1929

CHAPTER ONE

When spring came, Beau was seized again with the restless urge to travel, yet his deafness made him dependent on Angela and he could not seriously consider going alone. Angela was the only person who could handle his moods —he was more impatient than ever—and she often felt that she had changed from lover to nurse. Still, there was no way she could remain in Montreal when Beau was determined to sail for England.

Honey felt slightly relieved when they announced their plans. Over the years she had often given shelter to both her nephew and her niece, and she loved them, but they could be exhausting. The lashings of creativity and egocentricity, with the added burden of Beau's handicap, had become very wearing.

For her part, Angela's first thought was to seek out her grandmother in London, and as usual, Julia was only too pleased to scoop her up and take her in. She was not quite so eager to assume responsibility for Beau.

Because of Julia's attitude, it had taken firmness to convince her that Angela would not live either at Much Hadham or Upper Grosvenor Street—unless Beau was included in the plans. Julia, always a good general, knew when she had reached a stalemate. She promptly took a new approach to the problem. Not that she had changed her mind about Beau: He was totally unsuitable for Angela in her opinion and a selfish man. She could not ignore the fact that he was a brilliant musician with a great future. He might even be a genius. Many wealthy aristocrats had supported musical talents throughout history, and Julia was not beyond imagining her own salon. There were times when Beau could be charming. His appearance as a fascinator was beyond question, and Julia had always had a weakness for dashing but difficult men. One only had to consider Twickenham to realize that. Then there was Beau's deafness; only an ogre could have overlooked the fact that the boy needed help of some kind.

So, taking all these things into account, Julia capitulated. Angela moved into the Manor House with her grandmother, and Beau was given the Dower House—a miniature dwelling sitting neatly in its own garden on the Much Hadham estate. The Dower House had considerable beauty: a walled garden redolent of mignonette and nicotiana and night-scented stock, and colored by bold hollyhocks, sunflowers, and the stiff, unyielding pose of zinnias in season. No sooner had these arrangements been put into operation than Julia began to churn away on the issue of Angela's disastrous marriage and the fact that she must make a legal settlement.

"You must get an annulment," Julia said one day. "If that story you tell me about your honeymoon is true. Although *I* never had such a sordid experience myself. I'll find a solicitor to take the case."

"But I'm perfectly happy like this," Angela protested, dreading an exhumation of the whole painful encounter.

"No, you aren't, my dear. Nobody could possibly be happy in limbo. You will have to talk to Dorian and settle the whole question of the marriage. Then he'll stop writing."

"He's unhappy, poor man," Angela said meekly. "He's afraid of looking the fool. It happened to him before, you know."

"Angela, you will have to be strict. He must be made to see that the marriage is over or, better still, that it never existed. If that's what you want, of course. Unless you do something, your life is *too* untidy."

"Poor Dorian. He'll be miserable." Angela looked miserable just thinking about it.

"Dorian must face up," Julia said sternly. "I always did."

"Everybody isn't as strong as you are, Julia."

"I daresay," Julia allowed generously. "That's the trouble with the world. Too many weaklings."

Following this conversation, Julia rang up her London solicitor, Mr. Craddock, and made an appointment. She brooked no arguments and drove Angela personally to Horsham Station so there would be no slacking. From there it was only an hour and a half to Victoria Station and not really an exhausting journey. Nevertheless, Angela made it in a dismal mood.

She was naturally reluctant to face Mr. Craddock. The idea of consulting a man like him about an intimate marital problem terrified her. As she made a slow, foot-dragging pilgrimage along Fleet Street, she thought, *It's all Julia's doing. What difference does it make whether we're married or divorced or separated?*

She never wanted to see Dorian again as long as she lived. She had informed him of that in countless letters and in at least a dozen telephone calls. But Julia was so old-fashioned—such a stickler for the conventions. There were things one simply did not do, Julia had insisted severely; otherwise how could civilization possibly go on? Angela did not have the answer and did not care.

Having reached Chancery Lane, she turned left for the brisk walk toward Lincoln's Inn Gateway, one of the entrances to Lincoln's Inn, where Mr. Craddock had offices. Any solicitor Julia dealt with would have to be ensconced in Lincoln's Inn.

Once she was through the classic gate, the whole oppressively ancient ambience of the area weighed her down. She knew a little about the history of the four Inns of Court, because when she had lived in London the last time, she had studied some of London's old buildings. Here, amid carefully tended grass and mellow gray stones, breathed a law society that had actual records (the Black Books) dating back to 1422. Some buildings still stood on sites originally occupied by the society six hundred years earlier, when it rented private property for teaching, offices, and legal hearings from such landlords as Thomas de Lincoln, king's sergeant of Holborn and the bishop of Chichester. In fact, the Inn's coat of arms was said to have belonged to Henry de Lacy, earl of Lincoln, who died in 1311 and the Old Buildings dated from 1524 and 1613. The present chapel had been designed by Inigo Jones.

And here am I, Angela despaired silently, *coming to Mr. Craddock—pompous, stuffy Mr. Craddock—with my tawdry little twentieth-century problem. The bishop of Chichester will turn over in his grave.*

Outside the facade where Mr. Craddock no doubt crouched like a great gray spider, secure in his ancient trappings, she stopped to inhale some of the balmy June air. Above, the sky was a flat blue mirror. At her feet, the grass held a shimmer of shamrock-green. She would have liked to sit down and paint her surroundings, to transmute it into her own peculiar brand of gold. But there was no time for such frivolous notions. Mr. Craddock was waiting. Julia was insistent. Her marriage to Dorian Fraser must be terminated, or she must live with him and behave like a proper wife.

Mr. Craddock would not like what Angela had to tell him, though. There was no question in her mind about that. If it hadn't been the countess of Twickenham who called, with her unassailable social position and recognized wealth, not to mention her persuasive ways, Mr. Craddock would have shuddered and refused to take the case.

Once inside, she saw that Mr. Craddock's quarters were everything she had expected: They were silent, acerbic, hallowed. Mr. Craddock himself was a small man with a huge bald head. He was correctly attired, and his voice slid over his words like a silver flute. What he lacked in physical assets—he had no hair, needed thick lenses, and wore false teeth—he made up for in presence. He was a triumph of mind over matter.

"Do sit down, Mrs. Fraser," he said, indicating a chair with a wave of his hand.

Angela, who never thought of herself as "Mrs. Fraser," looked behind her, assuming somebody else was present. With a sharp little sting she realized that this was not the case. She *was* Mrs. Fraser whether she liked it or not. So she sat down, shaking inside, mouth dry, and stared back at Mr. Craddock with her huge, pansy eyes. Mr. Craddock, in turn, stared at her from behind his telescopic lenses.

"This is not the kind of case I usually handle," he said coldly, "but the countess prevailed upon me."

"Julia usually does prevail, doesn't she?"

Mr. Craddock raised his sparse eyebrows in apparent shock at the use of Lady Twickenham's first name. All his worst fears were realized, and he was reluctant to begin. Clearing his throat, however, he delicately moved forward to question Angela about dates and incidents. He scratched notes on an expensive piece of cream linen paper. Once or twice he murmured, "I see, I see," but it was clear that he did not see and that he did not care to see.

"Now about property settlement," he began, relieved that at last, they were able to speak about decent things, "what did you have in mind, Mrs. Fraser? What are you asking?"

"Nothing," Angela said.

"Nothing?" For the first time Mr. Craddock's voice cracked and took on an unpleasant veneer. Such disregard for material things, for real property, was unheard of. It was unbecoming. It was highly improper.

"That's ridiculous. You must ask for something."

"Nothing. Any property belonging to Mr. Fraser, anything that would remind me of the marriage, would revolt me. I have money of my own. I live with my grandmother. I don't need money from Dorian."

"That isn't the point. It's most irregular. You aren't thinking of the future, my dear lady, and as your solicitor, I must remind you, must advise you—"

"Sorry, Mr. Craddock, but I refuse to consider anything that belongs to Dorian. I earned nothing. I didn't live with him. I didn't love him. I did nothing but make him unhappy, actually. So it would be wrong of me to ask for property."

Mr. Craddock sighed and glanced away from his client. He spoke to the wall of legal books and informed them that he would abide by the wishes of his client. He would be in touch with Mr. Fraser's solicitor, he told the books, and perhaps an agreement could be reached.

"You can call me at Julia's. At Lady Twickenham's. I expect you have her number?" Angela offered.

"Yes, I do." Mr. Craddock reluctantly brought his myopic gaze back to the young woman before him. "If I need other information or signatures, I'll be in touch."

"Thank you, Mr. Craddock. You're very kind."

"Not at all, my dear. The countess is an old family friend."

Mr. Craddock rose. He courteously escorted her to the door, but she sensed his profound relief when she was outside his office. His sigh swept her down the silent, sacrosanct corridor and into the sheltering green that protected him from the great world.

Two Javan peacocks strutted under a black mulberry tree vainly searching for fallen berries. They adored mulberries. Their gold-green necks picked up every ray of clear October sun, and their crests shimmered like delicate auric antennae. Behind them six peahens hovered diffidently, echoing the neck stretches of their lords, then stopping

307

abruptly and moving backward in a tentative way as if they were afraid of stepping out of line.

The walled garden adjoining the Dower House was a favorite spot for both Angela and Beau. They often used it to reflect on creative problems, and Angela had begun a series of sketches of the peafowl for use in a large canvas. Today, she was delighted with their officious poses in the late afternoon light. They were not always so cooperative when people invaded the garden and would stalk off in haughty protest: huffy, disdainful, vaguely dissolute. Today, however, they lingered, and Angela hoped that one of the cocks might even condescend to spread his train, although so far, neither had given the matter a passing thought. It was odd, she noted as she drew, how coarse the bird's legs were in contrast to the vivid blue prowlike breasts and arrogant heads.

Beau paced along a narrow brick path that led to the frail gazebo, a white trellis-worked structure with a cupcake roof. At present, he was rewriting the love duet from *Héloïse and Abélard*: the part where the pair serenaded each other after a secret wedding ceremony had been performed. Actually, Beau had never been completely satisfied with some passages in the duet, and when Sir Thomas expressed his own lack of enthusiasm, Beau decided to rework the scene. The two melodic lines, crossing, dipping, sometimes merging, lacked tension in spots. He was determined to fix this, and now he walked thoughtfully, as if trying to catch sounds in his head that would solve the problem.

They often worked together like this—not speaking, of course, since Beau found it frustrating—yet companionable in their silence. If Angela spoke and he could not immediately grasp her meaning, he would become furious, and so it destroyed the mood. He had made some attempt to learn lip reading, and Angela suspected that he could do so fairly well when he put his mind to it. But he seemed to regard this as some form of "giving in" to his handicap. She would, occasionally, write him a note, but this, too, tended to release his rage.

As the air cooled, he looked up at the sky and saw that clouds were already forming. The light was changing, and he was not making much progress anyway, so he walked to where Angela sat sketching.

"Let's go inside. I'm cold," he said.

Angela looked up at him, smiled, and shook her head. The birds were so well-behaved today that she wanted to go on drawing as long as possible.

"You needn't act as if I'm an idiot," he said unreasonably.

"I wasn't," she said aloud. She shook her head again and indicated that the drawing wasn't finished. "*You* go in," she said, pointing to the main house.

He was not satisfied with her reply. The childishness that had always lurked just beneath the surface of his nature had flowered with his deafness. He fully expected Angela to respond to his every wish.

"You've done enough for today," he repeated. "Come along in, I'm cold. I want my tea."

Quite often Angela humored him because it made life so much simpler, but this time she was determined to finish her sketch of the peacocks. She was so close to accomplishing exactly what she needed for the large painting that it would be a shame to stop. There was no reason why Beau couldn't return to the house and ring for tea.

"Go on, Beau, ring for tea and I'll come along in a few minutes," she said.

She pointed at the face of her watch and indicated ten minutes. He glared at her, his green eyes banked with angry fires, his hands knotted together as if he were having trouble keeping them from tearing up her sketches.

"You are a selfish little thing!" he cried, his voice scattering the birds. They took fright and strode off in clouds of disapproval.

"*I'm* selfish?"

He could understand her meaning, although he could not hear the words. His eyes smoldered. His mouth took on a straight, hard line.

"You don't give a damn about my problems!"

"Beau, that's nonsense . . . I do . . . I try . . ."

"You only care about your damned pretty face and your family's money." (This was one of his favorite themes when he was in a temper, although all the evidence pointed in another direction.) "Dragging me off to the country to live off Julia . . . just so you could be comfortable. You can't bear to be poor like other artists, can you? No, you must have your luxuries. Painting is just a joke to you. You're a Court to your very soul, even if you *did* run away."

"I gave up my family for you!" she protested.

He was not trying to communicate. He merely wanted to plunge ahead and expend his own fury.

"Oh, you're a Court all right, let us not forget that. Power, money, pride. That's all you know. The world is supposed to grovel at your feet because you're a Court, worship you because you're beautiful. You have a right to be fed and admired while you play with your paintbox. Take care of me! Love me! Bow down and worship me! You're all the same. Every damned Court is the same. Vain, selfish, lusting for power and money. The whole bunch of you are just like those damned peacocks! Beautiful and parasitic! Meet the Courts, ladies and gentlemen, the golden peacocks!"

This ugly outburst was interrupted by a sharp voice from the garden gate. An unfamiliar voice. A stranger, breaking into their most private quarrel like an obscenity scrawled on a bathroom wall. Angela stood up and swung around to see who it was.

"Trouble in Eden?" asked the sarcastic male voice.

"Dorian!" Angela said, horrified at this intrusion.

"Yes, your husband, my dear. I'm so glad you recognize me after all this time. I thought you might have forgotten what I looked like."

"What are you doing here?" She had temporarily forgotten about Beau, Dorian's appearance in the garden was so outrageous.

"Shouldn't a husband visit his wife?"

"How did you find me?" Cold anger now in her voice.

"I assumed you were living with the countess. When you weren't at the Manor House, I was bold enough to come here. I could hear you both shouting, so I knew I was going in the right direction."

"What do you want? Didn't my solicitor get in touch with you?"

"That's why I'm here. I don't want you to ask for an annulment. I want you to live with me. I don't want any kind of public scandal about my private life. So, I've come for you."

"Dorian, you must be mad."

A chill spread through her. A chill that was in no way

connected with the late afternoon temperature, or the rising wind in the withering rosebushes. Dorian's face was peculiar, and the way he was standing, one hand behind his back, made her nervous. He looked unnatural.

"I can't allow you to go on with the annulment, Angela. Surely you can understand why? I've been humiliated before. I won't have it again."

"Who is going to find out?"

"Ah, everybody knows what an annulment means."

Dorian moved closer, coming into the garden. He walked slowly but with great deliberation. So far, he had ignored Beau entirely, and Beau could not follow the conversation at all. With strangers, he retreated.

"People have a way of finding out details," Dorian went on.

"I can't help that. That's a chance we'll have to take."

"No, it is a chance we are *not* obliged to take. I won't have it. I've been made to look a fool twice—first by Lady Maryanne and then by you when you left me. But at least the real truth of the matter is not public knowledge. Not yet. Now, you propose to ask for an annulment. Another public humiliation. I won't have it. Please, Angela, come home with me and we'll start again."

"I'm not going anywhere with you. You'd better leave. You can deal with my solicitor."

Beau stepped closer to Angela, interrupting them.

"Who is this man?"

"Dorian," Angela said, forming the word so that Beau could see her lips. Beau instantly became furious.

"Get out of here. Get out!" he shouted.

But Dorian ignored him.

"I'd like to be civilized about this, Angela. That's why I came personally. Get your clothes and come with me. I have the car. Just bring one bag, you can send for your other things later."

"My God, Dorian, don't be so stupid! You must have lost your mind. I told you, I don't love you. I can't live with you. I love Beau."

"That's a lie. I heard you screaming at each other."

"Oh, we fight . . ." Angela's voice fell off, as if exhausted. "I can't explain, but it has nothing to do with love. Didn't you read my letters? I explained everything in them. I'm sorry I married you, it was wrong of me to do that.

Beau is the only man I could ever love, or live with. I'm sorry. Truly sorry."

"Does that make it all right? Just saying you're sorry? Does that make it all right to publicly announce to the world that I'm not a man?"

Angela groaned and shook her head.

"That isn't what I said. Don't blame me."

"I blame you if you make me a public spectacle."

"Dorian, go away. Have your solicitor call mine. I don't want any of your property. Didn't he tell you that?"

"Property? What good is property? *You're* my property."

He walked toward them, eyes as cold as the evening air. Beau hesitated, not sure what was being said, not sure how he ought to deal with the situation.

"Dorian, get out!" Angela screamed. She saw his rage flare up then, and he brought the handgun from behind his back. It was a .38 revolver.

"If I can't have you, neither can your precious Beau! Nobody will have you."

He aimed the gun at Angela's head, and just as he fired, Beau dived at her, knocking her to the ground. Her face hit the gravel and she lay breathless, stunned. Beau threw himself at Dorian.

"Give me that gun, you fool!"

Dorian backed away, but now his rage was gone and he had turned to stone.

"Keep back. Keep back," he warned.

Beau could not hear the words. He stopped, however, again uncertain about what Dorian would do and how he ought to act. The man was mad and armed. As he hesitated, Dorian abruptly placed the gun under his own chin. Beau leaped forward to prevent him firing; Dorian pulled the trigger. The sound of the shot was mixed with the spray of blood and flesh and bits of bone. Dorian fell before him, almost at his feet, and Beau was overwhelmed with nausea. The tableau held briefly and then Beau turned to Angela and picked her up. She was unconscious, her face bleeding from the fall. He walked slowly toward the gate, leaving the garden and Dorian behind.

Near the Manor House Angela recovered enough to ask, "Beau? Did I hear a shot? What's happened? Why is my cheek bleeding?"

He heard Angela speak. That was the staggering thing.

Suddenly, he *heard* Angela speak. He heard a peacock cry—shrill, high-pitched, bizarre. He remembered hearing the shot.

"Did I fall?" Angela was saying.

"Yes, you fell."

"Beau! You heard me!"

"I heard you, Angela. I can hear. Thank God, I can hear again!"

They both began to cry as Beau carried her into the front hall. He heard Julia's anxious footsteps clattering on the parquet of the upstairs hall. He heard Angela breathing.

"Now that the police have taken your statements," Julia was saying rapidly, "we must make a plan. You've got to leave here immediately. I must think clearly. I must keep my head."

They were in the library. Julia had cleaned Angela's face before the police had arrived, and now she insisted on Angela drinking some brandy. She began to pace on the magnificent Savonnerie carpet.

"Why must we leave? Whatever do you mean, Julia?"

Julia looked stern.

"To avoid the newspapers. My dear child, don't you understand that once they get hold of this thing, they'll make such a juicy item out of it? It'll be all over the papers in no time. Prominent architect shoots himself over estranged wife. In garden of Countess Twickenham."

"Oh, Julia!" Angela groaned. "I couldn't bear it."

"And with your lover," Julia went on, "a promising, brilliant musician. What a lovely tidbit for the tube riders. And the newspapers *will* find out . . . I swear they have jungle drums. Every time I was divorced, it was the same thing. When Twickenham ran off to Argentina, they took pictures in Buenos Aires. You two must leave here before they show up with cameras."

"Newspaper pictures?" Angela cried, horrified at the prospect.

"Newspaper pictures," Julia pronounced.

"We must stop that. It would be bad for my career," Beau said. "Sir Thomas wouldn't like it."

"No, he wouldn't. He'd be appalled. It's in such bad taste, you see. Too sordid. And with your premiere scheduled for next spring, quite impossible. You have no choice but to hare it to London . . . or somewhere. Let me think."

"You're right," Beau said.

"Of course, I'm right," Julia said impatiently. "Twickenham always used to say, 'Buy time.' He meant that scandal died a natural death if you could get far enough away from it. I just wish he were here now to advise me. Twickenham always had his wits in an emergency, you know. Let me see. Whom do I know? Where can I send you?"

She continued to pace, frowning.

"We did tell the police everything," Angela said. "You don't think they'll want to keep us here, do you?"

"There'll be an inquest. But I'm going to speak to the district superintendent myself about that. Perhaps we can arrange to have it held in such a way the press won't have time to show up. That's the next step, but meanwhile, there is the question of tomorrow. The police have called Dorian's mother, but I'll speak to her myself later, when we settle what to do about the two of you. I knew her when she was lady-in-waiting to the queen."

Angela lay back on a small sofa, quite exhausted. Beau sat beside her, holding her hand, but he was distracted. Panic had begun to take hold. At first he had done what had to be done with some calmness, but the shock was catching up. He could still hear the sound of the gun and see Dorian's shattered head lying on the grass. He tried to concentrate on the fact that his hearing had been restored. What a wonderful thing! But the wonder of it kept escaping him and sinking into horror.

"Twickenham always said, 'Hide a book in a bookshelf.'" Julia said, still trying to hatch a plan. "What he meant was, try the obvious. I have it! A public meeting ground, a weekend party, filled with powerful and famous people. No ordinary newspaperman would think to look in such a place, do you think? Cliveden. Nancy Astor is an old friend of mine. I'm sure if I call up and explain our difficulty, she'll say, 'Come along.' The house is large, overflowing with people day and night, but especially at weekends. We could drive to London and hire some kind of boat and go up the river. It's right on the Thames, you know. I seem to remember a guest house down by the water. Perhaps Nancy could put Beau in there. You go up and pack a bag, Angela. I'll call Nancy right this minute. Beau, find Whitefield and have him bring round the Daimler in half an hour."

When Julia left the room, Beau and Angela agreed that she was probably right. They should flee Much Hadham even for the dubious pleasures of Cliveden. "People," Julia assured them from the doorway, "have such short memories. Thank God. So we must buy time, as Twickenham said. He was usually right about these things."

CHAPTER TWO

Despite disasters in many quarters of the globe, a particularly virulent form of airship fever had infected America. Ever since the first glimpse of menacing but romantic zeppelins during the Great War, many eager supporters of air travel had envisioned airships as the vehicles of the future. If only they could be made safe, vast numbers of paying passengers could be transported quickly and luxuriously from country to country, and time and space would significantly shrink. This beguiling notion refused to die without a struggle.

As recently as 1922 there had been the fiery death of the *Roma* near Langley Field, Virginia. She was an Italian-built, semirigid aircraft bought by the United States Army, and after three brilliant test flights the *Roma* (carrying a crew of forty-five officers and men) sailed majestically into the February sky on her fourth test flight.

For more than half an hour the supership, fueled by a million cubic feet of highly combustible hydrogen, performed like a prima ballerina. Then the rudder cables broke and the ship dived like a stricken bird. The crew desperately unloaded sandbags to stop her plunge, and it might have worked except that the *Roma* struck high-tension wires near the landing strip and burst into flames. Eleven men jumped—and lived. Thirty-three died.

After this grisly affair American enthusiasm for airships cooled considerably. It was revived by a decision on the part of naval authorities to substitute helium for hydrogen in all future aircraft. Helium would not burn, and though it provided much less lift, safety came first.

In Christmas week 1923 a French airship, the *Dixmude*,

vanished mysteriously over North Africa. Apparently she had been snatched up by a vicious storm. Several days later bits of her wreckage surfaced off the coast of Sicily, but none of her crew was ever seen again. A few romantic diehards speculated that a section of the damaged ship had floated over Tunis and survivors might even then be living with remote desert tribesmen. Nothing came to light to support this legend, and in France, at least, airships went out of fashion.

But back in America Admiral Moffett was pushing hard for completion of the ZR-1, soon to be rechristened the *Shenandoah*, a lyric and catchy name that would appeal to supporters across the country. Moffet even foresaw flying the *Shenandoah* over the North Pole. When these stories emerged, the taxpayers cheered.

The *Shenandoah* (translated, the name was even more melic—for it was "daughter of the stars") would be fueled by helium, was 682 feet long, carried a crew of forty plus, and had five engine cars and a control car suspended from her hull. Her bow was strengthened to permit mast landings—specially designed masts were to be built at crucial points across the continent—and she had a walkway along the outside top of her hull fitted to allow valving of her gas supply in an emergency. Her designers considered her invincible.

Her first test took place during a grueling winter windstorm while she was still snugly moored to the mast at Lakehurst, New Jersey. She emerged from this intact. Later, on a cross-country tour under Commander Zachary Lansdowne, the most experienced airshipman in America, she first battled storms over the midwest and then neatly wound her way through the narrow and treacherous passes of the Rockies to reach the California coast. Cheers for the gallant ship resounded across the United States. The Daughter of the Stars became the newest national heroine.

By late summer 1925 the *Shenandoah* had made fifty-seven successful flights and logged twenty-five thousand miles. Commander Lansdowne was, at that point, handed an assignment he did not like. The *Shenandoah*, he was told, would visit Scott Field, St. Louis, spice up a state fair in Minneapolis, and touch Dearborn, Michigan, where a new mooring mast had been constructed by Henry Ford at his own expense.

Lansdowne had been born in Ohio and he was only too familiar with the early autumn storms that blew up so suddenly over the Midwest. Perhaps the most treacherous was the line squall—a meeting of two individual storms, which invariably sucked up anything unfortunate enough to lie directly beneath. Lansdowne requested a postponement until early October. His superiors were not listening. Not only were they anxious to fly the *Shenandoah* again to see how she performed, but they were looking to Congress for future large appropriations. After all, more ships would be built, they hoped. Therefore, the fifty-eighth flight of the Daughter of the Stars would take place as planned in the first week of September.

At noon on September 2 the sky over Lakehurst was overcast. Thick gray clouds hung like huge stones above the dirigible as she nosed up to her mooring mast. Sometimes a gust of wind tossed her a little, but she always settled back completely level, totally stable. When sunlight managed to strain through heavy clouds around noon, it was feeble. Still, the ship would wait patiently until two o'clock before casting off in order to take advantage of every degree of warmth the day had to offer. The heat would give her extra lift, which she badly needed.

On a farm near Lakewood, New Jersey, ten miles from the airfield, Clarissa St. Amour had just come in from her morning ride. Around noon she brought her filly, Lady Burleigh, to the stable and then made her way up the path to the farmhouse. She and Michel had said good-bye early that morning. The decision not to go to see him off had been made then. Now, however, Clarissa regretted it. She felt distinctly restless. Among airshipmen it was considered unlucky for wives or sweethearts to watch the ship leave the mooring, and if women did happen to be present, they were expected to turn their backs. Peering up at the sullen sky, Clarissa felt cross about such childish superstitions. It was probable that the commander's wife would send him off, and she did not see, upon further consideration, why she should not drive over herself. There was still plenty of time. After washing up and brushing her hair, she went into the kitchen to prepare herself tea and a ham sandwich and to think over her plan.

"Damn their superstitions," she muttered to the teapot. "I think I'll go to the field anyway."

She looked at her wristwatch. Only twelve twenty, and if she didn't stop to bathe or change, she could easily arrive before the *Shenandoah* lifted off. She would go.

Clarissa adored Michel, still. Although she would have preferred him to choose the safe life of a gentleman farmer, she had known he was mad about airplanes when she married him. He had made it plain from the outset that marriage would not change his fascination with flight, and she had accepted that. Consequently, she had encouraged him in his career, introducing him to Admiral Moffet through her father's connections and, earlier, to the president of Fokker Aircraft in Brussels. Throughout the marriage Clarissa had provided enough income to keep them no matter how little money Michel earned. Her father had always been extremely generous with her allowance. When Michel had secured a berth on the *Shenandoah*, Clarissa had willingly crossed the Atlantic to be with him. She had set about finding, renting, and furnishing the farmhouse so they could live comfortably close to the airfield where Michel was in training. Living on the farm suited Clarissa very well—it had a spacious nineteenth-century brick house, stables, and grazing for the horses. In England she had always preferred her father's country place in Surrey to the great halls of Burleigh House, in London.

Although Michel had flown Fokker biplanes during the Great War and later tested new designs for the Fokker Aircraft works in the Netherlands, he had been glad to take on the position of weather officer when it meant flying with the *Shenandoah*. Actually, he would have signed on as a rigger if necessary. Airships had excited him since he saw his first zeppelin over France, and he had managed one trip aboard the *Dixmude* before her last, and fatal, flight.

As Clarissa drove alongside the field in her little Ford coupe, she saw the graceful lines of the *Shenandoah* floating like a pale panetela in the sky. It was thrilling, she had to admit, but still she felt doubtful about the flight. Michel, having discussed the entire seasonal weather picture with Commander Lansdowne earlier in the week, had warned her about the strong possibility of storms. She wished the authorities had seen fit to postpone the trip for a few weeks.

She parked the car conveniently near Hangar Number One. A handful of officers, including the commander and some of the land crew, were huddled for a final conference at the foot of the mast. Michel was among them, carrying a sheaf of papers in his hand. He caught sight of the car and then Clarissa and waved. Leaving the group, he hurried toward her, grinning a welcome. His thinness, dark hair, moustache, and the black energetic eyes appealed to her as much as when she had first met him. She felt a burst of good spirits at the sight of him.

"Clarissa!"

He held out his arms to her and hugged her, laughing. She was as tall as he, with brown hair, light blue eyes and a pleasant smile. She was not pretty but rather had a wholesome look; rangy and casual in well-tailored riding breeches.

"Darling, I just had to come," she said. "I hope you don't mind."

"Mind? I was hoping you would."

"Why didn't you say so at breakfast, then?"

"Custom. But it doesn't matter. You're here now. Look, I haven't quite finished over there—we're having a final conference. Just wait a moment, and I'll be back."

He turned away from her and returned to the cluster of officers by the mast. From above, one of the hatches in the ship opened and a crewman called down to warn them it was time to get aboard. Lansdowne responded and they hurriedly finished their meeting.

Clarissa had sighted Commander Lansdowne's wife, Betsy, and spoke to her and then to Lansdowne himself. The men were social friends as well as fellow officers.

"I don't much like your weather, Zach," Clarissa said.

"Don't worry, it'll be better when we're a few miles west," Lansdowne said, easily. "Michel will keep us informed. We depend on him to help us miss any storms that come along."

Another shout from the ship made the officers scatter.

"Coming aboard!" Lansdowne shouted and then kissed his wife good-bye. He stepped into the elevator that would carry him up to the control car.

Michel gave Clarissa a last hug and whispered, "Pray to

the Virgin for me, darling. I'd rather have her watching the storms than some of our weather forecasters here at Lakehurst."

Then he joined Lansdowne in the elevator and they went up to the control car. When the great ship was loosened from her mooring mast at last, and lifted off, the women turned their backs according to custom. There was no point in tempting fate.

By eight thirty that night the *Shenandoah* was cruising nicely over Chambersburg, Pennsylvania. To the west the dark hills of the ancient Alleghenies unfolded sullenly beneath them. With the first watch over, many of the crewmen had taken to the bunks slung along either side of the triangular tunnel that cut straight down the center of the hull. An eight-inch catwalk with guide ropes on either side connected the bow area to the stern, and under that only the fabric envelope protected men from the empty air outside. Control car and engine cars were attached to the keel area by ladders: The control car ladder was enclosed, but the other five ladders were open to the elements. During the day, with hatches open and light filtering through the unpainted bottom of the fabric cover, the keel area was luminous, but at night the ship's belly was pitch black. Then, only the phosphorescent numbers painted on girders to indicate working stations and the daring fireflies of the riggers' flashlights punctured the ultimate darkness.

At fifteen minutes past midnight, Radio Officer Cole handed a weather report from Lakehurst, New Jersey, to Lieutenant Mayer, one of the duty officers in the control car. Mayer read it briefly and passed it along to Weather Officer Michel St. Amour. Michel then drew up his own weather report to include the new information. Outside the control car clouds piled up around them like gray eiderdown.

"Thunderstorms over the Great Lakes," Michel said to Commander Lansdowne, "but they may not drift this far south. We'll probably miss them."

From their vantage point at three thousand feet the mountains slid away beneath the duty crew, flattening out gradually into undulating plains. Michel handed his finished report to Commander Lansdowne.

"Looks pretty good now," Zacharv Lansdowne said optimistically. "I'm going off watch. Don't wake me unless something urgent comes up. If anything arises, you can decide among yourselves what to do."

As he watched Lansdowne climb the ladder from the control car to the keel, Michel felt distinctly uneasy. He would have liked to discuss the weather report with Zach in more detail, but the commander looked weary and, besides, it was time for Michel himself to go off duty. What did he have to add when you came right down to it? His distrust of the weather was based only on a hunch so far. Nothing in the official reports offered cause for alarm. Storms were building up in the northwest. that was true, but they were still far away. Yet Michel would have felt easier if Lansdowne had ordered the ship to turn south, where the sky was clear.

Commander Lansdowne had no immediate worries. Originally, he had not liked the risk of seasonal storms, but at the moment local reports were reasonable. He went to bed with some feeling of confidence. All his officers for this trip had been chosen with great care. Lieutenant Commander Hancock, the officer left in charge of the ship when Lansdowne went off watch, was intelligent and experienced. The same could be said of Mayer. Lansdowne climbed the enclosed ladder from control car to keel and found an empty bunk in the officers' ward. He fell asleep quickly.

The *Shenandoah* ploughed effortlessly through the skies. Weather, she implied, meant nothing to her. Men in the crew space slept soundly while riggers on their duty rounds checked gasbags. In the engine cars, all five of them, there was a satisfactory purr from the motors, and in the control car everything was dark except for the glow from the instrument panel. The elevator man Allely (responsible for raising and lowering the ship's altitude) stared fixedly into the west. Far in the distance lightning cut through the sky, and Allely pointed it out to Lieutenant Mayer as a matter of routine.

Michel had retired shortly after Commander Lansdowne. At three o'clock somebody tugged at his shoulder, dragging him out of a fitful sleep. He was wanted immediately in the control car.

By the time Michel arrived, Lansdowne was once more

in command. Lightning in the northwest was more insistent and the wind had risen.

"We're bucking strong headwinds, Michel," Lansdowne said. "We aren't moving much. What do you think of those stormclouds ahead?"

Michel pulled out his earlier report and studied it again. Behind the ship in the east, fierce lightning chased their tail. From the northwest stormclouds moved ever closer. The only clear space was due south. As they struggled against the wind, Cambridge, Ohio, twinkled below, but almost as soon as they sighted the town, the lights blacked out.

"They're having a power failure down there," one of the men muttered. "The storm is severe."

Within minutes Cambridge was alight again. But the Shenandoah could not seem to leave the town behind. She was making very little headway against powerful westerly winds. As the men watched, Cambridge's lights went off a second time.

"I don't like that cloud, sir," Michel said to Lansdowne. The cloud lay directly before them. "We're going to cut right into it soon. I suggest we change course slightly south, sir."

"We just did," Lansdowne said. "As much as I care to turn."

Michel, staring at the threatening cloud, made the quick decision that the blackness was shadow rather than rain. He felt relieved at his own diagnosis and said so. Lansdowne, taking his cue from Michel, changed the ship's course back to due west. He, too, felt a sense of having been somehow saved from danger. Then he tried a variety of tactics to move the ship faster—different altitudes and combinations of engine speeds. Nothing made any appreciable difference. The ship seemed to be anchored over Cambridge, where the lights had once more come on to reveal the location of the town.

At last the Shenandoah began to move slightly forward and slowly passed under the northern edge of the huge cloud to break through safely. The altimeter registered twenty-five hundred feet and all engines were at cruising speed. Lansdowne ordered the motors stepped up, but still the ship made little progress.

"Why not bring her down to a thousand feet?" Michel suggested.

"Too dangerous," Lansdowne said without explanation. However, he compromised with an order to lower the ship to two thousand feet.

Clouds now began to mass in the west and northwest as if they were holding a convention. Lightning wrote brilliant, unreadable messages across the blackness of the night. Michel said suddenly, "That whole storm is backing up toward us, sir. I think we should turn due south."

Lansdowne was still optimistic. He felt the storm in the northwest was a long way off, and in his view the *Shenandoah* was committed to fly over a well-publicized course. He knew that thousands of people would be out along the route staring up at the sky for a sight of the fabulous ship. His superiors in naval command had given him orders, and he had a strong feeling of responsibility toward everybody who supported the airship program.

Michel would have liked to argue with the commander but instead turned away. Lansdowne explained apologetically, "I want to hold our regular course unless I see very real danger. You know how it is, Michel. So many people are waiting for a glimpse of the *Shenandoah*—they've been waiting for days. I can't disappoint them without good reason."

"Yes, sir," Michel said. He was distinctly unhappy about Lansdowne's decision.

A few miles to the west of the ship, near Caldwell, Ohio, sharp gusts of wind tossed around anything that wasn't nailed down. Trees bent double before the impetuous air. The atmosphere was, at the same time, ponderous with damp foreboding. When the *Shenandoah* passed over the area, a few observers on the ground noticed a menacing cloud riding right over her like a furtive hitchhiker. But in the control car below the ship, officers worried about the storm that lay ahead. A line squall was forming directly on top of them, and they could not see it.

By five o'clock in the morning all engines were running badly, yet not a single engineer or mechanic could explain why. To make things worse, a fresh fund of lightning had spawned in the northwest and was ripping up the sky. Standing beside Michel, Colonel Hall, an army observer traveling with them as a courtesy, said, "Aren't we rising rather suddenly?"

They were. Allely, still manipulating controls, confirmed

this. He pulled at the wheel, trying to turn it clockwise, an action calculated to bring the ship down. She would not respond, and as he fought the wheel, he began to perspire heavily.

"She's rising, sir," he said to Lansdowne, with just a hint of panic, "and I can't check her!"

Lansdowne ordered all motors speeded up, but the *Shenandoah* continued to rise dangerously fast. Her nose pointed down at an uncomfortable angle and her tail was up.

"I can't level her. I can't hold her down, either," Allely reported.

"We'll stop the rise, don't worry," Lansdowne said calmly.

Despite Lansdowne's assurance, the ship continued to climb steeply and then began to pitch and roll. After a sickening lurch she swung in a wide, crazy arc.

"Still rising two meters per second, sir," Allely called out.

They were now at fifty-five hundred feet.

After a quick conference Lansdowne gave orders to open the maneuvering valves. This would let out precious helium but would have the effect of bringing the ship down to a safer level. The sky had closed around them like a sodden gray blanket. By now, everybody in the control car suspected that the rapid rise probably meant they were caught in the eye of a line squall. Nothing else could explain the ship's erratic behavior.

Valving off thousands of cubic feet of helium slowed her rate of climb, but even so, she was at six thousand feet and still rising. Lansdowne knew from experience that the upward current would eventually desert them, and without the helium they would plunge downward. The solution was to slip emergency tanks. He gave Michel orders to mount the ladder into the keel area and pass the word: Stand ready to dump the heavy tanks.

When Michel came back to the control car, he reported to Lansdowne that he felt an icy blast as he stood by an open hatch. This merely confirmed what everyone had long suspected: They were, indeed, caught in a squall. The rise stopped at sixty-three hundred feet, and the *Shenandoah* trembled, then plunged like a huge rock toward the earth. In less than five minutes she had dropped down to twenty-six hundred feet, and then she stopped with a terrible jolt and leveled off. For a brief time it seemed to the officers that the ship might have conquered the storm.

But somewhere deep in the keel area a wire snapped like a rifle shot. In the control car Colonel Hall called out that the south was clear. Lansdowne gave in, at last, and ordered the ship turned in that direction.

The decision came too late. A shrill whistle of wind sent the *Shenandoah* shooting upward once again. This second rise, Lansdowne knew, would end quickly, and they would make yet another terrible drop. They now lacked the means to stop any dangerous descent unless the slip tanks were released.

At five forty-five the ship lurched so violently that crewmen were tossed about like rag dolls. There was a loud roar amidships and an immense hole opened in the bottom of the ship's envelope. Four crewmen vanished and hurtled downward to their deaths.

From the control car officers could feel the entire ship spinning like a giant top. Abruptly, her tail was yanked upward while her nose was twisted to the right. Two powerful opposing winds were tearing the *Shenandoah* as if fighting for possession. The nerve-shredding grind of shattered metal shuddered through the ship.

"There she goes," Michel said.

The control car quivered as the struts that held it to the mother ship were seized in a fierce grip. Soon the metal car would be wrenched off, taking everybody within on a fatal fall to earth.

"Colonel Hall, Michel, Cole, out of the car at once!" Lansdowne shouted. "That's an order! You can't help here. You may be able to help somebody up in the keel."

"Cole, Michel! You heard the order!" Colonel Hall cried, making for the ladder himself. "Out of here!"

Both men hesitated briefly and glanced at the remaining officers for confirmation. A scream split the air as the struts tore away and all three scrambled up the ladder to the tentative safety of the keel.

The *Shenandoah* shook like a whale in pain while a nauseating smell of burning cloth blew through her crumpled hull. The control car broke loose and dropped downward into a swirling wind to leave a second hole in the envelope. Standing in the bow section, Michel felt the catwalk crack beneath his feet. All around him girders collapsed like wooden toothpicks and one struck him on the head as it fell. He was suddenly dizzy, half-blind. The catwalk under him split before he had time to scramble away. And he was left dangling out in space, straddled helplessly over the narrow wooden platform. He clung to two wires that had spewed out from the bowels of the ship. The ground spun a thousand feet below while he clutched desperately at his fragile bridge. Even a shift of weight seemed perilous, and to breathe normally appeared excessive. The tiniest movement might snap the ragged bit of catwalk—all that stood between him and death.

The *Shenandoah* had split into two parts almost amidships. Each section sailed off in a different direction: Each had an open end, and the men who were left could see their colleagues clinging like monkeys to anything that would prevent them from falling into space. The bow section, where Michel hung suspended, soared higher than the tail, shooting upward like a bit of flotsam. A wrenching sound signaled yet another split in the doomed ship. The open end of the bow broke off from the nose. The crew space located amidships when the *Shenandoah* had been whole floated off alone, open at both ends. Four stunned crewmen clung to the girders. The ship now drifted in three distinct pieces, each scudding helplessly before an antic wind.

Four men riding the crewspace watched with a certain awe as the tail faded from view, bits of torn fabric streaming in its wake. Their own section was being dragged down at frightening speed by the weight of two engines still attached. Unless the engines broke loose of their own accord, the men would surely die. The weird piece of wreckage made a jagged descent until a welcome, high-pitched protest of breaking metal told them the miracle had occurred. Both engines dropped off. The crewspace stopped its plunge and almost like a feather began to drift easily on its few remaining gasbags.

The bow had reached five thousand feet and was circling madly while the tail was aimed at some low-lying hills. In the tail eighteen men gripped anything they could lay hands on and began to pray that the three engines would drop off. Two of them did. Still weighed down by one engine, the tail dragged itself in a heavy, crippled path across wooded hills and finally jammed into a slope. Men began to jump out and run downhill, pursued freakishly by wreckage that seemed impelled by a crazy intelligence. It chased them as it rolled over and over down the hill. One man, unable to get out of its maniacal path, lay down and let the wreck bounce over him. Airmen picked themselves up and began to count their losses. Fifteen of them had survived, most of them injured. Three were dead.

The bow was still aloft. Michel, on his precarious perch, felt seasick from the pitching and the height. Wind shrilled about his head, wreckage creaked above him, and for some time he was sure he was alone on one part of a derelict ship. As the bow gradually sank lower, eventually nosing under the wind rush, the noise dwindled. Finally there was only the eerie flapping of torn canvas and a thin whistling sound that he could not explain. Then, as if by a miracle, he heard a man's voice and recognized Lieutenant Mayer. Next he heard Colonel Hall answer from some spot high in the nose.

"Hey! It's Michel! I'm over here, but I can't move."

Mayer cried out, "Try to hang on. We'll come for you."

"Hurry. I don't know how long I can hold."

Mayer found a rigger to help him, and between them they secured a heavy rope and crawled gingerly toward the hole where Michel hung suspended. They were still several hundred feet from the ground, and the swaying motion suggested that they might sweep upward again on the whim of a gust of wind. Michel did not dare look down. His head hurt from the blow he had taken earlier, and he began to fear that he might faint and slip off. His hands were numb with cold.

"Hang on," Mayer shouted, "we'll lower you a line."

The two men peered down at him and dangled the rope, but he dared not let go of the wire to make a grab for it. Mayer slowly retrieved the rope. He began to fashion a makeshift lariat.

"I'm going to try something else," Mayer said. "Years ago I worked on a ranch. Let's see if I can still remember . . ."

He tried to put the lasso around Michel's head but each time he swung, the wind caught it and tossed it aside. On the third try it mercifully settled over Michel's shoulders.

"Take it easy," Mayer said. "You've got to get your arms through the loop, get the rope under your armpits. Let go of the wires carefully, one at a time."

All three stopped breathing. With excruciating slowness, when it seemed that the catwalk must surely break off, when a slight shift threatened to pitch him into eternity, Michel managed to get one arm through the loop. Timidly he manipulated the other arm through the rope, and at last Mayer was able to tighten it.

"Okay, we've got you. Now we're going to pull you up. Be ready to grab anything that looks secure."

They inched him back up to the edge of the hole and then across the keel area to a spot in the bow that seemed safe. He lay gasping while around him some of the survivors along with Colonel Hall went about slashing gasbags to force the wreck to land. As the bow sank lower, they made ready to jump out. Michel, overanxious and half-stupefied, crawled out on a flying strut as the wreck came close to the earth. Suddenly he felt himself caught by what seemed to be a vast, canvas-wrapped pair of arms. Part of the ship's envelope had caught in a tree, and he struggled to loosen himself. He struck the ground feet first, and unbelievable pain shot up each leg from foot to thigh. The pain drove him into unconsciousness.

Not far from where Michel lay with two broken ankles, the debris of Engine Cars Number Four and Five was snarled in a tangle of wires and girders. Four men lay twisted in grotesque postures among the wreckage. At the other end of the same field the control car had gouged out a deep hole when it fell. Seven officers and men lay sprawled nearby. They were stars upon the fresh, churned earth. The death of the *Shenandoah* had cost fourteen lives and multiple injuries.

The rescuers came first. They were the helpful ones, aiding the wounded and the shocked, telephoning for ambulances and police, and driving some of the injured to hospitals in the area.

The looters came next. They came in old cars and new cars, in broken-down buggies and rattling buckboards, on horseback and on foot. Thousands of people appeared like maggots to consume a corpse. They seized scraps of torn fabric, tools, canned goods, chunks of metal, useful blankets, valuable instruments, and useless pieces of junk. Enlisted men had been left on guard, but they seemed unable to stop the pillage. The raiders were implacable, avaricious, curious, gloating. National Guardsmen eventually threatened to open fire, but the looting went on until only the bare bones of the once-proud *Shenandoah* were left. Her remains were spread out obscenely upon the grass, over the fields, across the hillside. The dream she had created, so promising and proud, died with her.

Two weeks after the crash Michel was moved by ambulance and train to Montreal. He had suffered crushed ribs and bilateral ankle fractures. He wore a cast that extended from the ball of the foot to above the knee and was strapped to a stretcher. A nurse had been hired to travel with him. He was going home to Edenbridge, where between them, Honey and Clarissa would see him through a painful and tedious convalescence.

If she could not have her daughter, it seemed that fate had sent Honey back her son. Fortunately, he would not be crippled. It might be a year before he could walk again in comfort, but at least he had been spared permanent injury. Edenbridge was an ideal place in which to recover.

CHAPTER THREE

When the call came through, North had just returned from a meeting with Lord Court. (He still found it hard, even after all these months, to think of the old man as anything but "Sir Simon.") As he picked up the telephone, his mind was caught in the two major projects of the meeting: the miraculous production of the Court gold mine, which would soon overtake Hollinger Consolidated in output, and the fact that Lord Court had suggested North begin the first tentative moves in his political career.

There was no sense, Lord Court had pointed out, in North attempting to run for office in the October election that year. (North hadn't given the matter a thought.) Protocol demanded that he put in time as a party worker, no matter how influential his sponsor. Therefore, North could sit in on backroom strategy, give considerable time to organizing campaigns in various Montreal ridings, and help with fund raising. Perhaps next time around, a safe riding might be found for him, and he could stand for election. Lord Court had made up his mind that at least one member of his family should enter government directly, and North, with his charm and magnificent voice, was the obvious choice.

Since North always found the Courts exhausting, he was tired. He had never completely acclimatized himself to the Court zeal, the grandiose schemes, the phenomenal energy. It was now almost four o'clock, and he was ready to stop work for the day. Sinking back in his black leather armchair, he lighted up a cigarette and looked out of the window, momentarily seeing himself as a member of Parliament and wondering if he would like it.

Despite these preoccupations he was careful to let his voice sink into a warm flow as he spoke into the telephone.

"North Grenville-Court, here."

"My," said the voice, "aren't you impressive? Hello, North, it's Susan."

Her voice startled him. Susan never telephoned him, and lately Susan and David had been seen at Pride's Court less and less. Mildred had managed to discourage most invitations to the Mulqueens even when Lord Court personally put up their names.

"Susan!" He forced himself into enthusiasm. "Nice to hear your voice. How are you?"

Even as he said the words, he was wondering why in hell she had called and what she wanted. It was something of a shock.

"Rotten, thanks. I'm pregnant, you know."

"Sorry, I'd forgotten. Congratulations. Are you well?"

"North, don't you ever *listen*? I said, I feel *rotten*."

He recognized impatience in her voice. She sounded remarkably like Mildred when she spoke like that. Mildred was often short-tempered with him lately. Rex's premature birth had been a worry in the beginning, and North had felt guilty. But the boy was healthy now, a handsome little fellow, and he had managed to set aside any feelings of responsibility in the matter. North was not one to dwell upon the past.

"Oh, that's too bad," he said quickly, letting just the proper touch of concern color his voice. He dragged deeply on his cigarette and continued to stare out of the window. The first trace of serious worry about Susan's motives rumpled his usual complacency.

"I didn't call to discuss my health, North. That's too boring. In fact, I'm very bored. I'm calling from the farm because you promised to come out and see the horses. Why don't you drive out this afternoon for a drink? David will be along later. It won't take you more than an hour. It's a lovely day."

If by lovely she meant cool and bright, it had been that. It was also windy and was now clouding over. He did not particularly relish the idea of driving out to the farm late in the afternoon for a drink. Especially since Mildred had planned a dinner party for tonight and he had promised to be home to help entertain.

"It's clouding over here," North said, his tone becoming a little fretful. "It may rain."

"What's a little weather?" she asked ingenuously.

"Are you living at the farm? Is David driving into the city every day?"

"No, no, I just come out here often to check things. We have a trainer and two grooms living in the outbuildings and a couple who clean the house. But you must see Ondine, our newest horse. She's the most beautiful thing I've ever owned."

"I'd like to come out, but Milly is having dinner guests tonight. She expects me home early."

He heard the short, irritated sniff on the other end of the line and was aware, as he had been so often before, that Susan despised Mildred. Susan was also wilful, and when she demanded something, she was intolerant of anything that stood in her way. He could imagine her brown eyes curdling with temper and her pretty little mouth forming a hard, unforgiving line.

"I happen to have something to tell you, North."

Her voice was alarming—the tone demanding and brittle.

"Look, Susan, I'd love to come, really, but Milly is depending on me. You know how it is."

"David and I seem to be off Milly's list these days," Susan said coldly, attacking from a new angle. "You know how much I like to see my grandfather. He's just as much *my* grandfather as he is Milly's, you know. I don't much like being left out of things."

"We don't entertain as often these days. With two small babies," North said defensively.

"She's having guests tonight, isn't she? You just said so."

He felt trapped. Yet he could not for the life of him figure out why he ought to feel obliged to Susan in any way. Thinking back reluctantly on that nonsense at Christmastime, he thought it only fair to observe that she had been every bit as eager to make love as he. They had both been a little drunk at the time. Now she was trying to hold it over him in some subtle form of blackmail that he could not translate. Perhaps she was just bored, as she said. Women, after all, were impossible. On the other hand, they were necessary and delightful.

"Tonight just isn't a family affair, Susan. Strictly business. One of your grandfather's ideas, actually . . . political. You know what he's like."

"I know better than you do," she said with acidity. "He happens to be my grandfather, not yours. You may have changed your name, but you are not a Court. You might remember that."

So she had turned nasty. He would have liked to hang up, but he was afraid to do that and make her angrier still. Susan was a tough-minded, acquisitive little bitch, a fact he had recognized from the very beginning. At present she had her eye on the farm and thought her grandfather ought to give it to her just because he had deeded Drake House to North and Mildred. My God, but she was transparent!

"I don't mean to sound unfriendly, Susan, but you can see how things are, can't you? Put yourself in Milly's place."

"You promised to come out months ago." Now she sounded as if she were pouting. "Doesn't that mean anything to you?"

"And I have every intention of coming out, but not tonight because—"

"Leave the office early. Leave right now. What's the use of being so damned important over there if you're tied to your desk like some ordinary little clerk? Come out and have a drink, North."

He felt waves of unease, even fear. There was something so insistent about her tone, about the way she was forcing him to act. What could she want from him? She was pregnant, for one thing, so she could not be trying to set up some assignation, surely?

"I suppose if I left now . . ." he began uncertainly.

"Then, you'll come?"

"Actually, I shouldn't—"

She cut sharply into this fresh piece of indecision with a more strident speech.

"I *must* see you, North. It's important or I wouldn't call you like this. You're so damned thickheaded you can't see that, I suppose, so I might as well spell it out. Come out here. I must see you."

"I don't understand."

"Let me put it another way. If you don't come out, I'll have to pay an unexpected call at Pride's Court. Whether Milly invites me or not."

An uncomfortable scene flashed through his mind: Susan arriving unannounced with some kind of wretched demand to make, though what, he had no idea, and Mildred telling her to get out of Pride's Court and never come back. Then Lord Court would find out about the whole distasteful mess and North's position as one of his favorites would be forever jeopardized. It had an ugly edge to it. If Susan actually told Milly about Christmas and the scene in the bedroom, Milly would be furious. She might even throw him out. Lord Court, if he found out about the desecration of the shrine, would be so horrified he might have a stroke. At best, he would turn a cold shoulder on North. No man could be expected to put up with such behavior on the part of a family member. Inwardly, North groaned. How could he ever have been so foolish as to get mixed up with Susan like that, and in Pride's Court? He lighted a second cigarette on the butt of the first.

"Don't think about that, Susan. I'll come out. I'll leave now and be there in about an hour. But I can't stay too long. I told you why."

"Oh, we all know about poor old Milly's jealousy, darling. No wonder. She's so plain and you're so charming, North. And after you've made yourself such a comfy nest at Pride's Court, we wouldn't want to upset anything, would we?"

"I'm leaving now, Susan. See you in an hour."

He hung up, feeling as if he'd run a mile. He was actually perspiring. If he left this minute, he might just make it to the farm for a drink and get back without losing much precious time. He'd find out what was on her mind and take a quick look at the stables. That way, he could be back

333

in the city by seven thirty. If David showed up, he'd tell Milly where he'd been, and if David didn't, he'd ask Susan to share his secret. It was better not to stir up memories in Milly's mind. As he left the office, he gave his secretary some last-minute tasks and asked her to call Mrs. Grenville-Court to say he'd be a bit late but home in plenty of time to dress for dinner.

Once he was over Victoria Bridge, the highway was clear. On the gravel road to Caughnawaga he met few cars, but the wind had definitely risen and the sky had turned heavy and gray. All the brilliant crispness of late September had vanished, and in its place the air was heavy with foreboding. He reached the farm gates without incident and turned into the private trail that wound through strands of birch and maple, all scarlet and orange and yellow, with just a touch of green to remind one of reality. Then the house emerged with its steep roof and careful stonework. It was a paintable pastoral scene—a combination of loneliness, the uncertainty of trees bent by the wind, and old-fashioned charm. But North did not find himself capable of appreciating beauty. His heart was pounding unnaturally as he wondered why Susan wanted to see him.

She met him in the huge kitchen that was half sitting room. A blazing fire warmed the place, and she stood before the huge mantelpiece in a cinnamon wool gown that hung in folds from a yoke, hiding some of her pregnancy. She was still pretty and neat. She kissed him on the cheek in a distinctly cool manner.

"How nice of you to come, darling," Susan said, her voice trimmed in icicles. "Sit by the fire and warm up. I'll get you a drink. Scotch and soda, isn't it?"

"Please. You look well, Susan. As lovely as ever."

She smiled, but it was not a merry smile. At the long mahogany and pine sideboard where they kept the bar she mixed his drink silently. North, watching, could not resist a comparison with Mildred, who when pregnant always managed to look like a large and awkward peasant.

"Thank you for the compliment," Susan said, handing him a glass. "I'll share the fire with you. Isn't this nice?"

He did not think so. They faced each other, each occupying a fine French Canadian armchair of the Louis XIII *os de mouton* type—an unusual pair that Lord Court had picked up at an auction years earlier and that Susan coveted.

"This is boring, this waiting. I hate being pregnant." She tossed her head, shaking up the smooth cap of hair. "Anyway, let's not talk about that. When we've had a drink, you must come out and take a look at Ondine."

"Fine. Well"—he raised his glass to her—"cheers. To the new baby!"

"That's very funny, North. That is so funny." But she did not laugh.

"Funny? Why is it funny?"

"Never mind. It just is."

Suddenly her mood turned sour. He could not begin to follow all these changes and thought he ought to get off personal things and onto the subject of horses. So they discussed David's purchases and his plans to race one of the geldings at Sarasota, in New York State.

"David wants to buy this farm," she said next. "He wants to build and improve the stables, but when he doesn't own it . . ." She shrugged.

"Perhaps your grandfather will sell it cheaply to David. He's fond of you."

They talked more about family, exchanging bits of news and gossip in a desultory fashion: Lord Court's newest obsession with his gold mine, young Simon's passion for living in the north and his coming marriage to a local girl up there, Mildred's two babies and the difficulty of keeping good help.

"I suppose you heard about Michel being injured in the dirigible? The Ohio crash?"

"Everybody heard about it. How is he?"

"In a cast . . . one on each leg. He can't walk. But he'll walk again eventually, the doctors say. Broken ankles do heal apparently. I hear that Mother is delighted to have him home at Edenbridge, but I haven't been to see him. I don't know . . . I don't feel close to them . . . the whole scene over there seems so foreign to me. Poke up the fire, will you, North? Throw more wood on. I feel chilly."

He got up willingly because he wanted something to do. It seemed to him that they had reached the end of polite conversation. He looked at his watch. Almost time to go. Outside it was now darkening.

"I must go soon. Is David coming out?"

"No, he rang to say he'd stay in town. But I'll stay over. I often do."

North raised his eyebrows questioningly. He wasn't sure he liked the way things were going. He thought he'd better have one more scotch, neat this time. When he came back from the bar, he lighted another cigarette and Susan brought out a long black holder, fitted her own Players cigarette into it, and waited for a light. He obliged. She sat back and stared at him.

"You aren't thinking of confessing to David, are you?" North asked nervously.

"Not really, darling."

"I mean, there isn't any evidence, and it would just make trouble in every direction."

"Especially in your direction. But there's evidence."

North felt cold. So she *did* have something to tell him, and it had a remarkable resemblance to blackmail, judging by the tone of her voice.

"What in hell do you mean, evidence?"

"I mean, darling, that I've kept our little secret a long time, but now I'm tired of worrying about it all by myself. Of feeling guilty all by myself. Why should I? So I'm going to share it with you."

"Susan, I know our little secret. I share it, believe me."

"Afraid not," Susan said. "It's ever so much more riveting than you think, North. Ever so much more fascinating. And worrying."

"Suppose you tell me."

"The baby, darling, is *yours*."

"Oh, come on!" The first shock was followed by disbelief. "One time? We made love one time and we got caught? How can you be so sure?"

"First, because David and I were using precautions. I didn't want another baby. Also, it was the right time of the month. You and I didn't bother with any precautions, North. Surely you remember how spontaneous it all was? How passionate? That's how I know."

He stared into his empty glass, then walked over to the bar and poured himself another neat scotch. At last, he managed to get his voice to form words, but they stuck a little. even then.

"Why didn't you . . . do something about it?"

"You mean an abortion?"

"Yes, I guess that's what I mean. When there's enough money, anything can be found out, anything can be bought. Surely that would have been a better solution than this. We'll be reminded of it for the rest of our lives! One mistake . . . one drunken, rather silly incident and we're likely to lose everything. Oh, it isn't just me . . . what about you and David?"

"I never considered an abortion. Perhaps it's still a bit of the old training. I may be a *lapsed* Catholic, but I think abortion is a sin. I couldn't do it."

"Oh, hell."

"I'm perfectly serious."

He saw that she was. He felt a sick, falling sensation as if a chasm had opened up in the bottom of his secure, tight, comfortable world and he were about to fall through it into a horrible pit.

"We may get away with it," Susan was saying, "if you can keep your nerve. David is blond, but most of my St. Amour relatives are dark. So if the poor darling baby takes after you, North, and has dark hair and dark eyes, I could explain it away as a throwback, don't you think? So convenient, darling. I must say, it's the most useful thing my French relatives have ever done for me."

"Jesus," North said.

"Quite a pill to swallow, isn't it? Now, would you like to go with me to see Ondine? Put on your coat, North, it's turned quite nasty. I'll get us each a flashlight."

The wind had swelled into a cheeky bluster. Susan walked ahead through the damp darkness, leading the way with her flashlight. She was scrunched down into her muskrat-lined coat, one hand thrust into a pocket while the other held the light. North tramped somewhat woodenly behind her, his mind a numb pool of wretched information. He tried to reject the news Susan had told him—perhaps it was some kind of joke. But underneath, his good sense told him that Susan would never perpetrate such a miserable, tasteless trick. What in hell were they going to do? The shadow of scandal pressed down upon him as he leaned into the wind. He felt physically ill.

A clump of evergreens mixed with an odd maple or birch screened the barns from the farmhouse. As they rounded the turn, both barns were outlined against the sky and Susan shone her light at them. Instantly both North and Susan became painfully alert. Smoke sifted toward them on the thick wind—not the comforting scent of burning wood but an acrid, nasty stink of material not meant for burning. At the exact moment when they picked up the scent, a tongue of flame stabbed the night. It came from one of the tackroom windows.

"Fire! My God, North, the horses!" Susan screamed. She began to run toward the barns, and her voice came back to him on the wind. "Ondine! Ondine! We must get Ondine out!"

North caught up with her and passed her. One of the grooms, Rhodes, emerged from a barn. He was leading a gelding, Dapper Jack. Rhodes saw them but continued to hurry toward the other barn, pulling the horse behind him. Horses often tried to get back into a burning barn, back into their stalls. So Dapper Jack had to be safely stabled before Rhodes could return to rescue others.

There was no sign of the other groom, Kerner, or the trainer, McMichael. Susan, struggling toward the barn door, wondered briefly where they were and why they weren't here to help.

"Ondine—at the far end!" Susan gasped.

North dashed into the black, smoke-filled barn. His flashlight made a small, piercing hole in the gloom. He could hear the horses neighing wildly on either side and crashing about in the wooden stalls. They were hysterical. Overhead an ominous crackle of dry hay warned him that the fire had reached the loft. Soon the roof would collapse. Behind him a dog barked.

He flashed his light about desperately and then decided Ondine was in the last stall on the left. He opened it, and grabbed at her bridle, missed it, then said something to soothe her. Remembering what he'd heard about horses in fires, he tore off his coat and threw it over Ondine's head. Then, gasping for fresh air, he managed to grasp her bridle and began to tug at her. She dug in, not wanting to budge, terrified. But finally she allowed him to drag her forward, along the length of the building and out the door. North took a gulp of air. His lungs felt squeezed beyond endurance. Rhodes seized Ondine's bridle and North felt grateful for that. He remembered Susan.

"Susan?" he bellowed. "Susan?"

He knew then that she was in the barn. The little fool had gone inside to rescue another horse. He staggered back into the smoke, this time trying to breathe in a shallow way. His flashlight scarcely penetrated the thickening smoke.

"Susan!"

"Here, over here!" she cried. "I can't get this horse to stand still! He won't let me near him."

"Come out, Susan, for Christ's sake, come out of there!"

He began to cough but forced himself to go deeper into the barn and found her by one of the open stalls, grabbing for the animal she was trying to save. The horse was thrashing about like a maniac.

"He's crazy. He won't let me near."

North made an attempt to take her arm and pull her toward him, but she eluded him. By this time he was coughing, barely able to breathe, and his nose was burning inside.

"Don't be a fool. Come out."

"Make him stop!" Susan cried hysterically.

She was crying. He could hear her sobbing. The animal was still careening about in the stall like a rocking horse gone mad. His hoofs were flying in a mindless, lethal pattern. Susan lurched again toward the horse, flailing at the smoky air and not being able to grasp anything at all. The gelding was shrieking with fear.

North caught Susan's shoulder and managed to seize a handful of her cloth coat, but she escaped him. Then he heard the whistle of a hoof as it shot through the air. A sickening thud. Susan fell to the cement floor in a heap. The horse had caught her hard enough to knock her down. He abandoned all thought of the animal now and picked Susan off the floor. She felt as heavy as stone and he wondered if she might be dead. As he staggered with his burden to the open door, a bundle of flaming hay dropped from the loft and grazed his shoulder. The fire seared his arm through his shirt. He stumbled on toward the door, while behind him the gelding continued to scream like a human. Just as the roof collapsed in a thunderous roar of blazing debris, North and Susan reeled out into the night air. He felt himself sinking to the ground. Rhodes took Susan from him. The last thing North remembered was a shattering pain in his left arm.

North lay in the hospital bed. His left shoulder and arm was loosely bandaged so that only the well-shaped fingers poked out upon the stiff bedsheet. His face was pallid and he breathed with a faint wheeze. When Mildred came into the room, North's brown eyes were pools of mixed self-pity and childlike pleading for sympathy. He had been caught in what might appear to be a compromising situation, and he wanted forgiveness. After all, he had redeemed himself, surely, by his rescue of Susan as well as the valuable horse. He projected this petition without giving it conscious thought.

Mildred, upon first catching sight of him, was almost overcome with a wave of affection. She wanted to rush to him, to kiss him on the mouth, to stroke his face, to assure him of immediate comfort.

"Hello, sweetheart."

Even now, the voice was melodious and low, though it was overlaid with just a whisper of rasp from the smoke inhalation.

"Oh, North," she managed to say helplessly.

"I'm sorry I spoiled your dinner party."

"That isn't the p-p-point. That isn't the p-p-point of *anything*."

She had begun to stammer again, as she sometimes did under stress. North detected both suspicion and fear fighting with her natural affection for him. Even in the slack, amorphous state of his half-drugged mind, North's instinct to preserve position, to survive, was not completely lost.

"Come and give me a kiss," he said. He was genuinely in need of approval, of assurance, of love. The theme of an old nursery rhyme ran through his head: *The sky has fallen, the sky has fallen.*

The sky had indeed fallen on him, and he desperately wanted Mildred to say that she loved him, forgave him, that his life was back in place. Just as it had been that same morning when he left for work.

She walked across the room and stood beside the bed, aware of the smell of medicine and illness. Standing on his right side, his uninjured side, she bent over the dark and handsome face and put her lips on his. His mouth was slack, pliable. Even under sedation he was willing to burrow into the pleasures of the flesh to escape pain. She kissed his

cheek and put one of her large, capable hands on his forehead to brush away the thick hair.

"Does it hurt a lot, darling?"

"It hurts. But they gave me a painkiller earlier."

"You were brave," she said next. "I was talking to the
doctors, as well as Rhodes, and they told me you saved
Susan. And a horse, too."

North closed his eyes against realities. He allowed a faint
hiss of self-deprecation to escape his lips. Mildred drew up
a chair, holding his right hand in hers.

"How is Susan?" he asked without opening his eyes.

"Very ill. David is with her. The horse kicked her."

The drug was making him sleepy, but he needed to know
if he were safe, if Mildred intended to raise a terrible row
over his visit to the farm. His mind could not hold any one
thought. He muttered something and turned his head.

"Darling, you seem delirious," Mildred said.

"Hold my hand, darling. I adore it when you hold my
hand."

She pressured his fingers. North had such beautiful
hands, she thought. He was such a beautiful man. Why was
he so unreliable? Why couldn't she trust him? Why was
everything so difficult? Why had he been out at the farm
in the first place? A prick of anger supplanted her affectionate contemplation. She frowned.

"You didn't tell me you were going to the farm," Mildred
said. She wished she didn't have to ask this now, that she
could ignore it. But something drove her on. "You promised
to come home early."

"Susan telephoned," he muttered, letting his voice go
thin with exhaustion. "My God, this arm hurts. I wonder if
they gave me enough painkiller. Do you think I could get
more?"

Mildred's hand loosened from his.

"I doubt if they'll give you more. Why did you go out
there?"

He groaned and shifted his head restlessly to one side.
Then he opened his eyes and stared at his wife. He tried to
marshal his wits, to fix them on what would seem a reasonable excuse for his behavior.

"Susan called. She wanted me to have a drink."

"So I gathered. But why?"

Why? Why, indeed? He could not think why, or what it

341

was all about. Susan had wanted something. Definitely. Oh yes, Susan had been annoyed because she was cut off Milly's guest list. That was it. He dragged this fact to the top of his mind.

"She wanted me to ask you why she's cut off. She wanted me to speak to you about having the two of them over more often . . . she wants to talk to her grandfather about the farm—"

"But why *you*?"

Mildred detected the truth in North's answer, but still it didn't make a great deal of sense to her. She wished she would not force this issue now, that she would stop asking North about it.

"She thought I had some influence with you, darling."

He turned away from her in a special, childlike way he had, making himself out to be innocent, misunderstood. Even though Mildred had seen him do it dozens of times, it stirred in her the maternal instinct, and the old familiar urge to love him, to possess him, swept over her.

"But I guess she was wrong," North said lamely. "I told her she was wrong, Milly, that I couldn't help her. She was angry. Then we went to the barn."

"North . . . you d-d-do have influence with me. I l-l-love you, you know that. Susan was stupid to do it that way. Why didn't she come to m-m-me?"

"I don't know."

"After last Ch-Ch-Christmas, you c-can't expect me to—"

"Don't start all that again, Milly. I'm ill."

Mildred hesitated.

"It sounds like one of Susan's silly sch-schemes," she said, retreating. She leaned over North and kissed his cheek. Her eyes were hazy with tears and love. A bittersweet tide rolled over her. "Darling, darling . . . forgive me. I love you so m-m-much I can't b-b-bear to think about you and Susan, that's all. I was crazy at Christmas . . . overtired . . . too much wine. I don't know. North, just tell me that you and Susan didn't—"

North listened as best he could. He thought he heard the sound of victory. He slowly opened his dark eyes and tried to focus on Mildred's tear-stained face.

"I love *you*, Milly," he managed to say. "I swear, I love you. Don't cry Milly. I adore you."

The sky was back in place, he thought wearily. He had pushed it back off his face. It had been smothering him.

Milly was sobbing when the door opened. She looked toward it, startled. One of the doctors to whom she had spoken earlier came in and, seeing how distraught she was, seemed equally startled.

"I'm sorry to interrupt, Mrs. Grenville-Court, but you did ask me to let you know about Mrs. Mulqueen."

Mildred sniffled and dabbed her eyes, feeling rather foolish. The doctor must think her some kind of idiot. After all, North was in no danger. It was Susan who was critically ill.

"Yes, of course. We both want to know how she is."

"Mrs. Mulqueen is still very sick. She suffered shock and smoke inhalation as well as the kick from the horse, but we feel sure she'll recover. There is some bad news, though. She's lost the baby. I thought you'd want to know that, being part of the family."

"How terrible!" Mildred said, genuinely moved by this. "Poor Susan, that's terrible, really. Is David still with her?"

The doctor said he was. Both were surprised by a sudden groan from the patient, as if he had suffered an acute pain. Mildred bent toward North instantly.

"Darling, what's the matter? Is the pain worse?"

"The medication should be keeping him calm," the doctor said. "He ought to be relatively free from pain right now." He walked to the bed and took up the unbandaged wrist to feel the pulse.

"Pain," North muttered.

"He seems all right. I'll have a nurse check his temperature, but he doesn't seem feverish to me. I think you ought to go, though. Give the sedative a chance."

"I'd like to stay here tonight," Mildred said. "Can you arrange that, doctor? I'm sure it would help if he should wake and know I'm here."

"We can arrange it if you like, but there's not too much you can do. He isn't critically ill, you know. The pain has to be controlled as much as possible, that's all."

"Still, that's what I'd like. Just in case."

"Very well. I'll speak to the nurse about having a cot sent up here."

When the doctor had gone out again and closed the door, Mildred sat on the hard wooden chair looking down upon her husband. North had fallen into a drugged sleep; his handsome face was slack, the eyes closed, the mouth child-ish, vulnerable. Mildred, who had been worrying away at her doubts like a dog with a bone, suddenly felt all her pro-tective barriers give way. An orgy of emotion overwhelmed her. North, to her, looked completely lovable and he had been so brave. She heard the rattle of his breathing and looked with pity at the bandaged arm and hand.

Just for a second in eternity Mildred had the blinding notion that she had stumbled on the secret of life—that somehow she held the key to the world. All the puzzles of the universe unraveled before her—all made ridiculously simple by the perverse strength and outrageous fragility of a *man*. Then, as quickly as it had come upon her, the vision faded. The electric moment vanished and she was once more Mildred Grenville-Court, who knew very little about life, after all.

Yet on the palimpsest of her mind the tracing had been made. And she was more deeply committed, more in thrall, than she had been before.

On Honey's first visit to the hospital Susan was so heavily sedated that she scarcely was aware. Honey was shocked when she saw her daughter lying so pale and thin. This did not seem to be the same girl she remembered. There were purple shadows under Susan's eyes, and her hair (always bright and shining) looked lifeless and mussed upon the pillow.

Honey sat down beside the bed and looked at Susan, remembering her as a small child. Cheerful, energetic, seemingly very much a part of the St. Amour family. She had been such a pretty little thing, like a doll. The change came when Susan was about fourteen, Honey recalled. She had become sullen and easily irritated, stubborn about go-ing to church and family gatherings. She had become highly critical of the French Canadian culture. She had talked more and more about her English relatives, the Courts, and expressed a desire to see inside Pride's Court and visit with her grandfather. It was then that Honey and Susan had first drifted apart, unable to communicate ex-cept about the simplest, most practical things. Later came the outright hostility.

Now Honey felt useless as she looked down upon her

only daughter. She had so wanted to be close to Susan. She had been separated from her own mother by her runaway marriage, and her mother on her deathbed had said how much she regretted that separation, how much she missed Honey. She had never dreamed that circumstances would repeat themselves. Susan was now on "the other side," never visited the St. Amours and didn't seem to care about her brother, Michel. Still, when Honey had heard about Susan's accident at the farm and that she'd lost the baby, she was driven to see her daughter again. Perhaps it wasn't too late to patch things up, she thought.

A week later, she visited Susan again, and this time her daughter was awake and propped up in bed. While she was incredibly pale, Susan looked stronger and she was, Honey noticed, reading *The Green Hat* by Michael Arlen.

"Darling, you're feeling better?" Honey asked, leaning over to kiss Susan on the cheek.

"Quite a lot, thanks, Mother." Her voice, however, was dispirited. Her eyes were still dull, and her hair had lost its shine despite the fact that she'd had a hairdresser come in to style it.

"May I sit down?" Honey asked. Susan did not seem particularly enthusiastic about her unexpected visitor.

"Please do, Mother. My manners aren't very good. How are things in the great world of politics and newspapers?"

"Busy as always. The prime minister will have a run for his money after the customs scandals, but he's trying to make up for that. Meighen has his own problems—his earlier speeches about rushing to England's defense in case of war in the Middle East have harmed him a lot."

"I suppose Mathieu is running again?"

"Naturally, nothing could stop him. The St. Amours are behind him. You know how they are."

"I know how they are," Susan said wearily. "It's the same at Pride's Court. Grandfather is backing a candidate in Westmount. North was to work on the campaign, but now, I suppose, he's too ill."

"He's gone home to convalesce. I inquired about him. But I imagine you knew that. You're fortunate he was there when the fire broke out. We're all grateful to him."

"I'm grateful to him, too," Susan said. "How is Michel?"

"He's not walking yet, but the doctors have said he'll definitely be able to get around by Christmas. The casts will be on for about six weeks, you see. He's thinking about his future a lot. It's doubtful if he will ever qualify again for aircrew, so he has some scheme about starting a business of his own up here. Flying a small plane and carrying private passengers. Your father and I would love it if he and Clarissa settled in Montreal."

"I suppose Clarissa still dotes on him."

"Yes, she does. How is Anthony? I haven't seen him for a long time. Do you still have Starkey?"

"He's fine. He's really a good little boy. Starkey's wonderful with him, too. We're fortunate."

"Starkey has been with *some* member of the Court family for a good many years." Honey said. She hesitated then said lightly, "Susan, I wondered if you'd like to convalesce at Edenbridge? It's a bit like a hospital, now, with Michel there but a jolly one, with good food. We have plenty of help. It might be fun for you."

Susan was amazed at this offer. She had never at any time thought of asking her mother to take her in while she recuperated. She could easily go home, since Starkey had Anthony under her care and David was capable of managing the house.

"There's Anthony. And Starkey," she said.

"We've plenty of room. That wouldn't be a problem, dear. I thought it might be pleasant for you and Michel to get to know each other again."

"Really, it's good of you." Susan said, looking extremely doubtful. In the back of her mind she had wondered about convalescing at Pride's Court. Mildred might be difficult, but it would put such a good face on things if the family seemed casual about the circumstances surrounding the fire. It might, also, be a way to get back into Pride's Court and close to her grandfather.

"I'll probably just go home." Susan added.

"It was just an offer." Honey said, withdrawing a little before her daughter's coldness. Susan appeared to have no desire to reunite with the St. Amours.

"Yes, I know. It's kind." she said again.

"It was meant as more than kindness." Honey said. "Susan, I have to say this . . . no good can possibly come of the way you constantly pursue the Courts."

"I *am* a Court!" Susan cried sharply, showing the first signs of energy since her mother had come into the room.

"Just as much as Mildred, or Landry, or any of them. More than Mildred, if it comes to that. She's so plain and stupid. Or those frightful twins! They're like strangers. Nobody understands them—or that little sneak Charity, either."

This outburst shocked Honey.

"I thought you loved the Courts! You talk about them as if they were horrible. What do you want from them if you don't love them?"

"Love them?" Susan seemed genuinely puzzled.

"Love them."

"It's Pride's Court I love," Susan said. It was the first time she had realized this truth. Her attachment wasn't connected with her relatives but with the great house and all it represented. Actually, she had never given much thought to her feelings for the Courts as people, except possibly for her grandfather. She supposed, now that she thought about it, she did love him, but it was mixed with admiration and even awe.

Inwardly Honey recoiled. She could not understand how she had come to raise such a callous, selfish, unfeeling child. Susan was a complete mystery to her. She rose and drew on her gloves, masking her disillusionment as best she could.

"I must leave," Honey said.

"Good-bye, Mother," Susan said awkwardly. "I'm sorry."

But she was *not* sorry, only impatient. When Honey had gone and the door was closed, she thought about Pride's Court, and her irascible, powerful old grandfather. Yes, it was Pride's Court she loved, if she loved anything in this world. That was her goal. And she must set about reaching it more cleverly than she had done in the past.

CHAPTER FOUR

Within a week of the fire, North was home in Pride's Court, convalescing. His arm was still loosely covered with bandages and he could not use it, but it was his left arm, so he was able to draft letters for his secretary to type up at the office and make telephone calls. The Courts provided him with work to do on behalf of the Conservative party fund-raising committee. Lord Court was extremely sympathetic if a bit mystified. A hero was a hero to him, and he was pleased with the way North had "ploughed right in there," as he put it. He wasn't at all sure why North had been out at the farm in the first place, but other things took priority in his mind and he soon forgot such details.

On North's first night home Lord Court and Charles happened to be out at a political rally, and so Mildred was able to arrange an intimate dinner in the small dining room just for herself and North. She had told Peters to bring up a Chablis Grand Cru—one of North's favorites. It would go well with the chicken *herbes*. The table was set with the Worcester service (wreaths of apricots, borders of gold) and lemon-colored candles that matched the fat chrysanthemums.

As he took his place at the end of the table, North offered his wife his most winning smile.

"Darling, it's wonderful to be home. If I ever get sick again, don't let me die in hospital, will you? Promise me I'll be kept here at home. The food in that place is awful."

"If you go around rescuing horses, you might be in more danger of dying than you think," Mildred said with a touch of asperity.

"Now, sweetheart, it wasn't that dramatic. Is the Chablis to be poured all through dinner?"

"Yes, I thought so. Unless you want another wine brought up as well."

"No, no. This is wonderful. You always are so good about little touches, Milly."

Peters poured North's wine and then set the bottle in the bucket of ice by his place, as Milly had ordered.

"That's fine," North said appreciatively, after he'd tasted the Chablis. "Thank you, sweetheart, for going to all this trouble." He waved his right hand at the table appointments and at the fashionable dress she had chosen.

The gown was the same color as the apricots on the dinnerware. She had become more and more conscious of colors that flattered her skin. The candlelight enhanced her looks, too, and though she looked no more than her twenty-seven years, she was imposing rather than pretty.

Despite Mildred's seemingly pleasant mood and the careful arrangements she had made for dinner, North was apprehensive. If she started questioning him again about the farm, he felt doomed. He was not too sure what he'd said when he was drugged. In the back of his mind he felt guilty about Susan losing the baby, although it was convenient. How much interest ought he to show in Susan's predicament, he wondered? To ignore the situation might be equally suspect. The mere mention of Susan's name, though, seemed to turn Mildred to ice.

He had been having trouble sleeping, and in the dark of night he worried about Susan having a nervous breakdown because she had lost the baby. What if she went mad and began to babble about the baby and about North? As this thought prickled through his mind, North emptied his wine glass rather hurriedly. He lifted out the chilled bottle and refilled his glass.

"More wine, darling?" he asked, suddenly remembering Mildred.

"Not yet, thank you."

"Well, *I* need it. This is like getting out of jail. You wouldn't believe the awful slop in that place, Milly. And the way they're always pushing you around. Every minute there's something else they want—shoving a thermometer in your mouth—taking your pulse—taking off the bandages —asking the most intimate questions. Awful. Is this the tomato soup with gin that I like?"

"Yes, darling. I wanted to have some of your special dishes tonight. North . . . don't drink *too* much . . ."

"I won't, don't worry. Relax. This is a celebration."

"I know, but . . ." She wanted to strike a note somewhere between concern and panic. "North, did you go in to see Susan before you left the hospital?"

"No, I didn't. I asked about her. They said she was improving."

He had not been able to confront Susan. He had not felt strong enough to handle it, and he had had visions of her beginning to weep and saying things that others might overhear. God knows what she might have said or how she might have acted. He knew that Milly had done the right thing (as usual) and sent masses of flowers. He had reasoned that it wasn't necessary for him to go in to see Susan. Just thinking of what might transpire—the awful risks that lay out there like ragged reefs—made him shiver.

Mildred noticed his involuntary shudder and thought he was cold.

"Darling, are you cold? Shall I get a sweater to put over your shoulders?"

"No, I'm all right. I'll warm up with more wine. Ring for Peters, will you, sweetheart, and tell him to bring another bottle."

She did so reluctantly. Knowing North's tendency to drink throughout a whole evening, she did not like such an aggressive beginning.

"Let's forget about my accident and enjoy dinner," North suggested. "Here we are alone, thank God. You've gone to so much trouble. I like your dress. You look so pretty."

When the meat course had been served, North waited until Peters was gone and then said, "Darling, will you cut up my chicken for me? I can't manage."

Mildred instantly rose and went to his place, where she arranged his food so he didn't need to use a knife and kissed him fondly on the cheek. He lifted his right hand to touch her face and let his fingers trail along her neck, making a kiss with his mouth at the same time. Mildred always responded to that.

As Mildred felt the familiar twinge of sexual excitement North always seemed to generate in her, she warned herself not to talk about the fire. Not tonight. She ought not to raise the questions in her mind about Susan and spoil what could be a warm and loving evening. When she sat down again at her own place, she steered the conversation along general lines, and they chatted about relatives and how North would handle his work at home. By the time they reached the chocolate mousse, however, her doubts had resurfaced. She had taken more wine than she intended. She saw, through the pleasant haze of candlelight, North's handsome face. He looked pale, but for her, at least, madly desirable. She could easily see why Susan wanted him. Her fears refused to lie dormant.

"Why on earth did you go out to the stupid farm, anyway?" she burst out. "You haven't explained that to me."

"Yes, I have," he said defensively. "Susan wanted me to speak to you about her invitations to Pride's Court. She thinks you're jealous and she wanted me to reassure you that—"

"Jealous with good reason," Milly said grimly, all her inner vows now forgotten. "Do you think I don't know

350

about last Christmas? I never saw anybody look more guilty in my life. You'd been drooling after Susan for months . . . years . . . how do I know?"

"I wasn't with Susan last Christmas."

He wore his put-upon expression, like a child unjustly accused. His mouth turned down a little at the corners and his eyes pleaded for understanding.

"I smelled her perfume on you! I saw how you looked at her all evening. I never should have gone to bed and left you two alone. But I thought it was safe in our own house."

"Do you think I drove out to the farm to make love to a pregnant woman?" North demanded. "For Christ's sake, Milly, I'm not a monster!"

He seldom raised his voice and she knew she had gone too far, that she had provoked him to anger, and after that, he would retreat to a place in his mind where she could not reach him. She bit her lip, furious with herself for her lack of control. She asked him for more wine in a polite, conciliatory way.

He rose, heaved himself out of his chair by his good arm, and ambled along the table to refill her glass. He did not, however, speak to her or touch her. As they finished dessert, Mildred leaving most of hers to be taken away by Peters, he sat sullenly drinking up the remainder of the bottle.

"Where would you like to have coffee?" Mildred asked. Having made the mistake of ruining the mood at the dinner table, she was now eager to smooth things over, to begin again. "How about the Red Sitting Room? There's already a fire going. Brandy? Courvoisier?"

North looked at her absentmindedly, almost as if she were not present. It was an infuriating habit he had and one he often fell back upon when he did not like the way things were going.

"Any brandy will do. What do I care?"

He refused to discuss anything further but sat slumped in his chair sipping his drink and staring into the fire. He was in full retreat. At these times Mildred knew that he was lost to her. The only thing that might bring him out of his black mood was more alcohol, and then he would be in danger of having had so much that he would be incapable of making love to her. It was a poor choice, Mildred thought wearily, and why she had been dumb enough during dinner to spoil

351

things escaped her. Poor North had been ill, after all, and had been on medication. He had suffered considerable pain and wretched hospital food. Why couldn't she have left him alone? Now she had ruined the whole evening.

"I'm sorry I asked about Susan, darling. I'm sorry I even brought up that business about Christmas," Mildred said. Her coffee tasted bitter.

"Forget it."

After three brandies, however, his face softened again and he came out of his sulk. He talked about the election and the investigation being conducted by the Protective Association into the whole question of smuggling and the Customs Ministry. Whether the information would be available in time to use in the present campaign was not clear, but when the scandal broke into the open, North assured her, the Liberals would be exposed in all their rottenness.

"If we don't get a Conservative government soon," North said, pouring himself a fourth generous brandy, "the country will collapse. We'll lose all the momentum we gained after the war. Things are bad in some sectors of the economy now, you know, and people are just sticking their heads in the sand. King can't bail us out. He's a ridiculous man."

She could feel North relaxing again. Once he became talkative, he was on the way to a better mood. At last he got up and crossed the room.

"Sorry about all the drinking, but it kills pain," North said. "This arm is still bothering me."

"Let's go up to bed, darling," Milly said.

"Good idea. All this lying around in bed has made me horny. I was ready to attack the nurses," North said, his voice deep and soft in her ear. He ran his tongue around her earlobe as if investigating honeyed possibilities. Mildred succumbed.

"Help me upstairs," North said, reaching for her hand. "I'm feeling a bit shaky. Take my good arm, Milly."

As they crossed the Great Hall, Peters passed them making the rounds to lock up the house. Everything but the front door, for Lord Court and Charles were still out. Mildred and North said good night to Peters and began the formidable climb up the marble stairs.

"Your grandfather ought to install an elevator in this

place," North complained. "I've mentioned it to him often. These stairs are torture."

Mildred agreed in principle, although she considered the climb good exercise. Once they were inside their apartment, North became quite affable and disappeared into the bathroom while Mildred pulled down the silk embroidered spread and folded back the sheets. She turned out every light except a small one in the corner with a blue shade. Then she went into the dressing room to fetch her nightgown.

North came out of the bathroom still dressed.

"Can't manage, darling," he said, holding up his good arm. "You'll have to undress me."

"Sit down, then, until I come out of the bathroom," Mildred said. He obeyed her, now completely amenable and well behaved.

"Don't bother with the nightgown!" he called after her, but he knew she could not hear him through the closed door. The bidet was running. When she came out, he repeated what he had said, his voice velvet with persuasion. She smiled and began to undress him. He sat, helplessly, as if he could do nothing. He was floating pleasantly; his head tilted back, eyes hooded with sexual intent, like a swimmer lolling on loving water.

"How do I look wearing only a bandage?"

"Very sexy, darling."

"Then take off your nightgown, Milly so I can see all of you."

He watched her slowly slip the gown over her head. Despite the amount of alcohol he had consumed, he was apprehensive. Their lovemaking had been erratic since that disastrous scene the Christmas before. Mildred was sometimes friendly but seldom passionate. Often she refused him. Or she would argue during the evening and make him feel angry and used so that he no longer wanted to make love to her. Nothing had ever been the same since that night with Susan—since the birth of their second son, Rex.

Mildred came close to him and stood between his legs as he sat on the edge of the bed. He buried his face in her full breasts, trembling with need and hunger after what seemed an eternity of deprivation, of worry, of pain. He ran his tongue over the dark nipples and then took each one separately between his fingers, pinching lightly. The way

Mildred liked it. He heard Mildred sigh voluptuously as she stroked his hair. He bent his head still further and pushed his tongue between her thighs.

Wrapped in the shadows of blue light, Mildred looked a bit barbaric. She was overdone, lush, like a moist rose. She swayed slightly from the combination of wine and desire. It robbed her of balance. She steadied herself carefully with her hand on North's unbandaged shoulder. North leaned back, at last, so he could look up at her face, consume visually the large and welcoming breasts.

"Do you like that, darling?"

Mildred's eyes were closed, lids covering raw sexuality, the fresh bruise of desperate need.

"Darling? Darling?"

His voice purred with anticipated pleasure as he savored her skin on his skin, tasted the sweetness of his secret explorations, that intimate geography. How well he knew the honeyed territory between Mildred's thighs!

"You know I love it."

He eased himself gently back onto a mound of pillows to support his bandaged shoulder. Mildred knew she would have to make love to him tonight, that he could not bear to put any weight on his damaged arm, but she did not mind.

"Kiss me, Milly, kiss me," he murmured. And she knelt between his legs and kissed his mouth. Her tongue slid around his tongue. Her lips trailed slowly around the edges of his forehead, his eyebrows, over closed lids, across his beard-roughened cheeks, over his insatiable mouth, and then at last inside his mouth so that the kiss never seemed to end. Down his neck on his right side, across his chest (tip of tongue ferreting diffidently through the hair), down the stomach to the treasured place below. Milly's lips, sliding, sliding over the warm cushions that supported the stiffened phallus. When he could bear the pleasure no longer he begged her to take him inside, but instead, she ran her tongue around the hard shaft, flicking softly at the pink, delicate ridge. North groaned deliriously. He was wiping out past pain and future fears. He moved involuntarily and, without realizing he was climaxing, flooded her mouth. He was alarmed. But Milly would not listen to his apologies. With an abandon he had never witnessed, she swallowed his seed as if it were some primitive sacrifice.

With a curious harsh stroke Mildred wiped her mouth.

Her cheek was sticky, she could feel it drying, crusting. The muzzy thought drifted through her mind that she had possessed North as no other woman could. She had made him part of herself. The shrill ecstasy of ultimate pleasure and pain shook her.

North lay back, exhausted, wallowing in comfort and release. Mildred lay against him, her legs entwined with his, and she slid one foot over his calf. They lay silent for a few minutes, and then Mildred began to move her feet over him, playfully, smoothly. He became excited again, and this time she took him inside.

"It's never been as great as this, Milly," he muttered before he fell asleep. "Not even on our honeymoon."

Mildred, floating in a sea of lovely peace, agreed.

CHAPTER FIVE

Honey had given the small sitting room at Edenbridge a serene mood of mixed blues and greens with just a touch of warm beige. She had selected most of the pictures herself—for example, the two Francesco Zuccarellis that whispered of blue skies, lush feathery trees, and sunny European villas. The paintings were an indulgence, as were the important ornaments (a Meissen jar with gilt metal mounts and rare Chinaman finial, a splendid creamy sea-green jade bowl) sitting in the two elegant wall niches. Comfortable upholstered chairs and sofas were complemented by a pair of antique Georgian semicircular tables in sycamore banded with tulipwood that Honey had picked up on Mount Street in London. The room, at first glance, was casual, but it had been planned with great care.

The St. Amours gathered in the room for a predinner drink and grave discussion of Mathieu's campaign in the coming federal election. Once again he was running on the Liberal ticket in Outremont. The family had always been deeply involved in politics, and when Corbin Dufours (Helene St. Amour's husband) had run for Parliament thirty years earlier, the family had given him their whole-hearted support. Corbin was now an influential senator and advisor to the prime minister, so it was his turn to help Mathieu. Consequently, Corbin and Helene had come down from Ottawa for the weekend and were guests at Edenbridge. It was expected that Corbin would bring firsthand news of the Liberal campaign in the capital.

No other family members were present. Justine and Timotheé had remained on the farm, but Justine had telephoned to pledge twenty thousand dollars to Mathieu's campaign fund. Now that he was a bishop, Marc felt compelled to stay out of such family meetings. At one time, the bishops of Quebec had been extremely active in politics, but those days were past. Bishops no longer issued orders to their parish priests to preach politics from the pulpits, and they did not publish edicts making a Liberal vote a mortal sin. That had been at the turn of the century and times had changed.

While Armand offered drinks to his guests, Honey studied her nephew, Mathieu Dosquet. He seemed out of place in the fragile atmosphere of the sitting room. He was far too large and awkward, too dark, too vigorous in his movements for the pastel cocoon she had so lovingly created. She watched him pace about on the fine Nain rug with its faded hunting scene and feared he might damage her treasures with his flailing, demonstrative arms. He had always been accident-prone, although he had never been seriously injured. Even on his wedding night he'd had to suffer a sprained ankle because of an upset in his car.

She thought now that she would have been better advised to serve drinks in the Long Gallery, where at least Mathieu would have plenty of room for his histrionics. She glanced with sudden alarm at the pair of Ch'ien Lung spaniels with their stupid black stare and bright brown bodies. They had cost her four thousand pounds, and the idea that Mathieu might mindlessly break one made Honey shudder.

"Well, Corbin," Armand said by way of opening the discussion, "tell us the news. What is the prime minister saying in his speeches? What are the issues he wants to push?"

Corbin, still slim and handsome in a gray, distinguished way, reveled in his position as family pundit. Because he was one of King's advisors on strategy, he was always listened to with great respect. He cleared his throat and said in a theatrical manner, "King is hammering away at lower tariffs, of course. To stimulate trade, he says. He needs that bait to sell the West. It's the only hope he has out there, you know. He's also talking Senate reform. Although most of us hope he'll forget *that* issue, quickly. There's no appeal in that for the common man, and in my opinion, the Senate is fine the way it is."

"What about this damned Customs scandal?" Armand said, referring to the recent trial of the customs officer, Bisaillon, and his connection with a boatload of contraband alcohol that was smuggled into Canada.

"He ignores it."

"I'll bet he does," Honey interrupted angrily. "That whole mess is a disgrace to the party. Letting gangsters smuggle thousands of gallons of alcohol into Canada so it can be made legally into liquor and sold back in the United States illegally. Their prohibition is past a joke, of course, but it's their own business. Now that it's been exposed and the Customs minister himself is involved—"

"And King is protecting his Cabinet minister. What has Jacques Bureau got on King? That's what I'd like to know. And what has Bisaillon got on Bureau that he's willing to cover him? I don't understand it," Mathieu said.

"Nobody knows," Helene assured him. "And the less the said about it the better, I think."

"King was a fool to appoint Bureau to the Senate, just the same," Armand observed. "It looks like a reward for bad behavior. No wonder the prime minister won't talk about it in the campaign."

"But the Tories *will* talk about it," Honey pointed out. "They'll talk of nothing else. I've already heard two of their candidates speak, and they're screaming about the fact that a minister is involved in illegal activities and that he is not only let off but rewarded."

"It's their best ammunition," Armand said. "And smuggling is hurting a lot of big businesses."

"Yes, they'd like the liquor traffic stopped all right," Mathieu said gloomily. "In a way, I see their point."

"It's difficult to ignore those stories in my newspaper," Honey said. "No matter how loyal a Liberal a publisher is, a story like that is public property. I think King is a disgrace, and I wish we had another leader."

"Corbin, why does King ignore the situation? Does anybody know?" Mathieu demanded.

"Nobody knows," Corbin said with a shrug. "We've all

tried to talk sense to him, and he simply doesn't listen. We told him to dump Jacques Bureau months ago, long before this thing blew up. What his reason for protecting Bureau is, I don't know. But he must have a good one."

"Money," Armand said with finality. "It always comes down to money in the end, doesn't it?"

"You mean bribery," Honey said.

"Right. Well, no party is free of people who take bribes, that's the truth," Corbin agreed. "But it's shortsighted. And dangerous."

"I'd like to expose some things myself," Honey said crossly. "Even if they *are* bad for the Liberal party. The Treasury loses millions of dollars a year in revenue—because no duty is paid on smuggled alcohol."

"Now, *ma chérie*, you can't print that sort of thing. Just stick to the issues on which the Liberal party is right and ignore the rest. That's what *Le Monde* must do."

"Sometimes I hate politics and politicians," she said.

"Let's discuss my campaign funds," Mathieu began impatiently, "and forget all about rumrunners and the prime minister. Let's worry about getting me elected. I hate to sound crass, Uncle Armand, but have you decided how much you can contribute to my fund?"

Armand suddenly looked grim.

"Yes, I have. It's very important to me to see you elected. I need all the help I can get from you and Corbin and anybody else you can recruit. So I'm putting in two hundred thousand."

"Very generous. Thank you, Uncle Armand."

"It's damn well more than I can afford right now, that's the truth. My situation is a little desperate. I'm sure you've gathered the sugar market in Canada is a disaster. But you don't know how deeply it is affecting my finances."

"Do you think this is the time to mention it?" Honey asked.

She did not really know the details about the refinery. She did know that Armand was in financial trouble, however. As he stood there surveying his relatives, Honey noticed how tired he looked. Still handsome but disillusioned and exhausted. Armand had not been sleeping well lately. He had taken to relying on sleeping powders night after night.

"They might as well know," Armand said. "I want

Corbin to realize how important this sugar question is. How much I need his influence with the Board of Commerce."

"I don't know much about the Board of Commerce," Corbin said, "except that they certainly haven't subsidized the refineries as they promised."

"I'd like to know why they've gone back on their word," Armand said.

"Probably lack of action," Mathieu said. "It's easier to do nothing than something."

"If they don't help us out in the next few months, we're all likely to go under. We can't ask consumers to pay a decent price because the board won't let us. We're losing millions. We can't export. We're tied."

Armand went on to explain that as early as 1919 the Canadian government had forced sugar refiners to keep their prices down to protect Canadian consumers in a rising market, guaranteeing that they would assist the refineries if they began to lose money. Within a year, refiners had lost twenty million dollars, but consumers had benefited by the low prices. At the same time American and Cuban sugar was dumped on the Canadian market as competition. Refiners were caught between high prices for sugar futures and the inability to raise the consumer price to make a profit. Still, nothing was done to help them.

"The situation is desperate," Armand said. "Pressure must be brought to bear on the Board of Commerce and on the Trade Commission, or we'll go down the drain."

"But surely, Armand, all your capital isn't tied up in the refinery?" Corbin inquired.

"Roughly seventy percent."

Corbin looked surprised and said he failed to understand why Armand had allowed his finances to get into such a dangerous situation.

"Because I bought the stock cheaply. I thought the government would keep its promise. I see now that I was wrong."

They went on to discuss posters and pamphlets for Mathieu's campaign and how they could best be distributed. Mathieu said he had rented an empty store in Outremont as campaign headquarters and that a telephone was soon to be installed. He wanted somebody to take charge of the office and the telephone.

Clarissa came in during the final drink. It was her custom to do that before joining Michel in his upstairs sitting room for his evening meal. He still could not manage the stairs.

"You all look so gloomy!" Clarissa said, giving her smile to all of them at once. "Surely Mathieu hasn't lost the election yet?"

"Do come in and have a sherry, darling," Honey said warmly, pulling herself together with an effort. "You're just in time."

"The usual, *chérie*?" Armand asked.

"Yes, please, Armand."

Clarissa had always called her in-laws by their first names. She was not a sentimental girl who could have slipped into a familiar "Mother" and "Father." Since childhood she had called her own parents "Marr" and "Farr" as a family joke.

"I see you haven't converted to Canadian rye whisky," Corbin said.

"Awful stuff," Clarissa said, making a face.

"Papa always said rye was only good for one thing—pouring on the ground," Honey said.

"He was right," Clarissa agreed.

"Not looking for a job, are you, Clarissa?" Mathieu asked suddenly. "I need some help."

"Why, Mathieu, of course. I never thought of offering. What do you want me to do?"

"What about my headquarters? Would you consider taking it over, answering the telephone and talking sweet to visiting strays?"

"Love to, Mathieu, if you think I could. I used to help Farr when he was backing a candidate in Sussex, you know. He was a very big wheel in the Tory party. Made all his children work like slaves. Farr had no conscience whatsoever about child labor. We used to tell him that if Shaftesbury had been alive, he'd have had Farr's scalp."

This seemed to strike a rather happier note, but it did not completely alleviate the heavy mood at dinner.

The after-dinner meeting to discuss the coming campaign was over by ten o'clock. Mathieu leaped into his two-year-old Mercedes convertible and ground the gearshift so furiously that it groaned and creaked in protest. With a roar he took off down the Edenbridge driveway and headed for Park Avenue, a route that eventually would lead him to his house in Outremont.

When he arrived home, he found Nora sitting in the parlor with Rose. They were drinking thick, black coffee. His resentment of Rose came to the surface as soon as he saw her curly red hair, her moist pink mouth. When he and Nora had first been married, he had not objected to their friendship, but now that he was in government, he found it unsuitable. It was distasteful. Rose Starkey was, after all, a servant. She was a nanny, and the whole thing was ridiculously complicated by the fact that she worked for Susan, his Aunt Miel's daughter.

He had hoped Nora would voluntarily give up the relationship, but there was no sign of it. Now that Nora was once again pregnant, he was inclined to avoid scenes, so he had not mentioned his idea, but still it annoyed him.

He made no move to enter the room but stood in the doorway and said coldly, "Good evening, my dear. Good evening, Rose."

"Hello, Mathieu."

They both responded to him at the same time like puppets. He found this highly annoying. A couple of ignorant women if he'd ever seen any.

"Aren't you up late, Nora? I thought you were tired, with the baby coming. And you haven't been sleeping well. Why are you drinking coffee?"

"I don't know. I felt like it."

He stared pointedly at Rose. Rose blushed uncomfortably.

"I was about to go, Nora," Rose said.

"Oh, don't go yet, Rose," Nora said quickly. "Stay a little while longer. I'm sure Mathieu is going upstairs to his study, aren't you?"

"Yes, I am. But you ought to go to bed, Nora."

"I can't sleep anyway."

He gave up. He was impatient to go upstairs, and he did not wish to waste his time talking to two women who were, he felt, beneath him. A restlessness, which always preceded sexual need, had begun to make him think of Marie-Claire, up on the third floor in her small bedroom.

"I have a speech to write," Mathieu said. "I'll see you later, Nora, but I hope you won't stay up too long."

"There's coffee made if you want some," Nora said,

trying to placate him a little. She was aware that he wanted Rose to leave, but she was equally determined to keep Rose for another few minutes.

Nora sank back into her chair as soon as Mathieu was gone. She had often thought of giving up her friendship with Rose because the idea that her guilt might produce yet another abnormal child was sometimes almost too frightening to bear. Yet she had been unable to do so. When Rose failed to show up because she was working or ill, Nora was flooded with despair. She had become dependent upon Rose for comfort, advice—for pleasure, even. It had become a drug. She could not imagine life without those sweet, smooth fingers that aroused her sensuality, those moist pink lips foraging upon her own, the peach-colored cheek pressed against hers.

Yet the possibility of punishment for her sin was never far from her mind. What if this baby, too, was born deformed? The question tormented her. But she could not bear life with Mathieu on any other terms. Many nights she lay in bed peering into the blackness, knowing Mathieu was up on the third floor with Marie-Claire when he pretended to be in his study. She had heard him padding softly up the narrow staircase, having checked (as he thought) to see if Nora was asleep first.

Mathieu had been gone half an hour, and they had chatted casually about many things, when Rose got up to leave. She had a long walk home, and it was getting late. Knowing that, Nora was always reluctant to coax Rose to stay as long as she would have liked. She followed Rose into the darkened front hall to help her into her coat. No sound came from upstairs, but she knew Mathieu had left his study. When he was in there, she could often hear his chair move or a drawer slam. She was always aware of his presence in that room. What a fool he must think her, pretending to be working, shutting the door and leaving the light on, and sneaking up to Marie-Claire.

Nora did not bother to turn on a light. Rose took her woolen mackinaw down from the coat rack and placed it on a chair. Nora's attention was divided between Rose, here in the shadows of the hall, and Mathieu up there in the dark bedroom on the third floor. Though she despised him, Nora felt a thrill of anger at Mathieu's crude behavior. He was insulting her when he did not take the trouble to conceal his romps with Marie-Claire.

Rose said softly, "Do you think you can sleep, Nora?"

"I doubt it. I'm not sleeping at all well these days."

"You're angry because he's up there with *her*, aren't you? Don't think about the brute. He's horrible. Making love to that little slut. She's nothing but a body, really, Nora, she has no brains. Mathieu is like all men. He's a pig."

"I don't really care," Nora said. "Except that he throws it in my face. He's doesn't even try to hide it."

"Don't think about Mathieu," Rose whispered, drawing Nora into her arms. She began to kiss Nora's cheek and then let her lips caress Nora's neck. She slipped one hand into the top of Nora's gown and found the nipples already erect, waiting. Nora shifted, leaning back against the wall and thrusting out her hips toward Rose. They were taking some risk in making love like this in the open with Mathieu in the house, but that very risk made it more exciting. Nora sensed that Rose felt the same way. It was as if they were directly punishing Mathieu for his own liberties with the maid. As if they were challenging him to find them out. Nora thought about that and moved a little so Rose could touch her. She wore no underclothes. This, too, was part of the game. For if Mathieu ever found out, he would suspect something—that kind of behavior was not acceptable. Only tarts would go about with no underclothing. Nora felt the tingle of danger as some sounds sifted down from above. A door opening? Mathieu coming downstairs to see what Nora was doing, why she wasn't in bed? But the house settled again into quiet. Rose did not take her hand away, and Nora leaned back, eyes closed, yielding herself up to those delightful caresses.

CHAPTER SIX

The October election of 1925 carried with it a strange air of lethargy. Many of the issues were clouded, and aside from one or two sharp outbursts about the smuggling trade, nothing emotional or exciting transpired on the hustings. Despite this apparent lack of interest, voters returned King and his Liberal party in a slightly weaker position than before—only 101 seats in the House of Commons. They had lost 16 previously held seats. The Conservatives, on the other hand, were jubilant. They had shot up from 49 to 116. The future looked promising. But neither party held a majority, and Lord Byng, still governor general, offered King the chance to pull a government together if he could convince the third party, the Progressives, to rally behind him.

King's personal stock in his party was at an all-time low—it was his second near-defeat. On top of that, he had lost his seat and could not take his place in the House. He was forced to stage-manage his party and his government from the lobbies. Still, he accepted Byng's proposal, and the Progressives propped him up for the next six months. By March 1926 he had won a safe seat in a western by-election. Now, he was ready to fight the Conservatives—muckraking, as he saw it, among the rumrunners. Smuggling was the largest single issue he had to face.

Lord Court was happy about the election. He saw a great renaissance for the Conservatives and for the country. It was obvious that the voters had come to their senses at last and that it was only a matter of time before King was defeated.

A coming-out ball for Flora and Fenella was overdue. Lord Court had deliberately postponed it until after the election—the twins were still eighteen, and he felt he was slipping nicely under the wire. But in late November he was ready, and Pride's Court was aglow and welcoming guests.

"Here they come," Lord Court hissed in Mildred's ear as they stood together in the short receiving line. "Steady yourself, my girl, and keep smiling. The mob is upon us."

"Don't worry, Grandfather, everything will be fine." She was amused at his pretense. There was nothing he enjoyed more than a big splurge.

Next to her in line stood Fort and Sydney, as parents, and then North and Mary. The younger Courts had been excluded from receiving. Charity was only fifteen and considered too young. Simon II had refused to come down from the North, and if Landry, as the girls' brother, stood in the receiving line, then Noel must be included as well.

As the first wave of guests swept toward them, Mildred

was amused by her grandfather's *sotto voce* remarks. It was all right for *him* to make fun of society, of course, but she well knew he would not have put up with it from anyone else. She did not mind his hypocrisy. She was extremely fond of her grandfather.

There had never been any question about where the ball would be held—Pride's Court was the obvious place. Mellerstain was an impressive house, of course, but it could not provide the grand setting, and while Sydney and Fort were consulted about arrangements and were expected to provide a proper guest list for Mildred's scrutiny, they had little to do with the actual plans. As usual Simon Court was only too delighted to foot the bills for an important family affair. He could not honestly say he communicated very well with the twins, but he could see that they were stunning and a credit to him. What more reason did he need than that?

Now the formal greetings began in earnest. Mildred, imperious in coral-colored crepe marocain draped from one shoulder and caught up in a knot at one side of the hip to create a jagged hem, looked magnificent. She wore a heavy gold bracelet and chain that supported a huge emerald. Lord Court had given it to her the previous Christmas.

Behind them, marshaled at the foot of one branch of the marble staircase, a string orchestra played romantic tunes by Irving Berlin and Sigmund Romberg. Later there would be dance music. But first, champagne and caviar and, for the serious drinkers, whisky. After the twins had been presented to the lieutenant governor, they would dance the first waltz with their father and brother, Landry. The lieutenant governor would partner Mildred while Lord Court would squire the lieutenant governor's wife. After that, cards would be filled by those who wished to dance until a late supper was served.

With his usual flair for the theatrical, Simon Court had asked his granddaughters to remain upstairs until time for the presentation. He visualized them coming down the stairs while all the guests were assembled below. Without question they would be startling, and he fully expected it to be a dramatic moment.

The crowd had swelled until all three hundred guests were present. Romantic melodies from Victor Herbert's

Naughty Marietta mixed pleasantly with the clink of glasses, the murmur of well-trained servants moving about, the shrill laughter of glittering women, and the subterranean rumbles of powerful men. At exactly nine o'clock Lord Court suggested to an aide-de-camp that the lieutenant governor's party assemble for the presentation. Looking up, he saw that the twins were approaching the landing, walking together in perfect step, absolutely indistinguishable, one from the other.

The orchestra stopped playing. Guests gazed expectantly at the stairs, realizing this was a high point of the evening. Under the brilliance of the chandelier the twins slowly descended, like goddesses from another planet. They were gowned in pale green tissue, with wide skirts that did not quite reach slim ankles. Their narrow bodices were molded of tiny feathers dyed various shades of green, yellow, and blue and were held up by wide straps that curled under the bust in silver loops. A mist of green sheer draped over bare shoulders. Light brown hair was smoothed back from each oval face and held in place at the crown by a gold ring. A shining fall of hair hung down each back in an Oriental effect. Small green velvet slippers poked out from beneath the provoking rustle of skirts.

Flora and Fenella wore no makeup. Their flawless skin, tilted green eyes, and pouting, suggestive mouths were enough to enforce a brief silence on the assembly. They moved gracefully down the stairs, not quite touching fingers but joined by an invisible force. Nobody could have discerned with any amount of accuracy which was Flora and which Fenella. They moved like dancers across the Great Hall to be introduced to the lieutenant governor and his party.

As the orchestra struck up the first notes of the "Blue Danube Waltz," they moved off with their partners and the guests watched, smiling, fascinated. In the ranks of the eligible young men there was a curious stir. The twins were now formally available for proper dates, but their beauty, while intriguing, carried with it a rather chilling air of oddness.

Sydney, watching her daughters from the rim of spectators while Fort swirled Flora about in a haze of green silk and brown flying hair, frowned. Suddenly she felt afraid for them and afraid for herself. Something about them intimidated even her.

But the dramatic moments were not yet over. As the waltz ended, four guests arrived in the Great Hall. If anybody had noticed earlier that Susan and David were not present, they had failed to comment upon it. But now here she was, Susan Mulqueen, looking a tiny bit wan after her ordeal but hair sleek again, shining, slim body encased in a tight brown velvet tube and topped with an orange feather boa wound loosely about the neck. David stood beside her fair-haired and cool in his tails, looking vaguely bored. Beside them stood two staggeringly handsome, yet darkly mysterious young men.

Lord Court hurried toward the newcomers. He'd been too busy to miss Susan, but now he realized that she was late. A momentary flash of pleasure came over him when he saw her. He was fond of the girl. He admired her spirit, dammit. It was only when he fetched up directly in front of the Mulqueens that he realized what was bothering him, for his eyes were not what they had once been and he could not see in the distance. The two young strangers were introduced to him, and he felt an electrical charge of warning pass through him. Susan had Lord Court's own flair for drama he thought, for she had topped his own little show with one of her own! By God, you had to hand it to Susan!

The two young men, tall, dark, almost wickedly good-looking, were identical twins. They were tall—probably six feet—with heavy shoulders and necks beneath the crisp white starch of evening shirts and elegantly cut tails. Not only was the skin olive colored (but not unpleasantly swarthy), but the hair was black, thick, with just enough curl to keep it shaped to the head. They could have been actors. The eyes were rather narrow and set above prominent cheekbones, the lips curved and wide, just missing what might have been obvious sensuality. The chins were firm—not heavy, but definitely strong. The combination was patrician; acceptable but still carrying a touch of the exotic.

"Grandfather," Susan said, kissing him on the cheek, "I've brought two guests. I knew you wouldn't mind. May I introduce Kevin and Keith March? They're from Boston. I met them when I was visiting the clinic down there. This is my grandfather, Lord Court."

Lord Court offered his hand. He was not a man given to mysticism or belief in premonitions or any silly nonsense like that, but he had an uncanny feeling of unease as he examined the twins for the first time.

"Sorry to spring this on you, sir," David Mulqueen said lightly, "but Susan wanted to make it a surprise. I humored her."

"Perfectly all right. Susan always has a bit of style," Simon Court said, smiling now, relaxing again. "Come along and have some champagne. Or perhaps you prefer something else? We'll be having supper a bit later. As you see, dancing has just begun."

"The boys will be dying to dance," Susan said brightly. "I'm not quite up to that, yet. Unfortunately."

Other guests were looking at the March twins with curiosity now. A waiter came by with a tray and Susan took a glass.

"Mmmmm. Good. As always, Grandfather. Kevin and Keith would like to meet *our* twins. Shall I do it, or would you like to?"

"I'll do the introductions, my dear. Of course. Ah, there they are, off the floor now. And looking at their cards, if I'm not mistaken."

"Yes, they are," David confirmed.

Simon Court led the way around the edge of the dancers to where Flora and Fenella stood close together. A ripple of interest followed in his wake. People had noticed, were waiting expectantly for the two pairs of twins to meet. Flora and Fenella looked up, saw Lord Court approaching, and then caught sight of Kevin and Keith March.

The air was heavy with the breathless quality that precedes a storm. Pressure, invisible but palpable, built up around the party. Lord Court felt a buzzing in his head. He stared at his granddaughters and noticed that they no longer seemed aware of anybody but the March twins. Eyes locked into eyes. Then the shock passed. Faces returned to smiles, to charming masks.

Lord Court made the introductions with his usual air of grandeur, but he had scarcely finished when he saw that one of the young men had taken Flora's hand, the other Fenella's, and they led them to the floor. The music was a bit of romantic fluff from *Maytime*, a popular operetta, and the two sets of twins began to waltz like perfectly trained dancers on a stage. Everybody else stopped dancing and moved off the floor to stare in fascination. The two couples were graceful, facile, never missing a step, never hesitating, never taking their eyes from each other's faces. In a few minutes, the tension broke and people began to talk again, drink, and dance again, but somehow the chemistry of the ball had changed in some subtle way. Nothing was ever quite the same again.

Supper had not yet been served when Fort took Sydney aside. He found her watching the dancers. She had just seen the strange twins whisk Flora and Fenella to the dance floor, and she turned to her husband with a puzzled, wary look.

"Who *are* they? How odd."

"I have no idea. Susan brought them, I believe."

Sydney felt as if fate had somehow taken events out of her hands as she looked at the two mirror-image couples on the floor. On the surface there was nothing amiss. The March twins were handsome, impeccably dressed, and they would not have come to the ball unless somebody brought them and properly introduced them to this society. Perhaps it was the memory of a frivolous conversation she had held with Flora and Fenella on this very subject only a few months earlier. Being precocious, they had already looked into the question of meeting identical male twins.

"You can appreciate how much we'd like to marry exactly the same man," Flora had pointed out one morning over the breakfast table. "We'd be bound to fight if one of us found Prince Charming first. We might even cut him in half."

"Bloodthirsty little beast!" Fenella had cried, throwing a wicked look at her sister. "But of course she's right. Do you think I'm getting fat? Should I diet? Should I go on a fast?"

"Fasting is good for the soul. And fashionable, too," Flora agreed. "The new styles demand an absolutely flat figure. Do you think men like that, Mother? I shouldn't think so myself. Am I too fat?"

"You aren't too fat. Eat up and don't be so silly," Sydney replied impatiently.

"All I can say is, good thing old Milly snagged North when she did or we might have cut *him* in half, don't you think so? Right down the middle, poor thing," Flora said, reverting to the earlier theme of men. "What a sexy man he is!"

"That's a very coarse way to talk," Sydney had protested, but she did find the girls mildly amusing at times. "North is far too old for you even to look at. He must be at least twenty-seven."

"I read in the paper just the other day that some girls have been swallowing tapeworms to get thin," Flora said.

"Revolting. No tapeworms for me," Fenella assured her. "I have my own method of keeping thin. I drink a cup of vinegar every night before I go to bed. Cook smuggles it in for me by the gallon, you know. But getting back to men —Mother, don't you realize that older men are just what we need? How can we learn about life if we only talk to boys our own age? They know less about life than we do. It doesn't make sense."

"But we do know the answer to our problem," Flora said, giving her mother a stern look. "Identical twins! Imagine. That would prevent any chance of a massacre. Why can't we have raspberries every single day of our lives? Mmmm. I love them. I'll bet they have raspberries every day at Pride's Court. Lucky Milly to live there, don't you agree, Fenella?"

"Why, oh, why didn't Grandfather take a fancy to *us*?" Fenella cried, rolling her eyes. "We're much more fascinating than Milly. How does she manage to have all the luck? Pride's Court and North as well. It simply isn't fair. And she's the size of a horse."

"Speaking of horses, let's go out to the farm soon and look at those beautiful horses Susan and David have. What do you say? Susan invited us."

"Perhaps we could. But the awful truth is—getting back to men—we need to find identical twins who are dashing, rich, and older. But where? Do you know what the odds are?" Fenella demanded of her mother.

"No, I haven't thought about it. Rather astronomical," Sydney said.

"You're right," Flora said. "We've tried to calculate. For example, statistics show that only one out of every six hundred sets of identical twins is actually *identical*. Think of that. So alike even their dear mother can't tell them apart. Now, the chances of us finding look-alikes who are adorable and rich and possibly even clever are probably in the millions."

"Billions," Fenella corrected.

"Then I'd forget about it if I were you," Sydney suggested. "Are you riding this morning, girls?"

"Definitely. Must keep in shape. Also, it helps our restlessness, you know," Flora said, darkly. "Young girls have their own problems."

"There's always the chance that we might meet our Perfect Knights on the bridle path, too," Fenella added.

Tonight, watching the dancers go through the intricacies of the tango, Sydney could not help shuddering at the uncanny arrival of the March twins on the night of the coming-out ball. It was as if fate had taken rather too definite a hand in the lives of her children.

When she followed Fort to the reception hall, she found he had already brought her mink coat from the cloakroom.

"Sydney, I have a surprise for you tonight."

"Tonight? But this is the girls' night—not mine. Are we going out?"

"Yes, out. I've arranged a very special surprise. It took a great deal of planning, so I hope you'll come with me."

She was puzzled, but she saw that he was unusually excited. She could not imagine what he had in store for her, or where they could be going.

"Did I tell you how lovely you look?" Fort was helping her on with the fur. She had braided her hair with a silk daisy chain and wound it into a crown on top of her head.

"Here, put this on."

"But we can't go out," Sydney protested.

"Yes, we can. I've asked Dodgson to warm up the car. He's waiting outside now."

"Fort, I can't leave the ball. What will people think?"

"They won't notice. Please, Sydney, it's important or I wouldn't ask you to do it. I think you'll be pleased."

"But where on earth are we going?"

"To the Windsor Hotel. Now, come with me. Trust me."

She allowed him to put on his own coat while she took the gloves out of her own pocket, and during all this, she was so surprised by Fort's unusual behavior that she said no more. He guided her outside and helped her into the car. When they reached the hotel, they passed through the lobby to the elevators without meeting anyone they knew.

Fort had her by the elbow, steering her as if he thought she might run away. At the fifth floor they got out and he led her to one of the larger suites. He knocked and then opened the door himself, as if the person inside had been expecting him. From the entrance she could not see the entire sitting room.

"Someone here wants to meet you," Fort said.

"Fort, why are you being so mysterious?"

"You'll see. I'm going down to the lobby to wait for you. Come when you are ready."

Before she could argue, he had gone. The door closed behind him. She was curious, and yet she knew Fort would not do anything that would harm her. So she walked into the sitting room to see who was waiting there. A man stood quietly beside a large side table on which a tray of drinks and an ice bucket rested. She stared at him, but he was a complete stranger. He appeared to be in his seventies, with broad shoulders, a rather solid build and thick, white hair. Despite an air of familiarity about his face and manner, she had never seen him before in her life.

"Who are you? Should I know you?"

"My dear," he said in a gentle voice. "How beautiful you are!"

She detected an English flavor to his pronunciation. His voice was light but pleasant, and when she looked closer, she could see that he was older than she had thought at first. Yet the eyes were blue and alert, the eyelids folded down into relaxed creases. He wore spectacles with gold frames.

She saw, too, that his hands were clenched as if he might be nervous. He smiled, however.

"My name is Jamie Ackroyd. Does that mean anything to you?"

"Jamie Ackroyd!"

How peculiar the name sounded now that she had said it aloud. Of course it meant something to her! She looked at him in a different way now, taking in every detail, the balanced features, the intelligent glance, the deep chin. She saw that his clothes were well cut although not as expensive as those worn by the Court men.

"Jamie Ackroyd. My *father*!" she whispered, although she did not know why.

"Yes, Sydney. Your father."

"You really are my father," she repeated. "That's incredible. How did you get here? I don't understand—"

"Your husband arranged everything. He came to see me the last time he was in England. He thought this meeting might be important to you. I'm not in good health, my dear, but he kindly saw that I had good accommodation on a Court ship. Otherwise, I might not have made the journey."

"Fort did that?"

"My dear Sydney . . . I hope I may call you Sydney? If this meeting distresses you, say so and I'll not trouble you again. You see, your husband begged me to come. But there is no need to create a problem. I can book back to England again in a few days."

"Oh, no. You mustn't leave. Not yet. I want to understand what this means, to look at you. It's so hard to believe after all these years, and then, I didn't know you were alive until just a few years ago . . . did Fort tell you that?"

"He told me. He explained how he found me."

"I see."

She sat down and took off her gloves, as if that somehow settled things, but she kept staring at Jamie Ackroyd.

"Could I offer you a brandy?" he asked. "There is some good cognac here."

"Yes, please."

He poured some in a snifter and handed it to her.

"Thank you for coming," he said.

She accepted the drink and saw that his hands were well kept. She sipped the cognac gratefully, trying to find her bearings, to decide how she felt about this. Finally she asked if he were staying in the hotel, although it seemed self-evident. He said he was and that Fort had felt this the best arrangement until after the meeting. He had known about the ball for the twins, but again, Fort and he together decided that he ought not to appear until Sydney accepted or rejected him. He was anxious to see his granddaughters, he pointed out, and his grandson, but he would force nothing. Sydney finished the brandy and set down the empty glass. Then she stood up.

Sydney had never been a woman given to weeping easily. Her background, the harsh life in London's slums when she was a child, the struggle for survival in a world she could barely comprehend, had made tears a luxury. Weeping, she had noticed, solved nothing. It only seemed to make women look less attractive. But now the choked feeling that always prefaced a good cry almost overcame her. For years she had worried about the existence of this man, and then she refused to see him. Before Fort found out about Jamie Ackroyd, Sydney had often imagined her father as a raving lunatic, a transient, a criminal, perhaps a murderer. Yet here he was, looking perfectly normal and intelligent and kind. A shell of long-corroded fear dropped away as she looked into Jamie's affectionate gaze. Tears blurred her vision.

"You must come to Mellerstain," she said, holding out her hand to him. "You must come back to Mellerstain."

They had decided that Jamie Ackroyd would meet his grandchildren and move into Mellerstain the next day. To introduce this complication into the coming-out ball seemed far too dramatic and dangerous to all of them. It had been such an exhausting night that Fort did not press Sydney for a discussion. When they returned home after the ball, he went to his own room.

Sydney was pleased that Fort had made no demands upon her. It seemed that she had had enough turmoil for one day. She was totally exhausted, she thought, as she retired to her own bedroom to undress. The twins had stayed over at Pride's Court, as arranged, so that there would be no problem about escorts seeing them home. The emergence of the devastating Bostonians was such an added touch that Sydney had decided not to think about it until morning.

In the peace of her own room she undressed and put on a blue silk nightgown with full sleeves and a gathered bodice. She slipped into her own comfortable bed and lay staring up at the celing. Yet she was so tense that she could not seem to close her eyes. Her legs felt numb. Nerves, she decided, that was what was the matter. Far too much excitement for one day. Her mind spun around the events of the evening and she began to feel grateful to Fort. He had taken the risk of bringing her father to see her, taken the risk of yet another rejection from her. She felt a flood of gratitude toward him. Or was it love? She wanted to tell him how much she appreciated his thoughtfulness, how delighted she was actually to meet her father. She sat up in bed and then swung her feet to the floor. As she stood hesitantly on the carpet, she remembered a night long ago—the first night she had allowed Fort to make love to her after they were married. He had taken her out to the Court farmhouse and, when she did not respond, left her there in the frigid December weather to amuse herself as best she could. But he had not forced her. That had been their agreement and Fort had stuck to it. One night, as she lay shivering in the cold bedroom, she had felt so desperately lonely that she had torn off the heavy nightgown, and, naked, run across the hall to Fort's bedroom and thrown herself into his arms.

Now, in the warm cocoon of Mellerstain, she had the same sweeping need to feel Fort's arms around her, to have the assurance of his love. She ripped off the silk nightgown and tossed it to the floor. Then she walked through the shared bathroom into Fort's bedroom. Although the lights were out, she could distinguish his form lying perfectly still upon the bed. She walked naked toward him.

"So you've come, Sydney," he said.

"Yes, I've come."

"I've been waiting. I've been waiting such a long time, darling."

He lifted the covers (as he had done so many years before) and she slid between them and into his arms. He folded her close, his embrace warm and gentle. His arms tightened.

"Sydney, darling, welcome home."

CHAPTER SEVEN

"Since nobody will be downstairs for another half hour," Lord Court said, helping himself to kippers from the serving table, "we may as well have a brief meeting."

By some unfortunate trick of fate, North had arrived in the breakfast room at exactly the same time as Simon Court. This was unusual: Most mornings North appeared just as Lord Court was about to leave the table. When he timed it properly, North could manage a few minutes alone with his newspaper between the old man's departure and Mildred's arrival.

As he followed Lord Court to the sideboard (the Courts dispensed with table service at breakfast except for fresh pots of tea and coffee brought in by Peters), North groaned silently. Heaping his plate with bacon and eggs from the covered silver dishes and plucking lukewarm toast from a rack, he braced himself to face Lord Court's high-volume pontifications on various aspects of the financial stratosphere.

Looking out of the tall church-style windows into the depressing gray of a November morning, North decided that it was certainly not his day. First thing was not his idea of a proper time for a business meeting with Simon Court. He did not relish the meetings at any time, but at least if they took place in the afternoon, he had had sufficient time to adjust.

North preferred to approach his day slowly and slip easily into his routine without shocking his system. Usually, he drank two cups of coffee before holding any lengthy discussions with anybody about anything. He counted on reading the financial section of his newspaper undisturbed. He liked (if he could arrange it) to absorb the stock market quotations and business news painlessly and let the information sift gently down into his memory like silt settling in a pond. As he confronted the grisly necessity of concentrating on Lord Court's every word, he retreated.

"How's your arm?" Lord Court asked surprisingly.

"Healing well, thank you. It's still sore, though."

"Glad to hear it's improving. I like a man who acts promptly in an emergency. You'd have made a good soldier. We were all glad you weren't seriously hurt."

He sat down at his own end of the table and put on his spectacles to eat his fish.

"Dangerous things, kippers," he observed, lifting out the backbone and placing it carefully to one side. "Now, let's get down to business before Mildred arrives. I meant to find a space in my schedule this morning to talk to you. This saves valuable time."

"Certainly. What's on your mind?" North pumped up his enthusiasm with considerable effort. He left his paper lying unopened by his place, reluctantly abandoning the commodities market until a more appropriate time.

"I expect you've kept up with the changes in banking—the recent merger between the Standard Bank and the

Sterling—and between the Bank of Montreal and Molson's Bank?"

"Yes, of course. I meant to ask your opinion about the shrinking number of chartered banks in this country. Is it a bad thing, do you think?"

"No, no, it's a stabilizer. As a matter of fact, that's what I want to tell you. The Empire Bank is merging with the Royal."

North was taken by surprise. There hadn't been a single rumor about the merger around the Empire. For Lord Court to have pulled it off so secretively was quite a feat.

"Not a word leaked out. This is the first I've heard," he said.

"Good, good." Lord Court looked pleased. "I'm carrying on as a director at the Royal Bank. I'm also remaining in my office. I told them from the start that I wouldn't talk merger unless they agreed to let me keep my office. I'm too old to move now."

North waited. He knew Simon Court intended to enlarge on the subject, possibly even touching on the effect this would have upon North's career.

"I suppose you're wondering what I plan for you? Whether you're to stay on at the Royal or move to one of my other companies? Am I right?"

"Naturally, I'm concerned—"

"Don't worry, my boy. I have just the spot for you. A new business, a new challenge. I like your work, and you know how I appreciate you and Milly. She runs this place like an army camp. Ha. Ha. I'm making you president of Crown Tobacco."

"But I don't know anything about the tobacco business."

"You know something about money. You know how I like things done. That's what counts. Crown isn't my largest holding, but you're young. It has been suffering because of these damnable smugglers, but I think we can survive, with the right methods. There's money to be made in tobacco, you know."

"What about Jeffreys?" Jeffreys was president of Crown Tobacco at the present time. "Are you letting him go?"

"Moving him over to Court Mines. Don't you worry about Jeffreys, he will be all right. You won't run into hostility from management, if that's what you're afraid of. I'm backing you all the way, North. I want you to hire an advertising manager. Have you seen those colored cards they put in Turret cigarettes—the ones people collect? When they get a full set, they win a prize or some such thing. Now, I like that kind of idea. We might try something similar."

North tried to fix his mind on the entirely new prospect of selling tobacco and cigarettes. Other than buying them when he ran out and selecting the best cigars from Lord Court's humidors, the subject had occupied little of his attention.

"We're going to solve this smuggling thing one way or another," Lord Court was saying. "The Protective Association has been running a little investigation of its own, and we've got the goods. Just you wait until the House sits next January and we'll see some action. But that isn't what I want to talk to you about now, North. Before you take over Crown Tobacco, I have another job I want you to do. You'll have to go to Ottawa."

"What's going on there? The House isn't sitting, is it?"

"No, no, but there's some business as usual, you know. I need specific information about members of the Board of Commerce and the Trade Commission," Simon Court said. "You find out who they are and why they haven't supported the sugar refiners. Once we know that, we may be able to buy somebody off. It's that simple."

"Sorry, I don't follow."

"I'm out to get St. Amour. That man has done more damage to this family, caused me more agony than any man alive. I mean to have his scalp."

Every member of the Court family was familiar with Simon Court's attitude toward Armand St. Amour. But even when North had ferreted out facts and figures about St. Amour's financial situation three years earlier, he had not realized how emotionally involved the old man was. As he stared across the table at Lord Court, he saw a maniacal gleam in the cold blue eyes and primitive vengefulness in the expression that bordered on madness. He saw, exposed for the first time in his life, raw hatred.

"I've found a way to do it," Lord Court went on. "You can help me. I already know that the bulk of his capital is tied up in his refinery. He's always been a half-wit about investments. This goes well back before your time, North, but Armand was once in partnership with a man called

378

Max DeLeon. Max had all the brains. It goes without saying. That's how St. Amour bailed out of his financial troubles after his father died. But after De Leon died, St. Amour was on his own. He has another partner now, but it isn't the same thing. Everybody knew the bottom had fallen out of the sugar business in Canada, but St. Amour picked up this refinery for nothing, thinking the government would subsidize the industry. The gamble hasn't paid off."

"Why do you think the government backed down?"

"Who knows why they do *anything*? St. Amour has a brother-in-law who's a senator and a nephew who just got reelected to the House. I think he'll try to bring pressure to bear on the Board of Commerce. It only makes sense. Get my point? And by God, it might work. Well, two can play at that game. We'll bribe somebody on the Board—more than one if necessary—to do absolutely nothing. If things go on like this much longer, the sugar refineries will go under. St. Amour will be going under with them."

"How much are you prepared to pay?"

"Just between us, a million dollars doesn't look too high. But naturally, I'd like to spend a great deal less. See what you can find out. It depends who we must buy, and how many men are involved."

North was a little staggered. A million dollars to ruin somebody! The old man was obsessed. North wondered if Lord Court might be getting dotty.

"Your scheme will bring down all the refineries if it succeeds, not just St. Amour."

"That is possible. Not necessarily, but possible. And be damned to them. They sell molasses to the distilleries and next to the distillers I hate the sugar refiners. They all encourage gangsterism, rumrunning. We all know that the rumrunners are damaging business in many fields. That's no secret. So be damned to them. You just find out who we can pay off, that's all you have to do."

"I'll do the best I can."

North agreed because he felt he had to agree. But the whole proposition was disturbing. When he had looked into Armand's affairs three years earlier to gain a bargaining position for Simon Court, it had been different. Armand held a piece of land the Courts needed, and he refused to sell. Business was a dog-eat-dog affair, after all.

But to set out deliberately to ruin a man was another thing. Yet he was caught in the Court trap. How could he refuse something Lord Court wanted him to do? He wasn't willing to move out of Pride's Court and begin again on his own. The idea of falling into disfavor with Milly's grandfather was frightening. Milly wouldn't stand for it.

"This time, I'm going to put St. Amour in his place. He can't hold out for more than six months, perhaps not even that. His other interests won't support his style of living; I know what it costs to live the way he does. And that rag my daughter publishes won't support them either, though she makes a small profit on it."

"It will affect your daughter, too."

"Let *her* worry about that. She didn't think about money when she ran away from Pride's Court. From everything I stand for!"

He would have gone into a tirade except that Mildred appeared at that moment and interrupted his train of thought.

"Good morning, darling." She kissed North. "Good morning, Grandfather. You both look very grim so early in the morning."

She did not really wait for an answer but selected a small helping of scrambled eggs and one slice of toast and sat down at her own place with a pad and pencil. She always made notes about her household chores and appointments over the breakfast table.

"Milly, I want to speak to you," Lord Court said, turning his attention from North. "It's about Susan."

"Susan? What about her?" Mildred's voice was sharp.

"Now, Milly," her grandfather said in what he fondly imagined to be a placating tone but which actually came out like a voice in a megaphone, "I'd like to see Susan and David here more often." (There was a surprising choking sound from North's direction, as if he had swallowed his coffee the wrong way.) "She's had a bad time between the fire and losing the baby. We ought to cheer her up. I know North agrees with me on this. I thought she looked quite exhausted at the ball, didn't you?"

"I thought she looked fine," Milly said coldly.

"No, no, she didn't. You were too busy to notice, that's all. She might feel better if she saw more of the family.

But she managed to give us all a rare jolt when she sprang those twins on us, eh?"

"It was mischievous," Mildred said, pouring out her coffee with a vengeance. "She ought to have told me about extra guests."

"It was only a bit of drama," Simon Court said. "Susan always had a flair for the dramatic."

"I call it poor manners," Mildred said sullenly, "and thoughtless, too. Aunt Sydney wasn't pleased, either. Just the sight of the four of them is upsetting. I can't explain it. But—"

North put down his paper and said, chuckling, "All your guests thought they were drunk. Double vision."

"That isn't funny," Mildred said. She was irritated with both men.

"Susan told me they come from a good Boston family," Lord Court said. "Good, as far as American families go."

"Yes, I inquired about them, too," Mildred said, "and that's true. The March family ranks with the Rockefellers and the Morgans. Their ancestors were among the first fur traders. It's all very impressive, but it doesn't excuse Susan's behavior."

Lord Court ignored that now, delighted with Mildred's attitude.

"Looked them up, did you? Good for you. Just what I was going to do myself when I had a minute."

"At least I know how to behave," Mildred said point-edly.

"Oh, Susan is a good girl. Don't be hard on her. By the way, Simon is coming down from Courtsville next week and bringing that girl he plans to marry. We'll have to arrange some kind of quiet wedding. He doesn't want any fuss, and under the circumstances, it probably isn't ap-propriate. I thought you could invite them to stay here, Milly, instead of with Mary in the coach house. There isn't much room there."

"Certainly, that's all right. I always like to see Simon. Though it's odd he'd pick a country girl for a wife."

"I'm not sure it isn't for the best. She loves to live up north and so does Simon. If he married a Montreal girl, she'd want to live in the city. Simon's been much better since he went up there, you know. It agrees with him."

"I suppose you're right," Mildred agreed reluctantly.

"Gold is up," North announced from behind his newspaper, which he had finally opened. "So is copper and silver and zinc. I hope this boom lasts."

"It'll last awhile," Simon Court said confidently, "but don't buy anything speculative. There's a lot of paper floating around that's utterly worthless. Are you ready to go, North? Might as well ride with me."

"Yes, of course. Thank you."

In winter North drove a two-tone Ford sedan. He liked to drive himself to work, but this morning it was clear that Lord Court wasn't going to allow that. The business meeting was to continue, and so he yielded to the old man's suggestion with as good grace as he could manage.

As they left the room, Lord Court began to explain his latest maneuver.

"We're buying into Brazilian Traction. It's never looked back since Sir James Dunn put it on its feet some years ago. I'm sending Charles down there soon. Let me tell you how we managed this deal, North. . . ."

During the first week in December Sydney telephoned Mildred.

"I'd like to ask a favor of you, Milly," Sydney said, "though I know you're busy. The twins from Boston are back in Montreal for a few days, and I should have a dinner party, but I wondered if you'd consider giving it at Pride's Court . . ."

"I could manage that, if you like."

"Are you sure? With Christmas coming, it seems unfair to load it on you. But if I send some extra help over—"

"There's no need for that, Aunt Sydney. We have plenty of staff."

"You're always so well organized, Milly."

Mildred was pleased. She always felt gratified when somebody noticed how efficiently she ran Pride's Court.

"When did you want to have the dinner party?"

"Next week, if you can work it in."

"Wait until I look in my book, Aunt Sydney. Here . . . Tuesday looks good. How is that for you, and for the girls?"

"Perfect for us. Now, is there anything I can do?"

"Not really. Who is on your list, Aunt Sydney?"

"There'll be your mother, of course. Landry is home for

Christmas, and we could match him up at the table with Charity. That'll even it out, don't you think? What about Susan and David?"

"If you like." Mildred tried not to sound cold. "Susan did bring the boys to the ball, didn't she? So I guess the introductions were her idea."

"That would make twelve at the table. This is awfully good of you, Milly. I knew you'd see why I'd prefer to have the dinner at Pride's Court. Both North and your grandfather do enjoy entertaining . . ."

"Yes, of course they do. Don't worry, Aunt Sydney, I'll manage it just fine."

"How are the boys?"

"Both well, thank you."

"Let me know if there's anything you want, Milly. I could send flowers for the table if you like."

"No, I'll get something out of the gardener. Poinsettias would be nice, and I know he has them. We bought a beautiful Christmas dinner service last time we were in London. I'll use that."

"Thank you, darling, this *is* good of you. See you Tuesday."

An air of apprehension hung over the dinner party. Every conversation seemed shot through with double meanings, cross-currents that were almost palpable. Landry, for example, was more noticeably languid. His hair was long, as if he were about to play a role on stage, and his mannerisms had become fussy for such a young man. Lord Court had talked to him for a few minutes before dinner, asking about his work at the western experimental station, but he had soon become irritated and walked away. Even Sydney had noticed this disturbing softness in her son. She felt beleaguered—wasn't it enough to be saddled with the extraordinary March twins?

For her part, Mildred did not like having Susan in the house. Consequently, when she wasn't supervising drinks or checking on dinner arrangements, she found herself glancing secretively at her cousin and then at North. Susan had recovered from her invalid look and now appeared quite bright. Her voice, however, was uncommonly shrill. She wore a fashionable black silk gown with a long necklace of fake pearls. Mildred thought the beads were appalling, but several family members seemed mildly amused. This irritated Mildred even more. She noticed that North was drinking too fast and that he appeared to be highly nervous. She now regretted her generosity in offering to give the dinner when her aunt had telephoned. But of course, it was too late.

Sitting at table, the two sets of twins had been deliberately separated to reduce the effect of double vision. Even so, the four young people seemed to draw every eye. Reluctantly, everybody looked from one to the other constantly, trying to solve some vague puzzle. In fact, the twins were an irresistible magnet. Keith and Kevin seemed to operate on the same invisible connection that had always existed between Flora and Fenella. They, too, finished each other's sentences and glanced frequently at each other for confirmation or denial.

Everyone was startled, as well, at the sudden transformation of Charity from child to young woman. Relatives who had thought of her as chubby and preadolescent were suddenly confronted with a tall coltish young woman with the confidence of a tiger. Her long legs seemed to go on forever, her arms were stylishly slender, and her head featured a huge mane of streaky blond hair. She had a bony face, with full lips and storm-tossed dark eyes. She wore a number of cheap, gawdy rings, flashing them as a sign of independence. There was an odd ageless quality about her—she looked fifteen and twenty-one at the same time.

The Courts struggled through dinner, torn between the interesting mannerisms of the two sets of twins and the unexpected apparition of a new Court beauty. By the time port was served, they had reached no conclusions but were ready to retire from the table. However, one of the twins from Boston rose and directed his attention to Lord Court. This departure from ritual amazed everyone. A strained hush fell upon the table.

"Since this is a family dinner, sir," the twin Kevin said, glass in hand, "my brother and I thought it might be appropriate to make an announcement. I do hope I have your permission, Lord Court? And yours, Mrs. Grenville-Court?"

A wave of *déjà vu* swept around the table: They had all been here before, they knew what would be said. Lord

Court nodded, taken aback when things appeared to be wrested from his hands at his own table. Now, the second twin stood, also with a glass in his hand.

"Keith and I," Kevin said, "have asked Flora and Fenella to marry us. That is"—and here he smiled winningly at them—"Keith has asked Flora, and I have asked Fenella. They have accepted. We hope the family will approve."

This strange statement was greeted with silence, as eyes turned toward Lord Court. Nobody spoke for a few seconds. Then Lord Court coughed, drew himself together with an effort, and stood.

"A most unusual way to do things. But I suppose things have changed since I was young, eh? Since you've already decided, what can I say? What can any of us say, except we offer our congratulations to you two young men, and our loving good wishes to Flora and Fenella."

"Thank you, sir. We aren't planning a wedding until next spring. Kevin and I must make plans to move to Montreal. We've spoken to our father about taking over one of his companies up here . . . Northern Pulp and Paper. I'm sure you've heard of it? We need time to move, to buy a house—"

A house. It was the use of the singular that struck the Courts as unusual. A house.

"A house?" Fort asked. "One house? Or one house each?"

"Oh, one large house," Keith said brightly. "No sense in having two houses. We'd always be running back and forth. Flora and Fenella feel the same way, so there's no problem. We're looking for an older, established house here on the Mountain. So if anybody knows one that's for sale—"

"Yes, one large house," Kevin agreed. "We prefer not to build. Too exhausting. We'd much rather take over one that's standing."

"Oh, yes," Fenella said.

"Of course," Flora echoed.

The air thickened with nameless doubts. Yet not one person could have said why or what it was they found objectionable about the whole idea of the two pairs of newlyweds sharing a house. Essentially, there was nothing wrong with it. After all, Mildred and North had moved into Pride's Court to share the house with Charles and

Lord Court. Many years before, Charles and his bride, Venetia, had come here, and after that, his second wife, Polly. Why was it different?

It was Charity, oddly enough, who put her finger on it when she said lightly, "That ought to be just about the most confusing arrangement in the whole world. You'll all have to wear name tags!"

CHAPTER EIGHT

For the first six months of 1926 Canada's Parliament seethed with suspicion, cynicism, and outright distrust. Prime Minister Mackenzie King held no seat, an arrangement that was not only awkward but threw King into apoplectic rages. In February the Liberals asked for an adjournment—ostensibly to secure a safe seat for their chief in a carefully controlled by-election. But doubting Conservatives decided there was more to the request than *that*. When had the wily King ever done anything quite so obvious?

Since the Conservatives were busily preparing a grand exposé of the customs scandal, they feared the Liberals might be planning a coup—a modest *mea culpa* confession of slight wrongdoing in low places in order to soften the blow and protect rather extensive wickedness in high places.

The Commercial Protective Association (made up chiefly of powerful business interests in Montreal and Toronto) used private investigators to gather together a damning dossier of payoff and corruption in the Liberal camp. Longtime Conservative Member Harry Stevens had been carefully selected to put the matter before the House. Conservatives outmaneuvered the adjournment, and instead, a parliamentary committee was convened to look into the whole messy question of bootlegging, smuggling of manufactured goods into Canada from the United States, and possible bribery of high officials. On this uncertain note the business of the country creaked along from January until June.

As for the long-promised support for the suffering sugar industry, it was not forthcoming. Every day that government aid was denied, Armand St. Amour came closer to disaster. So that by the end of April he was desperate. His other interests were safe enough, but with more than half his capital tied up in the refinery he could not hope to maintain his present standard of living. Nothing could save the refinery now, and yet he found it almost unbearable to face selling Edenbridge. He searched about somewhat wildly for a way to recoup his financial losses.

On June 1 the refinery declared bankruptcy and closed its doors. It was his son, Michel, who told Armand that Angus McKie was in town. McKie was an American associate of Armand's old partner, Max DeLeon, who still held interests in many Canadian mining ventures. McKie, Michel said, was on his way to northwestern Quebec, where a supposedly fabulous gold mine was in the early stages of development.

As soon as he could walk comfortably, Michel had once again taken to the air and at present owned a small shuttle service out of Haileybury in northern Ontario. His flying boat (as it was called) was capable of carrying its pilot and two passengers on short-range flights, and the adventurous users of his plane were mostly mining engineers and potential investors who were anxious to look at the scene of the most recent gold strike in northern Canada—Noranda and Rouyn. Michel had agreed to fly Angus McKie into Noranda, and remembering his father had once known the New Yorker, informed him about McKie's residence in the Ritz-Carlton Hotel.

When he heard Armand's voice on the telephone, McKie instantly invited him up to the hotel for a drink and a chat. Armand found the former prospector still lively, still ambitious, still believing in the riches of the north. He was a small, bald man with two missing front teeth and a taste for ill-fitting tweed suits, but when he spoke, he was so knowledgeable that his physical handicaps vanished.

"Well, laddie, we meet again!" Angus thrust out his hand and pumped Armand's with genuine enthusiasm. "You're looking well."

"So are you, Angus. I'm surprised you're still willing to rough it up north. I thought you and Max might have let all the claims lapse."

"We let some lapse, yes. But I've kept an eye on things

up there, just the same. I'm not completely out of it. I always played my hunches, you know. I think Noranda is a big one."

"Really that good, is it?"

"Brandy? I still drink the same old thing," Angus said.

"That's fine, Angus, thank you. But isn't it trying, going up there? The place is pretty crude, from what I hear. Barely opened up."

"Well, this flying helps." He raised his glass in a silent toast to their old friendship. "I guess if I had to make the train trip and then the long haul from the end of the rail, I wouldn't be so keen. But your son's plane lands right on the lake—right on the doorstep of Number One Shaft."

"You aren't nervous about flying, then?"

"After all I've been through in life? Not me. Better to die doing the only thing I care about—assessing mines. I'm excited about this one, Armand. Maybe you ought to get into it."

"What makes you so sure about this one?" Armand asked.

"Several things. That's why I'm going up there to see for myself. If it looks as good as I think it is, I'm going to invest. I'd like to see you get a piece, Armand."

"So would I," Armand said. "I made a bad investment in sugar three years ago, and I've lost a hell of a lot of money."

"Sugar?" Angus McKie cried, shaking his head. "Dammit, laddie, you should have known better than that. Bottom fell out of the sugar market in Cuba and the States and has never recovered. Canada's just a convenient dumping ground. You can't make money that way, my boy."

"So I found. My refinery went into bankruptcy and a chunk of my capital vanished along with it. I'm seriously looking for a way to make up my losses."

"There's always a way, but this Noranda thing may take some time. Mines are often slow to develop, as you well know. Right now, it depends on how soon they build a smelter. See, when Horne first staked his claims at Noranda, he was looking for gold and he found it. When there's copper in the ore, it makes refining more difficult, but if it's commercial copper and there's enough of it, it can be worthwhile. Right now, the price of copper is high and going higher."

386

"What stage is Noranda at, exactly? Looking for development money?"

"That's right, laddie, and they're off to a good start. One of the things I like is that Noah Timmins believes in it. Last year Timmins was in for five hundred shares of Noranda. The capital of the company was increased to a million and a half shares, and stockholders of record received a hundred shares of new stock for one of the old. Timmins then had fifty thousand shares. But they were still looking for money. American Metals Company in New York got involved; they offered to invest three hundred and fifty thousand, but the Noranda syndicate wanted half a million. Then American Metals was invited to build a smelter on the site. A report from mining engineers up there said two hundred and fifty thousand tons of ore were already blocked out at a depth of two hundred feet. And there was plenty more lower down. American Metals agreed to build the smelter but on the condition they had one of their own engineers take a look and turn in a report."

"And what was the result of that?"

"Thumbs down. In polite terms, of course, but some goddamned fool said Noranda hadn't developed enough ore to justify building a smelter. He said he found the whole mine disappointing and gave facts and figures to prove his case. He was worried about whether the smelting process would yield enough to turn the mine into a moneymaker. Off the record what he said was a little more graphic: 'I wouldn't piss on it' is what he said privately."

Armand laughed.

"Then, why are you so sure it's a winner?"

"Have another brandy, laddie, and I'll tell you. This stupid bugger certainly cooled off his principals in New York, so there was no money coming from there, and no smelter, either. But I was following the thing because I was one of those principals—I was outvoted. But I didn't agree with the engineer and I still don't. So we'll see. Next thing I knew Noah Timmins, as Hollinger Gold Mines, actually put up three million dollars for buildings, plant, machinery—the works. Bonds to secure the loan were issued in the name of Horne Copper—that's the Noranda holding company. They're ten-year bonds redeemable at any time at a hundred and five plus accrued interest and secured by a mortgage deed, under which they become first charge against all properties and franchises. Except for land, power, and rail rights. It's too complicated to go into the whole thing right now, but Hollinger gets thirty thousand shares of Noranda as a bonus. Now, what I'm saying is, if Timmins believes in the mine to that extent, I'm inclined to believe in it, too."

"I've got to find money before I can invest," Armand said.

"Find it."

"That's all very well, Angus, but the banks won't lend me anything after this sugar disaster. I hate like hell to sell my shares in the asbestos mine, they're the only sound thing I have."

"Think about it while I'm gone. There's always a way. When I get back from Noranda, if I'm as excited as I think I will be, you be ready to tell me you've found some money. Horne was right. He figured there had to be a big strike there because it's in direct line with the Kirkland Lake deposits in Ontario. He said he didn't think the vein would stop at an imaginary boundary line between Ontario and Quebec because some surveyor drew it. Noranda is just inside the Quebec border, you know. Everything about the layout is right."

"I'm listening to you, Angus, believe me. I'll raise money somewhere. I'll think about it. When you come back, we'll talk."

"If that son of yours can fly that crate he's got, I'll be back in a week."

Armand took the call. Family matters were not uppermost in his mind, and when he heard Justine's voice, he was impatient.

"I wanted to tell you first, Armand," Justine began in her strong, sure voice. "Timothée and I have sold the farm."

Admittedly, he was surprised. He had been accustomed for so many years to thinking of Justine living on the farm that he had never expected a change.

"That *is* news," he said. "We didn't know you were thinking of selling, Justine. You've never mentioned it."

"Timothée wants to retire. We're moving into the city,

so we'll be looking for a suitable house. In Outremont, I think."

"You've given it a great deal of thought, Justine?" he began, but then he realized that was a ridiculous question. Justine was such a positive, self-assured woman, she would have weighed all the possibilities.

"Naturally," she said. "It seems to me that it's time I was closer to everybody. I'd like to see more of Marc and Camille. He's too busy now to come out to the country much."

"That's understandable, yes."

He steeled himself for a lengthy conversation. Justine was a woman who liked to talk, to give speeches. Now that she had a subject worthy of her attention, she'd be loath to let it go.

"The family will be pleased," Armand offered. He was not sure this was entirely true, but as he listened to his sister on the other end of the instrument, he decided that his first reaction was probably accurate enough.

"Nora is expecting her second baby soon, too. She's got nobody but servants around her, and that's not right, Armand. Starkey, and that Marie-Claire—they seem to be the only women she ever sees. I don't know what Mathieu was thinking about, bringing that girl in from the country."

Armand allowed himself a grin. If Justine didn't know, every other family member did. And that included poor Nora.

"I've talked to Mathieu," Justine went on, "and he seems pleased. He agrees that I ought to move right into the house until after the baby comes and we find a nanny. Timothée will stay on the farm awhile to sell things, pack things up. It won't be easy to move after all these years, you know."

"Your whole arrangement sounds reasonable. Nora will be delighted to have you, Justine. She must be worried about this baby after the way the first one died."

"Some kind of punishment, I suppose," Justine said heavily. "Mathieu defied his church and his family in his marriage. Well, she converted, we all know that, but it isn't the same. One never knows how *sincere* they are when they convert. It may be only lip service. Then, too, Mathieu is in Ottawa so much, Nora must get lonely."

Armand was a little amused at the idea that Mathieu

might be punished for marrying a Protestant. Justine was positively medieval in her thinking, and it was odd to hear such a biblical cast put upon ordinary events.

"We can't live other people's lives for them," Armand said, wishing he could get off the line.

"We have a duty, nevertheless, to the family," Justine said pompously. "Mathieu is my son."

"Nobody questions that."

"Another thing, Armand, I'll be looking for a broker. I have some money to invest, and I thought you might be able to find the right person to handle my affairs."

"Certainly, I'll give it some thought. When are you coming into town?"

"Next week. I'll call you when I get to Mathieu's place. We'll be house hunting, too."

His mind was already projecting that she might be able to lend him some money. But he would have to be careful how he approached her about such a matter. When he finally hung up, Armand was a little more cheerful than he had been earlier. It was possible that Justine might be helpful to him in his business affairs and that he might yet find a way out of his present difficulties.

CHAPTER NINE

After he had driven Nora to the hospital, Mathieu returned home exhausted. He unlocked the door and stepped gratefully into the dim shadows of his own front hall. Outside, the early June heat had made the city stifling, but so far it had failed to penetrate the cool sanctuary of the house. He removed his suit jacket and loosened his tie. A glass of wine was what he wanted. A glass of the Beaujolais he considered his own personal wine—it came from a place called St.-Amour, and despite the small difference in spelling, he associated it with his mother's family name.

He went directly to his study, where only that morning he had thoughtfully put out two bottles of the wine along with a half-empty bottle of brandy. As he worked the corkscrew, he noticed that Marie-Claire had left the window open. A warm breeze disturbed the algid air. Mathieu set down the opened bottle and crossed the room to bang shut the window. In no time the house would be a furnace, he thought crossly. With his wine, he sat down in his comfortable workchair in an attempt to regain some composure.

Marie-Claire would have heard him come in. She would be waiting for him up there on the third floor—incredibly nubile, impossibly stupid. But his rattled nerves were not yet sufficiently cured by wine to let his sexual appetites surface. She would keep. Tonight, for once, there was no need to hurry, no need to sneak around or take precautions. He had taken Nora to hospital in the first stages of labor and his mother, Justine, wasn't due to visit until noon next day. He and Marie-Claire had the house all to themselves tonight.

Doctor Fremeau had shooed Mathieu home from the hospital: No point in haunting the waiting room all night, he had insisted. There would be no baby before morning, perhaps not even then. Mathieu would be smart (the doctor advised in a kindly way) to get some sleep and prepare for what the morning might bring. Consequently, Mathieu had gratefully fled the place. But as he approached his own house, screeching around corners in his black Mercedes convertible, he dwelt with mixed feelings upon the imminent arrival of his mother coming to take charge of his household in Nora's absence.

It was convenient to have his mother move in while Nora was ill and even for a time after the baby arrived. Yet from years of experience Mathieu knew that Justine would try to run his life. She would be hard on Marie-Claire, too, knowing in her heart what was really going on. Justine's religious ardor now overruled any personal lapses she might have had in the past. If she ever gave a thought to her long-ago affair with the herdsman, Timothée Fitzgerald, she showed no sign. She had, apparently, wiped that out by marrying Timothée after Laurent Dosquet died. Her judgments on other people were inclined to be harsh and her attitudes rigid, so he could expect no mercy when she came.

He was once more overcome by nagging doubts. Just allowing himself to think about the new baby was frightening. *What if it should happen again?* What if he were forced to endure the ultimate obscenity—a second monster?

No, he rejected that. It was an unbearable thought. He poured himself a second glass of wine.

His enormous energy was still making him churn inside, even after the mad drive home and the wine. As usual he had almost caused two accidents, having nearly knocked down a meandering old lady crossing Sherbrooke at a snail's pace and later coming within an inch of flattening a misguided cat on St.-Denis.

He began to walk up and down on the carpet. What did he want to do now? Did he want supper? Should he drink more wine? Did he want to make love to Marie-Claire? His thoughts strayed to the maid's room upstairs, and he conjured up an image of the plump Marie-Claire, with her smooth olive skin, thick braid, and cunning black eyes. She was a simple animal, really, except for those surprising flashes of manipulation. Look how she had tricked him into bringing her to Montreal. Now and then she managed to sway him, bring him round to her way, but for the most part he considered her foolish and vapid.

Finishing off the second glass of wine, he decided to go upstairs and see what she was doing. It would be hot on the third floor. Should he bring her down to his own bedroom? A twinge of guilt made him hesitate, and yet, he reasoned, Nora did not love him. She didn't care a damn about him or what he did. Moreover, it was his house.

When he reached the second floor, he could hear movement in his bedroom and realized Marie-Claire was already downstairs. So she had beat him to the idea, then! She had decided to test him, no doubt, to see if he would send her back. How like her! But what did it matter in the end? He would take her, do as he liked, use her, and throw her aside. This notion gave him a feeling of power.

From the doorway he saw her posing in front of the oval pier glass. With a delicious shock he saw her nakedness in the thinned-out light of evening. She wore nothing but a pair of pink rayon step-ins that she obviously had taken from one of Nora's lingerie drawers. They were fighting a losing battle against the voluptuous ivory globes of her behind. She had pinned up her long hair in a hastily contrived knot so that little wisps of it clung to her damp neck.

She saw his reflection in the glass and gave him a sly smile. Then, slowly, she turned to face him, presenting him with a full view of her round, succulent breasts, crowned with large dark red nipples, and the slight satin curve of her stomach, the gauze-wrapped crotch. A sudden rush of blood to his groin stiffened him instantly, and his lips moved in hungry anticipation.

"I was only trying them on," Marie-Claire said meekly. "I've never had pretty underwear like these."

His mouth watered.

"I'll buy you some."

"Will you, really?" A child's voice now, innocent as an ice cream cone. "I'd wear them for you, if you did."

"Mmmmmmmm."

"You aren't cross, Mathieu?"

"Hell, I'm not cross."

He was, rather, suffocating with need. The room had become a vacuum: Lust had sucked up every ounce of breathable air. His hands reached out like those of a blind man searching. His mouth puckered for the feast.

"Let me look," Mathieu said, pausing just a few inches from her. "Very nice. Very nice."

He was mesmerized by the frail armor of ill-fitting silk. Being Nora's, the step-ins were too small to conceal the spring sable furze between her thighs. It crept out, eloquently inviting. His hand moved to touch the proffered fruit. The narrow shaft of silk was caught in the triangle, wedged, moist even before his fingers touched it. Marie-Claire closed her eyes rhapsodically as he tore aside the pink shard. He unfastened his shirt and trousers and shoved her down on the carpet, pushed inside, without waiting for niceties. But Marie-Claire did not expect niceties, she was a creature of the moment.

Afterward, as they lay breathless, staring at the plaster ceiling from their separate islands of thought, Marie-Claire decided that the moment had arrived to impart her news.

"Mathieu."

"Um?"

"There's something I have to tell you."

"Not now, for Christ's sake."

"It can't wait. I must tell you."

"God, you are an irritating little bitch."

"I'm sorry"—meekly, childlike, innocent once again—"but I really must tell you. It's important."

What would Marie-Claire consider important? When he

asked the question, his voice was still foggy with satisfaction. "All right, what is it, then?"

"I'm sorry to bother you," she said apologetically.

His instincts told him she was posing and that whatever it was she had on her mind, it could be troublesome. Perhaps she wanted a small gift or a raise, and if so, he would accommodate her. She must not babble to his mother or to Nora when she came home. Naturally, he would deny everything, but it would still create an uncomfortable situation.

"Go ahead, tell me. What is it?"

He was now getting dressed again, tidying himself up.

"You won't be angry?"

"How the hell would I know? If you don't tell me, how can I say?"

He stood up, looming over her as she sat upon the floor. Marie-Claire scrambled to her feet defensively.

"Mathieu, I'm pregnant."

"Pregnant?"

The idea was unacceptable. If he had ever thought about the risks, he had thrust them aside. Sometimes he had taken precautions but not consistently. His nature did not allow that.

"What are we going to do?" she was asking.

He would have liked to strangle her. His temper exploded and he began to shout. He tottered as he stood there raging, glaring at her with half-mad eyes.

Scandal. What if there were a scandal? It would not only ruin his marriage but his political career as well. Everything he'd worked to build could be wiped out by this stupid little peasant. What in hell had he been thinking of all this time? His fury at himself was quickly transferred to the girl-child. But after a while, he expended his wrath and became calmer.

"Go and get dressed. Wash up and then make me something to eat. I'll have to think."

He rushed off to the bathroom to wash. What he needed was another drink. Probably several drinks. When he came back to the bedroom, Marie-Claire was bending over to pick up her dress. He could see the silk step-ins lying where she had thrown them after they made love.

"Pick up those damned things and take them away.

Wash them. Don't leave them lying around, for God's sake!"

She did as she was told, but she was sulky.

"Did you hear me ask you for some supper?" he inquired.

"I heard."

She walked to the door, and he shouted after her, "And don't get any dumb ideas about an abortion."

Suddenly a new and even more frightening apparition reared its ugly head. He saw Marie-Claire dying at the hands of some filthy old woman or a wretched back-street butcher. He had heard of things like that. Not only scandal but mortal sin heaped upon his head. He turned white at the thought.

"Abortions are dangerous and wicked. Remember that!" he bellowed at her.

"Yes, I know."

She went downstairs and left him. He stared about the bedroom wildly, his imagination in full flight. What if she were stupid enough to try to arrange an abortion? He'd better reassure her, give her some support, try to keep her confidence so that she wouldn't go sneaking around doing something both of them would regret.

He ran downstairs and followed her into the kitchen, where he found her cutting ham on a wooden board. She was arranging a cold plate for him. The kettle was already on the wood stove.

"Now listen. You listen to me," he began. "Make yourself a plate as well, and we'll sit in the kitchen. I'll bring the wine in here and we'll talk. I'll think of something, don't worry. Just give me time to think."

She nodded in an absentminded way and brought out another china plate. He could not figure out whether she was pleased or whether she did not care about his new, friendly attitude. He poured some wine for her.

"Here, drink this, Marie-Claire. Now sit down and listen to me. You can trust me. We'll find a solution to this problem. Together."

Justine arrived in time for lunch. Already, Mathieu had begun to pace up and down in the library, waiting for news from the hospital. It seemed to him that this nightmare had gone on for years and years. He was about to suggest that they drive to the hospital and wait there when the telephone rang. It was Doctor Fremeau.

"M'sieur Dosquet? Doctor Fremeau, here. We have wonderful news! You have a son!"

A wave of sweet relief almost drowned Mathieu's words, but he did manage to repeat, "A son?"

Justine beamed at him. "That's wonderful, Mathieu."

"He's healthy. A fine boy. Weighs seven pounds. Congratulations."

"Thank you, thank you."

"And Madame," the doctor went on. "Madame has had a difficult time, though we knew that last night. As I told you. It was a long and difficult birth. She is tired. But after a good rest, we are sure she will recover."

The fact that the doctor had mentioned the word *recover* alerted Mathieu to danger. He felt there must be some doubt if it had to be mentioned at all.

"She is sick, then?"

"Yes, she's weak. There was a considerable loss of blood and other problems as well . . . I can't go into that. But I'm sure that in a day or two—"

"If we drive over, may we see her?"

"Come late this afternoon. Perhaps around five o'clock. Who is with you, m'sieur?"

"My mother. Nora has no parents. Will we be able to see my son then, too?"

"There's no reason why you can't see the baby."

"Thank you for calling, then."

"Now, don't worry, m'sieur. Your wife will be fine. It may take a little time, that's all. We must be patient."

When he was off the telephone Mathieu explained to Justine that Nora was ill. Justine looked grave but brightened immediately.

"What a blessing that the baby is fine. I must give thanks to the Virgin."

"I was so afraid . . ." Mathieu said, not finishing the sentence. "Let's drink a toast to my son."

"Have you decided on a name?"

"André-Pierre."

"I like that, dear. I like that very much."

A sign on the door of Nora's room read NO VISITORS, but the floor nurse had told Mathieu and Justine they could go in. They found Nora lying flat upon the bed, incredibly thin, her skin grayish white. Her hair was stuck in strands about her face as if she had been perspiring heavily. There were deep shadows under her eyes.

"Well, Nora, you have a fine son," Mathieu said heartily. "I'm happy about that. How are you feeling now?"

"Tired. Have you seen the baby?" Her voice was little more than a whisper.

At this, Nora shivered so violently that the bed shook. Justine looked alarmed. But the spasm passed quickly. Nora looked whiter than she had when Justine and Mathieu had appeared, and as she bent over Nora, Justine could see that her lips were bluish. Justine dispatched Mathieu to find a nurse. Almost immediately after the chill passed, Nora became hot and feverish to the touch.

"I'm so hot," Nora said.

"We've sent for the nurse, my dear. You have a little temperature, that's all." She poured water from a decanter into a glass and inserted a glass tube. Nora managed to swallow some water.

While she was not a nurse, Justine had assisted patients from time to time, including her husband when he had died of cancer. She had fully expected Nora to look exhausted and pale, but she knew that a fever following childbirth was a bad symptom. Mathieu came back with the news that a nurse was on the way.

"You're going to be fine," Mathieu said. "After all, Doctor Fremeau did tell me you had a hard time. So naturally you feel tired and hot."

"You mustn't worry, Nora," Justine said. "I'm going to look after the house and the baby until you're well. We'll begin looking for a nanny right away."

Even now Nora was intimidated by Justine. When she had visited the farm the first time, with Mathieu, she had been careful to try to please her future mother-in-law. She had never completely lost her feeling of being a servant. The birth of Jean-Baptiste had been such a disappointment, such a disgrace, that she felt her position had sunk even lower in Justine's eyes. She turned away from her mother-in-law, facing the wall.

"She's very hot," Justine said, touching Nora's forehead.

A nurse came bustling in. She picked up Nora's wrist to record the pulse (and found it racing), and then she marked it on the chart at the foot of the bed. After that, she put a thermometer in Nora's mouth and waited.

"She's exhausted, poor dear," the nurse said. "I'm afraid you'll have to leave."

"We're going," Mathieu said quite willingly. "We want to see the baby."

"Now, you go along, m'sieur. We'll call you at home if there is any news."

Mathieu and Justine visited the nursery, where Mathieu expressed himself as highly pleased by the sight of a short, plump, black-haired little monkey with a red face. On their way through the hospital, they met Doctor Fremeau.

"My wife is quite ill," Mathieu said. "I wonder if you'd go in and see her again? She's running a fever."

"I'm on my way to check her now," the doctor said hurriedly. "Now you go along home and don't worry. She'll be fine."

"If there is any need for extra nursing care, don't hesitate," Mathieu assured him. "You understand, there is no problem about money."

Outside, Mathieu helped his mother into the Mercedes. She held her hat with one hand as they sped off down the road amid shrieking tires. Over his mother's protests he guided the car along the streets; it careened and squealed as if it would fall into a thousand parts in the middle of traffic. Justine shouted at him and grimaced, but he paid no attention. When they finally reached the house, she felt as if she had been saved from the jaws of death by a miracle.

Over dinner Mathieu's conversation turned to politics.

"I've got to get back to Ottawa as soon as possible," he said. "We're under attack over this customs scandal, and every vote counts. The Tories will bring down the government if they can. I can't understand how King could have allowed such a mess to develop . . ."

He went on talking, and Justine enjoyed listening to him. She had always been interested in politics, and besides, it kept her mind off the hospital and what might be happening there.

Within a few days Nora's condition had deteriorated alarmingly. She often fell into delirious fevers; sometimes a chill seized her and she shook for minutes at a time. Her hands now flew to her face to scratch at bright red patches of rash on either cheek. The room had a terrible smell—a pervading rottenness that even the antiseptics could not hide. A special nurse sponged her face and arms with tepid water throughout the day and night.

Nora's temperature reached 104, the rash appeared on several areas of her body, and unless she was prevented, she tore the skin off. She had severe diarrhea.

"There must be more than this . . . why can't you do more?" Mathieu demanded angrily. "I know she's had a blood transfusion, but is that all there is to do?"

Doctor Fremeau looked worried.

"We're doing all we can."

"What exactly is wrong? Why can't you tell me—?"

"We weren't sure—sometimes the diagnosis isn't accurate. It's very difficult to be sure, you see. These symptoms are present with many illnesses—typhoid fever, meningitis, pneumonia, peritonitis—all sorts of conditions. But this is a general infection . . . it starts with torn tissues and they become infected. It spreads throughout the blood system. That's what we have here."

The doctor stepped back defensively. Mathieu looked ready to grab him by the lapels of his white coat and shake him.

"But is there nothing you can do?"

"We've given blood. That's about all we can do. We're trying to make her drink liquids, trying to keep her cool—"

"She is dying," Mathieu said.

"That's an extreme view," Doctor Fremeau said, but he did not deny the accusation. "She may make a recovery yet."

"What chance is there, can you tell me that?"

"I don't know. I simply don't know. She's very weak."

Doctor Fremeau knew that Nora had little chance of getting well. Her symptoms had not abated—irregular fever, progressive anemia, diarrhea, the bright red peeling tongue. Now there was pleurisy in one lung. Her heart would be affected soon.

Feeling helpless and totally frustrated, Mathieu went back to the sickroom. When he bent over Nora, the fruity, sweet odor of her breath made him draw back. He had not had much experience with death, but he felt the wrench of certainty as he stared down at her. She was so thin now that she was little more than a skeleton, it seemed to him, and her face was ravaged by the infected wounds she had made by clawing at the rash. He knew he must bring a priest. It occurred to him that his Uncle Marc might come in such an emergency. He hurried out to telephone the bishop at home.

Rose Starkey stood alone in the hospital corridor. She was terrified by the air of doom about the place—by the antiseptic sting in the air and the authoritative whisper of starched uniforms. She had tried to see Nora, but the nurses refused her permission. When she caught sight of Mathieu coming around the corner, his mother on one arm and his Uncle Marc just behind him, she thought she might ask permission of *them*. Then she noticed that the bishop was followed by his chaplain, and that the chaplain carried a tray. That would be wine and oil for the Last Rites. Nora was dying.

She leaned against the cream-painted wall and began to weep. If only she could see Nora once again, if only she dared speak to Madame Fitzgerald and ask if she would intercede. She *must* see Nora again, somehow. Did nobody understand that? She looked at Justine, who was standing outside the hospital room door, but Justine refused to recognize Rose. She looked very stern. When the bishop disappeared inside, Rose tried to find the courage to speak to the family, but she could not seem to do it. Then she spied Lady St. Amour just coming into view.

Rose felt briefly hopeful. Lady St. Amour had always been kind, understanding, and gentle. In her own way, of course, she was a strong-minded woman, and she was not afraid of Madame Fitzgerald. Rose moved forward, and when Honey glanced in her direction, Rose looked at her questioningly. Honey detached herself from her St. Amour relatives and walked to where Rose was standing.

"Rose, what are you doing here?"

"I want to see Nora."

Honey saw that the girl had been crying. Her eyes were red, and she was sniffling and dabbing at her face with a bit of damp cotton.

"That's not possible, Rose. Nora is very, very ill. You saw the bishop? He is giving her the Last Rites. This is a difficult time for the family, and so I don't think—"

"I must see her. They won't let me. Nobody will listen to me, but I thought you might understand, Lady St. Amour. I must see her again, just once."

"Now, Rose, try to be calm. You and Nora were close friends, I know, but it just doesn't seem the time . . ."

Rose began to cry again, sobbing noisily, all control apparently gone. Honey was rather alarmed and touched her arm consolingly.

"Here, let me give you a fresh handkerchief." She offered Rose one of her own monogrammed linen squares. "Try to pull yourself together, Rose. Please do."

Rose ignored these remarks and said, "The nurses wouldn't allow me in. But if you would speak to Madame Fitzgerald, it would be all right. Please, please ask her if I may see Nora. If she says so, everybody will agree, even Mathieu."

Rose was clutching Honey's arm.

"I'll speak to Justine," Honey said quickly. "But do try to straighten up, Rose. This kind of thing doesn't help. Please, don't cry."

Rose began mopping at her eyes again. Honey walked back to the family group outside the sickroom door and spoke to Justine. Justine, however, appeared to be horrified at the idea.

"Certainly not! Whatever is the girl thinking of?"

"For a moment, surely? It wouldn't hurt. They were awfully good friends, and Rose helped so much when Jean-Baptiste was ill. It seems to me, Justine, that—"

"She is a servant."

"She is the only friend Nora has," Honey corrected, now rather more on Rose's side than she had been earlier. Justine's hostility wasn't becoming.

"Unfortunately."

Mathieu now took an interest in the proceedings and glanced over at Rose. A woman making a spectacle of herself, he concluded, and no more than he would have expected from somebody of Rose's type. She ought not to be here. The image of his wife with a servant as her best friend was less attractive now than it had been before. After all, he was a member of Parliament. It was all rather tasteless.

"Tell her to go away," Mathieu said, speaking directly

to Honey. "She oughtn't to be here. She's making a fool of herself."

Honey turned away from Mathieu. When he had been a child, he had always been rash, given to scenes and tantrums, wildly enthusiastic and energetic and often unmanageable, but she had taken the view that children had to learn. She had been indulgent. Mathieu was a man now, and it seemed to her that he was vindictive and selfish. The traits that had seemed mildly acceptable when he was young were no longer forgiveable. She was profoundly disappointed in his attitude and in Justine's, having expected more compassion.

"I think you'd better leave, my dear. They don't want you to see Nora. I'm terribly sorry, but I couldn't persuade either of them."

"I knew *he'd* say no," Rose said, stifling her sobs with some difficulty. "But I thought she might understand."

"Justine is upset. Whatever the case, there's nothing more we can do. Why don't you go home, Rose, and have a good sleep?"

"I couldn't sleep."

As they talked, Marc came out of Nora's room and handed the tray to his chaplain. Then he turned to his nephew and took his arm. Both Honey and Rose could hear his words quite clearly in the still corridor.

"I'm sorry, Mathieu, but she's gone. I just had time to give her Extreme Unction. Then I realized that she had . . . died. At least her soul is free from sin, you must look at it that way."

Marc grasped his nephew's arm. Justine took Mathieu's other arm, and together they walked into the room where Nora lay. A nurse went off to fetch a doctor. As the door closed upon them, Rose gave a shrill cry and fled from the corridor. Honey felt a stab of fear and apprehension when she heard the sound. It had an animal quality that was violent and disturbing.

The Robillard Funeral Home was a small one. In the quiet of midmorning the building seemed empty. Rose Starkey, wearing a black dress she had just purchased and a close-fitting black hat, walked into the foyer. A visitor's book was open on an oak table. She ignored it. She saw no sign of anybody and heard nothing. On either side of the foyer was a parlor where, presumably, bodies were laid out in coffins for viewing. On this particular morning neither room was occupied, nor were there any flowers, nor any sign of activity.

Rose walked purposefully to the back of the foyer. A heavy oak door separated the public section of the mortuary from the more practical areas that lay behind. She opened the door, went through, and let it swing shut behind her. A small anteroom, empty of furniture, led to a larger laboratorylike area. The sweet scent of formaldehyde was heavy in the close air. She drew back but then, after waiting just a moment, went forward to the lure of gleaming white tiles, counters covered with tubes, jars, and instruments. In the center of the room under a bright light a man bent over a figure lying on a china slab.

"Nora!" Rose cried, flinging herself past the astonished mortician. "Nora, let me see you! What have they done to you?"

For Rose had not seen Nora in the hospital and did not realize that her face was disfigured by lesions. The undertaker was even then trying to cover the ugly scars with cream and powder, to lessen the dark red scabs on the torn and infected cheeks.

Mr. Robillard himself was working on the body of Madame Dosquet. There was a great deal of work to do if the family wished to see the deceased, and he was a man who took great pride in his work. The intrusion of this unknown, apparently mad, woman attacking him and trying to get close to the body was unnerving. He merely grabbed her by the arms and thrust her back. She struggled with him, still peering at the unfortunate young woman on the slab, trying desperately to free herself. He managed to wrestle her away from the table to the door.

"Ralph! Ralph! Come here and give me a hand!"

An assistant came running from the backyard and, seeing the odd tableau, pitched in without question. No strangers were allowed in this area, and therefore the woman must be dealt with. He needed to know nothing more than that.

"You cannot come in here, madame," Mr. Robillard said sternly. The two men forced Rose out into the front of the funeral home. "This is out of the question!"

Mr. Robillard breathed heavily and wiped his forehead

with his sleeve. Really, such behavior was absolutely without precedent! He was shocked as well as out of breath from the effort.

"I must see her," the woman was saying over and over. She actually made some attempt to return to the mortuary but the men took hold of each arm and forced her to the front door.

"You can see her at the funeral," Mr. Robillard said. "You can't stay here, so I suggest you go along. Talk to the family. Unless you *are* part of the family, in which case, you'll know about the funeral."

"Nobody will let me see her."

"I know nothing about that. But you certainly can't see her before she is prepared for burial. Ralph, you take this lady outside, will you? See that she goes along. . . I've got to get back to work."

Ralph took Rose outside and watched her as she walked along the street. She seemed to be in a daze. The whole thing was most extraordinary, and he went back inside shaking his head. This was, indeed, a funny business.

Rose sat in the very last pew in Notre-Dame church. She was dimly aware of the splendid gilt and paint in the chancel, of the size of the place. The day had become quite sullen, and outdoors it was gray and threatening, yet inside the church there was a richness that seemed almost too warm, too welcoming.

Rose sat alone, her expression completely covered by a mourning veil she had bought to wear over the black hat. She felt more secure that way. Noises at the door made her swing around, and there was the priest (who, she supposed, was in charge of the service), wearing a black cope. He met the coffin at the church door. It was carried up the center aisle, feet toward the altar. She watched as the pallbearers carefully set it down at the front of the church. Mass began. The priest made the sign of the cross.

"In the name of the Father, and of the Son, and of the Holy Spirit, Amen. I will go to the altar of God."

The server responded with, "The God of my gladness and joy."

"Do me justice, O God, and fight my fight against a faithless people; from the deceitful and impious man rescue me."

The server responded, in Latin this time.

The service continued. When it was over, Rose followed the mourners to the mountaintop cemetery in a taxicab and arrived after they were assembled.

Mathieu was flanked by his mother and his stepfather, Timothée. Just behind them stood Camille, with Armand and Honey. As well, there was a handful of people Rose did not recognize. Marc, as the celebrant, blessed the grave.

"Let us pray, O God, by whose mercy rest is given to the souls of the faithful . . ." he began to intone in French. When the prayer was over, he sprinkled both coffin and grave with holy water and then incensed them.

The droning (so it seemed to Rose) went on and on. As she stared at the coffin, the last remembrance she would have of Nora, she saw again the ravaged face she had first noticed at the undertaker's establishment. She could not understand, even now, why Nora was disfigured.

"They should have let me see her in the hospital," she muttered over and over. "I wanted to see her then."

"Dearest brothers," Marc was saying, "let us faithfully and lovingly remember our sister, whom God has taken to himself from the trials of this world. Lord have mercy, Christ have mercy, Lord have Mercy, Our Father . . ."

Complete silence except for the rustle of trees. Mourners bowed their heads in quiet prayer. Rose Starkey refused to bow her head. She stared stonily at the gathering of St. Amours and Dosquets in their cold and haughty cluster. Hatred surged through her from head to foot. Inside that box, cold and still, lay Nora, ugly and mutilated. An intolerable pain consumed Rose.

Marc moved forward to sprinkle holy water over the coffin. In a moment Nora would be lowered into the ground, and then men would come and shovel earth over the box and that would be the end. Rose would never see her again. Poor, beautiful Nora, tormented, scarred, murdered by Mathieu's passions.

Rose screamed. She flung herself over the grass toward the open grave and fell upon the coffin, her arms clasping the unyielding wood.

"Don't leave me, Nora! I love you, Nora!"

The mourners, momentarily stunned, came to life. Rough hands grasped Rose and tore her away from the coffin. Then they carried her from the cemetery, still screaming, while tears fell like burning salt upon her face and hands. Eventually, a merciful hand closed her mouth and put a stop to the obscene sounds.

CHAPTER TEN

Mildred had anticipated the call. She smiled rather indulgently when she heard the voice of one of her twin cousins on the line.

"Hello, Milly, it's Flora here. How are you? How are those adorable little boys?"

"Everybody is fine, thank you, Flora. The boys are a handful for Nanny Redman, but we're managing. I hear you two girls are seen around town these days with those handsome twins?"

"Rather too much night life for us, Milly. We like things quiet. But we're humoring the boys. Have you a minute to spare for a chat? Because Fenella and I would like to talk weddings."

"What about weddings? Have you set the date?"

Flora laughed. "Now don't pretend you can't guess, Milly. Are you sitting down, just in case it is a shock?"

"Nothing about you two comes as a shock to me. But yes, I'm sitting down. Now, what do you want to talk about?"

"We're asking you for a favor, and you'll have our undying devotion if you say yes. That's fair, isn't it?"

"Go ahead, Flora. I think I can guess, but spell it out for me."

"You don't know quite *all* we want. Not yet. What do you think it is, Milly?"

"You'd like to have the wedding in Pride's Court."

"Clever Milly! Isn't she clever, Fenella?" (Fenella was beside her sister. They always made telephone calls together.)

Fenella seized the telephone.

"Fenella here, Milly. You do see our point, don't you? Mellerstain is fine, we don't deny it. But it's no place for the grand affair when Pride's Court is just sitting there waiting to be inhabited by *us* in our wedding finery. You know Grandfather loves occasions, and we don't mind if he wants to run the show practically. Not that we want anything even approaching *your* wedding, Milly. What wedding could be as grand as that? Even the czarina of all the Russias couldn't have had anything more splendid. But then, she probably married a scruffy man who never bathed. Not like you, with heavenly North."

Here, Flora grabbed the telephone from her twin.

"That's another thing, Milly, we hope you'll talk to us about our terrible fate. We're absolute virgins, you know. Mother won't give us any details . . . she's medieval, as we all know. You wouldn't believe the difficulties we're having, so we want to talk to you privately. Being closer to our own age, you can confess all. We need a really serious chat, Milly, with plenty of delicious details. So you must promise to tell."

Fenella repossessed the instrument and said, "Otherwise, we'll go to our marriage beds in abysmal ignorance. Our whole lives may be ruined for lack of information. And since you have North, we assume it's divine. Milly, you can't say no."

"Why me?" Mildred protested, though she wasn't in the least angry with the twins for asking. If anything, she was flattered.

"Anyway, we'd like to have the ceremony in the Great Hall, right at the foot of the stairs, with old Great-grandfather Cathmor giving us his steely eye from his gilt frame. We first saw Kevin and Keith there, so it would be romantic," Fenella explained.

"Perfect," Mildred said, "very dramatic. I don't see why not, and I'll speak to Grandfather about it right away. How many guests?"

"Not more than two hundred, not really large. The boys have a few people from Boston and New York on their list."

"When? What date?"

"Ah, that's the next point, Milly. Now we need your permission for this, so are you ready?"

"Don't be silly, of course I'm ready. What on earth are you fussing about?"

"Flora again, Milly. Are you there? Fenella says I'm to ask this because I'll do it best. That isn't true, of course, but it's about the actual day. We thought we'd like it August 19, but since that's your anniversary, we thought we'd better ask. We don't want to interfere with your celestial memories."

Mildred laughed. They were a strange pair! Yet she rather liked the touch about having the wedding on the same date as hers and North's.

"I think it's wonderful. I'm sure North will, too. That gives us about a month to get ready. Not a bit too much."

"Anything you want from Mother, just ask. Flowers, wine, kitchen help . . . Just one or two other small things, Milly, before you go. We're planning to keep the attendants in the family—Landry and Noel. Also, Susan and Charity. How does that strike you?"

This was the first suggestion which *did* upset Mildred. Why Susan? She was still fighting a losing battle to keep Susan out of Pride's Court. Everybody seemed to be on Susan's side, however, and she did not want to make her objections too obvious.

"I wouldn't interfere in any way with that. It sounds fine," Mildred said, not managing much enthusiasm.

Flora caught Mildred's cool note and said briskly, "We know you don't like Susan much, Milly, and we don't blame you. The way she ogles North is past a joke. I would have poisoned her long ago if I had been in your place, but there's nobody else in the family. It means bringing somebody from outside. Fenella and I don't have many friends, and no close ones at all. So you see? You'll be too busy being the grand hostess. What with Angela's defection to the other side, it's difficult. Angela would have been perfect, but Grandfather hasn't made any noises about inviting her back here. Don't you wish you knew what she did that was so awful? We've tried to imagine, but we can't. So it seems to us, Milly, that we're doing the right thing."

"That's another thing, Milly," Fenella said, interrupting. "Can you just tell us, without details, of course, whether it's any *fun*? Please say it is. We figure it must be, otherwise, why are people doing it all the time?"

Mildred assured them that sometimes married life was fun and sometimes it wasn't. That was not a subject that she cared to discuss at the moment. She agreed to meet with the twins and Sydney soon to talk about dresses. She supposed, with a despairing heart, that Susan would have to be invited. Susan was supposed to know everything about fashion.

Despite the fact that Lord Court had ordered a two-manual organ installed for the ceremony, the importance of the guests, the masses of imported and local flowers, there was a whimsical, uncertain air about the wedding. It was not (as Lord Court said himself) that you could actually put your finger on what was wrong. That was the difficulty. What could possibly be wrong with a well-planned family wedding at Pride's Court?

Who could find fault with the guests—the cream of Montreal society? What criticism could be leveled at the Great Hall shimmering with flowers and the sounds of "Jesu, Joy of Man's Desiring" echoing from the walls?

There was nothing theatrical about the arrangements; the colors were subdued, and the clothes muted. The two couples, creating their handsome and impossible double image, were framed in the half-circle of the vast divided stairway. Enfolded on three sides, by banks of waxy white calla lilies and sea-green orchids, wrapped in the soothing sounds of Bach, the two princesses stood with their knights. Flora and Fenella were gowned in faded lilac silk with elaborate puffed sleeves bound tightly around the upper arms and wrists. On the long light hair little caps of seed pearls were their only ornaments. Susan and Charity wore dull purple raw silk made like a bishop's dalmatic—long loose shirts with bell sleeves hanging loose—and bands of ivory silk across the forehead pinned with a single purple iris. At the same time, Keith and Kevin might have been fauns escaped from a medieval tapestry except for the white tie and tails, which were so completely contemporary. Noel and Landry looked real enough, but their impact was not sufficient to counteract the total effect of the others.

Most guests seemed relieved when the ceremony was over and they could wander freely about the house and gardens with a glass of Taittinger in hand. Seeing the duplicate couples was arresting but created tension. Lord Court, satisfied with arrangements, wandered out to the rose beds and found himself trapped by his grandson Landry. Landry was not his favorite relative. He inquired politely about the boy's future.

"The project at the Manitoba station has been canceled," Landry said, pleased to corner his grandfather for a chat. "We had no luck with a new hard wheat. Anyway, they've just licensed one called Garnet that Doctor Saunders developed at the Ottawa Experimental Station a few years ago. It's an earlier ripener, so that seems to be that. Actually, I'm looking for something to do."

"Were you thinking of coming into one of the family businesses, then?" It was a natural idea.

"Not really. I'm not suited to business." He looked over his grandfather's shoulder and saw Miles Flanders approaching. "Come over here, Miles. We can tell my grandfather about our idea."

Lord Court swung sharply about to look at the newcomer. Like Landry, Miles wore his hair too long. His handshake was soft. Without pinpointing the reason, Simon Court had a whiff of indigestion. Perhaps, upon reflection, Landry *would* be better off away from the family business. When the two young men stood close together, something about their stance enraged him. Yet, Landry had been caught trying to make love to his own cousin! Surely that meant he was . . . well, a *man*. On the other hand, it was probably that awful event that turned him against women. Angela, the trollop, had seduced him. The boy had felt ill about it. Guilty. Yes, it was all Angela's fault! How wrong he had been to show mercy.

"I've been meaning to try to see you at the office," Landry was saying. "I talked it over with Father, and he advised me to see you. Miles and I want to mount an expedition to the Amazon."

"To the Amazon?" Lord Court considered this just another form of insanity. "What in hell for? Nothing there but rubber, bugs, and headhunters."

"To collect specimens. Plants and insects. We could present it to the university," Landry explained quickly. He was sure he could convince his grandfather and his father to put up at least half the money if he went about it the right way. McGill was one of their pets—they gave money to it in large quantities. Really, it was to amuse Miles that he had thought up the scheme; Miles was so fickle.

Landry was aware that Miles was always looking for a touch of the exotic and that he had been profoundly bored with England, then France. Montreal he considered dreary in the extreme. Upon reviewing his own career, Landry had come up with the notion that he might become known as a botanist. The way to do that would be to travel in unknown territory and discover some new species. Almost as soon as he had thought of it, he broached it to Miles. Miles had taken the bait.

Landry began to outline his plan to his grandfather, keeping the name of the university on the tip of his tongue. If such a collection were done properly and presented, then McGill would be delighted to accept. (He had no idea whether they would accept it or not. He had left that part of the investigation until he was assured that Lord Court would help finance the expedition.)

As he listened to Landry talk, Lord Court gathered that it would take considerable cash outlay and (this suddenly struck him as appealing) two or three years of planning and traveling. As this aspect of the matter sank into his mind, Simon Court changed like a chameleon. The more he studied the two young men, the more attractive the Amazon became as a distant repository for their persons. Although his worst suspicions were unproven, the more he watched them, the more he listened, the more convinced he became of the utterly unspeakable truth. They were a couple of pansies. Once he had recognized this, he saw the beguilement of faraway places. No doubt it was a harebrained scheme, but if it got the two of them out of his sight, it would be worth every penny spent. Also, it had an air of philanthropy. If McGill University wanted a collection of foreign bugs, let them have it. Such things were beyond his ken.

"Tell you what we'll do, Landry," he said, making an effort to sound reasonable. "You come in next Wednesday morning around ten. We'll talk money then. Meanwhile, get some commitment from the university. Have you done that?"

"No, because I wasn't sure I could raise the money. I have to do my share. Miles can't pay for the whole expedition."

"Go ahead and contact them. Ask your father or your Uncle Charles for the name of the right person. Or my secretary, if you have to."

The more he thought of it, the more the great Amazon-ian jungle bewitched him. There was, he understood, plenty of it. Millions of acres of mosquito-ridden, snake-infested forests. Riddled with ferocious cannibals and starving alligators. Disease, he believed, was rampant. Yes, it sounded like paradise.

Having arranged the appointment, Lord Court left Landry and Miles to their own devices (whatever those might be) and went off in search of Mildred. He wanted to see if all was going well with the supper she planned. Now, there was a sensible, acceptable human being. She ran this place like a clock and had her head screwed on her shoulders in exactly the right way. It was odd that some of the handsomer Courts were so eccentric. Why this should be was utterly beyond his power to understand, but he thought it was just one more cross he had to bear.

North was not pleased. Now that he had met the man Kay Prince had brought along as her escort, he wondered if he had made a social error. The fellow was not suitable. Not suitable at all. When he'd first formed the idea of inviting Kay to the wedding, he had been delighted because he was trying to impress her. He had been trying to seduce her for some time, and he wasn't at all sure he was making progress. Kay had resources of her own and, since she was divorced (a little risqué, of course), numbers of suitors. She was wealthy. She was attractive. She had no need to sneak around, and for the most part, he could offer nothing but elaborate assignations.

The wedding of the Court twins had caused considerable curiosity in the city, and an invitation was something of a cachet. North thought if he managed an invitation for Kay, she would be impressed and pleased. With this in mind he had approached Keith (or he *thought* it was Keith, the whole thing was too exhausting to sort out) and asked him to put Kay Prince on his personal invitation list. Keith could say he'd met her through the paper company.

The March twin had grinned at him and said confidentially, "Better make it two invitations, North. You can't expect your friend to come without an escort. Besides, it it will look better in every way."

North had agreed with him. Mildred wasn't likely to question Kay's presence if she was on the March twins' list and if she brought some man along with her. Having

414

seen Kay's choice, however, he was having second thoughts. Philip Norman didn't look like the sort of man with whom Kay would associate. Her description of him (when he'd queried her beforehand about her escort) had sounded perfectly all right. "I'm bringing Philip Charles Norman," she'd said. "He does a financial column for *The New York Times*. Everybody reads it. On Wall Street they think he's a prophet."

"Never heard of him," North had said gruffly.

"Oh, he's *very* well known. Right now he's in Montreal interviewing mining promoters about gold and copper discoveries. Some kind of special assignment about Canadian mining stocks for the New York scene."

"Has he talked to Lord Court?"

"Darling, I simply don't know. I just met him at a cocktail party the other night. Since I'm not the least bit interested in him, I thought you'd approve."

Today, in the midst of the festivities, Kay smiled upon her new friend and then upon North as she made the introductions. She seemed unaware of the fact that Norman looked out of place. This irritated North. Kay Prince was a woman of taste, after all, or he wouldn't have been interested in her himself. She was one of those fashionable, determined, pretty women with a well-shaped face and fraudulently liquid eyes who at one and the same time suggest vulnerability and vast inner strength. North was intrigued, but he felt hamstrung by his own situation.

He looked at the newcomer as if he were a rare animal in a zoo. Something about Philip Charles Norman made him uncomfortable. North's instinct for his own class was unimpeachable; he could sniff out a commoner just as he could spot a man who belonged to his own elitist cabal. And Norman was all wrong.

To the quick eye Philip Charles Norman suggested the solitary wisdom of a reclusive sage. He had cultivated the habit of standing somewhat apart from any social group in which he was involved—seemingly to imply that he was a little above the affairs of ordinary mortals. While he was reasonably tall and slim (a cunning tailor had concealed the rounded shoulders, the indented chest, the slightly thickened waist), he gave an impression of greater height, of inherited elegance that did not bear inspection. A second, more considered inventory would have revealed a predatory quality that was most unsavory. He had a habit of hunching, drawing in his longish neck with its obtrusive Adam's apple like a hungry cat about to pounce on some hapless rodent. In fact, everything about Norman was disconcertingly out of proportion: his prehensile fingers, badly managed feet in their hand-lasted shoes, gangling arms, and recklessly plunging nose. Even his brownish-red hair (what there was left of it, for he was almost bald) draped about his neck in lank strands. A man with less vanity and more taste would have spoken sharply to his barber.

Only his eyes were attractive: such a deep brown that they were almost black, heavy-lidded, almond-shaped. They hinted at dark passions, old pleasures best forgotten, promises too rich to bear fruit. And over the eyes hung luxuriant brows that attempted without much success to shelter his most private thoughts.

Philip was awkward in conversation and his voice so light and soft that it was often difficult to hear what he said. In public he spoke very little—which only served to convince people that he was clever beyond words. Actually, he was pitifully concerned about revealing even the smallest mistake in pronunciation. He had arrived in America at fourteen and had learned the English language late. But he was obsessed with the need to speak perfect English and, even more, to *look* American in the Anglo-Saxon sense. He would have adored to be taken for a bona fide descendant of the Pilgrim Fathers (which was quite impossible) and, failing this, contented himself with seducing women of that persuasion. In this field Philip Charles Norman was remarkably sucessful, considering his obvious handicaps.

The conversation between Norman, Kay Prince, and North was struggling for survival when Mildred arrived and a new round of introductions began. North lifted a glass of champagne off a passing waiter's tray for Kay Prince.

"Taittinger, your favorite champagne. I saw the bottles myself."

"How lovely!" Kay took the glass and gave him an all-encompassing smile.

Even in the bustle of the moment Mildred noticed. How did North know so much about Kay Prince's tastes? She said to Philip, "You're an old friend of the March twins? Did you know them in New York or Boston?"

"I don't know them. Kay brought me."

"I see . . . I somehow thought—"

Kay, sensing disaster, interceded hastily, "I've always longed to see the inside of this house. This probably isn't a convenient time for a tour, but—"

"How about a *short* tour?" Mildred said, grasping at the lifeline Kay had so helpfully offered. "I'll show you one or two special things if you like." ·

"How marvelous. Excuse us, will you?"

Mildred led Kay to the reception hall to look at the sculpture. As they abandoned North with Philip, Mildred caught his look of despair. *Well*, she thought angrily, *let him exercise his charm on that. It ought to keep him busy for a while.* The two women threaded their way carefully between guests until they found some space in the octagonal room with its graceful wall niches and alabaster figures. Mildred began to describe their origins when one of the March twins scurried by. He brushed Kay's shoulder, jiggling her glass, stopped to apologize profusely, and then, smiling warmly, moved along. Mildred felt the second stab of painful knowledge. The March twins did not know Kay Prince. For if one twin knew a person, so did the other. If Philip did not know the twins either, who had invited them to the wedding? Why was this woman here? She heard the telltale phrase ringing in her head, "Taittinger, your favorite champagne." North might as well have left a love letter from Kay on her dressing table or a monogrammed lighter, Mildred thought.

So North had been seeing Kay Prince. Had, in fact, been buying her champagne. Had been trying to make love to her. Mildred's imagination soared off in a wild and silent scream: She saw North kissing Kay as only North could kiss, his hands on that slim, curvaceous body, his lips foraging over that pretty face. Nausea almost overcame her as she stood there. She mumbled quickly, "I just remembered something I must do. Please excuse me."

Without waiting for a reply, Mildred fled to the powder room. At least in this place she could be alone for a moment to repair her face, to gather up what was left of her composure in order to see the remainder of the evening through. She longed to go up to her own apartment and lock the door and weep. Or shriek at North to tell him what a fool he was to play such a childish, insensitive trick. How could he do that to her? She leaned against the cold wall of the washroom, so perfectly appointed with its rose-festooned porcelain, its gold-plated taps. How could he do that to her? To all of them? If she had ever entertained a single doubt about Susan, this washed them all away. She felt used. Betrayed. She felt a thousand years old.

North felt deserted. In business he was forced to associate with almost every kind of person, but socially he was choosy. He did not want to talk to this man Norman. He gave Mildred a melancholy look as she left and then scanned the crowd rather helplessly, hoping for a savior, somebody he had to speak to instantly. He spied Susan. He caught her eye, raised his eyebrows (a signal for help), and she came over.

"I want you to meet one of our guests," North said. "Philip Norman. He writes for *The New York Times*. This is Susan Mulqueen, a cousin of my wife's. Lord Court's granddaughter."

Susan offered her hand to Philip Norman and gave him a pleasant, interested smile. She was still wearing the purple raw silk. Her hair was pulled back smoothly, into a shining little bob. She wore a "kiss-curl" on each cheek.

"What kind of writing?" Susan was asking. "I'm afraid I don't read the *Times*."

"He knows all about money. The stock market," North said. "Ask him anything."

His distaste for the man was showing, and he regretted that. Let Susan deal with him. He looked around for yet another escape, so he could leave Susan and Philip together.

"Why are you in Montreal?" Susan asked.

"We're preparing a story on Canadian gold mines. Whether or not they are a good investment. Are they really the El Dorados they seem to be? That kind of thing."

"I didn't know we were so important up here. Imagine the *Times* wanting to do a story on us," Susan said, pretending surprise.

"Gold is important no matter where it happens to be," Philip said.

"Another drink? Let me get you something," Susan said.

"It's just ginger ale," Norman said. "I don't usually drink alcohol."

North made a distressed sound.

"I see somebody I have to speak to," he said hastily and left them to carry on.

Susan was glad to see North go. She did not like being reminded of their affair and the results of it. Her whole association with Pride's Court was colored by seeing him. At any rate, she was intrigued by this newcomer, Philip Norman. Not because he was physically appealing, because he wasn't. But there was a quality about him that she had found lacking in so many of the men she met. He was intense. He gave her his full attention, bringing to bear upon her all the power of his mind. She was the only woman in the room, his attitude seemed to say, in the house, in the city.

"Your family must have connections with mining promoters," Philip said.

"Probably. I've never thought about it. Why?"

"Perhaps you could introduce to me to some people I ought to interview. Sometimes a personal recommendation can be valuable. They might be freer when they talk to me if they thought I had a friend like you."

Susan was pleased. Until this moment the party had bored her. But here at last was a new interest. An important writer, a man who worked for one of the great newspapers of he world. He must know all sorts of famous people.

"First, there's my grandfather. I'll introduce you to him. After that, I'll think. My husband, David, will know some names."

"I'd like to talk to some of the powerful Conservatives about tariffs, too. As I said to Coolidge only a month ago, I really believe that his policy of laissez faire in business is partly responsible for our present prosperity in the United States."

Susan's brown eyes widened. She realized with fascination that he meant Calvin Coolidge, the President.

"Well, I don't know anything about tariffs," Susan said. "I only know that Tories like high ones and Liberals like low ones."

419

"Is there a place we could sit and talk quietly? I'm not much for crowds and loud conversation."

"Sure, come with me. I know this house very well. I used to be here a great deal, before North and Mildred moved in." She led him away. She could not remember when she had felt so elated. Imagine being with a man who talked with Presidents! And to whom Presidents listened! He probably knew everybody worth knowing in New York. Somehow, she had managed to capture the most fascinating guest at the party.

They sat in the card room, where Philip invited her to lunch with him next day at the Ritz-Carlton. There, he suggested, they could make a list of people she knew, and if she would like to help him further, she might read some copy he had just written about the Canadian north. Susan was hypnotized.

"My opinion won't be worth much, but I'd love to read what you've written."

"Don't put down your opinion. It could be valuable. As a Canadian, as a woman, you have a point of view. Don't forget that."

She could not believe her luck. She hung on his every word, even to his description of his "perfect" marriage. He and Althea, he explained, lived in the fabled Dakota Apartments on Central Park West. Susan had heard of that luxurious fortress, of course. A piece of German Renaissance gingerbread with great style and greater pretensions. The Normans entertained powerful bankers (he knew several Rockefellers, Morgans, and had even met some Rothschilds in London), writers like the up-and-coming Hemingway and Faulkner. He had lunched at the Algonquin with Dorothy Parker and George S. Kaufman.

"And your marriage? It's really happy?" he asked.

"Fine, I guess," and she shrugged as if that were not important. "We get along. David took over one of his father's companies. We have horses. We had a terrible fire last winter and lost some, but we've started over again. Life is as good as I can expect."

"You sound secure. But everybody needs a little escape once in a while, no matter how wonderful life is. Don't you think so?"

She did. She most certainly did.

* * *

By eleven o'clock the newlyweds were packed into the Court Rolls-Royce and driven to the dock where the *Queen Alexandra*, newest ship of the Court Line, was waiting to sail for France. The two pairs of twins were spending two weeks at Cannes followed by a sail on a private yacht around the Italian coast. Simon Court had arranged it; he had fixed ideas about honeymoons, and one of them was that they ought to be spent at sea. Nobody in the family knew where he got this notion, but since he was willing to do all the booking, calling, and expediting, nobody protested.

After all the guests had left Pride's Court, Lord Court had a nightcap with his sons and with North. Over brandy in the library, he beamed at all of them.

"We're drinking a toast to something else," he said, "besides the twins' marriage."

"Thank God. We've had enough toasts to the newlyweds," North said fervently. "What's the occasion?"

"A personal triumph," Lord Court said. "We've brought about that French bastard's downfall! He's admitted failure. They're moving out of Edenbridge! Can't afford to live there. Ha. Ha. They have to rent. Can you imagine having to *rent* your house to some stranger?"

Put in Lord Court's derisive and ringing tones, the idea of renting one's house became a circle in Dante's Inferno. One close to the very center of the pit and offering the most unimaginable tortures. (Not that Lord Court would have made that comparison, since he had no real classical education.)

"He's lost just about everything, I hear," Lord Court went on, gloating as he sniffed his brandy. "Put his shares of the asbestos mine on the market. Trying to cut his losses, I daresay, or pay his damned bills. Moving out the end of August. I hear these things. People tell me things." (It was another of Simon Court's delusions that he had a fantastic natural spy system—that people told him secrets and advance news of world-shaking events.)

The Court sons, and North as well, did not really share in Lord Court's delight. While they did not like Armand particularly, they were fond of Honey. Armand's problems would most certainly affect her life, and that they did not relish.

"Where will they live? Did your spies tell you that?" Fort inquired.

"In an apartment, I'm told. An apartment in a publicly rented building. It's hard to believe, isn't it? Well, St. Amour deserves it."

North was glad to escape at last. He felt extremely guilty about his own share in Armand's bankruptcy. He had loathed the idea of bribing officials in Ottawa right from the start but had felt compelled to rally out of loyalty to the old man and consideration for Mildred. As he climbed the stairs, he felt remarkably sober, considering the amount of wine and scotch he had consumed during the evening. In the back of his mind he sensed that he was in trouble with Mildred. He walked into the bedroom hesitantly and found her standing beside the big double bed, ready to retire.

"Hello, sweetheart," he said, testing the ground diffidently. "You did a magnificent job of the wedding. As always."

Mildred stared at him grimly.

When she did not answer, he knew that his instincts had been right and that she was angry. It remained to be seen just how bad things were, whether or not he could bail out with kisses and charm.

"I know about Kay Prince."

"Know *what* about her?" North asked innocently. He began to undress. "Oh, about that man she brought. Well, that was too bad. I admit he wasn't suitable. She ought to have had more taste."

"The March twins have never met Kay Prince," Mildred added.

"They haven't?"

"So how did she get invited to the wedding?"

"Darling, I'm exhausted. Why don't we talk this over in the morning? You must be tired yourself. That old devil kept us down there drinking brandy . . . I didn't want any more but—"

"North, the March twins don't know that woman and Philip Norman doesn't know *them*. So how did they get invited?"

"I have no idea. Why should I know anything about it? I didn't make up the guest list."

"You knew about her taste in champagne."

"I'd been talking to her earlier, that's all. She said she liked Taittinger. Is that some kind of crime?"

"Don't lie. You're having an affair with Kay Prince."

"I am not having an affair with Kay Prince. Mildred, you're crazy. I hardly know the woman."

"I'm crazy, but not in the way you think. I'm crazy to love you so much. I'm crazy to believe anything you say. Do you think I don't know why you married me? I'm ugly and fat. You never loved me, you don't love me now. It will always be like this . . ."

She began to weep. North made a move to touch her, but she pushed him away.

"Don't come near me. Don't ever come near me again. Find somewhere else to sleep. I won't share this bed with you!"

"Sweetheart, be reasonable. Where would I find a bed this late at night? Where would I go?"

"Go to a guest room. Go to some other woman's room. How should I know? Sleep anywhere. I don't gave a damn about it."

"Now, sweetheart . . ." he began placatingly, having no idea what arguments he might use, what weapons he had. But then it came to him, as he looked about at the comfort of his bedroom, as he let all the expensive and beautiful things sink into his vision. "We'll have to preserve some kind of front, Milly. Your grandfather will be horrified if this marriage seems to be coming apart. You know how much he values us . . . the two of us. Our children . . . the way you run the house, Milly."

Mildred hesitated. North was right. They must never, never let Grandfather know the truth. North's behavior was threatening their whole position here.

"I don't care," she said. But her voice was brittle. It held no conviction.

"Now, sweetheart, let's not make fools of ourselves . . . let's not let everybody know we've had a quarrel. If I sleep somewhere else, it's bound to get out. I'm sorry if you're upset. You're tired."

"I'm tired because I'm pregnant again."

"Sweetheart!"

She heard the concern in his voice, the appearance of affection in the way he moved toward her. She did not believe him.

"All right, you can sleep here, North, but stay on your own side of the bed. I'll think of some arrangement . . . some way so we can have separate beds. I'll redecorate. There has to be a way. You're despicable, and I hate you. Don't come near me now, I warn you."

"You'll get over this, Milly. It's all nonsense. I wouldn't look at Kay Prince. I didn't know you were pregnant again, darling. That's wonderful news—"

"Stay on your own side of the bed. Don't speak to me. Don't touch me. Don't ever touch me again."

CHAPTER ELEVEN

It was Justine's idea to hold the small, very private wedding at Edenbridge. A united family front was needed, and since Armand and Honey planned to rent out the house in October, it seemed that Edenbridge was an appropriate spot. It was not a decision she had arrived at easily—this wedding of Mathieu's to a servant girl. Only after she had weighed all the options did Justine give her approval.

She had taken into account Mathieu's career in politics. A more suitable wife ought to have replaced Nora, of course (God knows, Nora had been inadequate enough), but other, more frightening possibilities took precedence. Marie-Claire could not be trusted. She might run off and find an abortionist—a path so sordid and dangerous Justine was scarcely able to think about it in a reasonable way. Or, she might simply run away (for example, to Quebec City) and lose herself, live with some distant relative, or hire herself out as a maid, taking Mathieu's child with her. What would stop her gossiping tongue if once she slipped through their fingers? Mathieu's baby. Out in the world without a name, without a father, with a mother barely more than a child herself. Who knew what stories Marie-Claire might spread once she was free of the St. Amour influence?

No, the best thing to do was face facts and have Mathieu marry the girl. She would arrange to hire a housekeeper and a nanny for the small baby Nora had left behind and for the new baby Marie-Claire would undoubtedly produce.

Justine herself would train Marie-Claire to run a proper household. In the end, it would work out, but, Justine reflected, it was true that the Lord worked in mysterious ways his wonders to perform.

Only the family would be present at the wedding and Marc would officiate at the ceremony. Helene and Corbin had already declined to come down from Ottawa, since Corbin had suffered a mild heart attack and was taking a rest.

While Justine stage-managed the wedding, Honey was grievously unhappy. Moving out of Edenbridge was extremely painful for her. She had come to love the house and had furnished it with care. She sympathized, too, with Armand in his private dilemma. The move was a public admission of defeat at a time when everyone around them seemed to be making more and more money as the stock market skyrocketed daily. Armand must surely be one of the few Montreal businessmen who was losing rather than gaining a fortune.

The other sugar refiners were suffering, too. Another Montreal refinery had closed down, and the others were losing money. Armand had sold his controlling interest in the asbestos mine at Thetford and had borrowed money from both Justine and Clarissa to buy heavily into Noranda Mines. Altogether he had raised half a million dollars, and on the advice of Angus McKie it was all invested in Noranda shares. He trusted Angus. But even if the scheme worked, it would take time, and meanwhile, the St. Amours had to live more economically.

In the midst of preparations for the wedding and moving out of the house, Honey became obsessed with the idea of making up with Susan. She had tried when Susan was in the hospital and had found her daughter cold. At the time she thought she would never make another attempt, but now she could not help thinking how much it would mean to Armand if Susan came back into the St. Amour fold. He would be delighted, she knew. This notion became uppermost in her mind, so she finally called Susan three weeks before Mathieu's wedding.

"Hello, dear," Honey began when she had Susan on the line, "how are you? How is Anthony?"

"Why, hello, Mother." Susan was obviously surprised at

the call. "We're all fine. I'm trying to hire a new nanny, since Starkey was taken away."

"That was an awful thing for you, Susan. I wanted to call you at the time and talk to you about it. We were all shocked. Starkey had been around the family a lot. She was such a good friend to Nora when her first baby was so sick. How could we have guessed?"

"It was revolting, Mother. Absolutely revolting. But it must have been ghastly at the funeral. To think we had a woman like that actually living in the house, looking after Anthony . . ."

"Now, dear, don't think of it anymore. At least she was good with Nora's baby, and with Anthony, too. She's in an institution, I believe."

"That's right. She had a complete breakdown. How is Mathieu? I suppose he's terribly depressed by all these things."

"That's what I'm calling about."

"You are? Why would you call me?" Susan appeared to be retreating.

"Mathieu is getting married. Now, don't be startled, though you might well, I suppose. We're having the wedding here at Edenbridge and I thought—"

"Married? How could he? Even Mathieu is rushing it a bit, isn't he?"

"I'm afraid it's necessary. Justine has arranged everything and, believe me, with good reason. We won't go into that. I'd like you and David to come. The wedding is going to be very small, very quiet. Your father is so depressed these days, Susan, it would be a great kindness if you made up— if you visited us again. You know we're moving out of the house?"

"I heard. I'm sorry."

"So am I," Honey said with a sigh. "I love the house and so does your father. But we have to do it right now. We've rented the house to a man called Lowestoft. An importer. I doubt if you'd know him."

"The word gets around. I'm sorry to hear Father is feeling down, though I'm not surprised. Everybody else in town is *making* money."

"There's no way I can explain. What I really want to know is, will you come?"

There was a moment's silence on the telephone. Susan

did not want to commit herself until she knew more about the situation.

"When is Mathieu's wedding?"

"August 19."

Susan felt relieved. Well, that solved that problem rather neatly. She was an attendant at the wedding of the Court twins, so there was no way she could attend Mathieu's wedding. She would have to decline.

"Sorry, Mother, I won't be able to make it. Flora and Fenella are being married that day at Pride's Court. I'm an attendant."

"My dear, I already know that. I was talking to Charles yesterday, but I thought under the circumstances, you might change your plans. Surely the twins would understand. It's the last large gathering we'll have in Edenbridge for some time."

The idea of giving up the Court wedding would never have entered Susan's mind. In the first place it would be too fascinating, and it was thought to be one of the social events of the summer. In the second, she was not at all sure she wanted to "make up" with her family, as her mother put it.

"But I couldn't do that," she cried, her voice a little sharper than she had intended. "I mean, just seeing the twins married is a big event, even if I weren't in the wedding party. It's quite a large affair, and the girls would have to look around for a replacement for me."

"I see."

"Well, you do understand, don't you?"

"Oh, I understand, Susan. I understand quite well."

Honey's spirits plunged. But she knew that her hopes had been unreasonable because Susan had not indicated in any way that she wanted to see her French relatives. She ought to have accepted Susan's rejection when she visited the hospital. She wished she could hang up without another word, but decency prevented her.

"If it had been some other time," Susan was saying.

"Yes. Well, dear, I hope you find a new nanny. And that Anthony will be fine."

Somehow, they got through the deflated good-byes. When she was finally free, Honey collapsed beside the table, staring at the telephone. Why had she thought it possible that Susan would come to Mathieu's wedding? A sense of coldness enveloped her.

I'll never ask her for anything again as long as we both live, Honey thought dully. *In fact, I don't even want to see her again.*

After the wedding Susan and Philip enjoyed two exploratory lunches at the elegant Ritz before he returned to New York to work on the mining story. After that, Susan received several brief notes asking questions about Montreal mining magnates, brokers, and promoters. Susan, feeling she was suddenly part of a larger world, responded.

The notes were handwritten on pale brown paper with the name Philip Charles Norman embossed in darker brown at the top. No address, or telephone, or title, but he had instructed her to send her replies to the *Times*. (He made spasmodic and rather grandiose appearances there.)

By the following spring correspondence between them had become regular, although it was still formal. Each time a note arrived, Susan was freshly shocked by Philip's deplorable hand (she had been accustomed to men whose penmanship was neat and precise), but she found the contents sufficiently exciting to carry on the communication. Philip often referred to members of the Cabinet by their first names: He had been chatting with Frank (Kellogg), Andrew (Mellon), or Herbert (Hoover). He was still generous in his praise of the Coolidge business policies, which, he said, were monumentally foresighted. He mentioned the mounting excitement in New York over Lindbergh's plan to fly solo across the Atlantic. Susan found all these references quite heady after what she considered the parochialism of Montreal.

As their correspondence increased, Philip threw in more and more names of the famous and powerful. Ezio Pinza had been engaged by the Met, he reported. Bruno Walter had attended one of Althea's soirées. Artur Rubinstein was touring America to sell-out crowds. He gave examples (as did so many other people) of Sir Thomas Beecham's witticisms: He had called Bruno Walter "malodorous" and had said of Koussevitsky, "I doubt if he can read a score at all." During rehearsals Beecham was supposed to have told one player with a short attention span, "We do not expect you to follow us all the time, but if you would

have the goodness to keep in touch with us occasionally
. . ." And so on.

In June Susan managed to organize a shopping trip to
New York, where she booked into the Plaza and had her
first truly secret luncheon with Philip in the Palm Court.
Against a backdrop of violins, which wailed insistently of
love's sweet mysteries, their relationship took a sharply
personal turn.

They had finished discussing diet (Philip confessed to
eating only fish, chicken, and one or two Italian dishes) and
had come to the crab and avocado salad when he took her
hand on top of the table and squeezed it intimately. He
looked into her light brown eyes with his dark ones.

"I'm lonely," he said. "I've been looking for a long, long
time for a woman who could really share my thoughts."

It was an ambush. She had never thought of the brilliant, renowned Philip Charles Norman as "lonely." From
his letters and conversation he was constantly meeting
the potent, rich, achieving people. His wife appeared to
organize around him a fairly gregarious life, and what time
was left over he needed in order to write. How could such
a man be lonely?

"I find that hard to believe," she said.

"Oh, you can be with people and still be alone," he
said, giving back her hand. "Surely you noticed that? In
the night, when I wake up and begin fighting my own
personal demons, it seems to me that man is not afraid
of death but of loneliness. Of nothingness. That's what
Moby Dick is all about. That's the greatest book ever
written."

"I'm sorry, I haven't read it."

"You should. As part of your education. After you've
read it, we'll talk. I'll tell you about Ahab's relationship
with the white whale."

"Will you really?"

She was touched that he wanted to spend precious
time in trying to educate her, in trying to introduce
thoughts that were beyond the concern of ordinary people.

"Certainly. It would be a privilege. We must exchange
our ideas . . . our most private thoughts . . . I trust
you . . . I'm not afraid of you. I'm afraid of my wife
. . . I was afraid of my mother . . . I'm not afraid of

you. Have you ever wanted to completely share another person's consciousness?"

Here he began to ceremoniously light his pipe. He sucked upon it contemplatively.

"That sounds dangerous."

"Very dangerous. Uncharted waters are always dangerous. Tell me about your marriage to the blond Viking David."

This reference made Susan smile. Without effort Philip had made David's good looks sound silly, presumptuous, while his own appearance, which was dark and brooding and, to be truthful, *old*, had become preferable.

"Boring. A boring marriage. But safe and comfortable. I guess I thought it would always be as exciting as it was at the beginning . . . when David and I first met. I've been childish. Hopelessly romantic."

"I'm a romantic. Don't apologize for it. Even after two marriages, both less than successful . . ." he broke off and smiled engagingly. He had a broad smile: Thin lips exposed a full set of even, not-very-white teeth. "I still look for that one great love. The Tristan and Isolde complex, I call it."

"But your life sounds so exciting," Susan said, still surprised at these frank revelations. "All the parties, the famous people, it all seems like a dream to me."

"On the outside, yes," Philip said in his soft, scarcely discernible words. "But Althea and I . . . it isn't really a marriage. It hasn't been for a long time. She isn't interested in sex, not in me or any other man. She's a terrible prude. We have a charade, that's all. Oh, she's a great hostess, and people think she's wonderful. So intelligent, so knowledgeable. But when they all go home, *I'm* left with her. She's cold. Full of problems."

"And don't you like having the important people around you?"

"Yes, but they all go home eventually."

He looked sad. As if he saw the endless parade of greats and near-greats who touched his life, lighted it briefly, and then moved on, leaving Philip Charles Norman lonelier and more isolated than ever.

"But you always say such romantic things about her publicly," Susan said. "I read one or two."

"I do that to keep Althea happy. She likes people to think ours is a wonderful marriage. Public opinion is important to her. She doesn't gossip, herself. When I'm in New York, I'm careful about seeing other women. I seldom indulge."

"What do you do, then? I mean for romance?"

He smiled one of his deprecating smiles that revealed nothing but hinted at indescribable depths of pain.

"Once in a while, I take a chance and see a woman, but believe me, it's rare. Our lunch today in a public restuarant is an exception. I could explain you as research, up to a point. But then, after one or two it would have to stop. Usually I see women in London or Paris."

Susan was intrigued by such circumspect behavior. She was much more apt to approach a problem head-on no matter what the risks, as she had done with North, and regret it later.

"Yes, Paris and London are fairly safe. Even Berlin. Although I don't like Berlin these days."

His eye took on a glazed look as he remembered. In his mind he saw the naked young women offered for his inspection. He felt again that first heady moment when he saw a new woman for the first time: her breasts, her pubic hair, all so different, no two the same, every one a stranger. What it lacked in subtlety, in the pleasures of the hunt, it made up for in the sheer luxury of being able to pick any of the girls, any size, any shape, any color, any age, and have them do exactly as he wished. Without question. Without apologies.

"And what would Althea think of it if she knew?"

"She'd be shocked. Althea doesn't understand anybody's need for sex. She only used to let me make love to her when she'd had too many drinks."

These revelations destroyed the tattered remains of pretense and formality. Philip had confessed to Susan things he had kept secret even from his wife. Philip and Susan were, astonishingly, in league against Althea. They were against David, too.

Her own good taste prevented her from discussing David's sexual habits, and she was a little perturbed that Philip would talk about Althea like that. Yet the excitement of a new, strange adventure with such a prominent man was something she could not reject. She was both stimulated and afraid. The time had come to take the perilous road or firmly resist Philip's advances.

"I'd like to see you tonight, but we can't go out to dinner. I'd love to be seen with you, you're beautiful, charming. But it isn't safe."

"I hadn't thought much about it," Susan said.

Philip leaned toward her, speaking very softly, bending all his persuasiveness upon her in a melancholy plea.

"We have to think of *them*—your husband and son —my wife and daughter. We don't want to hurt them unnecessarily. There are six people's lives involved here. We must be careful not to jeopardize everything we have."

Susan was forced to agree with that reasoning. She had no intention of risking anything. So when he mentioned dining in her suite, she thought that was the best thing to do. Either that or refuse to see Philip in the evening. In which case she would be bored, curious, and dissatisfied.

"I'll be manageable," Philip said. "We'll talk. I want to discuss so many things with you. We'll have champagne. I don't usually drink, but for you—bootleg champagne. Do you see how imporant you are to me already? If you get tired or frightened, ask me to leave. I'll go. I promise."

She gave in. She could not resist such a supplication. Philip arrived at precisely eight o'clock, looking slightly withdrawn as if he had a great deal on his mind. He wore a gray suit with a small pattern, a stark white shirt, and a solid slate gray tie. He looked like a banker. He brought with him a gift box from Cartier's. When she opened it, she found inside a gold chain with a Maltese cross. There was a garnet in the center. A hint of Byzantium.

Susan accepted the gift and fastened it around her neck. It hung snugly against the deep maroon of her silk dress, accentuating her small, firm breasts.

"I think crosses are sexy. I don't know why," Philip said.

They ordered champagne before dinner and sat on separate chairs. The window overlooked Central Park. Outside, it was purple-dusk. Philip asked permission to light his pipe.

"So peaceful," he said. "You bring peace with you. Peace and sanity. You have no idea how marvelous it is to be with somebody calm and sane. Althea's so nervous. So high-strung. I don't know if I told you—she goes to a psychiatrist. That's the new thing these days. Go and have yourself analyzed. Let a doctor take you apart and put you back together in a more acceptable pattern."

Susan felt a quiver of apprehension. Such things, which were evidently part of the larger city, the broader scope of social life here, made her nervous. Life was simpler at home. Susan herself had retreated to boats and horses when she became bored, and at the very worst, she would have an affair.

"Well, is she unbalanced, then?"

"She says not. I'm not so sure. She often screams at me. Throws things at me. Whatever's handy. Pots and pans, things like that. Once she actually lay across my desk to try to stop me from writing my column. She said I paid no attention to her, only to my work."

"That's ridiculous. You're making that up."

"I swear I'm not. She knew I wasn't capable of hitting her in return. So she had the advantage, you see. But sitting here with you, I feel so calm. So serene. It's like going outdoors after a rain—I'm seeing the world anew—fresh and vivid."

"What a lovely thing to say," Susan said, forgetting about Althea.

"You see, it would cost me a great deal of money to leave Althea."

"But I don't want you to leave Althea!" Susan said, alarmed. "I hadn't thought of such a thing. If we did get involved . . . in any way . . . it's just an affair, after all."

"Naturally, that's all we would be doing. I just mentioned that to illustrate why I put up with the wrangling —the bitching—the awful way she treats me in private. I make quite a lot of money between my column, my books, my speaking engagements. But it takes every cent to live the way we live."

Susan was shaken by all this intimate information. She had thought it would be fun. If anything happened, it was supposed to be gay, to make up for the dreariness of life. She did not want to be saddled with somebody else's problems.

Philip saw he had said too much. When the illegal cham-

433

pagne came, he pressed it upon her. He began to talk about the movie stars, the concert singers he knew. He mentioned the rich—the Morgans had invited him for a weekend to an exclusive island off the coast of Georgia. Eventually, he rose and stood, looking thoughtfully out of the window. Silence fell. After an interval he came to her chair and took one of her hands to pull her to her feet.

"Look at me," he said.

She stared up into the fathomless eyes. She felt the power of his mind, of his will. She forgot that he was not physically attractive—certainly not by *her* standards. The air he carried with him, that brilliance of mind, that cloying scent of power aroused her.

"Sex is the root of which intuition is the foliage and beauty the flower. A woman is at her loveliest when sex rises softly to her face, as a rose to the top of a rosebush. D. H. Lawrence," he said with a twitch of an eyebrow, which told her Philip may have just fed her a line.

But it didn't matter. She surrendered. She was surprised at the force with which he made love. If she had given it any thought, she had imagined something quite different: the soft voice, the cool approach, the tentative manner, indicated a gentle attitude toward sex. Instead, he was primitive and coarse: attacking with little finesse but a driving, raw sensuality. It was so unexpected that her secret pool of response was taken unawares.

Certainly there was nothing soft or inadequate about the implacable member, with which he penetrated her. His machinelike movements were at once greedy and insatiable. His appetite was overpowering, and his quick recoveries were astonishing. There was a touch of ugliness about Philip's sexuality, but this only seemed to excite her more.

Before he had left her that first night, he had said, "The angel of silence has flown over us."

She assumed it was original and was oddly affected by it. The first flicker of rebellion against family and position had set in, too, when she reflected upon Philip's way of life, the important people he knew, his knowledge of foreign places. She had lost hope of being mistress in Pride's Court—Mildred was solidly entrenched and no one could say she didn't run the place well. Mildred might be dull, but she was efficient and Lord Court admired her

434

tremendously. Unless the earth opened and swallowed North and Mildred, there was little chance of Susan ever living there. She was part of the Court clan, but not as intimately as she had hoped. North didn't want her around, and Mildred was decidedly suspicious and cold. Might it not be a triumph to leave them all, to come to New York and be part of an international set, rather than the inbred parochialism she had so admired until she had met Philip?

She began to think seriously about the cost of leaving David.

CHAPTER TWELVE

In the spring of 1928 *Héloïse and Abélard* was being rehearsed at the Paris opera on the Place de l'Opera. The official opening was scheduled for early April, and it was to be the last offering of the season, a substitute for *Tosca*, which, due to the impossible demands of the diva who was to have played the lead, had been regrettably postponed. Even in London Beecham heard about the disaster and hastened to offer Beau's new work. He would conduct and direct it himself, he said, and also secure suitable performers for the two principal parts. By virtue of considerable bullying and much money he managed to sign up Richard Tauber, a thirty-five-year-old tenor at his peak, and Kirsten Flagstad, a powerful Wagnerian soprano who seldom, if ever, ventured out of Norway. Sir Thomas prevailed. She would temporarily desert the mystic fjords for the boulevards of Paris. Both singers were rather overpowering for the romantic roles of the much-abused but intellectual tutor and the lovesick future abbess, but their names lent weight to the project. In musical circles, where Paris was still the most respected operatic center, word of the new opera stirred up a great deal of interest. Beecham was delighted. The splendid voices of his stars gave him a solid challenge: He always felt compelled to drown out singers if he could.

As a consequence Beau had moved to Paris in March, where he had taken an old but elegant flat on the Rue Bonaparte. Angela, still living with Julia, had accepted an assignment to design sets for the Sadler's Wells Ballet and was currently working on *Polovtsian Dances* by Borodin. This charming task had helped keep her mind off Beau's absence.

The unexpected telegram arrived at Much Hadham around teatime on a particularly raw April day. Julia took it from the maid suspiciously and examined it with a practiced eye. It boded no good, she was sure. She had been pleased to see Beau go off to Paris because she had plans for Angela herself. As soon as Beau was gone, she had instantly begun a fierce campaign in favor of a middle-aged duke who was both rich and reliable.

"After all, my dear, you are thirty-one years old," Julia had pointed out to Angela. "Hardly a child. And if you don't marry soon, how can you possibly have any children? The chance gets more unlikely every passing year. And that would be a pity. Now, take the duke. Just imagine how he'd adore to have an heir. He had no children by his first wife, and I happen to know it wasn't *his* fault. One hears these things, you know." (Julia *did* hear these things, though it was never clear to anybody just how she managed to find out things that were not public fact.)

"Well, I don't want to marry the duke. He's rather a dear, but after all, Julia, he is fifty-two. And besides, he hasn't asked."

"Fifty-two isn't old. As for asking, he's just waiting for some kind of signal. The poor dear doesn't want to be rejected. One can't blame him. He's sweet, the way he comes here to call. And sends all those bushels of roses. Not very original, but still you can't expect originality in a duke. That's icing on the cake."

Angela laughed.

"I don't mind the roses. But I can't imagine going to bed with him, that's all. Julia, you ought to know about things like that with all your experience."

Julia chose to ignore that and went on rambling,

"Terribly kind the way he overlooks your scandalous behavior with Beau. Oh, don't think people don't know you lived with Beau before I took over your life! Just a couple of gypsies. People *do* know." Julia sighed elaborately. "It would be quite lovely to be a duchess. You might think about that."

Julia had given similar speeches fairly often. She was genuinely concerned about Angela's future, and at the same time she was lonely herself. She missed Twickenham and, although she would never have admitted it, would have taken the earl back on almost any terms. Julia's life lacked a real center. If only Angela would marry, she could become embroiled in plans for houses, for the wedding itself, for prospective great-grandchildren. She had been deprived of all this.

And so she handed the telegram to Angela as if it had come straight from some local pesthouse.

"No doubt it's some unsavory little summons from The Great Genius," she said sarcastically. "I suppose Beau would like you to cross the Channel and take that awful train from Calais just to make his tea."

Angela opened the telegram nervously. It was unlike Beau to communicate in this way. She read the brief message with amazement. It said: "Will you marry me? Please come at once. Love, Beau."

It was as if a heavy weight had been lifted from her shoulders. She felt as if she wanted to laugh and cry at the same time. She smiled brilliantly at Julia.

"Read this. Read it!"

Julia accepted the piece of paper, frowning. She adjusted her reading glasses on their gold chain. Her expression turned from puzzlement to anger.

"He expects you to drop everything when he snaps his fingers," Julia cried. "To go *just like that!*"

"Yes, just like that."

"And I suppose you're going to rush off like some peasant?"

"I'm going to rush off, though I don't know if it will be like some peasant. I love Beau. I've wanted to marry him for a long, long time. I know it's right."

"Angela, please reconsider this. You're throwing yourself away, don't you see? Do you think marriage will change Beau? Do you think he'll behave better because some priest mumbles a few words over you? I suppose he'll want you to become a Catholic."

"I don't know about that. He's never mentioned it. But yes, I think marriage will change Beau and I have reasons. He's always been against the idea, so if he's changed his mind, then something inside has changed. But I can't expect you to see it."

"My dear child, *men never change*," Julia said wearily. "This is one of the notions that has undone women for centuries. *I* ought to know. I've had three husbands. It's always been the same story."

"Beau is different."

"Only in that he's worse. What about your sets for the ballet? Are you going to let somebody else take over?"

"I'm almost finished. It will be quite easy to have them completed by somebody else. It's just filling in paint now."

"You're wasting your life. How can I make you see? Throwing away a promising career, as well as a promising marriage, to follow this man around like a galley slave. He's selfish and impossible, and he has shown that time and again. You might as well marry a drunk. It's the same thing. Their promises to reform mean nothing because the damage is inside. It's not *who* they marry or *who* helps them that makes a difference. No amount of glue, no amount of shoring up, can change the fact that they're flawed. Beau is like that. You'll remember what I've said someday."

Angela was already wolfing down her tea. She wasn't listening. She was thinking only of packing, of making arrangements to get to London and from there to the Channel boat. Julia might as well have been talking to herself.

When Angela arrived in Paris, there was no one to meet her at the station. She was not surprised, although she had hoped Beau would be somewhat better organized. She found a porter to struggle with her bags, and he put her in a taxi. Her French was passable, and so she had no difficulty directing the driver to the flat on rue Bonaparte.

The flat was in an old house, and Beau had the ground floor. The tall, narrow windows were protected by louvered shutters, and it was cool and faintly musty inside. She found that Beau was not alone. He embraced her and kissed her and helped her off with her coat. He was quite casual as if this were just another meeting.

"We're going out again shortly, but come and wash up

and have a glass of wine first," he said. "John is here, and this is Renée, John's friend."

The four of them drank burgundy in the cool green room. She noticed that the furnishings were expensive, the carpet was Aubusson, and there were some good French landscapes on the walls. A concert grand, a Pleyel, took up much of the room.

"How did you find such a pretty flat?" Angela asked.

"It's one Sir Thomas rented," Beau said. "Belongs to a friend of his. Do you want to go and wash up before we drive off?"

"Yes, please. I feel so grubby. You know that boat train, it's a horror."

"Renée will show you where the bathroom is."

Renée led her down the hall and switched on a light.

"I think you'll find everything you need here."

She was a short, black-haired girl with full lips and clever eyes. She wore expensive clothes, and Angela decided John Leach's taste in women had improved since they had last met.

"I'll be out as soon as I can. Do you know where we're going?"

Renée laughed.

"How like Beau not to tell the bride," she said in French. "We're going out into the country to a monastery. You're to be married tonight."

"Tonight?"

"Beau wants the wedding to be secret. It's some new idea he has inside his head. I suppose he'll explain it all to you later."

She closed the door and left Angela in the large bathroom. It had an enormous pink porcelain sink on a pedestal. There were mirrors everywhere. Angela washed and brushed her hair. To arrive like this and find Beau waiting to whisk her off to a secret wedding ceremony seemed terribly theatrical. She wondered if he had gotten carried away with his work at the opera house.

When she emerged from the bathroom, she found them with their coats on, ready to leave. But she was not quite willing to fall in with Beau's plans. Not without some kind of explanation.

"Beau, you *must* tell me what's happening! Why are we

going off into the night like this, to be married secretly? Couldn't we talk alone for a few minutes?"

"We don't need to be alone. John and Renée know about my plans. John helped me arrange for the ceremony out at the monastery."

"If I'm to be a bride, I'd like to know why we have to do it secretly. Why at a monastery?"

"There are good reasons, one of them being that Father Cousteau isn't asking any questions about whether or not you're a Catholic." Beau consulted his watch. "We have a few minutes to spare. I told Father Cousteau ten o'clock, and it's only an hour in the car."

"Then please explain," Angela begged.

"One thing is that I'm completely immersed in my opera, in the story. I feel as if I *am* Abélard sometimes. That's what convinced me we ought to go through with the ceremony. He was absolutely brilliant . . . one of the great philosophers, and so if he thought it all right to marry Héloïse, I began to see that my resistance to marriage was childish."

"So I have Abélard to thank, have I?" Angela could see some humor in the situation. "How long has he been dead?"

"Seven hundred and eighty-six years."

"And it takes a man who's been dead seven hundred and eighty-six years to convince you that marriage is a good idea? Really, Beau, I don't know whether to laugh or cry."

"Don't do either, just come along," Beau said. He did not appear to think his ideas at all strange. "Héloïse and Abélard got married secretly, so I just thought it would be a good idea. We certainly don't want an elaborate ceremony, with people there, news reporters . . . they'd be bound to bring up . . . Dorian's death. Don't you see? We don't want anything in the newspapers about our wedding. It would only be disastrous for me."

"Oh, dear. And are you going to become a monk, as well?"

"No darling, certainly not. After all, Abélard was turned into a eunuch, and I'm not planning to live like that. Far from it."

"Thank goodness for something. I hope your identification will stop with the ceremony. They did have a child, didn't they?"

"They had a son," Beau said. "So, if you feel you'd like to follow that part of the story, it will be quite all right."

He seemed so caught up in the melodrama of the occasion that Angela felt she might have been a stuffed dummy. Still, it was not the moment that held her now but the future. For her there was something immensely appealing about their wedding night. She was still slightly stunned that the dream she had clung to for so long had become a reality. She was Beau's wife: Madame Dosquet. Angela Dosquet. That would take some getting used to, but she was gloriously happy. She felt that all the days of her life had led up to this one, perfect night. Her destiny had been played out at last. She was home.

Day after day, Angela sat in the back of the opera house watching rehearsals. The painful, sweet story of Héloïse and Abélard was spun out before her eyes. She saw Beau caught up in the magic of it; Abélard hired by the canon of Notre Dame to tutor his niece, the beautiful Héloïse, their love, the birth of a son, the secret wedding ceremony in the country performed by a cooperative priest, and, later, the canon's *idée fixe* that Abélard meant to abandon Héloïse, the ambush by ruffians in which Abélard was castrated, and the later separation of the lovers as Abélard became a monk and built his own hermitage near Troyes, while Héloïse became an abbess and founded a sisterhood.

"I don't understand why the uncle turned so nasty," Angela said one day to Beau during rehearsals. "After all, he seemed friendly to the lovers at first."

"He was a churchman of the old school, and Abélard was a rebel. Once Abélard began to teach a different set of beliefs, he became a danger. It was a question of politics. A man, or a woman for that matter, will do anything to protect his way of life if it's threatened. Look at Julia. She hates me. She wanted you to live the way she did and to accept her standards. I represented a threat—"

"Yes, I suppose so. But poor Julia had no intention of having you emasculated, darling. She's not at all bloodthirsty. Though it's a marvel Grandfather didn't think of it!"

They laughed, but Angela had now completely cut herself off from both sides of her family. Or so it seemed. She was content, though, to watch Beau and listen to his music. He spent every waking minute either at the opera house, consulting with Beecham, or rewriting bits of the music. He disliked Flagstad as Héloïse. "She has no heart," he said.

When she wasn't watching the opera unfold, Angela worked on small canvases at the flat. She had no proper studio and no time to find one. Beau was terribly thin, he seldom had time to eat, and sometimes his fierce fights with Beecham almost drove him to bed. He despaired of the principal singers and several times threatened to kill himself over the way Beecham conducted the music.

But on opening night Angela and Beau appeared, more romantic, more haunted, than the lovers in the new opera. He was black with anxiety, glowering from mad green eyes, mouth voluptuous with the desire for perfection in his work. Angela was remote, cool in gray silk that wrapped around her in the new draped fashion and with a gray fox circling her throat. Julia had surrendered and arrived in time for opening night. She was astonishing in red satin by Worth and an ermine cape. She declared the music radical and destructive, but she loved the attention she received. It was only later at supper, when she sat with Beecham (an old friend) and they both indulged in character assassination of mutual acquaintances, that she mellowed slightly.

The opera was hailed by the critics as an unqualified success. One went so far as to say that Beau Dosquet, "this unknown French Canadian," was the "heir to Saint-Saëns. *Héloïse and Abélard* compares with Saint-Saëns's opera *Samson et Dalila*. It has the same excruciating pain, the same poignant melodies. . . ."

CHAPTER THIRTEEN

They had moved into Philip's apartment in the Dakota. Since they never saw anybody who lived there, the fact that they were not married was completely irrelevant. It was only a question of time before they both obtained divorces—David was naming Philip as corespondent, and

Althea, Susan—and then their relationship would become as conventional as that of everybody else they knew.

Naturally, Susan would not have listened to Philip's pleas if he had not offered marriage. Nothing else could possibly have pried her loose from the security of her marriage to David, the status she enjoyed as part of the Courts' entourage. But Philip offered something more global in scale: a glittering life among the *haut monde*. Not a local, insular scene like the one from which Susan came, but something with a style beyond even *her* imaginings.

As for Philip's friends, some appeared indifferent to the situation and others did not invite Philip to private parties or dinners anymore. Philip was not a man with close friends, in any event. Susan soon began to notice that the people who had helped them when secrecy was so essential—Philip's part-time secretary, for example, and an economist with whom he'd gone to Harvard and whom he trusted—soon disappeared from their lives. Once these people were no longer useful, they were dispensable. Not only that, but Phillip was exceedingly disloyal. He told her personal things, intimate confessions these people had made to him and which they had never dreamed would be repeated to anyone. (She had first noticed this tendency when he talked about Althea, of course, but had chosen to ignore the warning.)

It was no common liaison; it was supposed to be the grand passion. A passion for which Philip had catapulted himself out of a long and grueling marriage (paying handsomely for the privilege) and for which Susan had relinquished a lifetime of comfortable security. Philip had limited access to his daughter, Abigail, but Susan was entirely cut off from Anthony—relegated to that terrible Siberia of the "fallen woman."

On an April evening in 1928 Susan stood dutifully at the huge front door of the apartment to bid Philip good-bye. He was speaking at a dinner that evening, every guest a top industrialist and none below the rank of president or chairman of the board. It was black tie. Susan noticed once again how old his dinner suit looked—a bit green around the braid—as if some antique patina had blown over it in a high wind and settled in the crevices. Why didn't Philip buy a new suit? As she received his kiss and felt his cheek pressed to hers, she felt the dry, dusty grit of face powder.

The first time she had noticed this, he had explained, "It's because I'm so sallow. And I'm bald. It helps reduce the shine." He rubbed Pond's face cream into his skin at night. She could never get used to any of these seemingly effeminate habits.

Sex had first drawn her to Philip, and she could not deny that. But now she realized that his lovemaking lacked sweetness, affection, any thoughtful tenderness. His kisses were actually cold, his hands artful without being kind. After the first flush of excitement had passed, she had to admit she did not really like his flesh. She had no wish to pat him, or stroke him, or even look upon him lovingly. He was sexually stimulating without generating any sense of devotion. She found it rather degrading that she could still respond.

After two months Susan began to think about leaving Philip. There were times when she thought wistfully of Montreal, of David's dullness, of the beauty of Pride's Court, of her grandfather's wonderful tantrums. Even of Mildred and North, whom she had been glad to put behind her.

She had no money of her own and no way of earning anything. She was not trained to do anything useful. Having deserted David, she now communicated with him only through a lawyer. David had made it clear he did not wish to see her or speak to her. She had dealt him a terrible blow, and he did not care to risk another. Each time she reviewed her situation, the nettles stung her afresh.

And when Philip was gone, her mind drifted back, as it always did, to the beginning. She could remember so clearly how excited she had felt that first time in the Plaza, when she and Philip had luncheon together and he had first broached the idea of an affair. And later that night in her hotel suite, when Philip had seduced her. She recalled only too well how stimulated she had been, how she had thought of it as a wonderful luxury—like eating Swiss chocolates or buying a piece of jewelry she didn't need. They had meant it to be that way. They had agreed that it would be only an affair. As Philip had said, "Let's be friends and occasional lovers." Somehow it had gotten out of control. For no sooner had she returned to Montreal after that New York meeting than the letters began to arrive. Philip had taken a postal box in New York and had told her to do the same in Montreal. That way they could write anything they wished and not worry about it. "I thought I could resist writing to you," he had said, "that I could wait until I saw you again, but I find that impossible."

The letters, the gifts, the cards poured across the border in what appeared to be an endless stream. She saw herself as a mistress to genius—Byron's lover, Lady Caroline Lamb; Elizabeth Barrett Browning; and George Sand. She was inundated with protestations of despair—he could not live without her, could not write without her, could not carry on his life without some hope that she would join him. Bits of poetry:

> Sometimes at night
> the devils come to me
> and I sit up in bed
> to listen.

> It is the sound and smell of you
> and I feel drawn
> to your sensuality
> like the home of a bird
> a thousand miles away.

Susan had never before received passionate love letters. David had written quite conventional ones, telling her pieces of news, what he was doing, or what he hoped to do. He had sometimes admitted that he missed her, but there had been no flights of fancy, no exquisite yearnings of the soul, no suggestion that he might die for love of her.

Philip had once written:

> In the damp parades of my solitudes
> I saw the whisky moon,
> And felt your pussywillow sweetness.
> But the sunrise has too often blinded me
> and I have crawled on my knees
> Looking for my hands.
> By the nails of Christ, I miss you.

On another occasion he had become quite whimsical: "I feel like a wild faun, caught eating broccoli."

Susan had been enchanted. They made arrangements to hold long-distance telephone calls. She would go to the main exchange in Montreal and call him at work at some specified time—they took no chances on any calls being traced. It was all beautifully contained.

But the letters and notes became more furiously demanding. The books he sent became more elegant, more touching. The pieces of jewelry, the scarves, the perfume, more expensive. They arranged more weekends together and the sexual ferment did not lessen but only seemed to increase until neither of them could think of anything else. She was in New York when Lindbergh was given a tumultuous tickertape welcome. Philip had arranged for her to watch it from the office window of some business acquaintance. Every time they were together, Philip moaned about Althea, that she was killing him. His doctor, he reported, had said he would have a heart attack if he stayed with Althea much longer. Between their sexual encounters Philip would take inventory of his maltreatment at Althea's hands. She was a virago. She had nearly broken his ankle when she threw a frying pan at him. She had tossed a lemon roll in his face. She was insane.

"She's been seeing a psychiatrist for two years and nothing ever improves," he told Susan. "I talked to the psychiatrist, trying to sort things out. But he told me the marriage was hopeless. I'll have to leave Althea."

This kind of *Sturm und Drang* formed part of every conversation they held. Philip could not get off the subject. He was obsessed, it seemed, with two things: sex with Susan and Althea's cruelty. When they were together, they seldom appeared in public because it was too risky. This meant that they spent most of their time in hotel suites, where they ambled from bed to bathtub.

His list of complaints about Althea was endless. She was crazy with jealousy, seeing in his every move some other woman. She refused to give him up not because of love but because of the people he knew, the celebrities he could invite to parties. Sometimes she told him to leave. This proved that she was unstable and neurotic. She had threatened suicide many times. Not only that, but she hated his mother. She was very rude to his old mother and screamed at her. It had come to the point where she would not allow the old lady in the apartment. This last touch bothered

Susan, who had been brought up to accept all family members, no matter how eccentric.

By early 1928 Susan had escaped to New York for yet another clandestine meeting. All around them were signs of an incredible, expanding prosperity. Money literally seemed to be growing on trees. Philip studded his conversation with references to the clubs of the elite. "They are saying at the Century Club . . ." he would begin. Or, "I saw David Gardiner at the Brook and he said . . ." When she asked Philip what would happen if Coolidge failed to run for President, he said it didn't matter, Herbert Hoover would achieve the same thing. No end was in sight as the spiral continued upward at a dizzying pace. Philip assured her and himself that the American government "could not afford" to let anything prick the balloon. Following her January visit Philip arranged for a meeting with his lawyer. She must leave David, they both told her, or Philip would collapse. Everything had come to a climax. He was going to leave Althea, and she must leave David. She did not need to worry about money; Philip would marry her and take care of her. In the meantime he was making out his will to her.

Susan took care to point out to Philip that she could have no more children, but that, he said, was unimportant. He did not need any more children. He did not need children to reinforce his masculinity the way some men did. He proposed to her on the telephone and she accepted, although they had already gone through that formality in front of his lawyer. Back in Montreal it was one of Philip's desperate notes that finally triggered her flight. It read:

> We never really wanted this to happen. But somehow we've come to sense in each other a paradoxical combination of mutual peace and excitement that we have both missed in difficult and wrenching lives.
>
> With you, and only you, do I feel the final shattering of solitude. A cathedral intensity of feeling I've never experienced before.
>
> Lightning flashes of pain and pleasure break and illuminate my separations from you. There are oh so many things I need to tell you. To explain the battles I've fought with music and the inner ear, with seeing and feeling, with the ethics of decision. (I walk the

streets enchanted with thoughts of striking back at the angels of savage Christendom, and they know the pleasure of striking hard.)

I live for that longed-for moment when I can see you again. When I can see you again and say: The rude and raging fact is this. Susan, I love you.

Her response was foreordained. She surrendered completely. There was no way she could hold out against such formidable ammunition.

As it turned out, she left David on Valentine's Day, although that was not by intent. It just happened by accident. She took a train to New York to join Philip. He had arranged to take over the apartment from Althea, and Susan moved in. One of the first surprises came when Althea began to telephone regularly, usually before breakfast. An hour of screaming would result—demands for more money, more time, more of everything. This certainly seemed to support Philip's contention that Althea was a little crazy. But Susan wondered why Philip did not simply hang up.

It was only as the days turned into weeks and the weeks into months that Susan began to think Althea may not have been so crazy after all. Philip's mother had a serpentine quality that was most alarming. When she first met Susan, she was friendly, even warm, kissing her when she arrived and when she left, complimenting her. But it soon turned into coolness, dislike, and total disapproval. Then, too, Philip expected all of life to revolve about his requirements. His eating habits were peculiar (he scooped sauerkraut out of a jar as if it were a bowl of nuts), and he refused to eat most ordinary dishes. He lacked gaiety, even after Althea was gone from his life. What Susan had taken for depression due to the fact that he was unhappily married turned out to be part of his personality.

The small things mounted. Until she longed to laugh and be foolish. She longed for a man who would eat rare roast beef with hot mustard. For a man who would, once in a while, drink too much wine. She longed for home.

CHAPTER FOURTEEN

March of 1929 saw the wildly inflated stock market totter and fall back as if struck by an invisible plague. This brief touch of financial fever was cooled by some careful propaganda from the big banks on Wall Street and the patient recovered. (Or appeared to recover.) A flurry of fresh activity indicated that the market was stronger, more vibrant than it had been before the illness.

Philip was desperate for money. His settlement with Althea had been expensive, more so than he had expected, and he still liked to live well. He had been investing heavily. To her astonishment, Susan discovered that Philip was inept about money and that his personal finances were always like a cat's cradle. Ironic, she thought sourly, that he continued to make pedantic speeches to Wall Street financiers and anybody else who cared to listen while he couldn't balance his own checkbook. His broker was beside himself. But Philip reiterated his theory that "there's always more money. Somehow it all works out."

Susan had been raised in an atmosphere where money was made but respected. In the Courts' world every move was planned: Money was fertilized, watered, and carefully pruned. It was not cast to the winds. With Philip, she was living on financial quicksand. Every month Althea made more demands. She needed a specific sum for this or that—an unremembered debt to be paid, an education fund for Abigail, extensive repairs upon her nutria coat. Always something. The telephone would ring, and it would either be Althea screaming at Philip about money or his mother screaming about her building superintendent. Philip would report that Althea had called him a "creepy bastard," whereupon he would call her a bitch. But not when she could hear him. He was craven when it came to Althea. After one of these difficult conversations Philip was quite likely to be reduced to tears. Sometimes he cried when he was happy (which was awful), sometimes when he was angry (which was degrading). Susan had never in her life had to contend with such an emotionally volatile man. Though her French Canadian relatives had sometimes been demonstrative, they were not given to much crying. As for the Courts, with them it was the stiff upper lip.

At first, Susan thought both Althea and Mrs. Norman to be ruthless hags bent on destroying Philip. She accepted Philip's assessment of Althea, and it had never occurred to her that Philip might have contributed to his wife's apparent hatred. His mother, he explained, had always blamed him for everything ever since he could recall. Probably because he was an only child.

The odd thing was that the sexual side of their relationship seldom suffered. Occasionally Philip would be too distraught to make love, but those times were rare. His sexual drive was strong, having survived his mother's lifelong passion to consume him and his wife's briefer attempt to emasculate him.

The scene was confusing to Susan, however, who had foolishly assumed that once he freed himself of Althea, Philip would be happy. She had not expected Althea to be part of her life with Philip. After all, she had left David behind, as well as her son. For good or bad, she had committed herself to life with Philip.

By early September, the market was booming again and Philip was solvent. He was optimistic about his own finances as well as those of the world. He bought Susan a Chanel original and some expensive nautical antiques for the apartment; he even discussed buying a new car.

At breakfast on the first of October he informed Susan that they would attend a friend's wedding in Westchester and asked her to be dressed and ready to drive out in mid-afternoon. It was a small affair, but Susan looked forward to a change of scene. She often found the Dakota confining after her life on the farm and in Montreal. The country air was sharp with the scent of harvest—pumpkins, squash, and corn and grain stalks cut off near the earth. The farmhouse where the ceremony was held was pleasantly furnished, and the guests stood about in the drawing room for the informal ritual. Immediately afterward, Philip took Susan aside and said conspiratorially, "Let's sneak away. I don't feel much like staying, do you?"

"But what about your friend? Won't he mind?"

"They won't notice. Come along, let's go before they serve the supper."

"All right, if you like."

"We'll drive back to the city and I'll take you to Luigi's for dinner. Just the two of us."

That sounded good and she was rather pleased that Philip didn't want to stay. She didn't know anybody, and they didn't look too interesting, anyway. A wave of nostalgia almost overwhelmed her when she thought about her own snug circle of friends in Montreal, where she was considered important, stylish, attractive. Here she had been nobody. She had sensed an air of disapproval as well.

They reached the restaurant by nine o'clock. A small group was playing passable jazz. She ordered red wine and chicken cacciatore. Philip had soda water and chicken. As she was taking her first sip of wine, Philip said casually, "You know, while I was standing there listening to the wedding ceremony, I came to an important decision."

"What was that?"

"I don't think I'll ever marry again."

At first the words did not register with her. They were like the words one heard in a dream, not to be taken seriously. One would wake up, and then everything would be safe and real again. It would not have occurred to her that Philip could be so insensitive as to tell her such a shattering thing in a public place. One did not say things that might destroy another person's composure in front of strangers. She was conscious of people at the next table, of a waiter passing by, of the orchestra making music.

"What did you say?"

Her mouth had gone dry. She took another sip of wine, but it didn't help. She felt numb. This is what it must feel like when you were shot, she decided, and realized that you were wounded. You saw blood, but the pain has not yet reached the brain.

"I said, I don't think I'll ever marry again."

"But Philip . . . where does that leave me?" Her voice was not much above a whisper. Although inside her head, she was screaming. "What about me?"

"I'm sure we can work something out," Philip was saying, as if he were discussing a play. "After all, we haven't talked about it yet. I don't mean we have to live apart . . . we can live together, if you like, but I don't want to marry you. That's what I'm saying."

"But I have no money . . . no place, then. You told me

to leave David, you and that lawyer . . . you said I had to—"

"Now, don't be old-fashioned, Susan. What does it matter whether or not we get married? We can go on living together. Just as we are. You do have a place."

"That isn't what you said . . . that isn't why I left David. And my son."

"After all, Susan, people change their minds. They do it all the time. You weren't really happy with David, or you would never have left. Be reasonable."

"Reasonable? I wasn't perfectly happy, no. But I hadn't even considered leaving . . . David and I had worked things out. You know that. All those speeches you made . . . your letters . . . you and your lawyer. You said you couldn't go on if I didn't move out and come to New York. You said all those things . . . I have the letters."

"Everybody makes mistakes." His voice was cool. "Let's not argue about it. That won't help."

His eyes had retreated into dark caverns where she could not reach him. He did not seem to realize that she was on the verge of hysteria in a public place.

"This is rather an important mistake," she pointed out.

"We'll work something out. Eat up."

"No thanks. I'm not hungry."

Philip ate his chicken. Susan drank her wine and ordered another decanter, but she remained sober. A lump of ice had formed where her lungs used to be, making it very difficult to breathe. The wine did not thaw the ice.

In Pride's Court word of the toppling stock market below the border was received with very little surprise. Lord Court had been predicting some kind of catastrophe. He had no holdings that were not solidly backed by gold, copper, railroads, and shipping lines. Some of his enterprises might suffer, but his investments were so diversified, in so many parts of the world, that he did not foresee a personal crisis. If the Court income was cut, then so would prices be cut. It would cost less to live in the way he believed to be correct.

Lord Court felt reasonably safe against the blights of the world. He had his family about him. At least, he had those parts of it that had not fled for some inexplicable and foolish reason. He seldom thought of Angela now. Susan had made a grave error, but then, she had not had the advantages of a Court upbringing for her whole life. As for Landry, he did not care to think deeply about *him*: Suffice it to say he was off in the Amazon on some lunatic expedition.

North and Mildred were a comfort to him. They had three children, having added a daughter, Sarah. They were a truly wonderful couple and a credit to him. Simon II had married, too, and had a son. Another Court. And Noel was considering marriage. There was a bit of a problem with Charity, he realized that. But no doubt she would pull out of her flightiness. It was not much more than that. The girl was too pretty. Beauty was always a problem. One only had to think of Venetia, and Angela, to know that. Much better to be plain, like Mildred. These women seemed to get down to the business of living rather well.

Yes, he was ready to dig in for whatever would be the duration of this unfortunate "crash," as people were calling it. He could hold out for an indefinite period of time. Perhaps for the remainder of his lifetime. But that wasn't enough. He must see that the future of the Courts was secure. The whole loyal tribe. There must be no end to the Courts.

Part Three

1930–1935

CHAPTER ONE

He lay in a hammock slung between the two poles that held up the hut's thatched roof. He found it difficult to breathe. The thick moist air pressed down upon his face, and the jungle night wrapped him in soft black velvet. How impossible it would be to describe such heat and dampness, Landry thought. It made the skin ache. Yet it was beautiful, the jungle, beautiful beyond reason. And, at times, deadly.

Around the makeshift camp glossy bacaba palms, colossal assacus, and broad-leaved marantaceas stirred with hidden life. From their possessive branches shrill parrots accused one another of murder, and closer to the wet earth, secret rustles whispered of pitiless snakes and carnivorous beetles. Vampire bats sliced through the firelight. The constant whine of mosquitos and the spasmodic signals of green and scarlet cicadas shimmered against the nerve ends.

Earlier in the evening the Indian guides had built a fire to discourage bats and bugs (although the strategy really didn't work), and now they were sitting around sipping homemade cassava brew. Landry could see their hunched naked forms through the film of white net that Miles had draped over his hammock to protect him.

He had been desperately ill for a week, but the first sign of his sickness had appeared two months earlier when he and Miles were still downriver in Manaus buying equipment and hiring guides. A doctor there had told him one injection might cure the disease, but as it turned out, that was not the case. Landry had not been particularly impressed with Doctor Alvarez from the first minute he entered the wooden shack Alvarez called an office. Everything in Manaus was in such terrible repair that it was hard to tell whether a building was being thrown up or whether it was in the process of falling down. Doctor Alvarez's office was typical. The doctor stank of rum at three o'clock in the afternoon, and it seemed that he had not laundered his cotton shirt for some time.

Landry's quick assessment was not far wrong—Carlos

Alvarez had been discredited in Lisbon over an abortion scandal ten years before and had fled to South America to finish out his professional life. He had chosen the squalid town at the forks of the Amazon and Negro rivers because he was needed there and no questions were asked. Manaus, nine hundred miles from the Atlantic, had seen better days. Before the Great War, during the big rubber boom, the town had been both rich and pretentious. It had boasted an opera and a cathedral. But now it was an outpost, a dreary shipping point for Brazil nuts, certain kinds of hardwoods, skins of cattle from the savannas of the Rio Branco, and a small supply of rubber from the interior.

Thinking back, Landry recalled how Doctor Alvarez had stood slightly aloof from him during the examination, head tilted away, not touching the single ugly red fungus growing on Landry's upper lip. Then he had felt cautiously around the jaw line beneath the ear. He had found a swelling.

"You've got yaws. One of our more charming tropical diseases," Doctor Alvarez said in excellent English. "That's my diagnosis."

It was one of Doctor Alvarez's more notable accomplishments that he spoke several languages. He sat down on a rough wooden chair behind his rickety desk and surveyed the young Canadian through the softening haze of too much rum and too much heat. Disillusionment clung to him like moss.

Landry, unable to stand up any longer because of the heat and his own feelings of inadequacy, collapsed on the only other chair in the room.

"Yaws? What in hell is that?"

"That, my dear sir, is one of a thousand blights in this hellhole, this anus of the world. There are some diseases so filthy that not even a doctor can accept them without the aid of some good Barbados rum."

He brought out a bottle, poured a splash of dark liquor into a dirty glass, and drank it down.

"The Indians," Doctor Alvarez went on, "come in here from the back of beyond and they're rotten with syphilis, or deformed with elephantiasis—feet like washtubs and testicles down to their ankles. When they're that far gone, I can't help them much. But they *will* wait."

"Are you saying that yaws is like syphilis?"

"Yaws and syphilis are closely related. Take a Wasserman and yaws will give you a positive test. It gets into the bloodstream through a small cut on the skin, usually around the mouth or genitals. You might have picked it up in Belém a month ago. It takes that long to incubate."

"I don't see how."

But he did see how. In Belém he had cut himself while shaving. It had been slow to heal. While they were in the seaport, Miles had gone to the bars around the docks and picked up a young sailor. The two had come back to the hotel room drunk and Miles had passed out and left Landry to settle with the sailor. When the fellow tried to make love to Landry and later asked for money, there had been an ugly scene. Landry could not remember all the details, but he could, unfortunately, recall the smell of sweat and rum and dirt.

"I don't care how you caught it," Doctor Alvarez was saying quite casually. "But you have it, I'm afraid. That's the point. Sometimes it's called frambesia—French for raspberry."

Landry stared at him miserably.

"What can you do for me?"

"We use the same treatment for yaws as we do for syphilis. An injection of arsenic compound."

"Arsenic?" He'd always thought arsenic was a poison. "Will that cure me?"

"One shot might cure you, but you really ought to have two to be sure. How long will you be here?"

"We planned to leave tomorrow on the *Dolphin*."

He knew that Miles would want to push on up the river. The *Dolphin* sailed for Iquitos the next day. Already Miles hated Manaus and was restless and irritable.

"What are you doing here, anyway?"

"My friend and I are on a private expedition—collecting insects and plants for a university. But it's a private expedition, we financed it ourselves. Do you know the *Dolphin*? We've hired a couple of guides here in Manaus and bought some of the supplies, but we expect to pick up more in Iquitos."

"I'd stay here a week and have another shot, if I were you. But you can do as you like. I don't care."

Doctor Alvarez got up with apparent difficulty and walked into an adjoining room to prepare a needle. Watching him, Landry saw no sign of any sterilizing equipment. Alvarez was speaking to him from the next room. "It's up to you. You're a young fellow, so you might recover with one injection. I wouldn't rush to get to Iquitos. If you think Manaus is a pigsty, just wait."

"I've been told it's quite a large port," Landry protested.

"It's a pesthole."

"We don't plan to stay there. We're going into the jungle to find rare specimens of equatorial insects."

Landry decided not to look when Alvarez gave him the needle. He had no choice but to take whatever medication the doctor offered, so the less he thought about it, the better. The needle was dull and hurt. But of course, all this had taken place weeks ago. Now he was sick again, and he knew that the disease had not been cured.

The lesions appeared around his mouth and around his genitals. There were rashes and outbreaks under his armpits and stomach as well. The growths on his face had begun as small pimples, but these had later enlarged and ulcerated. They secreted a puslike yellow liquid and then dried to form ugly crusts that built up into crimson lumps about his mouth.

As soon as he first noticed the pimples, Landry felt alarm. He knew, although he did not want to admit it even to himself, that he was in serious trouble. He was days from medical help. His temperature rose and swellings appeared once more under his ears. The rashes increased and were terribly itchy, adding to the scores of bites he had suffered from mosquitos, black flies, and dozens of nameless tormentors. No matter how much oil he spread over his arms and legs and face, the insects still attacked him, until finally, every inch of his body was infected in one way or another. When he fell into a fever, he raved. He had periods when he was calm and lucid, and then he knew that the disease that had struck him was lethal. He was thirsty all the time, and Miles had placed a pail of boiled river water beside the hammock where he could reach it. Miles refused to touch him.

"You look disgusting," Miles had said more than once. "I can't bear to look at you."

It seemed very late at night when Miles came into the hut to give him his nightly dose of quinine—the bitter white crystals that helped reduce his fever. Miles gingerly lifted

460

back the net to reveal Landry's face, now a cruel mass of suppurating sores. His mouth was only a slit, his eyes were almost closed. The hammock and the air around it smelled like rotten vegetation.

"I've brought you a tablet to help you sleep," Miles said. "And some whisky to wash it down."

"Thank you, Miles."

Landry took the cup and pressed it to his mouth. He saw Miles turn away so that he would not have to watch. Landry wanted to weep when he thought how painful it was to have a contagious, ugly illness. His loneliness was like some prolonged agony that vibrated through his gut. Even the Indians refused to come near him but sometimes stood in the doorway of the hut to stare at him. He was grateful for the sleeping tablet, though, because he might have a short time free of pain and self-disgust.

"What time is it?" he asked Miles.

"Nine o'clock. Dinner time in London. Dinner time in any place that's civilized. Do you know what I ate tonight? Boiled monkey. *Boiled monkey*. Christ, I feel like a cannibal. I hope we don't run out of whisky. I guess I could drink that miserable brew the Indians make, but it tastes like poison. I hate this place."

"I'm sorry I talked you into coming, Miles."

The party had been marooned at this temporary camp a week. From Iquitos they had paddled five dugout canoes along the north shore of the Amazon. It was flood season and the swift-flowing, dark red water ate away the banks around the roots of trees and small bushes. At some point they veered north along a marshy, shapeless tributary, and after several days they had turned east to follow the course of a sluggish stream rimmed with alligators rattling their brittle armor.

The Indians had promised exotic insects in this back-water. From the descriptions given by the two guides who spoke a little English, Landry had deduced that this territory was the home of the longicorne, with its slender body and long antennae decorated with tufts of hair, and the *Coremia hirtipes*, which sported fringes of down like little cockades along its hind legs.

Miles, left without anybody to talk to, found the Indians just as inscrutable as literature had always suggested. There was no way to reach them, and he never had the least idea what was going on behind their expressionless masks. On the surface they seemed quite gentle and even languid—the black eyes serene, the mouths slack, the skin a pretty polished rosewood. But an air of indefinable cruelty clung to them. They were cold and, at times, callous.

When Landry had first fallen ill, he and Miles had pretended it would only last a day or two. Miles had immediately given him quinine, and then, later, one of the guides had mixed a vile potion from herbs that he swore would cure every disease in the jungle. Landry sank quickly after that and was soon too weak to travel. Neither Miles nor the Indians wanted to share a canoe with him, anyway. Landry decided he was going to die and the rest of the party were merely waiting.

Miles was profoundly bored. Nothing had gone according to plan. This godforsaken hellhole was not his idea of paradise, or thrilling adventure. He wondered why he had ever agreed to come. But the surprising thing was how well he managed in the jungle, considering his delicate skin. As long as he kept covered from the sun and protected himself against marauding insects, he remained healthy. He seemed to be able to take the staggering heat and moisture. Landry's disgusting disease and the boredom of the camp drove him to drink. He knew the guides were watching him and wondered if they were hatching some scheme to abandon both white men and make off with the supplies. He began, therefore, to weigh the wisdom of splitting off a portion of the party and going back to Iquitos for help.

This was the night he planned to leave with two Indians and one canoe and a fair share of the supplies. He was leaving one of the English-speaking guides in charge of the camp, but he did not tell Landry because he knew it would frighten him. As Miles watched Landry swallow the tablet and the whisky, he breathed a little gasp of relief. Then he walked to the corner of the hut, where his personal luggage was piled, and began to sort out the things he wanted to take with him on the trip back to Iquitos.

From the hammock Landry could hear Miles sifting through the bags and was too sleepy to question him. His mind gradually slackened and dissolved into wayward, dreamlike ideas. The jungle night sounds began to whisper to him, and he imagined inside his mind how beautiful it was out there. He could see the myrtles, the wild guava with their smooth yellow stems, the plumes of the tall palms waving overhead. He could visualize the mahogany trees alive with brilliant birds—purple-headed tanagers, saffron-tailed toucans, luminescent hummingbirds, and scarlet parrots. Butterflies that were as large as birds and metallic blue, clustering delicately at the water's edge, trembling with fear and light.

Yes, he and Miles had collected some fine examples before he fell ill with fever. In the chests they had spiders the size of teacups, matted with black hair, eyes like suspicious grapes. He hoped Miles was looking after the specimen boxes, because you couldn't trust the Indians. They had no sense of values. As he sank lower in his sea of mild discomfort, Landry dreamed of taking these miraculous objects back to Montreal, presenting them to the university. How impressed his family would be! Everybody would be surprised. He might even find an entirely new species.

He drowsed off just as Miles left the hut to join the Indians. It was marvelous how Miles survived the jungle when you realized how small he was, how thin, how delicate his reddish coloring. But then Miles had always been an exceptional young man.

Miles had chosen an English-speaking guide and one other Indian to help with the paddling. He spoke about a selection of supplies to take with them on the journey, and he instructed the guide who was staying behind that he should wait for help. Unless, of course, Landry recovered sufficiently to travel. There was only one water route to Iquitos, so the parties couldn't possibly miss each other along the way.

All the Indians seemed agreeable. Miles had offered a generous bonus of cigarettes, coarse cotton cloth, a few axes, and some harpoons. All in addition to their regular wages. His own guide slyly asked for Miles's camera—a folding Kodak that took postcard-size photographs and had cost him fifty pounds in London. Miles refused. The Indian regarded it merely as a toy.

They set aside a light load. Miles had found that the jungle Indians could always hunt something for the cooking pot. They were adept at shooting birds and monkeys with their blowguns and they fished efficiently with both nets and harpoons. They ate wild fruits that were plentiful in the jungle: guavas, which they made into paste, and papayas, which they ate raw or boiled as a vegetable. So it was only necessary to carry the bare essentials: the two specimen boxes, Miles's guns and ammunition, a medical kit, tea, sugar, pots and pans, matches, kerosene for the lamps, tools, and tarpaulins. He was close to the end of his French cigarettes, but they were only a week or so from Iquitos, and he could make them last that long.

While Miles supervised the packing, the chief guide went down to the edge of the stream with a load of tarpaulins and storm lanterns for the boat. There was only a narrow strip of beach left at this time of year, although in the dry season the broad, fine sand beach acted as a landmark in the area.

The guide came back with a disjointed report about the state of the boats. Miles could not quite make out what the man meant, so he left the Indians to pack some small crates and, taking his powerful flashlight, loped down the path leading to the river. He could see the encouraging glow of the storm lanterns that had been hung on the boat.

The dugout was intact, so the guide could not have been talking about a leak, and the lanterns appeared to be secure. Miles counted the paddles and checked on the tarpaulins, which lay in the bottom of the canoe. In fact, he could find nothing wrong and was just about to climb back up the bank to the camp when he heard a soft rustle close by in the bushes overhanging the stream. He ignored it. The night was filled with alarming sounds—sighs, screeches, whispers, whines, distant crashes. He thought of the Indians, on whom he now depended, and wondered if he could trust them. Especially the ones he was leaving behind. They might easily steal off with as much goods as they could carry and leave Landry to die.

Miles heard the rustling noise again, closer this time, more insistent. He flashed his light in the direction of the sound. Then he bent over double to part the bushes where they drooped toward the water. He froze.

The snake was coiled with a few feet of its body erect, the huge head level with his own as he leaned down. In the swift moment of his inventory he did not comprehend the size of the animal although he had heard stories about forty-foot anacondas. They were known to eat whole antelope and regurgitate them because they couldn't digest the horns. Once in a while, they ate a boy or a small man, although the natives agreed that this was rare.

Snakes, so the story went, did not attack men who were upright unless they happened to be particularly hungry. But if a man was unfortunate enough to be lying down, injured perhaps, or kneeling, they might easily decide to make a meal of him.

Miles saw the gaping jaws and the needle-sharp teeth as they lunged toward him. He felt the teeth pierce his shoulder and tried to tear himself loose, to straighten up. The snake's grip was tenacious. Already, blood was streaming down his shirtfront. He tried to scream for help as the first coil wound around his chest, but the sound came out as a mumbled gasp. Slowly, every ounce of air was squeezed from his lungs as the great snake's muscles contracted. He could hear his own ribs breaking with a sickening crunch. The second coil wrapped about his waist. Inside his chest and in his arms and the fleshy parts of his thighs arteries burst one after the other like pricked balloons. Blood drowned his lungs and throat, so that he began to choke, gurgle, and finally sink to the moist earth, still within the slippery vise of the scaly body. When the third coil completed the work begun by the first two, he was unconscious.

The snake hesitated. Carefully it loosened the perfect muscles so that the man's body slid free. Then, tentatively, it sniffed at its prey to make sure it was dead. Finding that, the snake unlocked upper and lower jaws from their natural linkage, and the mouth yawned, making ready for the meal.

Higher on the river bank the guides had heard the disturbance and came rushing down the path, swinging their lanterns and uttering sounds of dismay, calling Miles's name. Near the water they caught the actors in a circle of light—the hovering snake, wide-mouthed and deliberate, the broken body of the man. The snake stared stupidly at the light, astonished at the interruption.

The Indians, armed with hatchets, began to attack it around the head and on the underside of the neck, where it was vulnerable. After the first two natives more came to join the fight, and with its belly open the snake collapsed at last.

The chief guide examined Miles.

"He is dead," he pronounced. "Take him up to the fire."

Among them they distributed the long weight of the snake and the easier burden of the dead man. The snake-skin was valuable, and they could eat some of the meat before it spoiled.

From inside the hut Landry heard extraordinary noises around the fire. There was something distinctly odd and fearsome in the cries of the Indians. He forced himself to waken from his drugged sleep. With great difficulty he heaved out of the hammock, almost falling to his knees as he did so. He was burning with fever, but he managed to stagger to the door. Leaning against the pole, he saw through slitted eyes a nightmare scene.

At first he thought he might still be hallucinating. He often did that nowadays. He saw the natives with the huge, mangled snake, obviously excited. Then, not far off, the body of a man, all crumpled but bloody around the neck and shoulders.

Landry shook his head to clear his vision, but nothing changed. Everything was just the same. He moved out to take a better look at the upturned face. It was Miles. The English-speaking guide came to him and said, "What will we do?" Pointing at Miles. The guide stared at him, waiting for instructions.

Landry closed his eyes. His legs crumpled, and he slid to the matted, fetid earth. A tidal wave of loneliness, of utter hopelessness, carried him back into a fever dream. Nothing was real. He had no idea what to do, what to say to the guide. He was ill and isolated and without so much as a prayer.

Landry began to cry.

The Catholic mission was situated about half a mile from the harbor, on the south shore of the river. Father Agustín inhabited a sparsely furnished two-room cottage with a screened verandah, where he could sit in the evening to catch any stray breeze that might come along and at the same time be free of mosquitos. The church itself was built in an architectural style indigenous to the area— bamboo poles and palm-thatched roof. There was also an outbuilding connected with the mission—a kind of shed— used by visiting Indians. Quite often natives asked for medical rather than spiritual aid. (Father Agustín was not at all certain that even when the Indians were converted, they understood what Christianity was all about. There were so many different tribes and they had so many varying dialects and customs that he was unable to communicate with most of them.) However, he was adroit at treating simple cuts and abrasions, minor infections, stomach upsets, and, in an emergency, setting a broken bone.

Father Augustín was a man who *looked* as if he had a vocation. His spare body in its black soutane (which he wore even on the hottest days as a matter of principle) and his hollow cheeks and deep-set eyes suggested stringent self-denial. His appearance implied that he shunned eating and drinking. The truth was that he did not eat much because of the heat and because he often lacked funds. Most wine imported into the area was rough, and he considered it undrinkable. He bore the heat and the humidity, the nagging insects, the surrounding filth and poverty, the dread parade of fruitless days and nights, with a gaunt stoicism. His tall, willowy figure, sallow skin, and abundant dark hair gave him a faintly romantic air.

At the moment Father Agustín was worried. The two young scientists who had gone upriver were very much on his mind, and he had even begun to mention them in his prayers. When they had been gone almost four weeks and he had heard nothing, he wondered what he ought to do: if he ought to speak to somebody at the police station or the government offices. Not that the expedition was his responsibility. Far from it. He had no delusions about that because the men weren't even Catholics, but Church of England. He had known them only briefly. He could not be responsible for every transient who drifted through the sulky port of Iquitos. But these two, so young, so obviously inexperienced, so out of place, had become through their gestures and trust a small part of his own life.

He was holding a letter for Landry Court from his father in Montreal. Landry had asked if he and Miles might use the mission as a mailing address, and Father Agustín had been glad to offer that small service. He had also undertaken to mail letters for both young men, which they had written during the day they visited with him at the mission. They had brought him gifts of beef, fresh vegetables, and a bottle of good French wine from their own stores. He appreciated this because of the novelty.

Landry had taken Father Agustín's picture with an expensive, folding camera. The priest was delighted because he was anxious to send a snapshot to his sister, who lived in Madrid. He hadn't seen her for seven years, and he would have liked to assure her that he was well. He looked forward to the day when Landry would have the roll of film developed and would show him the results.

He told himself that the party was well equipped and that the Indians, as far as he could tell from his casual contact with them that day, were as reliable as most. Yet he knew that the jungle was treacherous. He had noticed that if one thing went wrong, a series of fatal events often followed. Consequently, when he was next in Iquitos checking on mail and buying food and kerosene, he was tempted to go the authorities.

As he walked along the steaming and malodorous main street leading directly down to the riverfront, he thought he recognized an Indian who was coming toward him. The man definitely looked like one of the guides Landry and Miles had hired. Yet sometimes even Father Agustín could not be sure of identities, despite his long stay in the territory. He was about to dismiss the notion (admitting to himself that the subject of the two men was uppermost on his mind and that he might easily be imagining the resemblance) when he caught sight of the camera. It hung by its own leather strap attached to a piece of twine wound around the Indian's waist. There was no mistaking the Kodak. No Indian could afford one, and he wouldn't have known what it was for if he had somehow acquired one. Therefore, it must have been a gift and he would regard it as some kind of magical toy.

Father Agustín had the sharp, nauseating stab that signals impending disaster. He stopped the Indian, who because of the priest's garb was quite agreeable to a chat. Father Agustín spoke to him for several minutes and then gently persuaded the fellow to go with him to the police station, where he could tell his story to the proper authorities.

Father Agustín identified Landry and Miles when the bodies were brought into Iquitos from the jungle, and then he cabled the families in Montreal and London. (He had taken the addresses from the backs of the letters Landry and Miles had asked him to mail. It was something he usually did in such cases because his personal view of the jungle was unalterably fatalistic.) He received a cable from the Courts asking him to make all necessary arrangements to have Landry's body shipped home. Fort sent a large sum of money by cable to cover expenses and as a donation to the mission. Mr. Andrew Flanders, an uncle of Miles, responded in much the same manner, although his gift was considerably less.

The tragedy brought Fort and Sydney even closer together. They were shocked by Landry's death, and it was fortuitous that they had patched up their own marital differences some years before. The twins, Flora and Fenella, eyes veiled, retreated without comment into the mysterious caverns of their marriages. Exactly what they felt or thought about their brother's death was never clear to the rest of the family.

Lord Court had powerful but mixed emotions. On the one hand, he regretted the death of *any* male Court who might have carried on the dynasty. And he said so. But on the other hand, within the privacy of his own mind, he thought perhaps death was better than dishonor. He had entertained the feeling for a long time that in Landry's case, dishonor was just over the horizon. He did not make this observation to anybody, but it was a thing that made his grandson's death a little more supportable.

CHAPTER TWO

By the summer of 1930 a pall had descended upon people in every part of the world. Britain alone had three million unemployed, and hunger marches on Parliament were a common sight. The National Socialists were a major power in Germany, and Mussolini had become undisputed dictator of Italy with the somewhat pompous title, *Il Duce.* In Canada thousands of poor were "on relief," a scattered, disorganized sort of dole that no level of government wished to claim as its own.

For the rich of the Western world, taking the sun had become fashionable. To be tanned was to be terrific.

Everybody who was *anybody* showed up at Cannes, Antibes, and the Venice Lido, and American beauties of unbridled bounty sported mahogany skins, sparse little costumes, and flashing white teeth. (There were, it was noted by the cognoscenti, few *French* at Cannes.) Those with international tastes and the international bank accounts to support them now flew between London and Paris instead of suffering a wretched Channel crossing and then taking an even more risky boat train. Popular songs had a slightly risqué flavor: "Let's Do It" and "I Can't Give You Anything But Love, Baby" were good examples. Cocktails were old hat. They had never been embraced by more conservative socialites, anyway, since *they* had always taken the position that a known quantity was good, while the untested or faddish was déclassé. Dancing, on the whole, was slower and bosoms were back. The phrase *sex appeal* had been around for a couple of years.

Even for the most impeccable of women, makeup was now acceptable. *Vogue* was advocating foundation cream overlaid with two layers of powder (one light, one dark) plus vaseline rubbed into the eyelids. Mascara was not entirely out of the question.

The Canadian election of 1930 had a certain Alice-in-Wonderland flavor. In the Conservative corner, wearing a plug hat, tail coat, and striped trousers, and looking for all the world like the bloated capitalist that he was, stood the millionaire Richard Bedford Bennett. In the Liberal corner, wearing a thin smile and no longer suited up in the glistening armor of the Brave White Knight, stood Prime Minister Mackenzie King.

As Bennett expounded in his somewhat florid and swift-flowing style, he made only the vaguest promises to come to grips with the Great Depression. On the other hand, King's noisy vows were rather too specific. When the over-burdened provincial governments asked for financial aid from the federal piggy bank to relieve their poor, King flew into a rage and swore that they would not get a "five-cent piece." The "five-cent-piece" speech haunted King throughout his campaign, and no matter how brilliant or lofty his arguments concerning new power projects on the St. Lawrence River or vast public works to employ the unemployable, he was met with jeers and catcalls and reminders of the "five-cent piece." If ever a man had cause to regret a thoughtless outburst, it was Prime Minister Mackenzie King.

Now, by some ironic twist of fate, the rich Mr. Bennett, natural enemy of low tariffs and high wages, had become champion of the common folk. In Westmount Lord Court greeted this development with obvious glee. The Courts were putting all their weight behind their favorite Conservative candidate—North Grenville-Court—and a vote for Bennett was a vote for the Courts in their eyes. Even the fact that the Liberal candidate running against North was Mathieu Dosquet failed to dampen Lord Court's ardor.

Simon Court, by one of those curious juggling acts for which he was famous, took Mathieu's candidacy as a "good sign." When victory was his (that is, the Conservative party's and North's), Lord Court would find the hour sweetened by the fact that he had beaten a nephew of Armand St. Amour. To North, however, the identity of his opponent was immaterial: The riding had always gone Conservative, he believed, and King's ridiculous posturings only made a Conservative victory more certain with each passing day.

At the committee rooms on Argyle Avenue, North had just come out of a meeting after a long and dreary session concerning his next public appearance. The outer rooms were empty except for the presence of one volunteer worker, Laura Balfour.

North glanced at his wristwatch to confirm the fact that it was past six o'clock. These days, he reminded himself, he did not have to be concerned about time as much as he had in the past. It was marvelous how being a candidate laboring under the stress of political sciamachy relieved him of any responsibility at Pride's Court. Everything was clearly understood. Everything was forgiven. He wondered why he had not seen the advantages in patriotic gladiatorism earlier in his career.

"Would you like a lift home?" Laura asked, "or do you have your car with you?"

"That's kind of you, but I have my car outside."

He wished he had not driven the Dusenberg today. It would have given him a good excuse to ride with Mrs. Balfour. Ordinarily, of course, nothing would have induced him to leave his car behind. (It was new—a barrelside phaeton, creamy beige in color with maroon trim. The top was canvas, which made it a summer car.) He had wanted the Dusenberg desperately the moment he saw it, and though it had cost eighteen thousand dollars, he had bought it. At the moment, however, looking down at Laura Balfour, he would have gladly caused the automobile to vanish.

Laura Balfour was a young widow. Her husband, Victor, had been a lumber tycoon who had made a considerable fortune from the forests of New Brunswick on the East Coast and British Columbia on the West. Victor had been only thirty-seven years old when he died just after the Crash. It had come as a shock to his friends. Laura still lived in a fairly modest stone house on Cedar Avenue. The twelve rooms were cleverly designed and elegantly furnished. Laura was much like her house: correct, well-groomed, but not lavish.

Therein lay her charm for North. He had discovered when he was a much younger man that he preferred women with a modest helping of mind and a generous one of good taste. Women who were for hire, waitresses with shrill voices, girls who ate with the fork in the right hand, women who had careers, left him unmoved. He was seduced by luxury, beauty, refinement. He liked genuine fabrics and expensive perfume, real jewels and *couturier* clothes.

("I like *good* things," he had often told Mildred in the days when they had been close and she had hung on his words as if they were gospel.)

Laura Balfour was a small neat blonde. Her hair was drawn smoothly back from a high forehead and held by a narrow tortoiseshell bandeau (exchanged for a velvet or gold one in the evening), and it curled up at the ends just below her ears. She had the natural blonde's pale skin, finely textured, lineless over good strong bones. (When she was very old, she would look distinguished, possibly a bit skeletal.) Her eyes were China blue, and though not unusually large, they offered such a steady gaze that she often made her companions uncomfortable. Her chiseled nose and full lips suggested, to those with an artistic leaning, the famous head of Nefertiti—with its breathtaking balance.

On this warm afternoon she wore a light summer dress that she had picked up in Biarritz. It was fashioned of

472

white silk piqué, and she wore it with a matching lemon-yellow sweater, trimmed with the same white silk.

"Well." she said to North in her cool voice, "perhaps you'd like to come to the house anyway? For a drink. You look exhausted."

He noticed with approval that she did not invite him to have a *cocktail*, a term he loathed. A drink was a drink as far as he was concerned.

"I'd love to. Shall I follow you in my car, then?"

"You know where I live, I think."

"Yes, I do. It's kind of you to ask me."

Once inside, he found the Balfour house to be more commodious than it had appeared from the street. The drawing room formed an entire wing that stretched like the stem of the letter *T* from the back of the house into the garden. Thick white carpeting covered the floor from wall to wall, and small antique carpets were laid on top of that. The furniture was upholstered in shades of blue. Here and there a strategic ornament—a rare famille rose porcelain horse only five inches high, a terra cotta amlash from Persia, a flower painting from Brod in London—provided a bright accent. The blend created an air of mathematical tranquillity—rather like a Mozart serenade.

While Laura made them each a whisky and soda. North wandered about the room examining her choice of antiques. The amlash, she told him, was ninth century B.C., and she had bought it in Milan on her honeymoon. Victor had always liked it. The details of the room reinforced his earlier conviction that she had excellent taste.

Eventually, they sat side by side on a powder blue sofa with down-filled cushions and their conversation circled around the coming election, North's plans to mesh Ottawa and Montreal in his life, and whether or not Laura ought to sell the house.

All during their talk, North's mind was plagued by thoughts of the terrible waste he saw before him—Laura Balfour without a lover. He found it frustrating that he could offer no real solution to her dilemma. She would want an unattached man, surely? Not a man like himself, who would be forced to hide. Even if he did not love Mildred and was not sharing her bed very often, North could never have freed himself from the tangled web of Court finances. To abandon his position in the Court kingdom would be madness.

As a matter of fact, it was dangerous for him to stray in even the most casual way. Each new adventure had become a trick—a magician's sleight of hand. As he watched Laura Balfour now and saw the full pink lips fold hungrily over the thin edge of crystal, felt the devastating drench of her studied gaze, saw the graceful hands flash diamonds in some small gesture, he allowed himself the even greater luxury of glancing down at the pleasant, seductive breasts under the white silk gown. His mind began to do sly, quick turns. She was, he felt certain, a *real* blonde. He speculated on what that meant in terms of intimate anatomy. A nest of spun gold just waiting to be inhabited. How he longed to take up occupancy there—like some invading, rampant magpie. Without effort he could discern the fine blue capillaries on the inside surface of her wrists and underneath her upper arms when she raised them slightly to illustrate some new point. The pattern would be repeated, he felt sure, in delicate embroidery over the delicious breasts.

He had not had any sexual release in weeks—God knows, he did not count the wearisome expeditions into onanism—those forced marches into old memories that stimulated him to climax in the privacy of the shower. How could his own hand perform the same miracle as a partner's searching tongue, the exotic motherings of warm breasts, the moist maroon velvet funnel designed to receive him?

On his second whisky he felt obvious stirrings, embarrassing rallies that he was able to conceal only by getting up and walking across the room away from Laura. Through tall windows that faced west, he viewed the purple evening shot through with rosy clouds. Sunset. Light in the room became oddly translucent. He turned toward Laura and heard her catch her breath in a charming little gasp, felt waves of response reach out to him, real, almost visible in the shimmering air. He closed the ground between them quickly and seized her hand.

"I'd better go," he said, hoping she would bid him stay.

"Yes, I think so." She did not take away her hand.

He raised her hand to his lips and kissed the tips of her fingers.

"If you want me to go, I will," he offered. His voice was blurred with ignominious lust in the sudden quiet of the pretty room. "I don't want to make a fool of myself."

"Don't worry," she assured him softly, "I won't let you make a fool of yourself."

"What if I fall in love with you?"

"You aren't going to fall in love with me."

He kissed her tentatively at first, slowly tasting the fresh strange mouth and then moving swiftly to an eager scooping of her tongue into kinship with his own. Again, she let him have his way without protest—not yielding, exactly, but not pushing him away, either. He let one enterprising hand slide along the side of her neck, then down into the open front of her dress until he had actually touched a nipple. Still, she did not move. He felt the flesh rise slowly to the lure. At last she did push him away (but not before he had tasted the hors d'oeuvres) and said breathily, "I don't know, North. It's so terribly risky. I simply don't know."

They broke apart. He finished his drink without looking directly into her face again, without braving that fastidious stare. When he left the house, he felt frustrated and confused. They had come to no decision. She had asked for time to think things over, and it seemed to him that whatever conclusion she reached, the link between them had been forged. Nothing would significantly change in the next week, or month, or even year.

As he drove home, his personal life assumed vast proportions in his mind, thrusting out all thought of the election and his business commitments. Laura was the first woman who had attracted him sexually in a long time, and he wondered if he were willing to gamble with his future. At the age of thirty-five he felt seventy. He sat grimly at the wheel of the graceful Dusenberg (normally he basked in driving the car about the city because it drew so much admiration) and headed toward the loneliness of Pride's Court. He could recall with some irony the days when just thinking of Pride's Court and knowing that it was his own address gave him twinges of delight. Now, there was absolutely no anticipation in his heart.

* * *

Mildred did not make a habit of drinking alone. Most days when the Court men came in before dinner, she would listen to their conversation and join them for a sherry. But normally, alcohol was not an important factor in her daily life. For one thing, it put on weight. For another, it was more likely to make her feel tired than elated.

Today she felt unaccountably depressed. There was no obvious reason for it. She had done all the usual things—supervised the children's supper in the nursery, waited while Nanny Redman ran a bath for little Sarah, listened to the boys' stories of school and adventure.

She was a fond mother. Most days she genuinely enjoyed her hours with the children before dinner and had made it a rule from the time Nicholas was born that North should also spend time with them each day. It would have been so very easy for him to ignore them in Pride's Court. Since the election campaign began, however, she could no longer demand punctuality from North. There always seemed to be a meeting, a visiting dignitary, a last-minute change of strategy. Once North was elected, she would have to face the fact that he would be in Ottawa a great deal. Perhaps it was this realization that had brought on her gloomy mood.

In the past two years, the cutting edge had softened and she had stopped mourning her love for North, although she often felt a sense of futility about her life and her marriage. She had been forced to acknowledge that North would always look at other women, always indulge in some stupid little flurry outside his marriage. She had tried to accept the idea and integrate it into her thinking, but because she still loved him, it was difficult. She could be reasonable as long as his indiscretion remained an abstract, as long as it was labeled "tomorrow," as long as she could put no face or name to his diversion. When he had brought Kay Prince to the wedding, that had altered things, had put a whole different complexion upon the matter. It was unforgivable to bring another woman into *her* territory. It had opened up all the old wounds, displayed all the old possibilities for pain. Since that day she had not slept with North, although on one or two occasions he had managed to seduce her through alcohol and her own desperate need. When they were with family—in front of Lord Court, Charles, Fort and Sydney—when they were at family dinners or together in the nursery, Mildred and North kept up a pleasant front. Alone, they seldom spoke except to discuss the children, specific social engagements, or household expenses.

Mildred descended the nursery stairs to the broad upper halls and paused before making the final journey down the marble staircase to the sitting room. She glanced angrily at Sir Cathmor as she passed, a splendid and solitary monarch in his gilt-edged lodging. She thought that for him, like all men, life must have been secure and filled with pleasure.

Damn the Court men, anyway! Damn all of them! She went directly to the Red Sitting Room and found it empty. Not one man was home yet. The drinks tray had been placed on top of the commode, she saw, so at least she wouldn't have to ring. She supposed wearily that they were all off at a meeting connected with the campaign. Richard Bennett, the party leader, had been in Montreal for two days, and naturally, all the Courts had been dancing attendance. He was an old friend of Lord Court's and represented the family thinking. They had listened to his speeches, aided in organizing his program, and lunched with him at the Mount Royal Club. Life these days was structured so completely around politics that Mildred was utterly bored with the election. She poured herself a scotch and soda instead of her usual sherry.

Looking out through the sitting room windows into the rose garden, she saw that an unusual sunset was spreading pink and orange phantasmagoria across the sky. The light in the room tingled with life, electrifying everything with a glowing ember-red.

She would have liked to take pleasure in the room, but she could no longer do that. When she and North had first been married, the idea of being mistress of this great house had seemed to her the pinnacle of success. Now she stared about her with disenchantment. What did money, position, and power mean? It they were so important, why did she feel so empty?

Her mind trailed halfheartedly over scenes from her childhood—hot August days at Drake House, the willow-hung swimming pool, the broad, cool verandahs. Every summer since Drake House had been deeded to them, North and Mildred had opened it, installed the children there with servants, and completely rearranged their lives for two months of the year. The election had changed all that. This year they were staying in town.

Thinking back, dreaming, Mildred decided that life had been far more exciting when she was a child than it was now. Interesting relatives came and went, family feuds took place that the children only sensed or knew about from spying on the grown-ups. Romantic and powerful figures like Aunt Hannah (who had eloped with a Frenchman and been disowned by Grandfather), Aunt Venetia (a legendary beauty who had set fire to the house and killed herself), and the tyrannical Sir Simon himself, who had managed to terrify all of them, were part of daily life.

Life had seemed majestic and consequential in those days. Now it was common. Oh, there had been her own mad passion on North and her splendid wedding. That had been exciting, she had to admit, and learning to run Pride's Court had been an achievement. But somehow people were diminished. Nothing was as marvelous as she had thought it would be. Even her recollection of the twins' wedding (for which she had worked so hard) had been marred by North's behavior. She had been angry then, and she could become angry again just at the thought of his betrayal. Yet how she had adored him once!

She poured herself a second strong drink and stared miserably into the fading pink light. Blue shadows now fell in the room. She did not turn on a light but rather sat staring into space. Where was North at this very moment? Was he really working on the campaign, or was he with some woman? How disillusioned Grandfather would be if he knew the truth about his protégé.

Why couldn't North have been faithful and loving? Why couldn't he have been a devoted father and an adoring husband? Why had he turned out to be a spoiled, irresponsible, faithless, but totally charming delinquent?

Mildred knew it was useless to plough up this same well-worn ground, but she could not seem to rid her mind of her complaints. She poured herself yet another drink and continued to brood. She conjured up visions of the way North had made love to her in the days when they had first been married, when she had still worshipped him, when their sensual explorations had been so graphic. Mental images began to generate a strong current of need—a current that always lurked just below the surface of Mildred's nature. She relished past delights, the waves of lascivious frenzy that had once inundated her. Making love to North had always produced such wild pelvic intoxications, every one deliciously wicked, forbidden yet available because the sacred stamp of marriage had been placed upon it.

On her third scotch Mildred felt so fevered that she became extremely restless. She ought not to have allowed herself to dwell upon those past pleasures, she thought, or on her private and rather dangerous addiction to North's sexuality. Yet her mind would not stay still. It kept slipping away to wallow in legal lust until she finally forced herself to her feet and began to walk from the room, hot and trembling, to the privacy of her own apartment. She was desperate now for sexual release, even though it would have a sterile touch without North's body to feed the flame.

Once inside her own bathroom, Mildred hastily stripped off her clothes and stood before the full-length mirror. She knew that she was drunk, but the urgent impulse was greater than the sense of having behaved badly.

She began to examine her body, lids hooded, trying to decide whether she was, in fact, too fat. She lifted up the large breasts, and her nipples responded to the touch. North, she remembered, had always adored her breasts, finding in them an elusive comfort. The hunger inside sharpened. She stared with glazed interest at the dark patch, the greedy port between her legs.

Then she crossed the tiled floor to the bidet and carefully adjusted the taps, making certain with trailing fingers that the water was soothingly warm. She sat on the bidet at a certain angle she had discovered long before, so that the spray struck her with tireless velvet fingers. She turned the tap that controlled the spray to a perfect pressure and then, eyes closed, hovered yearningly over the play of water.

North's voice interrupted her voluptuous reverie. She looked up, startled, not knowing how long he had been there watching her.

"Milly!" he cried, his voice tight with the excitement of the righteous voyeur. "What in hell are you doing?"

He knew exactly what she was doing, and he did not expect an answer. Instead, he began to tear off his own clothes so that in seconds he was standing in front of her, marvelously erect. Milly did not hesitate but opened her mouth, leaned forward, and took him in. They stumbled to the bed eventually, and momentarily, at least, the prize of satisfaction became the whole world.

Afterward North fell asleep. Mildred, lying beside him, began to weep. As she surveyed that vulnerable body stretched out upon the bed in complete relaxation—the dark hair framing a profile turned away into shadows, manhood now appealingly innocent—she knew that she had never loved North more. She pressed her lips to the fine hair along his forearms, and North did not stir. Even when she put her mouth to his shoulder, his ear, his cheek, he was oblivious to her. He slept trustfully, as a child sleeps. Mildred was once again swamped with the familiar tidal wave of pain and love North had so long inspired in her. She had surrendered to him once again (without a struggle), opened up her defenses without a shred of dignity, and he would never even realize what it had cost her. This was her offering to his maleness. He would never question his right to that gift.

North, she knew, was incapable of a sustained passion. While Mildred had been burdened with a vision of her lover, layer by layer and dimension by dimension, so that she had adored his sexuality along with every nuance of his male striving. She had tasted his need to be strong and dominant, to win. In business and politics his urgency was to succeed, and in love it was a mindless path through a waiting flock of females. Each layer had only made him more precious to her. The dangerous appetite that had always ravaged her had gone far beyond mere sex and had become a personal absorption. She had reached that point where she would have given up her life for him— given it up just to ensure that this boy-warrior could continue the battle.

CHAPTER THREE

The prime minister, campaigning in the province of Quebec to shore up local candidates, liked to have French-speaking aides about him. Consequently, Mathieu (who was completely bilingual) was traveling with the King entourage. It had been a gritty, sweltering day in Lower Town, the oldest part of Quebec City, and by five o'clock, when the sun was just beginning to surrender, Mathieu was ready to escape to his hotel.

Lower Town could be charming, of course: in autumn, when frost crisped the foliage along the St. Lawrence; in spring, when fresh rains washed restless ships at anchor; or in winter, when a fleecy curtain covered some of the insidious decay. But summer brought the inescapable smell of ancient buildings, dirty harbor water, and gutters abused by cheeky dogs.

Mathieu was relieved when at last he was free to board the funicular on St.-Anne Street, which would take him smoothly up to Dufferin Terrace at the top of the cliff. In the old days it had been steam-driven and open to wind and rain, but for many years now, the car had been enclosed and it had been run by electricity. As he slid neatly up the forty-five-degree track, Mathieu wrestled with another evening of dreary banquet food and political promises. He hated sitting still for any length of time, and other men's speeches always bored him. When he stepped onto the terrace, a welcome breeze from the river made him pause.

The Château Frontenac loomed over him, a delightfully overdone fortress that was at once lushly Victorian and madly pretentious as any castle on the Rhine. Under the copperclad towers rooms were every shape and size and the decor included rococo mantelpieces, marble fixtures, and heavy oak furniture. By coincidence, Marc St. Amour was attending a conference of bishops in Quebec City, and Mathieu was sharing his uncle's suite in the main tower. Camille was along as well. This made more spacious accomodation practical: Each had a bedroom, and they could all make use of a shared sitting room hung with damask curtains and provided with fine carpets and old English prints.

Mathieu had always been a hero worshipper. Usually his gods were political figures, but his Uncle Marc held a special place in his esteem: an independent, hardworking priest who had risen within the Church despite a falling out some years ago with his bishop over political allegiance. When Nora died, Marc had been especially consoling. It was admirable, too, the way Marc had stood by his blind sister, Camille. In Mathieu's opinion the bishop had rare spiritual qualities.

His mind turned from his uncle to his own problems. In previous elections he had run in Outremont, considered a safe Liberal seat. This time he had been thrust through no fault of his own into an English stronghold. He was fighting not only the Conservative establishment but the Court family as well. His own family stood behind *him* and Mathieu did not consider it wrong for the Courts to bring influence, every ounce of prestige, to gain the victory. But the combination—a predominantly English-speaking riding with the fabled Court power and the undoubted charm of their candidate produced such a formidable obstacle to Mathieu's aspirations that he was extremely wary. He smelled defeat.

If he lost, however, he did have an alternative. He could give up federal politics and run in the next municipal election. His childhood dream of becoming mayor of Montreal had never completely faded, and he could make the switch if it became necessary. God knows, he had plenty of good connections on the municipal level. He would then be a big fish in a small pond instead of a small fish in the bigger pond of the capital city. The vision of himself as His Honor the Mayor, wearing the chain of office, wielding almost immediate local power, presiding at the clandestine meetings that often affected the workings of Montreal and sometimes even the country as a whole, did not displease him.

Trying to unload some of the tension, Mathieu decided he would like to relax over a glass of claret and think out his next moves. This crusade with the prime minister had sidetracked him from his own campaign, but he had been unable to refuse the request to come along. King liked to travel with a flock of supporters when he electioneered, and in Quebec he needed men about him who spoke French fluently, who shared a rapport with the French population. Later this evening there was to be a banquet, where the provincial premier, Taschereau, would be principal speaker, and Mathieu groaned inwardly at the thought of sitting through another series of windy, meandering monologues.

He unlocked the door to the suite and walked through the square entrance hall and into the comfortable sitting room. The beige patterned carpet was soft, the furniture rather heavy but giving off a comfortable flavor. A drinks tray had come up from the bar downstairs, although nobody was in sight. Before pouring himself some wine, he observed that his aunt's bedroom door was slightly ajar. Perhaps he ought to knock and announce that he was back, he decided. It seemed a little greedy to pour himself wine before he had inquired whether anybody else was about to join him. With this in his mind, he walked to Camille's door and raised his hand to knock. He could see a wall mirror through the opening of the door, and in it he caught a glimpse of a reflection that transfixed him. His hand froze in midair, his mouth fell open in amazement. He did not actually knock.

Camille was apparently dressing for dinner, judging by the long lavender silk gown. She was struggling to adjust a fastener at the waist and had not yet pulled the bodice up over her shoulders. He could see that she wore a pink satin brassiere. But it was not the sight of his aunt's dishabille that unnerved him but the fact that the bishop stood beside her, assisting in the dressing ceremony.

Just as Camille was about to tug the dress up over her shoulders, the bishop bent over and kissed her neck. It was not a brotherly kiss, Mathieu thought, a wave of electric shock passing through his system. The bishop slid one hand into the satin and lace of the brassiere. Camille did not protest, nor did she seem surprised, but instead, a look of sensuous pleasure spread across the normally placid features. The bishop moved around to face his sister and then lowered the straps of the lingerie to reveal the white breasts. He closed his mouth smoothly over one prominent nipple. Camille still did not move; she remained an eyeless statue, head tilted back at an angle, seemingly lost in fantasy. Her mouth grew loose as she stroked her brother's gray-black hair. Mathieu, whose incendiary nature was never far from the kindling point, caught the musky odor spawned of deprivation. He watched, mesmerized, as Marc carefully replaced each bathycolpian toy in its covering. He saw his aunt move somewhat suggestively as if she were ready to be taken then and there, and the magnetism of her craving moved invisibly toward him.

Yet he backed away from the door by instinct, his own sex hard with the heady sin of voyeurism (his aunt, his uncle, his bishop!) so that he could easily have made love to her himself had the sinfulness of it not made him ill at the same time. He fled to his own room, pulled as much by shock as fear. He closed the door firmly, shutting out the sight he had just witnessed, and leaned against the wood, breathing hard as if he had run for miles. Desire ebbed as disenchantment swept over him. His bishop indulged in not only the pleasures of the flesh but in the forbidden one of incest. Mathieu was riddled with disbelief, yet he knew well what he had seen, what he had felt. He could not deny the reality of that tableau.

He knew he had to leave. Not only that, he would have to leave without saying good-bye. He could not face either of them so soon after the revelation. Marc would assuredly read knowledge in his eyes, and he did not know when, if ever, he could face them without shame. Shame for their flaws, shame for his own awareness of those flaws. He began to look desperately about the room, as if he expected to be caught before he could get away. He would have to telephone somebody on the committee and tell them he'd had an urgent message from home—some family crisis that required his presence back in Montreal. He would also have to leave word of his departure.

Mathieu began to throw clothes into his bag and, after he had crammed it shut with difficulty, found a sheet of stationery on which he could write a note to his uncle. Let the bishop assume anything he wished, Mathieu thought with a touch of panic, just as long as he did not suspect the truth. He then left as quietly as he could through the door that led directly from his bedroom out into the corridor. At the front desk he paid his share of the bill and asked to have his car brought around. When at last he steered the automobile under the arch and out into

St.-Louis Street, he forced himself along the narrow street with his usual recklessness. Despite wheeling around corners and nosing through a line of children out for a walk with supervising nuns, he could not keep his mind off the sensuous mime he had seen. Such intimacy wasn't new. He was aware of that. Perhaps it had been going on a lifetime, he thought with horror. He pressed down upon the accelerator, thrusting the car into the blackness of the country night.

Some forty miles from the city he came upon one of many level crossings. To his right he could see the familiar power beam of an engine's cyclops eye, thundering down toward him. He could easily beat the train, he knew. He jammed his foot hard on the gas pedal, taking a grim pleasure in the challenge.

The glare of the headlight from the train illuminated the interior of the car. He felt the front tire hit the track and then catch. The train was closer than he had thought, and he could not believe that the tires were caught and spinning, that the engine was roaring in protest and the car was not moving. In the shrill light and deafening rumble of the train wheels he did not hear his own scream.

The train hit the car broadside and carried it along the track. Metal was fused with metal, and when the rescuers congregated, they found Mathieu dead. His skull was crushed to a bloody pulp, his body mutilated.

The St. Amours gathered to bury their dead hope. At first, Justine was wild with anger and disbelief—screaming like a virago about the loss of her son and demanding an answer from God. None was forthcoming. Later she sank into a trance; she became like a sleepwalker. Armand and Honey made all the funeral arrangements, and Timothée consulted with them while Justine behaved like a robot. Mathieu had been her future, her hope for a stake in the game of political chance. She had meant to guide him, to supervise his career and rule his home life. She did not get along with her daughter, Nicolette, and seldom saw her. Beau, her other son, was in Europe. Mathieu was everything. She could not believe that this purpose had been stolen from her. She did not recover from her stupor until she stood by the graveside.

When she saw Marie-Claire sniveling and apparently

incompetent, she roused herself and recalled that there was a house to be run and two small children left in this girl's care. Justine came to life. The girl, the children, must be taken in hand. Mathieu's house must be sold, and Marie-Claire must be moved along with the babies to Justine's house. That would be best for everybody. Then Justine could keep a firm control of the way the little boys were raised, she could make sure they were schooled properly, that they were given the benefit of the Church's teachings. They were Mathieu's sons, and her grandsons. This became the purpose of her life and she saw it clearly as she stood by the grave and watched the casket containing Mathieu's body lowered into the ground.

R. B. Bennett and his Conservatives won the election with a clear majority. Prime Minister King and his Liberals retired in a sulk. One hundred and thirty-eight seats went to the Tories, twenty-five in the province of Quebec. In Westmount North Grenville-Court won an easy victory.

Lord Court suddenly embraced a Divine Providence. Right, he told anyone who would listen, always triumphed in the end. He had always paid his respects somewhat grudgingly in Christ Church Cathedral, but age and success had made him mellow. At a victory dinner for North he told the family that Mathieu Dosquet's death was foreordained. God had seen fit, through the accident, to show his political leanings. And God was a Conservative.

They took off from Cartierville Airport on the other side of the Mountain, in clear, cold air. The Fokker F-14 roared with such vigor that they could not carry on a conversation but had to content themselves with a shout or gestures. Michel was delighted to see how flushed his mother's face was; she was excited and her blue eyes shone with anticipation. He had expected her to be pleased but not ecstatic. This was her first flight.

Until recently Michel had confined his flying to a regular shuttle service between Haileybury and Noranda mostly for prospectors, mining engineers, and promoters from Montreal, Toronto, and New York. At times he had accepted short-term contracts for large pulp and paper companies to carry aerial photographers and surveyors over thousands of miles of untracked forest. In fact, one of his clients had been Northern Pulp and Paper, a huge producer managed by the March twins. Michel had heard something of the twins from his mother, and he had been keen to meet them, although when his dealings with them were over, he was no closer to distinguishing one from the other than he had been at the beginning.

This year Michel was forming an airline company with scheduled passenger and freight service. North East Airlines had already obtained a Royal Mail contract to fly between Montreal, Quebec City, and Rimouski. Six Fokker Super Universals were now on order, and he had every hope of adding future mail contracts in parts of the Maritimes.

He was even beginning to think wistfully of that one-hour-and-fifteen-minute flight from Haileybury in Ontario to Noranda and Rouyn in Quebec as if it were old history. The fare had been a flat sixty dollars and each passenger was allowed only one modest piece of baggage. He had loved that kind of flying with its soupçon of risk, its scent of danger. A crash into one of the myriad icy lakes, getting lost in the endless miles of thick trees or quaggy flats was always just a breath away. And while he had been flying, he had watched Noranda grow from a single shaft to a huge and successful operation. In one year the original Noranda Mine had tripled in value, and another mine owned by Noranda, Waite-Ackerman-Montgomery, had been brought into production. Noranda had already begun construction on a huge copper refinery, while deep in the mine itself, at lower and lower levels, great deposits of gold and copper lay waiting for the harvest.

Gold carried its own magic. In world markets the value of copper (which was often found along with gold) was almost a legend. Fortunately, Michel thought, he had managed to find a little cash to invest in Noranda stock when he could afford it. But most of his capital had been tied up in the flying boat he had used on that run and to pay his assistant pilot.

When Michel turned to watch his mother's reaction to her first glimpse of Montreal from the air, he could not help feeling a bit smug. His life had taken the right direction as far as he was concerned, and he had every reason to be pleased with himself.

For her part Honey could not imagine why she had waited so long to take her first flight. Down below she could see the city's abundant trees and curving streets, the milling of traffic as it seemed to drain steadily down the Mountain toward the old section of the city, toward the docks and the toy boats floating so brightly on the broad river.

Roads wound like fine gray ribbons through regiments of stiff, pompous buildings and the hundred-foot illuminated cross on the eastern tip of Mount Royal, which had always seemed to loom when seen from below, now looked like a rather insignificant bit of religious jewelry. She understood, at last, why Michel was addicted to the air. Why he had dedicated his life to this. She felt young again, she felt as if she could do anything and that the petty concerns of daily life were far behind. All her burdens were down there among the earthlings.

When they had made a successful landing back at Cartierville, Michel helped roll the small plane into a hangar. Honey was absorbed in watching the busy mood of the little airport. Everybody had such a sense of future, of "going somewhere," and there was a startling vitality about the place.

As they walked toward the car for the drive back to the city, Honey said, "Michel, I want to take flying lessons. Will you have time to teach me?"

"Mother!" Such an idea had never occurred to him. He had been showing off, like the child he was, to his mother. But he had not expected the spirit of adventure to be catching.

"Don't look so shocked, darling. I was one of the first women in Montreal to drive a car. Why shouldn't I fly?"

"No reason. I wasn't expecting it, that's all. If your eyesight is adequate, and your health is good, I suppose—"

"Michel," she said, laughing, "my eyesight is excellent and so is my health. Look at Amelia Earhart! Wasn't it wonderful when she crossed the Atlantic with all those men? The story is that she's planning to fly solo within a year or two. What do you think of that?"

"She is a bit younger," he demurred.

"Amelia Earhart's age isn't the point. Will you give me lessons, or shall I find another tutor?"

"What will Father say?"

"There you go! Men are all the same. Even my own son. I know exactly what your father will say . . . he'll say I've gone mad. Like the rest of the Courts. But he won't stop me. I can handle him."

"I've never doubted that for a moment," Michel said, grinning.

"How much would a small plane cost?"

"Good God, you mean you want to buy a plane? Even before you find out if you can fly?"

"Oh, I'll be able to fly. Naturally, I want my own plane. What's the use of learning how to fly if I don't have anything to fly?"

"Well," he said, doubtful again, "an Avian is small. That's a good plane. Used in some small runs. I guess you could afford that . . ."

"Is it safe? Is it good?"

"I'd say so, yes," Michel said, still surprised by his mother's enthusiasm. "You certainly don't need a plane as large as the Fokkers I just ordered. Perhaps I could sell you this one . . ."

"Now, that's something we could discuss. When can we start my lessons, darling? I'm eager to begin," Honey said. "I'll pay you whatever the going rate is for lessons, no favoritism. We may as well take advantage of the summer weather, don't you think?"

"You're incredible."

"I'd hardly say that. But I'm far from dead, as you seem to think. There's plenty of spirit left in me yet. You know, I don't find the newspaper quite as exciting as I did years ago. I need a new interest in life."

When Honey arrived at the apartment to change her clothes before going in to Le Monde, she found Armand at home. She wore the breeches, shirt, and scarf that Michel had recommended for the flight.

"Been riding?" Armand asked as she came into the front hallway. "That doesn't look like a proper riding habit to me."

"It isn't. I've been flying."

"Flying? You mean you went up with Michel?"

"Yes, and I haven't felt so wonderful in years. Armand

489

". . . I have to tell you something, but . . ." She paused, suddenly realizing that he seemed to be anxious to speak. "What are you doing here, anyway? Why aren't you at the office?"

"I have wonderful news," he said, smiling at her. "Truly great news, *chérie*! I couldn't wait until dinnertime to tell you."

"But what is it, Armand?"

"We've done it! We've done it! We can move back to Edenbridge. We can repair the roof . . . redecorate the house . . . move in . . ."

"Oh, Armand, that's splendid. I'm so glad."

"Thank God I took McKie's advice about Noranda . . . the dividends have been announced and the future looks so good . . . I can't tell you. I'm not going to wait another year to move back to the house . . . I'm going to take that chance right now."

Honey flung her arms around Armand and kissed him. He exulted as he felt her kiss upon his cheek and knew a buoyant sensation, the feeling of relief combined with success.

"That's the best news you could possibly bring!"

"You're really pleased, then?"

"Enormously pleased, my darling. You know I am."

"I've hated to see you in this cramped place," he said, glaring furiously around the apartment. "And I've hated knowing you had to scrimp and save all the time . . . no decent reception rooms to entertain . . . an excuse for a library . . . I know what it's been for you . . . I felt like such a failure."

"Never a failure, Armand," she said, kissing him again.

"Could we have lunch here, *chérie*, and talk? I'd like to make plans. There is so much to decide . . ."

"Of course we can, Armand. Let me wash up and speak to Cook. Then we can have a drink to celebrate. What a wonderful idea! Just give me a few minutes, will you, darling?"

"Hurry up, then, Miel. We must decide about the tenants in the house, and about furniture . . . there is the lease to consider, you know. I'll make you a drink while you're gone."

She smiled, realizing that already his plans were far advanced in his mind and that he would really only want her to agree with him. But Armand was happy again. Happier than she had seen him in some years. However, as she issued orders in the kitchen and went into the bedroom to change, her mind was not on Edenbridge but on her new project. She wondered how she could extract the price of a small plane from the profits of *Le Monde* without infuriating Armand now that he was set on moving back to the house. The focus of her life had dramatically altered.

CHAPTER FOUR

Susan had returned to Montreal because she did not know what else to do. After only ten days in the Ritz-Carlton Hotel she was swimming in boredom and self-pity, doubtful about calling most of her friends, afraid to call her relatives. She had no desire to see her mother (and listen to some highly moral lecture about her shortcomings), and the mere idea of facing her irascible old grandfather made her tremble. She longed to see her son, Anthony, and had called David and then his lawyer. So far she had had no direct communication from either one. Sometimes she thought about a possible reconciliation with David.

Living in a hotel, cut off from any semblance of regulated life, she felt like a refugee, a stranger in her own city. Was it only two years since she had been such an integral part of society's fabric? One of its arbiters? In those days everybody had considered her chic, beautiful, and rich. She had been confident inside and fashionable outside. She had been like a rare jewel set in the gold security of family. Now, she was a woman who had made a social error and been publicly rapped on the knuckles for it.

She pined for all the things she had once taken for granted. She missed her son and the large house on the Mountain. She yearned for the farm on the South Shore, with its stables filled with horses and its groves of trees and river views. She could have cried every time she thought of the yellow Hispano-Suiza that probably sat unused in David's garage. She even thought wistfully of the gargantuan dinners at Pride's Court. Most of all, she regretted her loss of "place," that indefinable, invisible possession she had accepted without thought but which was now more precious because it seemed to be lost forever.

Tonight she had agreed to join the Rodriguez party because it was the only invitation she had received and she could not bear to dine alone. She did not like Ramón Rodriguez and suspected that many of his tastes were perverted if not actually criminal. Rodriguez was a retired film star—a man with an exotic past and an empty future. His meteoric rise to fame had ended abruptly at the age of thirty-five—one of the disasters laid at the doorstep of talking pictures. In Ramón's case, the reason for his failure had been rather more complicated than the quality of his voice.

True, Rodriguez had rather a thin voice and sound did not improve his sultry Latin image, but even more telling was the fact that he could not act. When Rodriguez first flashed upon the silent screen, he had been the essence of the exciting Latin lover: dark, lithe, and sexually suggestive. Smooth but masculine. Cajoling but still powerful. In the days when acting on the screen had been mainly a matter of the extravagant gesture and the flairing nostril, he had made women swoon from coast to coast. They had lapped it up and cried for more. Collected his photographs and mobbed him when he appeared in public. But the vogue for him passed when sound came in, and Rodriguez joined the restless legion of the bored and rich, the scavengers who roam the world seeking new thrills. Susan had first met Ramón at a cocktail party given by Gloria Swanson in a penthouse overlooking Central Park. Philip had taken her there and had introduced her. She had thought no more about Rodriguez until she met him in Montreal walking along Sherbrooke. He had explained to her rather glibly that his third wife had been French Canadian and that she had left him a house in the city when she died. (She had taken an overdose of drugs combined with alcohol, and it had all been rather messy.) He often brought a group of friends up during the summer to spend a few days in the house and float about, tasting the French flavor without taking the trouble to go to France.

So far, Susan had managed to keep her relationship with Rodriguez on a casual basis and had gone to some trouble to meet him in places where she would not be likely to run into family or friends. In her present dark mood, however, she had tossed aside caution and had told him to meet her in the Ritz Hotel's Palm Court.

The maître d' showed Susan to a table against the wall. Glancing about, she saw no one she recognized—only a scattered dozen tea drinkers gossiping over plates of tiny sandwiches—the usual watercress and cucumber, she thought irrelevantly. She ordered tea because it was the thing to do. At least the room was a pleasant place in which to wait: all soft grays and pinks, upholstered comfortable chairs and rose-shaded lights. A shallow flight of stairs led to the formal dining room beyond, and on the landing potted palms gave the place a Victorian air. A string orchestra was playing the "Merry Widow Waltz."

The music turned her mood bitter. Better a widow than a deserted woman. Every little incident was a reminder of her colossal error in judgment, of the security she had given up, of her loneliness. When she thought of Philip Charles Norman these days, it was with resentment—often hatred. Once he had been exciting, the treasured lover, but now she saw him stripped: a shoddy opportunist, nimble liar, unbathed Philistine, and crude pretender. His writing talent, viewed in this light, was minimal indeed.

He had wrapped himself in a cloak of false power and cool intellectualism, and it had suddenly vanished. Seen up close, Philip could not maintain his own image.

Being a user of people, Philip did not understand the nature of friendship. Susan was frequently shocked by Philip's betrayal of the confidence men had placed in him. Those few friends who had been loyal to him when he finally left Althea were discarded like paper handkerchiefs as soon as they were no longer needed.

Near celebrities Philip fawned. He inquired about their health or offered to write reviews for the *Times* or small squibs for obscure musical publications. Anything to ingratiate himself with a musician. He always ended up behaving like an unemployed headwaiter. Susan's sensibilities, sharpened on a different stone, made her cringe. She often noticed an embarrassed expression flit over a famous face.

If he was not a social success, neither was he fashioned for intimate, day-to-day living. His taste in food was crude, and he despised people who used alcohol while he himself swallowed huge quantities of sedatives to sleep or stimulants to stay awake. She had even known him to dress for dinner without taking a shower. As Susan came to mean less and less to Philip, he shed skin after skin like a lizard in the sun. Nothing about him had ever been real: All had been illusion. Even the gifts he had given her were (she gradually discovered) books sent to the newspaper for review or jewelry that had been placed in a more expensive box.

His poetry and bits of philosophy would not have passed muster in a high school journal. It had been his talent that first attracted her. He seemed to have such a broad knowledge of books, poetry, music, and art. She had desperately needed to believe he was brilliant, perhaps even a genius. Now, shorn of her dreams, she saw that his scraps of wisdom were nothing but theatrical trash.

Once he had written to her, "The organ grinder looks up all day at heaven. But all the coins come out of the windows." Upon reflection it meant nothing at all. He had compared her to a "wild faun caught eating broccoli" and later she had seen the same description applied, in one of his columns, to a powerful politician. "Sex," Philip had once written to her, "is a question of communicated fire." She knew now there was no fire and no communication. Philip's lust was sprinkled with a handful of tinsel stars to make it shine. He must convince himself each time that his was the great love.

He had been an only child and had gradually made that his avocation. Other people's pain meant nothing to him. He thought every person who crossed his path, who entered the drama of his life, was fuel for his creative fire. Yet even that fire was false: nothing more than a kerosene-soaked rag upon which he had idly dropped a match.

Susan stirred her black Bohea moodily, and in the midst of her reverie, it came as a distinct shock to see her young cousin Charity Court approaching. She was with a non-descript young man.

"Susan, what are you doing here alone?" Charity cried. She was much the same as she had been at the twins' wedding, Susan noticed, tall, slim, with enormous doe eyes, and thick blond hair.

"Charity, how nice to see you!" Susan said, forcing a smile. "You look divine. So smart."

"And so do you. I didn't know you were in town." Charity introduced the young man as Rod Bainbridge.

"How could you leave New York? Wasn't it exciting? May we sit down? Thanks. I want to hear all about your wicked life. Have you really left the famous columnist?"

They spent the next few minutes catching up on family gossip. Rod ordered tea. Charity told Susan that the twins had each had a baby daughter. "Same day. Same hour. Naturally, they're identical. The whole thing is eerie. I can't stand it. You always feel that your eyes are playing tricks."

"Have you seen David lately?" Susan could not resist asking.

"Not recently. But he looked fine the last time I saw him. He hasn't married again. He lives in the house with Anthony and a housekeeper. He seldom shows up at Pride's Court."

Susan felt cold. Her loss seemed magnified by her cousin's casual attitude, by hearing Anthony's name again. She saw in Charity all the old assurance that had once been her own. How comforting it was to belong!

"Are you waiting for someone?" Charity asked, finally.

"I'm expecting a friend."

"Why so mysterious? Is he married? A gangster?"

"Don't be silly. You wouldn't be interested."

"Try me. Come on, Susan, don't be stingy. I'll bet he's fabulous . . . some New Yorker, probably."

"I met him there, yes. But he isn't really a New Yorker."

"Well, who is he? Gosh, you're mean, Susan. I'm not going to let you get away with this. Who is he?"

"If you must know, a star of silent movies. He just happens to be here in Montreal. I don't like him much, actually, he isn't a man you ought to know."

"Movie star?" Charity cried, large eyes getting larger. "And you don't want me to meet him? Tell me who, Susan."

"All right," Susan said, giving in with a shrug. "Ramón Rodriguez."

"Ramón Rodriguez? But I've got a photo of him on my wall! Really, Susan, I'll bet you're just kidding me."

"I wish I were."

"*I'm* not moving until I meet him, so you might as well relax. Why is he in Montreal?"

"He owns a house here. Says his wife left it to him. I

495

don't know, Charity, I just don't care. I don't like him. I wish I hadn't agreed to meet him."

"I'm glad you did."

Charity asked for another pot of tea and a plate of sandwiches. Rod was agreeable. He seemed in no hurry to move along to the dinner party they had planned to attend.

"Don't get interested in Ramón, Charity, I warn you. He's no good. I wish you'd go to your party."

"No thanks. I *have* to meet him. I used to be in love with him when I was younger. But now I have a crush on Richard Barthelmess."

"He's not nice," Susan repeated. "He's into all sorts of things. He makes my flesh creep."

"Well, we aren't exactly saints ourselves," Charity said eagerly. "Are we, Rod? We've tried hashish. But I didn't like it much. We aren't lily white. I like booze better, anyway."

"You ought to keep away from all those things," Susan said, cross at having to sound like a maiden aunt. "Anyway, remember I've warned you about Ramón."

"So why are *you* meeting him, then?"

Susan gave her cousin an angry look and crushed out her cigarette as if to punish it. She brought out another one immediately, however, and fitted it into her long black holder. Rod leaned forward to offer a light.

"Thank you, darling," Susan said with a patronizing inflection. "I'm having dinner with Rodriguez and his friends because I'm bored, if you must know."

"You'd better make up with David," Charity said with the directness of the very young. "Have you tried to see him? Have you called Grandfather?"

"Not yet. I'm afraid to call Grandfather."

"He was pretty upset when you left. He's a bit frailer, but he can still shout and roar. He was furious when he heard about you running off like that. He called your friend an "upstart and a bounder." And all sorts of other things. My, he was angry! But you can't stay in the Ritz forever."

Charity was right. Her words only made Susan feel more downhearted, and she found herself sitting in the middle of the bar feeling like a tired gypsy.

She was saved from further self-examination by the arrival of Ramón and his friends. They swarmed into the lounge like colorful buzzing insects, glittering and flashing and alighting at tables in the midst of a hum of conversation. Rodriguez wore an ice-cream silk suit and carried a goldheaded cane. He looked very dashing, and confident. His dark hair was liberally laced with gray streaks, and he still wore his sideburns long, as he had done in films. His eyes darted restlessly about; he moved with quick, jerky gestures as if he were on strings. At his elbow an aging blond Adonis hovered solicitously. This was his longtime secretary and companion, Gerald Barrett. As they entered, Rodriguez cast his frantic gaze around the room and finally found his target. He and Barrett descended upon Susan's table with cries of welcome and surprise as if they had not planned this meeting.

"Well, well," Ramón said smoothly. "And who is *this* beauty?" His eyes scooped up Charity with obvious appreciation.

"My cousin," Susan said coolly, "my very *young* cousin. Charity Court. And this is Rod Bainbridge."

"Drag up a couple of chairs, will you Gerald?" Ramón said, leaning on his cane. "My dear, I can't stop looking! I'm mesmerized by such beauty. Such youth! You've been keeping secrets from me, Susan! Isn't that right, Gerald?"

Gerald gave the group an angry look and put down two chairs so that they were all crowded together in a circle. It was apparent that he did not share his employer's enthusiasm for young girls—even such nubile examples as Charity Court. Ramón began to chatter and invited Charity and Rod to come on to dinner with the party. They had found a new restaurant on Mountain Street, he said, where the food was sublimely Parisian. Much to Susan's relief, Charity declined. But Rodriguez did not give up easily. He produced an engraved card and gave it to her and suggested that she might like to call at the house later in the evening. He was giving a little party, he said, and the time did not matter. They would be welcome, no matter how late.

Charity was smitten. She could not take her eyes off Rodriguez—the incarnation of a screen hero—a man whose photograph she had long admired but whom she had never expected to meet. She had never been so close to a bona fide celebrity before. She noticed how he kept the gold serpenthead of his cane under his hand, caressing it, fondling it, even while he was seated. As if he did, indeed, lean upon it. She was fascinated.

At last Rod insisted that they go to the private dinner, but Charity was reluctant to leave. Susan was swept with relief when at last Charity disappeared through the wide doors leading to the foyer of the hotel. She felt a twinge of guilt, as if she were personally responsible for exposing Charity to something evil. After dinner she returned to the hotel and took a sleeping tablet. Her thoughts drifted toward David and a possible reconciliation, but at the same time, little intrusions disturbed her, and she felt distinctly uneasy when she thought that Charity might see Rodriguez again.

Charity could be so strong-minded at times that even Rod Bainbridge felt he could not be bothered to fight her any longer. This evening was a fine example: She insisted on going to the Rodriguez party, although he did not wish to go. With a mixture of anger and resentment he let her off on Atwater. "I'm not going," he said. "I don't like those people. And I wish you wouldn't either."

Charity's reply had been short and pithy. She had employed a vulgar but very graphic expression that sent Rod on his way, shaking his head. They had both had too much wine at dinner.

She had no trouble finding the right house. A single light burned in an old Chinese lantern over the front door. Most of the windows were dark, as if the curtains had been pulled. When she rang the bell, she could hear a resonant gong sound somewhere deep inside. After what seemed a long time, the door opened and Gerald appeared. He looked unhappy to see her.

"I've come to the party," Charity said. "Ramón asked me. Remember?"

"I remember." He hesitated and then stepped back to let her in. "I don't know where Ramón is at the moment. There are people all over the house."

Actually, he knew exactly where Ramón was. He always knew. He had the lover's instinct for keeping in touch. He not only knew where Ramón was, but he knew his mood, anticipated his whims. Right from the beginning he had recognized the fickle quality in Ramón, and he had accepted it because he could not help doing so. It was his nature to be faithful, just as it was Ramón's to be a philanderer. There had been other men. There had often been young girls. Ramón had married three times, each more disastrous than the last, and all very young women. This, too, was part of Ramón's personality, for he had the Pygmalion complex.

Over the years Gerald had watched and persevered, torn by pain and love. Often despairing, often deliriously happy. There was no other life for him, he had decided, because without Ramón, Gerald would have been dead. He had endured years of shame, of agony, even of ridicule at Ramón's hands. His face was furrowed with the lines of Ramón's excesses.

As he viewed this latest threat to his serenity, Gerald wondered if he could possibly shunt the girl off into a corner where Ramón would overlook her, and he was juggling this pleasant prospect when Ramón suddenly materialized in the foyer. He was swinging the goldheaded cane in a dashing way.

"Ah, the beautiful Miss Court! So fresh, so young, so untouched! Don't you agree, Gerald? Youth is the elixir of life, and we must never forget it. Come in, come, my darling, and let me show you the delights of my little home."

He took Charity by the arm and she felt his hand, dry upon her flesh. He darted forward, pulling her with him, powered by an unnatural flood of energy.

"What about your other guests?" Gerald asked nastily. "Are you abandoning them?"

"Certainly not. We'll be back shortly. It's only a tour, Gerald. I want Charity to see the house, that's all."

Charity, fascinated and swept up on a cloud of Ramón's attention and too much wine, was willing to follow. She sensed that Gerald was merely a lackey, and her upbringing had prepared her to dismiss such people as insignificant.

"You entertain them, Gerald," Ramón said over his shoulder, poking a curtain aside with the cane. "I have better things to do."

"Can't you leave *any* young girl alone? Do you have to go on taking and taking when you have—"

"When I have *what*, Gerald?" Ramón's voice took on a dangerous edge. "Go on, Gerald, tell me what I have.

499

Tell me what I have that compares with this beauty. She is Goya's Maya . . . she is Aphrodite . . . she is Psyche . . . she is Delilah . . . she is Salome. Come along, my dear, and see my collection."

Charity listened to this speech in amazement. She had never thought of herself as any of those women. This was like a movie, and she was an actress in a film.

"If you think I'm stupid enough to believe you are only interested in showing her around," Gerald began again.

"Believe whatever you like," Ramón said. "I don't give a damn what you believe. If you don't like it here, get out."

"You know I can't do that!" Gerald cried. "Why do you torture me like this when you know—"

He had gone too far. He saw that he had bridged that abyss over which it was dangerous to cross. He had revealed to a stranger some of the dark secrets of their relationship. Ramón let go of Charity's arm and raised his cane in a curiously threatening way, but he did not bring it down. He shuddered a bit and his voice was filled with sinewy anger.

"Don't ever embarrass me like this again! If you do, Gerald, I'll kill you."

"Why don't you fire me, instead?" It was a taunt.

"All right, then, I'll fire you. Get your things and get out. You can leave tonight. Forget the guests, just leave me alone."

Gerald began to speak quickly, protesting that he could not leave. He could not go tonight. They could talk this over in the morning when they were both sober.

"No, go right now. Call a taxi. Go to a hotel. I'm sure you have money, Gerald. You've been milking me for years. Yes, go. Consider yourself fired."

Then he pulled at Charity's arm again, muttering that he didn't like the atmosphere. Charity felt afraid. Somehow, without meaning to, she had started a quarrel, and she did not like the overtones. She glanced backward to see that Gerald was standing as still as a stone statue. Some of the magic of the meeting with a movie idol vanished, and fear dribbled into her mind through the alcoholic haze. She shook her head as if that would clear her mind. In front of her, in a dim reddish glow, she saw two huge blackamoor figures bearing silver trays piled high with fruit and vegetables. In that light (or was it really the creator's intention) the gourds were tumescent, the peaches had become women's breasts, and somehow, the halved, purple, furrowed flesh of plums had been transformed into something sexually suggestive.

"Come, my lovely, we'll begin here," Ramón was saying in his light, accented voice. "Come and see my beautiful collection."

"It's a strange house," she said uneasily.

Ramón did not reply but offered her vodka from a decanter on the sideboard. His smile was now electric and his fingers possessive. The familiar drink gave her an unexpected jolt.

"All this is part of your education," he said. "You're fortunate you met me. Come and see the moths. The butterflies."

In the center of the room glass cases contained brilliantly colored insects set on dark voluptuous cloth. Ramón hovered over them to extoll the beauties of the great moths of the tropics. Here was the moss green and toasted russet of the *Darapsa versicolor,* the iridescent pinks of the *Herse cingulata,* the gossamer yellow of the *Anisota,* the startling twin eyes etched on the wings of the *Automeris io,* and the graceful swooping tails of the seagreen *Luna*— all there, pinned forever against a black velvet night.

"Don't you think it's cruel to kill such lovely things and stick pins through them?".

"No worse than pinning people to their wives, or to their jobs, or to their place on earth," Ramón said glibly. "But those of us who have the money ought to bring our fantasies to life—we are mediators between creative souls and the dull world. King Ludwig was one of those. He ought to have been made a saint for building those fairytale castles of his. They inspired the artists and poets of his day. The extravagances of Isadora Duncan were responsible for some divine music, and the pitiless Salome has lived two thousand years in song and story. Some of us, by virture of our follies, provide the poets with fuel."

"You consider this house a folly, then?"

"I hope it is. Or I have failed."

For a moment his impatience overshadowed desire. Young women were all so stupid. It was a pity they were so delicious. Was he getting too old to find teaching an aphrodisiac? Perhaps he needed another touch of the elixir he had dissolved in the vodka.

He was about to take her to another room where the dancing was in progress when she stopped to look at the tapestries. At first glance they had appeared to be medieval forests inhabited by shapeless hunters, horsemen, and a smattering of damsels in distress, but upon closer inspection Charity found them riveting.

Some mad weaver had fashioned these wild scenes in an extraordinary blend of Western and Oriental foliage. With a total disregard for time and place, the concoction of humans and animals was a nauseating brew of fanciful pagodas and formidable castles. Panthers and unicorns strolled among enormous camphor trees and monstrous flowers dripping blood. Swans with ebony heads and storks with bright blue breasts cavorted drunkenly in infested bogs. Crocodiles were bloated with half-swallowed babies and giant spiders with human faces crawled through maggot-ridden corpses. Herculean men supporting impossible erections poised ready to rape frail women spread beneath them on carpets of dead lilies. Everywhere, in every direction, prancing women wearing only the shreds of tattered veils besought passing riders to seduce them. The sirens were screaming and swooning among the peach trees, in the midst of fleshy cacti, paper-white narcissus, and putrescent purple violets.

Overhead, hibiscus vines loaded with dank orange flowers reached down hungrily to strangle absent-minded victims while hunters, bows drawn, slaughtered deformed children among the rigid swords of black iris and the yellow tendrils of nepenthes tipped with oozing acid. Vulvoid orchids, avid with mold, rooted obscenely in the foreheads of drowning women.

But there was worse. Among all this perverted beauty were terrible tableaux of torture: men slowly roasting on spits, warriors with their heads lopped off, the skulls of living humans pierced through with iron nails, worm-riddled bowels spilling from ragged wounds, fingernails torn out with sizzling pincers, eyeballs flopping from gaping sockets.

Charity, staring upon this consummate horror for the first time, was stabbed to the heart with a pain that sank lower and lower till it finally struck her sexually. A kind of mindless frenzy gripped her.

"Drink up, darling," Ramón said calmly. "Don't be afraid of the pictures."

"But the torture! Why would you want to look at such evil?"

"Evil has its place in the world. Anything forbidden is evil, but is also attractive. Don't you see what I mean? As soon as we are told not to do something, we want to do it more than ever. You only have to remember Eve in the garden. Every time a law is broken by somebody, it produces an orgasm."

"I don't believe that."

"Don't turn away, my sweet. It's true. That's why perversion is so popular. If we said it was perfectly all right for women to sleep with their fathers, or if men could enjoy their sisters, we'd lose a great deal of life's sensuality."

"No, no, I don't believe you."

He took her hand and led her away from the tapestry into another room where a dozen people were gathered about in semidarkness watching two women dancers in a patch of orange light. From these shadows came a tango, the music merely a growl and a beat.

The sweet smell of hashish stung her nostrils. She felt lethargic now and no longer angry and abruptly sat down on a floor cushion in the middle of the guests. Ramón stood behind her. Once, when she turned to look at him, she saw him sniffing from a tiny spoon. A thrill of recognition spun through her mind, and she heard him sneeze. When she caught his gaze, his eyes glittered in the gloom. The dancers were naked except for thin red silk scarfs tied about their necks and high, black shiny boots. They moved gracefully through the movements of the dance, slithering flesh on flesh, touching and swaying and leaning like lovers in the wind.

A rustle of disturbance drew her eyes once more to Ramón. He was standing at the door and Gerald was with him. Gerald was making angry motions with his hands, and Charity could hear the timbre of a tear-stained voice above the music. Ramón turned away, impatient, and gave Gerald a push with the head of the cane. Then he sat beside Charity and they watched the dancers. She had no idea how much time went by. Eventually some of the guests danced. People came and went. There was laughter and music, there was drinking, there was incense and smoke. She only knew that it seemed very late when Ramón took her upstairs. "We must get away from all these people," he said. "I think Gerald is discouraged. He seems to have gone."

Charity seemed to fly up the carpeted stairs as if she were a few feet above the ground. On the wide upper landing Ramón opened one of the heavy carved doors and led her into a large bedroom that was all gold and pink and white. The door closed, cutting off the sounds from below. She saw the bed, set on a throne in an alcove of golden pillars. An immense circular dome on the ceiling shed pink light on the carpet. Around the dome hung naked priapic cupids, cunning as if their shame were merely naughty and not wicked. There were photographs on the walls, huge, larger than life, of Ramón Rodriguez looking incredibly handsome, and these were multiplied by mirrors. In some he was naked. In some he was with a barbaric woman. In some he was with a man. Over the white-painted mantel there was an oil painting of a hunter in a garden among the bloodied corpses of his catch. His arrow was aimed at the bottom of the canvas where a fleeing doe looked shattered with doom.

Then she saw the dog. A live German shepherd sitting with his tongue hanging out, his eyes bright with a sense of mission, was posed by the bed. He gave a low burry sound as Charity advanced into the room.

"What's the dog doing here?"

"Satyr is my watchdog. Don't be afraid of him. He's very obedient."

He put the goldheaded cane in a stand by the door and shouted to the dog, "*Stay*, Satyr, *stay!*"

"He looks ferocious," she said uncertainly. "As if he'd like to eat me."

"Probably he would. Some women like dogs," Ramón said, laughing.

"Couldn't he go somewhere else? He makes me nervous."

"In that case out he goes. I'll shut him in the dressing room."

She was afraid of dogs. She could not remember how

it had started or why she crackled with fear when she came close to one. Ramón took the dog by the collar and led him away, saying he was going to get them each a robe.

Charity examined the room, thinking about Ramón, drawn to his larger-than-life pictures on the wall. Part of her was curious to find out what Ramón was like, to have some real contact with such a sophisticated man. Yet, part of her withdrew from the scene, fluttering with youth and inexperience. She was still standing in the center of the room when Ramón came back carrying two silk robes —a royal purple one for himself and a gold one for her.

"Take this gown and go into the bathroom over there," Ramón said, pointing to a painted door in a far corner of the room. "Change into the gown. Here's another vodka to cheer you up. You look a bit sad. Don't take too long, my lovely, I'll be waiting. We must get on with your education."

She accepted both the robe and the drink. The bathroom was large, all black porcelain and white rug, with gold taps and splendid mirrors. Flagons of perfume, boxes of powder and antique jars of face cream were lined up on the dresser. She saw herself reflected over and over in the mirrors from every possible angle.

When she came out, the bedroom lights had been turned off and she could hear the seductive sound of a young boy's voice singing from some distant point. She could smell roses in the air. Ramón was standing by the bed wearing his purple robe and holding out his hand to her. He had lighted a candle and she could see the flame moving gently.

"Ah, you are more beautiful than I dreamed."

"I'm not sure I want to do this."

"You're not a virgin, surely?"

She looked startled. The big doe eyes widened, the mouth fell open. Somehow, she had lost the ability to make decisions. She let him push her to the bed where her long legs formed sinuous curves under the transparent gold of the robe. He lay beside her and pulled the robe away from her breasts, began to caress her with lips as old as time. The words were not important, it was the tone he used as he spoke. She sank in a warm and silken ocean, consumed, enfolded, limp with pleasure.

And then a voice severed the brooding miasma, cutting it with a swish of hatred. Filthy words split the delicate air like an axe on an egg. Gerald sprang toward them brandishing the goldheaded cane. Ramón leaped off the bed to defend himself, flailing with both arms. He lunged toward Gerald to seize the cane. Gerald held it grimly by the tip using the golden serpent's head as a club, and he brought it down on Ramón's shoulder and upper arm with a crash that sent Ramón reeling to his knees. Ramón scrambled to his feet, crying for help, trying to grab the cane with his undamaged arm while the other hung limply inside the purple silk sleeve.

Charity could hear the dog scratching at the closed door. Satyr began to bark. If only she could get to the door and let the dog out, he would defend Ramón. She willed herself to slide from the bed, to crawl to the door, but her body did not move an inch. She was caught in the web of nightmare, focusing her will toward action but not actually moving an inch. All her strength of will was useless. The drugs had taken effect and she lay like a patient in a coma, paralyzed from the heart down.

The two men wrestled. Furniture flew, pictures and vases crashed down in a carillon that was tuneless and sharp, echoing about the room while Gerald swung the cane to split Ramón's skull again and again. Blood streamed down Ramón's face and into his eyes, into his mouth. He tried to raise his unbroken arm to ward off some of the blows, but he could not see. He was on his knees. The swish of the cane, the sickening thud of the golden serpent's metallic weight cracking human bone, the dog's bark, Ramón's terrified cries, all blended together in a cacophony of bloody sound.

Somebody arrived and threw open the door. Somebody seized Gerald from behind and took away the cane. Ramón lay on the carpet drowning in blood. Charity did not remember anything after that.

The police found Ramón Rodriguez lying in an everwidening pool of blood. The purple silk robe was sodden and caught up under him so that he was indecently naked, vulnerable. One side of his skull was crushed so completely that a grayish-pink matter oozed through jagged cracks. Hair was matted with clots of blood. Above the body the painted hunter aimed his arrow directly at Ramón Rodriguez.

Lord Court summoned three lawyers, Charles, Fort, and North to a conference in his boardroom office. When they were all assembled, he fixed them with a furious eye and said it was clear to him that the first line of defense was offense. And by offense, he meant attack the newspapers. The dailies must be prevented from exaggerating this filthy murder into a yellow-press sensation. They could just as well cover it with a paragraph buried in the back. The newspapers controlled by his own friends, that is the English-speaking ones, would be approachable. He had done them all favors from time to time. The French press would be another matter, since they were almost all Liberal in sympathy and anti-English by nature. *Le Monde*, that scurrilous rag owned by his daughter, was probably the most difficult.

"Somebody will have to speak to Hannah immediately," he boomed, giving them all the benefit of his most savage look. "How can we hope to instill some sense of decency in that woman? She'll want to turn the whole front page over to it."

In the past Honey had muffled reports that would have blackened the Court name, but Lord Court's memory was conveniently faulty when it came to his defecting daughter. He visualized her, at this moment, as a woman ready to sacrifice a young girl's future to a trivial past complaint.

"I'll call Honey," Charles offered, deliberately using Honey's nickname as a small reprimand to his father. "I talk to her every now and then. She's been remarkably loyal in the past."

"*Loyal?*" Simon Court cried. "*Loyal?*"

Charles could see that he had only confused matters by trying to defend his sister. He regretted his words instantly. He ought to have confined himself to agreeing to call Honey and not introduced side issues.

"Good idea, Charles, you do it," Fort said hastily.

"I leave that to you, Charles," Lord Court said, dispensing with a diatribe on loyalty that had sprung to mind. "Let's get on with other things. Charity is the main concern here. She's under age. Can we use that to keep her from being called as a witness at the inquest? She's still a minor. On top of that, she claims to have forgotten. Isn't there a name for that?"

"Amnesia," one of the lawyers supplied. "We'll have to get a psychiatrist's report. Perhaps more than one. Medical testimony, you see."

"Then get them. That should be easy. Look into it, will you, Gillies?" The lawyer so named wrote down his instructions.

"Good idea, Papa," Charles said, astonished that his father had embraced such a new science as psychiatry.

"You needn't be so surprised. I'm not dead yet. I'm far from being dead, if you want to know. You're not dealing with one of these decadents now, you know . . . *I* haven't lost my wits by taking drugs and wallowing in sin."

It had not astonished him in the least to learn that foreigners indulged in evil practices. He had come, over the years, to expect that sort of behavior from them. The French, he had always said, were the dregs of humanity, but it was now clear that he had overestimated them—it was the Latins who could lay claim to that title. When one considered the Spanish Inquisition, of course, and the way the Incas slaughtered young girls for gold, it all seemed obvious.

"What I can't understand is how a man like Rodrigwez would be allowed to own property in the city," he went on, mispronouncing the name to show his contempt for the Spanish language, "Is there no law against that kind of thing?"

Mr. Gillies looked shocked but Charles said easily, "I'm afraid not, Papa. If a man has enough money, he can buy property no matter where he comes from. It's all quite legal."

Lord Court was momentarily lost in disbelief. This was not his idea of British justice. On second thought, though, it showed how *fair* the English were to let these people in. He picked up his next item with renewed vigor.

"I leave the details to you, gentlemen. Call me as soon as you have some news. You can call me at home. Now, we have another problem, and I wanted to give you all the benefit of my thinking. I propose to correct a situation that is out of control. For the good of the family. You all know that Susan is living at the Ritz-Carlton Hotel, I suppose? It was through her that Charity met this—this Rodrigwez—and that is because Susan is out there like a nomad—an orphan. If she'd been part of the family, this tragedy would have been avoided. Do you follow me?"

They were not quite sure whether or not they did. Every man in the room turned his attention to Lord Court's words in the hope that they would soon catch his drift.

"I see you don't understand the ramifications," Lord Court said with a touch of satisfaction. "I will explain. Susan was mixing with trash because she's alone. I wish David would take her back. I thought of approaching him about that. What do you think?"

Nobody knew what to think. The Court men, while they saw how convenient it would be to have Susan taken back into David's keeping, could not bring themselves to say that he ought actually to do so.

Noticing the pause, Lord Court hurried on.

"Not that I blame him. We'll see. Next to patching up her marriage, we can make her a comfortable allowance on the understanding that she leave Montreal. I don't want her in England, because I have a notion to send Charity to boarding school over there. Wouldn't want to take a chance on them meeting. I thought of Paris. If she'd agree to live in Paris, we could make her a good, solid financial commitment. It's like remittance men in reverse. Ha. Ha."

Again, they were stunned. But finally Fort said that he agreed with the principle, but he saw a flaw in the reasoning. Lord Court was mystified.

"Susan has a father and mother of her own. Have you forgotten? You're only her grandfather, after all. Why don't you get Sir Armand to pay her an allowance or take her in and chaperone her life?"

"Ha. Because you don't understand the French mind. That's your trouble, always has been. First, Susan would have gone back of her own accord if she'd wanted to. I happen to know that Hannah tried to make up with her several times. Then, there is the question of money. *Sir Armand*"—spoken heavily, to denote great sarcasm—"hasn't enough money. Oh, they're back in the house, I know that. But it will take him all his time to keep up. Believe me, he can't afford this kind of extra spending."

"Perhaps you're right," Fort said, surrendering. "But they have more responsibility in the matter, just the same."

"Sir Armand and Lady St. Amour are not responsible people. Why look for miracles? He's witless. I always knew it. Susan rejected them because at one time she had good taste. Later, of course, she made a mistake. Going off with that American. Anyway, I won't have Susan interfering with this family. Bringing us to the brink of scandal. A young girl like Charity, perhaps damaged forever . . ."

He was about to go off in a tirade, and the Court men gradually calmed him down and brought him back to the main issue. As it turned out, Charity did have to attend the inquest, but they managed to keep it closed to the public. Very little appeared in the newspapers and the Court name was kept out of the case almost entirely. By September Charity was on her way to a stuffy and expensive boarding school in the Midlands: a place with cold bedrooms, wretched food, and impossible rules. Susan had agreed to live in Paris.

Lord Court had, he thought with great satisfaction, solved the family's problems as usual in a swift and brilliant manner. He had no idea, he confessed to Charles one evening, what they would all do when he died. Still, dying was the last thing on his mind. He was only eighty-eight and in remarkably good health.

CHAPTER FIVE

The abandoned monastery of St.-Benedict lay just north of Toulon, in Provence. Many years earlier, the monks had been forced to disband for lack of financial support: Benefactors who might have kept them going had either died or gone bankrupt themselves. St.-Benedict had been a contemplative order, and consequently, the monks had no means of raising funds for themselves. The most practical thing they had ever done was to produce enough vegetables for their table, keep a handful of goats for milk and cheese, and cultivate a small vineyard that had yielded a rough red wine of astonishing potency. Otherwise, they spent their days in prayer, study, and occasional attempts to shore up the ancient buildings.

The twelve monks and their prior had dispersed to a wide variety of areas in France, where they had been absorbed by various religious institutions. The property (which still belonged to the Church) was leased to anyone eccentric enough to want such a secluded life and who had certain credentials. What these credentials were was never made clear, but they had much to do with the opinion held by the Sacristan, an ex-monk who now took care of the property. This system of rental, along with the location, created a rather strange and fluctuating cluster of renters.

Late one summer afternoon Susan stopped the black Isotta-Fraschini in a spurt of dust beside the front gate. She had picked up the car cheaply in Paris—a stunning little coupe with silver trim, cobra radiator cap, brown leather seats, and a V-shaped windshield divided by a metal rod.

As the dust settled around the cream wire wheels, Susan turned to look at her passenger. He was withdrawn, pale, sulky when he spoke and made little nervous gestures with his hands when he was silent. Obviously, he was under strain at the idea of this meeting.

Although she had known Beau from childhood—they were first cousins—he had become a stranger to her when they were grown-ups. Beau had moved into the house on St.-Denis Street so that he could take piano lessons in Montreal and because he was unhappy on the farm. Susan had thought him peculiar even then, and an intruder as well. Sibling rivalry was only increased by his presence and Michel hadn't liked him, either. Denys, her other brother, had not objected quite so much, but then Denys had always been calmer, and after his death in the war, Beau had become more than ever like a son to the St. Amours. *But not like a brother*, Susan thought now. *Never like a brother.*

It struck her as amazing when she saw Beau's name in the newspapers along with such famous people as Sir Thomas Beecham, Dimitri Mitropoulos, Gieseking, Rubinstein. As if she were living in some kind of dream. Still, she had many days in which she was profoundly bored, and so, eventually, she looked him up. He had an apartment in Paris and did not seem to be living with Angela or his small son. At least, not very often.

Only a week ago they had taken dinner together on the Champs Elysées, and Beau had indicated that he was soon going to America on tour.

"Aren't you going to see Angela first?" Susan had asked. She did not care, it was just a funny way of doing things, she decided.

"Yes, of course. Did you say you were driving to the south coast soon, Susan?"

"Next week," Susan had told him. "Actually, I'm going to St.-Tropez to meet a friend. A Russan prince. Or he *says* he is. I know what Grandfather would say . . . you can buy titles from a wheelbarrow in Italy and Russia. I suspect he's right. Anton is very, very bogus. Should I go by way of that place Angela's living in and pay her a visit?"

"I was going to ask if I could drive down with you," Beau said, looking unhappy.

"Say, that's a good idea. Why not? I'd love to have company. Where did you say it was, exactly?"

"Near Toulon. Can you go there?"

"Why not? That's a great idea. I'd kind of like to see Angela living in this monastery, it sounds a bit eerie to me. But I guess painters and musicians are different."

"It's a beautiful spot. A good place for Angela to paint and look after the child."

"Are you serious? Because if you are, let's make plans right now."

So here they were, arriving in the late afternoon, at the stone wall of the monastery with only the sound of birds and a kind of glow from the dipping sun to point up the chapel tower. Beau got out and pulled the bell rope. As they stood together, waiting, Susan could hear footsteps—the slap of leather sandals on hard tile. Then the top half of the weathered wooden gate opened with a creak to reveal a melancholy face. The sacristan looked neither surprised nor pleased to see them. He wore a brown woolen robe tied at the waist with a frayed belt.

"What do you want?" he asked in French.

"It's Beau, Brother Evraud. Beau Dosquet."

Beau's voice was edgy with annoyance. He whispered to

512

Susan, "He knows perfectly well who I am, the old fool. He likes to play games."

"Ah yes, yes, I'll open the gate."

Beau snorted with impatience as the chains rattled and a bolt was pulled on the other side. The wooden gate swung in and they went through into a cool courtyard that had lost the sun.

"Come this way, Susan," Beau said. He carried both their bags. Still, he moved swiftly across the cracked paving past a fountain that was now merely a bird bath.

They reached one of the cells that opened off the cloisters, and Beau set down the bags to turn the doorknob. He was impatient with detail now that he had arrived and began shouting for Angela. Susan thought grimly that all men were a bit mad and wondered why women put up with such crazy behavior.

Angela flew out from some inner room, all gray eyes, black curls, and pale skin. She looked as lovely as ever, Susan thought, but totally ill groomed. That was what came from living in such an isolated dump. Probably there were no bathtubs, no hairdressers for miles, no point in dressing or making up anyway, where would one go?

"Beau!" Angela cried, flinging herself at him and not even seeing Susan, who stood hesitantly a few feet behind Beau. Then they broke apart. Angela smiled happily. *Not even criticizing him for staying away, for not letting her know he was returning*, Susan thought.

Then, at last, Angela's eyes fell upon her cousin.

"Susan! It is Susan, isn't it?"

"Yes. I'm sorry we didn't let you know, but Beau said it would be all right. That you could find a bed for me overnight. I drove him down from Paris."

"That's all right, Susan, we'll manage. If you can put up with it. It isn't a hotel, exactly. Lots of space, but not much else."

The child came running from an inner room and threw chubby arms around his father's legs. He was a beautiful little boy—a cherub stepped down from a medieval painting, all dark curls, bright eyes, dimpled smile. Susan thought, with a sharp pain, of her own son. She had only seen him once when she was in Montreal. He had been like a stranger to her. Even if Angela was miserable with Beau, she *did* have her son.

They sat around a wooden table, and Angela brought wine and cheese and bread. Susan explained that she was driving on to St.-Tropez in the morning. As she watched them, she could not help reflecting on how far they had both come in ten years. How she had envied Angela her secure place in Pride's Court! She had even tried to help destiny force Angela out because she wanted so badly to be Sir Simon's favorite, to rule in the big house and enjoy all the prestige that the Court name could bring. And yet, she had thrown it all away when the time came. She was worse off than Angela in many respects, still. Angela had fled the Courts and so had she, but at least Angela had her son, and, at times, her husband. She also had her painting, Susan thought with a touch of anger. And Susan had nothing. Nothing but stupid parties, with chattering mindless people who drank too much, who sometimes experimented with drugs, who bought yachts and were too bored to sail, who traveled but always saw the same people.

She heard Beau telling Angela his plans. Dimitri Mitropoulos was turning from the piano to conducting and would be in Paris for a while before going to America. He wanted to premiere Beau's Second Symphony in Philadelphia the following spring.

"Tell me what *you're* doing, Susan," Angela said, at last. "We hear from your mother sometimes, but it's months since I had news about you. I gather you don't see your mother?"

"No." Susan lighted a cigarette and drew on it a little ostentatiously. "We don't get along. I don't want to be part of that . . . of their life. And I've given up my rights to the life I had with the Courts, apparently. Grandfather wanted me out of the country. I suppose you heard about Charity meeting that awful old pig Rodriguez? It was my fault. But I didn't want her to see him, I warned her." Susan shrugged.

"So Grandfather doesn't want you around?"

"He thinks I'm a bad influence. Of course, if David had been willing to take me back and make me an honest woman again, it might have worked out. But David wouldn't have any of that. So here I am. Living in Paris, flitting about, not doing much of anything. You're lucky.

You have your painting. I see your pictures in Paris sometimes. You seem to be quite important."

"I don't know how important I am," Angela said, as if it didn't matter. "But I do love to paint. Now that my grandmother is dead . . . you heard about Julia, I suppose? I don't have any reason to go to London. So I just stay on here. I work. It's comfortable."

"Have you an ashtray?" Susan asked, looking about for a place to flick the ash from her cigarette.

"Oh, sorry. Here, this tin lid will do."

Susan looked at the piece of tin, and then around the stone walls of the room, and the bare floor, at the fading light filtering through portholes that were a foot thick, at the paintings hanging here and there. It was so far removed from her own world. It was hard to believe such a place existed.

They talked about family and gossip and Montreal and New York and Paris until late in the evening.

"I'm leaving right after breakfast," Susan assured Angela. "So please don't think I'm going to be a nuisance."

She would have driven off that night if she hadn't been so tired. She could not imagine how Angela could bear to live in a vacuum like this. It was incomprehensible. She would have gone mad in two days if she'd had to stay in a monk's cell. Thank God she had the allowance from Grandfather! Even the phony prince began to look good as she fell asleep on the hard trestle bed.

After Susan had driven off and the sacristan had taken little Piers for a walk outside the monastery, Beau sank on a chair by the kitchen table to stare into his coffee cup. He was tense, restless, angry, afraid.

Angela could feel the waves of revolution reaching out to her.

"More coffee, Beau?"

"Yes, please. Sit down. I have some things to discuss."

"This is a good time. I want to talk to you, too. What are we going to do about our lives?"

There, it was out. She had forced the issue. She trembled, waiting for him to respond, knowing he disliked being put in that position. But surprisingly, he said flatly, "I have plans." He looked past her, at the wall.

"Then tell me what they are. I've tried to be reasonable.

515

Not to put pressure on you. We've been alone and we've had time to think about things. But this can't go on much longer."

"You're fair, Angela. I don't criticize you for that."

"What do you want to do, then?"

"I can't live here. It doesn't suit me."

"Perhaps I ought to move to Paris, then. I could work there. We can afford a larger apartment now—"

"No, that isn't it. It's the idea of marriage, of losing my freedom, that bothers me."

"You wanted to marry me, Beau."

"Well, I was wrong. I'm admitting that. I was wrong."

"But you *are* free! You do exactly as you wish."

"It isn't the same. Anyway, something's come up. I've got an offer to do a ballet in New York. It's exactly what I need right now, and I'm going."

"New York?"

"A major ballet. You know how important that is. I have to go."

Angela poured herself more coffee and carefully laced it with milk as if the proportions were important. She neglected to drink it.

"Why couldn't I pack up and take Piers? We could all go."

He rose then, flinging his body upward in protest. He began to pace around the room.

"My God, Angela, I wish I could say that's what I want! But it isn't. Look, it isn't being here, or in Paris, or London, or anywhere. The trouble is, I feel trapped. It preys on my mind. I feel guilty . . . as if I were committing a crime. Yet I can't live with you. I want out of the marriage, Angela. I can't work. I'm desperate."

"You don't want us?" She was numb.

"You aren't listening to me, Angela. It isn't that I don't want you. Or that I do want you, for that matter. I love you as much as I can love any woman, but I don't want responsibility. And I don't want guilt."

"What about Piers? Don't you love your son?"

"You know I love Piers. But I can't look after him, and you can. I have no fears about that. You've got your work, so concentrate on that."

They argued for an hour, but nothing changed. Beau knew exactly what he wanted. His plans were made.

When the sacristan returned, Beau made arrangements to leave with a food supply truck. It would take him to Toulon. By late afternoon he was gone. Angela struggled through the dinner hour and finally put Piers to bed. In the stillness of the evening she was afraid that despair would engulf her. Only the thought of abandoning Piers kept her from doing something desperate.

She would have to find a way to end her dreadful servitude, to kill her passion. It was degrading to be caught in an emotional storm, tossed about by someone else's needs, most of which were entirely selfish. She must stop loving Beau.

The cell was filled with memories, the whole landscape of the monastery was touched with the magic she had shared with Beau. She would have to leave. She could go to England. But eventually she would return to Montreal seeking solace in the carefully structured life of the St. Amours. If she could keep her mind on that, keep her thoughts off Beau, she might just survive. She must get rid of her love once and for all.

CHAPTER SIX

By five o'clock an implacable winter dark had fallen over the house and garden. Outside, smooth blue snow slopes turned to charcoal dust in bitter little squalls. The spruce and pine branches rattled with thin ice wafers, and the temperature had dropped so much that frost had formed on the glass panes of the bedroom windows. Inside, it was a warm cocoon with a lively fire and the scent of expensive scotch mixed with the more elusive one of passion. North and Laura lay on the generous bed propped up against a fat mound of satin pillows while North smoked and drowsed and Laura simmered in satisfaction.

Yes, he thought, he had the most convenient arrangement imaginable. His mistress was beautiful, wealthy, and politically alert. She was socially apt and sexually choreographed to amuse him. She poured his drinks, fed him snacks, dried him on thick Turkish towels after his shower, kissed his cheek, and listened to his rondelet of woes. Laura loved him. How could he doubt it?

When he turned his dark eyes upon the gold wisps of hair lying on the pillow so close to his face, he felt an unfamiliar rush of gratitude. With one well-shaped finger he traced a strand of golden hair downward to where it lay against Laura's cheek. He waited for her usual response.

To his surprise, she did not react. She did not nibble playfully on his finger or put her lips to the inside of his wrist or nuzzle against his forearm. Instead, she stared straight ahead into the fire. A warning light flickered in the depths of his mind comfort. Taking instant precautions, North deliberately sank his well-submerged voice right down to sea bottom.

"You're too quiet. Is something wrong, sweetheart? Weren't you happy when we made love? Wasn't I a good lover?"

"You're always a good lover, North," Laura said in a peculiar flat tone that only increased his alarm. "You're always a beautiful lover. I've never complained about the quality, only the quantity."

"Oh. I suppose you're saying I don't see you often enough. I can't come any oftener, Laura, you know that. I'm in Ottawa so much now and then I always have some damn thing to do for Lord Court, and I try to keep Mildred calm. I have to spend a little time with the children. There just aren't enough days in the week."

"Exactly. There isn't enough time."

"Is that what you're upset about?"

"I'm going to tell you, North. I have every intention of telling you what I'm upset about."

Pause. He had come, over the years, to fear pauses almost as much as long sermons and angry accusations. Pauses usually meant that a woman was simply taking time to mount a campaign. That she was laying the groundwork before firing the cannon. God, he only had to recall some of his scenes with Milly to know that. And with Kay Prince, too. He heaved a self-pitying sigh, as if he were being punished wrongly. He wanted to get up and pour himself another drink, but he was afraid this would seem too self-indulgent. He gave in, after a short internal argument.

"Tell me what the problem is, then," he said encouragingly, although he did not want to know. "Don't keep me in suspense. We're good friends, aren't we? Surely you know we can talk about anything. Anything at all."

They could not talk about quite *anything*, he silently amended. They could not talk about Milly, or about his resentment at being a mere pawn of the Courts, or about the fact that he was drinking more and more.

"We'll talk about *us*, North. It's time, don't you think? You've said exactly the things I've been thinking—that you don't have time for me. Not really. It's a pleasant diversion for you because you have another life. I don't have another life."

"I have another life and it's a pile of crap." He very seldom spoke like that to Laura because he knew she did not like vulgarity. He came back to bed with his drink, raising his eyebrows as if he were amazed that she would think otherwise. "You have a great social life, hell, dinners here, lunches there. Committee work . . ."

"It isn't quite the same thing as having a husband to plan one's life around, or a lover who is at least free to take one to dinner parties. Or to have somebody to travel with. I had to go to Nassau alone. You know I loathe Christmas and New Year's."

"Right. It isn't the same thing." He said this humbly, falling into a well-worn pattern that had always served him well in the past. Admit guilt. Be sorry. Do not deny one's own rottenness, but seem staggered that somebody else, who is presumably fine and generous, can be bothered to put up with it for even a moment. "I'm a louse, Laura. I don't deserve you. But what can I do?"

"You can leave."

"Leave?"

Now it was his turn to pause. The word *leave* shimmered between them a barely visible thread. Its meaning vibrated and hung there like a word from Sanskrit. He tried to marshal his thoughts so that he could be sure of saying the right thing. He had had too much scotch, he was too relaxed from making love, to be alert.

"Yes, I said *leave*. Why wouldn't you leave? God knows, you don't love Mildred. You live in an atmosphere of constant aggravation—either at Mildred or your relatives. You're always being sent off on some piece of business you hate. You didn't want to run for office. There's no dignity, no self-respect for you at Pride's Court. You must know that, North. Everybody knows you married Milly for money and position. Do you think it's a secret?"

He did not answer. The word *leave* rolled around his mind like a water ball. Just for a moment he tried to think what life would be like if he did not live in Pride's Court, if he did not have that incredible status, security, extension of power that the Courts provided. He tried to imagine life on some lesser scale—inhabited by mortals who lived closer to the earth. He tried to think about days without Milly (whom he did not love but who still provided a sense of reality, of knowing where he was, like a surveyor's stake stuck in the middle of a trackless forest). He tried to think about not seeing the children—not that he saw them very much anyway, but they were part of his past and his future. He envisioned life in a smaller house (even this one seemed cramped when he had just come from Pride's Court), without the servants, the expensive cars, the rare wines, the precious china and silver and glass. The whole royal ritual of that great house.

Memories of Susan flitted through his mind and he dwelt momentarily on her disastrous choice. Susan had left the shelter of the Courts and had almost been destroyed in the process. He did not envy her, living as an outcast on a Court allowance. Just thinking of Susan's fate was enough to turn his stomach to jelly. He couldn't hope to buck the Court power any more than Susan. Nobody could go against them and gain a victory. The family remained united and strong even if one broke away—like Angela— like Susan. The nucleus held, as if Lord Court by his own fantastic will kept them in his orbit to play out their roles. And in return family members had a certain clout, dignity, luxury, that only a vast fortune could provide.

"You want me to leave Mildred?" he repeated.

He knew that he sounded stupid. His voice had croaked unpleasantly. He knew that he must stall and that he must not lose his power over her, his charm.

"Yes, leave. That's what I'm suggesting. I'm throwing you a lifeline, North. You're drowning. Drowning in hostility, self-hatred, indignity, and boredom. And alcohol, of course. Let's not forget the alcohol. You'll be a physical wreck in ten years if you go on like this. You'll be finished before you're fifty."

"Hell, it isn't that bad," he protested. "I'm not a drunk."

"Aren't you? I think it *is* that bad. If you aren't a drunk now, you will be eventually. You think Milly loves you? She's a leech. You make her feel grand and important. She's nothing. She'd be nothing without that money and family."

"You're a bit hard on Milly," he remonstrated. Milly did love him. He was sure of that.

"I don't think I'm hard on Milly. Anyway, I don't really care a damn about her. It isn't as if you'd be marrying a nobody if you left the Courts for me. My family and my husband's family are important here, too. There's enough money to live comfortably and you could choose something to do—I don't care what. You don't need the Court money. This house is not as grand as Pride's Court, but still it isn't exactly a tenement."

"Laura, for God's sake, don't make an issue of this!"

"Milly is a spoiled brat," Laura went on fiercely. "You're just a plaything she bought. A handy robot to take her out to dinner, a man who sits properly dressed at the head of the table, who knows how to behave in public. Charming, handsome, *useful* North."

It was the first time Laura had ever attacked Milly, and he was stunned. He was convinced that she was wrong. Wrong about the motives she ascribed to Milly. Milly loved him. He had not behaved too well in some cases, but Milly had forgiven him. Milly had had three children by him, and he owed her some loyalty. Milly had often been passionate, and he had felt some kind of passion in return.

"Leave Milly out of this."

"Why? She's very much a part of all this. Do you think she doesn't know about me? Do you think she doesn't tolerate your liaisons? Of course she does! A woman of principle would have told you to get out long ago. She's weak and silly. She's shallow. She doesn't know what love is."

"There are the children," he offered.

"Are you trying to tell me you spend a lot of time with your children? What do you do for them, North? Do you think they'd miss you? There are three other Court men all waiting to be father figures. And that's all you are. A *figure*. You wouldn't miss the children one bit, so don't give me that pious, stay-for-the-children act. Keep that for Milly. She might buy it. She's stupid enough."

521

"Let's not make an issue out of this . . . Why do we have to talk about it now? Why tonight, when everything was so pleasant?"

"We have to talk about it sometime. You only think of yourself, North, and your own comforts."

He got out of bed for the second time and poured another drink. He drank some scotch neat and then turned to face her.

"If you think I'm so damned selfish, why do you want me?"

Laura looked miserable and began to pluck at the silk sheet like a child.

"Don't you think I've asked myself that a thousand times? I don't know. Dammit, I don't know. I hate to sound trite, but I feel some kind of chemical attraction to you . . . you excite me. I feel good inside when you touch me. I like to touch you. I haven't felt that way about a man for years. I never did feel that way about poor Victor, by the way. He was sweet and kind, but he didn't excite me. You do."

He finished off the scotch, set down the glass, and climbed back into bed beside her. He reached toward her bare shoulders and tried to take her in his arms. He let his lips run over her cheek and found her mouth. His tongue found her tongue. His fingers broke new trails through the gold strands of hair upon the pillow. He felt her loosen beneath him and he hardened: thick with blood rush. He moved to mount her.

Laura rolled away from him, pushing him away with the palms of her hands. Her voice sounded icy.

"Oh, stop it! There's no point in making love, North. Please go. I want you to go right now and never come back. Don't call me. I don't want to discuss this."

"I'm not going. Not like this."

She began to weep.

"Yes, you are. I won't endure any more pain. It's ridiculous. I won't have the half-ration you dole out. I'm going to change my whole life. I'll find a man who is all mine. I don't want any more of Milly's leftovers, or Lord Court's crumbs. Go away, North, and don't come back. Don't ever come back."

He tried to talk to her. He tried every trick he knew to break down this frightening reserve that she had manufactured from some secret source. She remained adamant, however, cold as the snow outside on the evergreens. At last, exhausted, he gave up. He slowly dressed, feeling strangely sober and very, very old. The glow from the scotch and the loving had dissipated. All the creamy calm that sex had deposited inside his chest had been washed away. He felt as if he had not known love for a thousand years. Finally, because she would not speak, he went downstairs and put on his coat. He walked out into the biting December night. It was over.

He put the Packard away himself. Dodgson was in the garage doing some work on the Rolls-Royce, and they exchanged a few words. North was numb. When he came from the cloakroom after having rid himself of his hat and coat, Peters met him in the Great Hall.

"His Lordship would like you to join him in the library. He asked me to tell you the minute you came in. They're having a meeting before dinner, sir."

"Some people don't have holidays." North said, making the remark for Peters's benefit. Peters gave him a sympathetic look.

"Oh, His Lordship never stops working."

"Where is Mrs. Grenville-Court?"

"In her apartment, sir. She ordered a tray upstairs."

"Thank you, Peters."

After Peters had gone, North stood in the middle of the Great Hall and looked about as if he were seeing it for the first time. Or perhaps, the last. The high vaulted ceiling, the enormous marble staircase, the portrait of Sir Cathmor presiding from the landing, the whole bloody, smothering, awesome aura of the place swooped down to enfold him. He stood rigid for a moment, breathing it in. It was magnificent. It was lethal.

Reluctantly he made his way to the library, past the priceless paintings, the lustrous antiques; he trod upon the imported carpets, over the marble floor, to open the library door, knowing how the scene would look. Lord Court stood near the fire pontificating on yet another Court venture or on the economy or on the Crash of the year before; it did not really matter which subject he happened to be handling.

Around him, listening attentively while they nursed the

best scotch in crystal glasses, were Charles and Fort and Noel (who had come down for Christmas). Simon II had decided to stay in Courtsville. North spoke briefly to everybody and headed for the bar. Behind him he heard them talking about Ottawa, about specific Cabinet members. He took a place across from Charles, now cold sober, and impeccably dressed. But he scarcely heard a word they were saying—the meaning of the words did not really engage his mind. Phrases drifted by: "that block of Brazilian Traction," "the power project on the St. Lawrence is up in the air," and "the price of copper is up." Up and up. He knew he was expected to take part, but everything in him had turned to sawdust. After two scotches he got up and excused himself from the company, pleading illness. Lord Court bristled. "Aren't you going to have dinner?"

"I'm sorry, sir. I'm not well. I think I'll go upstairs. Maybe it's influenza."

"What's wrong with everybody these days? Milly said the same thing. I never get sick."

"If you'll excuse me—"

"I haven't finished the meeting—" Simon Court began, but North was already out the door.

"I'm sorry," he said again and closed the library door behind him.

He wondered now how he could go on living like this. He wondered if he could stand another day of them, of their obsession with making money, of buying people off, of obeying the old man as if he were some kind of tin god, their greed. He walked slowly up the staircase and stood for a moment looking at Sir Cathmor's steely stare. It was, he thought in a small flight of fancy, like one of the Stations of the Cross.

In the apartment he found Milly reading in bed.

"Hello, Milly," he said wearily.

She put the book down and her expression was cold. She looked sallow and exhausted.

"You decided to come back? How nice."

"I was tied up."

"I'm sure you were. Business, of course."

"Yes, business."

Her voice changed.

"You expect me to believe that?" Her tone was dangerous, almost threatening.

"I expect you to believe that, yes."

He took off the suit jacket and walked to the dressing room to hang it up. He was a tidy man. He made the decision to get into pajamas and housecoat, to send for drinks up here.

"You're a liar," she said when he came out again.

"I'm going to have my dinner up here. Do you want anything to drink? I'll ring for Peters."

"Did you hear what I said?"

"I heard you."

He rang. He knew he ought to try to pacify Milly, to reassure her somehow, but he had no strength left. He sat down in the sitting room until Peters came and then gave instructions for a decanter of scotch to be brought up, along with a supper tray. When he found he could no longer concentrate on his book, he walked back into the bedroom.

"Milly, I don't know what you think I've been doing but—"

"I know exactly what you've been doing."

Alarm cut sharply through the numbness that had settled upon him like a suit of armor.

"What's that supposed to mean?"

"Just what it says. Don't be stupid. I know you've been with Laura Balfour."

The numbness fell away and he was left with fear. Why was she doing this now, when he had just broken off with Laura? It was ironic that Mildred would confront him with an affair that was already in the past.

"What in hell do you mean?" he said defensively.

"I've had you watched. I know."

He stared at her, too stunned to feel the fear anymore. Nobody, that is nobody *they* knew, would do such a thing. His mind raced over the recent meetings with Laura, the rendezvous they had kept. He felt injured, even martyred.

"Watched? That's a rotten thing to do."

"Is it? More rotten than your cheating?"

"You're crazy, Milly."

"Oh, stop lying, you make me sick."

She had put down her book and the anger showed in the way her hands had tensed. She began to stammer.

"I l-l-loved you, North. I l-l-loved you so much."

"And I love you, Milly," he said automatically. The words were like the coins that are fed into a slot machine to produce a winning combination.

"Oh, North, you d-d-don't know what l-love means."

"Thank you, Milly." Sarcastically, trying desperately to grab something to keep himself afloat.

"You'd b-b-better listen to me, North."

"I'm listening. I'm in shock."

"You sh-sh-should be."

He was gathering up the strands of dignity, but his heart was still pounding as if he were in grave danger.

"Say it, whatever it is. Let's get it over with."

"Either s-s-stop seeing her, or get out. If you don't stop, I'll tell Grandfather. I'll tell him everything. You'll be out . . . of everything . . . the b-b-business, and the house. You can never live on what you m-m-make as a m-m-member. See how you like it."

"I'm not seeing Laura."

"If you do, I'll find out. Remember that."

"I'm not seeing Laura."

"All right, North. But remember what I said. If you d-d-do see her again, I'll tell Grandfather. I'll d-d-divorce you and name her as correspondent. Would you l-l-like that?"

"I'm not seeing Laura." It was the only truth he had.

"Go away, please. I don't want to t-t-talk to you. And don't sleep in here—sleep out there on the sofa. Don't come near me."

She began to sob.

He turned away and closed the door. As he did so, Peters came in with both trays and the decanter, on a trolley.

"I'll take it to Mrs. Grenville-Court. She isn't well. Just leave everything here with me, Peters. I'll take care of it."

When Peters had gone, he poured out some scotch and drank it thirstily. He thought he would have at least two drinks before he took in the tray. Then perhaps he wouldn't notice, wouldn't feel any of the guilt, or fear, or even the milder sensation of disgust. A drink was definitely called for in a situation like this.

CHAPTER SEVEN

When Mussolini's troops marched into Ethiopia in October 1935, it was, from his point of view, not war but a renaissance. It was obvious to the clairvoyant dictator that a vigorous Italian Empire could only do good: It would restore the image of the Caesars and at the same time create a Promethean prosperity in the homeland. Ethiopia, as it turned out, was conveniently close (on the northwest corner of Africa) and pleasingly defenseless.

In Geneva news of the invasion forced the doddering League of Nations to begin rehearsals for an ill-timed trapeze act: Big powers like Britain and France now threatened to impose economic sanctions (a blockade) against Italy if she persisted in her aggressive behavior. They would, they said sternly, be forced to place an embargo on iron, steel, coal, and oil, thus cutting off vital life-giving energy to Mussolini's war machine.

Due to a complicated set of circumstances Canada's representative, Dr. Walter Riddell, had come to sponsor the embargo act when he was appointed by the Bennett government. But no sooner had Mussolini's army goose-stepped across the Ethiopian border than Bennett lost the fall election to Mackenzie King. Receiving no counter-order, Riddell continued to foster the embargo bill.

Canada's parochial politicians now began to take a more global view of the Italian-Ethiopian conflict. More than twenty-five raw materials essential to the proper execution of even the most insignificant war were about to be placed on the embargo list. Copper was one of them, and copper just happened to be a by-product of the flourishing gold industry. Canadian mining magnates with heavy investments saw the light—this kind of international games-playing simply would not do. The country's economy might be jeopardized if the market for their wares became seriously depressed, and Italy was a major buyer. In high places enthusiasm for sanctions against Italy began to fade rather rapidly.

Then there was the question of geography. It suddenly occurred to the more astute members of the Canadian Parliament that Rome was in Italy, that the Vatican was in Rome, and that the pope was the spiritual leader of Canadian Roman Catholics. Might not a hostile attitude toward Italian Roman Catholics be construed as a hostile attitude toward French Canadian voters? The bishops took no official stand on the sanctions, but it was clear that they could not be expected to whip up any genuine zeal among their flock when it came to punishing Mussolini for his transgressions.

Unrelated but odd things began to happen in the city. A parade by a band of Silver Shirts led by a Fascist called Adrien Arcand hailed *Il Duce* in the streets of Montreal and booed the League of Nations. Well, that could be taken with a grain of salty humor, but there was also the matter of ex-mayor Camillien Houde. Houde was a city slicker whose role of "lovable scamp" was richly embroidered with the threads of fatherly concern. French Canadians often laughed at Houde's peccadilloes and shook their heads in wonder, but they listened to his words of wisdom just the same. And Houde was telling Canadians in general and French Canadians in particular that if Britain went to war against Italy over some hapless African shire, the province of Quebec would be on Italy's side. That was bad news, indeed, for Liberals, who depended heavily on support from the residents of Quebec.

In the Liberal camp a certain amount of fancy footwork took place as well as considerable dissection of the individual conscience, but in the end, it seemed that Catholics came down firmly on the side of an antiembargo platform. Protestant English Conservatives, most still loyal to the Crown, had an even more difficult time. If they had large investments in northern mines, they devoutly wished to keep up the market value of copper and iron. Yet the spectacle of a helpless little nation (no matter how distant) being bombed by Fascist aircraft was hard to ignore.

In Edenbridge the question of economic sanctions against Italy was reduced to a personal level. Since Sir Armand and Lady St. Amour had moved back into the house, Honey had carefully restored the placid pastels of the small sitting room: The Zuccarellis had been rehung on the walls, and she had added a small view of Venice by Guardi that was all vivid blues and creamy-colored clouds. On this particular evening she sat before the coffee tray and poured a demitasse from the French porcelain pot. She offered it to Armand with a smile. But the room's serenity did not, evidently, encompass her husband's mood. He looked extremely agitated.

"Now that we've finished dinner, *ma chérie*, there is something important I wish to discuss with you," Armand began.

"I suspected as much. You look restless."

She gave him an encouraging smile. It was so like Armand to wait until they had finished dinner before bringing up something unpleasant. He had the gentleman's view of a meal: It was to be a relaxing, warm experience never marred by abrasive arguments or unsavory subjects.

"We know each other too well to hide anything," Armand said, shrugging, "so I won't try."

"Not money again?" Honey asked. "Not so soon, surely? Oh, Armand, I can't bear it if we have to start counting pennies again, watching every dollar."

"Not exactly money in that sense. At least not yet."

"Then what do you mean, *not yet*? I hate having to scrimp and save and argue about the cost of everything . . . it's so degrading."

· She looked tired. More and more, the newspaper was taking all her energy and leaving her feeling that it wasn't worthwhile. Her flying was the only thing that seemed to justify the work, the problems that life presented. When she was in her plane, she felt free and exuberant, young again.

"Yes, you are a Court," he said rather sarcastically. "Used to the best of everything. Used to money. It is degrading for a Court to have to think about expenses. Are you enjoying your new airplane?"

She had just bought a new Fairchild and was delighted with it. But she did not like Armand's tone of voice.

"Don't be cross, Armand. I know it's terribly extravagant of me, but flying is the most exciting thing . . . I love it."

"So I gathered. You also like to buy new paintings. I saw the bill for that little extravagance," he said, pointing to the Guardi, which she had so recently hung. "Then there was the bill for redecorating this house."

"We couldn't move in here after other people without having it completely done over."

"No, my darling, I appreciate your fastidiousness. Yet

it costs a great deal of money to do these things. True, I'm doing well, but we could easily find ourselves in financial difficulties once again if you aren't more careful."

"Oh? I thought Noranda was pouring out gold and making all the investors richer and richer."

She knew what he was about to say, but she did not want to admit that she could have gone ahead with her own plans, knowing it might distress Armand. So she pretended, at least momentarily, to be rather dense.

"Noranda is one of the greatest gold mines in the world," he said slowly, putting down his coffee cup. "Nobody would doubt that who knows anything about it. I thank the Virgin that I listened to Angus McKie and bought the shares when I had the opportunity."

"Well, then, what is the trouble? I'm making a small profit at the paper, so it isn't costing you anything."

"The newspaper is the problem. You must stop campaigning for economic sanctions. The other French newspapers are pro-Italian. Only *Le Monde* is suggesting that Canada continue to support the embargos."

"Really, Armand, you can't expect me to support that ugly brute's bombing a lot of poor, defenseless natives! Have you seen the pictures of those tribesmen being bombed? That's not war, Armand, that's murder."

"I can't argue that point," Armand said. "But you are ill informed, just the same. The cold, hard fact is that copper is next on the embargo list. Did you know that? You must know it, you read enough, and you are quite intelligent."

"Thank you," she said angrily.

"Have you examined my list of investments?" he went on. "No, you haven't time. Yet you should know that copper and iron are two of them. And where does the money come from to redecorate this house? To buy your paintings? Your airplane? From copper. Gold. Iron. Not from your trivial newspaper, Miel. I thank God that you are making even a marginal profit, but it doesn't support your idea of how we ought to live . . . it is a toy that—"

"Toy?" she cried. "Toy? Your precious Liberal party finds *Le Monde* useful enough at election time. I hardly call it a toy."

"Nevertheless, run as you are running it, the paper is dangerous. I think you ought to stop being a hypocrite."

"Hypocrite?" she shouted incredulously. "How can you call *me* a hypocrite when I'm only trying to tell the truth? While you and your charming French friends close your eyes and ally yourself with that ghastly pope? Willing to sell out to a madman because he's Italian and Catholic! And you say *I'm* a hypocrite."

"Yes, you're a hypocrite," he said grimly. "Don't shout at *me*, Miel. I'm not one of the lackeys at your newspaper!"

"I have no lackeys," she said through clenched teeth.

"Is that so? That isn't the impression I get when I visit your office, my dear. Now, since you are so fond of the truth, let me tell you a few that reflect on your own life. Then perhaps you can drop your role as Joan of Arc— a role for which you are so ill prepared. Your whole way of life depends upon my investments, much in the gold mines. If copper and iron go on that embargo list, the prices will drop. Then we'll be close to where we were a few years ago, living in an apartment, with one car and no cook. You can sell your newest painting then to buy clothes, if you like. Do you understand me? So stop trying to look like a saint on the one hand while benefiting from the very things you deplore."

"That's the cruelest thing you've ever said to me, Armand. I wasn't aware that I was playing a role. That I was living off the blood of those people. That murder supports my way of life. I've always had money and you know that! It has nothing at all to do with the Ethiopians or any other foreigners—"

"Oh, yes, it has. You've always had money and you've always depended, whether you knew it or not, upon foreign markets. Upon immigrants for your papa's ships and materials being sold abroad. You just don't want to see the truth. You were brought up that way."

"And *your* upbringing was perfect, I suppose? You've lost more money at cards than I've ever spent on a painting or a plane or a house! How can you accuse me of this?"

"I'd forget that line of argument if I were you."

"Do you really believe that what I print in my newspaper makes any difference to the League of Nations?" she demanded, taking another tack.

"It might influence members of government. They read your paper. And they are directing the Canadian representative at the League meetings. The government will assume that the paper reflects the opinion of some part of the population, yes. And they mean by that, voters."

"I don't believe that my newspaper will make any difference to world events."

"If Canada withdraws sponsorship of the embargos, the bill may die."

"I see. So will thousands of innocent Ethiopians, if we let Il Duce have his way. What about them? You will sell copper, and the Fascists will kill the natives. It sounds very attractive. You ought to listen to yourself."

"For your information, Miel, every major power is in exactly the same position," Armand said wearily, as if he were talking to a child. "France sells steel to Italy and Spain sells iron. Norway, Poland, and Rumania have had orders for war materials for a long time, and they're just waiting to deliver. The United States is not in the League, but while she declares sympathy to the embargos, Secretary of State Hull has said that American scrap iron, oil, tractors, and various war goods are already on order. What do you think is happening in the world? Are you really so naïve?"

"And you want our prime minister to withdraw support in the League, is that it?"

"Yes, and he won't find it so hard. He didn't sponsor the bill originally, it was Prime Minister Bennett and his Conservatives who did that. King merely inherited the mess. He can easily back out of it that way."

"Convenience is the most important thing, then. Frankly, I hate that position. I find it intolerable."

"But you don't hate money."

"One of the reasons I like owning a newspaper, why I like to be a publisher, is that I can say worthwhile things, things I believe to be the truth. Important things. I happen to think that telling the truth to people about Mussolini's barbaric invasion is important. I can't change my position on that, even for you, Armand."

"That's unfortunate."

"Yes, it is. I'm sorry. But I have to live with myself as well as with you."

"You may end up living by yourself, Miel. Be careful."

"Are you threatening me?"

"I am merely making a suggestion."

"I won't change my editorial position."

"Power has obviously gone to your head. It's appalling."

"Misuse of power is more appalling."

"I'm going to the library to do some work."

"Good night, Armand."

He walked out of the room rigidly—angry and worried at the same time. As she watched him close the sitting room door, she felt the space between them widen and knew it would be difficult to patch up the quarrel they had had tonight, even if she capitulated. She could not easily accept his cold attitude, and it was impossible to make that image fit the Armand she loved. But despite the danger, she must print the truth. She knew that. She could not give up the newspaper, either, although she did not extract the same pleasure and sense of challenge as she had when she was younger. She would not give up the newspaper now, or at any time, as long as she was strong enough to manage it.

"Just because we have a lunatic running the country doesn't mean we ought to abandon the ship," Lord Court said, mixing his metaphors and drawing heavily on his cigar. "Somebody's got to impress upon King what's best. And what is best is for Canada to withdraw from supporting the ridiculous economic sanctions against Italy."

He gathered about him all the Court men. Charles, Fort, and North were present, and even Noel and Simon II, who had made one of his rare expeditions down to civilization. They sat about the library and listened to the old man who even now could thunder and flash lightning from his blue eyes although arthritis had crumpled his hands and squeezed his hip joints so that he walked with discomfort. Not one of them could bear to think of his death, not one of them could escape a feeling of fear at the thought of losing his leadership.

"But if England supports the sanctions, how can we back down?" Charles asked reasonably. "I don't see that, Papa. We can't leave England out on a limb."

"Ha, that's all you know! England *wants* out! I have it on the best authority because I telephoned Sir Samuel Hoare yesterday—he's foreign secretary, you know. I knew his father well. Used to go grouse shooting with him. Hoare says England and France are trying to find a plan that will make the sanctions unnecessary. In London they wish our delegate would shut up. Hoare put it more delicately, but that's what he meant."

"Funny that London should agree with the French press here," Noel said. "Every paper but *Le Monde* wants Canada to withdraw from support of the proposal."

North looked at him with barely concealed distaste. There had been a time when Noel had not figured in his life, other than as a peripheral relative. But that had changed the year before, when Noel had, surprisingly, married Laura Balfour. Now, looking at Noel and thinking how wasted Laura's charms were upon this rather ordinary-looking fellow, and how he had given up all hope of possessing them himself, North could only feel dissatisfaction, irritation, and a hint of anger. It was especially difficult to bear when Noel and Laura came to dinner at Pride's Court and he was forced to entertain them and be civil. Now, he looked away from his brother-in-law and stared out of the window, as if to dissassociate himself from the whole proceedings.

Lord Court, however, jumped to the bait. To find himself in agreement with the French press was imcomprehensible. To find himself in disagreement with *Le Monde* would, at most times, have seemed to him a natural thing. He had never minded agreeing with the bishops because they had allied themselves with the Conservative party right from the beginning of the English occupation, realizing that their only hope of retaining power lay with the English ruling class. Power they understood. Liberalism, independence of spirit, was not a thing the bishops had ever been keen to sell, even when the proponents were French Canadian.

For Lord Court to agree with Liberals (and he was forced to do so on the matter of economic sanctions) was enraging. He somehow felt that Honey was right and that he was wrong, yet the economics of the thing dictated otherwise. That she had found the courage to fly in the face of material considerations was infuriating. He well knew that Armand St. Amour's holdings were almost entirely in gold and copper and iron. The Court holdings (while so diversified that the family fortune could never be wholly destroyed) included the lucrative Court gold mines and a new iron mine just developing in northern Quebec on the Labrador border.

"My daughter is a fool and a dangerous one," Lord Court said, dismissing Honey with a wave of his hand. "The real problem is, how serious is this? I want figures on how much copper we have been selling to Italy and what our contracts are at this time. Do we sell iron there? How much are the sanctions going to cost us, *that's* what I must know. Simon, look into that and come up with some figures by tomorrow. Also, where can we sell if Italy is cut off? There must be other markets, but I don't seem to know where we stand. Are we trying to find new markets? I just wish I were younger!"

Simon II allowed himself a smile. His grandfather was a dinosaur, but you had to admire the old man's spirit and energy.

"I'll have the figures, Grandfather."

"Good. Charles, there's a meeting of mining people tomorrow. We're all in the same boat, so a handful of the top chaps are getting together. They want me to go, but I said I'd send you. My secretary has called yours with the details."

"All right, Papa. I have a full day tomorrow, but I can cancel something, I guess."

"Cancel anything. This is what matters at the moment. After that meeting we'll figure out how to pressure King into withdrawing support. If he needs it. Maybe he's not completely witless, but I wouldn't count on it."

"What do you want me to do, Grandfather?" Noel asked. "You must have a job for me, surely?"

"Find out about iron. I know the mines aren't producing that much, but the potential is there. Get the forecast. Let me see it by tomorrow."

"That'll be easy."

"Then there's shipping. Fort, you know most about that side. If we stop sending copper and iron to Italy, how will that affect our cargos?"

He moved on, then, to agonize about the election they had just lost. With the Conservatives in power, it would have been simpler for the Courts to deal with the present situation. Bennett had belonged to some of the same clubs as Lord Court. But now, with a renegade in charge of the ship of state, the whole thing was reduced to a bureaucratic level that struck the old man as unbelievable. There was no meeting ground.

"Papa, I'd like to try to convince Angela to come home," Charles said, introducing a new note. "This Ethiopian thing may spread. Have you really looked at the situation in Germany and Italy? Sure, they may be satisfied with a few plums here and there. But how do we know? How do we know there won't be a war over there?"

Lord Court halted in the middle of a rather grisly picture he had been imagining—somehow he had managed to line up the entire Liberal Cabinet before a firing squad —and glared at his eldest son. Then the blue eyes glistened, and softened a little, as if he could suddenly see Angela's lovely face in front of him. When he spoke, his voice was unusually mellow.

"Perhaps you're right." (It was one thing for Lord Court to exile relatives who offended him, quite another for foreigners to put the lives of those relatives in jeopardy.) "She ought to come home. Is it true that the Frenchie abandoned her and her son?"

"I don't know if you'd call it abandoned," Charles said. "They happen to be separated, according to Angela's letters . . . I think he sends money. Although Angela is selling her paintings over there for a great deal of money. She's living in a monastery and—"

"A *monastery*?"

The old man was horrified. Bad enough to have married a French Roman Catholic, but to live in a monastery, a source of popery, as it were, seemed to him the bottom of a very deep well. How could anybody brought up in Pride's Court, with Angela's background, bring herself to live in such a place? He could not believe it. He saw before his mind's eye vast parades of black-frocked monks all chanting horrible pagan rites. He saw his great-grandson schooled in the ways of wickedness and heathenism. He found it difficult to speak, but with an effort he cried from the heart, "She must be saved!"

"Well, Papa, I think—" Charles began.

"She must be gotten away from the clutches of those . . . monks!"

"There aren't any monks there now. The place is abandoned, Papa. The order had no funds . . . they ran out of money."

"Ran out of money? Best news I've heard today. Angela must be gotten out of France. You can't trust Europeans not to fight. The Germans are always spoiling for a fight, you know. And the Italians seem to be about the same, nowadays. Hitler sounds like a madman. Have you heard any of his speeches on the radio? Sounds like gibberish. Can't understand a word he says!"

Fort stifled a laugh.

"He's speaking German, Papa."

"*That's German?* No wonder they're such a difficult race!"

"But I agree that he sounds hysterical," Fort added.

"Charles, you'd better send for her. Find somebody to go over there. After we settle this thing about the sanctions, of course."

"How about Susan?" Fort said helpfully. "She's in Paris. Why don't we contact Susan—she's more reasonable—and have her talk to Angela. Susan ought to come back as well. They could come together."

"Susan was a wonderful girl until she ran off with that . . ." Words failed him when it came to Philip Charles Norman. *There* was a man who had raided his house, seduced his favorite granddaughter, and then left her to fend for herself. "*Immigrant*," he finished off.

He stopped to wonder, as he had wondered so often in the past, why so many of the women in the family left to go off with hopeless men. Not only hopeless but foreigners. Beau had been Canadian, but he had been French Canadian, and there you were. Same thing as St. Amour. All untrustworthy. All unstable, when it came to that.

Charles was pleased that he had his father's permission to bring Angela back home. It only remained to convince her. He and Fort exchanged looks. North had turned away. He felt nothing now for Susan. It did not matter to him where she was, except that when she was away, things seemed safer. With old secrets (hopefully buried) one never knew what to expect. There could always be a resurrection.

CHAPTER EIGHT

When the weather was fine, Angela walked through the breathless cloisters every evening. The graceful arches, the ancient stones, seemed to give off an air of peace, and she was able to absorb that mood—almost as if she could take on some of the wisdom from the thoughtful monks who had walked the corridors before her. Shadows shifted in the courtyard, and birds assembled at the fountain looking for crumbs and rainwater that had accumulated in the basin.

She had come to a crossroads. Back in Paris her last show had been both a critical and commercial success. Two of her larger works had sold to American museums of art, and the major Parisian art critics had put her in the same rarefied atmosphere as Dali, Ernst, and Duchamp. The years in the monastery had been lonely at times (she seldom ventured to Paris except for her openings and for some erratic shopping), but there were always other tenants, and the sacristan remained and also a cook who hired herself out. Her son, Piers, was of an age when he ought to be in a proper school, although the Sacristan had taught him French and Latin and she had taught him English and some arithmetic. He was a bright little boy, but he had very few friends his own age unless a temporary tenant happened by with young children.

Beau had been living in London with occasional visits to Paris. He wrote to her occasionally and sent large checks at random, but Angela did not ask for any kind of regular commitment from him. She needed very little money, living as she did, and her paintings now brought sizable prices. At times she longed to see Beau, and yet her emotions had been tamped down, kept below the surface, so that only in her work did they erupt at times, in brilliant splurges of passion.

As she walked on this evening, watching the twilight descend and the birds sputter to a halt, she longed for home. This was an ususual feeling for Angela. Yet she recognized that she was weary of the climate and of her associates here in the monastery, tired of the whole dreary procession of homogeneous days and nights. Her longing took the form of wanting to go back to Montreal, for Julia had died four years before and Angela no longer had any desire to live in England. It was Montreal she thought about, Pride's Court she saw in her mind's eye. She could even imagine Piers in the big house, could see herself showing him its treasures, and could hear her grandfather's gruff pleasure in the little boy. She thought of her father and felt a sting of nostalgia. He must be lonely, poor man. He had lost the two women he had loved, after all, and rattling about in that vast cavern of a house must be gloomy.

The question was, would Grandfather have forgiven her by now? Would he have forgotten, perhaps, what their quarrel had been about? Landry was dead. He had been dead five years. Surely there was no use carrying on a vendetta that had outlived one of the causes!

The courtyard was chilly now. It was October and the air was clean and cold. Leaves rustled on the paving stones, crumpled and dry, blowing in a fitful breeze. The quiet was broken by the sound of a car drawing up to the gate. It was not the time for deliveries from the village, and Angela stopped in her pacing, wondering if some kind of emergency had arisen.

She saw the sacristan ambling slowly to the gate when he heard the bell jangle, and through the grayish-purple light she saw the gate swing open. She caught her breath.

He was outlined sharply against the faded gray stone walls—his velvet topcoat black, his hair ruffled, the thrust of his head belligerent. She could feel his eyes hot with unspent passion cutting across the space that separated them. He was as slim and tense as he had been the day he left.

"Beau!"

Her first instinct was to run toward him, but instead, she stood stolidly on the paved ground under the cloisters, not moving. He came toward her, striding, anxious, taut. Then he threw out his arms to her.

"Angela, darling."

She felt his embrace as if she were in a dream, but the scent of his thick black curls pressed against her cheek, and then the hot mouth journeying over her face was very real. His grip was fierce.

"I've come for you," he said as if they had talked about it, as if he had written to her, perhaps, or had in some way communicated his plans.

After they had embraced, he asked to see his son.

"He's in his bedroom," Angela said. "But not asleep. always give him an early supper and then he reads."

"Good. I'll visit with him, and we'll talk."

"Have you had dinner? Surely not, if you drove from Toulon."

"I'd like something light and some wine. Once we settl Piers and I've had my visit, there are some things we ough to discuss."

"Yes, I imagine there are," Angela said, making a little face at him. Beau was a bit humorless, she thought, and s driven that he failed to see how his actions might appear t anybody else. The world was supposed to stop when he appeared.

Angela stood in the doorway and watched Beau as h approached the narrow trestle bed. Piers was reading by lamplight. He looked up, his dark eyes suddenly alert and questioning. His brown curls tumbled about his face. When he recognized Beau (so it seemed), he gave a merry smile.

"Papa!"

Beau picked him up and hugged him. Then he sat down on the bed with the book Piers was holding to read a few pages from Robinson Crusoe.

"That's all. We'll put out the lamp. More tomorrow,' Beau said briskly. "And don't disturb us. Your mother and have things to talk about."

Piers was oddly grown-up in his manner. He looked at his father gravely, without surprise or resentment, and agreed to go to sleep. He lay quite still, looking with a very penetrating eye upon the two adults who stood in the doorway.

Back in the living-dining room, which was the central room of the cell Angela rented, they sat over red wine, and after three glasses Beau relaxed enough to tell her what was really on his mind.

"I think you ought to move from here," he said. "Things in Europe look very unsettled. I've been traveling, a brief concert tour that included Berlin. I don't like what I see."

"Actually, I've been thinking about home."

"Have you? That's your instinct at work, darling. I should think you have no reason to live in England now. With Julia gone."

"That's right, I haven't, although I'm sure Julia would have liked me to live in one of her houses. She left the

540

country place to Twickenham, you know, and the town house to me. But I'm not interested in living in London. I have a strong feeling that I want to go back to Montreal and that Piers would be best there."

"That's good. I agree. What do you think about writing to Aunt Miel? She might take you into Edenbridge. Wouldn't that be marvelous for Piers?"

"Yes, it would, Beau. Of course, I've thought of that. I've also wondered whether Grandfather—"

"Might forgive and forget?"

"Something like that. My father must be lonely, even though Mildred is running the house and I'm sure there are people around all the time. But it isn't the same—as having somebody of your own."

Beau looked away from her then, sensing in her words a rebuke. He did not take criticism well, even indirect criticism.

"I've been talking to Susan," Beau said, breaking the short silence rather abruptly. "And *she's* going home, as well. That's partly why I came here now. To tell you that there's word from your grandfather—he wants you back. Susan was talking to your father on the long-distance telephone. From what I gather, the family had had one of its world-shaking meetings and decided to have you back. Susan is being taken off probation as well. She can come back to Canada and still keep her allowance."

He laughed. The tyrannies of the Court family always amused him, since he had never buckled under to them in any way.

"Beau! Is that true?"

"Yes, that's why I was so interested when you voiced the idea by yourself. Before you heard what I had to say."

"Oh. . . I think I really do want to go back!"

Beau looked pleased.

"Then you'll like my plan. Susan has booked the four of us on the *Île de France*, sailing from Le Havre the first week in November. What do you think of that? The classiest boat—oh, not the largest—but the best, so everybody says. Trust Susan to think of that. So I want you to arrange for your paintings to be packed and shipped. You can decide whether you want to write to Aunt Miel about taking you in at Edenbridge or whether you want to brave the storm and go back to Pride's Court. Of course, you know, Mildred runs the place, so it would mean living with her and her family. So I'd think about that."

"And you?"

He looked away from her momentarily as if to gather his thoughts.

"I'm going home, too."

"But you don't want to have a house? You don't want us to live like a family?"

"I haven't been able to figure that out. First, I'll be away on tour a lot. The New York Philharmonic is going to premiere my Third Symphony. The first thing is to get Piers and you and Susan home, where it's safe."

"All right, Beau."

Between the surprise of seeing him and considering such a drastic change in her life, she felt tired. She could not help remembering how he had left her the last time, so desperate and lonely. She had thought then of leaving and going to London or Montreal, but inertia had done its work and she'd decided against it. Today, circumstances had changed. Beau was making definite arrangements and there was the question of war and Piers's safety.

"I'm going to bed," Angela said. "I've given you my room. I'll sleep on the cot in Piers's room."

He looked astonished.

"But Angela, for God's sake . . ."

He came close and tried to take her in his arms. She pushed him away wearily. There was no feeling where her heart was supposed to be. He was the same man, still attractive, still compelling, but she could not respond. Perhaps in time she would recover some of that excitement, but it was not going to happen so easily as Beau imagined.

"Good night, Beau. We'll talk again in the morning."

He did not beg. He picked up a lamp and left her abruptly, to disappear into the room she had assigned. Angela walked in the other direction, frail as a ghost. She felt nothing, neither love nor pain, not even hope.

CHAPTER NINE

When Susan emerged from the Windsor Hotel, a bitter wind was blowing up Peel Street. Having lived in various cozy corners of Europe for a long time, flitting from oasis to oasis, she had come to regard the weather as a manageable commodity. The sting of cold air shocked her. She hesitated, unsure of her direction.

She had parted from Beau and Angela and little Piers the day before. After the ocean voyage on the *Île de France* and the train journey to Montreal, she had checked into the Windsor Hotel. Angela and Beau had decided to stay with Justine. Now, she was alone again. It seemed to her that her life for the last few years had been a jolting series of rushed parties, mad weekends, pointless travel always punctuated by periods of terrible loneliness. She slept ten hours, breakfasted in her room, and then decided to walk. There was really nothing else to do.

As she looked down Peel Street, whipped by a gust of icy air from the river to the south, a flood of nostalgia drove her to walk to the old part of the city and St.-Denis Street. The house had been sold and was probably lived in by a strange family, or perhaps it had been abandoned. But she wanted to see it anyway.

Suddenly it seemed important to find out why she had rejected her upbringing, her loving family, so easily. Just as, later, she had abandoned her husband and son and the security of Pride's Court in, what seemed now, a mindless way. What had she been trying to find? What *was* this elusive dream she had been so relentlessly pursuing? She could not remember anymore, but she had reaped only loneliness and despair.

By the time she reached St.-Denis Street, her face felt frozen. The house looked smaller than she had remembered, and there was no sign of life. At some windows she could see curtains, however, so there must be someone living there. Eventually, shivering, she trudged away, drawn by the curious notion that she must visit Notre Dame Church. When she reached the steps, she hesitated, then walked up to the huge dark doors, pulled one open, and entered.

The church was too cavernous to be actually warm, but at least there was no cold wind. It was still. A scattering of parishioners knelt in the soft light and she took a back pew, wanting to be inconspicuous. Sitting in the comfort provided by almost two thousand years of implied support, she came to rest. It was here, rather than at the old house, that memories of her childhood swept over her.

So many little details came back to haunt her: services that had seemed endless, priests mouthing words she did not understand, the sweet smell of incense (stifling, expected), the terror of her first mass, arguments with her friends about the sacramental wine actually becoming Christ's blood, her pathetic confessions. Peace enveloped her, hope seeped back into her mind. She thought she would seek out Uncle Marc. Perhaps he would know what she ought to do.

Marc was uneasy. After a light dinner he excused himself from Camille and retired to his study to meditate. Even in that restful, comforting room, surrounded by polished wood and mellow leather and the smell of good books, he managed only to stare into space. Nothing constructive occurred to him. Susan had telephoned that morning to request an appointment, and he was bewildered. He had assumed she would go to Edenbridge now that she was back in Montreal. Either that, or to Pride's Court.

Because it was unusual for Susan to seek him out, he felt a heaviness around his heart. As if something sad were about to happen. He wished that his Uncle Eustache were alive, but the old bishop had died the year before. It was at times like this that he missed his uncle—missed his wisdom and compassion. Uncle Eustache had been the senior male member of the St. Amour clan, and as such he had always been the one to direct, to take hold. Now, Marc had assumed that role, and he was not sure he was equal to the task. Yet, try as he would, he could not pin down exactly what worried him about Susan's visit. He was her uncle, and, if she had remained in the Church, he would be her bishop. He paced back and forth for a while, but that yielded no results. He really must be calm, he reasoned, until he found out what Susan wanted of him.

Marc settled himself in his comfortable armchair behind the massive desk upon which he worked. He saw the piece of paper lying there, and his heart gave a familiar tug when he recognized Camille's handwriting. She wrote in large, scrawling letters. It was a poem which she was giving him, the note said, as a pre-Christmas gift.

He adjusted the desk lamp and began to read. The poem was entitled "Passion." It went:

> Those who seize a moment
> as it flies by,
> and cage it,
> turn it to dust. It is not love.

> Those who let the moment go,
> watch it flee,
> cannot then
> dismember it. Those who truly love are always late.

It was a long time since Camille had shown him any poetry, he thought. He had wondered at times if the flame in her had really been extinguished; if perhaps she no longer felt that terrible drive, that consuming need that they had shared for so long. He saw now that the spirit was still alive. And he experienced a sharp pain of longing for her.

The front doorbell jarred him from his trance. He could hear his housekeeper, Mrs. Carlisle, walking toward the hall to answer it, and he knew it would be Susan. He tried desperately to bring his mind to bear upon the problem Susan would present to him.

When she came in, he thought at first that she did not look very different from the girl he had seen years before —he caught the gleam of polished hair, the expensive scent of French perfume, the rustle of fine fabric, the whole air of an elegant, glossy woman. (So few of his parishioners shared that aura that he only recognized it from his occasional excursions into the world of Armand and Honey.) A second glance, however, revealed that the girl looked pale and tired. She wore a black woolen suit that looked expensive to him. It was trimmed with mink at the cuffs and collar, and she wore a small, jaunty fur hat and a matching muff. He walked around the desk to greet her and felt her cold cheek pressed against his and smelled the sweet effluence of flowers. He offered her a chair.

"Nothing's changed, has it?" she said, looking around the room and waving one hand with long, brilliant red nails. "You look well, Uncle Marc."

"So do you," he lied. "Welcome, my dear. We all knew you were coming, but I certainly didn't expect to be one of your first stops."

He smiled tentatively at her, fastening her gaze with his dark, brooding eyes. Her nervousness was catching. He found himself fiddling with a pen.

"Neither did I."

"How's Paris?"

"Exciting, if you have money and friends and position. I'm happy to be back here, though. No, that's a lie! It's just that I felt I *had* to come back."

She began to fish about inside the muff and finally produced a packet of Gauloises. She looked at him for permission and he brought her an ashtray. Her hands trembled as she fitted the cigarette into the holder, lighted it, and deposited the match in the tray with a theatrical gesture.

"What are your plans, Susan?"

"That's what I've come to see you about, Uncle Marc. I hope you can help me . . . help me sort things out. I don't know where to turn . . ."

A trickle of despair leaked from her voice into the room.

"What can I do to help? Tell me."

"I want to know about Mother . . . how she feels about me."

Suddenly all the false courage dropped away from her, and she leaned toward him, big-eyed, young, extremely vulnerable.

"Honey is the kind of person who loves without conditions," Marc said. "Do you think she would have taken her love away, or destroyed it? Come now, Susan—"

"You don't know the things that have happened between us . . . or you wouldn't say that, Uncle Marc. I've behaved badly, no, worse, I've behaved like a bitch. Excuse me, but that's the right word. Oh, you know about the wedding at Pride's Court, and you know how I always

546

wanted to be with the Courts, but there are other things . . ."

"What other things? Perhaps if you told me, you'd feel better, my dear."

"Mother wanted to make up our quarrel even when I was in the hospital. After the fire, you know. But I treated her so coldly then, I can't imagine that she'll have forgotten. I thought I didn't want my French relatives . . . that part of my life. Well, you know I left the Church. You know I've lost even that, even my faith."

"Faith can be restored." (He sounded like Uncle Eustache, he thought with a jolt. Had he inherited some of the old man's talent for weighing matters, and rendering judgment?)

"Can it? I hope so. Everything I've done seems to be wrong. My marriage, my relationship with the Courts, running away from David, not making up with Mother . . . and there's plenty more. I can't bear to think of all the things I've done . . ."

He looked into those candid young eyes and felt the twist of pain that he usually associated with Camille. The sensitivity to agony that cannot be pushed aside or hidden but must be borne. *My God, why is there so much pain in the world?* he cried inside.

"The Church bored me," she went on. "I had no time for it. I was a hypocrite at the services, going through all that ritual and thinking inside that it was rubbish. That's why I left . . . because I couldn't bear to be so two-faced about it. What's the use of religion if you're not a believer?"

"Perhaps you were right to leave, then," Marc heard himself saying although he knew that to leave the Church could not be considered right, and that it was, in fact, a step toward hell itself.

"At the time, I thought so. I was such a hypocrite!" she repeated.

"Being a hypocrite isn't fatal, especially once you've recognized the condition."

"No, I guess not. Sinners can always repent, can't they? After all, there was the Prodigal Son. Well, I guess maybe I'm the Prodigal Daughter, but I don't know if Mother will be ready to put on a banquet for me."

"Do you still feel it would be hypocritical to go to church?"

"I don't know, honestly. I thought I might confess, take communion again and see how I felt." She said this hesitantly. "Sort of test it out, if you see what I mean."

"An excellent idea."

"I want to see Mother." She said it in a forlorn voice, like a small child who is lost in a storm. He felt great pity for her, a sweep of fatherly affection.

"Of course you do. That's perfectly natural."

"Will you speak to her? Will you find out?"

"Why don't you speak to her yourself?"

"Because . . ." Her voice had fallen to a point where he had to strain to hear. "Because I can't live through another rejection. If she said no . . . to my face . . . perhaps I couldn't bear it."

"I think I see what you mean."

"Oh, I feel so lonely . . ."

Her shoulders sagged in the rich fabric of her suit. She drooped in the chair as if she were going to double up.

"You ought to try to make up with your mother, Susan, and become part of the family again. You can't go on living alone . . . in and out of hotels. It isn't right. I'll see what I can find out for you . . ."

"Oh, yes, please. I can't just go banging on the door like some beggar, saying 'Take me in, take me in.' I feel so alone. . . . I've been in hotels and apartments for the last few years, running around Europe . . . it's all so silly. The people are all so empty, and they're afraid, too. Do you know that? They're afraid."

"I'm not surprised, but Susan—"

"I'm so terribly depressed," she cut in, not listening to him now but caught up in her own emotional cloud. "I think I'll go mad sometimes, Uncle Marc, or kill myself. Yes, I often think of killing myself . . . I . . ."

"Susan!" he said, shocked into speaking sharply.

"It's true! I miss everything I had . . . I didn't like my life . . . I wanted to get away where things would be exciting. But they aren't, you know. It's lonely. . . . I think if I spend another night alone, I'll jump out of the window, or cut my wrists. . . . I'm so alone . . ."

"My dear, listen to me . . . I'm your uncle . . . your friend . . . your bishop still, although you may have forsaken the Church. Do you think you would feel better if we prayed?"

"Uncle Marc, I want . . ." she was crying now, reaching for a square of linen buried somewhere in the fur muff. "I want to confess . . . will you hear it?"

Marc, feeling strangely out of his depth, closed the study door and locked it. They remained locked in the room for an hour, during which Susan became once again the child she had been so long ago, and although her confession was far from the innocent ones she had recited in the past, at the end of it she felt stronger. Marc, more moved than he had been by any other emotional scene in his life except those that involved his sister, was exhausted when it was over, but he knew then what he must do. Susan would move into his house until such time as her life could be sorted out. He sent Mrs. Carlisle to the Windsor to pick up Susan's clothes and had Camille arrange a bedroom for her. In the morning it would be time to consider calling Honey, time to talk about this important reunion.

Honey heard about the flight in her own office. Michel himself called to her that he had agreed to fly 600,000 units of diphtheria antitoxin up to Kirkland Lake and Courtsville, where an epidemic was already imminent. The town doctor had requested the antitoxin immediately because even a single day's delay might affect the spread of the disease.

It had happened quite coincidentally. Michel happened to be in the Cartierville Airport when somebody from the Royal Victoria Hospital staff requested a pilot who could fly that same afternoon. Since he was between runs and his plane, a Fairchild Super 71, was already ski-equipped and even gassed up, Michel agreed to go at once. He called Clarissa first and then, knowing she would hear about the mercy flight through the newspaper, his mother.

"I'll be back tomorrow, Mother, so don't worry. It's just a routine flight except for the cargo, and you know the Fairchild, it's the best plane there is."

"What does Clarissa have to say?" Honey asked, feeling frustrated in the face of Michel's enthusiasm.

"Go ahead, naturally."

Yes, *she would*, Honey thought with unreasoning anger.

Clarissa had that British do-or-die attitude, which was always remarkable and often foolhardy.

"Then I suppose you have to go."

"They need the stuff right away. For God's sake, Mother, your own nephews might be in danger! It's an emergency, and I'm the guy who happens to be right here. No choice."

That stopped her. Simon II and Noel were both potential victims, especially Simon. Noel did not stay up north but traveled back and forth constantly. Simon's wife would be susceptible as well. She felt another wave of resentment, however, because no matter how hard she tried to escape, she was always and forever mixed up with her relatives.

"There's no use my saying such a stupid thing as 'Be careful,' I suppose?" Honey said, her voice a little feeble with the effort to be casual.

"Not much. I'm an experienced bush pilot . . . who do you know that's any better? Other than you." He said things like that as a joke, of course. She was a good pilot, but she was not experienced in the bush. Bush pilots were a different breed.

"I know you are, darling. Have you checked the weather up there?"

"Yes, and it isn't encouraging." There was no use lying because she could easily ask for a report.

"I see."

"But the weather is never good up north, you know that, and a blizzard is just as likely to come on whether they announce it or not. Just don't worry. I'll see you tomorrow."

Michel had delivered the antitoxin, stayed overnight, and then flown out of Courtsville early in the morning. He had touched down at a trading post on Lac-Doumaine, gassed up, and headed southeast once more. He was due at two o'clock in the afternoon at Cartierville Airport, and by four there was no sign of him. By five it was getting dark and people were becoming concerned. Clarissa telephoned Honey at the office.

"I'm out at the airport," Clarissa said. "Nobody knows what to do at the moment. We can't possibly expect a rescue party to go out before morning."

"Stay there, darling, and I'll drive out."

"But there's not much you can do."

"I can keep you company. And talk to somebody."

"Yes, all right. But driving is bad, so do be careful. Perhaps you ought to ask Armand to drive out with you?"

"I'm a better driver than Armand," Honey said. "Just stay there and wait for me."

At the airport, however, there was no news, and nothing to be done before morning, everybody agreed, except to locate planes that might be used in the search. Blizzards had been reported over scattered areas of northern Quebec and Ontario, some in the flight pattern that Michel ought to have taken.

"Get my plane ready," Honey said to one of the mechanics. "I'm going out with the search party in the morning. If it's necessary. Perhaps we'll hear something before then."

At home she found Armand restlessly drinking scotch and pacing around the library. At midnight they went to bed, but sleep was not forthcoming, and long before light had broken, they were both in the kitchen making coffee and discussing what must be done.

"I suppose there's no trying to talk sense into you," Armand said, without any preamble. "You're determined to do this?"

"I'm as good a flyer as most of them. I have a plane. It's ready. I have to go."

"You are also a woman," Armand said. "And my wife."

He did not want to say what was in both their minds. That he might have already lost a son, and therefore, it would be doubly painful if he lost a wife as well.

"Darling, I know what you're thinking. I know why you're thinking it. But it doesn't make any difference. Don't you see that?"

"Well, I can't stop you."

"I'd find it easier to do something to help than to stay on the ground and worry or wish I were up there doing something."

Action. Yes, he understood that. The situation made him uncomfortable because he had never wanted to learn to fly and had never fully appreciated Honey's interest. Now, *she* could go (when it counted) and he had to stay on the ground, helpless as a baby.

"That I can't argue with."

"You know I must go. They need every plane. They'll section off the map in the area he might possibly have come down in—and every pilot will take a square. Then we'll just crisscross the square looking for Michel."

"It's a large order. He may have been blown off course or gotten lost if there was a blizzard."

"Flying is risky, we all know that. Michel had to do it, because it gave meaning to his life. But remember, darling, he came through the airship crash. This may not be nearly so bad."

Michel had to be somewhere south of Lac-Doumaine, where he had landed and gassed up without incident. At that time the sky had been clear, but farther south there had been smatterings of heavy snow. By eleven o'clock the following morning nothing had been heard, and six planes were ready to begin the search. One of the pilots was Honey.

Armand and Clarissa were there to wish her luck. The parting was a little tearful, but at the same time, Honey was impatient to take off. To do something, especially something as useful as searching actively, was preferable to waiting. She wore a heavy flying suit, helmet and gloves.

The Fairchild lifted off the snowy field without difficulty. The air was bright with frost and sun, but half an hour out of the airport the sky became grayish and leaden with snowy masses. She headed for Lac-Désert, the area she had been assigned, but kept an eye on the ground below, just in case Michel had made it this far south. Near the Coulonge River the storm sifted toward her, and the wind got up and began pushing the plane around. At times she lost sight of the ground.

She began to circle the area, then still hardly able to see the ground for blowing snow, began a crisscross pattern as she had been instructed. At times the earth appeared, scarcely discernible from the whitened sky. Black patches indicated rock face or clumps of trees. Her own determination to find Michel, rather than have somebody else save him, drove her back and forth with a kind of relentless pressure, although she knew she might be covering some of the same ground more than once. She checked her gas, calculated how much she needed to take her back to Cartierville, and realized that she had used up her quota. A sense of loss and desperation made her enlarge the search area she had been assigned—a kind of reasoning based on nothing more than wild hope. She saw the gas gauge getting lower but found herself unable to turn the plane in the direction of Cartierville. One more chance, she told herself, what if he were out there? What if he were only a few miles away? Only a mile? And she turned away?

She was stiffening with cold and nervous exhaustion when the motor began to cough. She looked at the gas gauge and saw that it was almost empty. A numbness grew like a plant inside her, reaching out along the nerves and blood vessels, paralyzing every part of her. She tried to remember her training, her instructions. *Stall the motor.* That was it! Stall the motor and look for trees to break the impact of the crash against frozen earth or rock.

The plane was coming down, and she had lost control, but if she could just glide . . . if there were trees . . . she saw the black shapes of evergreens skimming up toward the nose. Thank God, they would break the fall, catch the bottom of the aircraft, and drag it to a halt. But as she waited for the grinding of the fuselage on tree branches, she realized with a flash of panic that she was overshooting the trees and coming down on flat white surface that might be a lake or river. She was strapped in, and she put her arms over her head and waited for the whiteness to turn black.

Standing in the hospital corridor, Doctor Frampton looked first at Armand and then down toward the window, which opened on a courtyard, as if he saw something fascinating there. It was snowing lightly. The window outlined a white square.

"I'm sorry, Sir Armand. There's nothing more I can do."

"You mean, there's no hope?"

"Even if she did recover, by some miracle"—and here the doctor waited for a moment, choosing his words—"even if she did recover, she would be unable to walk again. There would be many complications."

"I see."

In the silence that followed, Armand reviewed the knowledge he had of the plane crash. The engine had slid back to pin Honey to the seat, to smash bones and flesh from the waist down. She had lost a great deal of blood, and there had been shock and cold before she had been found.

"Believe me, I've done everything I could. We can't give her any more blood."

"I understand. I wasn't questioning your judgment."

"You'd better go in and see her now. I can't promise how long . . . she's got . . . I don't know."

"Yes, yes, of course. I'll go in now."

The strange thing was he felt nothing. As he pushed open the door and walked into the room, he felt calm. He observed the nurse. He saw Honey lying white and flat upon the high bed.

Any moment now, he supposed, he would feel the full impact. He steeled himself, glancing at the nurse inquiringly. Her eyes were noncommittal. He walked forward to the bedside and looked down upon the bruised face, the closed shadowed lids, the damp forehead. The nurse stepped back.

"Would you like to watch over her for a while? There's really nothing more I can do right now."

"Thank you, nurse. Yes, I'll watch her. I'll call you if . . . if we need you."

"All right, Sir Armand. I'll be just outside."

After the door had closed upon the rustle of starched uniform, he was alone with Honey in the quiet room. He could hear the faint rise and fall of her breathing. Her blond hair was damp—perhaps with perspiration—perhaps it had been wiped clean to take away blood from the bruises. Only the face bones remained as he remembered them: fine, carefully sculpted under the clammy skin. And the eyelashes, of course, black and perfectly patterned on the dark circles beneath. Age had receded, drained away with the blood she had lost. She looked pathetically young and vulnerable. He wanted to protest about that helpless look and picked up one hand to comfort her. The abrasions had been painted with some pink disinfectant.

"Miel?"

She opened her eyes and gazed at him from a blue distance. Then she recognized him and seemed to come closer, like a person walking slowly down a road.

"Armand . . . darling." It was only a whisper.

"*Ma chérie*, I love you."

He was surprised that his voice was level.

"I love you, Armand. Always."

She was quiet, gathering her forces for the next question. Finally it came, but with some effort.

"Michel? They found him?"

"He's safe, darling. They found both of you almost at the same time. You crashed quite close to where he came down. Michel's going to be all right."

"Thank God."

At the mention of God, he wondered if he ought to bring in a minister, perhaps the rector of Christ Church. Yet she looked so exhausted that he doubted the value of it. Michel was heavily sedated, and there was not much sense in asking the doctor if he could be wheeled in. He had no idea what he should do or whether there was anybody else she would want to see. He clung to her hand tightly, pinching the fingers. Realizing this, he relaxed his grip and raised her fingers to his lips. The tears came to his eyes and fell slowly down his cheeks. He made no attempt to wipe them away.

He was still struggling for control when the door swung open and he looked up, expecting to find Doctor Frampton or the nurse. Instead, he saw his daughter, Susan. A new shock ran through him as he noticed how pale and lost she was—how frightened.

"I came as soon as I heard," Susan said, staring at the figure on the bed. And then with a gasp: "Mother, you can't die now!"

She ran across the room and grasped Honey's hand. Armand stepped back as Susan leaned over the bed.

"Mother, can you hear me?" Susan cried desperately. "Mother, I came back to . . . to see you, and that's when they told me. About the accident. I came to ask you to forgive me. You must get well . . . please, get well, Mother . . ."

Honey seemed to take on an unexpected strength. She looked at Susan and smiled a little, focusing on her face with difficulty.

"I'm glad you're home, Susan. You must come to Edenbridge. You must help your father . . ."

"I'm home. I'm sorry, Mother, for all the awful things I did . . . I was so stupid and wrong. I want you to forgive me . . . please say that you'll forgive me."

She lifted the flaccid hand to her mouth and kissed it. She was crying.

"There's nothing to forgive. I love all my children. But Susan, your father is going to need you. Do you understand? He'll be so lonely."

"No, no, you're coming back to Edenbridge soon. The doctors will make you well. You'll see . . ."

"Darling, I'm not. I know that." Her voice was so low that both Armand and Susan had to bend over to hear what she said.

"You must take my place. Promise me that you will try to take my place, there."

But that wasn't possible, Susan thought. How could she ever be strong like her mother? She had no talent for business, for running a newspaper, for taking up important causes, for politics.

"How could I take your place?"

"You're my daughter. And Armand's daughter," Honey said. "And you *will* be able to do many things . . . you're young, Susan. You can learn."

After this long speech she fell silent. Armand drew up a chair for Susan, and they sat watching, waiting for Honey to speak again. Armand rested his hand on Susan's shoulder as if to give her support. They waited like that.

Susan began to pray, that Honey would be spared them, that some miracle would take place, but she had little faith in that, really. And as Honey seemed to recede even more, into shadows that reflected in the very stillness of her face, Susan began to pray for something else. That she could be strong, that she could go on and make her life useful, that she would truly be a support to her father when he needed her so desperately. She was going home to Edenbridge, and if she were given another chance and did well, perhaps even David might consider a reconciliation.

Give me the kind of strength she *had*, Susan begged silently, looking down at her mother.

Honey looked as if she were in a deep sleep. Armand spoke her name softly, close to her ear.

"Miel? Miel?"

Honey did not open her eyes this time. Her voice was faint. Armand and Susan, straining, could scarcely hear.

"Susan . . . look after your father."

The stillness was a hammer blow. Armand knew that Honey was dead. He had no need to call Doctor Frampton to confirm it. He knew it as surely as if it had been his own death. He was hollow.

When Doctor Frampton entered the room, he found Sir Armand St. Amour and his daughter standing at the foot of the bed looking down at the patient. They were holding hands, but they did not speak.

Lord Court walked along the thickly carpeted hall toward the enclosed staircase that led to the tower. He looked fiercely at his pocket watch as if daring it to betray him. He had not climbed up to the fourth floor for many years, but it seemed appropriate to do so now.

North, climbing the marble staircase with Mildred, hesitated at the top step when he caught sight of the old man. Lord Court looked most peculiar, he thought, as if he did not know where he was. North was about to speak, but Mildred took his hand to stop him. He and Mildred then stood still and watched the old man go up the narrow, curving flight of stairs until he was no longer visible. For some reason North held tightly to Mildred's hand. A cold wind had blown across his heart, and he clutched at the only strength left to him.

As she saw her grandfather slowly mount the steps, Mildred sensed what he was about to do. She kept her hand in North's warm one, gripping him until she felt pain. In that one gesture she took him back and knew with a sweep of desolation that nothing had changed and that it would never change for her. She had loved him from the beginning, and she loved him now. There was no escape from that.

Lord Court had not seen his relatives. He was consumed with his mission. When he had first planned this great house, the tower had had a very important function: From the tower he could watch his own ships sweep up the St. Lawrence to the docks. He savored the pride of ownership and power, pride of plans fulfilled and of a mighty fortune amassed by his own shrewd abilities. He had delighted in the prospect of leaving it to his sons and to his beautiful daughter.

The stairs made him short of breath, but at last he reached the square little room with its four windows. A heavy snowfall cut his view somewhat, but he could still see the streets below, the gray stone of houses, the weighted branches of the trees in winter. His breathing clouded the cold glass panes as he stared down at the city.

With his cuff he brushed the steam from the glass. Yes, there it was, coming along the street, winding slowly up the Mountain to the Protestant cemetery. The black limousine first, with its marker, and then the polished ebony hearse, long as a yacht, silent as a ghost. A trail of cars streamed after it, climbing, each bearing relatives or friends. Taking Hannah Court to her resting place.

As he watched the cars, his mind dropped back into the past: He saw Honey as a pretty blond doll, bright, blue-eyed, charming, with the world at her feet. Nothing was too good for her, she could reach the pinnacle of society. She was a Court, she had breeding and background, and money and beauty. She could have been a duchess, he often thought, or even a princess. Why not? His own family was ancient and important, exquisitely loyal to the Crown, intensely loyal to the country.

Yes, she could have been a princess.

And now she was dead, gone from him forever. All the quarrels, the bitter words, the hours of agony, the icy breath of loss, all drowned him now in a torrent that tore at his heart. The pain seized him so that he thought he could not bear to live, certainly he could not bear to look anymore at that funeral cortege as it unraveled gently up the Mountain.

He clenched his fists and pounded the windowsill.

And he cried out, to the chill December day, "I should have loved you more!" Pounding again and again, eyes blank with tears, "I should have loved you more!"

Dell Bestsellers

At your local bookstore or use this handy coupon for ordering:

Dell **DELL BOOKS**
P.O. BOX 1000, PINEBROOK, N.J. 07058

Please send me the books I have checked above. I am enclosing $ _____
(please add 75¢ per copy to cover postage and handling). Send check or money
order—no cash or C.O.D.'s. Please allow up to 8 weeks for shipment.

Mr/Mrs/Miss _____

Address _____

City _____ State/Zip _____

THE PASSING BELLS

by

PHILLIP ROCK

A story you'll wish would go on forever.

Here is the vivid story of the Grevilles, a titled
British family, and their servants—men and wom-
en who knew their place, upstairs and down, until
England went to war and the whole fabric of British
society began to unravel and change.

"Well-written, exciting. Echoes of Hemingway,
Graves and *Upstairs, Downstairs.*"—*Library Journal*

"Every twenty-five years or so, we are blessed with
a war novel, outstanding in that it depicts not only
the history of a time but also its soul."—*West
Coast Review of Books.*

"Vivid and enthralling."—*The Philadelphia Inquirer*

A Dell Book   **$2.75   (16837-6)**

At your local bookstore or use this handy coupon for ordering:

| **Dell** | **DELL BOOKS**   THE PASSING BELLS $2.75   (16837-6) |
| | **P.O. BOX 1000, PINEBROOK, N.J. 07058** |

Please send me the above title. I am enclosing $ _____
(please add 75¢ per copy to cover postage and handling). Send check or money
order—no cash or C.O.D.'s. Please allow up to 8 weeks for shipment.

Mr/Mrs/Miss _____

Address _____

City _____ State/Zip _____